# THE SAVAGE DETECTIVES

# THE SAVAGE DETECTIVES

## ROBERTO BOLAÑO

**TRANSLATED FROM THE SPANISH BY NATASHA WIMMER**

FARRAR, STRAUS AND GIROUX / NEW YORK

Farrar, Straus and Giroux
19 Union Square West, New York 10003

Grateful acknowledgment is made for permission to reprint the following material:

"The Vampire," by Octavio Paz, translated by Samuel Beckett, from *Anthology of Mexican Poetry*, © 1970 by Calder & Boyars. Reprinted by permission of John Calder. All rights reserved.

"A Philosophical Satire," translated by Margaret Sayers Peden, from *Sor Juana Inés de la Cruz: Poems*, © 1985 by Bilingual Press/Editorial Bilingüe, Arizona State University, Tempe. Used by permission. All rights reserved.

Library of Congress Cataloging-in-Publication Data
Bolaño, Roberto, 1953–
    [Detectives salvajes. English]
    The savage detectives / Roberto Bolaño ; translated from the Spanish by
Natasha Wimmer.— 1st American ed.
        p.   cm.
    ISBN-13: 978-0-374-19148-1 (hardcover : alk. paper)
    ISBN-10: 0-374-19148-4 (hardcover : alk. paper)
    I. Wimmer, Natasha.   II. Title.

PQ8098.12.O38D4813 2007
863'.64—dc22

                                                    2006022176

Designed by Jonathan D. Lippincott

www.fsgbooks.com

3   4   5   6   7   8   9   10

This work has been published with a subsidy from the Directorate-General of Books,
Archives and Libraries of the Spanish Ministry of Culture.

For Carolina López and Lautaro Bolaño,

who have the good fortune to look alike

"Do you want Mexico to be saved? Do you want Christ to be our king?"

"No."

—Malcolm Lowry

# MEXICANS LOST IN MEXICO

## (1975)

## NOVEMBER 2

I've been cordially invited to join the visceral realists. I accepted, of course. There was no initiation ceremony. It was better that way.

## NOVEMBER 3

I'm not really sure what visceral realism is. I'm seventeen years old, my name is Juan García Madero, and I'm in my first semester of law school. I wanted to study literature, not law, but my uncle insisted, and in the end I gave in. I'm an orphan, and someday I'll be a lawyer. That's what I told my aunt and uncle, and then I shut myself in my room and cried all night. Or anyway for a long time. Then, as if it were settled, I started class in the law school's hallowed halls, but a month later I registered for Julio César Álamo's poetry workshop in the literature department, and that was how I met the visceral realists, or viscerealists or even vicerealists, as they sometimes like to call themselves. Up until then, I had attended the workshop four times and nothing ever happened, though only in a manner of speaking, of course, since naturally something always happened: we read poems, and Álamo praised them or tore them to pieces, depending on his mood; one person would read, Álamo would critique, another person would read, Álamo would critique, somebody else would read, Álamo would critique. Sometimes Álamo would get bored and ask us (those of us who weren't reading just then) to critique too, and then we would critique and Álamo would read the paper.

It was the ideal method for ensuring that no one was friends with anyone, or else that our friendships were unhealthy and based on resentment.

And I can't say that Álamo was much of a critic either, even though he talked a lot about criticism. Really I think he just talked for the sake of talking. He knew what periphrasis was. Not very well, but he knew. But he didn't know what pentapody was (a line of five feet in classical meter, as everybody knows), and he didn't know what a nicharchean was either (a line something like the phalaecean), or what a tetrastich was (a four-line stanza). How do I know he didn't know? Because on the first day of the workshop, I made the mistake of asking. I have no idea what I was thinking. The only Mexican poet who knows things like that by heart is Octavio Paz (our great enemy), the others are clueless, or at least that was what Ulises Lima told me minutes after I joined the visceral realists and they embraced me as one of their own. Asking Álamo these questions was, as I soon learned, a sign of my tactlessness. At first I thought he was smiling in admiration. Later I realized it was actually contempt. Mexican poets (poets in general, I guess) hate to have their ignorance brought to light. But I didn't back down, and after he had ripped apart a few of my poems at the second session, I asked him whether he knew what a rispetto was. Álamo thought that I was demanding *respect* for my poems, and he went off on a tirade about objective criticism (for a change), a minefield that every young poet must cross, etc., but I cut him off, and after explaining that never in my short life had I demanded respect for my humble creations, I put the question to him again, this time enunciating as clearly as possible.

"Don't give me this crap," said Álamo.

"A rispetto, professor, is a kind of lyrical verse, romantic to be precise, similar to the strambotto, with six or eight hendecasyllabic lines, the first four in the form of a serventesio and the following composed in rhyming couplets. For example . . ." And I was about to give him an example or two when Álamo jumped up and cut me off. What happened next is hazy (although I have a good memory): I remember Álamo laughing along with the four or five other members of the workshop. I think they may have been making fun of me.

Anyone else would have left and never gone back, but despite my unhappy memories (or my unhappy failure to remember what had happened, at least as unfortunate as remembering would have been), the next week there I was, punctual as always.

I think destiny brought me back. This was the fifth session of Álamo's workshop that I'd attended (but it might just as well have been the eighth or the ninth, since lately I've been noticing that time can expand or contract at will), and tension, the alternating current of tragedy, was palpable in the air, although no one could explain why. To begin with, we were all there, all seven apprentice poets who'd originally signed up for the workshop. This hadn't happened at any other session. And we were nervous. Even Álamo wasn't his usual calm self. For a minute I thought something might have happened at the university, that maybe there'd been a campus shooting I hadn't heard about, or a surprise strike, or that the dean had been assassinated, or they'd kidnapped one of the philosophy professors. But nothing like that was true, and there was no reason to be nervous. No objective reason, anyway. But poetry (real poetry) is like that: you can sense it, you can feel it in the air, the way they say certain highly attuned animals (snakes, worms, rats, and some birds) can detect an earthquake. What happened next was a blur, but at the risk of sounding corny, I'd say there was something miraculous about it. Two visceral realist poets walked in and Álamo reluctantly introduced them, although he only knew one of them personally; the other one he knew by reputation, or maybe he just knew his name or had heard someone mention him, but he introduced us to him anyway.

I'm not sure why they were there. It was clearly a hostile visit, hostile but somehow propagandistic and proselytizing too. At first the visceral realists kept to themselves, and Álamo tried to look diplomatic and slightly ironic while he waited to see what would happen. Then he started to relax, encouraged by the strangers' shyness, and after half an hour the workshop was back to normal. That's when the battle began. The visceral realists questioned Álamo's critical system and he responded by calling them cut-rate surrealists and fake Marxists. Five members of the workshop backed him up; in other words, everyone but me and a skinny kid who always carried around a book by Lewis Carroll and never spoke. This surprised me, to be honest, because the students supporting Álamo so fiercely were the same ones he'd been so hard on as a critic, and now they were revealing themselves to be his biggest supporters. That's when I decided to put in my two cents, and I accused Álamo of having no idea what a rispetto was; nobly, the visceral realists admitted that they didn't know either but my observation struck them as pertinent, and they said so; one of them asked how old I was, and I said I was seventeen and tried all over again to explain what a rispetto was; Álamo was red with rage; the members of the workshop said I was being pedantic (one of them

5

called me an academicist); the visceral realists defended me; suddenly unstoppable, I asked Álamo and the workshop in general whether they at least remembered what a nicharchean or a tetrastich was. And no one could answer.

Contrary to my expectations, the argument didn't lead to an all-around ass-kicking. I have to admit I would have loved that. And although one of the members of the workshop did promise Ulises Lima that someday he would kick his ass, in the end nothing actually happened; nothing violent, I mean, although I responded to the threat (which, I repeat, was not directed at me) by letting the threatener know that he could have it out with me anywhere on campus, any day, any time.

The end of class was surprising. Álamo dared Ulises Lima to read one of his poems. Lima didn't need to be asked twice. He pulled some smudged, crumpled sheets from his jacket pocket. Oh no, I thought, the idiot is walking right into their trap. I think I shut my eyes out of sheer sympathetic embarrassment. There's a time for reciting poems and a time for fists. As far as I was concerned, this was the latter. But as I was saying, I closed my eyes, and I heard Lima clear his throat, then I heard the somewhat uncomfortable silence (if it's possible to hear such a thing, which I doubt) that settled around him, and finally I heard his voice, reading the best poem I'd ever heard. Then Arturo Belano got up and said that they were looking for poets who would like to contribute to the magazine that the visceral realists were putting out. Everybody wished they could volunteer, but after the fight they felt sheepish and no one said a thing. When the workshop ended (later than usual), I went with Lima and Belano to the bus stop. It was too late. There were no more buses, so we decided to take a *pesero* together to Reforma, and from there we walked to a bar on Calle Bucareli, where we sat until very late, talking about poetry.

I still don't really get it. In one sense, the name of the group is a joke. At the same time, it's completely in earnest. Many years ago there was a Mexican avant-garde group called the visceral realists, I think, but I don't know whether they were writers or painters or journalists or revolutionaries. They were active in the twenties or maybe the thirties, I'm not quite sure about that either. I'd obviously never heard of the group, but my ignorance in literary matters is to blame for that (every book in the world is out there waiting to be read by me). According to Arturo Belano, the visceral realists vanished in the Sonora desert. Then Belano and Lima mentioned somebody called Cesárea Tinajero or Tinaja, I can't remember which (I think it was when I was shouting to the waiter to bring us some beers), and they talked about the Comte de Lautréamont's *Poems*, something in the *Poems* that had to do with this Tinajero woman, and then Lima made a mysterious claim. According to him, the present-day visceral realists walked backward. What do you mean, backward? I asked.

"Backward, gazing at a point in the distance, but moving away from it, walking straight toward the unknown."

I said I thought this sounded like the perfect way to walk. The truth was I had no idea what he was talking about. If you stop and think about it, it's no way to walk at all.

Other poets showed up later on. Some were visceral realists, others weren't. It was total pandemonium. At first I worried that Belano and Lima were so busy talking to every freak who came up to our table that they'd forgotten all about me, but as day began to dawn, they asked me to join the gang. They didn't say "group" or "movement," they said "gang." I liked that. I said yes, of course. It was all very simple. Belano shook my hand and told me that I was one of them now, and then we sang a *ranchera*. That was all. The song was about the lost towns of the north and a woman's eyes. Before I went outside to throw up, I asked them whether the eyes were Cesárea Tinajero's. Belano and Lima looked at me and said that I was clearly a visceral realist already and that together we would change Latin American poetry. At six in the morning I took another *pesero*, this time by myself, which brought me to Colonia Lindavista, where I live. Today I didn't go to class. I spent the whole day in my room writing poems.


NOVEMBER 4

I went back to the bar on Bucareli, but the visceral realists never showed up. While I was waiting for them, I spent my time reading and writing. The regulars, a group of silent, pretty grisly-looking drunks, never once took their eyes off me.

Results of five hours of waiting: four beers, four tequilas, a plate of tortilla *sopes* that I didn't finish (they were half spoiled), a cover-to-cover reading of Álamo's latest book of poems (which I only brought so I could

7

make fun of Álamo with my new friends), seven texts written in the style of Ulises Lima, or rather, in the style of the one poem I'd read, or really just heard. The first one was about the *sopes*, which smelled of the grave; the second was about the university: I saw it in ruins; the third was about the university (me running naked in the middle of a crowd of zombies); the fourth was about the moon over Mexico City; the fifth about a dead singer; the sixth about a secret community living in the sewers of Chapultepec; and the seventh about a lost book and friendship. Those were the results, plus a physical and spiritual sense of loneliness.

A couple of drunks tried to bother me, but young as I may be, I can take care of myself. A waitress (I found out her name is Brígida; she said she remembered me from the other night with Belano and Lima) stroked my hair. She did it absentmindedly, as she went by to wait on another table. Afterward she sat with me for a while and hinted that my hair was too long. She was nice, but I decided it was better not to respond. At three in the morning I went home. Still no visceral realists. Will I ever see them again?

NOVEMBER 5

No news of my friends. I haven't been to class in two days. And I don't plan to go back to Álamo's workshop either. This afternoon I was at the Encrucijada Veracruzana again (the bar on Bucareli), but no sign of the visceral realists. It's funny the way a place like that changes from afternoon to night or even morning. You'd think it was a completely different bar. This afternoon it seemed much filthier than it really is. The grisly night crowd hadn't shown up yet, and the clientele was—how should I put it—more furtive, less mysterious, and more peaceable. Three low-level office workers, probably civil servants, completely drunk; a street vendor who'd sold all his sea turtle eggs, standing next to his empty basket; two high school students; a gray-haired man sitting at a table eating enchiladas. The waitresses were different too. I didn't recognize the three who were on duty today, although one of them came right up to me and said: you must be the poet. This flustered me. Still, I was flattered, I have to admit.

"Yes, I'm a poet, but how did you know?"

"Brígida told me about you."

Brígida, the waitress!

"And what did she tell you?" I asked, not daring to use the informal *tú* with her yet.

"That you wrote some very pretty poems."

"There's no way she could know that. She's never read any of my work," I said, blushing a little, but increasingly satisfied by the turn the conversation was taking. It also occurred to me that Brígida might have read some of my poems—over my shoulder! That I didn't like so much.

The waitress (her name was Rosario) asked me to do her a favor. I should have said, "It depends," as my uncle had taught me (to the point of exhaustion), but that's not the way I am. All right, then, I said, what?

"I'd like you to write me a poem," she said.

"Consider it done. One of these days I promise you I will," I said, using *tú* with her for the first time and finally getting up the courage to order another tequila.

"It's on me," she said. "But you have to write it now."

I tried to explain you can't just write a poem that way, on the spot.

"Anyway, what's the hurry?"

Her explanation was somewhat vague; it seemed to involve a promise made to the Virgen de Guadalupe, something to do with the health of someone, a very dear and longed-for family member who had disappeared and come back again. But what did a poem have to do with all that? It occurred to me that I'd had too much to drink and hadn't eaten in hours, and I wondered whether the alcohol and hunger must be starting to disconnect me from reality. But then I decided it didn't matter. If I'm remembering right (though I wouldn't stake my life on it), it so happens that one of the visceral realists' basic poetry-writing tenets is a momentary disconnection from a certain kind of reality. Anyway, the bar had emptied out, so the other two waitresses drifted over to my table and then I was surrounded, in what seemed (and actually was) an innocent position but which to some uninformed spectator—a policeman, for example—might not have looked that way: a student sitting with three women standing around him, one of them brushing his left arm and shoulder with her right hip, the other two with their thighs pressed against the edge of the table (an edge that would surely leave a mark on those thighs), carrying on an innocent literary conversation, but a conversation that might look like something else entirely if you saw it from

9

the doorway. Like a pimp in conference with his charges. Like a sex-crazed student refusing to be seduced.

I decided to get out while I still could, and doing my best to stand up, I paid, sent my regards to Brígida, and left. When I stepped outside the sun was blinding.

## NOVEMBER 6

Cut class again today. I got up early and caught the UNAM bus, but I got off at an earlier stop and spent the rest of the morning wandering around downtown. First I went into the Librería del Sótano and bought a book by Pierre Louys, then I crossed Júarez, bought a ham sandwich, and went to read and eat on a bench in the Alameda. Reading Louys's story, plus looking at the illustrations, gave me a colossal hard-on. I tried to get up and go someplace else, but with my dick in the state it was in, I couldn't walk without attracting attention and scandalizing not just whoever passed by but pedestrians in general. So I sat down again, closed the book, and brushed the crumbs off my jacket and pants. For a long time I watched something I thought was a squirrel climbing stealthily through the branches of a tree. After ten minutes (more or less), I realized that it wasn't a squirrel at all—it was a rat. An enormous rat! The discovery filled me with sadness. There I was, unable to move, and twenty yards away, clinging tightly to a branch, was a starving, scavenging rat, in search of birds' eggs, or crumbs swept by the wind up to the treetops (unlikely), or whatever it was he was looking for. Anguish choked me, and I felt sick. Before I could throw up, I got up and ran away. After five minutes of brisk walking, my erection had disappeared.

I spent the evening on Calle Corazón (the street one block over from mine), watching a soccer game. The people playing were my childhood friends, although *friends* is maybe too strong a word. Mostly they're still in high school but some have left school and gone to work with their parents or don't do anything. When I started college, the gulf between us suddenly deepened and now it's as if we're from different planets. I asked if I could play. The light on Calle Corazón isn't very good, and you could hardly see the ball. Also, every once in a while cars would go by and we'd have to stop. I got kicked twice and slammed once in the face with the ball. Enough. I'll read a little more Pierre Louys and then turn out the light.

10

## NOVEMBER 7

There are fourteen million people living in Mexico City. I'll never see the visceral realists again. And I'll never go back to the university or to Álamo's workshop either. I don't know what I'm going to tell my aunt and uncle. I finished *Aphrodite*, the book by Louys, and now I'm reading the dead Mexican poets, my future colleagues.

## NOVEMBER 8

I've discovered an amazing poem. They never said anything about its author, Efrén Rebolledo (1877–1929), in any of our literature classes. I'll copy it here:

### The Vampire
Whirling your deep and gloomy tresses pour
over your candid body like a torrent,
and on the shadowy and curling flood
I strew the fiery roses of my kisses.

As I unlock the tight rings
I feel the light chill chafing of your hand,
and a great shudder courses over me
and penetrates me to the very bone.

Your chaotic and disdainful eyes
glitter like stars when they hear the sigh
that from my vitals issues rendingly,

and you, thirsting, as I agonize,
assume the form of an implacable
black vampire battening on my burning blood.

The first time I read it (a few hours ago), I couldn't help locking myself in my room and masturbating as I recited it once, twice, three times, as many as ten or fifteen times, imagining Rosario, the waitress, on all fours above me, asking me to write a poem for her long-lost beloved relative or begging me to pound her on the bed with my throbbing cock.

Now that I've gotten that over with, I've had some time to think about the poem.

There can be no doubt, I think, about the meaning of "deep and gloomy tresses." The same isn't true of the first line of the second stanza: "As I unlock the tight rings," which could refer to the "deep and gloomy tresses" and to drawing them out or untangling them one by one, but the verb *unlock* might conceal a different meaning.

"The tight rings" isn't very clear either. Does it mean curls of pubic hair, the vampire's curly tresses, or the human orifices—*plural*? I.e., is he *sodomizing* her? I think I'm still haunted by my reading of Pierre Louÿs.

NOVEMBER 9

I've decided to go back to the Encrucijada Veracruzana, not because I expect to find the visceral realists there, but to see Rosario. I've written a few lines for her. I talk about her eyes and the endless Mexican horizon, about abandoned churches and mirages over the roads that lead to the border. I don't know why, but somehow I got the idea that Rosario is from Veracruz or Tabasco, possibly even Yucatán. Maybe she mentioned it, although I may have just made it up. Or maybe the name of the bar confused me, and Rosario isn't from Veracruz or Yucatán at all. Maybe she's from Mexico City. Anyway, I thought that some poetry evoking lands that are the diametric opposite of hers (assuming she is from Veracruz, which seems more and more unlikely) would be more promising, at least as far as my intentions are concerned. After that, whatever happens will happen.

This morning I wandered around downtown thinking about my life. The future doesn't exactly look bright, especially if I keep cutting class. But what really worries me is my sexual education. I can't spend my whole life jerking off. (I'm worried about my poetic education too, but one thing at a time.) Could Rosario have a boyfriend? If she does have a boyfriend, what if he's jealous and possessive? She's too young to be married, but you never know. I think she likes me; that much is clear.

NOVEMBER 10

I found the visceral realists. Rosario is from Veracruz. All the visceral realists gave me their respective addresses, and I gave them all mine. They meet at Café Quito, on Bucareli, a little past the Encrucijada, and at

12

María Font's house, in Colonia Condesa, or at the painter Catalina O'Hara's house, in Colonia Coyoacán. (María Font, Catalina O'Hara, such evocative names—but what is it they evoke?)

As for the rest of it, everything went fine, although it almost ended in tragedy.

Here's what happened: I got to the Encrucijada at eight. The bar was packed, the crowd grim and grisly beyond belief. In a corner there was actually a blind man playing the accordion and singing. All the same, I elbowed my way into the first opening I spotted at the bar. Rosario wasn't there. When I asked the girl behind the bar where Rosario was, she acted as if the question were somehow fickle, flighty, presuming. But she was smiling, as if she didn't think that was so bad. Honestly, I had no idea what she was trying to get at. Then I asked her where Rosario was from, and she told me that she was from Veracruz. I asked her where she was from too. From here, from Mexico City, she said. What about you? I'm a cowboy from Sonora, I said. I'm not sure why, it just popped out. In real life, I've never been to Sonora. She laughed, and we might have kept talking for a while, but she had to go wait on a table. But Brígida was there, and when I was on my second tequila, she came over and asked me how I was. Brígida is a woman with a frowning, melancholy, offended look. I remembered her differently, but I'd been drunk the time before, and this time I wasn't. Brígida, I said, how's it going, long time no see. I was trying to seem friendly, even cheerful, though I can't say I felt that way exactly. Brígida took my hand and pressed it to her heart, which made me jump, and my first impulse was to back away from the bar, maybe even just take off, but I restrained myself.

"Do you feel it?" she said.

"What?"

"My heart, you idiot, can't you feel it beating?"

With my fingertips I explored as much territory as I could: Brígida's linen blouse and her breasts, framed by a bra that seemed too small to contain them. But no trace of a heartbeat.

"I don't feel anything," I said with a smile.

"My heart, bonehead, can't you hear it beating, can't you feel it slowly breaking?"

"I'm sorry, I can't hear anything."

"How do you expect to hear anything with your hand, lamebrain, I'm just asking whether you feel it. Don't your fingers feel anything?"

13

"Honestly . . . no."

"Your hand is icy," said Brígida. "Such pretty fingers. It's obvious you've never had to work."

I felt watched, scrutinized, bored into. The grisly drunks at the bar had taken an interest in Brígida's last remark. Preferring not to confront them just yet, I announced that she was wrong, that of course I had to work to pay my tuition. Now Brígida was gripping my hand as if she were about to read my palm. That interested me, and I forgot about the potential spectators.

"Don't be cagey," she said. "You don't have to lie to me, I know you. You're rich and spoiled, but you're very ambitious. And lucky. You'll go as far as you want to go. Although here I see that you'll lose your way several times, and it'll be your own fault, because you don't know what you want. You need a girl to stand by you in good times and bad. Am I wrong?"

"No, that's perfect, keep going, keep going."

"Not here," said Brígida. "There's no reason these nosy bastards should hear your fortune, is there?"

For the first time I dared to take a good look around. Four or five grisly drunks were still hanging on Brígida's words, one of them even staring at my hand with unnatural intensity, as if it were his own. I smiled at all of them, not wanting to upset them, trying to let them know this had nothing to do with me. Brígida pinched the back of my hand. Her eyes were burning, as if she were about to start a fight or burst into tears.

"We can't talk here, follow me."

I watched her whisper to one of the waitresses, then she beckoned to me. The Encrucijada Veracruzana was full, and a cloud of smoke and the music of the blind man's accordion rose over the heads of the regulars. I looked at the clock. It was almost twelve; time is flying, I thought.

I followed her.

We went into a kind of long, narrow storage room piled with cartons of bottles and cleaning supplies for the bar (detergent, brooms, bleach, a squeegee, a collection of rubber gloves). At the back stood a table and two chairs. Brígida motioned me toward one of them. I sat down. The table was round and its surface was covered with gouges and names, mainly illegible. The waitress remained standing, less than an inch from me, watchful as a goddess or a bird of prey. Maybe she was waiting for

14

me to ask her to sit. Touched by her shyness, I did. To my surprise, she proceeded to sit on my lap. The situation was uncomfortable and yet in a few seconds I realized with horror that my instincts, taking leave of my mind, my soul, and even my most shameful wishes, were stiffening my dick to the point that it was impossible to hide. Brígida surely noticed the state I was in, because she got up and, after studying me again from above, offered me a blow job.

"What . . ." I said.

"A blow job, do you want me to give you a blow job?"

I looked at her blankly, although the truth, like a lone and flagging swimmer, was gradually making some headway in the black sea of my ignorance. She stared back at me. Her eyes were hard and flat. And there was something about her that distinguished her from every other human being I'd known up until then: she always (wherever you were, whatever the circumstances, no matter what was happening) looked you straight in the eye. Brígida's gaze, I decided then, could be unbearable.

"I don't know what you're talking about," I said.

"Baby, I'm talking about sucking your dick."

I didn't have time to reply, which was probably all for the best. Without taking her eyes off me, Brígida kneeled down, unzipped my pants, and took my cock in her mouth. First the head, which she nibbled, the bites no less disturbing for being light, and then, showing no signs of choking, the whole penis. At the same time, she ran her right hand over my lower abdomen, stomach, and chest, slapping me hard at regular intervals and giving me bruises I still have. The pain probably helped make the pleasure I felt even more exquisite, but it also prevented me from coming. Every so often, Brígida would lift her eyes from her work, although without releasing my member, and search for my eyes. Then I would close my own and mentally recite random lines from the poem "The Vampire," which later, when I reviewed the incident, turned out not to be lines from "The Vampire" at all, but an unholy mixture of poetry from different sources, my uncle's pronouncements, childhood memories, the faces of actresses I loved in puberty (Angélica María's face in black and white, for example), a whirlwind of spinning scenes. At first I tried to shield myself from the slaps, but once I realized that my efforts were futile, my hands went to Brígida's hair (dyed a light chestnut color and not very clean, as I discovered) and her ears, which were small and fleshy but almost unnaturally tough, as if they weren't made of flesh and blood at all, only cartilage or plastic, or no: barely tempered metal, from which hung two big fake silver hoops.

When the end was near, and in order not to cry out I had raised my fists and was shaking them at some invisible being slithering along the walls of the storage room, the door opened suddenly (but silently), and a waitress's head appeared, a terse warning issuing from her lips:

"Look out!"

Brígida immediately abandoned her task. She got up, looked me in the eyes with an expression of great suffering, and then, pulling me by the jacket, led me to a door I hadn't noticed before.

"See you next time, baby," she said, her voice much throatier than usual, as she pushed me through the door.

Suddenly, I found myself in the toilets of the Encrucijada Veracruzana, a long, gloomy, rectangular room. I stumbled around a little, still dazed by how quickly things had just happened. It smelled like disinfectant and the floor was wet, and partly flooded. The lighting was dim to nonexistent. Between two chipped sinks, I saw a mirror, and glancing sideways at myself, I caught an image in the mercury that made my hair stand on end. In silence, and trying not to splash in the rivulet that I'd just noticed trickling from one of the stalls, I turned back to the mirror, drawn by curiosity. The mirror revealed a cuneiform face, dark red and beaded with sweat. I sprang backward and almost fell. There was someone in one of the toilets. I heard him mutter, swear. One of the regulars, I assumed. Then someone called me by my name:

"Poet García Madero."

I saw two shadows next to the urinals. They were enveloped in a cloud of smoke. Two queers, I thought. Two queers who know my name?

"Poet García Madero. Come closer, man."

Although logic and prudence urged me to find the door and leave the Encrucijada without further delay, what I did was take two steps toward the smoke. Two pairs of bright eyes were watching me, like the eyes of wolves in a gale (poetic license: I've never seen a wolf; I have seen gales, though, and they didn't really go with the mantle of smoke that enveloped the two strangers). I heard them laugh. Hee hee hee. There was a smell of marijuana. I relaxed.

"Poet García Madero, your thing is hanging out."

"What?"

"Hee hee hee."

"Your penis . . . It's hanging out."

I patted my fly. It was true. I'd been so flustered I really had forgotten to tuck myself back in. I blushed, and thought about telling them to go fuck themselves, but I contained myself, fixed my pants, and took a step in their direction. They looked familiar, and I tried to pierce the surrounding darkness and decipher their faces. No luck.

Then a hand, followed by an arm, emerged from the globe of smoke around them. The hand offered me the end of a joint.

"I don't smoke," I said.

"It's weed, poet García Madero. Acapulco Gold."

I shook my head.

"I don't like it," I said.

I was startled by a noise in the room next door. Somebody's voice was raised. A man's. Then someone shouted. A woman. Brígida. I was sure the owner of the bar was hitting her and I wanted to come to her defense, although the truth is I didn't care all that much about Brígida (I didn't care about her at all, really). Just as I was turning back toward the door, the strangers' hands grabbed me. Then I saw their faces emerge from the smoke. It was Ulises Lima and Arturo Belano.

I sighed with relief, I almost burst into applause; I told them that I had been looking for them for days. Then I made another attempt to come to the aid of the shouting woman, but they wouldn't let me.

"Don't make trouble for yourself, those two are always at it," said Belano.

"Who?"

"The waitress and her boss."

"But he's hitting her," I said. The slaps were clearly audible now. "We can't just let him hit her."

"Ah, García Madero, what a poet," said Ulises Lima.

"You're right, we *couldn't* let him hit her," said Belano, "but things aren't always the way they sound. Trust me."

Clearly they knew all about the Encrucijada, and I would have liked to ask them some questions, but I didn't want to seem indiscreet.

When I came out of the toilets, the light of the bar hurt my eyes. Everybody was talking at the top of their lungs. Some people were singing along to the blind man's song, a *bolero*, or what sounded to me like a *bolero*, about a desperate love, a love that time could never heal, although with the passage of the years it became more humiliating, more

17

pathetic, more terrible. Lima and Belano were carrying three books apiece, and they looked like students, like me. Before we left, we went up to the bar, shoulder to shoulder, and ordered three tequilas which we downed in a single gulp, and then we went out into the street, laughing. As we left the Encrucijada, I looked back for the last time in the vain hope of seeing Brígida appear in the doorway to the storage room, but she wasn't there.

Ulises Lima's books were:

*Manifeste électrique aux paupieres de jupes,* by Michel Bulteau, Matthieu Messagier, Jean-Jacques Faussot, Jean-Jacques Nguyen That, and Gyl Bert-Ram-Soutrenom F.M., and other poets of the Electric Movement, our French counterparts (I think).

*Sang de satin,* by Michel Bulteau.

*Nord d'été naître opaque,* by Matthieu Messagier.

The books Arturo Belano was carrying were:

*Le parfait criminel,* by Alain Jouffroy.

*Le pays où tout est permis,* by Sophie Podolski.

*Cent mille milliards de poèmes,* by Raymond Queneau. (The Queneau was a photocopy, and the way it had been folded, in addition to the wear and tear of too much handling, had turned it into a kind of startled paper flower, its petals splayed toward the four points of the compass.)

Later we met up with Ernesto San Epifanio, who was also carrying three books. I asked him to let me make a note of them. They were:

*Little Johnny's Confession,* by Brian Patten.

*Tonight at Noon,* by Adrian Henri.

*The Lost Fire Brigade,* by Spike Hawkins.


NOVEMBER 11

Ulises Lima lives in a room on a roof on Calle Anáhuac, near Insurgentes. It's a tiny place, ten feet by eight, with books piled up everywhere. Through the only window, as small as a porthole, you can see the neighboring rooftops, where human sacrifices are still performed, according to Ulises Lima, who got it from Monsiváis. In the room there's only a thin mattress on the floor, which Lima rolls up during the day or when he has visitors and uses as a sofa; there's also a tiny table, its entire top taken up by a typewriter, and a single chair. Visitors, obviously, have to sit on the mattress or the floor or just stand. Today there were five of us: Lima, Belano, Rafael Barrios, and Jacinto Requena. Belano took the chair, Barrios and Requena the mattress, Lima stood the whole time (sometimes pacing around the room), and I sat on the floor.

We talked about poetry. No one has read any of my poems, and yet they all treat me like one of them. The camaraderie is immediate and incredible!

Around nine, Felipe Müller showed up; he's nineteen, so until I came along he was the youngest in the group. Then we all went to eat at a Chinese café, and we walked and talked about literature until three in the morning. We were all in complete agreement that Mexican poetry must be transformed. Our situation (as far as I could understand) is unsustainable, trapped as we are between the reign of Octavio Paz and the reign of Pablo Neruda. In other words, between a rock and a hard place.

I asked where I could buy the books they'd had with them the other night. The answer came as no surprise: they steal them from the Librería Francesa in the Zona Rosa and from the Librería Baudelaire on Calle General Martínez, near Calle Horacio, in Polanco. I also asked about the authors, and one after another (what one visceral realist reads is soon read by the rest of the group) they filled me in on the life and works of the Electrics, Raymond Queneau, Sophie Podolski, and Alain Jouffroy.

Felipe Müller asked if I could read French. He sounded a tiny bit annoyed. I told him that with a dictionary I could get along all right. Later I asked him the same question. You read French, don't you, *mano?* He answered in the negative.

NOVEMBER 12

Ran into Jacinto Requena, Rafael Barrios, and Pancho Rodríguez at Café Quito. I saw them come in around nine and motioned them over to my table, where I had just spent three good hours writing and reading. They introduced me to Pancho Rodríguez. He's as short as Barrios, and has the face of a twelve-year-old, even though he's actually twenty-two. It was almost inevitable that we'd like each other. Pancho Rodríguez never stops talking. Thanks to him I found out that before Belano and Müller showed up (they came to Mexico City after the Pinochet coup, so they weren't part of the original group), Ulises Lima had published a magazine with poems by María Font, Angélica Font, Laura Damián, Barrios, San Epifanio, some guy called Marcelo Robles I'd never heard of, and the Rodríguez brothers, Pancho and Moctezuma. According to Pancho, Pancho himself is one of the two best young Mexican poets, and the other one is Ulises Lima, who Pancho says is his best friend. The magazine (two issues, both from 1974) was called *Lee Harvey Oswald* and was bankrolled entirely by Lima. Requena (who wasn't part of the group back then) and Barrios confirmed everything Pancho Rodríguez said. That was how visceral realism started, said Barrios. Pancho Rodríguez thought otherwise. According to him, *Lee Harvey Oswald* should have continued. It folded just as it was taking off, he said, just as people were starting to know who we were. What people? Well, other poets, of course, literature students, and the poetry-writing girls who came each week to the hundred workshops blossoming like flowers in Mexico City. Barrios and Requena disagreed about the magazine, even though they both looked back on it with nostalgia.

"Are there a lot of poetesses?"

"It's lame to call them poetesses," said Pancho.

"You're supposed to call them poets," said Barrios.

"But are there lots of them?"

"Like never before in the history of Mexico," said Pancho. "Lift a stone and you'll find a girl writing about her little life."

"So how could Lima finance *Lee Harvey Oswald* all by himself?" I said.

I thought it prudent not to insist just then on the subject of poetesses.

"Oh, poet García Madero, Ulises Lima is the kind of guy who'll do anything for poetry," said Barrios dreamily.

Then we talked about the name of the magazine, which I thought was brilliant.

"Let's see if I understand. Poets, according to Ulises Lima, are like Lee Harvey Oswald. Is that it?"

"More or less," said Pancho Rodríguez. "I suggested that he should call it *Los bastardos de Sor Juana*, which sounds more Mexican, but our friend is crazy about anything to do with gringos."

"Actually, Ulises thought there was already a publishing house with the same name, but he was wrong, and when he realized his mistake he decided to use the name for his magazine," said Barrios.

"What publishing house?"

"P.-J. Oswald, in Paris, the place that published a book by Matthieu Messagier."

"And that dumbass Ulises thought that the French publishing house was named for the assassin. But it was P.-J. Oswald, not L. H. Oswald, and one day he realized and decided to take the name."

"The French guy's name must be Pierre-Jacques," said Requena.

"Or Paul-Jean Oswald."

"Does his family have money?" I asked.

"No, Ulises's family doesn't have money," said Requena. "Actually, the only family he has is his mother, right? Or at least I've never heard of anyone else."

"I know his whole family," said Pancho. "I knew Ulises Lima long before any of you, long before Belano, and his mother is the only family he has. He's broke, that I can promise you."

"Then how could he finance two issues of a magazine?"

"Selling weed," said Pancho. The other two were quiet, but they didn't deny it.

"I can't believe it," I said.

"Well, it's true. The money comes from marijuana."

"Shit."

"He goes and gets it in Acapulco and then he delivers it to his clients in Mexico City."

"Shut up, Pancho," said Barrios.

"Why should I shut up? The kid's a fucking visceral realist, isn't he? So why do I have to shut up?"

NOVEMBER 13

I spent all of today following Lima and Belano. We walked, took the subway, buses, a *pesero*, walked some more, and the whole time we never stopped talking. Sometimes they'd go into houses, and then I had to wait outside for them. When I asked what they were doing they told me that they were taking a survey. But I think they're making deliveries of marijuana. Along the way I read them the latest poems I'd written, eleven or twelve of them. I think they liked them.

NOVEMBER 14

Today I went with Pancho Rodríguez to the Font sisters' house.

I'd been at Café Quito for four hours, I'd already had three cups of coffee, and I was losing my appetite for reading and writing when Pancho showed up and invited me to come with him. I leaped at the invitation.

The Fonts live in Colonia Condesa, in a beautiful two-story house on Calle Colima, with a front yard and a courtyard in back. The front is nothing special, just a few stunted trees and some ragged grass, but the courtyard is another story: the trees are big, and there are enormous plants with leaves so intensely green they look black, a small tiled pool that can't quite be called a fountain (there are no fish in it, but there is a battery-powered submarine, property of Jorgito Font, the youngest brother), and a little outbuilding completely separate from the big house. At one time it was probably a carriage house or stables and now it's where the Font sisters live. Before we got there, Pancho gave me a heads-up:

"Angélica's father is kind of nuts. If you see something strange, don't be scared, just do whatever I do and act like nothing's happening. If he starts to make trouble, don't worry. We'll take him down."

"Take him down?" I wasn't quite sure what he meant. "The two of us? In his own house?"

"His wife would be eternally grateful. The guy's a total headcase. A year or so ago he spent time in the bin. But don't repeat that to the Font sisters. Or if you do, don't say you heard it from me."

"So he's crazy," I said.

"Crazy and broke. Until recently they had two cars and three servants, and they were always throwing these big parties. But somehow he blew a fuse, poor fucker, and just lost it. Now he's ruined."

"But it must cost money to keep up this house."

"They own it. It's all they've got left."

"What did Mr. Font do before he went crazy?" I said.

"He was an architect, but not a very good one. He designed the two issues of *Lee Harvey Oswald*."

"No shit."

When we rang the bell, a bald man with a mustache and a deranged look came to let us in.

"That's Angélica's father," Pancho whispered to me.

"I figured," I said.

The man came striding up to the gate, fixing us with a look of intense hatred. I was happy to be on the other side of the bars. After hesitating for a few seconds, as if he wasn't sure what to do, he opened the gate and charged. I jumped back, but Pablo spread his arms wide and greeted him effusively. The man stopped then and extended an unsteady hand before he let us through. Pancho walked briskly around the house to the back, and I followed him. Mr. Font went back inside, talking to himself. As we headed down a flower-filled outside passageway between the front and back gardens, Pancho explained that another reason for poor Mr. Font's agitation was his daughter Angélica:

"María has already lost her virginity," said Pancho, "but Angélica hasn't yet, although she's about to, and the old man knows it and it drives him crazy."

"How does he know?"

"One of the mysteries of fatherhood, I guess. Anyway, he spends all day wondering which son of a bitch will deflower his daughter, and it's just too much for one man to bear. Deep down, I understand him; if I were in his shoes I'd feel the same."

"But does he have someone in mind or does he suspect everyone?"

"He suspects everyone, of course, although two or three are out of the running: the queers and her sister. The old man isn't stupid."

None of it made any sense.

"Last year Angélica won the Laura Damián poetry prize, you know, when she was only sixteen."

I'd never heard of the prize in my life. According to what Pancho told me later, Laura Damián was a poetess who died before she turned twenty, in 1972, and her parents had established a prize in her memory. According to Pancho, the prize was very highly regarded "among the true elite." I gave him a look, as if to ask what kind of an idiot he was, but Pancho didn't notice. He seemed to be waiting for something. Then he raised his eyes skyward and I thought I noticed a curtain move in one of the windows on the second floor. Maybe it was just the breeze, but I felt watched until I crossed the threshold of the Font sisters' little house.

Only María was home.

María is tall and dark, with very straight black hair, a straight (absolutely straight) nose, and thin lips. She looks like a nice person, though it's not hard to see that her rages might be long and terrible. We found her standing in the middle of the room, practicing dance steps, reading Sor Juana Inés de la Cruz, listening to a Billie Holiday record, and absentmindedly painting a watercolor of two women holding hands at the foot of a volcano, surrounded by streams of lava. She received us coldly at first, as if Pancho's presence annoyed her and she was only putting up with him for her sister's sake and because, in all fairness, the little house in the courtyard wasn't hers alone but belonged to both of them. She didn't even look at me.

To make matters worse, I managed to make a banal remark about Sor Juana that prejudiced her against me even more (a clumsy allusion to the celebrated lines "Misguided men, who will chastise / a woman when no blame is due, / oblivious that it is you / who prompted what you criticize") and that I made worse when I tried again by reciting, "Stay, shadow of contentment too short-lived, / illusion of enchantment I most prize, / fair image for whom happily I die, / sweet fiction for whom painfully I live."

So suddenly there we were, the three of us, sunk in timid or sullen silence, and María Font wouldn't even look at Pancho and me, although sometimes I looked at her or the watercolor (or to be more precise, stole glances at her and the watercolor), and Pancho Rodríguez, who seemed completely unaffected by María's hostility or her father's, was looking at the books, whistling a song that as far as I could tell had nothing to do with what Billie Holiday was singing, until at last Angélica appeared, and then I understood Pancho (he was one of the men who wanted to deflower Angélica!), and I almost understood Mr. Font, although to be honest, virginity doesn't mean much to me. (I'm a virgin myself, after all, unless Brígida's fellatio *interrupta* is considered a deflowering. But is that making love with a woman? Wouldn't I have had to simultaneously lick her pussy to say that we'd actually made love? To stop being a virgin, does it only count if a man sticks his dick into a woman's vagina, not her mouth, her ass, or her armpit? To say that I've really made love, do I have to have ejaculated? It's all so complicated.)

But as I was saying, Angélica appeared, and to judge by the way she greeted Pancho, it was clear (to me at least) that he had some romantic possibilities with the prize-winning poet. As soon as he introduced me, I was ignored again.

The two of them set up a screen that divided the room in two, and then they sat on the bed and I could hear them whispering to each other.

I went over to María and said a few things about how good her watercolor was. She didn't even look up. I tried another tactic: I talked about visceral realism and Ulises Lima and Arturo Belano. I also analyzed (intrepidly: the whispers on the other side of the screen were making me more and more nervous) the watercolor before me as a visceral realist work. María Font looked at me for the first time and smiled:

"I don't give a shit about the visceral realists."

"But I thought you were part of the group. The movement, I mean."

"Are you kidding? Maybe if they'd chosen a less disgusting name . . . I'm a vegetarian. Anything to do with viscera makes me sick."

"What would you have called it?"

"Oh, I don't know. The Mexican Section of Surrealists, maybe."

"I think there already is a Mexican Section of Surrealists in Cuernavaca. Anyway, what we're trying to do is create a movement on a Latin American scale."

"On a Latin American scale? Please."

"Well, that's what we want in the long term, if I understand it correctly."

"Who *are* you, anyway?"

"I'm a friend of Lima and Belano."

"So why haven't I ever seen you around here?"

"I only met them a little while ago . . ."

"You're the kid from Álamo's workshop, aren't you?"

I turned red, although really I don't know why. I admitted that we had met there.

"So there's already a Mexican Section of Surrealists in Cuernavaca," said María thoughtfully. "Maybe I should go live in Cuernavaca."

"I read about it in the *Excelsior*. It's some old men who paint. A group of tourists, I think."

"Leonora Carrington lives in Cuernavaca," said María. "You're not talking about her, are you?"

"Um, no," I said. I have no idea who Leonora Carrington is.

Then we heard a moan. It wasn't a moan of pleasure, I could tell that right away, but a moan of pain. It occurred to me then that it had been a while since we heard anything from behind the screen.

"Are you all right, Angélica?" said María.

"Of course I'm all right. Go take a walk please, and take that guy with you," responded the muffled voice of Angélica Font.

In a gesture of annoyance and boredom, María threw her paintbrushes onto the floor. From the paint marks on the tiles, I could tell that it wasn't the first time her sister had requested a little privacy.

"Come with me."

I followed her to a secluded corner of the courtyard, beside a high wall covered in vines, where there was a table and five metal chairs.

"Do you think they're . . . ?" I said, and immediately I regretted my curiosity, which I'd hoped she'd share. Luckily, María was too angry to pay much attention to me.

"Fucking? No way."

For a while we sat in silence. María drummed her fingers on the table, and I crossed and recrossed my legs a few times and busied myself studying the plants in the courtyard.

"All right, what are you waiting for? Read me your poems," she said.

I read and read until one of my legs fell asleep. When I finished I was afraid to ask whether she'd liked them or not. Then María invited me into the big house for coffee.

In the kitchen, we found her mother and father, cooking. They seemed happy. She introduced me to them. Her father didn't look deranged anymore. He was actually pretty nice to me; he asked me what I was studying, how I planned to balance law and poetry, how good old Álamo was (it seems they know each other, or were childhood friends). Her mother talked about vague things that I can hardly remember: I think she mentioned a séance in Coyoacán that she'd been to recently, and the restless spirit of a 1940s *rancheras* singer. I couldn't tell whether she was joking or not.

In front of the TV we found Jorgito Font. María didn't speak to him or introduce us. He's twelve years old, has long hair, and dresses like a bum. He calls everybody *naco* or *naca*. To his mother he says no way, *naca*, no can do; to his father, *naco*, check it out; to his sister, that's my *naca* or *naca*, you're the best. To me he said hey, *naco*, what's going on?

*Nacos*, as far as I know, are urban Indians, city Indians. Jorgito must be using the word in some other sense.


NOVEMBER 15

Back at the Fonts' house today.

Things happened exactly as they did yesterday, with minor variations.

Pancho and I met at El Loto de Quintana Roo, a Chinese café near the Glorieta de Insurgentes, and after having several cups of coffee and something a little more substantial (paid for by me), we headed for Colonia Condesa.

Once again Mr. Font came to the door when we rang the bell, in the exact same state as yesterday; if anything, he was a few steps farther down the path to madness. His eyes bulged from their sockets when he accepted the cheerful hand Pancho offered him, unperturbed, and he showed no sign of recognizing me.

María was by herself in the little house in the courtyard; she was painting the same watercolor as before and in her left hand she held the same book, but it was Olga Guillot's voice, not Billie Holiday's, coming out of the record player.

Her greeting was just as cold.

Pancho, for his part, repeated the previous day's routine and took a seat in a little wicker armchair while he waited for Angélica to arrive.

This time I was careful not to make any value judgments about Sor Juana, and I occupied myself first by looking at the books and then the watercolor, standing near María but keeping a prudent distance. The watercolor had undergone significant changes. The two women beside the volcano, whom I remembered in a stern or at least serious pose, were now pinching each other's arms; one of them was laughing or pretending to laugh; the other one was crying or pretending to cry. Floating on the streams of lava (clearly lava, since it was still red or vermillion) were laundry detergent bottles, bald dolls, and wicker baskets full of rats; the women's dresses were torn or patched; in the sky (or at least in the upper part of the watercolor), a storm was brewing; in the lower part María had reproduced this morning's weather report for Mexico City.

The painting was hideous.

Then Angélica came in, glowing, and once again she and Pablo set up the screen. I spent a while thinking, as María painted: there was no longer the slightest doubt in my mind that Pancho had dragged me to the Fonts' house so that I could distract María while he and Angélica went about their business. It didn't seem very fair. Before, at the Chinese café, I'd asked him whether he considered himself a visceral realist. His reply was ambiguous and lengthy. He talked about the working class, drugs, Flores Magón, some key figures of the Mexican Revolution. Then he said that his poems would definitely appear in the magazine that Belano and Lima were putting out soon. And if they don't publish me, they can go fuck themselves, he said. I don't know why, but I get the feeling the only thing Pancho cares about is sleeping with Angélica.

"Are you all right, Angélica?" said María, when the moans of pain, exactly the same as yesterday's, began.

"Yes, yes, I'm fine. Can you go take a walk?"

"Of course," said María.

Once again we resignedly settled ourselves at the metal table under the climbing vine. For no apparent reason, my heart was broken. María started to tell me stories about their childhood, thoroughly boring stories that it was clear she was only telling to pass the time and that I pretended to find interesting. Elementary school, their first parties, high school, their shared love of poetry, dreams of traveling, of seeing other countries, *Lee Harvey Oswald*, in which they'd both been published, the Laura Damián prize that Angélica had won . . . Once she reached this point (I don't know why; possibly because she stopped talking for a minute), I asked who Laura Damián had been. It was pure intuition. María said:

"A poet who died young."

"I already know that. When she was twenty. But who was she? Why haven't I read anything by her?"

"Have you ever read Lautréamont, García Madero?" said María.

"No."

"Well, then, it's no surprise that you've never heard of Laura Damián."

"I'm sorry. I know I'm ignorant."

"That's not what I said. All I meant was that you're very young. Anyway, Laura's only book, *La fuente de las musas*, was privately published. It was a posthumous book subsidized by her parents, who loved her very much and were her first readers."

"They must have lots of money."

"Why do you think that?"

"If they're able to fund an annual poetry prize themselves, they have to have lots of money."

"Well, not really. They didn't give Angélica much. The prize is more about prestige than money. It's not even all that prestigious. After all, they only give it to poets under the age of twenty."

"The age Laura Damián was when she died. How morbid."

"It isn't morbid, it's sad."

28

"And were you there when the prize was awarded? Do the parents give it in person?"

"Of course."

"Where? At their house?"

"No, at the university."

"Which department?"

"The literature department. That's where Laura was studying."

"Jesus, that's so morbid."

"None of it seems morbid to me. If you ask me, you're the morbid one, García Madero."

"You know what? It pisses me off when you call me García Madero. It's like me calling you Font."

"Everybody calls you that, so why should I call you anything different?"

"Fine, never mind. Tell me more about Laura Damián. Didn't you ever enter the contest?"

"Yes, but Angélica won."

"And who won before Angélica?"

"A girl from Aguascalientes who studies medicine at UNAM."

"And before that?"

"Before that, no one won, because the prize didn't exist. Next year maybe I'll enter again, or maybe I won't."

"And what will you do with the money if you win?"

"Go to Europe, probably."

For a few seconds we were both silent, María Font thinking about unexplored foreign countries, while I thought about all the foreign men who would make love to her night and day. The thought startled me. Was I falling in love with María?

"How did Laura Damián die?"

"She was hit by a car in Tlalpan. She was an only child, and her parents were devastated. I think her mother even tried to commit suicide. It must be sad to die so young."

"It must be extremely sad," I said, imagining María Font in the arms of a seven-foot-tall Englishman, so white he was practically an albino, his long pink tongue between her thin lips.

"Do you know who you should ask about Laura Damián?"

"No, who?"

"Ulises Lima. He was friends with her."

"Ulises Lima?"

"Yes, they were inseparable, they were in school together, they went to the movies together, they lent each other books. They were very good friends."

"I had no idea," I said.

We heard a noise from the little house, and for a while we both sat expectantly.

"How old was Ulises Lima when Laura Damián died?"

María didn't answer for a while.

"Ulises Lima's name isn't Ulises Lima," she said in a husky voice.

"Do you mean it's his pen name?"

María nodded her head yes, her gaze lost in the intricate tracings of the vine.

"What's his real name, then?"

"Alfredo Martínez, something like that. I don't remember anymore. But when I met him he wasn't called Ulises Lima. It was Laura Damián who gave him that name."

"Wow, that's crazy."

"Everyone said that he was in love with Laura. But I don't think they ever slept together. I think Laura died a virgin."

"At twenty?"

"Sure, why not."

"No, of course, you're right."

"Sad, isn't it?"

"Yes, it is sad. And how old was Ulises, or Alfredo Martínez, then?"

"A year younger, nineteen, maybe eighteen."

"He must have taken it hard, I guess."

"He got sick. They say he was on the verge of death. The doctors didn't know what was wrong with him, just that he was fading fast. I went to see him at the hospital and I was there during the worst of it. But one day he got better and it all ended as mysteriously as it had begun. Then Ulises left the university and started his magazine. You've seen it, right?"

"*Lee Harvey Oswald*? Yes, I've seen it," I lied. Immediately I wondered why they hadn't let me have an issue, even just to leaf through, when I was in Ulises Lima's rooftop room.

"What a horrible name for a poetry magazine."

"I like it. It doesn't seem so bad to me."

"It's in terrible taste."

"What would you have called it?"

"I don't know. The Mexican Section of Surrealists, maybe."

"Interesting."

"Did you know that it was my father who laid out the whole magazine?"

"Pancho said something like that."

"It's the best part of the magazine, the design. Now everybody hates my father."

"Everybody? All the visceral realists? Why would they hate him? That doesn't make sense."

"No, not the visceral realists, the other architects in his studio. I guess they're jealous of how well he gets along with young people. Anyway, they can't stand him, and now they're making him pay. Because of the magazine."

"Because of *Lee Harvey Oswald?*"

"Of course. Since my father designed it at the studio, now they're making him responsible for anything that happens."

"But what could happen?"

"All kinds of things. Clearly you don't know Ulises Lima."

"No, I don't," I said, "but I'm getting some idea."

"He's a time bomb," said María.

Just then, I realized that it had gotten dark and that we could only hear, not see, each other.

"Listen, I have to tell you something. I just lied to you. I've never gotten my hands on the magazine, and I'm dying to take a look at it. Could you lend me a copy?"

"Of course. I'll give you one; I have extras."

"And could you lend me a book by Lautréamont too, please?"

"Yes, but that you absolutely have to return. He's one of my favorite poets."

"I promise," I said.

María went into the big house. I was left alone in the courtyard, and for a minute I couldn't believe that Mexico City was really out there. Then I heard voices in the Fonts' little house, and a light went on. I thought that it was Angélica and Pancho, and that in a little while Pancho would come out into the courtyard to find me, but nothing happened. When María returned with two copies of the magazine and the *Chants de Maldoror*, she too noticed that the lights were on in the little house, and for a few seconds she waited attentively. Suddenly, when I was least expecting it, she asked me whether I was still a virgin.

"No, of course not," I lied, for the second time that evening.

"And was it hard to lose your virginity?"

"A little," I said, after considering my response for a second.

I noticed that her voice had gotten husky again.

"Do you have a girlfriend?"

"No, of course not," I said.

"Who did you do it with, then? A prostitute?"

"No, with a girl from Sonora who I met last year," I said. "We were only together for three days."

"And you haven't done it with anyone else?"

I was tempted to tell her about my adventure with Brígida, but in the end I decided that it was better not to.

"No, nobody else," I said, and I felt so miserable I could have died.


NOVEMBER 16

I called María Font. I told her I wanted to see her. I begged her to come out. She said that she'd meet me at Café Quito. When she came in, around seven, several pairs of eyes followed her from the doorway all the way to the table where I was waiting.

She looked beautiful. She was wearing a Oaxacan blouse, very tight jeans, and leather sandals. Over her shoulder she was carrying a dark brown knapsack stamped with little cream-colored horses around the edges, full of books and papers.

I asked her to read me a poem.

"Don't be a drag, García Madero," she said.

I don't know why, but her saying that made me sad. I think I had a physical need to hear one of her poems from her own lips. But maybe it wasn't the place; Café Quito was loud with talk, shouts, shrieks of laughter. I gave her back the Lautréamont.

"You read it already?" said María.

"Of course," I said. "I stayed up all night reading. I read *Lee Harvey Oswald* too. What a great magazine, it's such a shame they had to fold. I loved your things."

"So you haven't been to bed yet?"

"Not yet, but I feel good. I'm wide awake."

María Font looked me in the eyes and smiled. A waitress came over and asked what she wanted to drink. Nothing, said María, we were just leaving. Outside, I asked whether she had somewhere to go, and she said no, she just wasn't in the mood for Café Quito. We went walking along Bucareli toward Reforma, then crossed Reforma and headed up Avenida Guerrero.

"This is where the whores are," said María.

"I didn't realize," I said.

"Give me your arm so nobody gets the wrong idea."

The truth is, at first I didn't see anything to suggest that the street was any different from those we had just been on. The traffic was heavy here too, and the people crowding the sidewalks were no different from the people streaming along Bucareli. But then (maybe because of what María had said) I started to notice some differences. To start with, the lighting. The streetlights on Bucareli are white, but on Avenida Guerrero they had more of an amber tone. The cars: on Bucareli it's unusual to find a car parked on the street; on Guerrero there were plenty. On Bucareli, the bars and coffee shops are open and bright; on Guerrero, although there were lots of bars, they seemed turned in on themselves, secret or discreet, with no big windows looking out. And finally, the music. On Bucareli there wasn't any. All the noise came from people or cars. On Guerrero, the farther in you got, especially on the corners of Violeta and Magnolia, the music took over the street, coming from bars, parked cars, and portable radios, and drifting from the lighted windows of dark buildings.

"I like this street," said María. "Someday I'm going to live here."

A group of teenage hookers was standing around an old Cadillac parked at the curb. María stopped and greeted one of them:

"Hey there, Lupe. Nice to see you."

Lupe was very thin and had short hair. I thought she was as beautiful as María.

"María! Wow, *mana*, long time no see," she said, and then she hugged her.

The girls with Lupe were still leaning on the hood of the Cadillac and their eyes rested on María, scrutinizing her calmly. They hardly looked at me.

"I thought you died," said María all of a sudden. The callousness of the remark stunned me. María's tact has these gaping holes.

"I'm plenty alive. But I almost died. Didn't I, Carmencita?"

"That's right," said the girl called Carmencita, and she continued to study María.

"It was Gloria who bit it. You met her, didn't you? *Mana*, what a fucking mess, but no one could stand that cunt."

"I never met her," said María with a smile on her lips.

"The cops are the ones who nailed her," said Carmencita.

"And has anyone done anything about it?" said María.

"*Nelson*," said Carmencita. "Do what? The bitch knew too much, she was in way over her head, there was nothing anyone could do."

"Well, how sad," said María.

"Say, how's school?" said Lupe.

"So-so," said María.

"You still got that hot stud running after you?"

María laughed and shot me a glance.

"My friend here is a ballerina," Lupe said to the other girls. "We met at Modern Dance, the school on Donceles."

"Yeah, sure," said Carmencita.

"It's true, Lupe hung out at the dance school," said María.

"So how did she end up here?" asked a girl who hadn't spoken before, the shortest one of all, almost a dwarf.

María looked at her and shrugged.

"Will you come have coffee with us?" she said.

Lupe checked the watch on her right wrist and then looked at her friends.

"The thing is, I'm working."

"Just for a little while, you'll be back soon," said María.

"All right, then. Work can wait," said Lupe. "I'll see you girls later." She started to walk with María. I walked behind them.

We turned left on Magnolia, onto Avenida Jesús García. Then we walked south again, to Héroes Revolucionarios Ferrocarrileros, where we went into a coffee shop.

"Is this the kid you've been fooling around with?" I heard Lupe say to María.

María laughed again.

"He's just a friend," she said, and to me: "If Lupe's pimp shows up here, you'll have to defend us both, García Madero."

I thought she was kidding. Then it occurred to me she might be serious and, frankly, the situation started to seem appealing. Just then I couldn't imagine a better way to look good in front of María. I felt happy. We had the whole night ahead of us.

"My man is heavy," said Lupe. "He doesn't like me to be running around with strangers." It was the first time she had looked directly at me when she spoke.

"But I'm not a stranger," said María.

"No, *mana*. Not you."

"Do you know how I met Lupe?" said María.

"I have no idea," I said.

"At the dance school. Lupe was Paco Duarte's girlfriend. Paco is the Spanish dancer who's the head of the school."

"I went to see him once a week," said Lupe.

"I didn't know you took dance lessons," I said.

"I don't. I just went there to fuck," said Lupe.

"I meant María, not you."

"Since I was fourteen," said María. "Too late to be a good ballerina. That's the way it goes."

"What do you mean? You're a great dancer! Weird, but the truth is everyone in that place is half insane. Have you seen her dance?" I said I hadn't. "You'd fall head over heels."

María shook her head to deny it. When the waitress came we ordered three coffees and Lupe also ordered a cheese sandwich, no beans.

"I can't digest them," she explained.

"How's your stomach?" said María.

"Not bad. Sometimes it hurts a lot, other times I forget it exists. It's nerves. When it gets to be too much, I just have a toke and it's fixed. So what about you? Aren't you going to the dance school anymore?"

"Not so often," said María.

"This idiot walked in on me once in Paco Duarte's office," said Lupe.

"I almost died laughing," said María. "Actually, I don't know why I started to laugh. Maybe I was in love with Paco and it was hysterics."

"Come on, *mana*, you know he wasn't your type."

"So what were you doing with this Paco Duarte?" I said.

"Nothing, really. I met him once on the street and since he couldn't come to me and I couldn't go to his house because he's married to a gringa, I'd go see him at the dance school. Anyway, I think that was what he liked, the scumbag. Fucking me in his office."

"And your pimp let you go that far out of your zone?" I said.

"My *zone*? What do you know about my *zone*? And who said I have a pimp?"

"I'm sorry, I didn't mean to offend you. It's just that a minute ago María said your pimp was the violent type, didn't she?"

"I don't have a pimp. You think just because I'm talking to you, you have the right to insult me?"

"Calm down, Lupe. No one's being insulted," said María.

"This dickhead insulted my man," said Lupe. "If he hears you he'll show you. Little punk. He'll take you down in a second. I bet you wish you could suck my man's dick."

"Hey, I'm not a homosexual."

"All of María's friends are faggots, everybody knows that."

"Lupe, leave my friends alone. When Lupe was sick," María said to me, "Ernesto and I took her to the hospital. It's amazing how quickly some people forget a favor."

"Ernesto San Epifanio?" I said.

"Yes," said María.

"Did he take dance lessons too?"

"He used to," said María.

"Oh, Ernesto, I have such good memories of him. I remember he lifted me up all by himself and put me in a taxi. Ernesto is a faggot," Lupe explained to me, "but he's strong."

"It wasn't Ernesto who got you into the taxi, stupid, it was me," said María.

"That night I thought I was going to die," said Lupe. "I was fucked up and suddenly I felt sick and I was vomiting blood. Buckets of blood. Deep down, I don't think I would have cared if I did die. I was just remembering my son and my broken promise and the Virgen de Guadalupe. I'd been drinking until the moon came up, little by little, and since I didn't feel good, that dwarf girl you saw gave me some Flexo. That was my big mistake. The cement must have gone bad or I was al-

36

ready sick, but whatever it was, I started to die on a bench on the Plaza San Fernando and that was when my friend here showed up with her partner the faggot angel."

"Lupe, you have a son?"

"My son died," said Lupe, fixing me with her gaze.

"But how old are you, then?"

Lupe smiled at me. Her smile was big and pretty. "How old do you think I am?"

I was afraid to guess, and I didn't say anything. María put her arm around Lupe's shoulders. The two of them looked at each other and smiled or winked, I'm not sure which.

"A year younger than María. Eighteen."

"We're both Leos," said María.

"What sign are you?" said Lupe.

"I don't know. I've never paid much attention to that kind of thing, to tell the truth."

"Well, then you're the only person in Mexico who doesn't know his own sign," said Lupe.

"What month were you born, García Madero?" said María.

"January, the sixth of January."

"You're a Capricorn, like Ulises Lima."

"*The* Ulises Lima?" Lupe said.

I asked her whether she knew him, afraid they would tell me that Ulises Lima went to the dance school too. For a microsecond, I saw myself dancing on tiptoe in an empty gym. But Lupe said she had only heard about him, that María and Ernesto San Epifanio talked about him a lot.

Then Lupe started to talk about her dead son. The baby was four months old when he died. He was born sick, and Lupe had promised the Virgin that she would stop working if her son recovered. She kept her promise for the first three months, and according to her the baby seemed to be getting better. But in the fourth month she had to start working again and he died. She said the Virgin took him away because she didn't keep her word. Lupe was living in a building on Paraguay at the time, near the Plaza de Santa Catarina, and she would leave the baby with an old woman who took care of him at night. One morning, when she got back, they told her that her son was dead. And that was it.

"It isn't your fault," said María. "Don't be superstitious."

"How can it not be my fault? Who broke her promise? Who said that she was going to change her life and didn't?"

"Then why didn't the Virgin kill you instead of your son?"

"The Virgin didn't kill my son," said Lupe. "She took him away, which is a whole different thing. She punished me by leaving me on my own, and she took him away to a better life."

"Oh, well, if that's how you see it, then what's the problem?"

"Of course, that solves everything," I said. "And when did you meet each other, before or after the baby?"

"After," said María, "when this girl here was running wild. Lupe, I think you wanted to die."

"If it hadn't been for Alberto, I would have called it quits," said Lupe with a sigh.

"Alberto is your . . . boyfriend, I guess," I said. "Do you know him?" I asked María, and she nodded her head yes.

"He's her pimp," said María.

"But he's got a bigger dick than your little friend," said Lupe.

"Are you referring to me?" I said.

María laughed. "Of course she's referring to you, stupid."

I turned red and then I laughed. María and Lupe laughed too.

"How big is Alberto?" said María.

"As big as his knife."

"And how big is his knife?" said María.

"Like this."

"That's ridiculous," I said, although I should have changed the subject. Trying to fix the unfixable, I said: "There aren't any knives that big." I felt worse.

"Ay, *mana*, how are you so sure about the knife thing?" said María.

"He's had the knife since he was fifteen, a hooker from La Bondojo gave it to him, some girl who died."

"But have you measured his thing with the knife or are you just guessing?"

"A knife that big gets in the way," I persisted.

"He measures it. I don't need to measure it, what do I care? He measures it himself and he measures it all the time, once a day at least, to make sure it hasn't gotten any smaller, he says."

"Is he afraid his weenie will shrink?" said María.

"Alberto isn't afraid of anything. I'm telling you, he's bad."

"Then why the knife? Honestly, I don't understand it," said María. "Plus, hasn't he ever cut himself?"

"A few times, always on purpose. He's good with the knife."

"Are you telling me that your pimp cuts himself on the penis sometimes for fun?" said María.

"That's right."

"I can't believe it."

"It's the truth. Just every once in a while, it's not like he does it every day. Only when he's nervous. Or fucked up. But the measuring thing he does all the time. He's says it's good for his manhood. He says it's a habit he learned inside."

"He sounds like a fucking psychopath," said María.

"You're just too high class, *mana*. You don't understand. Anyway, what's wrong with it? All these stupid men are always measuring their dicks. Mine does it for real. And with a knife. Also, it's the knife he got from his first girlfriend, who was almost like a mother to him."

"And is it really that big?"

María and Lupe laughed. In my mind, Alberto kept growing and getting tougher the more they talked. I had stopped wanting him to show up, or to risk my life for the girls.

"Once, in Azcapotzalco, there was this blow-job contest in a club, and this one slut always won. No one could get her mouth around all the dicks she could swallow. Then Alberto got up from the table where we were sitting and said wait a minute, I've got some business to take care of. The people who were at our table said that's the way, Alberto, you could tell they knew him. Inside, I was thinking the poor girl was already finished. Alberto stood in the middle of the floor, pulled out his huge dick, stroked it into action, and stuck it in the champion's mouth. She really was tough, and she gave it her best shot. She took it little by little and everyone was gasping in astonishment. Then Alberto grabbed her by the ears and pushed his dick all the way in. No time like the present, he said, and everybody laughed. Even I laughed, although the truth is I felt embarrassed too, and a little bit jealous. For the first few seconds it looked like the girl was going to do it, but then she choked and started to suffocate . . ."

"Jesus, your Alberto's a monster," I said.

"But keep telling the story, what happened next?" said María.

"Nothing, really. The girl started to hit Alberto, trying to pull away from him, and Alberto started to laugh and say whoah, girl, whoah, like he was riding a bucking bronco, know what I mean?"

"Of course, like he was in a rodeo," I said.

"I didn't like that at all, and I shouted let her go, Alberto, you're going to hurt her. But I don't think he even heard me. Meanwhile the girl's face was turning red, her eyes were wide open (she closed them when she gave head), and she pushed at Alberto's thighs, sort of tugging on his pockets and his belt. Of course, it didn't matter, because each time she tried to pull away from Alberto, he yanked her again by the ears to stop her. And he was going to win, you could tell."

"But why didn't she bite his thing?" said María.

"Because the party was all his friends. If she had, Alberto would have killed her."

"Lupe, you're crazy," said María.

"So are you. Aren't we all?"

María and Lupe laughed. I wanted to hear the end of the story.

"Nothing happened," said Lupe. "The girl couldn't take it anymore and she started to puke."

"And what about Alberto?"

"He pulled out a little before, right? He realized what was coming and he didn't want to get his pants dirty. So he sort of leaped like a tiger, but backward, and he didn't get a drop on himself. The people at the party were clapping like crazy."

"And you're in love with this maniac?" said María.

"In love, like really in love? I don't know. I'm crazy about him, that's for sure. You'd love him too, if you were me."

"Me? Not in a million years."

"He's a real man," said Lupe, looking out the window, her gaze lost in the distance, "and that's the truth. And he understands me better than anyone."

"He exploits you better than anyone, you mean," said María, pushing back and slapping the table with her hands. The blow made the cups jump.

"Come on, *mana*, don't be that way."

"She's right," I said, "don't be that way. It's her life. Let her do what she wants with it."

"Stay out of this, García Madero. You're looking in from the outside. You don't have a fucking clue what we're talking about."

"You're looking in from the outside too! For Christ's sake, you live with your parents, and you aren't a whore—sorry, Lupe, no offense."

"That's okay," said Lupe, "you couldn't offend me if you tried."

"Shut up, García Madero," said María.

I obeyed her. For a while the three of us were silent. Then María started to talk about the feminist movement, making reference to Gertrude Stein, Remedios Varo, Leonora Carrington, Alice B. Toklas (*tóclamela*, said Lupe, but María ignored her), Unica Zürn, Joyce Mansour, Marianne Moore, and a bunch of other names I don't remember. The feminists of the twentieth century, I guess. She also mentioned Sor Juana Inés de la Cruz.

"She's a Mexican poet," I said.

"And a nun too. I know that much," said Lupe.


NOVEMBER 17

Today I went to the Fonts' house without Pancho. (I can't spend all day following Pancho around.) When I got to the gate, though, I started to feel nervous. I worried that María's father would kick me out, that I wouldn't know how to handle him, that he would attack me. I wasn't brave enough to ring the bell, and for a while I walked around the neighborhood thinking about María, Angélica, Lupe, and poetry. Also, without intending to, I ended up thinking about my aunt and uncle, about my life so far. My old life seemed pleasant and empty, and I knew it would never be that way again. That made me deeply glad. Then I headed back quickly toward the Fonts' house and rang the bell. Mr. Font came to the door and made a gesture as if to say hold on a second, I'm on my way. Then he disappeared, leaving the door ajar. After a while he appeared again, crossing the yard and rolling up his sleeves as he walked, a broad smile on his face. He seemed better, actually. He swung open the gate, saying you're García Madero, aren't you? and shook my hand. I said how are you sir, and he said call me Quim, not sir, in this house we don't stand on ceremony. At first I didn't understand what he wanted me to call him and I said Kim? (I've read Rudyard Kipling), but he said no, Quim, short for Joaquín in Catalan.

"Okay then, Quim," I said with a smile of relief, even happiness. "My name is Juan."

"No, I'd better keep calling you García Madero," he said. "That's what everybody calls you."

Then he walked partway through the yard with me (he had taken my arm). Before he let me go, he said that María had told him what happened yesterday.

"I appreciate it, García Madero," he said. "There aren't many young men like you. This country is going to hell, and I don't know how we're going to fix it."

"I just did what anyone would have done," I said, a little tentatively.

"Even the young people, who in theory are our hope for change, are turning into potheads and sluts. There's no way to solve the problem; revolution is the only answer."

"I agree completely, Quim," I said.

"According to my daughter, you behaved like a gentleman."

I shrugged my shoulders.

"A few of her friends—but there's no point getting into it, you'll meet them," he said. "In some ways, it doesn't bother me. A person has to get to know people from all walks of life. At a certain point you need to steep yourself in reality, no? I think it was Alfonso Reyes who said that. Maybe not. It doesn't matter. But sometimes María goes overboard, wouldn't you say? And I'm not criticizing her for that, for steeping herself in reality, but she should *steep* herself, not *expose* herself, don't you think? Because if one steeps oneself too thoroughly, one is at risk of becoming a *victim*. I don't know whether you follow me."

"I follow you," I said.

"A victim of reality, especially if one has friends who are—how to put it—magnetic, wouldn't you say? People who innocently attract trouble or who attract bullies. You're following me, aren't you, García Madero?"

"Of course."

"For example, that Lupe, the girl the two of you saw yesterday. I know her too, believe me, she's been here, at my house, eating here and spending a night or two with us. I don't mean to exaggerate, it was just one or two nights, but that girl has *problems*, doesn't she? She attracts problems. That's what I meant when I was talking about magnetic people."

"I understand," I said. "Like a magnet."

"Exactly. And in this case, what the magnet is attracting is something bad, very bad, but since María is so young she doesn't realize and she doesn't see the danger, does she, and what she wants is to *help*. Help those in need. She never thinks about the risks involved. In short, my poor daughter wants her friend, or her acquaintance, to give up the life she's been leading."

"I see what you're getting at, sir—I mean Quim."

"You see what I'm getting at? What am I getting at?"

"You're talking about Lupe's pimp."

"Very good, García Madero. You've put your finger on it: Lupe's pimp. Because what is Lupe to him? His means of support, his occupation, his office; in a word, his job. And what does a worker do when he loses his job? Tell me, what does he do."

"He gets angry?"

"He gets *really* angry. And who does he get angry at? The person who did him out of a job, of course. No question about it. He doesn't get angry at his neighbor, though then again maybe he does, but the first person he goes after is the person who lost him his job, naturally. And who's sawing away at the floor under him so that he loses his job? My daughter, of course. So who will he get angry at? My daughter. And meanwhile at her family too, because you know what these people are like. Their revenge is horrific and indiscriminate. There are nights, I swear, when I have terrible dreams"—he laughed a little, looking at the grass, as if remembering his dreams—"that would make the strongest man's hair stand on end. Sometimes I dream that I'm in a city that's Mexico City but at the same time it isn't Mexico City, I mean, it's a strange city, but I recognize it from other dreams—I'm not boring you, am I?"

"Hardly!"

"As I was saying, it's a vaguely strange and vaguely familiar city. And I'm wandering endless streets trying to find a hotel or a boardinghouse where they'll take me in. But I can't find anything. All I find is a man pretending to be a deaf-mute. And worst of all is that it's getting late, and I know that when night comes my life won't be worth a thing, will it? I'll be at nature's mercy, as they say. It's a bitch of a dream," he added reflectively.

"Well, Quim, I'm going to see whether the girls are here."

"Of course," he said, not letting go of my arm.

"I'll stop in later on to say goodbye," I said, just to say something.

"I liked what you did last night, García Madero. I liked that you took care of María and you didn't get horny around those prostitutes."

"Jesus, Quim, it was just Lupe . . . And any friends of María's are friends of mine," I said, flushing to the tips of my ears.

"Well, go see the girls, I think they have another guest. That room is busier than . . ." He couldn't find the right word and laughed.

I hurried away from him as fast as I could.

When I was about to go into the courtyard, I turned around and Quim Font was still there, laughing quietly to himself and looking at the magnolias.

NOVEMBER 18

Today I went back to the Fonts' house. Quim came to the gate to let me in and gave me a hug. In the little house I found María, Angélica, and Ernesto San Epifanio. The three of them were sitting on Angélica's bed. When I came in they instinctively drew closer together, as if to prevent me from seeing what they were sharing. I think they were expecting Pancho. When they realized it was me, their faces didn't relax.

"You should get in the habit of locking the door," said Angélica. "He almost gave me a heart attack."

Unlike María, Angélica has a very white face, though the underlying skin tone is olive or pink, I'm not sure which, olive, I think, and she's got high cheekbones, a broad forehead, and plumper lips than her sister's. When I saw her, or rather when I saw that she was looking at me (the other times I'd been there she'd never actually looked at me), I felt as if a hand, its fingers long and delicate but very strong, was squeezing my heart. I know Lima and Belano wouldn't approve of that image, but it fits my feelings like a glove.

"I wasn't the last to come in," said María.

"Yes you were." Angélica's voice was assured, almost autocratic, and for a minute I thought that she seemed like the older sister, not the younger one. "Bolt the door and sit down somewhere," she ordered me.

I did as she said. The curtains of the little house were drawn and the light that came in was green, shot through with yellow. I sat in a wooden chair, beside one of the bookcases, and asked them what they were looking at. Ernesto San Epifanio raised his head and scrutinized me for a few seconds.

"Weren't you the one taking notes on the books I was carrying the other day?"

"Yes. Brian Patten, Adrian Henri, and another one I can't remember now."

"*The Lost Fire Brigade*, by Spike Hawkins."

"Exactly."

"And have you bought them yet?" His tone was mildly sarcastic.

"Not yet, but I plan to."

"You have to go to a bookstore that specializes in English literature. You won't find them in the regular bookstores."

"I know that. Ulises told me about a bookstore where you all go."

"Oh, Ulises Lima," said San Epifanio, stressing the *i*'s. "He'll probably send you to the Librería Baudelaire, where there's lots of *French* poetry, but not much *English* poetry . . . And who exactly are 'you all'?"

" 'You all'?" I said, surprised. The Font sisters kept looking at objects I couldn't see and passing them back and forth. Sometimes they laughed. Angélica's laugh was like a bubbling brook.

"The people who go to bookstores."

"Oh, the visceral realists, of course."

"The visceral realists? Please. The only ones who read are Ulises and his little Chilean friend. The rest are a bunch of functional illiterates. As far as I can tell, the only thing they do in bookstores is steal books."

"But then they read them, don't they?" I said, slightly annoyed.

"No, you're wrong. Then they give the books to Ulises and Belano, who read them and tell what they're about so the others can go around bragging about having read Queneau, for example, when all they've really done is *steal* a book by Queneau, not read it."

"Belano is Chilean?" I asked, trying to steer the conversation in a different direction, and also because I honestly didn't know.

"Couldn't you tell?" said María without lifting her eyes from whatever it was she was looking at.

"Well, I did notice that he had a slightly different accent, but I thought he might be from Tamaulipas or from Yucatán, I don't know . . ."

"You thought he was from Yucatán? Oh, García Madero, you poor innocent child. He thought Belano was from Yucatán," San Epifanio said to the Font sisters, and the three of them laughed.

I laughed too.

"He doesn't look like he's from Yucatán," I said, "but he could be. Anyway, I'm not a specialist in Yucatecans."

"Well, he isn't from Yucatán. He's from Chile."

"So how long has he lived in Mexico?" I said to say something.

"Since the Pinochet putsch," said María without lifting her head.

"Since long before the coup," said San Epifanio. "I met him in 1971. What happened was, he went back to Chile and after the coup he came back to Mexico."

"But we didn't know either of you back then," said Angélica.

"Belano and I were very close in those days," said San Epifanio. "We were both eighteen and we were the youngest poets on Calle Bucareli."

"Will you please tell me what you're looking at?" I said.

"Pictures of mine. You might not like them, but you can look at them too if you want."

"Are you a photographer?" I said, getting up and going over to the bed.

"No, I'm just a poet," said San Epifanio, making room for me. "Poetry is more than enough for me, although sooner or later I'm bound to commit the vulgarity of writing stories."

"Here." Angélica passed me a little pile of pictures that they had finished with. "You have to look at them in chronological order."

There must have been fifty or sixty photos. All of them were taken with flash. All were of a room, probably a hotel room, except for two, which were of a dimly lit street at night and a red Mustang with a few people in it. The faces of the people in the Mustang were blurry. The rest of the pictures showed a blond, short-haired boy, sixteen or seventeen, although he might only have been fifteen, and a girl maybe two or three years older, and Ernesto San Epifanio. There must have been a fourth person, the one taking the pictures, but he or she was never seen. The first pictures were of the blond boy, dressed, and then with progressively fewer clothes on. In picture number fifteen or so, San Epifanio and the girl showed up. San Epifanio was wearing a purple blazer. The girl had on a fancy party dress.

"Who is he?" I said.

"Be quiet and look at the pictures, then ask," said Angélica.

"He's my love," said San Epifanio.

"Oh. And who's she?"

"His older sister."

By about picture number twenty, the blond boy had begun to dress in his sister's clothes. The girl, who was darker and a little chubby, was making obscene gestures at the unknown person who was photographing them. San Epifanio, meanwhile, remained in control of himself, at least in the first pictures, which showed him smiling but serious, sitting in a leatherette armchair or on the edge of the bed. All of this, however, was only an illusion, because by picture number thirty or thirty-five, San Epifanio had taken off his clothes too (his body, with its long legs and long arms, seemed excessively thin and bony, much thinner than in real life). The next pictures showed San Epifanio kissing the blond boy's neck, his lips, his eyes, his back, his cock at half-mast, his erect cock (a remarkable cock too, for such a delicate-looking boy), under the always vigilant gaze of the sister, who sometimes appeared in full and sometimes in part (an arm and a half, her hand, some fingers, one side of her face), and sometimes just as a shadow on the wall. I have to confess that I'd never seen anything like it in my life. Naturally, no one had warned me that San Epifanio was gay. (Only Lupe, but Lupe also said that I was gay.) So I tried not to show my feelings (which were confused, to say the least) and kept looking. As I feared, the next pictures showed the Brian Patten reader fucking the blond boy. I felt myself turn red and I suddenly realized that I didn't know how I was going to face the Fonts and San Epifanio when I had finished looking through the pictures. The face of the boy being fucked was twisted in a grimace that I assumed was an expression of mingled pain and pleasure. (Or fake emotion, but that only occurred to me later.) San Epifanio's face seemed to sharpen at moments, like an intensely lit razor blade or knife. And every possible expression crossed the watching sister's face, from violent joy to deepest melancholy. The last pictures showed the three of them in bed, in different poses, pretending to sleep or smiling at the photographer.

"Poor kid, it looks like someone was forcing him to be there," I said to annoy San Epifanio.

"Forcing him to be there? It was his idea. He's a little pervert."

"But you love him with all your heart," said Angélica.

"I love him with all my heart, but there are too many things that come between us."

"Like what?" said Angélica.

"Money, for example. I'm poor and he's a spoiled rich kid, used to luxury and travel and having everything he wants."

"Well, he doesn't look rich or spoiled here. Some of these pictures are really brutal," I said in a burst of sincerity.

"His family has lots of money," said San Epifanio.

"Then you could have gone to a nicer hotel. The lighting looks like something from a Santo movie."

"He's the son of the Honduran ambassador," said San Epifanio, shooting me a gloomy look. "But don't tell anybody that," he added, regretting having confessed his secret to me.

I returned the stack of pictures, which San Epifanio put in his pocket. Less than an inch from my left arm was Angélica's bare arm. I gathered up my courage and looked her in the face. She was looking at me too, and I think I blushed a little. I felt happy. Then right away I ruined it.

"Pancho hasn't come today?" I asked, like an idiot.

"Not yet," said Angélica. "What do you think of the pictures?"

"Hard-core," I said.

"Hard-core? That's all?" San Epifanio got up and sat in the wooden chair where I had been. From there he watched me with one of his knife-blade smiles.

"Well, there's a kind of poetry to them. But if I told you that they only struck me as poetic, I'd be lying. They're strange pictures. I'd call them pornographic. Not in a negative sense, but definitely pornographic."

"Everybody tends to pigeonhole things they don't understand," said San Epifanio. "Did the pictures turn you on?"

"No," I said emphatically, although the truth is I wasn't sure. "They didn't turn me on, but they didn't disgust me either."

"Then it isn't pornography. Not for you, at least."

"But I liked them," I admitted.

"Then just say that: you liked them and you don't know why you liked them, which doesn't matter much anyway, period."

"Who's the photographer?" said María.

San Epifanio looked at Angélica and laughed.

"That really is a secret. The person made me swear I wouldn't tell anybody."

"But if it was Billy's idea, who cares who the photographer was?" said Angélica.

So the name of the Honduran ambassador's son was Billy; very appropriate, I thought.

And then, don't ask me why, I got the idea that it was Ulises Lima who had taken the pictures. And next I immediately thought about the interesting (to me) news that Belano was from Chile. And then I watched Angélica. Not in an obvious way, mostly when she wasn't looking at me, her head in a book of poetry (*Les Lieux de la douleur*, by Eugène Savitzkaya) from which she looked up every now and then to contribute to the conversation that María and San Epifanio were having about erotic art. And all over again I started thinking about the possibility that Ulises Lima had taken the pictures, and I also remembered what I'd heard at Café Quito, that Lima was a drug dealer, and if he was a drug dealer, I thought, then he almost definitely dealt in other things. And that was as far as I'd gotten when Barrios showed up arm in arm with a very nice American girl (she was always smiling) whose name was Barbara Patterson and a poetess I didn't know, called Silvia Moreno, and then we all started to smoke marijuana.

My memory is vague (though not because of the pot, which had practically no effect on me), but later someone brought up the subject of Belano's nationality again—maybe it was me, I don't know—and everybody started to talk about him. More accurately, everyone started to run him down, except María and me, who at some point more or less separated ourselves from the group, physically and spiritually, but even from a distance (maybe because of the pot) I could still hear what they were saying. They were talking about Lima too, about his trips to Guerrero state and Pinochet's Chile to get the marijuana he sold to the writers and painters of Mexico City. But how could Lima go all the way to the other end of the continent to buy marijuana? People were laughing. I think I was laughing too. I think I laughed a lot. I had my eyes closed. They said: Arturo makes Ulises work much harder, it's riskier now, and their words were stamped on my brain. Poor Belano, I thought. Then María took my hand and we left the little house, like when Pancho and Angélica kicked us out, except that this time Pancho wasn't there and no one had kicked us out.

Then I think I slept.

I woke up at three in the morning, stretched out beside Jorgito Font. I jumped up. Someone had taken off my shoes, my pants, and my shirt. I felt around for them, trying not to wake Jorgito. The first thing I found was my backpack with my books and poems in it, on the floor at the foot of the bed. A little farther away, I found my pants, shirt, and jacket laid out on a chair. I couldn't find my shoes anywhere. I looked for them under the bed and all I found were several pairs of Jorgito's sneakers. I got dressed and thought about whether I should turn on the light or go out with no shoes on. Unable to make up my mind, I went over to the window. When I parted the curtains, I saw that I was on the second floor. I looked out at the dark courtyard and the girls' house, hidden behind some trees and faintly lit by the moon. Before long, I realized that it wasn't the moon that was lighting up the house but a lamp that was on just below my window, slightly to the left, hanging outside the kitchen. The light was very dim. I tried to make out the Fonts' window. I couldn't see anything, just branches and shadows. For a few minutes I weighed the possibility of going back to bed and sleeping until morning, but I came up with several reasons not to. First: I had never slept away from home before without letting my aunt and uncle know; second: I knew I wouldn't be able to go back to sleep; third: I had to see Angélica. Why? I've forgotten, but at the time I felt an urgent need to see her, watch her sleep, curl up at the foot of her bed like a dog or a child (a horrible image, but true). So I slipped toward the door, silently thanking Jorgito for giving me a place to sleep. So long, *cuñado*! I thought (from the Latin *cognatus*, *cognati*: brother-in-law), and steeling myself with the word, I slid catlike out of the room down a hallway as dark as the blackest night, or like a movie theater full of staring eyes, where everything had gone pop, and felt my way along the wall until, after an ordeal too long and nerve-racking to describe in detail (plus I hate details), I found the sturdy staircase that led from the second floor to the first. As I stood there like a statue (i.e., extremely pale and with my hands frozen in a position somewhere between energized and tentative), two alternatives presented themselves to me. Either I could go looking for the living room and the telephone and call my aunt and uncle right away, since by then they had probably already dragged more than one tired policeman out of bed, or I could go looking for the kitchen, which I remembered as being to the left, next to a kind of family dining room. I weighed the pros and cons of each plan and opted for the quieter one, which involved getting out of the Fonts' big house as quickly as possible. My decision was aided in no small part by a sudden image or vision of

Quim Font sitting in a wing chair in the dark, enveloped in a cloud of sulfurous reddish smoke. With a great effort I managed to calm myself. Everyone in the house was asleep, although I couldn't hear anyone snoring like at home. Once a few seconds had passed, enough to convince me that no danger was hovering over me, or at least no imminent danger, I set off. In this wing of the house, the glow from the courtyard faintly lit my way and before long I was in the kitchen. There, abandoning my extreme caution, I closed the door, turned on the light, and dropped into a chair, as exhausted as if I'd run a mile uphill. Then I opened the refrigerator, poured myself a tall glass of milk, and made myself a ham and cheese sandwich with oyster sauce and Dijon mustard. When I finished I was still hungry, so I made myself a second sandwich, this time with cheese, lettuce, and pickles bottled with two or three kinds of chilies. This second sandwich didn't fill me up, so I decided to go in search of something more substantial. In a plastic container on the bottom shelf of the refrigerator, I found the remains of a chicken mole; in another container I found rice—I guess they were leftovers from that day's dinner—and then I went looking for real bread, not sandwich bread, and I started to make myself dinner. To drink I chose a bottle of strawberry Lulú, which really tastes more like hibiscus. I ate sitting in the kitchen in silence, thinking about the future. I saw tornadoes, hurricanes, tidal waves, fire. Then I washed the frying pan, plate, and silverware, brushed away the crumbs, and unbolted the door to the courtyard. Before I left, I turned out the light.

The girls' house was locked. I knocked once and whispered Angélica's name. No one answered. I looked back, and the shadows in the courtyard and the spout of the fountain rising up like an angry animal kept me from returning to Jorgito Font's room. I knocked again, this time a little harder. Waiting a few seconds, I decided to change tactics. I stepped a few feet to the left and tapped with my fingertips on the cold windowpane. María? I said, Angélica? María, let me in, it's me. Then I was silent, waiting for something to happen, but nobody moved inside the little house. In exasperation, although it would be more accurate to say in exasperated resignation, I dragged myself back to the door and slumped against it, sliding to the ground, staring into nothing. I sensed that I would end up there, asleep at the Font sisters' feet one way or another, like a dog (a wet dog in the inclement night!), just as I had foolishly and intrepidly wished a few hours ago. I could have burst into tears. To clear

51

away the clouds on my immediate horizons, I started to go over all the books I should read, all the poems I should write. Then it occurred to me that if I fell asleep, the Fonts' servant would probably find me there and wake me, saving me from the embarrassment of being found by Mrs. Font or one of her daughters or Quim Font himself. Although if it was the latter who found me, I argued hopefully, he would probably think that I'd sacrificed a night of peaceful slumbers to keep faithful watch over his daughters. If they wake me up and ask me in for a cup of coffee, I concluded, nothing will be lost; if they kick me awake and throw me out without further ado, there'll be no hope left for me. Besides, how will I explain to my uncle that I crossed the whole city barefoot? I think it was this line of reasoning that roused me, or maybe it was desperation that made me unconsciously pound the door with the back of my head. In any case, I suddenly heard steps inside the little house. A few seconds later, the door opened and a voice asked me in a sleepy whisper what I was doing there.

It was María.

"My shoes are gone. If I could find them, I'd go home right now," I said.

"Come in," said María. "Don't make a sound."

I followed her with my arms outstretched, like a blind man. All at once I ran into something. It was María's bed. I heard her order me to get in, then I watched her retrace her steps (the girls' house is actually pretty big) and silently close the door, which had been left ajar. I didn't hear her return. The darkness was total now, although after a few seconds—I was sitting on the edge of the bed, not lying down as she had commanded—I could make out the outline of the window through the enormous linen drapes. Then I felt someone get into bed and lie down, and then, how much later I don't know, I felt that person just barely sit up, probably leaning on an elbow, and pull me close. By the feel of her breath I realized that I was only fractions of an inch from María's face. Her fingers ran over my face, from my chin to my eyes, closing my eyes as if inviting me to sleep; her hand, a bony hand, unzipped my pants and felt for my cock. Why I don't know, maybe because I was so nervous, but I said I wasn't sleepy. I know, said María, me neither. Then everything turned into a succession of concrete acts and proper nouns and verbs, or pages from an anatomy manual scattered like flower petals, chaotically linked. I explored María's naked body, María's glorious naked body, in a contained silence, although I could have shouted, rejoicing in each corner, each smooth and interminable space I discovered. María was less reserved. Soon she began to moan, and her maneuvers, at first timid or restrained, became more open (I can't think of another word for it just now), as she guided my hand to places it hadn't reached, whether out of ignorance or negligence. So that was how I learned, in fewer than ten minutes, where a woman's clitoris is and how to massage or fondle or press it, always within the bounds of gentleness, of course, bounds that María, on the other hand, was constantly transgressing, since my cock, treated well in the first forays, soon began to suffer torments in her hands, hands that in the dark and the tangle of the sheets sometimes seemed to me like the talons of a falcon or a falconess, tugging on me so hard that I was afraid they were trying to pull me right off, and at other times like Chinese dwarfs (her fingers were the fucking dwarfs!) investigating and measuring the spaces and ducts that connected my testicles to my cock and each other. Then (but first I had pushed my pants down to my knees) I got on top of her and entered her.

"Don't come inside of me," said María.

"I'll try not to," I said.

"What do you mean you'll *try*, you jerk? Don't come inside!"

I looked to either side of the bed as María's legs laced and unlaced across my back (I would've been happy to keep going like that until I died). In the distance I glimpsed the shadow of Angélica's bed and the curve of Angélica's hips, like an island observed from another island. Suddenly I felt María's lips sucking my left nipple, almost as if she were biting my heart. I jumped, and pushed in all the way in one thrust, wanting to pin her to the bed (the springs of which began to squeak hideously so that I paused), while at the same time I kissed her hair and forehead with great delicacy and still managed to find the time to wonder how it was possible that the noise we were making hadn't woken Angélica. I didn't even notice when I came. Of course, I pulled out in time; I've always had good reflexes.

"You didn't come inside, did you?" said María.

I swore into her ear that I hadn't. For a few seconds we were busy breathing. I asked her whether she'd had an orgasm and her answer was perplexing:

"I came twice, García Madero, didn't you notice?" she asked in utter seriousness.

I was honest and told her no, I hadn't noticed anything.

"You're still hard," said María.

"I guess I am," I said. "Can we do it again?"

"All right," she said.

I don't know how much time went by. I pulled out and came again. This time I couldn't keep from crying out.

"Now do me," said María.

"You didn't have an orgasm?"

"No, not this time, but it was good." She took my hand, selected my index finger, and guided it around her clitoris. "Kiss my nipples. You can bite them too, but very gently at first," she said. "Then bite them a little harder. And put your hand around my neck. Stroke my face. Put your fingers in my mouth."

"Wouldn't you rather that I . . . suck your clitoris?" I said, vainly trying to find an elegant way to put it.

"No, not right now, your finger is enough. But kiss my tits."

"You have gorgeous breasts." I was unable to repeat the word *tits*.

I got undressed without getting out from under the sheets (suddenly I had begun to sweat) and immediately began to carry out María's instructions. First her sighs and then her moans got me hard again. She noticed and with one hand she stroked my cock until she couldn't anymore.

"What's wrong, María?" I whispered in her ear, afraid that I'd hurt her throat (squeeze, she kept whispering, squeeze) or bitten one of her nipples too hard.

"Keep going, García Madero," said María, smiling in the dark, and she kissed me.

When we were done she told me that she had come more than five times. To be honest, I had a hard time accepting that such an outrageous thing was possible, but when she gave me her word I had to believe her.

"What are you thinking about?" said María.

"About you," I lied; actually, I was thinking about my uncle and the law school and the magazine that Belano and Lima were going to publish. "What about you?"

"I'm thinking about the pictures," she said.

54

"What pictures?"

"Ernesto's."

"The pornographic pictures?"

"Yes."

The two of us shuddered in unison. Our faces were glued together. We could talk, vocalize, thanks to the space made by our noses, but even so I could feel her lips move against mine.

"Do you want to do it again?"

"Yes," said María.

"Well," I said, a little queasy, "if you change your mind at the last minute, let me know."

"Change my mind about what?" said María.

The insides of her thighs were drenched in my semen. I felt cold and I couldn't help sighing deeply at the moment I penetrated her again.

María whimpered and I started to move with increasing enthusiasm.

"Try not to make too much noise, I don't want Angélica to hear us."

"You try not to make noise," I said, and I added: "What did you give Angélica to make her sleep like that?"

The two of us laughed quietly, me against her neck and her burying her face in the pillows. When I finished, I didn't even have the energy to ask her if she'd enjoyed herself, and the only thing I wanted was to gradually drift off to sleep with María in my arms. But she got up and made me get dressed and follow her to the bathroom in the big house. When we went out into the courtyard I realized that the sun was already coming up. For the first time that night I could see my lover a little more clearly. María was wearing a white nightgown with red embroidery on the sleeves, and her hair was pulled back with a ribbon or a piece of braided leather.

After we dried ourselves I thought about calling home, but María said that my aunt and uncle would surely be asleep and I could do it later.

"And now what?" I said.

"Now let's sleep a little," said María, putting her arm around my waist.

But the night or day held a last surprise for me. Huddled in a corner of the little house, I discovered Barrios and his American friend. The two of them were snoring. I would've liked to wake them with a kiss.

We all had breakfast together: Quim Font, Mrs. Font, María and Angélica, Jorgito Font, Barrios, Barbara Patterson, and me. Breakfast was scrambled eggs, slices of fried ham, bread, mango jam, strawberry jam, butter, salmon pâté, and coffee. Jorgito drank a glass of milk. Mrs. Font (she kissed me on the cheek when she saw me!) made something that she called crêpes but that were nothing like crêpes. The rest of breakfast was prepared by the servant (whose name I don't know or can't remember, which is inexcusable). Barrios and I washed the dishes.

Afterward, when Quim went off to work and Mrs. Font began to plan her day (she works, so she told me, as a writer for a new Mexican family magazine), I finally decided to call home. My aunt Martita was the only one there, and when she heard my voice she started to scream like a crazy woman, then cry. After an uninterrupted series of prayers to the Virgin, appeals to duty, fragmented accounts of the night I had "put my uncle through," warnings in a tone more complicitous than recriminatory about the impending punishment that my uncle was surely pondering that very morning, I finally broke in and assured her that I was fine, that I'd spent the night with some friends and I wouldn't be home until "after dark" since I planned to head straight for the university. My aunt promised that she would call my uncle at work herself, and she made me swear that as long as I lived I would call home when I decided to spend the night out. For a few seconds I considered whether it might be a good idea to call my uncle myself, but in the end I decided that it wasn't necessary.

I fell into an armchair with no idea what to do. I had the rest of the morning and day at my disposal, which is to say, I was conscious that they were at my disposal and in that sense they struck me as different from other mornings and other days (when I was a lost soul, wandering around the university or in the grips of my virginity), but here at the first sign of change I didn't know what to do. I had so many possibilities to choose from.

The consumption of food—I ate like a wolf while Mrs. Font and Barbara Patterson talked about museums and Mexican families—had made me slightly sleepy and at the same time had reawakened my desire to have sex with María (whom I had avoided looking at during breakfast, trying when I did to adapt my gaze to the notions of brotherly love or disinterested camaraderie that I imagined were harbored by her father, who incidentally didn't seem the least bit surprised to see me at his table at such an early hour), but María was getting ready to go out, Angélica was getting ready to go out, Jorgito Font had already left, Barbara Patterson was in the shower, and only Barrios and the maid were wandering around the big library of the main house like the last survivors of a terrible shipwreck, so to stay out of their way and in a faint desire for symmetry, I crossed the courtyard for the millionth time and made myself comfortable in the sisters' little house, where the beds were still unmade (which was a clear sign that it was the maid or servant or cleaning lady—or the *naca* of steel, as Jorgito called her—who did the work, a detail that increased my attraction to María rather than lessening it, tainting her pleasantly with frivolousness and indifference), contemplating the still-damp scene of my gateway to glory, and even though I ought to have wept or prayed, what I did was lie down on one of the unmade beds (Angélica's, as I found out later, not María's) and fall asleep.

I was woken by Pancho Rodríguez hitting me (I think he may have been kicking me too, though I'm not sure). Only good manners prevented me from greeting him with a punch in the jaw. After saying good morning I went out into the courtyard and washed my face in the fountain (proof that I was still asleep), with Pancho behind me muttering unintelligibly.

"There's no one home," he said. "I had to hop the wall to get in. What are you doing here?"

I told him that I had spent the night there (I played it down, since I didn't like the way Pancho's nostrils were quivering, by adding that Barrios and Barbara Patterson had spent the night too), then we tried to get into the big house by the back door, the kitchen door, and the front door, but they were all locked tight.

"If a neighbor sees us and calls the police," I said, "how will we explain that we're not breaking in?"

"I don't give a shit. Sometimes I like to nose around my girlfriends' houses," said Pancho.

"And also," I said, ignoring Pancho's remark, "I think I saw a curtain move in the house next door. If the police come . . ."

"Did you have sex with Angélica, asshole?" asked Pancho suddenly, turning his eyes away from the front windows of the Fonts' house.

"Of course not," I assured him.

I don't know whether he believed me or not. But the two of us hopped the wall again and beat a retreat from Colonia Condesa.

As we walked (in silence, through the Parque España, down Parras, through the Parque San Martín, and along Teotihuacán, where the only people out at that time of day were housewives, maids, and bums), I thought about what María had said about love and about the suffering that love would bring down on Pancho's head. By the time we got to Insurgentes, Pancho was in a better mood, talking about literature and recommending authors to me, trying to forget about Angélica. Then we headed down Manzanillo, turned onto Aguascalientes, and turned south again onto Medellín, walking until we reached Calle Tepeji. We stopped in front of a five-story building and Pancho invited me to have lunch with his family.

We took the elevator up to the top floor.

There, instead of going into one of the apartments, as I had expected, we climbed the stairs to the roof. A gray sky, but bright as if there had been a nuclear attack, welcomed us in the middle of a vibrant profusion of flowerpots and plants spilling into the passageways and laundry space.

Pancho's family lived in two rooms on the roof.

"Temporarily," explained Pancho, "until we save enough for a house around here."

I was formally introduced to his mother, Doña Panchita; his brother Moctezuma, nineteen, Catullian poet and union organizer; and his younger brother Norberto, fifteen, high school student.

One room served as dining and TV room during the day, and as Pancho, Moctezuma, and Norberto's bedroom at night. The other was a kind of giant closet or wardrobe, which held the refrigerator, the kitchen supplies (they brought the portable stove out into the hallway during the day and put it back in the room at night), and the mattress where Doña Panchita slept.

As we were starting to eat, we were joined by a guy called Luscious Skin, twenty-three, rooftop neighbor, who was introduced as a visceral realist poet. A little before I left (many hours later; the time passed in a flash), I asked him again what his name was and he said Luscious Skin so naturally and confidently (much more naturally and confidently than I would've said Juan García Madero) that for a minute I actually believed that somewhere amid the back alley and swamps of our Mexican Republic there was actually a family named Skin.

After lunch, Doña Panchita sat down to watch her favorite soap operas and Norberto began to study, his books spread out on the table. Pancho and Moctezuma washed the dishes in a sink from which there was a view of lots of the Parque de las Américas, and behind it the threatening hulks—looking as if they'd dropped from another planet, and an unlikely planet too—of the Medical Center, the Children's Hospital, the General Hospital.

"The good thing about living here, if you don't mind the close quarters," said Pancho, "is that you're close to everything, right in the heart of Mexico City."

Luscious Skin (called Skin, of course, by Pancho and his brother—and even Doña Panchita!) invited us to his room, where, he said, he had some marijuana left over from the last big party.

"No time like the present," said Moctezuma.

Unlike the two rooms occupied by the Rodríguezes, Luscious Skin's room was a model of bare austerity. I didn't see clothes strewn around, I didn't see household things, I didn't see books (Pancho and Moctezuma were poor, but where they lived I'd seen books in the most unexpected places, by Efraín Huerta, Augusto Monterroso, Julio Torri, Alfonso Reyes, the aforementioned Catullus in a translation by Ernesto Cardenal, Jaime Sabines, Max Aub, Andrés Henestrosa), just a thin mattress and a chair—no table—and a nice leather suitcase where he kept his clothes.

Luscious Skin lived alone, although from remarks that he and the Rodríguez brothers made, I gathered that not long ago a woman (and her son), both pretty tough, had lived there and taken off with most of the furniture when they left.

For a while we smoked marijuana and surveyed the landscape (which, as I've said, basically consisted of the silhouettes of the hospitals, endless rooftops like the one we were on, and a sky of low clouds moving swiftly toward the south), and then Pancho started to tell the story of his adventures that morning at the Fonts' house and his meeting with me.

I was questioned about what had happened, this time by all three of them, but they didn't manage to get anything out of me that I hadn't already told Pancho. At some point they started to talk about María. From what I could gather, it seemed as though Luscious Skin and María had been lovers. And that Luscious Skin was banned from the Fonts' house. I wanted to know why. They explained to me that Mrs. Font had walked in on Luscious Skin and María one night as they were screwing in the little house. There was a party going on in the big house, in honor of a Spanish writer who had just come to Mexico, and at a certain point during the party, Mrs. Font wanted to introduce her older daughter—María, that is—to the writer and couldn't find her. So she went looking for her, arm in arm with the Spanish writer. When they got to the little house it was dark and from inside they could hear a noise like blows: loud, rhythmic blows. Mrs. Font surely wasn't thinking (if she'd thought first, said Moctezuma, she would've taken the Spaniard back to the party and come back alone to see what was going on in her daughter's room), but as it was, she didn't think, and she turned on the light. There, to her horror, was María, at the other end of the little house, dressed only in a shirt, her pants down, sucking Luscious Skin's dick as he slapped her on the ass and the cunt.

"Really hard slaps," said Luscious Skin. "When they turned on the light I saw her ass and it was all red. I actually got scared."

"But why were you hitting her?" I said angrily, afraid I would blush.

"Isn't he an innocent. Because she asked for it," said Pancho.

"I find that hard to believe," I said.

"Stranger things have happened," said Luscious Skin.

"It's all because of that French girl Simone Darrieux," said Moctezuma. "I know for a fact that María and Angélica invited her to a feminist meeting and afterward they talked about sex."

"Who is this Simone?" I asked.

"A friend of Arturo Belano's."

"I went up to them. I was like, how's it going, girls, and the little sluts were talking about the Marquis de Sade," said Moctezuma.

The rest of the story was predictable. María's mother tried to say something, but nothing came out of her mouth. The Spaniard, who, according to Luscious Skin, turned visibly pale at the sight of María's raised and proffered backside, took Mrs. Font's arm with the solicitude reserved for the mentally ill and dragged her back to the party. In the sudden silence that fell over the little house, Luscious Skin could hear them talking in the courtyard, exchanging hurried words, as if the horny Spanish bastard were proposing something unsavory to poor Mrs. Font as she leaned there on the fountain. But then he heard their footsteps fade away in the direction of the big house and María said that they should keep going.

"That I really can't believe," I said.

"I swear on my mother," said Luscious Skin.

"After you were interrupted, María wanted to keep making love?"

"That's how she is," said Moctezuma.

"And how would you know?" I said, getting more worked up by the second.

"I've fucked her too," said Moctezuma. "She's the wildest girl in Mexico City, although I've never hit her, that's for sure; I don't like that weird stuff. But I know for a fact that she does."

"I didn't hit her, man, what happened was that María was obsessed with the Marquis de Sade and she wanted to try the spanking thing," said Luscious Skin.

"That's very María," said Pancho. "She takes her reading seriously."

"And did you keep fucking?" I asked. Or whispered, or howled, I can't remember, although I do remember that I took several long drags on the joint and that they had to ask me several times to pass it on, that it wasn't just for me.

"Yeah, we kept fucking, or anyway she kept sucking my dick and I kept slapping her but less and less hard, and somehow I wasn't so into it anymore. I think her mother showing up had gotten to me, even if it hadn't gotten to her, and it was like I didn't feel like fucking anymore, like I'd cooled off and now I just wanted to get out and maybe see what was going on at the party, I think some of the famous poets were there, the Spanish writer, Ana María Díaz and Mr. Díaz, Laura Damián's parents, the poets Álamo, Labarca, Berrocal, Artemio Sánchez, the actress América Lagos from TV, and also I was a little afraid that María's mother would show up again, but this time with the fucking architect and then I was really going to get it."

"Laura Damián's parents were there?" I asked.

"The casta diva's parents themselves," said Luscious Skin, "and other celebrities. Believe me, I notice these things. I'd seen them before through the window and said hello to Berrocal, the poet. I'd been to his workshop a few times, but I don't know whether he remembered me or what. I think I was hungry too, and just imagining the things they were eating in the other house was making me drool. I wouldn't have minded showing up there, with María of course, and digging in. I felt really beat, it must have been the blow job. But I honestly wasn't thinking about the blow job, you know? I wasn't thinking about María's lips, or her tongue wrapping around my dick, or her saliva, which by that point was trickling down the hair on my balls . . ."

"Spare us," said Pancho.

"Cut the crap," said his brother.

"Make it snappy," I said so as not to be left out, although the truth was I felt completely drained.

"Well, so I told her. I said: María, let's do this next time or some other night. We usually fucked here, at my place, where we could take our time, although she never stayed all night, she always left at four or five in the morning, and it was a pain in the ass because I always offered to take her home. I couldn't let her go by herself at that hour. And she said keep going, don't stop, it's all right. And I thought she meant that I should keep slapping her ass. What would you have thought she meant? (The same thing, said Pancho.) So I started hitting her again, well, hitting her with one hand and stroking her clitoris and her tits with the other. Really, the sooner we finished, the better. I was ready. But of course, I wasn't going to come before she came. And the slut was taking forever and that started to make me mad, so I was hitting her harder and harder. Her butt, her legs, but also her cunt. Have you ever done it that way, boys? Well, I recommend it. At first the sound, the sound of the slaps, kind of doesn't seem right, it throws you off. It's like something raw in a dish where everything else is cooked. But then it kind of meshes with what you're doing, and the girl's moans, María's moans, mesh with it too, each time you hit her she moans, and the moans keep getting louder, and a moment comes when you feel her ass burning, and the palms of your hands are burning too, and your cock starts to beat like a heart, *plunk plunk plunk* . . ."

"You're laying it on thick, *mano*," said Moctezuma.

"I swear it's the truth. She had my cock in her mouth, but not gripping it tight, not sucking it, just teasing it with the tip of her tongue. She had it like a gun in a holster. See the difference? Not like a gun in the hand, but a gun in a sheath, under the arm or slung around the waist, if that makes sense. And she was throbbing too, her butt was throbbing and so were her legs and the lips of her vagina and her clitoris. I know because each time after I hit her I would stroke her, I felt her there and I noticed, and that really turned me on and I had to make an effort not to come. And she was moaning, but when I hit her she moaned more. When I wasn't hitting her she moaned a lot (I couldn't see her face), but when I was hitting her it was much more extreme, the moaning, I mean, like her heart was breaking, and what I wanted was to turn her over and screw her, but there was no way, she would've gotten mad. That's the problem with María. Things are intense with her but you always have to do it her way."

"And what happened next?" I said.

"Well, she came and I came, and that was it."

"That was it?" said Moctezuma.

"That was it, I swear. We cleaned ourselves up—well, I cleaned myself up, combed my hair a little, and she put on her pants, and we went out to see what was going on at the party. Then we got separated. That was my mistake. Letting myself get separated from her. I started to talk to Berrocal, who was alone in a corner. Then the poet Artemio Sánchez came over with some girl about thirty who was supposedly the deputy editor at *El Guajolote* and right there I started asking her whether she needed poems or stories or philosophical pieces for the magazine, I told her that I had lots of unpublished material, I talked to her about my buddy Moctezuma's translations, and as I talked I was looking for the hors d'oeuvre table out of the corner of my eye because all of a sudden I was fucking hungry, and then I saw María's mother show up again, followed by her father, with the famous Spanish poet a few steps behind, and that was the end of that: they threw me out and warned me never to set foot in their house again."

"And María didn't do anything?"

"No, she didn't. Nothing. At first I acted like I didn't understand what they were talking about, you know, like none of this had anything to do with me, but then, *mano*, there was no point pretending anymore. It became clear that they were going to boot me out like a fucking dog. I was sorry that they did it in front of Berrocal. Why not be honest, the bastard was probably laughing to himself as I backed away toward the door. I can't believe there was a time I actually sort of admired him."

"You admired Berrocal? You really are a dumbshit," said Pancho.

"The truth is that in the beginning he was nice to me. You don't know what it's like, you're from Mexico City, you grew up here, but I came here not knowing anyone and without a fucking peso. That was three years ago, when I was twenty-one. It was one hurdle after another. And Berrocal helped me out, let me into his workshop, introduced me to people who could hook me up with a job; I met María in his workshop. My life has been like a *bolero*," said Luscious Skin suddenly, in a dreamy voice.

"Well, go on: Berrocal was looking at you and laughing," I said.

"No, he wasn't laughing, but I thought he was laughing to himself. And Artemio Sánchez was looking at me too, but he was so bombed he didn't even know what was going on. And the deputy editor of *El Guajolote*, I think she was the most horrified, as well she should have been because the look on María's mother's face was enough to give you the chills. I swear I thought she might have a weapon on her. And despite it all I was backing out in slow motion, and that was because I still hoped that María would show up, that María would push through the guests and between her parents and grab me by the arm or sling her arm over my shoulders—María is the only woman I know who puts her arm around men's shoulders instead of their waists—and get me out of there with some decorum, I mean go with me."

"So did she come over?"

"Come over? No, at least not in the sense you mean. I did see her. Her head popped up for a second over the heads and shoulders of a bunch of assholes."

"And what did she do?"

"She didn't do a goddamn thing."

"Maybe she didn't see you," said Moctezuma.

"Of course she saw me. She looked me in the eye, but the way she does. You know how it is, sometimes she looks at you and it's like she doesn't see you or she's looking right through you. And then she disappeared. So I said to myself you lost this one, amigo. Go quietly and don't make a scene. And I started to move for real, and as I was backing away María's bitch of a mother lunges at me, and I thought the woman was going to kick me in the balls or slap me at least. All right, then, I thought, so much for the orderly retreat, I'd better run, but by then the bitch was on top of me like she was going to kiss me or bite me, and guess what she says to me . . ."

The Rodríguez brothers were silent. No doubt they already knew.

"Did she insult you?" I asked hesitantly.

"She said: shame on you, shame on you. That's all, but she said it ten times at least, and an inch away from my face."

"It's hard to believe that witch gave birth to María and Angélica," said Moctezuma.

"Stranger things have happened," said Pancho.

"Are you still her lover?" I said.

Luscious Skin heard me but didn't answer.

"How often have you had sex with her?" I said.

"I don't even remember," said Luscious Skin.

"What's with the questions?" said Pancho.

"I don't know, just curious," I said.

It was late that night when I left the Rodríguez brothers' house (I had lunch and dinner with them and I could probably even have spent the night, they were so generous). When I got to the bus stop on Insurgentes, I suddenly realized that I didn't feel strong enough or in the mood for the long, involved discussion waiting for me at home.

One by one, the buses that I should have taken kept going by, until at last I got up from the curb where I'd been sitting and thinking and watching the traffic (or rather, watching the headlights of the cars shining in my face) and set out for the Fonts'.

Before I got there I called. Jorgito answered. I told him to get his sister. In a few seconds, María came to the phone. I wanted to see her. She asked me where I was. I told her I was near her house, at Plaza Popocatépetl.

"Wait for a few hours," she said, "and then come. Don't ring the bell. Come over the wall and sneak in as quietly as you can. I'll be waiting for you." I sighed deeply and almost told her that I loved her (but didn't say it), and then hung up. Since I didn't have the money to go to a coffee shop, I stayed in the plaza, sitting on a bench, writing in my diary and reading a book of Tablada's poems that Pancho had loaned me. When two hours exactly had passed, I got up and set out for Calle Colima.

I looked both ways before I jumped, hauling myself up onto the wall. I dropped down, trying not to crush the flowers that Mrs. Font (or the maid) had planted on that side of the garden. Then I walked in the dark toward the little house.

María was waiting for me under a tree. Before I could say anything, she kissed me on the mouth, sticking her tongue down my throat. She tasted of cigarettes and expensive food. I tasted of cigarettes and cheap food. But both kinds of food were good. All the fear and sadness that I felt instantly melted away. Instead of going to her little house we started to make love right there, standing up under the tree. So that no one would hear the sounds she made, María bit my neck. I pulled out before I came (María said ahhhh: maybe I pulled out too quickly) and I guess I came on the grass and the flowers. In the little house Angélica was sound asleep, or pretending to be sound asleep, and we made love again. And then I got up, my whole body aching, and I knew that if I told her I loved her the pain would go away instantly, but I didn't say anything and I checked in every corner, to see whether I would find Barrios and the Patterson girl sleeping in one of them, but there was no one there except for the Font sisters and me.

Then we started to talk, and Angélica woke up and we turned on the light and the three of us talked until late. We talked about poetry, about the dead poet Laura Damián and the prize named after her, about the magazine that Ulises Lima and Belano planned to publish, about Ernesto San Epifanio's life, about what Huracán Ramírez must look like with his mask off, outside the ring, about a painter friend of Angélica's who lived in Tepito, and about María's friends from the dance school. And after lots of talk and many cigarettes, Angélica and María fell asleep and I turned out the light and got into bed and made love to María again in my mind.


NOVEMBER 20

Political affiliations: Moctezuma Rodríguez is a Trotskyite. Jacinto Requena and Arturo Belano used to be Trotskyites.

María Font, Angélica Font, and Laura Jáuregui (Belano's exgirlfriend) used to belong to a radical feminist movement called Mexican Women on the Warpath. That's where they supposedly met Simone Darrieux, friend of Belano and promoter of some kind of sadomasochism.

Ernesto San Epifanio started the first Homosexual Communist Party of Mexico and the first Mexican Homosexual Proletarian Commune.

Ulises Lima and Laura Damián once planned to start an anarchist group: the draft of a founding manifesto still exists. Before that, at the age of fifteen, Ulises Lima tried to join what remained of Lucio Cabañas's guerrilla group.

Quim Font's father, also called Quim Font, was born in Barcelona and died in the Battle of the Ebro.

Rafael Barrios's father was active in the illegal railroad workers' union. He died of cirrhosis.

Luscious Skin's father and mother were born in Oaxaca and, according to Luscious Skin himself, they starved to death.


NOVEMBER 21

Party at Catalina O'Hara's house.

This morning I talked to my uncle on the phone. He asked me when I planned to come back. Always, I said. After an awkward silence (he probably didn't understand my answer but didn't want to admit it), he asked me what I'd gotten myself mixed up in. Nothing, I said. Tonight I want to see you home where you belong, he said. Or else. Behind him I could hear my aunt Martita crying. Of course, I said. Ask him if he's on drugs, my aunt said, but my uncle said he can hear you and then he asked me whether I had money. I've got bus fare, I said, and then I couldn't talk anymore.

Actually, I didn't even have bus fare. But then things took an unexpected turn.

At Catalina O'Hara's house were Ulises Lima, Belano, Müller, San Epifanio, Barrios, Barbara Patterson, Requena and his girlfriend Xóchitl, the Rodríguez brothers, Luscious Skin, the woman painter who shared the studio with Catalina, plus lots of other people I didn't know and hadn't heard of, who came and went like a dark river.

When María, Angélica, and I made our entrance, the door was open. As we came in the only people we saw were the Rodríguez brothers, sitting on the stairs to the second floor sharing a joint. We said hello and sat down next to them. I think they were waiting for us. Then Pancho and Angélica went upstairs and we were left alone. From above came spooky music that was supposed to be soothing, full of the sounds of birds, ducks, frogs, wind, the sea, and even people's footsteps on the earth or dry grass, but the general effect was terrifying, like the sound track for a horror movie. Then Luscious Skin came in, kissed María on the cheek (I looked the other way, at a wall covered in prints of women or women's dreams), and started to talk to us. Why I don't know, maybe because I was shy, but while they talked (Luscious Skin was a regular at the dance school; he spoke María's language), I gradually tuned out, turning inward, and started to think about all the strange things I had experienced that morning at the Fonts'.

At first everything went smoothly. I sat down to breakfast with the family. Mrs. Font greeted me with a pleasant good morning. Jorgito didn't even glance at me (he was half asleep). The maid, when she arrived, waved in a friendly way. So far so good, and in fact for a moment I even thought I might be able to live in María's little house for the rest of my life. But then Quim appeared, and just the sight of him gave me the shivers. He looked as if he hadn't slept all night, as if he'd just emerged from a torture chamber or an executioners' den, his hair was a mess, his eyes were red, he hadn't shaved (or showered), and the backs of his hands were spotted with something that looked like iodine, his fingers stained with ink. Of course, he didn't greet me, although I said good morning to him as warmly as I could. His wife and daughters ignored him. After a few minutes, I ignored him too. His breakfast was much more frugal than ours: he swallowed two cups of black coffee and then he smoked a wrinkled cigarette that he pulled from his pocket instead of a pack, watching us in the strangest way, as if he were defying us but at the same time didn't see us. Finished with breakfast, he got up and asked me to follow him, saying that he wanted to have a word with me.

I looked at María, I looked at Angélica, and since nothing in their faces told me to say no, I followed.

It was the first time I had been in Quim Font's study, and I was surprised by the size of the room, which was much smaller than any of the other rooms in the house. There were photographs and plans tacked to the walls or scattered around any which way on the floor. A drafting table and a stool were the only furniture and they took up more than half the space. The study smelled like tobacco and sweat.

"I've been working all night," said Quim. "I couldn't sleep a wink."

"Oh, really?" I said, thinking that now I was in for it, that Quim must have heard me come by the night before, that he had seen María and me through the study's one little window, and now I was going to get it.

"Yes, look at my hands," he said.

He held his two hands at chest height. They were trembling considerably.

"On a project?" I said affably, looking at the papers spread out on the table.

"No," said Quim, "on a magazine. A magazine that's coming out soon."

I don't know why, but I immediately thought (or knew, as if he had told me so himself) that he meant the visceral realist magazine.

"I'm going to show them, everyone who's against me, yes, sir," he said.

I went over to the table and studied the diagrams and drawings, leafing slowly through the rough stack of papers. The mock-up for the magazine was a chaos of geometric figures and randomly scribbled names or letters. It was obvious that poor Mr. Font was on the verge of a nervous breakdown.

"What do you think?"

"Extremely interesting," I said.

"Those jackasses will learn what the avant-garde is now, won't they? And that's even without the poems, see? This is where all of your poems will go."

The space he showed me was full of lines, lines mimicking writing, but also little drawings, like when someone swears in the comics: snakes, bombs, knives, skulls, crossbones, little mushroom clouds. The rest of each page was a compendium of Quim Font's extravagant ideas about graphic design.

"Look, this is the magazine's logo."

A snake (which might have been smiling but more likely was writhing in a spasm of pain) was biting its tail with a hungry, agonized expression, its eyes fixed like daggers on the hypothetical reader.

"But nobody knows what the magazine will be called yet," I said.

"It doesn't matter. The snake is Mexican and it also symbolizes circularity. Have you read Nietzsche, García Madero?" he said suddenly.

I confessed apologetically that I hadn't. Then I looked at each of the pages of the magazine (there were more than sixty), and just as I was getting ready to leave, Quim asked how things were going between me and his daughter. I told him that things were fine, that María and I were getting along better and better every day, and then I decided to shut my mouth.

"Life is hard for parents," he said, "especially in Mexico City. How long has it been since you slept at home?"

"Three nights," I said.

"And isn't your mother worried?"

"I talked to them on the phone. They know I'm all right."

Quim looked me up and down.

"You're not in great shape, my boy."

I shrugged my shoulders. The two of us stood there pensively for a minute without saying anything, him drumming his fingers on the table and me looking at old plans tacked to the walls, plans for dream houses that Quim would probably never see built.

"Come with me," he said.

I followed him to his room on the second floor, which was about five times the size of his study.

He opened the closet and took out a green sports shirt.

"Try this on, see how it fits."

I hesitated for a second, but Quim's gestures were abrupt, as if there were no time to lose. I dropped my shirt at the foot of the bed, an enormous bed where Quim, his wife, and his three children could've slept, and I put on the green shirt. It fit me well.

"It's yours," said Quim. Then he stuck his hand in his pocket and handed me some bills: "So you can treat María to a soda."

His hand was trembling, his outstretched arm was trembling, his other arm, which was hanging at his side, was trembling too, and his face was twisting into horrible expressions that forced me to look anywhere but at him. I thanked him but said there was no way I could accept such a gift.

"Strange," said Quim, "everybody takes my money: my daughters, my son, my wife, my employees"—he used the plural, although I knew perfectly well that at this point he didn't have any employees, except for the maid, but he didn't mean the maid—"even my bosses love my money and that's why they keep it."

"Thank you very much," I said.

"Take it and put it in your pocket, damn it!"

I took the money and put it away. It was quite a bit, though I didn't have the nerve to count it.

"I'll return it as soon as I can," I said.

Quim let himself fall backward on the bed. His body made a muffled sound and then quivered. For a second I wondered whether it could be a water bed.

"Don't worry, boy. We were put on this earth to help each other. You help me with my daughter, I'll help you with a little cash for your expenses. Call it an extra allowance, all right?"

His voice sounded tired, as if he were about to collapse in exhaustion and sleep, but his eyes were still open, staring nervously at the ceiling.

"I like the way the magazine looks, I'll give those bastards something to talk about," he said, but his voice was a whisper now.

"It's perfect," I said.

"Well, naturally, I'm not an architect for nothing," he said. And then, after a moment: "We're artists too, but we do a good job hiding it, don't we?"

"Sure you do," I said.

He seemed to be snoring. I looked at his face: his eyes were open. Quim? I said. He didn't answer. Very slowly, I approached him and touched the mattress. Something inside it responded to my touch. Bubbles the size of an apple. I turned and left the room.

I spent the rest of the day with María and chasing María.

It rained a few times. The first time it stopped, a rainbow appeared. The second time there was nothing, black clouds and night in the valley.

Catalina O'Hara is red-haired, twenty-five, has a son, is separated, is pretty.

I also met Laura Jáuregui, who used to be Arturo Belano's girlfriend. She was at the party with Sofía Gálvez, Ulises Lima's lost love.

Both of them are pretty.

No, Laura is *much* prettier.

I drank too much. Visceral realists were swarming everywhere, although more than half of them were just university students in disguise.

Angélica and Pancho left early.

At a certain point during the night, María said to me: disaster is imminent.


**NOVEMBER 22**

I woke up at Catalina O'Hara's house. As I was having breakfast, very early, with Catalina and her son, Davy, who had to be taken to nursery school (María wasn't there, everyone else was asleep), I remembered that

71

the night before, when there were just a few of us left, Ernesto San Epifanio had said that all literature could be classified as heterosexual, homosexual, or bisexual. Novels, in general, were heterosexual, whereas poetry was completely homosexual; I guess short stories were bisexual, although he didn't say so.

Within the vast ocean of poetry he identified various currents: faggots, queers, sissies, freaks, butches, fairies, nymphs, and philenes. But the two major currents were faggots and queers. Walt Whitman, for example, was a faggot poet. Pablo Neruda, a queer. William Blake was definitely a faggot. Octavio Paz was a queer. Borges was a philene, or in other words he might be a faggot one minute and simply asexual the next. Rubén Darío was a freak, in fact, the queen freak, the prototypical freak.

"In our language, of course," he clarified. "In the wider world the reigning freak is still Verlaine the Generous."

Freaks, according to San Epifanio, were closer to madhouse flamboyance and naked hallucination, while faggots and queers wandered in stagger-step from ethics to aesthetics and back again. Cernuda, dear Cernuda, was a nymph, and at moments of great bitterness, a faggot, whereas Guillén, Aleixandre, and Alberti could be considered a sissy, a butch, and a queer, respectively. As a general rule, poets like Carlos Pellicer were butches, while poets like Tablada, Novo, and Renato Leduc were sissies. In fact, there was a dearth of faggots in Mexican poetry, although some optimists might point to López Velarde or Efraín Huerta. There were lots of queers, on the other hand, from the mauler (although for a second I heard mobster) Díaz Mirón to the illustrious Homero Aridjis. It was necessary to go all the way back to Amado Nervo (whistles) to find a real poet, a faggot poet, that is, and not a philene like the resurrected and now renowned Manuel José Othón from San Luis Potosí, a bore if ever there was one. And speaking of bores: Manuel Acuña was a fairy and José Joaquín Pesado was a Grecian wood nymph, both longtime pimps of a certain kind of Mexican lyrical verse.

"And Efrén Rebolledo?" I asked.

"An extremely minor queer. His only virtue is that he was the first, if not the only, Mexican poet to publish a book in Tokyo: *Japanese Poems*, 1909. He was a diplomat, of course."

Anyway, the poetry scene was essentially an (underground) battle, the result of the struggle between faggot poets and queer poets to seize control of the *word*. Sissies, according to San Epifanio, were faggot poets by birth, who out of weakness or for comfort's sake lived within and accepted—most of the time—the aesthetic and personal parameters of the queers. In Spain, France, and Italy, queer poets have always been legion, he said, although a superficial reader might never guess. What happens is that a faggot poet like Leopardi, for example, somehow reconstructs queers like Ungaretti, Montale, and Quasimodo, the deadly trio.

"In the same way, Pasolini redraws contemporary Italian queerdom. Take the case of poor Sanguinetti (I won't start with Pavese, who was a sad freak, the only one of his kind, or Dino Campana, who dines at a separate table, the table of hopeless freaks). Not to mention France, great country of devouring mouths, where one hundred faggot poets, from Villon to our beloved Sophie Podolski, have nurtured, still nurture, and will nurture with the blood of their tits ten thousand queer poets with their entourage of philenes, nymphs, butches, and sissies, lofty editors of literary magazines, great translators, petty bureaucrats, and grand diplomats of the Kingdom of Letters (see, if you must, the shameful and malicious reflections of the *Tel Quel* poets). And the less said the better about the faggotry of the Russian Revolution, which, if we're to be honest, gave us just one faggot poet, a single one."

"Who?" they asked him. "Mayakovsky?"

"No."

"Esenin?"

"No."

"Pasternak? Blok? Mandelstam? Akhmatova?"

"Hardly."

"Come on, Ernesto, tell us, the suspense is killing us."

"There was only one," said San Epifanio, "and now I'll tell you who it was, but he was the real thing, a steppes-and-snow faggot, a faggot from head to toe: Khlebnikov."

There was an opinion for every taste.

"And in Latin America, how many true faggots do we find? Vallejo and Martín Adán. Period. New paragraph. Macedonio Fernández, maybe? The rest are queers like Huidobro, fairies like Alfonso Cortés (although some of his poems are authentically fagotty), butches like León de Greiff, butch nymphs like Pablo de Rokha (with bursts of freakishness that would've driven Lacan crazy), sissies like Lezama Lima, a misguided reader of Góngora, and, along with Lezama, all the poets of the Cuban Revolution (Diego, Vitier, horrible Retamar, pathetic Guillén, inconsolable Fina García) except for Rogelio Nogueras, who is a darling and a nymph with the spirit of a playful faggot. But moving on. In Nicaragua most poets are fairies like Coronel Urtecho or queers who wish they were philenes, like Ernesto Cardenal. The Mexican Contemporaries are queers too . . ."

"No!" shouted Belano. "Not Gilberto Owen!"

"In fact," San Epifanio continued unruffled, "Gorostiza's *Death Without End,* along with the poetry of Paz, is the 'Marseillaise' of the highly nervous and sedentary Mexican queer poets. More names: Gelman, nymph; Benedetti, queer; Nicanor Parra, fairy with a hint of faggot; Westphalen, freak; Enrique Lihn, sissy; Girondo, fairy; Rubén Bonifaz Nuño, fairy butch; Sabines, butchy butch; our beloved, untouchable Josemilio P., freak. And back to Spain, back to the beginning"—whistles —"Góngora and Quevedo, queers; San Juan de la Cruz and Fray Luis de León, faggots. End of story. And now, some differences between queers and faggots. Even in their sleep, the former beg for a twelve-inch cock to plow and fertilize them, but at the moment of truth, mountains must be moved to get them into bed with the pimps they love. Faggots, on the other hand, live as if a stake is permanently churning their insides and when they look at themselves in the mirror (something they both love and hate to do with all their heart), they see the Pimp of Death in their own sunken eyes. For faggots and queers, *pimp* is the one word that can cross unscathed through the realms of nothingness (or silence or otherness). But then, too, nothing prevents queers and faggots from being good friends if they so desire, from neatly ripping one another off, criticizing or praising one another, publishing or burying one another in the frantic and moribund world of letters."

"And what about Cesárea Tinajero? Is she a faggot or a queer?" someone asked. I didn't recognize the voice.

"Oh, Cesárea Tinajero is horror itself," said San Epifanio.


NOVEMBER 23

I told María that her father had given me money.

"Do you think I'm a whore?" she said.

"Of course not!"

"Then don't take any money from that old nut-job!" she said.

This afternoon we went to a lecture by Octavio Paz. On the subway, María didn't speak to me. Angélica was with us and we met Ernesto at the lecture, at the Capilla Alfonsina. Afterward we went to a restaurant on Calle Palma where all the waiters were octogenarians. The restaurant was called La Palma de la Vida. Suddenly I felt trapped. The waiters, who were about to die at any minute, María's indifference, as if she'd already had enough of me, San Epifanio's distant, ironic smile, and even Angélica, who was the same as always—it all seemed like a trap, a humorous commentary on my own existence.

On top of everything, they said I hadn't understood Octavio Paz's lecture at all, and they might have been right. All I'd noticed were the poet's hands, which beat out the rhythm of his words as he read, a tic he'd probably picked up in adolescence.

"The kid is a complete ignoramus," said María, "a typical product of the law school."

I preferred not to respond. (Although several replies occurred to me.) What did I think about then? About my shirt, which stank. About Quim Font's money. About Laura Damián, who had died so young. About Octavio Paz's right hand, his index finger and middle finger, his ring finger, thumb and little finger, which cut through the air of the Capilla as if *our* lives depended on it. I also thought about home and bed.

Later two guys with long hair and leather pants came in. They looked like musicians but they were students at the dance school.

For a long time I stopped existing.

"Why do you hate me, María? What have I done to you?" I whispered in her ear.

She looked at me as if I were speaking to her from another planet. Don't be ridiculous, she said.

Ernesto San Epifanio heard her reply and smiled at me in a disturbing way. In fact everybody heard her, and everybody was smiling at me as if I'd gone crazy! I think I closed my eyes. I tried to join some conversation. I tried to talk about the visceral realists. The pseudomusicians laughed. At some point María kissed one of them and Ernesto San Epifanio patted me on the back. I remember that I caught his hand in the air or grabbed his elbow, and that I looked him in the eye and told him to back off, that I didn't need anybody's pity. I remember that María and Angélica decided to go with the dancers. I remember hearing myself shout at some point during the night:

"I earned your father's money!"

But I don't remember whether María was there to hear me or if by then I was alone.

### NOVEMBER 24

I'm back at home. I've been back to the university (but not to class). I'd like to sleep with María. I'd like to sleep with Catalina O'Hara. I'd like to sleep with Laura Jáuregui. Sometimes I'd like to sleep with Angélica, but the circles under her eyes keep getting darker, and every day she's paler, thinner, less there.

### NOVEMBER 25

Today I only saw Barrios and Jacinto Requena at Café Quito, and our conversation was mostly gloomy, as if something irreparably bad was about to happen. Still, we laughed a lot. They told me that Arturo Belano once gave a lecture at the Casa del Lago and when it was his turn to talk he forgot everything. I think the lecture was supposed to be on Chilean poetry and Belano improvised a talk about horror movies. Another time, Ulises Lima gave a lecture and no one came. We talked until they kicked us out.

### NOVEMBER 26

No one was at Café Quito and I didn't feel like sitting at a table and reading in the middle of the dreary bustle at that time of day. For a while I walked along Bucareli. I called María, who wasn't home, walked past the Encrucijada Veracruzana twice, went in the third time, and there, behind the bar, was Rosario.

I thought she wouldn't recognize me. Sometimes I don't even recognize myself! But Rosario looked at me and smiled, and after a while, once she had waited on a table of regulars, she came over.

"Have you written me my poem yet?" she said, sitting down beside me. Rosario has dark eyes, black, I'd say, and broad hips.

"More or less," I said, with an ever-so-slight feeling of triumph.

"All right, then, read it to me."

"My poems are meant to be read, not spoken," I said. I think José Emilio Pacheco claimed something similar recently.

"Exactly, so read it to me," said Rosario.

"What I mean is, it's better if you read it yourself."

"No, you'd better do it. If I read it myself, I probably won't understand it."

I chose one of my latest poems at random and read it to her.

"I don't understand it," said Rosario, "but thank you anyway."

For a second I waited for her to ask me back to the storage room. But Rosario wasn't Brígida, that much was immediately clear. Then I started to think about the abyss that separates the poet from the reader and the next thing I knew I was deeply depressed. Rosario, who had gone off to wait on other tables, came back to me.

"Have you written Brígida some poetry too?" she asked, gazing into my eyes, her thighs grazing the edge of the table.

"No, just you," I said.

"They told me what happened the other day."

"What happened the other day?" I asked, trying to seem distant. Pleasant, but distant.

"Poor Brígida has been crying over you," said Rosario.

"And why is that? Have you seen her crying?"

"We've all seen her. She's crazy about you, Mr. Poet. You must have some special thing with women."

I think I blushed, but at the same time I was flattered.

"It's nothing . . . special," I murmured. "Did she tell you anything?"

"She told me lots of things, do you want to know what she said?"

"All right," I said, although the truth is I wasn't very sure I wanted to hear Brígida's confidences. Almost immediately, I despised myself. Human beings are ungrateful, I said to myself, thoughtless and quick to forget.

"But not here," said Rosario. "In a little while I get an hour off. Do you know where the gringo's pizzeria is? Wait for me there."

I said I would, and I left the Encrucijada Veracruzana. Outside the day had turned cloudy and a strong wind was making people walk faster than usual or take shelter in the entrances to stores. When I passed Café

Quito I glanced in and didn't see anyone I knew. For a minute I thought about calling María again, but I didn't.

The pizzeria was full and people were standing up to eat the slices that the gringo in person cut with a big chef's knife. I watched him for a while. I thought that the business must bring in good money and I was happy because the gringo seemed nice. He did everything himself: mix the dough, spread tomato sauce and mozzarella, put the pizzas in the oven, cut them, hand the slices to the customers who crowded around the counter, make more pizzas, and start all over again. Everything except take money and make change. That job was handled by a dark kid, maybe fifteen, with very short hair, who constantly consulted with the gringo in a low voice, as if he still didn't know the prices very well or wasn't good at math. After a while I noticed another odd detail. The gringo never let go of his big knife.

"Here I am," said Rosario, tugging on my sleeve.

She didn't look the same out on the street as she did at the Encruci- jada Veracruzana. Outside, her face was less firm, her features more transparent, vaporous, as if on the street she were in danger of turning in- visible.

"Let's walk a little way, then you can treat me to something, okay?"

We started to walk toward Reforma. Rosario took my arm the first time we crossed the street and didn't let go.

"I want to be like your mother," she said, "but don't get the wrong idea, I'm not a slut like that Brígida, I want to help you, be good to you, I want to be with you when you become famous, darling."

This woman must be crazy, I thought, but I didn't say anything. I just smiled.

NOVEMBER 27

Everything is getting complicated. Horrible things are happening. At night I wake up screaming. I dream about a woman with the head of a cow. Its eyes stare at me. With touching sadness, actually. On top of it all, I had a little "man-to-man" talk with my uncle. He made me swear that I wasn't doing drugs. No, I said, I don't do drugs, I swear. None at all? he said. What does that mean? I said. What do you mean what does that mean! he roared. Exactly what I say, what do you mean? Could you please be a little more precise, I said, shrinking like a snail. At night I called María. She wasn't there, but I talked to Angélica for a while. How are you? she said. Not very well, really, I said, in fact, pretty bad. Are you sick? said Angélica. No, nervous. I'm not very well either, said Angélica, I can hardly sleep. I would've liked to ask her more, one ex-virgin to another, but I didn't.

NOVEMBER 28

Horrible things keep happening, dreams, nightmares, impulses I indulge that are completely out of my control. It's like when I was fifteen and always masturbating. Three times a day, five times a day, nothing was enough! Rosario wants to marry me. I told her I didn't believe in marriage. Well, she said with a laugh, married or not, what I'm trying to say is that I NEED to live with you. Live together, I said, in the SAME house? Well, of course, in the same house, or in the same ROOM, if we don't have enough money to RENT a house. Or even in a cave, she said, I'm not PICKY. Her face shone, whether from sweat or pure faith in what she was saying I'm not sure. The first time we did it was at her place, a crummy tenement building way out in the Colonia Merced Balbuena, near the Calzada de la Viga. The room was full of postcards of Veracruz and pictures of movie actors tacked to the walls.

"Is it your first time, *papacito*?" Rosario asked me.

I said yes, I don't know why.

NOVEMBER 29

I drift from place to place like a piece of flotsam. Today I went to Catalina O'Hara's house without being invited and without calling first. It so happened that she was there. She'd just gotten home and her eyes were red, an unmistakable sign that she'd been crying. At first she didn't recognize me. I asked her why she was crying. Man trouble, she said. I had to bite my tongue not to say that if she needed someone I was there, ready and willing. We had some whiskey—I need it, said Catalina—and then we went to pick up her son at nursery school. Catalina drove like a maniac and I felt sick. On the way home, as I played with her son in the backseat, she asked whether I wanted to see her paintings. I said yes. In the end we finished half a bottle of whiskey and after Catalina put her son to bed she started to cry again. Don't go near her, I told myself, she's a MOTHER. Then I thought about graves, about fucking on a grave, about sleeping in a grave. Luckily, the painter she shares the house and studio with came in a few minutes later and the three of us started to make dinner together. Catalina's friend is separated, but evidently she handles it better. As we were eating she told jokes. Painter jokes. I'd never heard a woman tell such good jokes (unfortunately I can't remember a single one). Then, why I don't know, they started to talk about Ulises Lima and Arturo Belano. According to Catalina's friend, there was a poet who was six and a half feet tall and weighed more than two hundred pounds, the nephew of an administrator at UNAM, who was looking to beat them up. Knowing he was after them, they'd disappeared. But Catalina O'Hara didn't buy it; according to her, our friends were off looking for Cesárea Tinajero's lost papers, hidden in archives and used bookstores around Mexico City. I left at midnight, and when I was outside all of a sudden I had no idea where to go. I called María, prepared to tell her everything about Rosario (and while I was at it, about the *affaire* in the storage room with Brígida) and ask her to forgive me, but the telephone rang and rang and no one answered. The whole Font family had disappeared. So I set off south, toward Ulises Lima's rooftop. When I arrived, no one was there, so I ended up heading downtown again, toward Calle Bucareli. Once I got there, before I went to the Encrucijada Veracruzana, I looked in the window of Café Amarillo (Quito was closed). At one of the tables, I saw Pancho Rodríguez. He was alone with a half-drunk cup of coffee in front of him. He had a book on the table, one hand flat on the pages to hold it open, and his face was twisted in an expression of intense pain. From time to time he grimaced, making faces that were terrifying to see through the window. Either the book he was reading was having a wrenching effect on him, or he had a toothache. At one moment he raised his head and looked all around, as if he sensed that he was being watched. I hid. When I looked in the window again, Pancho was still reading and the expression of pain had disappeared from his face. Rosario and Brígida were working that night at the Encrucijada Veracruzana. Brígida came up to me first. In her face I detected bitterness and resentment, but also the suffering of the rejected. Honestly, I felt sorry for her! Everybody was suffering! I bought her a tequila and listened without flinching to everything she had to say to me. Then Rosario came over and said that she didn't like to see me standing at the bar writing, like an orphan. There's no free table, I said and went on writing. My poem is called "Everybody Suffers." I don't care if people stare.

NOVEMBER 30

Last night something really bad happened. I was at the Encrucijada Veracruzana, leaning on the bar, switching back and forth between writing poems and writing in my diary (I have no problem going from one format to the other), when Rosario and Brígida started to scream at each other at the back of the bar. Soon the grisly drunks were taking sides and cheering them on so energetically that I couldn't concentrate on my writing anymore and decided to slip away.

I don't know what time it was, but it was late, and outside the fresh air struck me in the face. As I walked I started to feel like writing again, recovering the inclination if not the inspiration (does inspiration really exist?). I turned the corner at the Reloj Chino and started to walk toward La Ciudadela looking for a café where I could keep working. I crossed the Jardín Morelos, empty and eerie, but with glimpses of secret life in its corners, bodies and laughter (giggles) that mocked the solitary passerby (or so it seemed to me then). I crossed Niños Héroes, crossed Plaza Pacheco (which commemorates José Emilio's grandfather and which was empty, no shadows or laughter this time), and as I was about to turn up Revillagigedo toward the Alameda, Quim Font emerged or materialized from around a corner. The shock almost killed me. He was wearing a suit and tie (but there was something about the suit and tie that made them look all wrong together), and he was dragging a girl after him, her elbow firmly in his grip. They were going the same way I was, although on the other side of the street, and it took me a few seconds to react. The girl Quim was dragging after him wasn't Angélica, as I had irrationally supposed when I saw her, although her height and build added to my confusion.

Clearly the girl had no great desire to follow Quim, but neither could it be said that she was putting up much resistance. As I drew level with them, heading up Revillagigedo toward the Alameda, I couldn't stop staring, as if to make sure that the nocturnal passerby was Quim and not an apparition, and then he saw me too. He recognized me right away.

"García Madero!" he shouted. "Over here, man!"

I crossed the street, taking great precautions or pretending to (since at that moment there were no cars on Revillagigedo), possibly in order to put off my meeting with María's father for a few seconds. When I reached the other side of the street, the girl raised her head and looked at me. It was Lupe, whom I'd met in Colonia Guerrero. She showed no sign of recognizing me. Of course, the first thing I thought was that Quim and Lupe were looking for a hotel.

"You're exactly the person we wanted to see!" said Quim Font.

I said hello to Lupe.

"How're things?" she said with a smile that froze my heart.

"I'm looking for a safe place for this young lady to stay," said Quim, "but I can't find a decent goddamn hotel anywhere in the neighborhood."

"Well, there are plenty of hotels around here," said Lupe. "What you really mean is that you don't want to spend much."

"Money isn't a problem. If you have it, you have it, and if you don't, you don't."

Only then did I notice that Quim was very nervous. The hand with which he was gripping Lupe trembled spasmodically, as if Lupe's arm were charged with electricity. He blinked fiercely and bit his lip.

"Is there some problem?" I asked.

Quim and Lupe looked at me for a few seconds (both of them seemed about to explode) and then they laughed.

"We're fucked," said Lupe.

"Do you know of a place we can hide this young lady?" said Quim.

Nervous as he may have been, he was also extremely happy.

"I don't know," I said, to say something.

"I don't suppose we could use your house?"

"Absolutely impossible."

"Why don't you let me handle my own problems?" said Lupe.

"Because no one escapes from under my protection!" said Quim, winking at me. "And also because I know you can't."

"Let's go get some coffee," I said, "and we'll come up with something."

"I expected no less of you, García Madero," said Quim. "I knew you wouldn't let me down."

"But it was pure coincidence that I ran into you!" I said.

82

"Oh, coincidence," said Quim, sucking air into his lungs like the titan of Calle Revillagigedo. "There's no such thing as coincidence. When it comes down to it, everything is ordained. The goddamn Greeks called it destiny."

Lupe looked at him and smiled the way you smile at crazy people. She was wearing a miniskirt and a black sweater. I thought the sweater was María's, or at least it smelled like María.

We started to walk, heading right on Victoria to Dolores, where we went into a Chinese café. We sat down near a cadaverous-looking man who was reading the paper. Quim inspected the place, then shut himself in the bathroom for a few minutes. Lupe followed him with her eyes and for an instant she gazed at him like a woman in love. Suddenly I just knew they'd slept together, or were planning to momentarily.

When Quim returned, he'd washed his hands and face and splashed water on his hair. Since there was no towel in the bathroom he hadn't dried off, and water was running down his temples.

"These places bring back memories of the worst times of my life," he said.

Then he was quiet. Lupe and I were silent for a while too.

"When I was young I knew a deaf man. Actually, he was a deaf-mute," Quim went on after a moment of thought. "The deaf-mute was always at the student cafeteria where I would go with a group of friends from the architecture department. One of them was the painter Pérez Camargo. I'm sure you've heard of him or know his work. At the cafeteria we always saw the deaf-mute, who sold pencil cases, toys, cards printed with the sign-language alphabet. Trinkets, basically, to make a few extra pesos. He was a nice guy, and sometimes he would come sit at our table. In fact, I think some of us were stupid enough to consider him our mascot, and more than one of us even learned some sign language, just for fun. The deaf-mute may actually have been the one who taught us, I can't remember now. Anyway, one night I went into a Chinese café like this, but in Colonia Narvarte, and I bumped into the deaf-mute. God only knows what I was doing there. It wasn't a neighborhood where I spent much time. Maybe I was on my way home from some girlfriend's house, but anyway, let's just say I was a little upset, in the middle of one of my depressive episodes. It was late. The café was empty. I sat at the counter or a table close to the door. At first I thought I was the only customer in the place. But when I got up and went to the bathroom (to do my business or cry in peace!) I discovered the deaf-mute in the back half of the café, in a kind of second room. He was alone too, and reading the paper, and he didn't see me. The strange turns life takes. When I passed him he didn't see me and I didn't greet him. I guess I didn't think I could bear his happiness. But when I came out of the bathroom everything had changed somehow, and I decided to go up to him. He was still there, reading, and I said hello to him and jostled the table a little so that he would notice I was there. Then the deaf-mute raised his head. He seemed half asleep, and he looked at me without recognizing me and said hello."

"Jesus," I said, and the hair rose on the back of my neck.

"You get it, García Madero," said Quim, looking at me sympathetically, "I was scared too. The truth is, all I wanted was to get the hell out of that place."

"I don't know what you were scared of," said Lupe.

Quim ignored her.

"It was all I could do not to go running out of there screaming," he said. "The only thing that kept me from leaving was the knowledge that the deaf-mute hadn't recognized me yet and that I had to pay the bill. Still, I couldn't finish my coffee, and when I was out in the street I took off running, shamelessly."

"I can imagine," I said.

"It was like seeing the devil," said Quim.

"The guy could talk fine," I said.

"Perfectly fine! He looked up and said hello to me. He even had a nice voice, for God's sake."

"It wasn't the devil," said Lupe, "although maybe it was, you never know. But in this case I don't think it was the devil."

"Please, you know I don't believe in the devil, Lupe," said Quim. "It's a manner of speaking."

"Who do you think it was?" I asked.

"A narc. An informer," said Lupe, grinning from ear to ear.

"Well, of course, you must be right," I said.

"And why would he be friendly to us, pretending he was mute?" said Quim.

"Deaf-mute," I said.

"Because you were students," said Lupe.

Quim looked at Lupe as if he were about to kiss her.

"You're so smart, Lupita."

"Don't make fun of me," she said.

"I'm serious, damn it."

At one in the morning we left the Chinese café and went looking for a hotel. At around two we finally found one on Río de la Loza. Along the way they explained to me what had happened to Lupe. Her pimp had tried to kill her. When I asked why, they told me that it was because Lupe didn't want to work in the afternoons anymore; she wanted to go to school.

"Congratulations, Lupe," I said. "What are you going to study?"

"Contemporary dance," she said.

"At the dance school with María?"

"That's right. With Paco Duarte."

"But can you enroll just like that, without taking some test?"

Quim looked at me as if I were in some other dimension.

"Lupe has influential friends of her own, García Madero, and we're all prepared to help her. She doesn't need to pass any fucking test."

The hotel was called the Media Luna and contrary to my expectations, after Quim took a look at the room and spoke a few words in private to the night clerk, he told Lupe good night and warned her not even to think about leaving without letting him know. Lupe said goodbye to us at the door to her room. Don't see us out, Quim said. Later, as we were walking toward Reforma, he explained that he'd had to give the clerk a small tip to get him to take Lupe without asking too many questions, but especially, if it came down to it, not to give out too many answers.

"What I'm afraid of," he told me, "is that tonight her pimp's going to check every hotel in Mexico City."

I suggested that maybe the police could take care of the problem or at least issue some kind of restraining order.

"Don't be an ass, García Madero. Alberto has friends in the police. How else do you think he runs his rackets? All the whores in Mexico City are controlled by the police."

"Come on. That's hard to believe," I said. "Maybe there are some officers who take bribes to look the other way, but to say that all of them . . ."

"The prostitution business in Mexico City and all of Mexico is controlled by the police, get that into your head once and for all," said Quim. And after a while, he added: "We're on our own in this."

At Niños Héroes he caught a taxi. Before he got in he made me promise that the next day first thing I'd be at his house.

### DECEMBER 1

I didn't go to the Fonts' house. I spent all day having sex with Rosario.

### DECEMBER 2

I ran into Jacinto Requena walking along Bucareli.

We went to get two slices of pizza at the gringo's place. As we ate he told me that Arturo had ordered the first purge of visceral realism.

I was stunned. I asked him how many he'd kicked out. Five, said Requena. I assume I wasn't one of them, I said. No, not you, said Requena. The news came as a great relief. Those purged were Pancho Rodríguez, Luscious Skin, and three poets I didn't know.

While I was in bed with Rosario, it occurred to me that Mexican avant-garde poetry was undergoing its first schism.

Depressed all day, but writing and reading like a steam engine.

### DECEMBER 3

I have to admit that I have more fun in bed with Rosario than with María.

### DECEMBER 4

But whom do I love? Yesterday it rained all night. The building's outdoor stairways looked like Niagara Falls. I kept a tally as we made love. Rosario was amazing, but to preserve the integrity of the experiment, I didn't tell her so. She came fifteen times. The first few times she had to cover her mouth so she wouldn't wake the neighbors. The last few times I was afraid she was going to have a heart attack. Sometimes she seemed to swoon in my arms and other times she arched as if a ghost were tickling her spine. I came three times. Later we went outside and bathed in the rain spilling over the stairwells. It's strange: my sweat is hot and Rosario's is cold and reptilian, with a bittersweet taste (mine is definitely salty). In total we spent four hours fucking. Then Rosario dried me,

dried herself, tidied up the room in a heartbeat (it's incredible how industrious and practical the woman is), and went to sleep, because the
next day she had to work. I sat at the table and wrote a poem that I called
"15/3." Then I read William Burroughs until dawn.

### DECEMBER 5

Today Rosario and I had sex from midnight until four-thirty in the morning and I clocked her again. She came ten times, I came twice. And yet
the time we spent making love was longer than yesterday. Between poems (as Rosario slept), I made some calculations. If you come fifteen
times in four hours, in four and a half hours you should come eighteen
times, not ten. The same ratio goes for me. Are we already in a rut?

Then there's María. I think about her every day. I'd like to see her,
sleep with her, talk to her, call her, but when it comes down to it I'm incapable of taking a single step in her direction. And then, when I make
a cool assessment of my sexual encounters with her and with Rosario,
I have to admit that I have a better time with Rosario. If nothing else, I
learn more!

### DECEMBER 6

Today I had sex with Rosario from three to five in the afternoon. She
came twice, maybe three times, I don't know, and I'd rather leave the exact figure shrouded in mystery. I came twice. Before she went to work I
told her Lupe's story. Contrary to what I expected, she wasn't very sympathetic to Lupe or Quim or me. I told her about Alberto, Lupe's pimp,
too, and to my surprise she showed quite a bit of understanding for him,
only reproaching him, and then not severely, for working as a pimp.
When I told her that this Alberto could be a very dangerous person and
that there was a risk that if he found Lupe he would do her real harm,
she answered that a woman who abandoned her man deserved all that
and more.

"But you don't have to worry, darling," she said, "that's not your
problem. You have your true love by your side, thank God."

Rosario's declaration made me sad. For an instant I imagined the unknown Alberto, his huge cock and his huge knife and a fierce look on his
face, and I thought that if Rosario met him on the street she would be at-

tracted to him. Also: that in some way he was coming between María and me. For an instant, that is, I imagined Alberto measuring his cock with his kitchen knife and I imagined the notes of a song, evocative and suggestive, although of what I couldn't say, drifting in the window (a sinister window!) along with the night air, and all of it together made me extremely sad.

"Don't be gloomy, darling," said Rosario.

And I also imagined María making love with Alberto. And Alberto smacking María on the buttocks. And Angélica making love with Pancho Rodríguez (ex–visceral realist, thank God!). And María making love with Luscious Skin. And Alberto making love with Angélica and María. And Alberto making love with Catalina O'Hara. And Alberto making love with Quim Font. And in the final instance, as the poet says, I imagined Alberto advancing over a carpet of bodies splattered with semen (a semen of deceptive consistency and color, because it looked like blood and shit) toward the hill where I stood, still as a statue, although everything in me wanted to flee, go running down the other side and lose myself in the desert.


DECEMBER 7

Today I went to my uncle's office and told him everything.

"Uncle," I said, "I'm living with a woman. That's why I don't come home to sleep. But there's no need for you to worry because I'm still going to class and I plan to finish my degree. Otherwise, I'm fine. I eat a good breakfast. I get two meals a day."

My uncle looked at me without getting up from his desk.

"What money do you plan to live on? Have you found work or is she supporting you?"

I answered that I didn't know yet, and that for now, Rosario was in fact covering my expenses, which were modest anyway.

He wanted to know who this woman was I was living with, and I told him. He wanted to know what she did. I told him, maybe slightly glossing over the coarser aspects of the job of bar girl. He wanted to know how old she was. From then on, despite my initial resolve, everything was a lie. I said that Rosario was eighteen when she's almost definitely older than twenty-two, maybe even twenty-five, although that's only a guess, since I've never asked her; it doesn't seem right to seek out the information unless she volunteers it herself.

"Just so you don't make a fool of yourself," said my uncle, and he wrote me a check for five thousand pesos.

Before I left he urged me to call my aunt that night.

I went to the bank to cash the check and then I stopped by some of the downtown bookstores. I looked in at Café Quito. The first time I didn't see anyone. I ate there and went back to Rosario's room, where I sat reading and writing until late. After dark I went back and found Jacinto Requena dying of boredom. None of the visceral realists except for him, he said, were showing their faces at the café. Everybody was afraid of running into Arturo Belano, though their fears were unwarranted since the Chilean hadn't been there in days. According to Requena (who is definitely the most laid-back of the visceral realists), Belano had begun to kick more poets out of the group. Ulises Lima was remaining discreetly in the background, but apparently he supported Belano's decisions. I asked who'd gotten purged this time. He named two poets I didn't know and Angélica Font, Laura Jáuregui, and Sofía Gálvez.

"He's expelled three women!" I exclaimed, unable to help myself.

Moctezuma Rodríguez, Catalina O'Hara, and Jacinto himself were hanging in the balance. You, Jacinto? Belano hasn't been wasting any time, said Requena, resigned. And me? No, no one's said anything about you yet, said Requena, sounding unsure. I asked him the reason for the expulsions. He didn't know. He repeated his original opinion: temporary madness on the part of Arturo Belano. Then he explained to me (although this *I already knew*) that Breton recklessly indulged in the same sport. Belano thinks he's Breton, said Requena. Actually, all the *capi di famiglia* of Mexican poetry think they're Breton, he sighed. And the people who were expelled, what are they saying? Why don't they form a new group? Requena laughed. Most of the people who were expelled, he said, don't even know they've been expelled! And those who do know couldn't care less about visceral realism. You might say Arturo has done them a favor.

"Pancho couldn't care less? Luscious Skin couldn't care less?"

"Those two might care. The others have just been relieved of a burden. Now they're free to join the ranks of the peasant poets or go kiss up to Paz."

"What Belano is doing doesn't seem very democratic to me," I said.

"True enough. It isn't exactly what you might call democratic."

"We should go see him and tell him," I said.

"No one knows where he is. He and Ulises have disappeared."

For a while we sat watching the Mexico City night through the window.

Outside people were walking fast, hunched over, not as if they were expecting a storm, but as if the storm were already here. Still, no one seemed to be afraid.

Later Requena started to talk about Xóchitl and the baby they were going to have. I asked what they would call it.

"Franz," said Requena.


DECEMBER 8

Since I don't have anything to do, I've decided to go looking for Belano and Ulises Lima in the bookstores of Mexico City. I've discovered the antiquarian bookstore Plinio el Joven, on Venustiano Carranza. The Lizardi bookstore, on Donceles. The antiquarian bookstore Rebeca Nodier, at Mesones and Pino Suárez. At Plinio el Joven the only clerk is a little old man who, after waiting obsequiously on a "scholar from the Colegio de México," soon fell asleep in a chair next to a stack of books, supremely ignoring me. I stole an anthology of Marco Manilio's *Astronómica*, with a prologue by Alfonso Reyes, and *Diary of an Unknown Writer* by a Japanese writer from the Second World War. At Lizardi I thought I saw Monsiváis. I tried to sidle up next to him to see what book he was looking at, but when I reached him, Monsiváis turned around and stared straight at me, with a hint of a smile, I think, and keeping a firm grip on his book and hiding the title, he went to talk to one of the clerks. Provoked, I filched a little book by an Arab poet called Omar Ibn al-Farid, published by the university, and an anthology of young American poets put out by City Lights. By the time I left, Monsiváis was gone. The Rebeca Nodier bookstore is tended by Rebeca Nodier herself, an old woman in her eighties who is completely blind and wears unruly white dresses that match her dentures; armed with a cane and alerted by the creaky wooden floor, she hops up and introduces herself to everyone who walks into her store, I'm Rebeca Nodier, etc., finally asking in turn the name of the "lover of literature" she has the "pleasure of meeting" and inquires what kind of literature he or she is looking for. I told her that I was interested in poetry, and to my surprise, Mrs. Nodier said all poets were bums but they weren't bad in bed. Especially if they don't have any money, she went on. Then she asked me how old I was. Seventeen, I said. Oh, you're still a pipsqueak, she exclaimed. And then: you're not planning to steal any of my books, are you? I promised her that I would rather die. We chatted for a while, and then I left.

## DECEMBER 9

The Mexican literary mafia has nothing on the Mexican bookseller mafia. Bookstores visited: the Librería del Sótano, in a basement on Avenida Juárez where the clerks (numerous and neatly uniformed) kept me under strict surveillance and from which I managed to leave with volumes by Roque Dalton, Lezama Lima, and Enrique Lihn. The Librería Mexicana, staffed by three samurais, on Calle Aranda, near the Plaza de San Juan, where I stole a book by Othón, a book by Amado Nervo (wonderful!), and a chapbook by Efraín Huerta. The Librería Pacífico, at Bolívar and 16 de Septiembre, where I stole an anthology of American poets translated by Alberto Girri and a book by Ernesto Cardenal. And in the evening, after reading, writing, and a little fucking: the Viejo Horacio, on Correo Mayor, staffed by twins, from which I left with Gamboa's *Santa*, a novel to give to Rosario; an anthology of poems by Kenneth Fearing, translated and with a prologue by someone called Doctor Julio Antonio Vila, in which Doctor Vila talks in a vague, question mark–filled way about a trip that Fearing took to Mexico in the 1950s, "an ominous and fruitful trip," writes Doctor Vila; and a book on Buddhism written by the Televisa adventurer Alberto Montes. Instead of the book by Montes I would have preferred the autobiography of the ex–featherweight world champion Adalberto Redondo, but one of the inconveniences of stealing books—especially for a novice like myself—is that sometimes you have to take what you can get.

## DECEMBER 10

Librería Orozco, on Reforma, between Oxford and Praga: *Nueve novísimos*, the Spanish anthology; *Corps et biens*, by Robert Desnos; and *Dr. Brodie's Report*, by Borges. Librería Milton, at Milton and Darwin:

Vladimir Holan's *A Night with Hamlet and Other Poems*, a Max Jacob anthology, and a Gunnar Ekelöf anthology. Librería El Mundo, on Río Nazas: selected poems by Byron, Shelley, and Keats; Stendhal's *The Red and the Black* (which I've already read); and Lichtenberg's *Aphorisms*, translated by Alfonso Reyes. This afternoon, as I arranged my books in the room, I thought about Reyes. Reyes could be my little refuge. A person could be immensely happy reading only him or the writers he loved. But that would be too easy.

DECEMBER 11

Before, I didn't have time for anything, and now I have time for everything. I used to spend my life on the bus and subway, having to cross the city from north to south at least twice a day. Now I walk everywhere, read a lot, write a lot. Every day I make love. In our tenement room, a little library has already begun to grow from my thefts and visits to bookstores. Last on the list, the Batalla del Ebro: its owner is a little old Spaniard named Crispín Zamora. I think we've gotten to be friends. Naturally, the store is almost always deserted and Don Crispín likes to read but he doesn't mind spending hours at a time talking about any old thing. Sometimes I need to talk too. I confessed that I was making the rounds of Mexico City bookstores looking for two friends who had disappeared, that I'd been stealing books because I didn't have any money (Don Crispín immediately gave me a Porrúa edition of Euripides translated by Father Garibay), that I admired Alfonso Reyes because in addition to Greek and Latin he knew French, English, and German, and that I had stopped going to the university. Everything I tell him makes him laugh, except my not going to class anymore, because it's important to have a degree. He distrusts poetry. When I explained that I was a poet, he said that distrust wasn't exactly the right word and that he'd known some poets. He wanted to read my poems. When I brought them to him I could see he found them a little confusing, but when he was done reading he didn't say anything. All he asked me was why I used so many ugly-sounding words. What do you mean, Don Crispín? I asked. Blasphemy, swear words, curses, insults. Oh, that, I said, well, it must just be the way I am. When I left that afternoon, Don Crispín gave me *Ocnos*, by Cernuda, and urged me to study it, because Cernuda was also a poet with a difficult disposition.

After I walked Rosario to the door of the Encrucijada Veracruzana (all the waitresses, including Brígida, greeted me effusively, as if I'd become part of the club or the family, all of them convinced that someday I'd be an important person in Mexican literature), my feet carried me unthinkingly to Río de la Loza and the Media Luna hotel, where Lupe was staying.

In the shoe box–size lobby, much more sinister than I remembered it, the wallpaper patterned with flowers and bleeding deer, a squat man with a broad back and big head said there was no Lupe staying there. I demanded to see the register. The clerk told me it was impossible, that the register was absolutely confidential. I argued that it was my sister, separated from my brother-in-law, and that the reason I was there was to bring her money to pay the hotel bill. The clerk must have had a sister in similar circumstances, because he immediately became more understanding.

"Is your sister a thin little dark girl who goes by Lupe?"

"That's her."

"Wait just a second, I'll go knock on her door."

While the receptionist went up to get her I looked through the register. The night of November 30, someone called Guadalupe Martínez had arrived. That same day, a Susana Alejandra Torres, a Juan Aparicio, and a María del Mar Jiménez had checked in. Following my instincts, I decided that Susana Alejandra Torres, not Guadalupe Martínez, must be the Lupe I was looking for. I decided not to wait for the receptionist to come down and I took the stairs in threes to the second floor, room 201, where Susana Alejandra Torres was staying.

I knocked just once. I heard footsteps, a window closing, whispers, more footsteps, and finally the door opened and I found myself face-to-face with Lupe.

It was the first time I'd seen her with so much makeup on. Her lips were painted a deep red, her eyes lined with pencil, her cheeks smeared with glitter. She recognized me at once:

"You're María's friend," she exclaimed with undisguised happiness.

"Let me in," I said. Lupe looked over her shoulder and then stood aside. The room was a jumble of women's clothes strewn in the most unlikely places.

I could tell right away that we weren't alone. Lupe was wearing a green bathrobe and she was smoking furiously. I heard a noise in the bathroom. Lupe looked at me and then looked toward the bathroom door, which was half open. I was sure it must be a client. But then I saw a paper with drawings on it lying on the floor, the mock-up of the new visceral realist magazine, and the discovery filled me with alarm. I thought, rather illogically, that it was María in the bathroom, or Angélica, and I didn't know how I was going to justify my presence at the Media Luna to them.

Lupe, who hadn't taken her eyes off me, noticed my discovery and started to laugh.

"You can come out now," she shouted, "it's your daughter's friend."

The bathroom door opened and Quim Font came out wrapped in a white robe. His eyes were weepy and there were traces of lipstick on his face. He greeted me warmly. In his hand he was holding the folder with the plan for the magazine in it.

"You see, García Madero," he said, "I'm always hard at work, always paying attention."

Then he asked me whether I'd been by his house.

"Not today," I said, and I thought about María again and everything seemed unbearably sordid and sad.

The three of us sat on the bed, Quim and I on the edge and Lupe under the covers.

Really, the situation was untenable!

Quim smiled, Lupe smiled, and I smiled, and none of us could bring ourselves to say anything. A stranger would have assumed that we were there to make love. The idea was gruesome. Just thinking about it made my stomach lurch. Lupe and Quim were still smiling. To say something, I started to talk about Arturo Belano's purge of the ranks of visceral realism.

"It was about time," said Quim. "All the freeloaders and incompetents should be tossed out. The movement only needs the pure of heart, like you, García Madero."

"True," I said, "but the more of us, the better, it seems to me."

"No, numbers are an illusion, García Madero. For our purposes, five is as good as fifty. That's what I told Arturo. Make heads roll. Shrink the inner circle until it's a microscopic dot."

I thought he was going off the rails, and I kept quiet.

"Where were we going to get with an idiot like Pancho Rodríguez, tell me that?"

"I don't know."

"Do you actually think he's a good poet? Does he strike you as a model member of the Mexican avant-garde?"

Lupe didn't say a thing. She just watched us and smiled. I asked Quim whether there was any news of Alberto.

"We're few and soon we'll be fewer," said Quim enigmatically. I didn't know whether he was referring to Alberto or the visceral realists.

"They've expelled Angélica too," I said.

"My daughter Angélica? Good Lord, that is news, man. I had no idea. When was this?"

"I don't know," I said, "Jacinto Requena told me."

"A poet who's won the Laura Damián prize! That takes some nerve, it really does! And I don't say so because she's my daughter!"

"Why don't we go for a walk?" said Lupe.

"Quiet, Lupita, I'm thinking."

"Don't be a pain in the ass, Joaquín, you can't tell me to be quiet. I'm not your daughter, remember?"

Quim laughed softly. It was a rabbity laugh that hardly disturbed the muscles of his face.

"Of course you're not my daughter. You can't write three words without making a spelling mistake."

"What? You think I'm illiterate, you asshole? Of course I can."

"No, you can't," said Quim, making a disproportionate effort to think. A scowl of pain etched itself on his face, reminding me of the expression on Pancho Rodríguez's face at Café Amarillo.

"Come on, test me."

"They shouldn't have done that to Angélica. It disgusts me the way those bastards are toying with people's feelings. We should eat something. I feel sick to my stomach," said Quim.

"Don't be a prick. Test me," said Lupe.

"Maybe Requena was exaggerating, maybe Angélica asked to be let go voluntarily. Since they'd expelled Pancho . . ."

"Pancho, Pancho, Pancho. That son of a bitch is nothing. He's nobody. Angélica doesn't give a damn whether they expel him, kill him, or give him a prize. He's a kind of Alberto," he added in an undertone, nodding toward Lupe.

"Don't get so upset, Quim, I only said it because they were together, weren't they?"

"What are you saying, Quim?" said Lupe.

"Nothing that's any of your business."

"Test me then, man. What do you think I am?"

"Root," said Quim.

"That's easy, give me paper and pencil."

I tore a sheet out of my notebook and handed it to her with my Bic.

"I've shed so many tears," said Quim as Lupe sat up in bed, her knees raised, the paper resting on her knees, "so many and what for?"

"Everything will be all right," I said.

"Have you ever read Laura Damián?" he asked me absently.

"No, never."

"Here it is, see what you think," said Lupe, showing him the paper. Quim frowned and said: fine. "Give me another word, but this time make it really hard."

"Anguish," said Quim.

"Anguish? That's easy."

"I have to talk to my daughters," said Quim, "I have to talk to my wife, my colleagues, my friends. I have to do something, García Madero."

"Relax, Quim, you have time."

"Listen, not a word of this to María, all right?"

"It's between the two of us, Quim."

"How does that look?" said Lupe.

"Excellent, García Madero, that's what I like to hear. I'll give you Laura Damián's book one of these days."

"How's that?" Lupe showed me the paper. She had spelled the word *anguish* perfectly.

"Couldn't be better," I said.

"Ragamuffin," said Quim.

"Excuse me?"

"Write the word *ragamuffin*," said Quim.

"Yikes, that really is hard," said Lupe, and she set to work immediately.

"Not a word about this to my daughters, then. To either of them. I'm counting on you, García Madero."

"Of course," I said.

"Now you'd better go. I'm going to spend a little while longer giving this dunce Spanish lessons, and then I'll be moving along too."

"All right, Quim, see you around."

When I got up the mattress bounced back and Lupe murmured something but didn't lift her eyes from the paper she was writing on. I saw a few scratched-out words. She was trying hard.

"If you see Arturo or Ulises, tell them it isn't right what they've done."

"If I see them," I said, shrugging my shoulders.

"It isn't a good way to make friends. Or to keep them."

I made a noise like laughter.

"Do you need money, García Madero?"

"No, Quim, not at all, thank you."

"You know you can always count on me. I was young and reckless once too. Now go. We'll get dressed in a little while and then head out for something to eat."

"My pen," I said.

"What?" said Quim.

"I'm going. I'd like my pen."

"Let her finish," said Quim, glancing at Lupe over his shoulder.

"Here, how does that look?" said Lupe.

"You got it wrong," said Quim. "I ought to give you a spanking."

I thought about the word *ragamuffin*. I'm not sure I'd have spelled it right the first time either. Quim got up and went to the bathroom. When he came out he had a black-and-gold mechanical pencil in his hand. He winked at me.

"Give him back the pen and write with this," he said.

Lupe returned my Bic. Goodbye, I said. She didn't answer.


DECEMBER 13

I called María. I talked to the maid. Miss María isn't in. When will she be home? No idea, may I ask who's calling? I didn't want to give my name and I hung up. I sat at Café Quito for a while, waiting to see whether anyone else would come, but it was hopeless. I called María again. No one answered the phone. I went walking to Montes, where Jacinto lives. Nobody was home. I ate a sandwich in the street and finished two poems I'd started the day before. Another call to the Font

97

house. This time the voice of an unidentifiable woman answered. I asked whether it was Mrs. Font.

"No, it isn't," said the voice in a tone that made my scalp tingle.

It clearly wasn't María's voice. Nor was it that of the maid I had just spoken to. The only alternatives were Angélica or a stranger, maybe one of the sisters' friends.

"Who is this, please?"

"To whom do you wish to speak?"

"To María or Angélica," I said, feeling stupid and scared at the same time.

"This is Angélica," said the voice. "To whom am I speaking?"

"It's Juan," I said.

"Hello, Juan. How are you?"

It can't be Angélica, I thought, it simply can't be. But then I thought that everyone living in that house was crazy, so maybe it was possible after all.

"I'm fine," I said, shaking. "Is María there?"

"No," said the voice.

"All right, I'll call again," I said.

"Do you want to leave her a message?"

"No!" I said and I hung up.

I felt my forehead with my hand, thinking I must have a fever. At that moment, all I wanted was to be home with my aunt and uncle, studying or watching TV, but I knew that there was no turning back, that all I had was Rosario and Rosario's tenement room.

Without realizing it, I must have started to cry. I wandered aimlessly for a while, and when I tried to get my bearings I was in the middle of a bleak stretch of Colonia Anáhuac, surrounded by dying trees and peeling walls. I went into a place on Calle Texcoco and asked for a coffee. When it came, it was lukewarm. I don't know how long I spent there.

When I left it was night.

I called the Fonts again from another pay phone. The same woman's voice answered.

"Hello, Angélica, it's Juan García Madero," I said.

"Hello," said the voice.

I felt sick. Some kids were playing soccer in the street.

"I saw your father," I said. "He was with Lupe."

"What?"

"At the hotel where we have Lupe. Your father was there."

"What was he doing there?" The voice was uninflected; it was like talking to a brick wall, I thought.

"He was keeping her company," I said.

"Is Lupe all right?"

"Lupe's fine," I said. "It was your father who didn't seem to be doing very well. I thought he'd been crying, even if he was better by the time I got there."

"Hmm," said the voice. "And why was he crying?"

"I don't know," I said. "Maybe it was regret. Or maybe shame. He asked me not to tell you."

"Not to tell me what?"

"That I'd seen him there."

"Hmm," said the voice.

"When will María be home? Do you know where she is?"

"At the dance school," said the voice. "And I was just leaving."

"Where are you going?"

"To the university."

"All right, then, goodbye."

"Goodbye," said the voice.

I went walking back to Sullivan. When I crossed Reforma, near the statue of Cuauhtémoc, I heard someone call my name.

"Hands up, poet García Madero."

When I turned, Arturo Belano and Ulises Lima were there, and I fainted.

When I woke up I was in Rosario's room, in bed, with Ulises and Arturo on either side of me trying and failing to get me to drink some herbal tea they'd just made. I asked what had happened, and they told me I'd fainted, that I'd thrown up and then I'd started to ramble incoherently. I told them about calling the Fonts' house. I said it was the call that had made me sick. At first they didn't believe me. Then they listened carefully to a detailed account of my latest adventures and delivered their verdict.

According to them, the problem was that I hadn't been talking to Angélica at all.

"And you knew it too, García Madero, and that's why you got sick," said Arturo, "from the fucking shock."

"What did I know?"

99

"That it was somebody else, not Angélica," said Ulises.

"No I didn't," I said.

"Unconsciously you did," said Arturo.

"But who was it, then?"

Arturo and Ulises laughed.

"There's actually a simple answer, and it's funny too."

"Stop torturing me, then, and tell me what it is," I said.

"Think a little," said Arturo. "Come on, use your head. Was it Angélica? Clearly not. Was it María? Even less likely. Who's left? The maid, but she isn't there at the time of day you called, and anyway you'd already talked to her and you would've recognized her voice, right?"

"Right," I said. "It definitely wasn't the maid."

"Who's left?" said Ulises.

"María's mother and Jorgito."

"I don't think it was Jorgito, was it?"

"No, it couldn't have been Jorgito," I admitted.

"And can you see María Cristina putting on an act like that?"

"Is María's mother called María Cristina?"

"That's her name," said Ulises.

"No, I really can't, but who was it, then? There's no one left."

"Someone crazy enough to imitate Angélica's voice," said Arturo, and he looked at me. "The only person in the house who would pull a weird stunt like that."

I looked from one to the other as gradually the answer began to take shape in my mind.

"Warm, warmer . . ." said Ulises.

"Quim," I said.

"Who else," said Arturo.

"That son of a bitch!"

Later I remembered the story about the deaf-mute that Quim had told me and I thought about child abusers who had themselves once been abused as children. Although now that I write it, the cause-and-effect relationship between the deaf-mute and Quim's personality shift doesn't seem so clear. Then I went storming out into the street and wasted coin after coin on futile calls to María's house. I talked to her mother, the maid, Jorgito, and, very late that night, Angélica (this time it was the real Angélica), but María was never there and Quim would never come to the phone.

For a while, Belano and Ulises Lima kept me company. I gave them my poems to read while I made the first phone calls. They said the poems weren't bad. The purge of visceral realism is just a joke, said Ulises. But do the people who were purged know it's a joke? Of course not, it wouldn't be funny if they did, said Arturo. So no one is expelled? Of course not. And what have you two been doing all this time? Nothing, said Ulises.

"There's some asshole who wants to beat us up," they admitted later.

"But there are two of you and only one of him."

"But we aren't violent, García Madero," said Ulises. "At least, I'm not, and neither is Arturo, anymore."

Between phone calls to the Fonts', I spent the evening with Jacinto Requena and Rafael Barrios at Café Quito. I told them what Belano and Ulises had told me. They must be finding things out about Cesárea Tinajero, they said.

### DECEMBER 14

No one gives the visceral realists ANYTHING. Not scholarships or space in their magazines or invitations to book parties or readings.

Belano and Lima are like two ghosts.

If *simón* is slang for yes and *nel* means no, then what does *simonel* mean?

I don't feel very good today.

### DECEMBER 15

Don Crispín Zamora doesn't like to talk about the Spanish Civil War. So I asked him why he'd given his bookstore a military-sounding name. He confessed that he hadn't come up with the name himself. It was the previous owner, a Republican colonel who had covered himself in glory in the battle in question. I detected a hint of irony in Don Crispín's words. At his request, I talked to him about visceral realism. After he'd made a few observations like "realism is never visceral," "the visceral belongs to the oneiric world," etc., which I found rather disconcerting, he theorized that we underprivileged youth were left with no alternative but the literary avant-garde. I asked him what exactly he meant by underprivileged. I'm hardly underprivileged. At least not by Mexico City standards. But then I thought about the tenement room Rosario was sharing with me and I wasn't so sure he was wrong. The problem with literature, like life, said Don Crispín, is that in the end people always turn into bastards. By now, I had the impression that Don Crispín was talking just for the sake of talking. The whole time I was sitting in a chair while he kept scurrying around moving books from one place to another or dusting stacks of magazines. At a certain moment, however, he turned around and asked how much it would cost him to sleep with me. I've noticed you're short on cash, which is the only reason I'd venture to propose such a thing. I was stunned.

"You're making a mistake, Don Crispín," I said.

"Don't take it the wrong way, my boy. I know I'm old and that's why I'm suggesting a transaction. Call it a reward."

"Are you homosexual, Don Crispín?"

The word was scarcely out of my mouth before I realized how stupid it was and I blushed. I didn't wait for him to answer. Did you think *I* was homosexual? Aren't you? asked Don Crispín.

"Ay, *ay*, *ay*, I've really put my foot in it. Forgive me, my boy, for heaven's sake," said Don Crispín, and he started to laugh.

I stopped wanting to go running out of the Batalla del Ebro, which had been my first reaction. Don Crispín asked me to give up my chair because he was laughing so hard he was afraid he might have a heart attack. When he had calmed down, still apologizing profusely, he asked me to understand that he was a timid homosexual (never mind my age, Juanito!) and that he was out of practice in the art of hooking up, always difficult even when it wasn't downright mysterious. You must think I'm an ass, and rightly so, he said. Then he confessed that it had been at least five years since he'd slept with anyone. Before I left, he insisted on giving me the Porrúa edition of the complete works of Sophocles and Aeschylus to make up for bothering me. I told him that I hadn't been bothered at all, but it would have seemed rude not to accept his gift. Life is shit.


DECEMBER 16

I'm sick for real. Rosario is making me stay in bed. Before she left for work she went out to borrow a thermos from a neighbor and she left me half a liter of coffee. Also four aspirin. I have a fever. I've started and finished two poems.

## DECEMBER 17

Today a doctor came to see me. He looked at the room, looked at my books, and then took my blood pressure and felt different parts of my body. Afterward he went to talk to Rosario in a corner, in whispers, stressing his words with the emphatic motion of his shoulders. When he left I asked Rosario how she could have called a doctor without consulting me first. How much did you spend? I said. That doesn't matter, *papacito*. You're the only thing that matters.

## DECEMBER 18

This afternoon I was shivering with fever when the door opened and my aunt and then my uncle came in, followed by Rosario. I thought I was hallucinating. My aunt threw herself on the bed, covering me with kisses. My uncle stood stoically by, waiting until my aunt had unburdened herself, and then he clapped me on the shoulder. The threats, scolding, and advice followed soon after. Basically, they wanted me to come straight home, or if not, then go to the hospital, where they intended to have me undergo a thorough examination. I refused. In the end there were threats and when they left I was laughing hysterically and Rosario was sobbing.

## DECEMBER 19

First thing in the morning, Requena, Xóchitl, Rafael Barrios, and Barbara Patterson came to visit me. I asked them who had given them my address. Ulises and Arturo, they said. So they've appeared, I said. They've appeared and disappeared again, said Xóchitl. They're finishing work on an anthology of young Mexican poets, said Barrios. Requena laughed. It wasn't true, according to him. Too bad: for a moment I had hoped that they'd include some poems of mine. What they're doing is getting the money together to go to Europe, said Requena. Getting it together how? Selling pot left and right, how else, said Requena. The other day I saw them on Reforma with a backpack full of Acapulco Gold. I can't believe it, I said (but I remembered that the last time I'd seen them they had, in fact, been carrying a backpack). They gave me a little, said Jacinto, and he pulled out some weed. Xóchitl said that it wasn't good for me to smoke in my condition. I told her not to worry, that I was already feeling much better. You're the one who shouldn't smoke, said Jacinto, unless you want our baby to turn out retarded. Xóchitl said that there was no reason marijuana should hurt the fetus. Don't smoke, Xóchitl, said Requena. What hurts the fetus is bad vibes, said Xóchitl, bad food, alcohol, abuse of the mother, not marijuana. Don't smoke anyway, said Requena, just in case. Let her smoke if she wants, said Barbara Patterson. Fucking gringa, don't butt in, said Barrios. Once you've given birth, you can do whatever you want, but for now you'll have to go without, said Requena. While we smoked, Xóchitl went to sit in a corner of the room, next to some cardboard boxes where Rosario keeps the clothes she isn't wearing. Arturo and Ulises aren't saving money, she said (although they are setting a little aside, why deny it), they're putting the final touches on something that's going to blow everybody's minds. We looked at her, waiting to hear more. But Xóchitl was silent.

## DECEMBER 20

Tonight I had sex with Rosario three times. I'm better now. But I'm still taking the medicine she bought for me, more to make her happy than anything else.

## DECEMBER 21

Nothing to report. Life seems to have ground to a halt. Every day I make love to Rosario. While she's at work, I write and read. At night I make the rounds of the bars on Bucareli. Sometimes I stop in at the Encrucijada and the waitresses serve me first. At four in the morning Rosario comes home (when she's working the night shift) and we eat something light in our room, usually food that she brings from the bar. Then we make love until she falls asleep, and I begin to write.

## DECEMBER 22

Today I went out early to take a walk. I'd been planning to head to the Batalla del Ebro and spend the time until lunch with Don Crispín, but when I got to the store it was closed. So I started to wander aimlessly, enjoying the morning sun, and almost without realizing it I came to Calle

Mesones, where the Rebeca Nodier bookstore is. Although on my first visit I'd ruled the store out as a target, I decided to go in. No one was there. A sickly sweet, stuffy air hung over the books and the shelves. I heard voices coming from the back room, by which I deduced that the blind lady must be busy wrapping up some deal. I decided to wait and started leafing through old books. There was *Ifigenia cruel* and *El plano oblicuo* and *Retratos reales e imaginarios*, in addition to the five volumes of *Simpatías y diferencias*, all by Alfonso Reyes, and *Prosas dispersas*, by Julio Torri, and a book of stories, *Mujeres*, by someone called Eduardo Colín whom I'd never heard of, and *Li-Po y otros poemas*, by Tablada, and *Catorce poemas burocráticos y un corrido reaccionario*, by Renato Leduc, and *Incidentes melódicos del mundo irracional*, by Juan de la Cabada, and *Dios en la tierra* and *Los días terrenales*, by José Revueltas. Soon I got tired and took a seat in a little wicker chair. Just as I sat down, I heard a cry. The first thing that occurred to me was that someone was attacking Rebeca Nodier, and without thinking, I dashed into the inner room. A surprise awaited me behind the door. Ulises Lima and Arturo Belano were poring over an old catalog on a table. When I burst into the room they raised their heads and for the first time I saw them look truly surprised. Beside them, Doña Rebeca was gazing up at the ceiling as if she were thinking or reminiscing. Nothing had happened to her. It was she who'd cried out, but her cry was a cry of surprise, not fear.

DECEMBER 23

Nothing happened today. And if anything did, I'd rather not talk about it, because I didn't understand it.

DECEMBER 24

A miserable Christmas. I called María. Finally I got to talk to her! I told her what was going on with Lupe and she said she knew everything. What do you know? I said.

"Well, that she ran away from her pimp and that she's finally decided to study at the dance school," she said.

"Do you know where she's living?"

"At a hotel," said María.

"Do you know which hotel?"

"Of course I know. The Media Luna. I go see her every afternoon. She's awfully lonely, poor thing."

"No, she isn't awfully lonely, your father makes sure of that," I said.

"My father is a saint and he's killing himself for despicable brats like you," she said.

I wanted to know what she meant by killing himself.

"Nothing."

"Tell me what the fuck you're trying to say!"

"Don't shout," she said.

"I want to know where I stand! I want to know who I'm talking to!"

"Don't shout," she said again.

Then she said that she had things to do, and she hung up.

## DECEMBER 25

I've decided not to sleep with María ever again, but the Christmas holidays, the tension radiating from people on the streets downtown, poor Rosario's plans (she's all set to spend New Year's Eve at a nightclub—with me, of course, and dancing), only make me want to see María again, to undress her, to feel her legs on my back again, to slap (if she asks me to) the perfect tight curve of her ass.

## DECEMBER 26

"Today I have a surprise for you, *papuchi*," announced Rosario as soon as she got home.

She started to kiss me, saying over and over again that she loved me and promising that she was going to start reading a book every two weeks to be "up to my level," which only embarrassed me, finally confessing that no one had ever made her so happy.

I must be getting old, because her verbal excesses gave me goose bumps.

Half an hour later we went walking to El Amanuense Azteca, a public bathhouse on Calle Lorenzo Boturini.

That was the surprise.

"We have to be nice and clean now that the new year is coming," said Rosario, winking at me.

I would've liked to slap her right there, then walk away and never see her again. (My nerves are shot.)

And yet, when we had passed through the frosted glass doors of the bathhouse, the mural or fresco that arched over the front desk seized my attention with mysterious force.

The anonymous artist had painted an Indian scribe writing on paper or parchment, lost in thought. Clearly, he was the Amanuense Azteca. Behind the scribe stretched hot springs, where Indians and conquistadors, bathing in pools set three in a row, were joined by Mexicans from colonial times, El Cura Hidalgo and Morelos, Emperor Maximilian and Empress Carlota, Benito Juárez surrounded by friends and enemies, President Madero, Carranza, Zapata, Obregón, soldiers in different uniforms or out of uniform, peasants, Mexico City workers, and movie actors: Cantinflas, Dolores del Río, Pedro Armendáriz, Pedro Infante, Jorge Negrete, Javier Solís, Aceves Mejía, María Félix, Tin Tan, Resortes, Calambres, Irma Serrano, and others I didn't recognize because they were in the farthest pools, and those really were tiny.

"Cool, huh?"

I stood there with my arms at my sides. Ecstatic.

Rosario's voice made me jump.

Before we turned down the hallway with our little towels and soap, I discovered that at each end of the mural there was a stone wall surrounding the springs. And on the other side of the wall, on a kind of plain or frozen sea, I saw shadowy animals, maybe the ghosts of animals (or the ghosts of plants) lying in wait, multiplying in a seething but silent siege.


DECEMBER 27

We've been back to El Amanuense Azteca. A success. The private rooms are carpeted, with a table, coat rack, and sofa, and a cement stall where the shower and steam taps are. The steam jet is at floor level, like in a Nazi movie. The door between the room and the stall is heavy, and there's a creepy, perpetually fogged-up peephole at eye level (although I have to stoop since I'm taller than the average person it was designed for). There's restaurant service. We shut ourselves in and order cuba libres. We shower, take steam baths, rest and dry ourselves on the sofa, then shower again. We make love in the stall, in a cloud of steam that hides our bodies. We fuck, shower, let the steam smother us. All we can see are our hands, our knees, sometimes the back of a neck or the tip of a breast.

## DECEMBER 28

How many poems have I written?
   Since it all began: 55 poems.
   Total pages: 76.
   Total lines: 2,453
   I could put together a book by now. My complete works.

## DECEMBER 29

Tonight, while I was waiting for Rosario at the bar of the Encrucijada Veracruzana, Brígida came by and said something about time passing.

"Pour me another tequila," I said, "and tell me what you mean."

In her look I caught something that I can only call victory, although it was a sad, resigned victory, more attuned to small signs of death than signs of life.

"What I meant was that time goes by," said Brígida as she filled my glass, "and once you were a stranger, but now you're like part of the family."

"I don't give a shit about the family," I said as I wondered where the fuck Rosario had gone.

"I didn't mean to insult you," said Brígida. "Or pick a fight. These days I don't feel like fighting with anyone."

I sat looking at her for a while, not knowing what to say. I would've liked to say you're being an idiot, Brígida, but I wasn't in the mood to fight with anyone either.

"What I meant was," said Brígida, looking behind her as if to make sure Rosario wasn't coming, "that I would've liked to fall in love with you too, believe me, I would've liked to live with you, give you spending money, make your meals, take care of you when you were sick, but it wasn't meant to be. We have to accept things the way they are, don't we? But it would've been nice."

"I'm impossible to live with," I said.

"You are who you are and you have a cock that's worth its weight in gold," said Brígida.

"Thank you," I said.

"I know what I'm talking about," said Brígida.

"So what else do you know?"

"About you?" Now Brígida was smiling, and this, I guessed, was her victory.

"About me, of course," I said as I swallowed the last of the tequila.

"That you're going to die young, Juan, and that you're going to do Rosario wrong."


DECEMBER 30

Today I went back to the Fonts' house. Today I did Rosario wrong.

I got up early, around seven, and went out to roam the streets downtown. Before I left I heard Rosario's voice saying: wait a second and I'll make you breakfast. I didn't answer. I closed the door quietly and left the tenement.

For a long time I walked as if I were in a foreign country, feeling choked and sick. When I got to the Zócalo my pores opened at last. I started to sweat freely, and my nausea vanished.

Then suddenly I was starving and I went into the first cafeteria I found open, a little place on Madero called Nueva Síbaris, where I ordered coffee and a ham sandwich.

To my great surprise, there was Pancho Rodríguez, sitting at the bar. His hair was freshly combed (it was still wet) and his eyes were red. He didn't look surprised to see me. I asked him what he was doing there, so far from home and so early in the morning.

"I was out whoring all night," he said, "to see whether I was finally ready to get the fuck over you-know-who."

I guessed that he meant Angélica, and as I took the first sips of coffee I thought about Angélica, María, my first visits to the Fonts' house. I felt happy. I felt hungry. Pancho, on the other hand, seemed listless. To distract him I told him that I'd left my aunt and uncle's place and that I was living with a woman in a tenement straight out of a 1940s movie, but Pancho wasn't in the right frame of mind to listen to me or anybody else.

After he'd smoked a few cigarettes, he said he felt like stretching his legs.

"Where do you want to go?" I asked, although deep down I already knew the answer, and if he didn't say what I expected to hear, I was ready to get it out of him by any means necessary.

"To Angélica's," said Pancho.

"That's the spirit," I said and I hurried to finish my breakfast.

Pancho went ahead and paid my bill (which was a first) and we left. A feeling of lightness settled in our legs. Suddenly Pancho didn't seem quite so trashed and I didn't feel so clueless about what to do with my life. Instead, the morning light returned us to ourselves, refreshed. Pancho was cheery and quick again, gliding along on words, and the window of a shoe store on Madero reflected back a mirror image of my inner vision of myself: someone tall, with pleasant features, neither gawky nor sickeningly shy, striding along followed by a smaller, stockier person in pursuit of his true love — or whatever else came his way!

Of course I had no idea then what the day had in store for us.

For the first half of the trip, Pancho was enthusiastic, friendly, and extroverted, but after that, as we got closer to Colonia Condesa, his mood changed and he seemed to succumb again to the old fears that his strange (or rather histrionic and enigmatic) relationship with Angélica awakened in him. The whole problem, he confided, gloomy again, had to do with the social divide between his family, who were lowly and working-class, and Angélica's, firmly ensconced as they were in Mexico City's petit bourgeoisie. To cheer him up, I argued that although this would surely make it harder to *start* a relationship, the chasm of class struggle narrowed considerably once the relationship was already under way. To which Pancho replied by asking what I meant by saying the relationship was already under way, a stupid question I didn't bother to answer. Instead I responded with another question: were he and Angélica really two average people, two typical, rigid representatives of the petit bourgeoisie and the proletariat?

"No, I guess not," said Pancho pensively as the taxi we'd caught at Reforma and Juárez headed at breakneck speed toward Calle Colima.

That's what I was trying to say, I told him, that since he and Angélica were poets, what difference did it make if one belonged to one social class and the other to another?

"Plenty, I'm telling you," said Pancho.

"Don't be mechanistic, man," I said, more and more irrationally happy.

Unexpectedly, the taxi driver backed me up: "If you've already gotten what you came for, there's no such thing as barriers. When love is good, nothing else matters."

"See?" I said.

"No, actually," said Pancho, "not really."

"You go at it with your girl and forget that communist crap," said the taxi driver.

"What do you mean communist crap?" said Pancho.

"You know, all that social class business."

"So according to you social classes don't exist," said Pancho.

The taxi driver, who had been watching us in the rearview mirror as he talked, turned around now, his right hand resting on the back of the passenger seat, his left firmly grasping the wheel. We're going to crash, I thought.

"For all intents and purposes, no. When it comes to love all Mexicans are equal. In the eyes of God too," said the taxi driver.

"What a load of bullshit!" said Pancho.

"If that's what you want to call it," replied the taxi driver.

With that, Pancho and the taxi driver started to argue about religion and politics, and meanwhile I stared out the window, watching the scenery (the storefronts of Juárez and Roma Norte) rolling monotonously past, and I also started to think about María and what separated me from her, which wasn't class but experience, and about Rosario and our tenement room and the wonderful nights I'd spent there with her, though I was prepared to give them up for a few seconds with María, a word from María, a smile from María. And I also started to think about my aunt and uncle and I even thought I saw them, walking arm in arm down one of the streets that we were passing, never turning to look at the taxi as it zigzagged perilously away down other streets, the two of them immersed in their solitude just as Pancho, the taxi driver, and I were immersed in ours. And then I realized that something had gone wrong in the last few days, something had gone wrong in my relationship with the new Mexican poets or with the new women in my life, but no matter how much I thought about it I couldn't figure out what the problem was, the abyss that opened up behind me if I looked over my shoulder. All the same, it didn't frighten me. It was an abyss without monsters, holding only darkness, silence, and emptiness, three extremes that caused me pain, a lesser pain, true, a flutter in the stomach, but a pain that sometimes felt like fear. And then, with my face glued to the window, we turned onto Calle Colima, and Pancho and the taxi driver stopped talking, or maybe only Pancho stopped, as if he'd given up trying to win his argument, and my silence and Pancho's silence clutched at my heart.

We got out a few feet past the Fonts' house.

"Something strange is going on here," said Pancho, as the taxi driver drove happily away, with a few choice words about our mothers.

At first glance the street looked normal, but I too noticed something different about the place I remembered so vividly. Across the street I saw two guys sitting in a yellow Camaro. They were staring at us.

Pancho rang the bell. For a few long seconds there wasn't any movement inside the house.

One of the occupants of the Camaro, the one sitting in the passenger seat, got out and propped his elbows on the roof of the car. Pancho watched him for a few seconds and then repeated, in a low voice, that something very strange was going on. The Camaro guy was scary. I remembered my first few times at the Fonts' house, standing at the door, gazing at the garden, which to my eyes seemed to spread before us full of secrets. That hadn't been long ago, and yet it felt like years.

It was Jorgito who came out to let us in.

When he got to the gate he made a sign to us that we didn't understand and he looked over toward where the Camaro was parked. He didn't return our greeting and when we were through the gate he shut and locked it again. The garden looked neglected. The house seemed different. Jorgito led us straight to the front door. I remember that Pancho looked at me inquiringly and as we walked he turned around and scanned the street.

"Move it, man," Jorgito told him.

Inside the house Quim Font and his wife were waiting for us.

"It was about time you showed up, García Madero," said Quim, giving me a big hug. I hadn't been expecting such a warm welcome. Mrs. Font was dressed in a dark green robe and slippers and it looked as if she'd just gotten up, although later I learned that she'd hardly slept the night before.

"What's going on here?" asked Pancho, looking at me.

"You mean what *isn't* going on," said Mrs. Font as she stroked Jorgito's hair.

After he hugged me, Quim went to the window and looked out sur-reptitiously.

"Nothing new to report, Dad," said Jorgito.

Immediately I thought about the men in the yellow Camaro and I began to form a vague idea of what was going on at the Fonts'.

"We're having breakfast, boys, would you like some coffee?" said Quim.

We followed him into the kitchen. There, sitting at the table, were Angélica, María—and Lupe! Pancho didn't even blink when he saw her, but I almost jumped out of my skin.

It's hard to remember what happened next, especially because María greeted me as if we'd never fought, as if we could pick things up again from where we'd left off. All I know is that I said hello to Angélica and Lupe in a friendly way and that María gave me a kiss on the cheek. Then we had coffee and Pancho asked what was going on. The explanations were various and heated and in the middle of it all Mrs. Font and Quim started to fight. According to Mrs. Font, this was the worst New Year's holiday she'd ever had. Think about the poor, Cristina, replied Quim. Mrs. Font started to cry and left the kitchen. Angélica went out after her, which prompted Pancho to make a move, though it came to nothing: he got up from his chair, followed Angélica to the door, and then sat down again. Meanwhile Quim and María, between the two of them, brought me up to date. Lupe's pimp had found her at the Media Luna. After a scuffle, the particulars of which I didn't understand, she and Quim had managed to escape from the hotel and make it to Calle Colima. This had been a few days ago. When Mrs. Font found out what was going on, she called the police, and it wasn't long before a couple of officers showed up in a patrol car. They said that if the Fonts wanted to make a formal complaint they would have to go to the station. When Quim told them that Alberto and the other guy were there, in front of the house, the officers went to talk to the pimp, and from the gate Jorgito could tell that they seemed more like old friends than anything else. Either the guy with Alberto was also a policeman, according to Lupe, or the police had been given a handout big enough to make them look the other way. That was when the siege of the Fonts' house formally began. The officers left. Mrs. Font called the police again. Different officers came, with the same result. A friend of Quim's, who talked to Quim on the phone, recommended that they wait out the siege as best they could until the holidays were over. Sometimes, according to Jorgito, who was the only one with the guts to spy on the intruders, another car would come, an Oldsmobile that parked behind the Camaro, and Alberto and his companion, after talking to the new besiegers for a while, would drive off noisily, even threateningly, making the car tires squeal and honking the horn. Six hours later they were back and the car that had replaced them would leave. There was no question that these comings and goings were wearing down the house's inhabitants. Mrs. Font refused to go out for fear that she'd be kidnapped. Quim, faced with these new developments, wouldn't go out either. He said it was out of responsibility to his family, although I think it was really out of fear that he would be beaten up. Only Angélica and María had crossed the threshold, once and separately, and the outcome was ugly. Angélica was heckled and María, who walked boldly right past the Camaro, was groped and knocked around. By the time we got there, the only person who dared to answer the door was Jorgito.

Once we'd been informed of the situation, Pancho's reaction was immediate.

He was going to go and beat the shit out of Alberto.

Quim and I tried to dissuade him, but there was nothing to be done. So after speaking to Angélica in private for a quarter of an hour, Pancho headed outside.

"Come with me, García Madero," he said, and like an idiot I followed him.

As we walked out, Pancho's determination to do battle cooled by several degrees. We opened the gate with the keys Jorgito had given us. Turning around to look back at the house, I thought I saw Quim watching us from the living room window and Mrs. Font from a second-floor window. This bites, said Pancho. I didn't know what to answer. Who asked him to open his mouth in the first place?

"It's all over for me with Angélica," said Pancho as he tried the keys one by one, unsuccessfully.

There were three people in the Camaro, not two as it had seemed before. Pancho strode right up to them and asked them what they wanted. I lingered several feet behind, the figure of the pimp hidden from me behind Pancho. I couldn't see him and he couldn't see me. But I heard his voice, resonant as a *ranchera* singer's, arrogant but not entirely unpleasant, nothing like what I would've expected, betraying not a hint of hesitation. The contrast with Pancho's voice was cruel. Pancho had begun to stutter and talk too fast, slipping too quickly toward insult and aggression.

At that moment, for the first time since everything that had happened that morning, I realized that these were dangerous people and I wanted to tell Pancho that we should turn around and go back into the house. But Pancho was already challenging Alberto.

"Get out of the car, man," he said.

Alberto laughed. He made a remark I didn't hear. The passenger-side door opened and it was the other guy who got out of the car. He was of average height, very dark, on the fat side.

"Get out of here, kid." It took me a minute to realize he was talking to me.

Then I saw that Pancho had taken a step back and Alberto was getting out of the car. What came next happened too fast. Alberto stepped up to Pancho (it looked like he was giving him a kiss) and Pancho collapsed.

"Leave him there, kid," said the dark guy from the other side, leaning on the roof of the car. I ignored him. I pulled Pancho up and we went back to the house. When we got to the door I turned around to look. The two of them were back in the yellow Camaro and it looked to me like they were laughing.

"You got it good, huh," said Jorgito, popping out of the bushes.

"The bastard had a gun," said Pancho. "If I'd fought back he would've shot me."

"That's what I thought," said Jorgito.

I hadn't seen any gun, but I kept quiet.

Together, Jorgito and I helped Pancho toward the house. When we were on the flagstone path leading to the porch, Pancho said no, that he wanted to go to María and Angélica's little house, so we went around through the garden. The rest of the day was mostly miserable.

Pancho shut himself up with Angélica in the little house. The maid came late and started cleaning, getting in everyone's way. Jorgito wanted to go visit some friends but his parents wouldn't let him. María, Lupe, and I played cards in the corner of the garden where María and I had first talked. For a moment I had the impression that we were repeating the motions from when we'd first met, when Pancho and Angélica would

115

shut themselves in the little house and order us out, but now everything was different.

At lunchtime, at the kitchen table, Mrs. Font said she wanted a divorce. Quim laughed and shrugged as if to say that his wife had gone crazy. Pancho started to cry.

Then Jorgito turned on the television and he and Angélica sat down to watch a documentary on spiders. Mrs. Font served coffee to those of us who were still in the kitchen. Before the maid left, she announced that she wouldn't be coming the next day. Quim talked to her for a few seconds in the courtyard and gave her an envelope. María asked whether it was a plea for help. Please, sweetheart, said Quim, the phone line hasn't been cut yet. It was her end-of-year bonus.

I'm not sure exactly when Pancho left the house. I'm not sure exactly when I decided that I would spend the night there. All I know is that after dinner Quim took me aside and thanked me for the gesture.

"I expected no less of you, García Madero," he said.

"I'm at your service," I answered stupidly.

"Now let's forget all the silly stuff there's been between the two of us and concentrate on the defense of the castle," he said.

I didn't understand what he meant by silly stuff. I did understand what he meant about the castle. I decided to keep my mouth shut and nodded my head.

"It would be best if the girls slept in the house," said Quim, "for security reasons, you understand. In moments of grave danger it makes sense to gather the troops in a single spot."

We agreed on everything and that night Angélica slept in the guest room, Lupe in the living room, and María in Jorgito's room. I decided to sleep in the little house in the courtyard, maybe in the hope that María would pay me a visit, but after we'd said good night and gone our separate ways I lay there waiting in vain on María's bed, enveloped in María's smell, with an anthology of Sor Juana in my hands but unable to read, until I couldn't stand it anymore and I went out for a walk in the garden. The muted sound of a party came from one of the houses on Calle Guadalajara or Avenida Sonora. I went to the wall and looked over it: the yellow Camaro was still there, although I couldn't see anyone inside it. I went back to the house. There was a light in the living room window and when I listened at the door I heard soft voices that I couldn't identify. I was afraid to knock. Instead, I turned around and went in through the kitchen door. In the living room, sitting on the sofa, were María and Lupe. It smelled like marijuana. María was in a red nightgown, which I mistook for a dress at first, with a volcano, a river of lava, and a village on the verge of destruction embroidered in white on the bodice. Lupe hadn't put on her pajamas yet, if she even had pajamas, which I doubt, and she was in a miniskirt and black shirt, her hair a mess, which gave her a mysterious, attractive look. When they saw me, they were quiet. I would've liked to ask them what they were talking about, but instead I sat down beside them and told them that Alberto's car was still outside. They already knew.

"This is the strangest New Year's I've ever spent," I said.

María asked us whether we wanted coffee and then she got up and went into the kitchen. I followed her. As she was waiting for the water to boil I put my arms around her from behind and told her I wanted to sleep with her. She didn't answer. That must mean yes, I thought, and I kissed her neck and the nape of her neck. María's smell, a smell that had begun to seem strange to me again, aroused me so much that I started to shake. I instantly moved away from her. Leaning against the kitchen wall, I was afraid for a moment that I would lose my balance or pass out right there, and I had to make an effort to return to normal.

"You have a good heart, García Madero," she said as she left the kitchen carrying a tray with three cups of hot water, the Nescafé, and the sugar. I followed her like a sleepwalker. I would've liked to know what she meant by saying that I had a good heart, but that was the last she spoke to me.

I soon realized that my presence was unwelcome. María and Lupe had a lot to say to each other and none of it made any sense to me. For an instant it might seem as if they were talking about the weather and the next instant about Alberto, the evil pimp.

Back at the little house I felt so tired that I didn't even turn on the light.

I groped my way to María's bed, guided only by the dim light from the big house or the courtyard or the moon, who knows which, and I threw myself facedown without undressing and was asleep immediately.

I don't know what time it was or how long I slept that way. All I know is that it felt good and that when I woke up it was still dark and a woman was caressing me. It took me a while to realize that it wasn't María. For a few seconds I thought I was dreaming or that I was hopelessly lost in the tenement, with Rosario. I pulled whoever it was to me and searched for her face in the dark. It was Lupe and she was smiling like a spider.

DECEMBER 31

We had what you might call a family New Year's. All day long, old friends kept coming and going. Not many. A poet, two painters, an architect, Mrs. Font's younger sister, the father of the late Laura Damián.

The latter's visit was marked by extreme and mysterious behavior. Quim was in his pajamas and unshaven, sitting in the living room watching TV. I opened the door and Mr. Damián came in preceded by an enormous bouquet of red roses that he handed to me in a shy, clumsy gesture. As I took the flowers to the kitchen and looked for a vase or something to put them in, I heard him talking to Quim about the difficulties of day-to-day life. Then they talked about parties. They're not what they used to be, said Quim. They certainly aren't, said Laura Damián's father. You can say that again. Everything about the past was better, said Quim. We're getting old, said Laura Damián's father. Then Quim said something surprising: I don't know, he said, how you manage to keep on living. If I were you, I would've died a long time ago.

There was a prolonged silence, broken only by the distant voices of Mrs. Font and her daughters, who were putting up a piñata in the courtyard, and then Laura Damián's father burst into tears. My curiosity got the better of me and I came out of the kitchen, trying not to make a sound, an unnecessary precaution because the two men were intent on each other, Quim looking as if he'd just gotten up, his hair uncombed, circles under his bleary eyes, his pajamas wrinkled, his slippers dangling—he had dainty feet, as I could see, very different from my uncle's, for example—and Mr. Damián with his face bathed in tears, although the tears only made two furrows down his cheeks, two deep furrows that seemed to swallow up his whole face, his hands clasped, sitting in an armchair facing Quim. I want to see Angélica, he said. First wipe your nose, said Quim. Mr. Damián pulled a handkerchief from his jacket pocket and rubbed his eyes and cheeks with it, then blew his nose. Life is hard, Quim, he said as he got up suddenly and headed for the bathroom like a sleepwalker. He didn't even glance at me as he went by.

Then I think I spent a while in the courtyard helping Mrs. Font get ready for the dinner party she was planning to host that evening, the last night of 1975. Each New Year's Eve I have a dinner party for friends, she said, it's a tradition by now, although this year I'd just as soon skip it; I'm not in a party mood, as you can imagine, but we have to be brave. I told her that Laura Damián's father was there. Alvarito comes every year, said Mrs. Font, he says I'm the best cook he knows. What will we have to eat tonight? I said.

"I have no idea, dear. I think I'll make some mole and then go to bed early. This isn't exactly a year for celebrations, is it?"

Mrs. Font looked at me and started to laugh. I think the woman isn't quite right in the head. Then the bell rang insistently and Mrs. Font, after standing there waiting for a few seconds, asked me to go see who it was. As I passed the living room I saw Quim and Laura Damián's father, each with a glass in his hand, sitting together on the sofa watching another TV show. The visitor at the door was one of the peasant poets. I think he was drunk. He asked me where Mrs. Font was and then he went straight out to the courtyard, where she stood amid her wreaths and little paper Mexican flags, avoiding the sad spectacle presented by Quim and Laura Damián's father. I went up to Jorgito's room and from there I saw the peasant poet clapping his hands to his head.

And yet there were many phone calls. First some woman named Lorena, an ex–visceral realist, called to invite María and Angélica to a New Year's Eve party. Then a poet from the Paz camp called. Then a dancer named Rodolfo called wanting to speak to María, but she refused to come to the phone and begged me to tell him that she wasn't home, which I did mechanically, taking no pleasure in it, as if I were beyond jealousy now (which if true would be amazing, since jealousy does no one any good). Then the head architect from Quim's studio called. Surprisingly, after talking to Quim, he wanted to speak to Angélica. When Quim asked me to call Angélica to the phone there were tears in his eyes and as Angélica talked, or rather listened, he told me that writing poetry was the most beautiful thing anyone could do on this godforsaken earth. Those were his exact words. Not wanting to contradict him, I agreed (I think I said "right on, Quim," a moronic reply any way you look at it). Then I spent a while at the girls' little house, talking to María and Lupe or rather listening to them talk as I wondered when and how the pimp's siege would end.

As for fucking Lupe last night, the whole thing's still shrouded in mystery, although I can honestly say it's been forever since I had such a great time. At one in the afternoon there was a semblance of lunch: first Jorgito, María, Lupe, and I ate, then at one-thirty Mrs. Font, Quim, Laura Damián's father, the peasant poet, and Angélica ate. As I was washing dishes I heard the peasant poet threatening to go out and confront Alberto, only to be warned against it by Mrs. Font, who said: Julio, don't be a fool. Then we all gathered for dessert in the living room.

That afternoon I showered.

My body was covered in bruises but I didn't know who'd given them to me, whether it was Rosario or Lupe. In any case it hadn't been María, and strangely enough that hurt, although the pain was far from unbearable, as it had been when I first met her. On my chest, just under my left nipple, I have a bruise the size of a plum. On my collarbone there are scratches like tiny comet trails. I discovered some marks on my shoulders too.

When I came out everyone was having coffee in the kitchen, some sitting and others standing. María had asked Lupe to tell the story of the whore Alberto almost choked to death with his cock. Every once in a while someone would interrupt Lupe's story and say my God, or what animals, and a female voice (Mrs. Font's or Angélica's) even said can you believe it, as Quim was saying to Laura Damián's father: you see the kind of person we have to deal with.

At four the peasant poet left, and soon afterward Mrs. Font's sister appeared. Dinner preparations shifted into high gear.

Between five and six there was a flurry of phone calls from people saying they couldn't make it to dinner and at six-thirty Mrs. Font said that she'd had enough, started to cry, and went upstairs to her bedroom, closing the door.

At seven Mrs. Font's sister, with María and Lupe's help, set the table and put the finishing touches on the dinner. But a few ingredients were missing and she went out to get them. Before she left Quim called her into his study for a few seconds. When she came out she had an envelope in her hand, with money in it, I guess, and from inside the study I heard Mr. Font tell her that she should put the envelope in her bag, because otherwise there was a risk it would be stolen by the occupants of the Camaro, a suggestion Mrs. Font's sister seemed to ignore at first, but as she opened the front door and left, she followed his advice. As an additional safety measure, Jorgito and I walked her to the gate. The Camaro was still there, but the occupants didn't even move when Mrs. Font's sister went by, heading toward Calle Cuernavaca.

At nine we sat down to dinner. Most of the guests had made their excuses and the only people who showed up were an older lady, a cousin of Quim's, I think; a tall, thin man who was introduced as an architect, or ex-architect, as he himself hastened to point out; and two painters who had no idea what was going on. Mrs. Font emerged from her room dressed to the nines and accompanied by her sister, who after returning had spent the final moments helping her dress, as if taking charge of dinner hadn't been enough. Lupe, who was becoming increasingly prickly as the new year approached, said that she had no right to have dinner with us and would eat in the kitchen, but María firmly refused to let her and finally (after an argument that to be honest I didn't understand) she ended up sitting at the table with everyone else.

Dinner got off to an unusual start.

Quim rose and said that he wanted to give a toast. I guessed that it would be a toast to his wife, who under the circumstances had demonstrated incredible fortitude, but it was a toast to me! He spoke of my youth and my poems, he recalled my friendship with his daughters (when he said this he stared at Laura Damián's father, who nodded) and my friendship with him, our conversations, our unexpected encounters on the streets of Mexico City, and bringing his speech to a close—it was actually short but to me it seemed to go on forever—he asked me, now addressing me directly, not to judge him too harshly when I grew up and became a responsible adult citizen. When he stopped talking, I was red with embarrassment. María, Angélica, and Lupe clapped. The clueless painters clapped too. Jorgito crawled under the table and no one seemed to notice. When I snuck a glance at Mrs. Font, she looked as mortified as I was.

Despite this lively beginning, the New Year's Eve dinner was sad and silent. Mrs. Font and her sister busied themselves with serving; María hardly touched her food; Angélica sank into a silence more languid than sullen; Quim and Laura Damián's father generally kept to themselves, though they paid some attention to the architect, who spent the evening gently scolding Quim; the two painters only talked to each other and every once in a while to Laura Damián's father (it seemed he also collected art); and María and Lupe, who at the beginning of dinner had seemed the most inclined to have a good time, got up to help serve and finally disappeared into the kitchen. *Sic transit gloria mundi*, Quim said to me from the other end of the table.

Then someone rang the doorbell and we all jumped. María and Lupe looked in from the kitchen.

"Someone get the door," said Quim, but no one moved.

I was the one to get up.

The garden was dark and through the gate I could see two figures. I thought it must be Alberto and his policeman friend. I felt an irrational desire to fight and I headed purposefully toward them. When I got a little closer, however, I realized that it was Ulises Lima and Arturo Belano. They didn't say why they'd come. They weren't surprised to see me. I remember thinking: we're saved!

There was more than enough food, and Ulises and Arturo were seated at the table and Mrs. Font served them dinner while the rest of us had dessert or talked. When they were done eating, Quim took them into his study. Laura Damián's father soon followed.

A little while later Quim looked out the half-open door and called for Lupe. Those of us in the living room looked as if we were at a funeral. María asked me to come with her to the courtyard. She talked to me for what seemed like a long time but couldn't have been more than five minutes. This is a trap, she said. Then the two of us went into her father's study.

Surprisingly, Álvaro Damián had taken charge. He was sitting in Quim's chair (Quim was standing in a corner) and signing several checks to the bearer. Belano and Lima were smiling. Lupe seemed worried but resigned. María asked Laura Damián's father what was going on. Laura Damián's father looked up from his checkbook and said that the Lupe problem had to be solved as quickly as possible.

"I'm going north, *mana*," said Lupe.

"What?" said María.

"Here, with these guys, in your dad's car."

It didn't take me long to figure out that Quim and Laura Damián's father had convinced my friends to take Lupe with them and go wherever they wanted, thus lifting the siege of the house.

What surprised me most was that Quim was letting them take the Impala. That was something I certainly hadn't expected.

When we left the room, Lupe and María went to pack. I followed them. Lupe's suitcase was almost empty because when she fled the hotel she'd left most of her clothes behind.

After the countdown to midnight on TV we all hugged: María, Angélica, Jorgito, Quim, Mrs. Font, her sister, Laura Damián's father, the architect, the painters, Quim's cousin, Arturo Belano, Ulises Lima, Lupe, and I.

There came a moment when none of us knew whom we were hugging anymore or whether we'd hugged the same person more than once.

Until ten it had been possible to see the shapes of Alberto and his sidekicks through the gate. By eleven they weren't there anymore and Jorgito was brave enough to go out into the garden, look over the wall, and scan the whole street. They were gone. At twelve-fifteen we all made our way stealthily to the garage and the goodbyes began. I hugged Belano and Lima and asked them what would happen to visceral realism. They didn't answer me. I hugged Lupe and told her to take care of herself. In return I got a kiss on the cheek. Quim's car was a white Ford Impala, the latest model, and Quim and his wife wanted to know who the driver would be, as if at the last minute they were having second thoughts.

"Me," said Ulises Lima.

As Quim explained some of the finer points of the car to Ulises, Jorgito said that we should hurry up because Lupe's pimp had just come back. For a few seconds everyone started talking in normal voices and Mrs. Font said: the shame of it all, to be reduced to this. Then I hurried off to the Fonts' little house, got my books, and came back. The car's engine was already running and everyone looked frozen in place.

I saw Arturo and Ulises in the front seats and Lupe in back.

"Someone will have to go open the gate," said Quim.

I offered to do it.

I was on the sidewalk when I saw the lights of the Camaro and the lights of the Impala go on. It looked like a science fiction movie. As one car left the house, the other approached, as if the two were magnetically attracted to each other, or drawn together by fate, which the Greeks would say is the same thing.

I heard voices. People were calling my name. Quim's car passed me. I saw the shape of Alberto getting out of the Camaro and the next moment he was alongside the car my friends were in. His friends, still sitting in the Camaro, yelled at him to break one of the Impala's windows. Why doesn't Ulises hit the gas? I thought. Lupe's pimp started to kick the doors. I saw María coming through the garden toward me. I saw the faces of the thugs inside the Camaro. One of them was smoking a cigar. I saw Ulises's face and his hands, which were moving on the dashboard of Quim's car. I saw Belano's face looking impassively at the pimp, as if none of this had anything to do with him. I saw Lupe, who was covering her face in the backseat. I thought that the window glass couldn't withstand another kick and the next moment I was up next to Alberto. Then I saw that Alberto was swaying. He smelled of alcohol. They'd been celebrating the new year too, of course. I saw my right fist (the only one I had free since my books were in my other hand) hurtling into the pimp's body and this time I saw him fall. I heard my name being called from the house and I didn't turn around. I kicked the body at my feet and I saw the Impala, which was moving at last. I saw the two thugs get out of the Camaro and I saw them coming toward me. I saw that Lupe was looking at me from inside the car and that she was opening the door. I realized that I'd always wanted to leave. I got in and before I could close the door Ulises stepped on the gas. I heard a shot or something that sounded like a shot. They're shooting at us, the bastards, said Lupe. I turned around and through the back window I saw a shadow in the middle of the street. All the sadness of the world was concentrated in that shadow, framed by the strict rectangle of the Impala's window. It's firecrackers, I heard Belano say as our car leaped forward and left behind the Fonts' house, the thugs' Camaro, Calle Colima, and in less than two seconds we were on Avenida Oaxaca, heading north out of the city.

# THE SAVAGE DETECTIVES

## (1976–1996)

## II

**1**

**Amadeo Salvatierra, Calle República de Venezuela, near the Palacio de la Inquisición, Mexico City DF, January 1976.** My dear boys, I said to them, I'm so glad to see you, come right in, make yourselves at home, and as they filed down the hall, or rather felt their way, because the hall is dark and the bulb had burned out and I hadn't changed it (I haven't changed it yet), I skipped joyfully ahead into the kitchen, where I got out a bottle of Los Suicidas mezcal, a mezcal only made in Chihuahua, limited run, of course, of which I used to receive two bottles each year by parcel post, until 1967. When I returned the boys were in the front room looking at my paintings and examining some books and I couldn't help telling them again how happy their visit made me. Who gave you my address, boys? Germán, Manuel, Arqueles? At which they looked at me as if they hadn't understood and then one of them said List Arzubide. But sit down, I said, have a seat, ah, my good friend Germán List Arzubide, he's not one to forget me, is he still the same big old wonderful man? And the boys shrugged their shoulders and said yes—well of course he'd hardly have shrunk, would he? but all they said was yes—and then I said let's try this mezcalito and I handed them two glasses and they sat there looking at the bottle as if they were afraid a dragon might come shooting out of it, and I laughed, but I wasn't laughing at them, I was laughing for sheer glee, it made me so happy just to be there with them, and then one of them asked if they'd heard right, if that was really what the mezcal was called, and I passed them the bottle, still laughing, I knew the name would impress them, and I stepped back a little to get a better look at them, God bless them, they were so young, with their hair down to their shoulders and carrying all those books—the memories they brought

127

back!—and then one of them said are you sure this won't kill us, Señor Salvatierra? and I said what do you mean kill you, this is the essence of health, the water of life, drink it without fear, and to set an example I filled my glass and downed half of it and then I served them, and at first the rascals just wetted their lips, but little by little it grew on them, and they started to drink like men. Well, boys, how is it? I said, and one of them, the Chilean, said that he'd never heard of a mezcal called Los Suicidas, which struck me as a little presumptuous, there must be two hundred brands of mezcal in Mexico at the very least, so it would be hard to know them all, especially if you weren't from here, but of course the boy didn't realize that, and the other one said it's good, and then he said I've never heard of it before either, and I had to tell them that as far as I knew no one made it anymore, the factory went out of business, or burned down, or was sold and turned into a bottling plant for Refrescos Pascual, or the new owners didn't think the name was good for sales. And for a while we were quiet, the two of them standing and me sitting, drinking and savoring each drop of Los Suicidas and thinking who knows what. And then one of them said Señor Salvatierra, we want to talk to you about Cesárea Tinajero. And the other one said: and about the magazine *Caborca*. Those boys. Their brains and their tongues were interconnected. One of them could start to talk, then stop in the middle of what he was saying, and the other one would pick up the sentence or the idea as if he'd begun it himself. And when they spoke Cesárea's name I raised my eyes and looked at them as if I were seeing them through a curtain of gauze, surgical gauze, to be precise, and I said don't call me Señor, boys, call me Amadeo, which is what my friends call me. And they said all right, Amadeo. And they spoke the name Cesárea Tinajero again.


**Perla Avilés, Calle Leonardo da Vinci, Colonia Mixcoac, Mexico City DF, January 1976.** I'm going to talk about 1970. I met him in 1970, at Porvenir, a high school in Talismán. The two of us were students there for a while. He started in 1968, which was when he came to Mexico, and I started in '69, although we didn't meet until 1970. For reasons that are beside the point we both quit school for a while. Financial reasons in his case, I think, and inner turmoil in mine. But then I went back and he did too, or his parents made him go back, and then we met. This was

1970 and by then I was older than anyone in my class, I was eighteen, and I should have been in college, not high school, but there I was at Porvenir, and one morning, after the school year had already begun, he showed up, I noticed him right away, he wasn't a new student, he had friends, and he was a year younger than me, although he'd repeated a grade. At the time, he lived in Colonia Lindavista, but after a few months he and his parents moved to Colonia Nápoles. I became his friend. In the beginning, as I was getting up the courage to talk to him, I watched him play soccer in the yard. He loved to play. I watched him from the stairs and I thought he was the most beautiful boy I'd ever seen. Long hair was forbidden in high school, but he had long hair and when he played soccer he took off his shirt and played bare-chested. I thought he looked just like a Greek god from those magazines with tales of the Greek myths and at other times (in class, when he seemed to be asleep), a Catholic saint. I watched him and that was enough for me. He didn't have many friends. He knew lots of people, sure, he kidded around with everybody (he was always laughing), making jokes, but he had very few friends, maybe none at all. He didn't do well at school. In chemistry and physics he was lost. That surprised me because neither one was really hard. All you had to do to pass was pay the tiniest bit of attention, study a little, but obviously he hardly ever studied, or maybe never studied at all, and in class his mind was elsewhere. One day he came up to me, I was on the stairs reading Lautréamont, and asked me whether I knew who owned Porvenir. I was so startled that I didn't know what to say, I think I opened my mouth but nothing came out, my face crumpled, and I might even have started to shake. He was shirtless, carrying his shirt in one hand and a backpack, a dusty backpack full of notebooks, in the other, and he looked at me with a smile on his lips and I looked at the sweat on his chest that was drying fast in the wind or the late afternoon air (which aren't the same thing), and most classes were over, I don't know what I was doing at school, maybe waiting for someone, some friend, though that's unlikely since I didn't have many friends either, maybe I'd just stayed to watch him play soccer. I remember that the sky was a bright, damp gray and that it was cold or that I felt cold at the time. I also remember that the only sounds were of distant footsteps, muted laughter, the empty school. He probably thought I hadn't heard him the first time and he repeated the question. I don't know who it belongs to, I said, I don't know whether it has an owner. Of course it has an owner, he said, it's owned by Opus Dei. He must have thought I was a complete idiot, because I told him that I didn't know what Opus Dei was. A Catholic sect in league with the devil, he said, laughing. Then I understood and I told him that I didn't care much about religion and that I already knew that Porvenir was owned by the church. No, he said, what's important is which part of the church it's owned by: Opus Dei. And what kind of people belong to Opus Dei? I asked. Then he sat down beside me on the stairs and we talked for a long time and it bothered me that he wasn't putting his shirt on and it kept getting colder and colder. I remember what he said in that first conversation about his parents: he said they were naïve and that he was naïve too and he probably said they were stupid (he and his parents) and gullible for not having realized until now that the school belonged to Opus Dei. Do your parents know who's in charge here? he asked me. My mother is dead, I said, and my father doesn't know or care. I don't care either, I added, all I want is to finish high school and go to college. What will you study there? he said. Literature, I said. That's when he told me he was a writer too. What a coincidence, I said, I'm a writer. Or something like that. Not making a big deal out of it. I thought he was kidding, of course. That's how we became friends. I was eighteen and he had just turned seventeen. He'd been living in Mexico since he was fifteen. Once I invited him to go riding with me. My father had some land in Tlaxcala and had bought a horse. He said he was a good rider and I said this Sunday I'm going to Tlaxcala with my father, you can come with us if you want. What bleak country that was. My father had built a thatched adobe hut and that was all there was, the rest was scrub and dirt. When we got there he looked around with a smile, as if to say, I knew this wasn't going to be a fancy ranch or a big spread, but this is too much. Even I was a little bit ashamed of my father's land. Among other things, there was no saddle, and some neighbors kept the horse for us. For a while, as my father was off getting the horse, we wandered the flats. I tried to talk about books I'd read that I knew he hadn't read, but he hardly listened to me. He walked and smoked, walked and smoked, and the scenery was always the same. Until we heard the horn of my father's car and then the man who kept the horse came, not riding the horse but leading it by the bridle. By the time we got back to the hut my father and the man had gone off in the car to settle some business and the horse was tied up waiting for us. You go first, I said. No, he said (it was clear his mind was on other things), you go.

Not wanting to argue, I mounted the horse and broke straight into a gallop. When I got back he was sitting on the ground, against the wall of the hut, smoking. You ride well, he said. Then he got up and went over to the horse, saying that he wasn't used to riding bareback, but he vaulted up anyway, and I showed him which way to go, telling him that over in that direction there was a river or actually a riverbed that was dry now but that filled up when it rained and was pretty, then he galloped off. He rode well. I'm a good horsewoman, but he was as good as I was or maybe better, I don't know. At the time I thought he was better. Galloping without stirrups is hard and he galloped clinging to the horse's back until he was out of sight. As I waited I counted the cigarette butts that he had stubbed out beside the hut and they made me want to learn to smoke. Hours later, as we were on our way back in my father's car, him in front and me in back, he said that there was probably some pyramid lying buried under our land. I remember that my father turned his eyes from the road to look at him. Pyramids? Yes, he said, deep underground there must be lots of pyramids. My father didn't say anything. From the darkness of the backseat, I asked him why he thought that. He didn't answer. Then we started to talk about other things but I kept wondering why he'd said that about the pyramids. I kept thinking about pyramids. I kept thinking about my father's stony plot of land and much later, when I'd lost touch with him, each time I went back to that barren place I thought about the buried pyramids, about the one time I'd seen him riding over the tops of the pyramids, and I imagined him in the hut, when he was left alone and sat there smoking.

**Laura Jáuregui, Tlalpan, Mexico City DF, January 1976.** Before I met him I was dating César, César Arriaga, and I was introduced to César in the poetry workshop at the Torre de Rectoría at UNAM. That was where I met María Font and Rafael Barrios. That's also where I met Ulises Lima. His name wasn't Ulises Lima back then, or I don't know, maybe it already was but we called him by his real name, Alfredo something or other, and I met César too and we fell in love or we thought we'd fallen in love and the two of us wrote poems for Ulises Lima's magazine. This was at the end of 1973, I can't say exactly when. It was at a time when it was raining a lot, I remember, because we were always coming in wet to meetings. And then we put together the magazine, *Lee Harvey Oswald,* what a name, at the architecture studio where María's father worked. Those were gorgeous afternoons, we would drink wine and one of us always brought sandwiches, Sofía or María or I. The boys never brought anything, although actually they did, at first they did, but then the ones who brought things, the politer ones, quit the magazine, or at least stopped coming to the meetings, and then Pancho Rodríguez showed up and everything was spoiled, at least as far as I was concerned, but I kept working on the magazine, or anyway I still hung around in that crowd, mostly because César was part of it and mostly because I liked María and Sofía (I was never friends with Angélica, not real friends), not because I wanted my poems to be published, none were published in the first issue, though there was supposed to be a poem of mine in the second issue, "Lilith" it was called, but in the end I don't know what happened and it wasn't published after all. It was César who had a poem in *Lee Harvey Oswald*, a poem called "Laura and César," very sweet, but Ulises changed the title (or convinced César to change it) and in the end it was called "Laura & César." That was the kind of thing Ulises Lima did.

But anyway, first I met César, and Laura & César started dating, or something like that. Poor César. He had light brown hair and he was tall. He lived with his grandmother (his parents lived in Michoacán) and I had my first adult sexual experiences with him. Or actually, my last adolescent sexual experiences. Or second to last, now that I think about it. We would go to the movies and a few times we went to the theater. It was around then that I enrolled at the dance school and sometimes César would go there with me. The rest of the time we spent taking long walks, talking about books we were reading, and doing nothing together. And this went on for months, three or four months or even nine months, and one day I broke up with him. That I know for sure, I was the one who told him it was over, although I can't remember exactly why, and I remember that César took it very well, he agreed that I was right, he was in his second year of medical school then and I had just started at the university, studying literature. That afternoon I didn't go to class, I went to María's house, I had to talk to a friend, I mean in person, not on the phone, and when I got to Colima, to María's house, the gate was open and that surprised me a little, because it was always closed, María's mother was paranoid about it, and I went in and rang the bell and the door opened and a guy I'd never seen before asked me who I was looking for. It was Arturo Belano. He was twenty-one then, skinny and long-haired, and he wore glasses, horrible glasses, although his eyes weren't especially bad, he was just a little bit nearsighted, but the glasses were still horrible. We only exchanged a few words. He was with María and a poet called Aníbal who was crazy about María back then, but they were on their way out when I got there.

That same day I saw him again. I spent all afternoon talking to María and then we went downtown to buy a scarf, I think, and we kept talking (first about César & Laura, then about everything in existence) and we ended up having cappuccinos at Café Quito, where María was supposed to meet Aníbal. And Arturo showed up around nine. This time he was with a seventeen-year-old Chilean called Felipe Müller, his best friend, a tall blond kid who almost never spoke and followed Arturo everywhere. And they sat down with us, of course. And then other poets turned up, poets a little older than Arturo, none of them visceral realists, among other reasons because visceral realism didn't exist yet, poets like Aníbal who had been friends with Arturo before he left for Chile and so had known him since he was seventeen. They were actually journalists and government officials, the kind of sad people who never leave downtown, or certain downtown neighborhoods, sovereigns of sadness in the area bounded by Avenida Chapultepec, to the south, and Reforma, to the north, staffers at *El Nacional,* proofreaders at the *Excelsior,* pencil pushers at the Secretaría de Gobernación who headed to Bucareli when they left work and sent out their tentacles or their little green slips. And even though, as I say, they were sad, that night we laughed a lot. In fact we never stopped laughing. And then we went walking to the bus stop, María, Aníbal, Felipe Müller, Gonzalo Müller (Felipe's brother who was leaving Mexico soon), Arturo, and I. And somehow all of us felt incredibly happy, I had forgotten all about César, María was looking up at the stars that had miraculously appeared in the sky of Mexico City like holographic projections, and even the way we were walking was graceful, our progress incredibly slow, as if we were advancing and retreating to put off the moment at which we would inevitably have to reach the bus stop, all of us walking and looking up at the sky (María was naming the stars). Much later Arturo told me that he hadn't been looking at the stars but at the lights in some apartments, tiny rooftop apartments on Calle Versalles or Lucerna or Calle Londres, and that was the moment he realized nothing would make him happier than being with me in one of those apartments, eating a few sandwiches with sour cream from a certain street stall on Bucareli. But he didn't tell me that at the time (I would've thought he was crazy). He told me that he'd like to read some of my poems, he told me that he loved the stars of both hemispheres, north and south, and he asked me for my number.

I gave him my number and the next day he called me. And we made a date to meet, but not downtown, I told him I couldn't leave Tlalpan, where I lived, that I had to study, and he said perfect, I'll come visit you, that way I'll get to see Tlalpan, and I said that there was nothing to see, you'll have to take the metro and then a bus and then another bus, and then I don't know why but I was sure he'd get lost and I said wait for me at the metro stop and when I went to meet him I found him sitting on some crates of fruit, leaning against a tree, really, the best place possible. You're lucky, I said. Yes, he said, I'm extremely lucky. And that afternoon he talked to me about Chile, I don't know whether it was because he wanted to or because I asked him about it, although the things he said were mostly incoherent, and he also talked about Guatemala and El Salvador, he'd been all over Latin America, or at least to every country along the Pacific coast, and we kissed for the first time, and then we were together for several months and we moved in together and then what happened happened, or in other words we broke up and I went back to living at my mother's house and I began to study biology (I hope to be a good biologist someday, I want to specialize in biogenetics), and strange things started to happen to Arturo. That was when visceral realism was born. At first we all thought it was a joke, but then we realized it wasn't. And when we realized it wasn't a joke, some of us went along with him and became visceral realists, out of inertia, I think, or because it was so crazy that it seemed plausible, or for the sake of friendship, so as not to lose a whole circle of friends, but deep down no one took it seriously. Not deep down.

At the time I was beginning to make new friends at the university and I saw Arturo and his friends less and less. I think the only one I called or went out with occasionally was María, but even my friendship with María began to cool. Still, I always more or less kept track of what Arturo was doing, and I thought: of all the stupid things to come up with, how can he believe this junk, and suddenly, one night when I couldn't sleep, it occurred to me that it was all a message for me. It was a way of saying don't leave me, see what I'm capable of, stay with me. And then I realized that deep down the guy was a creep. Because it's one thing to fool yourself and another thing entirely to fool everybody else. The whole visceral realism thing was a love letter, the demented strutting of a dumb bird in the moonlight, something essentially cheap and meaningless.

But that wasn't what I meant to say.

**Fabio Ernesto Logiacomo, editorial offices of the magazine *La Chispa*, Calle Independencia and Luis Moya, Mexico City DF, March 1976.** I came to Mexico in November of 1975. This was after I'd been through a few other Latin American countries, living pretty much hand to mouth. I was twenty-four and my luck was starting to change. That's the way things happen in Latin America, which is as far as I'm willing to try to explain it. There I was moldering in Panama when I found out that I'd won the Casa de las Américas poetry prize. I was thrilled. I didn't have a cent, and the prize money got me a ticket to Mexico and food to eat. But the funny thing is, I hadn't entered the Casa de las Américas competition that year. Honest to God. The year before, I'd sent them a book and the book didn't even get so much as an honorable mention. And this year, out of the blue, I hear that I've won the prize and the prize money. When I first got the news I thought I was hallucinating. I hadn't been eating enough, to tell the truth, and when you don't eat enough it can have that effect. Then I thought it might be some other Logiacomo, but that would've been too much of a coincidence: another Argentinian Logiacomo, another twenty-four-year-old Logiacomo, another Logiacomo who'd written a book of poetry with the same title as mine. Well. In Latin America these things happen and there's no point giving yourself a headache trying to come up with a logical answer when sometimes there is none. Fortunately I really had won the prize, and that was that. Later the people at Casa told me that the book from the year before had gotten misplaced, that kind of thing.

So I was able to come to Mexico and I settled in Mexico City and a little while later I get a call from this kid telling me that he wants to interview me or something, I thought he said interview. And of course I said yes. To tell the truth, I was pretty lonely and lost. I didn't know any young Mexican poets and an interview or whatever seemed like a fantastic idea. So we met that same day and when I got to the place we were supposed to meet it turned out that instead of just one poet, there were four poets waiting for me, and what they wanted wasn't an interview but a discussion, a three-way conversation to be published in one of the top Mexican magazines. The participants would be a Mexican (one of them), a Chilean (also one of them), and an Argentinian, me. The other two tagging along were just there to listen. The topic: the state of new Latin American poetry. An excellent topic. So I said great, I'm ready whenever you are, and we found a more or less quiet coffee shop and started to talk.

They'd come with a tape recorder all ready to go, but at the crucial moment the machine conked out. Back to step one. This went on for half an hour, and I had two cups of coffee, paid for by them. It was clear they weren't used to this kind of thing: I mean the tape recorder, I mean talking about poetry in front of a tape recorder, I mean organizing their thoughts and expressing themselves clearly. Anyway, we tried it a few more times, but it didn't work. We decided that it would be better if each of us wrote whatever came to mind and then we put together what we'd written. In the end it was just the Chilean and I who had the discussion. I don't know what happened to the Mexican.

We spent the rest of the afternoon walking. And a funny thing happened to me with those kids, or the coffee they bought me, I noticed something strange about them, it was as if they were there but at the same time they weren't there, I'm not sure how to explain it, they were the first young Mexican poets I'd met and maybe that was why they seemed odd, but in the previous few months I'd met young Peruvian poets, young Colombian poets, young poets from Panama and Costa Rica, and I hadn't felt the same thing. I was an expert in young poets and something was off here, something was missing: the camaraderie, the strong sense of shared ideals, the frankness that always prevails at any gathering of Latin American poets. And at one point during the afternoon, I remember it like a mysterious drunkenness, I started to talk about my book and my own poems, and I don't know why but I told them about the Daniel Cohn-Bendit poem, a poem that was neither better nor worse than any of the others in the collection that had won the Cuban prize, but that ultimately wasn't included in the book, we were probably talking about length, about page count, because those two (the Chilean and the Mexican) wrote extremely long poems, or so they said, I hadn't read them yet, and I think they even had a theory about long poems, they called them poem-novels, I think it was some French poets who came up with the idea, though I can't remember exactly, and so I'm telling them about the Cohn-Bendit poem, why in the world I honestly don't know, and one of them asks me why isn't it in your book and I tell them that what happened was that the Casa de las Américas people decided to take it out and the Mexican says but they asked your permission, didn't they, and I tell him no, they didn't ask my permission, and the Mexican says they took it out of the book without letting you know? and I say yes, the truth is that I couldn't be located, and the Chilean asks why did they take it out? and I tell him what the people at Casa de las Américas told me, which was that Cohn-Bendit had just issued some statements against the Cuban Revolution, and the Chilean says was that the only reason? and like a dickhead I tell him I guess so, but the poem wasn't very good anyway (what had those guys given me to drink to make me talk that way?), definitely long, but not very good, and the Mexican says bastards, but he says it sweetly, he really does, not bitterly at all, as if deep down he understood everything the Cubans had been through before they mutilated my book, as if deep down he couldn't be bothered to despise me or our comrades in Havana.

Literature isn't innocent. I've known that since I was fifteen. And I remember thinking that then, but I can't remember whether I said it or not, and if I did, what the context was. And then the walk (but here I have to clarify that it wasn't five of us anymore but three, the Mexican, the Chilean, and me, the other two Mexicans having vanished at the gates of purgatory) turned into a kind of stroll on the fringes of hell.

The three of us were quiet, as if we'd been struck dumb, but our bodies moved to a beat, as if something was propelling us through that strange land and making us dance, a silent, syncopated kind of walking, if I can call it that, and then I had a vision, not the first that day, as it happened, or the last: the park we were walking through opened up into a kind of lake and the lake opened up into a kind of waterfall and the waterfall became a river that flowed through a kind of cemetery, and all of it, lake, waterfall, river, cemetery, was deep green and silent. And then I thought it's one of two things: either I'm going crazy, which is unlikely since I've always had my head on straight, or these guys have doped me. And then I said stop, stop for a minute, I feel sick, I have to rest, and they said something but I couldn't hear them, I could only see them coming closer, and I realized, I became conscious, that I was looking all around trying to find someone, some witness, but there was no one, we were in the middle of a forest, and I remember I said what forest is this, and they said it's Chapultepec and then they led me to a bench and we sat there for a while, and one of them asked me what hurt (the word *hurt,* so right, so fitting) and I should have told them that what hurt was my whole body, my whole being, but instead I told them that the problem was probably that I wasn't used to the altitude yet, that it was the altitude that was getting to me and making me see things.

**Luis Sebastián Rosado, La Rama Dorada coffee shop, Colonia Coyoacán, Mexico City DF, April 1976.** Monsiváis said it first: disciples of Marinetti and Tzara, their noisy, outrageous, overwrought poems did battle in the realm of simple typographic arrangement, never rising above the level of childish entertainment. Monsi was talking about the stridentists, but the same goes for the visceral realists. No one paid attention to them and they opted for indiscriminate assault. In December of '75, just before Christmas, I was unlucky enough to run into some of them here at La Rama Dorada. The owner, Don Néstor Pesqueira, will back me up: it was extremely unpleasant. One of them, the one in charge, was Ulises Lima; the second was a big fat dark guy called Moctezuma or Cuauhtémoc; the third went by the name Luscious Skin. I was sitting right here, waiting for Alberto Moore and his sister, and all of a sudden these three nuts surround me, sitting down one on each side of me, and they say Luisito, let's talk poetry, let's analyze the future of Mexican poetry, something like that. I'm not a violent person and of course I got nervous. I thought: what are they doing here? how did they find me? what scores have they come to settle? This country is a disgrace, it must be said, and so is Mexican literature, it must also be said. Anyway, we were talking for twenty minutes (I've never been so annoyed by the lateness of Albertito and his snotty sister) and finally we even managed to agree on several points. When it came down to it, ninety percent of the time we hated the same things. Of course I always stood up for what Octavio Paz was doing on the literary scene. And of course all they seemed to like was what they were doing themselves. Thank goodness. That being a lesser evil, I mean, since it would've been worse if they'd declared themselves disciples of the peasant poets or followers of poor Rosario Castellanos or disciples of Jaime Sabines (one Jaime is enough, in my opinion). And then Alberto got here and I was still alive, there'd been a little bit of shouting, some unpleasant language, a certain kind of behavior that was inappropriate in a place like La Rama Dorada, Don Néstor Pesqueira will back me up here, but that was all. And when Alberto arrived I thought I'd handled the situation well. But then Julia Moore comes right out and asks them who they are and what they plan to do that night. And the one called Luscious Skin is quick to say that they're not doing anything, that if she has any ideas she should say so, he's up for anything. And then Julita, oblivious of the looks her brother and I are shooting her, says that we could go dancing at Priapo's, an insanely vulgar place in Colonia 10 de Mayo or Tepito, I've only been there once and I've always done my best to forget it, and since neither Alberto nor I can say no to Julita, off we go in Alberto's car, with Alberto, Ulises Lima, and me in the front seat and Julita, Luscious Skin, and the guy called Cuauhtémoc or Moctezuma in the backseat. Honestly, I feared the worst, these people weren't trustworthy, somebody told me once that they cornered Monsi in Sanborn's, at the Casa Borda, but since Monsi did agree to have coffee with them, granted them an audience, you might say, it was partly his fault, because everybody knows the visceral realists are just like the stridentists and everybody knows what Monsi thinks about the stridentists, so he really couldn't complain about what happened, and anyway nobody or almost nobody knows what did happen, though occasionally I've been tempted to ask him, but I haven't, not wanting to pry or open old wounds, still, *something* happened to him during his meeting with the visceral realists, and everybody knows it, everybody who secretly loves or hates Monsi, and there were all kinds of hypotheses and theories, but anyway, that's what I was wondering as Alberto's car shot like lightning or crawled like a cockroach, depending on the traffic, toward Priapo's, and in the backseat Julita Moore kept talking and talking and talking to the two visceral realist bums. I'll spare you a description of the club itself. I swear to God I thought we wouldn't get out of there alive. All I'll say is that the furnishings and human specimens adorning its interior seemed arbitrarily plucked from Lizardi's *The Mangy Parrot*, Mariano Azuela's *The Underdogs*, del Paso's *José Trigo*, the worst novels of the Onda, and the worst fifties porn (more than one woman looked like Tongolele, who incidentally I don't think was making movies in the fifties, but should have been). So as I was saying, we went into Priapo's and sat at a table close to the dance floor and as Julita danced the cha-cha or a bolero or a *danzón*, I'm not exactly up on the annals of popular music, Alberto and I started to talk about something (what it was I swear I can't remember), and a waiter brought us a bottle of tequila or rat poison that we accepted without a murmur, that's how desperate we were. And suddenly, in less time than it takes to say "otherness," we were drunk and Ulises Lima was reciting a poem in French, what in the world for I don't know, but he was reciting it, I didn't realize he spoke French, English, maybe, I think I'd seen a translation of his somewhere of Richard Brautigan, a terrible poet, or John Giorno, whoever he is, maybe a stand-in for Lima himself, but French? that surprised me a little. Good enunciation, passable pronunciation, and the poem, how to put it, sounded familiar, very familiar, but because of my increasing drunkenness or the relentless boleros I couldn't identify it. I thought of Claudel, but none of us can imagine Lima reciting Claudel, can we? I thought of Baudelaire, I thought of Catulle Mendès (some of whose texts I translated for a university journal), I thought of Nerval. Ashamed as I am to admit it, those were the names that came to mind. In my defense I should say that soon, through the haze of alcohol, I asked myself what Nerval could possibly have in common with Mendès, and then I thought of Mallarmé. Alberto, who must have been playing the same game, said: Baudelaire. It wasn't Baudelaire, of course. Here's the poem. Let's see if you can guess:

> Mon triste coeur bave à la poupe,
> Mon coeur couvert de caporal:
> Ils y lancent des jets de soupe,
> Mon triste coeur bave à la poupe:
> Sous les quolibets de la troupe
> Qui pousse un rire général,
> Mon triste coeur bave à la poupe,
> Mon coeur couvert de caporal!
>
> Ithyphalliques et pioupiesques
> Leurs quolibets l'ont dépravé!
> Au gouvernail on voit des fresques
> Ithyphalliques et pioupiesques.
> Ô flots abracadabrantesques,
> Prenez mon coeur, qu'il soit lavé!

*Ithyphalliques et pioupiesques*
*Leurs quolibets l'ont dépravé*

*Quand ils auront tari leurs chiques,*
*Comment agir, ô coeur volé?*
*Ce seront des hoquets bachiques*
*Quand ils auront tari leurs chiques:*
*J'aurai des sursauts stomachiques,*
*Moi, si mon coeur est ravalé:*
*Quand ils auront tari leurs chiques*
*Comment agir, ô coeur volé?*

It's Rimbaud. Which was a surprise. Relatively speaking, that is. The really surprising thing was that he recited it in French. Anyway, I was a little angry not to have guessed it, since I know Rimbaud's work fairly well, but I didn't let it bother me. Another point in common. Maybe we *would* make it out of that hellhole alive. And after reciting Rimbaud, Ulises Lima told a story about Rimbaud and some war, which war I don't know, war not being a subject that interests me, but there was something, a common theme linking Rimbaud, the poem, and the war, a sordid story, I'm sure, although at the time my ears and then my eyes were registering other sordid little stories (I swear I'll kill Julita Moore if she drags me to another dive like Priapo's), disjointed scenes in which brooding young delinquents danced with desperate young cleaning girls or desperate young whores in a whirl of contrasts that, I confess, heightened my drunkenness, if such a thing is possible. Then there was a fight somewhere. I didn't see anything, I just heard shouts. A pair of thugs emerged from the shadows dragging a guy with blood all over his face. I remember I told Alberto that we should go, that things could take a turn for the worse, but Alberto was listening to Ulises Lima's story and he ignored me. I remember that I watched Julita dancing with one of Ulises's friends, then I remember dancing a bolero myself with Luscious Skin, as if it were a dream, but still, it might have been the first time I'd felt good all night, in fact, it was definitely the first time I'd felt good all night. Next, like someone waking up, I remember whispering into my (dance) partner's ear that what we were doing would probably offend the other dancers and spectators. It's not clear what happened next. Someone said something rude to me. I was, I don't know, ready to crawl under a table and fall asleep or curl up on Luscious Skin's chest and fall asleep there too. But someone said something rude to me, and Luscious Skin made a motion as if to leave me and turn to face the person who'd spoken (I don't know what he said, pansy or faggot, I'm still not accustomed to that sort of language, although I know I should be), but I was so drunk, my muscles were slack and he couldn't let go of me—if he had I would've fallen—and he just shot something back from the middle of the dance floor. I closed my eyes, trying to remove myself from the situation. Luscious Skin's shoulder smelled like sweat, a strange acidic smell, as if he'd just walked away unscathed from the explosion of a chemical plant, and then I heard him speak, not to one person but to several people, more than two at least, and people were raising their voices. Then I opened my eyes, my God, and what I saw wasn't the people surrounding us but myself, my arm on Luscious Skin's shoulder, my left arm around his waist, my cheek on his shoulder, and I saw or imagined I saw the malicious looks, the stares of born killers, and then, rising in sheer terror above my drunkenness, I wanted to disappear, O Earth, swallow me up! I begged to be struck by lightning, I wished, in a word, never to have been born. How completely mortifying. I was red with shame, I wanted to vomit, I had let go of Luscious Skin and I was hardly able to stand, realizing that I was the object of cruel mockery and under attack at the same time. My one consolation was that the mocker was also under attack. It was essentially as if, having been betrayed in battle (what battles, what wars, was Ulises Lima talking about?), I was begging the angels of justice or the angels of the apocalypse for a great wave to appear, a great miraculous wave, that would sweep both of us away, that would sweep us all away, that would put an end to the ridicule and injustice. But then, through the icy lakes of my eyes (the wrong metaphor, since it was sweltering inside Priapo's, but I can't think of any better way to say that I was about to cry and that at the exact moment of "about to" had changed my mind, backpedaling, but that a distorting layer of liquid still glazed my pupils), I saw the mirific figure of Julita Moore appear intertwined with Cuauhtémoc or Moctezuma or Netzahualcóyotl or whatever his name was, and he and Luscious Skin stood up to the people who were making trouble, while Julita put her arm around my waist and asked me whether those sons of bitches had done anything to me and got me off the dance floor and out of that revolting dive. Once we were outside, Julita led me to the car and in the middle of the street I started to cry and when Julita helped me into the backseat I asked—no, begged—her to leave with me. I wanted the three of us to go and leave the others there, with their own evil kind. Please, Julita, I said, and she said for fuck's sake, Luisito, you're spoiling my night, don't start, and then I remember that I said or shouted or howled: what they've done to me is worse than what they did to Monsi, and Julita asked what the fuck they'd done to Monsi (she also asked which Monsi I meant; she said Montse or Monchi, I can't remember), and I said: Monsiváis, Julita, Monsiváis, the essayist, and she said oh, not seeming surprised at all, my God, the fortitude of that woman, I thought, and then I think I vomited and I started to cry, or I started to cry and then vomited—in Alberto's car!—and Julita started to laugh and by then the others were coming out of Priapo's, I saw their shadows in the beam of a streetlight, and I thought what have I done? what have I done? and I was so ashamed that I collapsed on the seat and curled up in a ball and pretended to be asleep. But I could hear them talking. Julita said something and the visceral realists replied. Their voices sounded cheerful, not hostile at all. Then Alberto got in the car and said what the fuck is this, it stinks in here, and then I opened my eyes and seeking his eyes in the rearview mirror I said I'm sorry, Alberto, I didn't mean to, I feel really sick, and then Julita got in the passenger seat and said my God, Alberto, open the windows, it reeks, and I said do you mind, Julita, there's no need to exaggerate, and Julita said: Luisito, it smells like you've been dead for a week, and I laughed, not much, but I was already starting to feel better. At the end of the street, under the lighted sign for Priapo's, shadows were roving, but not toward our car, and then Julita Moore rolled down her window and kissed Luscious Skin and Moctezuma or Cuauhtémoc, but not Ulises Lima, who was standing away from the car looking up at the sky, and then Luscious Skin stuck his head in the window and said how are you, Luis, and I don't think I even answered, I just made a gesture as if to say fine, I'm fine, and then Alberto started the Dodge and we headed out of Tepito with all the windows rolled down, on our way back to our own neighborhoods.

**Alberto Moore, Calle Pitágoras, Colonia Narvarte, Mexico City DF, April 1976.** What Luisito says is true, up to a point. My sister is an utter lunatic, yes, but she's charming, only twenty-two, a year older than me, and an extremely intelligent woman. She's about to finish medical school and she wants to specialize in pediatrics. She's no ingenue. Let's get that clear from the start.

Second: I didn't speed like lightning along the streets of Mexico City. The blue Dodge I was in that day is my mother's and when that's the case I'm usually a careful driver. The vomiting thing was completely unforgivable.

Third: Priapo's is in Tepito, which is like saying a war zone, a no-man's-land, or the other side of the Iron Curtain. At the end there was almost a fight on the dance floor, but I didn't see anything because I was sitting at a table talking to Ulises Lima. There is no club in Colonia 10 de Mayo as far as I know; my sister will vouch for that.

Fourth and last: I didn't say Baudelaire. It was Luis who said Baudelaire, and Catulle Mendès, and even Victor Hugo, I think. I didn't say anything. It sounded like Rimbaud to me, but I didn't say anything. Make sure you get that straight.

The visceral realists weren't as badly behaved as we were afraid they might be, either. I hadn't met them before, only heard of them. Mexico City, as we all know, is a small town of fourteen million. And the impression they made on me was relatively positive. The one called Luscious Skin was trying to flirt with my sister, poor idiot. The other guy, Moctezuma Rodríguez (not Cuauhtémoc), was doing his best too. At some point during the night they even seemed to think they were getting somewhere. It was a sad sight, but there was something sort of sweet about it too.

As for Ulises Lima, he gives the impression of always being high and his French is decent. He told an amazing story too, about the poem by Rimbaud. According to him, "Le Coeur Volé" was an autobiographical text describing a trip Rimbaud took from Charleville to Paris to join the Commune. As he was traveling (on foot!), Rimbaud ran into a group of drunken soldiers on the road who first taunted him, then proceeded to rape him. Frankly, it was a pretty crude story.

But there was even more: according to Lima, some of the soldiers, or at least their leader, the *caporal* of *mon coeur couvert de caporal*, were veterans of the French invasion of Mexico. Of course, neither Luisito nor I asked him what evidence he had for that. But I was interested in the story (unlike Luisito, who was more interested in what was or wasn't going on around us) and I wanted to know more. Then Lima told me that in 1865 a column under Colonel Libbrecht, which was supposed to occupy Santa Teresa, in Sonora, stopped sending back reports, and that Colonel Eydoux, commander of the plaza that served as a supply depot for the troops operating in that part of northeastern Mexico, sent a detachment of thirty troops to Santa Teresa.

The detachment was under the command of Captain Laurent and lieutenants Rouffanche and González, the latter a Mexican monarchist. This detachment, according to Lima, reached a town called Villaviciosa, near Santa Teresa, on the second day's march, but never made contact with Libbrecht's column. All the men, except Lieutenant Rouffanche and three soldiers who died in the act, were taken prisoner while they ate at the only inn in town, among them the future *caporal*, then a twenty-two-year-old recruit. The prisoners, bound and gagged with hemp rope, were brought before the man acting as military boss of Villaviciosa and a group of town notables. The boss was a mestizo who answered indiscriminately to Inocencio and El Loco. The notables were old peasants, most of them barefoot, who gazed at the Frenchmen and then retired to confer in a corner. After half an hour and some hard bargaining between two clearly opposed groups, the Frenchmen were taken to a covered corral where their clothes and shoes were removed and a little while later a group of their captors spent the rest of the day raping and torturing them.

At midnight they slit Captain Laurent's throat. Lieutenant González, two sergeants, and seven soldiers were taken to the main street and bayoneted by torchlight by shadowy figures riding the soldiers' own horses.

At dawn, the future *caporal* and two other soldiers managed to break their bonds and flee cross-country. No one came after them, but only the *caporal* lived to tell the tale. After two weeks of wandering in the desert he reached El Tajo. He was decorated for bravery and remained in Mexico until 1867, when he returned to France with the army under Bazaine (or whoever was in command of the French at the time), which was retreating from Mexico, leaving the emperor to his fate.

**Carlos Monsiváis, walking along Calle Madero, near Sanborn's, Mexico City DF, May 1976.** No ambush, no violent incident, nothing like that. Two young men, who couldn't have been more than twenty-three, both of them with extremely long hair, longer than any other poet's (and I can testify to the length of *everybody's* hair), determined not to acknowledge that there could be anything good about Paz, childishly stubborn, I-don't-like-him-because-I-don't, perfectly willing to deny the obvious. In a moment of weakness (mental, I suppose), they reminded me of José Agustín, of Gustavo Sainz, but with nothing like the talent of those two outstanding novelists, in fact with nothing at all, no money to pay for the coffee we drank (I had to pay), no arguments of substance, no original ideas. Two lost souls, two empty vessels. As for myself, I think I was more than generous (coffee aside). At some point I even suggested to Ulises (I don't remember the other one's name, I think he was Argentinian or Chilean) that he should write a review of a book by Paz that we'd been discussing. If it's any good, I said to him, stressing the word *good*, I'll publish it. And he said yes, that he'd write it, that he'd bring it to my house. Then I said that he shouldn't bring it to my house, that my mother might be frightened if she saw him. It was the only joke I made. But they took me seriously (not a smile) and said they would send it by mail. I'm still waiting.

# 2

Amadeo Salvatierra, Calle República de Venezuela, near the Palacio de la Inquisición, Mexico City DF, January 1976. Ah, I said to them, Cesárea Tinajero, where did you hear about her, boys? Then one of them explained that they were writing a piece about the stridentists and that they'd interviewed Germán, Arqueles, and Maples Arce, and read all the magazines and books of the era, and that among all those names, the names of established figures and empty names that mean nothing anymore and aren't even an unpleasant memory, they'd found Cesárea's name. So? I said. They looked at me and smiled, both at the same time, damn them, as if they were interconnected, if that makes any sense. It struck us as odd, they said, she seemed to be the only woman, and there were lots of references to her, all saying that she was a fine poet. A fine poetess? I said, where did you read her work? We haven't read anything she wrote, they said, not anywhere, and that got us interested. Got you interested how, boys? Come now, explain what you mean. Everyone says either wonderful or terrible things about her, but no one published her. We've read González Pedreño's magazine *Motor Humano*, Maples Arce's directory of the avant garde, and Salvador Salazar's magazine, said the Chilean, and she doesn't show up anywhere except in Maples's directory. And yet Juan Grady, Ernesto Rubio, and Adalberto Escobar all mention her in separate interviews, and in very complimentary terms. At first we thought that she was a stridentist, a fellow traveler, said the Mexican, but Maples Arce told us she never belonged to his movement. Although it's possible that Maples's memory is failing him, added the Chilean. Which we obviously don't believe, said the Mexican. Well, he didn't remember her as a stridentist, but he did remember her as a poet, said the Chilean.

Blasted boys. Blasted youth. Interconnected. A shiver ran through me. Although he didn't have a single poem by her in his extensive library to support his claim, said the Mexican. To sum it all up, Mr. Salvatierra, Amadeo, we've been asking around, we've talked to List Arzubide, Arqueles Vela, Hernández Miró, and the result is always more or less the same, everyone remembers her, said the Chilean, to a greater or lesser degree, but no one has anything by her that we can include in our study. And this study, boys, what is it exactly? Then I raised my hand and before they could answer I poured them more Los Suicidas mezcal and then I sat on the edge of the armchair and in my very backside I swear I felt as if I'd perched on the edge of a razor.

**Perla Avilés, Calle Leonardo da Vinci, Colonia Mixcoac, Mexico City DF, May 1976.** I didn't have many friends in those days, but when I met him I didn't have a single friend. I'm talking about 1970, when the two of us were in school together at Porvenir. Not for long, really, which goes to show how relative memory is, like a language we think we know but we don't, that can stretch things or shrink them at will. That's what I used to tell him, but he hardly listened to me. Once I went home with him when he still lived near the school, and I met his sister. There was no one else there, just his sister, and we talked for a long time. Soon after that they moved, went to live in Colonia Nápoles, and he quit school for good. I used to say to him: don't you want to go to college? are you going to deny yourself the privilege of higher education? and he would laugh and tell me that in college he was sure he'd learn exactly what he'd learned in high school: nothing. But what are you going to do with your life? I'd say, what kind of work will you do? and he would answer that he had no idea and didn't care. One afternoon when I'd gone to see him at his house I asked him whether he did drugs. No, he said. Never? I said. And he said: I've smoked marijuana, but that was a long time ago. And nothing else? No, nothing else, he said, and then he started to laugh. He was laughing at me, but I didn't mind. In fact, I liked to see him laugh. Around that time he met a famous film and theater director. A fellow Chilean. Sometimes he would talk to me about him, telling me how he'd approached him at the door to the theater where one of the director's plays about Heracleitus or some other pre-Socratic philosopher was being performed, a loose adaptation of the philosopher's writings that caused quite a stir, Mexico being so straitlaced at the time, not because of anything in the play but because almost all the actors came onstage naked at some point. I was still in school at Porvenir, in the stench of Opus Dei, and I spent all my time studying and reading (I don't think I've ever read so much since), and my only entertainment, my greatest pleasure, was going to his house. I would visit him regularly, but not too often because I didn't want to be a bore or get in the way. I would come in the afternoon, or when it was already dark, and we would spend two or three hours talking, usually about literature, although he'd also tell me about his adventures with the director, it was clear he admired him greatly, I don't know whether he liked the theater, but he loved film, in fact now that I think about it, he didn't read very much back then, I was the one who talked about books, and I really did read a lot, literature, philosophy, political essays, but he didn't, he went to the movies and then every day or every third day, extremely often, really, he would go to the director's house, and once when I told him he had to read more, he said he'd already read everything that mattered to him. Such arrogance! Sometimes he would say things like that, I mean sometimes he was like a spoiled child, but I forgave him everything, whatever he did seemed fine to me. One day he told me that he'd fought with the director. I asked him why and he didn't want to tell me. Or rather, he said that it had to do with a difference in literary opinion and that was all. What I managed to get out of him was that the director had said that Neruda was shit and that Nicanor Parra was the greatest poet of the Spanish language. Something like that. Of course I could hardly believe that two people would fight about something so unimportant. Where I come from, he said, people fight about things like that all the time. Well, I said, in Mexico people kill each other for no good reason at all, but certainly not educated people. Oh, the ideas I had then about culture. A while later, I went to visit the director, armed with a little book by Empedocles. His wife ushered me in and shortly afterward the director in person came into the living room and we started to talk. The first thing he asked me was how I'd gotten his address. I said that my friend had given it to me. Oh, him, said the director, and right away he wanted to know how he was, what he was doing, why he never came to visit. I gave him the first answer that popped into my head, then we started to talk about other things. After that, I had two people to visit, the director and my friend, and suddenly I realized that my horizons were expanding imperceptibly and my life was being gradually enriched. Those were happy days. One afternoon, however, after the director asked about my friend again, he told me about their fight. The story he told me wasn't much different from what my friend had told me. The fight had been about Neruda and Parra, about the validity of their respective poetic visions, and yet there was a new element to the story that the director told (and I knew he was telling me the truth): when he fought with my friend and my friend couldn't come up with anything else to say in his desperate defense of Neruda, he started to cry. Right there in the director's living room, like a ten-year-old, without trying to hide it, although he was seventeen and had been for a while. According to the director, it was the tears that had come between them, that were keeping my friend away, since he must be ashamed (according to the director) of his reaction to what was otherwise a completely trivial and circumstantial disagreement. Tell him to come visit me, the director said that afternoon when I left his house. I spent the next two days thinking about what he'd said and about the kind of person my friend was and the reasons he might have had for not telling me the full story. When I went to see him I found him in bed. He had a fever and he was reading a book on the Templars, the mystery of the Gothic cathedrals, that kind of thing, I really don't know how he could read such trash, although to be honest it wasn't the first time I'd surprised him with books like that, sometimes it was thrillers, other times junk science, anyway, the only good thing about the books he read was that he never tried to get me to read them too, whereas whenever I read a good book, I immediately passed it on to him and sometimes I waited whole weeks for him to finish reading it so we could discuss it. He was in bed, he was reading the Templars book, and the minute I stepped into his room I started to shake. For a while we talked about things I've forgotten now. Or maybe we were silent for a while, me sitting at the foot of his bed, him stretched out with his book, the two of us sneaking looks at each other, listening to the sound the elevator made, as if we were in a dark room or lost in the country at night, just listening to the sound of horses. I could've sat there like that for the rest of the day, for the rest of my life. But I spoke. I told him about my latest visit to the director's house, I relayed the director's message, that he should go see him, that he was expected, and he said: then he'd better wait sitting down because I'm not going back. Then he started to pick up his Templars book again. I argued that just because Neruda's poetry was good it didn't mean that Parra's couldn't be. I was stunned by his reply. He said: I don't give a shit about Neruda's poetry or Parra's poetry. So why the big argument, then, why the fight? I managed to ask, and he didn't answer. Then I made a mistake. I came a little closer, sitting down beside him on the bed, and I took a book out of my pocket, a book of poetry, and I read him a few lines. He listened in silence. It was a poem about Narcissus and a nearly endless forest inhabited by hermaphrodites. When I finished he didn't say anything. What do you think? I asked. I don't know, he said, what do you think? Then I told him that I thought poets were hermaphrodites and that they could only be understood by each other. *Poets*, I said. What I would have liked to say was: *we poets*. But he looked at me as if the flesh had been stripped from my face and it was just a skull, he looked at me with a smile and said: don't be corny, Perla. That was all. I turned pale and flinched, only managing to move a little bit away, and I tried to get up but I couldn't, and all that time he sat there motionless, looking at me and smiling, as if all the skin, muscles, fat, and blood had slid off my face, leaving only the yellow or white bone. At first I was unable to speak. Then I said or whispered that it was late and I had to go. I stood up, said goodbye, and left. He didn't even look up from his book. When I crossed the empty living room, the empty hallway, I thought I would never see him again. A little while later I started college and my life took a ninety-degree turn. Years later, purely by chance, I ran into his sister handing out Trotskyist propaganda at the Faculty of Literature. I bought a pamphlet from her and we went to have coffee. By then I'd stopped seeing the director, I was about to finish my degree, and I was writing poems that almost no one read. Naturally, I asked about him. Then his sister gave me a detailed account of his latest adventures. He had traveled all over Latin America, returned to his native country, suffered through a coup. All I could bring myself to say was: what bad luck. Yes, said his sister, he was planning to stay there to live and a few weeks after he got there the military decides to stage a coup, pretty rotten luck. For a while we couldn't think of anything else to say to each other. I imagined him lost in a white space, a virgin space that kept getting dirtier and more soiled despite his best efforts, and even the face I remembered grew distorted, as if while I was talking to his sister his features melded with what she was describing, ridiculous tests of strength, terrifying, pointless rites of passage into adulthood, so distant from what I once thought would become of him, and even his sister's voice talking about the Latin American revolution and the defeats and victories and deaths that it would bring began to sound strange and then I couldn't sit there a second longer and I told her I had to go to class and we'd see each other some other time. I remember that for two or three nights I dreamed of him. In my dreams he was thin, all skin and bones, sitting under a tree, his hair long, his clothes ragged, his shoes ruined, unable to get up and walk.

**Luscious Skin, in a rooftop room on Calle Tepeji, Mexico City DF, May 1976.** Arturo Belano never liked me. Ulises Lima did. A person can sense these things. María Font liked me. Angélica Font didn't. It doesn't matter. The Rodríguez brothers liked me: Pancho, Moctezuma, and little Norberto. Sometimes they criticized me, sometimes Pancho said he didn't understand me (especially when I slept with men), but I knew that they still cared about me. Not Arturo Belano. He never liked me. I used to think it was Ernesto San Epifanio's fault. He and Arturo were friends before either of them was twenty, before Arturo went to Chile, supposedly to join the Revolution, and I'd been Ernesto's lover, or so they said, and I'd dumped him. But the truth is that I only slept with Ernesto a few times, so why should it be my fault if people got all worked up over nothing? I also slept with María Font, and Arturo Belano had a problem with that. And I would've slept with Luis Rosado that night at Priapo's, and then Arturo Belano would've kicked me out of the group.

I really don't know what I was doing wrong. When Belano heard what had happened at Priapo's, he said that we weren't thugs or pimps, but all I'd done was express my sensuality. In my defense I could only stutter (sarcastically, and not even looking him in the eye) that I was a freak of nature. But Belano didn't get the joke. As far as he was concerned, everything I did was wrong. And it wasn't even me who asked Luis Sebastián Rosado to dance. It was Luis, who was totally wasted and came on to me. I like Luis Rosado, is what I should have said, but nobody could say a thing to the André Breton of the Third World.

Arturo Belano had it in for me. And it's funny, because when I was around him I tried to do things right. But nothing ever worked out. I had no money, no job, no family. I lived off whatever I could scavenge. Once I stole a sculpture from the Casa del Lago. The director, that asshole Hugo Gutiérrez Vega, said it must have been a visceral realist. Impossible, said Belano. He probably turned red, he was so embarrassed. But he stood up for me. Impossible, he said, although he didn't know it had been me. (What would've happened if he had known?) A few days later Ulises told him: it was Luscious Skin who stole the sculpture. That's what he said, but without really thinking, like it was a joke. That's how Ulises is. He doesn't take these things seriously, they just seem funny to him. But Belano blew up, saying how could this happen, saying that the people at Casa del Lago had arranged for us to give several readings and that now he felt responsible for the theft. Like he was the mother of all the visceral realists. Still, he didn't do anything. He acted disgusted, that's all.

Sometimes I felt like kicking the shit out of him. Luckily, I'm a peace-loving person. Also, people said Belano was tough, but I knew he wasn't. He was eager, and brave in his own way, but he wasn't tough. Pancho is tough. My friend Moctezuma is tough. I'm tough. Belano just looked like he was tough, but I knew he wasn't. Then why didn't I let him have it some night? It must have been because I respected him. Even though he was younger than me and looked down on me and treated me like dirt, deep down I think I respected him and listened to him and was always waiting for some sign of recognition from him and I never lifted a hand against the bastard.


**Laura Jáuregui, Tlalpan, Mexico City DF, May 1976.** Have you ever seen a documentary about those birds that make gardens and towers and clearings in the bushes where they perform their mating dances? Did you know that the only ones that find a mate are the ones that make the best gardens, the best towers, the best clearings, the ones that perform the most elaborate dances? Haven't you ever seen those ridiculous birds that practically dance themselves to death to woo the female?

That's what Arturo Belano was like, a stupid, conceited peacock. And visceral realism was his exhausting dance of love for me. The thing was, I didn't love him anymore. You can woo a girl with a poem, but you can't hold on to her with a poem. Not even with a poetry movement.

Why did I keep hanging out with the same people he hung out with for a while? Well, they were *my* friends too, my friends *still*, although it wasn't long before I got tired of them. Let me tell you something. The university was real, the biology department was real, my professors were real, my classmates were real. By that I mean tangible, with goals that were more or less clear, plans that were more or less clear. Those people weren't real. The great poet Alí Chumacero (who I guess shouldn't be blamed for having a name like that) was real, do you see what I mean?, what he left behind was real. What they left behind, on the other hand, wasn't real. Poor little mice hypnotized by Ulises and led to the slaughter by Arturo. Let me put it as concisely as I can: the real problem was that they were almost all at least twenty and they acted like they were barely fifteen. Do you see what I mean?

**Luis Sebastián Rosado, lawn party with lights in the grass at the Moores' house, more than twenty people, Colonia Las Lomas, Mexico City DF, July 1976.** Against all the odds of logic or luck, I saw Luscious Skin again. I have no idea how he got my phone number. According to him, he called the editorial department of *Línea de Salida* and they gave it to him. Despite all the precautions dictated by common sense (but what the hell! aren't we poets supposed to do these things?), I agreed to meet him that same night, in a coffee shop on Insurgentes Sur where I sometimes used to go. The possibility of not showing up certainly passed through my mind, but when I got there (half an hour late), ready to turn around and leave if he was there with someone else, the sight of Luscious Skin alone, writing almost sprawled on the table, made a great warmth suddenly spread through my chest, which until then was icy, numb.

I ordered a coffee and told him he ought to order something too. He looked me in the eyes and smiled in embarrassment. He said he was broke. It doesn't matter, I said, get what you want, it's on me. Then he said he was hungry and he wanted some enchiladas. They don't make enchiladas here, I said, but they can bring you a sandwich. He seemed to think it over for a moment and then he said all right, a ham sandwich. He ate three sandwiches in total. I was supposed to call some people, and maybe see them, but I didn't call anyone. Or actually yes, I called my mother from the coffee shop to tell her that I'd be home late, and I blew off the rest of my plans.

What did we talk about? Lots of things. His family, the town he came from, his early days in Mexico City, how hard it had been for him to get used to the city, his dreams. He wanted to be a poet, a dancer, a singer, he wanted to have five children (like the fingers of a hand, he said, and he raised the palm of his hand, almost brushing my face), he wanted to try his luck at the Churubusco studios, saying that Oceransky had auditioned him for a play, he wanted to paint (he told me in great detail the ideas he had for some paintings). Anyway, at some point in our conversation I was tempted to tell him that I had no idea what I really wanted, but I decided to keep it to myself.

Then he asked me to come home with him. I live alone, he said. Quivering, I asked him where he lived. In Roma Sur, he said, in a room on the roof near the stars. I answered that it was after twelve now, really too late, and that I should go to bed because the next day the French novelist J.M.G. Arcimboldi was arriving in Mexico and some friends and I were going to arrange a tour of the sights of our chaotic capital. Who's Arcimboldi? said Luscious Skin. Those visceral realists really are ignoramuses. One of the greatest French novelists, I told him, though hardly any of his work has been translated, into Spanish, I mean, except one or two novels that came out in Argentina, but I've read him in French, of course. The name doesn't sound familiar, he said, and he insisted again that I come home with him. Why do you want me to come with you? I said, looking him in the eyes. I'm not usually so bold. I have something to tell you, he said, something that will interest you. How much will it interest me? I said. He looked at me as if he didn't understand and then he said, suddenly belligerent: how much what? how much money? No, I hurried to clarify, how much will what you have to say interest me. I had to stop myself from tousling his hair, from telling him not to be silly. It's about the visceral realists, he said. Oof, that doesn't interest me at all, I said. I'm sorry to have to tell you this, and don't take it the wrong way, but I couldn't care less about the visceral realists (God, what a name). What I have to tell you will interest you, I know it will, he said. They've got something big in the works. You have no idea.

For a moment, I admit, the idea of a terrorist act passed through my mind. I saw the visceral realists getting ready to kidnap Octavio Paz, I saw them breaking into his house (poor Marie-José, all that broken china), I saw them emerging with Octavio Paz gagged and bound, carried shoulder-high or slung like a rug, I even saw them vanishing into the slums of Netzahualcóyotl in a dilapidated black Cadillac with Octavio Paz bouncing around in the trunk, but I recovered quickly. It must have been nerves, or the gusts of wind that sometimes sweep along Insurgentes (we were talking on the sidewalk) and sow the most outrageous ideas in pedestrians and drivers. So I rejected his invitation again and he insisted again. What I have to tell you, he said, will shake the foundations of Mexican poetry. He might even have said Latin American poetry. But not world poetry, no. One could say he restricted himself to the Spanish-speaking world in his ravings. The thing he wanted to tell me would turn Spanish-language poetry upside down. Goodness, I said, some undiscovered manuscript by Sor Juana Inés de la Cruz? A prophetic text by Sor Juana on the fate of Mexico? But no, of course not, it was something the visceral realists had found and the visceral realists would never come anywhere near the lost libraries of the seventeenth century. What is it, then? I said. I'll tell you at my place, said Luscious Skin, and he put his hand on my shoulder, as if he were pulling me toward him, as if he were inviting me to dance with him again on the horrible dance floor at Priapo's.

I began to tremble and he noticed. Why do I have to like the worst ones? I thought, why do I have to be attracted to the most brooding, least cultured, most desperate ones? It's a question I ask myself twice a year. I still haven't found an answer. I told him that I had the keys to a painter friend's studio. We should go there, I said, it was close enough to walk, and along the way he could tell me whatever he wanted. I thought he wouldn't accept, but he did. Suddenly the night was beautiful, the wind stopped blowing, and only a gentle breeze accompanied us as we walked. He started to talk, but frankly I've forgotten almost everything he said. There was just one thought in my head, one wish: that Emilio wouldn't be in his studio that night (Emilito Laguna, he's in Boston now studying architecture, his parents had enough of his bohemian life in Mexico and sent him away: it's either Boston and an architecture degree or you get a job), that none of his friends would be there, that no one would come near the studio for—my God—the rest of the night. And my prayers were answered. Not only was no one at the studio but it was clean too, as if the Lagunas' maid had just left. And he said what a super studio, this place really does make you want to paint, and I didn't know what to do (I'm sorry, but I'm extremely shy—and worse than shy—in these situations) and I started to show him Emilio's canvases, I couldn't think of anything better, I set them up against the wall and listened to his murmurs of approval or his critical remarks behind me (he didn't know anything about painting), and the paintings just kept coming and I thought, wow, Emilio really has been working a lot lately, who would've thought, unless they were paintings by some friend of his, which was highly possible, since at a glance I could see more than one style, and a few red, very Paalen-esque canvases, especially, had a well-defined *style*. But who cares? The truth is that I didn't give a shit about the paintings, but I was incapable of taking the initiative, and when I finally had all the walls of the studio lined with Lagunas, I turned around, sweating, and asked him what he thought, and with a wolfish smile he said that I shouldn't have gone to so much trouble. It's true, I thought, I've made a fool of myself and now on top of it all I'm covered in dust and I stink of sweat. And then, as if he'd read my mind, he said you're sweating and then he asked me whether there was a bathroom in the studio where I could take a shower. You need one, he said. And I said, probably in a tiny voice, yes, there is a shower, but I don't think there's any hot water. And he said good, cold water is better, I always take cold showers, there's no hot water on the roof. And I let myself be dragged into the bathroom and I took off my clothes and turned on the shower and the gush of cold water almost knocked me out, my flesh shrinking until I could feel each and every bone in my body. I closed my eyes, I might have shouted, and then he got in the shower and put his arms around me.

The rest of the details I'd rather not disclose; I'm still a romantic. A few hours later, as we were lying in the dark, I asked him who had given him the name Luscious Skin, so suggestive, so fitting. It's my name, he said. Well yes, I said, all right, it's your name, but who gave it to you? I want to know everything about you. It was the tyrannical, slightly stupid kind of thing you say after you've made love. And he said: María Font, and then he was quiet, as if he'd suddenly been overwhelmed by memories. His profile, in the dark, seemed very sad to me, thoughtful and sad. I asked, maybe with a hint of irony in my voice (perhaps I'd been over-come by jealousy, and sadness too), whether María Font was the one who'd won the Laura Damián prize. No, he said, that's Angélica, María is her older sister. He said a few more things about Angélica that I can't remember now. The question burst from me as if of its own accord: have you slept with María? His reply (my God, what a sad, beautiful profile Luscious Skin had) was devastating. He said: I've slept with every poet in Mexico. What I should have done then was either be quiet or hold him, and yet I did neither, but kept asking him questions, and each question was worse than the one before and I lost a little ground with each one. At five in the morning we went our separate ways. I caught a cab on Insurgentes, and he walked off north.

**Angélica Font, Calle Colima, Colonia Condesa, Mexico City DF, July 1976.** That was a strange time. I was Pancho Rodríguez's girlfriend. Felipe Müller, Arturo Belano's Chilean friend, was in love with me. But I liked Pancho best. Why? I don't know. All I know is that I liked Pancho best. A little while before, I'd won the Laura Damián prize for young poets. I never knew Laura Damián. But I did know her parents and lots of people who'd known her, even people who'd been friends with her. I slept with Pancho after a party that lasted for two days. On the last night, I slept with him. My sister told me to be careful. But who was she to give me advice? She was sleeping with Luscious Skin, and with Moctezuma Rodríguez, Pancho's younger brother, too. She was also sleeping with someone called the Gimp, a poet and alcoholic in his thirties, but at least she had the courtesy not to bring him home with her. Really, I was sick of having to put up with her lovers. Why don't you go fuck in *their* pigsties? I asked her once. She didn't answer and then she started to cry. She's my sister and I love her, but she has no self-control. One afternoon Pancho started to talk about her. He talked a lot, so much that I thought she must have slept with him too, but no, I knew all her lovers. I heard them moan at night less than fifteen feet from my bed, and I could tell them apart by the sounds they made, by the way they came, quietly or noisily, by the things they said to my sister.

Pancho never slept with her. Pancho slept with me. I don't know why, but he was the one I chose and for a few days I even lost myself in fantasies of love, although of course I never really loved him. The first time was pretty painful. I didn't feel anything, only pain, but even the pain wasn't unbearable. We did it in a hotel in Colonia Guerrero, a hotel probably frequented by whores. After he came, Pancho told me that he wanted to marry me. He told me he loved me. He said he would make me the happiest woman in the world. I looked him in the face and for a second I thought he'd gone crazy. Then I realized that he was actually afraid, afraid of *me*, and that made me sad. I'd never seen him look so small, and that made me sad too.

We did it a few more times. It didn't hurt anymore, but it didn't feel good either. Pancho saw that our relationship was flickering out as fast as—as what?—something that blinks out very quickly, the lights of a factory at the end of the day. No, more like the lights of an office building eager to blend into the anonymity of night. It's a contrived image, but it's what Pancho would've chosen. A contrived image with two or three dirty words tacked on. One night after a poetry reading I realized that Pancho had realized what was happening, and that same night I told him we were finished. He didn't take it badly. For a week, I think, he tried unsuccessfully to get me back into bed. Then he tried to sleep with my sister. I don't know whether he succeeded. One night I woke up and María and some shadowy figure were screwing. That's enough, I said, I want to sleep in peace. Always reading Sor Juana, and then you act like a slut. When I turned on the light I saw that the person with her was Luscious Skin. I told him to leave that instant if he didn't want me to call the police. María, oddly enough, didn't complain. As he put on his pants, Luscious Skin asked me to forgive him for waking me up. My sister isn't a slut, I told him. I know my behavior was a little contradictory. Well, not my behavior, my words. Whatever. When Luscious Skin had gone I got in bed with my sister and hugged her and started to cry. A little while later I started to work for a university theater company. I had a manuscript that my father wanted to send to a few publishing houses, but I wouldn't let him. I wasn't involved in the activities of the visceral realists. I didn't want to have anything to do with them. Later María told me that Pancho wasn't part of the group anymore either. I don't know whether he was expelled (whether Arturo Belano expelled him) or whether he left on his own, whether he just didn't have the heart for anything anymore. Poor Pancho. His brother Moctezuma was still in the group. I think I saw one of his poems in an anthology. Anyway, they didn't hang around our house anymore. I heard that Arturo Belano and Ulises Lima had disappeared up north; my father and mother discussed it once. My mother laughed. I remember she said: they'll show up someday. My father seemed worried. María was worried too. Not me. By then the only friend I had left from the group was Ernesto San Epifanio.

# 3

**Manuel Maples Arce, walking along the Calzada del Cerro, Chapultepec Park, Mexico City DF, August 1976.** This young man, Arturo Belano, came to interview me. I only saw him once. He was with two boys and a girl, I don't know their names, they hardly said a word. The girl was American.

I told them that I abhorred tape recorders for the same reason that my friend Borges abhorred mirrors. Were you friends with Borges? Arturo Belano asked in a tone of astonishment that I found slightly offensive. We were quite good friends, I answered, close friends, you might say, in the far-off days of our youth. The American wanted to know why Borges abhorred tape recorders. Because he's blind, I suppose, I told her in English. What does blindness have to do with tape recorders? she said. It reminds him of the perils of hearing, I replied. Listening to one's own voice, one's own footsteps, the footsteps of the enemy. The American looked me in the eyes and nodded. I don't think she knew much about Borges. I don't think she knew my work at all, although I was translated by John Dos Passos. I don't think she knew much about John Dos Passos either.

But I've lost my train of thought. Where was I? I told Arturo Belano that I would prefer that he not use the tape recorder and that it would be better if he left me a list of questions. He agreed. He pulled out a sheet of paper and wrote the questions while I showed his companions some of the rooms in the house. Then, when he had finished the list, I had drinks brought in and we talked for a while. They had already interviewed Arqueles Vela and Germán List Arzubide. Do you think anyone is interested in stridentism these days? I asked Arturo Belano. Of course, maestro, he answered, or words to that effect. My opinion is that stridentism is history now and as such it can only be interesting to literary historians, I said. It interests me and I'm not a historian, he said. Well, then.

Before bed that night I read the list. Just the kind of questions an ignorant, zealous young man might ask. That same night I drafted my answers. The next day I made a clean copy. Three days later, as we had arranged, he came to pick up the list. The maid let him in, but following my express instructions, she told him I wasn't there. Then she handed him the package I had prepared for him: the list of questions with my answers and two books of mine that I was afraid to inscribe to him (I think young people today scorn such sentimentalism). The books were *Andamios interiores* and *Urbe*. I was on the other side of the door, listening. The maid said: Mr. Maples left this for you. Silence. Arturo Belano must have taken the package and looked at it. He must have leafed through the books. Two books published so long ago, their pages (excellent paper) uncut. Silence. He must have looked over the questions. Then I heard him thank the maid and leave. If he comes back to see me, I thought, I'll be justified, if he shows up here one day, without calling first, to talk to me, to listen to me tell my old stories, to submit his poems for my consideration, I'll be justified. All poets, even the most avant-garde, need a father. But these poets were meant to be orphans. He never came back.

**Barbara Patterson, in a room at the Hotel Los Claveles, Avenida Niño Perdido and Juan de Dios Peza, Mexico City DF, September 1976.** Motherfucking hemorrhoid-licking old bastard, I saw the distrust in his pale, bored little monkey eyes right from the start, and I said to myself this asshole will take every chance he gets to spit on me, the motherfucking son of a bitch. But I'm dumb, I've always been dumb and naïve, and I let down my guard. And the same thing happened that always happens. Borges. John Dos Passos. Vomit carelessly soaking Barbara Patterson's hair. And on top of it all the dumbfuck looks at me like he's sorry for me, as if to say these kids have brought me this pale-eyed gringa just so I can shit on her, and Rafael looked at me too and the fucking dwarf didn't even blink, like he was used to me being insulted by any old fart-breath, any constipated grand old man of Mexican literature who got the urge. And then the old bastard comes right out and says he doesn't like tape recorders, never mind how hard it was for me to get this one, and the ass kissers say okay, no problem, we'll write up a question sheet right here, Mr. Great Poet of the Pleistocene, yes sir, instead of pulling down his pants and shoving the tape recorder up his ass. And the old guy struts around listing his friends (all of them dead or practically dead), and he keeps calling me miss, as if that could make up for the puke, the vomit all over my shirt and jeans, and what can I say, I didn't even have the strength to answer him when he started talking to me in English, just yes, no, or I don't know, mostly I don't know, and when we left his house, which was a mansion, I said so where did the money come from, you dead-rat-fucking bastard, where did you get the money to buy this house? I told Rafael we had to talk, but Rafael said that he wanted to hang out with Arturo Belano, and I said you goddamn bastard I *need* to talk to you, and he said later, Barbarita, later, like I was some girl he fucked up the ass every night and not a woman who's three inches taller and at least thirty pounds heavier than he is (I have to go on a diet but who can *diet* with all this fucking Mexican food), and then I said I need to talk to you *now*, and the lousy prick, acting like the cocksucker he is, turns around and stares at me and says hey baby, what's wrong? some unexpected problem? and luckily Belano and Requena had gone on ahead and didn't hear him. It's especially lucky they didn't see me, because I guess my martyred face must have just collapsed, I could actually feel it changing. At any rate, I felt my eyes flare up with a lethal dose of hatred, and then I said go screw your mother, asshole, so I wouldn't say anything worse, and turned and left. I spent the afternoon in tears. I was supposedly in Mexico to do a postgraduate course on Juan Rulfo, but I met Rafael at a poetry reading at the Casa del Lago and we fell in love at first sight. Or at least that's how it was for me. I'm not so sure about Rafael. That very night I dragged him to the Hotel Los Claveles, where I still live, and we fucked until we dropped. Actually, Rafael doesn't have much stamina, but I do, and I kept him going until daylight came down along Niño Perdido, like something swooning or struck by lightning, dawn is so weird in this fucking city. The next day I stopped going to class and I spent my time having these endless conversations with the visceral realists, who back then were still more or less normal, more or less sick kids, and weren't calling themselves visceral realists yet. I liked them. They reminded me of the beats. I liked Ulises Lima, Belano, María Font. I liked that conceited bastard Ernesto San Epifanio a little less. Anyway, I liked them. I wanted to have a good time, and around them things were always lively. I met lots of people, people who gradually began to drift away from the group. I met an American, from Kansas (I'm from California), the painter Catalina O'Hara, but we never hit it off. A stuck-up bitch who thought she invented the wheel and acted like she was a revolutionary just because she'd been in Chile during the coup. Anyway, I got to know her a little after she separated from her husband and all the poets were dying to fuck her. Even Belano and Ulises Lima, who were obviously asexual and secretly got it on together (you know, I'll suck you, you suck me, just for a minute and then we'll stop), seemed to be wild for the fucking cowgirl. Rafael too. But I grabbed Rafael and said: if I find out you're sleeping with that bitch I'll cut your balls off. And Rafael laughed and said but baby, why would you cut my balls off? You're the only one I love. But even his eyes (which were the best thing about Rafael, Arab eyes, tents and oases) were saying the exact opposite. I'm with you because you give me money to pay the bills. I'm with you because you put up the cash. I'm with you because right now I don't have anyone better to be with or fuck. And I said: Rafael, you bastard, you stupid prick, you son of a bitch, when your friends disappear I'll still be with you, *I know it*, when you're left all alone and helpless, *I'm* the one who'll be by your side and who'll help you. Not some old bastard festering in his memories and literary quotations. And definitely not your second-rate gurus (Arturo and Ulises? he said, they aren't my gurus, you dumb gringa, they're my friends), who the way I see it are going to vanish one of these days. Why would they vanish? he said. I don't know, I said, out of fucking embarrassment? shame? mortification? insecurity? indecision? evasiveness? spinelessness? and then I had to stop because my Spanish wasn't good enough. Then he laughed at me and said you're a witch, Barbara, go on, get back to work on Rulfo, I'm leaving now but I'll be back soon, and instead of listening to him I threw myself on the bed and started to cry. They're all going to leave you, Rafael, I shouted from the window of my room at the Hotel Los Claveles as Rafael disappeared in the crowd, except me, asshole, except me.

**Amadeo Salvatierra, Calle República de Venezuela, near the Palacio de la Inquisición, Mexico City DF, January 1976.** So what did Manuel, Germán, and Arqueles say? I asked them. What did they say about what?

one of them said. About Cesárea, of course, I said. Very little. Maples Arce hardly remembered her. Neither did Arqueles Vela. List said he'd only heard of her. When Cesárea Tinajero was in Mexico, he lived in Puebla. According to Maples she was a very young girl, very quiet. And that was all they told you? That was all. And what about Arqueles? More of the same, nothing. And how did you find me? Through List, they said, he told us that you, Amadeo, must have more information about her. And what did Germán say about me? That you really had known her, that before you joined the stridentists you were part of Cesárea's group, the visceral realists. He also told us about a magazine, a magazine that he said Cesárea published back then, *Caborca* he said it was called. That Germán, I said and I poured myself another shot of Los Suicidas. At the rate we were going the bottle wouldn't last until dark. Drink up, boys, drink up and don't worry, if we finish this bottle we'll go down and buy another one. Of course, it won't be the same as the one we've got now, but it'll be better than nothing. Ah, what a shame they don't make Los Suicidas mezcal anymore, what a shame that time passes, don't you think? what a shame that we die, and get old, and everything good goes galloping away from us.

**Joaquín Font, Calle Colima, Colonia Condesa, Mexico City DF, October 1976.** Now that the days are going by, coldly, in the cold way that days go by, I can say without the slightest resentment that Belano was a romantic, often pretentious, a good friend to his friends, I hope and trust, although no one really knew what he was thinking, probably not even Belano himself. Ulises Lima, on the other hand, was much friendlier and more radical. Sometimes he seemed like Vaché's younger brother. Other times he seemed like an extraterrestrial. He smelled strange. This I know, this I can say, this I can attest to because on two unforgettable occasions he showered at my house. More precisely: he didn't smell bad, he had a strange smell, as if he'd just emerged from a swamp and a desert at the same time. Extreme wetness and extreme dryness, the primordial soup and the barren plain. At the same time, gentlemen! A truly unnerving smell! It bothered me, for reasons that aren't worth getting into here. His smell, I mean. Characterologically, Belano was extroverted and Ulises was introverted. In other words, I had more in common with Belano. Belano knew how to swim with the sharks much better than Lima did, no doubt about that. Much better than I did. He came across better, he knew how to handle things, he was more disciplined, he could pretend more convincingly. Good old Ulises was a ticking bomb, and what was worse, socially speaking, was that everyone knew or could sense that he was a ticking bomb and no one wanted him to get too close, for obvious and understandable reasons. Ah, Ulises Lima . . . He wrote constantly, that's what I remember most about him, in the margins of books that he stole and on pieces of scrap paper that he was always losing. And he never wrote poems, he wrote stray lines that he'd assemble into long, strange poems later on if he was lucky . . . Belano, on the other hand, wrote in notebooks . . . They both still owe me money . . .

**Jacinto Requena, Café Quito, Calle Bucareli, Mexico City DF, November 1976.** Sometimes they disappeared, but never for more than two or three days. When you asked them where they were going, they said in search of provisions. That was all. They never talked too much about *that*. Some of us, of course, those of us who were closest to them, knew what they were doing while they were gone, even if we didn't know where they were going. Some of us didn't care. Others thought it was wrong, saying that it was lumpen behavior. Lumpenism: the childhood syndrome of intellectuals. And others actually thought it was a good thing, mostly because Lima and Belano were generous with their ill-gotten gains. I was one of those. Things weren't going well for me. Xóchitl, my partner, was three months pregnant. I didn't have a job. We were living in a hotel that her father paid for, near the Monumento a la Revolución, on Calle Montes. We had one room with a bathroom and a tiny kitchen but at least we could make our meals there, which was much cheaper than going out to eat every day. Xóchitl's father had already had the room, which was actually more like a little apartment, long before she got pregnant, when he turned it over to us. He must have used it as a place to bring women or something. He let us have it, but first he made us promise to get married. I said yes right away, I think I even swore that we would. Xóchitl said nothing, just staring her father in the eyes. An interesting man. He was so old he could easily have passed for her grandfather, but he also had a look about him that gave you the shivers, the first time you saw him, anyway. I definitely got the shivers. He was big and hulking, huge, which is funny because Xóchitl is short and fine-boned. But her father was big and dark (in that sense, Xóchitl does take after him), with very wrinkled skin, and every time I saw him he was wearing a suit and tie, sometimes a navy suit, sometimes a brown one. Two nice suits, though they weren't new. Sometimes, especially at night, he wore a trench coat over the suit. When Xóchitl introduced me to him, the time we went to ask him for help, the old man looked at me and then he said come with me, I want to talk to you alone. Now we're in trouble, I thought, but what could I do? I followed him, prepared for the worst. But all the old man did was tell me to open my mouth. What? I said. Open your mouth, he said. So I opened my mouth and the old man looked at me and asked me how I'd lost the three teeth I'm missing. In a fight in school, I said. And my daughter met you like this? he said. Yes, I said, I already looked like this when she met me. Goddamn, he said, she must really love you. (The old man had stopped living with my partner's family when she was six, but she and her sisters would go see him once a month.) Then he said: if you leave her I'll kill you. He stared me in the eyes as he said it, his ratlike little eyes—even the pupils looked wrinkled in that face—fixed on mine, but without raising his voice, like a fucking gangster in an Orol movie, which was ultimately probably what he was. I, of course, swore that I would never leave her, especially now that she was going to be the mother of my child, and that was the end of our private talk. We went back to Xóchitl and the old man gave us the key to his place, promising us that we wouldn't have to worry about the rent, that he would take care of it, and handing us a wad of cash to keep us going.

It was a relief when he left, and it was a relief to know that we would have a roof over our heads. But soon we discovered that the old man's money was barely enough for us to live on. What I mean is, Xóchitl and I had some extra expenses, extra needs the paternal allowance didn't cover. It wasn't hard for us to get used to wearing the same old clothes, so we didn't spend money on that, but we spent it on movies, plays, buses, and the subway (although the truth is that living downtown we could walk almost everywhere), which we mostly took to get to the poetry work-shops at the Casa del Lago or the university. We weren't actually in school, in the formal sense of being in school, but there was no work-shop that we didn't check out at least once. We had a kind of obsession with workshops. We would make ourselves a couple of sandwiches and we'd just show up, as happy as could be. We'd listen to poetry, listen to the critiques, sometimes offer critiques of our own, Xóchitl more often than me, and then we would leave, and by that time it would already be dark, and as we headed to the bus or the subway or went walking home, we would eat our sandwiches, enjoying the Mexico City night, which I've always thought is gorgeous, the nights here are mostly cool and bright but not cold, nights made for walking or fucking, nights made for talking, which was what Xóchitl and I did, talk about the child we were going to have, the poets we'd heard, the books we were reading.

It was actually at a poetry workshop that we met Ulises Lima and Rafael Barrios and Luscious Skin. It was the first or second time we'd been there and the first time Ulises had showed up, and when the workshop was over we made friends and walked out together and then we took the bus together, and while Luscious Skin flirted with Xóchitl I listened to Ulises Lima and he listened to me, and Rafael nodded in agreement at what Ulises was saying and what I was saying, and it was honestly as if I'd found a soul mate, a real poet, a poet through and through, who could explain clearly what I'd only sensed and wished and dreamed, and that was one of the best nights of my life, and when we got home we couldn't sleep, Xóchitl and I, and we talked until four in the morning. Later I met Arturo Belano, Felipe Müller, María Font, Ernesto San Epifanio, and all the others, but none of them impressed me as much as Ulises. Of course, Luscious Skin wasn't the only one who tried to get Xóchitl into bed. Pancho and Moctezuma Rodríguez did their best too, and even Rafael Barrios. Sometimes I would say to Xóchitl: why don't you tell them you're pregnant? Maybe they'll give up and leave you alone. But she laughed and said she didn't mind being wooed. Fine, I said, it's up to you. I'm not the jealous type. But one night, I remember it clearly, it was Arturo Belano who tried to come on to Xóchitl, and that really did make me sad. I knew she wasn't going to sleep with anyone, but their attitude bothered me. It was basically as if they'd written me off because of the way I looked. It was as if they thought: this girl can't like that poor loser with the missing teeth. As if teeth have anything to do with love. But it was different with Arturo Belano. It amused Xóchitl to be courted, but this time it was different, it was much more than a diversion for her. We hadn't met Arturo Belano yet. This was the first time. We'd heard a lot about him before, but for one reason or another we still hadn't been introduced. And that night he was there and the whole group got on an empty bus in the early hours of the morning (a bus full of visceral realists!), heading to a party or a play or somebody's reading, I've forgotten now, and Belano sat next to Xóchitl on the bus and they spent the whole ride talking, and I could tell, I was sitting a few seats back, shaky, with Ulises Lima and the kid Bustamante, I could tell that Xóchitl's face looked different, that this time she really was enjoying herself, how to explain, that she was *delighted* that Belano was sitting there next to her, giving her one hundred percent of his attention, while everybody else, but especially everybody who'd already tried to get her into bed, watched what was going on out of the corners of their eyes, like me, still talking, still watching the semideserted streets and the door of the bus shut tight, like the door of a crematorium oven, still doing the things they'd been doing, I mean, but with every sense alert to what was happening in the seats where my Xóchitl and Arturo Belano were sitting. And at a certain moment the atmosphere became so fraught, everything on pins and needles, that I thought to myself these assholes must know something I don't, something strange is going on here, it isn't normal for the fucking bus to be circling the city like a ghost, it isn't normal that no one's getting on it, it isn't normal for me to start hallucinating for no reason. But I got a hold on myself, the way I always do, and in the end nothing happened. Then Rafael Barrios, the nerve of him, told me that Belano didn't know that Xóchitl was my partner. I answered that nothing had happened and that if anything had happened it was Xóchitl's business, Xóchitl lives with me, she's not my slave, I said. But now comes the strange part: after that night, the night Belano was all over Xóchitl on that lonely nocturnal journey (the only thing he didn't do was kiss her on the mouth), no one ever bothered her again. Absolutely nobody. As if the bastards had seen themselves reflected in their fucking leader and they didn't like what they saw. And something else I should add: Belano's flirtation only lasted the length of that interminable bus ride, in other words it was an innocent thing, so maybe he really didn't know that the gap-toothed guy a few seats back was the partner of the girl he was coming on to, but Xóchitl did, and the way she accepted the Chilean's flattery was different from the way she endured the flattery of Luscious Skin or Pancho Rodríguez, for example, by which I mean that with them you could see she was enjoying herself, having a good time, laughing, but with Belano her face, the angle of her face that I was able to see that night, betrayed very different emotions. And that night, at the hotel, it seemed to me that Xóchitl looked more pensive and distant than usual. But I didn't say anything. I thought I understood why. So I started to talk about other things: our child, the poems she and I would write; the future, essentially. And I didn't talk about Arturo Belano or any of the real problems in store for us, like me finding work or the two of us having enough money to rent a place and be able to support ourselves and our child. No, I talked about poetry, just as I did every night, about the creative act and about visceral realism, a literary movement that was a perfect match for my inner self and my sense of reality.

After that somehow disastrous night we started to see them almost every day. Wherever they went, we went. It was only a week later, I think, that they invited me to participate in one of the group's poetry readings. We didn't miss a single meeting. And the relationship between Belano and Xóchitl was frozen in polite ritual, not devoid of a certain mystery (a mystery that nevertheless cast no shadow over the steady growth of my partner's belly), but not going any farther. The truth is, Arturo never really saw Xóchitl. What happened that night, in the bus carrying only us along the vacant streets, the howling streets, of Mexico City? I don't know. Probably a girl whose pregnancy wasn't visible yet fell in love for a few hours with a sleepwalker. And that was all.

The rest of the story is fairly ordinary. Sometimes Ulises and Belano disappeared from Mexico City. Some people didn't like it. Others didn't care. I thought it was a good thing. Sometimes Ulises loaned me money. They had piles of money, more than enough, and I always needed it. I don't know where they got it from and I don't care. Belano never loaned me money. When they left for Sonora I had the sense that the group was about to fall apart. Kind of as if the joke had stopped being funny. It didn't seem like such a terrible thing to me. My son was about to be born and I'd finally found a job. One night Rafael called me and told me they were back, but that they were leaving again. Fine, I said, the money's theirs, let them do what they want with it. This time they're going to Europe, Rafael told me. Perfect, I said, that's what we should all do. But what about the movement? said Rafael. What movement? I said, watching Xóchitl as she slept. The room was dark and the hotel sign flickered through the window like something in a gangster movie. It was in these shadows that my son's grandfather had done his dirty business. What do you mean "what movement"? Visceral realism, said Rafael. What about visceral realism? I said. That's what I mean, said Rafael, what will happen to visceral realism? What will happen to the magazine we were going to publish, to all our projects? He sounded so pitiful that if Xóchitl hadn't been asleep I would've burst out laughing. We'll publish the magazine ourselves, I said, and we'll do the projects with them or without them. For a while, Rafael didn't say anything. We can't get off track, he murmured. Then he was quiet again. Thinking, I guess. I was quiet too. But I wasn't thinking. I knew perfectly well where I stood and what I wanted to do. And just as I knew what I wanted to do, what I planned to do from then on, I also knew that Rafael would end up finding his way. There's no point getting all upset, I told him when I got tired of standing there in the dark with the phone to my ear. I'm not upset, said Rafael. I think we should go too. I'm not leaving Mexico, I said.

**María Font, Calle Colima, Colonia Condesa, Mexico City DF, December 1976.** We had to put my father in an asylum (my mother corrects me and says psychiatric clinic, but there are words you can't gloss over: an asylum is an asylum) a little before Ulises and Arturo came back from Sonora. I don't know whether I've told you, but they left in my father's car. According to my mother, it was that act, which she describes as underhanded and even criminal, that triggered my father's collapse. I disagree. My father's relationship to his possessions, his house, his car, his art books, his bank account, was always distant and ambiguous, to say the least. It was as if my father were always unburdening himself, willingly or reluctantly, always getting rid of things, but with such bad luck (or so slowly) that he could never achieve the nakedness he longed for. And that, as you might imagine, ended up driving him crazy. But to get back to the matter of the car. When Ulises and Arturo came back and I saw them again, at Café Quito and almost by chance—although if I was at that horrible place, in the end it meant I was looking for them—when I saw them again, as I was saying, I almost didn't recognize them. They were with some guy I didn't know, a man dressed completely in white, with a straw hat on his sticklike head, and at first I thought they'd seen me but were pretending they hadn't. They were sitting in the corner by the window that looks onto Bucareli, next to the mirror and the sign that says "Roast Goat," but they weren't eating anything. They had two tall glasses of coffee in front of them and every once in a while they would take a few feeble sips, as if they were sick or exhausted, although the man in white was eating, not roast goat (every time I repeat the words *roast* *goat* I feel sick) but enchiladas, Café Quito's famous cheap enchiladas, and there was a bottle of beer in front of him. And I thought: they're pretending they haven't seen me, there's no way they couldn't have seen me, they've changed a lot, but I haven't changed at all. They don't want to talk to me. Then I started to think about my father's Impala and I thought about what my mother said, that it was completely shameless the way they'd stolen that car from him, really incredible, and that the best thing would be to report it and try to get the car back, and I thought about my father, who would mumble incoherently whenever anyone said anything to him about the car. For God's sake, Quim, my mother would say, stop babbling, I'm tired of going back and forth by bus or taxi, because in the end all those trips are going to cost an arm and a leg. And when my mother said that, my poor father laughed and said be careful, you'll end up crippled. And my mother didn't see the humor in it, but I did. Told the way I'm telling it, it probably isn't funny at all, but the way my father came out with it all of a sudden, more confidently than usual, or at least in a more confident voice, it really was clever and witty. In any case what my mother wanted was to report the theft of the Impala so we could get the car back and what I wanted was not to report it, since it would come back on its own (that's funny too, isn't it?). We just had to wait and give Arturo and Ulises time to come back, to return it. And now there they were, talking to the man in white, back in Mexico City, and they didn't see me or were avoiding me, so I had plenty of time to watch them and think about what I should say to them, that my father was in an asylum and that they should give the car back, although as time went by, I don't know how long I was there, the tables around me emptied and were filled again, the man in white never took off his hat and his plate of enchiladas seemed eternal, everything began to tangle in my head, as if the words I had to say were plants and all of a sudden they'd begun to wither, fade, and die. And it did me no good to think of my father shut up in the asylum, suicidally depressed, or my mother brandishing the threat or refrain of the police like a UNAM cheerleader (which she actually had been in her student days, poor Mom), because suddenly I began to wither too, to fall apart, to think (or rather repeat to myself, like a tom-tom) that nothing had any meaning, that I could sit at that table at Café Quito until the end of the world (when I was in high school we had a teacher who claimed to know exactly what he would do if World War III broke out: go back to his hometown, because nothing ever happened there, probably a joke, I don't know, but in a way he was right, when the whole civilized world disappears Mexico will keep existing, when the planet vaporizes or disintegrates, Mexico will still be Mexico) or until Ulises, Arturo, and the stranger in white got up and left. But none of that happened. Arturo saw me and got up, came over to my table, and gave me a kiss on the cheek. Then he asked whether I wanted to come and sit with them, or, better yet, wait for them where I was. I told him I would wait. All right, he said, and he went back to the man in white's table. I tried not to watch them and for a while I managed it, but finally I looked up. Ulises had his head bowed, his hair covering half his face, and he seemed about to fall asleep. Arturo had his eyes on the stranger and every once in a while he glanced at me, and both looks, the ones he gave the man in white and the ones directed at my table, were absent, or distant, as if he'd left Café Quito a long time ago and only his ghost was still there, restless. Later (how much later was it?) they got up and came to sit with me. The man in white was gone. The café had emptied. I didn't ask them about my father's car. Arturo told me that they were leaving. Going back to Sonora? I asked. Arturo laughed. His laugh was like a gob of spit. As if he were spitting on his own pants. No, he said, much farther. Ulises is off to Paris this week. How nice, I said, he'll be able to meet Michel Bulteau. And see the most famous river in the world, said Ulises. Very nice, I said. Yeah, not bad, said Ulises. And what about you? I said to Arturo. I'm leaving a little later, for Spain. And when do you plan to come back? I said. They shrugged their shoulders. Who knows, María, they said. I'd never seen them look so beautiful. I know it sounds silly to say, but they'd never seemed so beautiful, so seductive. Although they weren't trying to be. In fact, they were dirty, who knows how long it'd been since they'd showered, how long since they'd slept, they had circles under their eyes, and they needed to shave (not Ulises, because he never had to shave), but I would've kissed them both, I don't know why I didn't, I would've gone to bed with them both, fucked them until we passed out, then watched them sleep and afterward kept fucking. I thought: if we find a hotel, if we're in a dark room, if we have all the time in the world, if I undress them and they undress me, everything will be all right, my father's madness, the lost car, the sadness and energy I felt and that at moments seemed about to choke me. But I didn't say a word.

**4**

Auxilio Lacouture, Faculty of Literature, UNAM, Mexico City DF, December 1976. I'm the mother of Mexican poetry. I know all the poets and all the poets know me. I met Arturo Belano when he was sixteen years old and he was a shy boy who didn't know how to drink. I'm Uruguayan, from Montevideo, but one day I came to Mexico without knowing exactly why, or what for, or how, or when. I came to Mexico City, Distrito Federal, in 1967, or maybe it was 1965 or 1962. I can't keep track of the dates or my travels anymore; all I know is that I came to Mexico and I never left again. When I came to Mexico, León Felipe (what a colossus, what a force of nature) was still alive, and León Felipe died in 1968. When I came to Mexico, Pedro Garfias (what a great man, what a melancholy man) was still alive, and Don Pedro died in 1967, which means that I must have gotten here before 1967. So let's say I came to Mexico in 1965. I think it must have been 1965, though I may be wrong, and every day I'd go to see those universal Spaniards. I spent hours with them, as passionately devoted as a poetess and an English nurse and a little sister keeping tireless watch over her older brothers. And they would say to me in that odd Spanish accent of theirs, the way it circles around the z and the c and leaves the s more orphaned and libidinous than ever: Auxilio, stop fussing around the apartment, Auxilio, leave those papers alone, woman. Dust and literature have always gone hand in hand. And I would say to them: Don Pedro, León (isn't that funny! I used *tú* with the older one, the more venerable one, and yet the younger one intimidated me in some way and I couldn't drop the *usted*!), let me take care of this, you go about your business, keep writing, relax, and pretend I'm the invisible woman. And they would laugh. Or actually, León Felipe would laugh, although to be honest you could never be quite sure if he was laughing or clearing his throat or cursing, and Don Pedro wouldn't laugh (Pedrito Garfias, what a melancholy man), he wouldn't laugh, he would just look at me with his eyes like lakes at sunset, those lakes in the mountains that no one visits, those sad, peaceful lakes, so peaceful they seem otherworldly, and he would say don't trouble yourself, Auxilio, or thank you, Auxilio. And that was all. What a lovely man. So I would go see them, as I was saying, faithfully and without fail, not bothering them with my own poems and trying to be useful, but I did other things too. I worked. I tried to work. Because it's easy to live in Mexico City, as everybody knows or thinks they know or imagines, but it's only easy if you have money or a scholarship or a job, and I didn't have anything. The long trip to *la región más transparente* had drained me of many things, among them the energy to work at just any old job. So what I did was make the rounds of the university, specifically the Faculty of Literature, doing what you might call volunteer work: one day I might help to type Professor García Liscano's lectures, another day I'd translate some French texts in the French department, another day I'd cling like a limpet to a group that was putting on a play. I'd spend eight hours, without exaggeration, watching the rehearsals, going to pick up sandwiches, trying my hand at the lights. Sometimes I'd land a paying job: a professor would pay me out of his own salary to act as his assistant, say, or the department heads would arrange for themselves or the faculty to hire me for two weeks or a month to perform some vague task or another, mostly nonexistent, or the secretaries (they were such nice girls) would get their bosses to give me little jobs so I could make a couple of pesos. This was during the day. By night I led a bohemian life with my friends, which was extremely fulfilling and actually convenient because by then money was scarce and sometimes I didn't even have enough to pay for a furnished room. But usually I did. I don't want to exaggerate. I had money to live on. I was happy. During the day I lived at the faculty, like a little ant or actually more like a cicada, running back and forth from one cubicle to another, up on all the gossip, all the cheating and divorces, all the plans and projects, and at night I spread my wings, I turned into a bat, I left the faculty and wandered the DF like an imp (I'd like to say like a fairy, but it wouldn't be true) and drank and talked and attended literary gatherings (I knew every group) and advised the young poets who were already coming to me, although not as often as later on, and I lived, to make a long story short, in my time, I lived in the time I'd chosen and that surrounded me, aquiver, in flux, brimming over, happy. And then I hit 1968. Or 1968 hit me. Now I can say that I felt it coming, that I smelled it in bars, in February or March of '68 but before '68 really became '68. Oh, it makes me laugh to remember it. It makes me want to cry! Am I crying? I saw everything and at the same time I saw nothing. Does that make sense? I was at the faculty when the army violated the university's autonomy and came on campus to arrest or kill everybody. No. There weren't many deaths at the university. That was Tlatelolco. May the name be forever etched on our memory! But I was at the faculty when the army and the riot police came in and carted everybody off. It was the most incredible thing. I was in the bathroom, in the bathroom on one of the floors in the building, I think it was the fourth floor, though I can't say for sure. And I was sitting on the toilet, with my skirt hitched up, as the poem or the song goes, reading the exquisite poetry of Pedro Garfias, who had been dead for a year, Don Pedro, such a melancholy man, grieving for Spain and the rest of the world—who could've imagined that I would be reading in the bathroom at the very moment the filthy riot police entered the university? May I digress for a moment? I think that life is full of marvelous and mysterious things. And in fact, thanks to Pedro Garfias, to Pedro Garfias's poems and my long-standing habit of reading in the bathroom, I was the last to learn that the riot police had come in, that the army had come in, and that they were hauling away everyone they could find. Let's say I heard a noise. A rumble in my soul! And let's say that then the noise got louder and louder and by then I was paying attention to what was going on. I heard someone pull the chain in the next stall, I heard the door slam, heard footsteps in the hall, heard the clamor rising from the lawn, from the neatly cut grass that frames the faculty like a green sea wreathing an island, an island where there's always time for whispered confidences and love. And then the bubble of Pedro Garfias's poetry went pop and I closed the book and got up, pulled the chain, opened the door, said something out loud. *Che*, I said, what's going on outside? but no one answered me, everyone using the bathroom had disappeared, I said *che*, isn't anyone there? knowing beforehand that no one would answer. Maybe you know the feeling. And then I washed my hands and looked at myself in the mirror, and I saw a tall, thin, blond figure, a face with a few wrinkles already, too many wrinkles, the female version of Don Quixote, as Pedro Garfias once said to me, and then I went out into the hallway, and it was there that I suddenly realized something was going on, the hallway was empty and the shouting coming from downstairs was the kind that strikes you dumb and makes history. What did I do then? I did what anyone would do. I went over to a window and looked down, and I saw soldiers, and then I looked out another window and I saw tanks, and then out another one, at the end of the hallway, and I saw vans into which the captive students and professors were being herded, like something from a World War II movie crossed with a María Félix and Pedro Armendáriz movie of the Mexican Revolution, a dark canvas peopled with little phosphorescent figures, the kind of thing they say crazy people see, or people in the throes of fear. And then I said to myself: Auxilio, stay here. Don't let yourself be taken prisoner, baby. Stay here, Auxilio. Baby, don't let them write you into their script. If they want you let them come and find you. And then I went back to the bathroom and it was the strangest thing, not only did I go back to the bathroom but I went back into the stall, the very one I'd been in before, and I sat down on the toilet again, with my skirt up again, I mean, and my underwear pulled down, although I felt no physiological urgency (they say it's precisely in cases like this that the bowels loosen, but it wasn't true for me), and with Pedro Garfias's book open and despite not wanting to read, I started to read slowly, word by word, line by line, and suddenly I heard sounds in the hallway, the sound of boots? the sound of hobnailed boots? but *che*, I said to myself, isn't this a coincidence? and then I heard a voice saying something like everything is in order, though maybe it said something else, and someone, maybe it was the same bastard who'd spoken, opened the bathroom door and came in and I lifted my feet like a Renoir ballerina, my underwear dangling down around my skinny ankles and snagging on a pair of shoes I had back then, the most comfortable yellow moccasins, and as I was waiting for the soldier to check the stalls one by one, preparing myself, if it came down to it, not to open the door, to defend UNAM's last redoubt of autonomy—I, a poor Uruguayan poetess, who loved Mexico as much as anyone—while I waited, as I say, a special silence fell, as if time had fractured and were running in several directions at once, a pure time, not verbal or made up of gestures or actions, and then I saw myself and I saw the soldier who was staring entranced into the mirror, the two of us still as statues in the women's bathroom on the fourth floor of the Faculty of Literature, and that was all, then I heard his footsteps fading away in the distance, I heard the door close, and my raised legs returned to their former position as if of their own accord. I must've sat there like that for three hours or so, I'd say. I know it was starting to get dark when I came out of the stall. This was a new situation, I admit, but I knew what to do. I knew my duty. So I went over to the only window in the bathroom and looked out. I saw a soldier far off in the distance. I saw the outline of an armored troop carrier or the shadow of an armored troop carrier. Like the portico of Latin literature, the portico of Greek literature. Oh, I adore Greek literature, from Pindar to George Seferis. I saw the wind sweeping the university as if it was delighting in the last light of day. And I knew what I had to do. I knew. I knew I had to resist. So I sat on the tiled floor of the women's bathroom and in the last rays of light I read three more poems by Pedro Garfias and then I closed the book and closed my eyes and said to myself: Auxilio Lacouture, citizen of Uruguay, Latin American, poet and traveler, stand your ground. That was all. And then I started to think about my past the same way I'm thinking about my past now. I started to think about things that might not interest you in the same way as what I'm thinking now about Arturo Belano, the young Arturo Belano, whom I met when he was sixteen or seventeen, in 1970, when I was already the mother of the young Mexican poets and he was a kid who couldn't hold his liquor but felt proud that in his faraway Chile Salvador Allende had won the elections. I knew him. I met him in a noisy crowd of poets at the bar La Encrucijada Veracruzana, a ferret hole of a place where various promising young people and not-so-young people used to get together. I became friends with him. I think it was because we were the only two South Americans among all those Mexicans. I became friends with him despite the age difference, despite every conceivable difference! I taught him who T. S. Eliot was, who William Carlos Williams was, who Pound was. I took him home once, sick, drunk, his arms around my neck, his weight hanging from my narrow shoulders, and I became friends with his mother and his father and his very nice sister, all of them so nice. The first thing I said to his mother was: señora, I haven't slept with your son. And she said: of course not, Auxilio, but don't call me señora; we're practically the same age! I became friends with the family. A family of nomadic Chileans who had immigrated to Mexico in 1968. My year. I stayed as a guest at Arturo's mother's house for long stretches, once for a month, another time for two weeks, another time for a month and a half. This was because at the time

I didn't have money to pay for a furnished room or a place on a roof. During the day I lived at the university doing this, that, and the other and at night I lived the bohemian life and I slept at friends' houses, leaving my meager belongings scattered everywhere, my clothes, my books, my magazines, my pictures, I was Remedios Varo, I was Leonora Carrington, I was Eunice Odio, I was Lilian Serpas (oh, poor Lilian Serpas), and if I didn't lose my mind it was because I always kept a sense of humor, I laughed at my skirts, my stovepipe pants, my tights with runs in them, my Prince Valiant haircut rapidly growing whiter than blonde, my blue eyes peering into the Mexico City night, my pink ears listening to the university stories, the rises and falls, the put-downs, the slights, the fawning, the flattery, the false praise, shivering beds that were disassembled and reassembled against the night sky of Mexico City, that sky I knew so well, that churning, unreachable sky like an Aztec cauldron under which I moved in perfect bliss, with all the poets of Mexico and Arturo Belano, who was sixteen or seventeen and who began to grow up as I watched and who in 1973 decided to return to his homeland to join the revolution. And I was the only one, besides his family, who went to see him off at the bus station, since he was traveling overland, a long journey, extremely long, plagued with dangers, the journey of initiation of all poor Latin American boys, crossing this absurd continent, and when Arturito Belano looked out the window of the bus to wave goodbye to us, it wasn't just his mother who cried, I cried too, and that night I slept at his family's house, more to keep his mother company than anything else, but the next morning I left, though I had nowhere to go except the same old bars and coffee shops, but still I went. I don't like to overstay my welcome. And when Arturo returned, in 1974, he was a different person. Allende had fallen and he had done his duty, or so his sister told me. Arturito had done his duty, and his conscience, the terrible conscience of a young Latin American male, had nothing with which to reproach itself. He had presented himself as a volunteer on September 11. He had mounted absurd guard in a deserted street. He had gone out at night; he had seen things. Then, days later, he had been arrested at a police checkpoint. They didn't torture him, but he was held captive for a few days and during that time he behaved like a man. Waiting for him in Mexico were his friends, the Mexico City night, the poets' life. But when he got back he wasn't the same. He started to go out with other, younger people, snot-nosed kids of sixteen, seventeen, eighteen, he met Ulises Lima (a bad influence, I thought so from the first time I saw him), he started to make fun of all his old friends, look down on them, see everything as if he were Dante and he'd just returned from hell, or not Dante, I mean, but Virgil himself, such a sensitive boy, and he started to smoke marijuana, that vulgar weed, and deal substances I'd rather not even think about. But deep down he was still as nice as ever, I know he was. And so when we met (purely by chance, because we didn't see the same people anymore), he would say how are you Auxilio, or he'd shout help, help! help!! from the sidewalk on Avenida Bucareli, jumping around like a monkey with a taco or a piece of pizza in his hand, always with that Laura Jáuregui, who was gorgeous, though her heart was blacker than a black widow's heart, and Ulises Lima, and that other little Chilean, Felipe Müller, and sometimes I would even bring myself to join his group, but they spoke in *glíglico*, like in *Hopscotch*, you could tell they liked me, you could tell they knew who I was, but they spoke in *glíglico* and that made it hard to follow the ins and outs and ups and downs of the conversation, which ultimately drove me off. Let no one think they laughed at me! They listened to me! But I didn't speak their *glíglico* and the poor kids were incapable of giving up their slang. Those poor abandoned kids. Because that was the situation: no one wanted them. Or no one took them seriously. Or sometimes a person got the impression that they took themselves too seriously. And one day someone said to me: Arturito Belano has left Mexico. And then: let's hope this time he doesn't come back. And that made me really angry because I had always loved him and I think I probably scolded the person who said it (mentally, at least), but first I had the presence of mind to ask where he'd gone. And whoever it was couldn't tell me: Australia, Europe, Canada, someplace like that. And then I started to think about him, and I started to think about his mother, who was so generous, and about his sister, about the afternoons we made empanadas at his house, and about the time I made noodles and we hung them all over the place so they would dry, in the kitchen, in the dining room, in the little living room they had on Calle Abraham González. I never forget anything. That's my trouble, they say. I'm the mother of all Mexican poets. I'm the only one who stuck it out at the university in 1968, when the riot police and the army came in. I stayed at the faculty all alone, shut up in the bathroom, with nothing to eat for ten days, fifteen days, I don't remember anymore. There I was with a book by Pedro Garfias and my bag, dressed in a white shirt and a pleated blue skirt, and I had all the time in the world to think and think. But I couldn't think about Arturo Belano back then because I didn't know him yet. I said to myself: Auxilio Lacouture, stand your ground, if you come out they'll throw you in jail (and probably deport you to Montevideo, because naturally you never got your papers in order, you fool), they'll spit on you, they'll beat you. I prepared myself to resist. To resist against hunger and loneliness. I slept for the first few hours sitting on the toilet, the same toilet I'd been on when everything began, and that, vulnerable as I was, I believed brought me luck, but sleeping sitting on a toilet stool is extremely uncomfortable and I ended up huddled on the tiles. I had dreams. Not nightmares. Musical dreams, dreams of transparent questions, of sleek, safe airplanes crossing Latin America from end to end in a cold, bright blue sky. I woke up frozen stiff and I was starving. I looked out the window, out the little bathroom window, and in pieces of campus like puzzle pieces, I saw the morning of a new day. That first morning I spent crying and thanking God in heaven that no one had shut off the water. Don't get sick, Auxilio, I said to myself, drink all the water you want, but don't get sick. I slid to the floor, my back against the wall, and I opened Pedro Garfias's book again. My eyes closed. I must have fallen asleep. Then I heard footsteps and I hid in my stall (that stall is the cubicle I never had, that stall was my trench and my Duino palace, my epiphany of Mexico). Then I read Pedro Garfias. Then I fell asleep. Then I looked out the little window and I saw very high clouds, and I thought about Dr. Atl's paintings and *la región más transparente*. Then I began to think about pleasant things. How much poetry did I know by heart? I started to recite it, whispering the poems I remembered, and I would've liked to write them down, but although I had a Bic I didn't have paper. Then I thought: you fool, you've got the best paper in the world right here. So I took some toilet paper and I started to write. Then I fell asleep and dreamed, oh, how ridiculous, about Juana de Ibarbourou, I dreamed about her book of poetry *La rosa de los vientos*, from 1930, and also about her first book, *Las lenguas del diamante*, such a pretty title, a gorgeous title, almost as if it were the title of a book of avant-garde poetry, a French book from last year, but it was published in 1919, in other words when Juana de América was twenty-seven. What an interesting woman she must have been back then with the whole world at her feet, all those gentlemen ready to graciously do her bidding (gentlemen who no longer exist, although Juana does), all those modernist poets ready to die for poetry, all those lingering looks, all those pretty words, all that love. Then I fell asleep. Then I woke up, and for hours, maybe days, I cried for lost time, for my childhood in Montevideo, for faces that still trouble me (that trouble me now even more than before) and that I'd rather not talk about. Then I lost track of the days I'd been confined. From my window I saw birds, trees, branches extending from invisible places, bushes, grass, clouds, walls, but I didn't see people or hear any noise, and I lost track of how long I'd been inside. Then I ate toilet paper (part of me was maybe remembering Charlot), but just a little piece, I didn't have the stomach to eat more. Then I discovered that my appetite was gone. Then I took the toilet paper that I'd written on and I threw it in the toilet and pulled the chain. The sound of the water startled me, and I thought I was lost. I thought: despite my cleverness and all my sacrifices, I'm lost. I thought: what a poetic act to destroy my writings. I thought: I should have swallowed them instead, because now I'm lost. I thought: the vanity of writing, the vanity of destruction. I thought: because I wrote, I stood my ground. I thought: because I destroyed what I wrote they're going to find me, beat me, rape me, kill me. I thought: the two acts are related, writing and destruction, hiding and being found. Then I sat on the toilet and closed my eyes. Then I fell asleep. Then I woke up. My body was a mass of cramps. I moved slowly around the bathroom, looked in the mirror, combed my hair, washed my face. Oh, how awful my face looked. The way it looks now, to give you some idea. Then I heard voices. I think it had been a long time since I heard anything. I felt like Robinson Crusoe when he discovers the footstep in the sand. But my footstep was a voice and a door slamming shut, an avalanche of stone marbles suddenly tossed down the hall. Then Lupita, Professor Fombona's secretary, opened the door and we stood there staring at each other, both of us with our mouths open and unable to say a word. From the shock of it, I think, I fainted. When I opened my eyes again I was in Professor Rius's office (what a brave, handsome man Rius is and was!), among friends and familiar faces, among university people, not soldiers, and that seemed so wonderful to me that I started to cry, unable to give a coherent account of what had happened, despite the urging of Rius, who seemed at once grateful for and shocked by what I'd done. And that's all, my young friends. The legend spread on the winds of Mexico City and the winds of '68, fusing with the stories of the dead and the survivors and now everybody knows that a woman stayed at the university when its freedom was violated in that beautiful, tragic year. And I've heard others tell the story many times, and in their telling, the woman who spent fifteen days shut in a bathroom without eating is a medical student or a secretary at the Torre de Rectoría, not a Uruguayan with no papers or work or place to lay her head. And sometimes it isn't even a woman but a man, a Maoist student or a professor with gastrointestinal troubles. And when I hear these stories, these versions of my story, I don't usually say anything (especially if I'm not drunk). And if I am drunk, I try to play it down. That's nothing, I say, that's university folklore, that's urban legend, and then they look at me and say: Auxilio, you're the mother of Mexican poetry. And I say (or if I'm drunk, I shout): no, I'm not anybody's mother, but I do know them all, all the young poets of Mexico City, those who were born here and those who came from the provinces, and those who were swept here on the current from other places in Latin America, and I love them all.

**5**

**Amadeo Salvatierra, Calle República de Venezuela, near the Palacio de la Inquisición, Mexico City DF, January 1976.** Then I said to them: all right, boys, what do we do if the mezcal runs out? And they said: we'll go down and buy another bottle, Señor Salvatierra, Amadeo, don't worry. And thus assured, or encouraged, at least, I took a good swig, emptying my glass. They used to make some fine mezcal in this country, yes sir, and then I got up and went over to my library, my dusty library—how long had it been since I gave those shelves a cleaning!—not because I didn't care about books anymore, certainly not, but because life makes us so fragile and anesthetizes us too (almost without our noticing it, gentlemen), and some people, though this hasn't happened to me, are even hypnotized or end up with the left hemisphere of their brains split down the middle, which is a figurative way of describing the problem of memory, if you follow me. And the boys got up from their seats too and I felt their breath on the back of my neck, figuratively, of course, and then, without turning around, I asked them whether Germán or Arqueles or Manuel had told them what my job was, what I did for a living. And they said no, Amadeo, none of them said anything to us about that. And then I said, pompously, that I wrote, and I think I laughed or coughed for a few long seconds, I write for a living, boys, I said, Octavio Paz and I are the only ones in this goddamned country who make a living that way. And they, of course, remained touchingly silent, if you'll permit me the expression. Silent in the way people say Gilberto Owen was. And then, with my back still to them and my gaze fixed on the spines of my books, I said: I work nearby, in the Plaza Santo Domingo, I write petitions and prayers and letters, and I laughed again and dust rose from the books with the force of my laugh, and then I could see the titles better, the authors, the files where I kept the unpublished material of my day. And they laughed too, a brief laugh that brushed my neck, such discreet boys, until at last I managed to find the folder I was looking for. Here it is, I said, my life and incidentally all that's left of Cesárea Tinajero's life. And then comes the funny part, gentlemen: instead of pouncing greedily on the file to rifle through the papers, they just stood there and asked me whether I wrote love letters. Everything, boys, I told them, setting the file on the floor and filling my glass with Los Suicidas mezcal again, letters from mothers to their children, letters from children to their fathers, letters from women to their husbands in prison, and letters from lovers, of course, which are the best, either because they're so innocent or so steamy, everything mixed together as it is at the druggist's counter and sometimes the writer adds something of his own devising. Well, what a wonderful job, they said. After thirty years under the arches of Santo Domingo it isn't quite what it used to be, I said as I opened the file and began to rummage through the papers, looking for the only copy I had of *Caborca*, the magazine Cesárea had edited with so much secrecy and excitement.

**Joaquín Font, El Reposo Mental Health Clinic, Camino Desierto de los Leones, on the outskirts of Mexico City DF, January 1977.** There are books for when you're bored. Plenty of them. There are books for when you're calm. The best kind, in my opinion. There are also books for when you're sad. And there are books for when you're happy. There are books for when you're thirsty for knowledge. And there are books for when you're desperate. The latter are the kind of books Ulises Lima and Belano wanted to write. A serious mistake, as we'll soon see. Let's take, for example, an average reader, a cool-headed, mature, educated man leading a more or less healthy life. A man who buys books and literary magazines. So there you have him. This man can read things that are written for when you're calm, but he can also read any other kind of book with a critical eye, dispassionately, without absurd or regrettable complicity. That's how I see it. I hope I'm not offending anyone. Now let's take the desperate reader, who is presumably the audience for the literature of desperation. What do we see? First: the reader is an adolescent or an immature adult, insecure, all nerves. He's the kind of fucking idiot (pardon my language) who committed suicide after reading *Werther*. Second: he's a limited reader. Why limited? That's easy: because he can only read the literature of desperation, or books for the desperate, which amounts to the same thing, the kind of person or freak who's unable to read all the way through *In Search of Lost Time*, for example, or *The Magic Mountain* (a paradigm of calm, serene, complete literature, in my humble opinion), or for that matter, *Les Misérables* or *War and Peace*. Am I making myself clear? Good. So I talked to them, told them, warned them, alerted them to the dangers they were facing. It was like talking to a wall. Furthermore: desperate readers are like the California gold mines. Sooner or later they're exhausted! Why? It's obvious! One can't live one's whole life in desperation. In the end the body rebels, the pain becomes unbearable, lucidity gushes out in great cold spurts. The desperate reader (and especially the desperate poetry reader, who is insufferable, believe me) ends up by turning away from books. Inevitably he ends up becoming just plain desperate. Or he's cured! And then, as part of the regenerative process, he returns slowly—as if wrapped in swaddling cloths, as if under a rain of dissolved sedatives—he returns, as I was saying, to a literature written for cool, serene readers, with their heads set firmly on their shoulders. This is what's called (by me, if nobody else) the passage from adolescence to adulthood. And by that I don't mean that once someone has become a cool-headed reader he no longer reads books written for desperate readers. Of course he reads them! Especially if they're good or decent or recommended by a friend. But ultimately, they bore him! Ultimately, that literature of resentment, full of sharp instruments and lynched messiahs, doesn't pierce his heart the way a calm page, a carefully thought-out page, a technically perfect page does. I told them so. I warned them. I showed them the technically perfect page. I alerted them to the dangers. Don't exhaust the vein! Humility! Seek oneself, lose oneself in strange lands! But with a guiding line, with bread crumbs or white pebbles! And yet I was mad, driven mad by them, by my daughters, by Laura Damián, and so they didn't listen.

**Joaquín Vázquez Amaral, walking on a university campus in the American Midwest, February 1977.** No, no, no, of course not. That boy Belano was an extremely nice person, very polite, not hostile at all.

When I was in Mexico in 1975 for the launch, if you can call it that, of my translation of Pound's *Cantos*, a book that in any European country would have attracted much more attention (it was published in a handsome edition, by the way, by Joaquín Mortiz), he and his friends came to the event, and later, and this is important, they stayed to talk to me, to keep me company (when you're a stranger in a city in some way foreign, you appreciate these things), and we went to a bar, I've forgotten which one it was, but it must have been downtown, near Bellas Artes, and we talked about Pound until very late. In other words, I didn't see familiar faces at the launch, I didn't see the famous faces of Mexican poetry (if they were there I didn't recognize them, I'm sorry to say), all I saw were those kids, those eager, idealistic kids, you understand? and that, as a foreigner, I appreciated.

What did we talk about? About the maestro, of course, and his time at Saint Elizabeth's, about that strange man Fenollosa, about the poetry of the Han dynasty and the Sui dynasty, about the poetry of Liu Hsiang, Tung Chung-shu, Wang Pi, Tao Chien (Tao Yuan-ming, 365–427), the Tang dynasty, Han Yu (768–824), Meng Hao-Jan (689–740), Wang Wei (699–759), Li Po (701–762), Tu Fu (712–770), Po Chu-I (772–846), the Ming dynasty, the Ching dynasty, Mao Tse-tung — in other words, about Pound things that none of us knew anything about, not even the maestro, really, because the literature he knew best was European literature, but what a show of strength, what magnificent curiosity Pound had, to root around in that enigmatic language, am I right? What faith in humanity, wouldn't you say? And we also talked about Provençal poets, the usual ones, you know, Arnaut Daniel, Bertrán de Born, Guiraut de Bornelh, Jaufré Rudel, Guillem de Berguedà, Marcabrú, Bernart de Ventadorn, Raimbaut de Vaqueiras, the Castellan of Coucy, the towering Chrétien de Troyes, and we also talked about the Italians of the Dolce Stil Novo, Dante's compadres, as they say, Cino da Pistoia, Guido Cavalcanti, Guido Guinizelli, Cecco Angiolieri, Gianni Alfani, Dino Frescobaldi, but most of all we talked about the maestro, about Pound in England, Pound in Paris, Pound in Rapallo, Pound in Saint Elizabeth's, Pound back from Italy, Pound on the verge of death . . .

And then what happened? The usual. We asked for the check. They insisted that I contribute nothing at all, but I refused point-blank. I was young once too, and I know how hard it is to make ends meet at that age, especially if you're a poet, so I put my money on the table, enough to pay for everything we'd had (there were ten of us: young Belano and eight friends of his, among them two lovely girls whose names I've unfortunately forgotten, and me), but they, and now that I think about it, this was the only strange thing that happened all night, they picked up the money and returned it to me, and I put the money back on the table and they returned it to me again, and then I said kids, when I go out for drinks or Coca-Colas (ha ha) with my students I never let them pay, and I delivered my little speech very affectionately (I love my students and I assume they return the sentiment), but then they said: don't even think about it, maestro, and that was all: don't even think about it, maestro, and at that moment, as I decoded that very polysemous (if I may) sentence, I was watching their faces, seven boys and two beautiful girls, and I thought: no, they would never be my students. I don't know why I thought it when really, they'd been so polite, so nice, but I thought it.

I put my money back in my wallet and one of them paid the bill and then we went out. It was a beautiful night, without the daytime crush of cars and crowds, and for a while we walked toward my hotel, almost as if we were drifting along, we might just as easily have been getting farther away, and as we proceeded (but toward where?), some of the kids said goodbye, shaking my hand and heading off (the way they said goodbye to their friends was different, or so it seemed to me), and little by little the group began to dwindle, and meanwhile we kept talking, and we talked and talked, or now that I think about it, maybe we didn't talk much, I would say instead that we thought and thought, but I can't believe it, at that time of night no one thinks much, the body is begging for rest. And a moment came when there were just five of us aimlessly wandering the streets of Mexico City, possibly in the deepest silence, a Poundian silence, although the maestro is the furthest thing from silent, isn't he? His words are the words of a tribe that never stops delving into things, investigating, telling every story. And yet they're words circumscribed by silence, eroded minute by minute by silence, aren't they? And then I decided that it was time to go to bed, and I hailed a taxi and said goodbye.


**Lisandro Morales, Calle Comercio, in front of Jardín Morelos, Colonia Escandón, Mexico City DF, March 1977.** It was the Ecuadorean novelist Vargas Pardo, a man who always does just as he likes and who was working as a copy editor at my publishing house, who introduced me to this Arturo Belano. A year before, the same Vargas Pardo had convinced me that it would be worth the publishing house's while to finance a magazine that would serve as a forum for the best writers in Mexico and Latin America. I listened to him and launched it. They gave me the title of honorary director and Vargas Pardo and a couple of his cronies appointed themselves to the editorial board.

The plan, at least as they sold it to me, was for the magazine to promote the books of the publishing house. That was the main goal. The secondary goal was to put out a quality literary magazine that would reflect well on the house, as much for its content as for its contributors. They talked to me about Julio Cortázar, García Márquez, Carlos Fuentes, Vargas Llosa, the leading lights of Latin American literature. Always prudent, not to say skeptical, I told them that I would be happy to get Ibargüengoitia, Monterroso, José Emilio Pacheco, Monsiváis, Elenita Poniatowska. They said yes, of course, that before long everyone would be begging to be published in our magazine. All right, let them beg, I said, let's do good work, but don't forget the main goal: promoting the house. That would be no problem, they said. It would be a presence on every page, or every other page, and before long the magazine would be turning a profit too. And I said: gentlemen, I leave its fate in your hands. In the first magazine, as anyone can see for themselves, there was no sign of Cortázar, or García Márquez, or even José Emilio Pacheco, but we had an essay by Monsiváis, which rescued the issue, in a sense; otherwise, there was a piece by Vargas Pardo, an essay by an exiled Argentinian novelist and friend of Vargas Pardo, two excerpts from novels that we were about to publish, a story by a forgotten fellow countryman of Vargas Pardo. And poetry, too much poetry. In the review section, at least, I found nothing to object to. Most of the attention was focused on our new releases and was generally favorable.

I remember I talked to Vargas Pardo after reading the magazine and said: I think there's too much poetry, and poetry doesn't sell. I still remember his response: what do you mean it doesn't sell, Don Lisandro, he said, look at Octavio Paz and his magazine. All right, Vargas, I said, but Octavio is Octavio, and there are luxuries the rest of us can't afford ourselves. What I didn't say was that I hadn't read Octavio's magazine for ages, nor did I rectify my use of the word *luxuries*, which I had meant to describe not poetic endeavors but Octavio's tedious publication, since ultimately I think publishing poetry isn't a luxury but utter foolishness. That was as far as it went, anyway, and Vargas Pardo was able to put out the second and third issues, and then the fourth and fifth. Sometimes I heard talk that our magazine was becoming too aggressive. I think it was all Vargas Pardo's fault, that he was using the magazine as a weapon against those who'd snubbed him when he first came to Mexico, as the perfect vehicle for settling a few scores (some writers are so vain and touchy!), and to tell the truth, that was all right with me. It's good for a magazine to generate controversy, it means it's selling, and it struck me as miraculous that a magazine with so much poetry could be selling. Sometimes I asked myself why that bastard Vargas Pardo was so interested in poetry. He wasn't a poet himself, I knew, but a fiction writer. So how did he come by his interest in verse?

For a while, I admit, I engaged in all kinds of speculation. I came to suspect he was a queer. He might have been. He was married (to a Mexican, incidentally), but you never know. What kind of queer? A platonic, starry-eyed queer who got his kicks, shall we say, on a purely literary level? Or did he have a Mr. Right among the poets he published in the magazine? I don't know. To each his own. I don't have anything against queers. There are more of them every day, though. In the forties, the number of queers in Mexican literature was at an all-time high, and I thought that was as far as things could go. But today there are more of them than ever. I suppose the fault lies with the education system, the increasingly common tendency of Mexicans to make a spectacle of themselves, the movies, music, who knows what. Even Salvador Novo himself once mentioned to me that he was taken aback by the behavior and language of some of the young people who visited him. And Salvador Novo knew what he was talking about.

So that was how I met Arturo Belano. One afternoon Vargas Pardo told me about him, about how he was putting together a fantastic (was that the word he used?) book, the definitive anthology of young Latin American poets, and was looking for a publisher. And who is this Belano? I asked. He writes reviews for our magazine, said Vargas Pardo. These poets, I said, secretly watching him for his reaction, are like hustlers desperately seeking new women to pimp, but Vargas Pardo took it in stride and told me the book was very good, the kind of book another house would pick up if we didn't publish it ourselves (ah, what an interesting use of the plural). Then, watching him surreptitiously again, I said: bring him in, schedule me a meeting with him, and we'll see what can be done.

Two days later Arturo Belano showed up at the publishing house. He was wearing a denim jacket and jeans. The jacket had unpatched rips on the arms and the left side, as if someone had been shooting him full of arrows for fun or spearing him. The pants, well, if he'd taken them off they would've stood up on their own. The tennis shoes he wore were frightening just to look at. He had hair down to his shoulders, and probably he'd always been skinny but now he was even skinnier. He looked like he hadn't slept for days. Good God, I thought, what a wreck. At least he seemed to have showered that morning. So I said: let's see this anthology you've put together, Mr. Belano. And he said: I already gave it to Vargas Pardo. Off to a bad start, I thought.

I picked up the phone and told my secretary to send Vargas Pardo to my office. For a few seconds neither of us said a word. Damn it, if Vargas Pardo took any longer to get here the young poet was going to fall asleep on me. At least he didn't look like a queer. To kill time I explained to him that poetry collections, as he probably realized, were published by the dozen, but hardly ever sold. Yes, he said, they're published by the dozen. My God, he was like a zombie. For a moment I wondered whether he was on drugs, but who can tell? So, I said, was it hard to put together your anthology of Latin American poetry? No, he said, it's all friends. The arrogance. Well then, I said, there should be no problem with authors' rights, you have the permissions. He laughed. Or rather, let me explain, he twisted his mouth or curled his lip and showed a few yellowish teeth and made a sound. I swear that his laugh made the hair rise on the back of my neck. How to describe it? An otherworldly laugh? The kind of laugh you hear when you're walking down the deserted corridors of a hospital? Something along those lines. And afterward, after the laugh, we seemed about to sink back into silence, into one of those embarrassing silences between people who've just met, or between a publisher and a zombie (which happened, in this case, to be the same thing), but there was no way I wanted to be caught in that silence again, so I kept talking, talking about Chile, where he was from, about my magazine, where he'd published reviews, about how hard it could be to unload a stock of poetry books. And Vargas Pardo was nowhere to be seen (he was probably on the phone gabbing away with another poet!). And then, at that very moment, I had a kind of insight. Or a presentiment. I realized that it would be better not to publish that anthology. I realized that it would be better not to publish *anything* by this poet. To hell with Vargas Pardo and his brilliant ideas. If other publishing houses were interested, let them take him on, not me. In that second of clarity I realized that publishing a book by this kid would bring me bad luck, that having this kid sitting across from me in my office, looking at me with those vacant eyes, close to sleep, would bring me bad luck, that bad luck was probably already gliding over the roof of my publishing house like a vulture or an Aerolíneas Mexicanas plane fated to crash into my offices.

And suddenly there was Vargas Pardo, brandishing the manuscript of Latin American poets, and I woke from my trance, but very slowly, at first I couldn't even really hear what Vargas Pardo was saying. All I heard was his laugh and his goddamn booming voice, cheerful as can be, as if working for me was the best thing that ever happened to him, a paid vacation in Mexico City, and I remember being so confused that I stood up and offered Vargas Pardo my hand, my God, I offered that bastard my hand like he was the boss or the general manager and I was a goddamn lackey, and I remember too that I looked at Arturo Belano and that he didn't get up from his seat when the Ecuadorean came in, and not only did he not get up, he didn't even pay attention to us, didn't even look at us, would you believe, and I saw the hairy back of his neck and for a second I thought that what I was seeing wasn't a person, not a living, breathing human being with blood in his veins like you or me, but a scarecrow, a bundle of ragged clothes on a body of straw and plastic, something like that. And then I heard Vargas Pardo saying everything's ready now, Lisandro, Martita will be here in a second with the contract. With what contract? I stammered. With the contract for Belano's book, of course, said Vargas Pardo.

Then I sat back down and said wait a minute, wait a minute, what is this about a contract? The thing is, Belano is leaving us the day after tomorrow, said Vargas Pardo, and we have to get this resolved. Where is he leaving us for? I said. Europe, said Vargas Pardo, to get himself some Scandinavian pussy (crassness, for Vargas Pardo, is synonymous with frankness, even honesty). He's going to Sweden? I said. More or less, said Vargas Pardo, Sweden, Denmark, over there where it's cold. And can't we send him the contract? I said. No, you see, Lisandro, he's going to Europe with no fixed address and anyway he wants to get this resolved. And that bastard Vargas Pardo winked at me and brought his face close to mine (I thought he was going to kiss me, the big undercover faggot!) and I couldn't back away, didn't know how to back away, but all Vargas Pardo wanted was to say something in my ear, complicitly whisper a few words. And what he said was that we didn't have to pay an advance, that I should sign, sign right away, so Belano wouldn't back out of the deal and let the competition have the book. And I would have liked to say: I don't give a shit if he lets the competition have the book, I hope he does let them have it so they go broke before we do, but instead of telling him that, I only had the strength to ask, in a thin little voice: is this kid on drugs, or what? And Vargas Pardo burst out laughing. Then, whispering again, he said: something like that, Lisandro, something like that, you never really know, but the important thing is the book, and here it is, so let's sign the contract before it's too late. But is it wise . . . ? I managed to whisper back. And then Vargas Pardo removed his enormous face from mine and answered me in his usual voice, his booming Amazonian voice, as he himself, in an unbelievable display of narcissism, called it. Of course, of course, he said. And then he went over to the poet and slapped him on the back. How's it going, Belano, he said, and the young Chilean looked at him and then looked at me, and an idiotic smile lit up his face, the smile of someone mentally impaired, of someone who'd been lobotomized, for God's sake. And then Martita, my secretary, came in, and she put two copies of the contract on the desk, and Vargas Pardo went looking for a pen so Belano could sign, come on, right here, but I don't have a pen, said Belano, a pen for the poet, then, said Vargas Pardo. As if by common accord, all the pens had disappeared from my office. I had a couple in my jacket pocket, of course, but I didn't want to offer them. No signature, no contract, I thought. But Martita searched through the papers on my desk and found one. Belano signed. I signed. I shook the Chilean's hand. I watched his face. He was smiling. He was about to collapse from exhaustion, and he was smiling. Where had I seen that smile before? I looked at Vargas Pardo as if to ask him where I'd seen that goddamn smile. The ultimate defenseless smile, the kind that drags us all down. But Vargas Pardo was saying goodbye to the Chilean. He was giving him advice about what to do in Europe! The faggot was reminiscing about his youth in the merchant marines! Even Martita was laughing at his stories! I could see there was nothing to be done. The book would be published.

And I, who'd always been a brave publisher, took the blow to my pride on the chin.

**Laura Jáuregui, Tlalpan, Mexico City DF, March 1977.** Before he left, he came to my house. It must have been seven in the evening. I was alone, my mother had gone out. Arturo told me that he was leaving and he wouldn't be coming back. I wished him luck, but I didn't even ask where he was going. I think he asked me about my studies, how I was doing at the university, in biology. I said great. He said: I've been to the north of Mexico, to Sonora, and Arizona too. That's what I think he said, but I'm not sure, and then he laughed. A short, dry laugh, a rabbity laugh. Yes, he did seem high, but I know for a fact that he never did any drugs. Ulises Lima did. He would try anything, and the funny thing was that you couldn't even tell when he was high and when he wasn't. But Arturo was different. He didn't get high. If anybody should know, it's me. And then he told me again that he was leaving. And before he could say another word, I told him I thought that was a fantastic idea, there was nothing like traveling and seeing the world, different cities and different skies, and he said the sky was the same everywhere, cities changed but the sky was the same, and I said he was wrong, I told him I didn't believe it, and that in one of his own poems he talked about the skies painted by Dr. Atl, different from any other skies in art or on the planet. Something like that. The truth is that I didn't feel like arguing. At first I'd pretended I wasn't interested in his plans, his talk, anything he had to say to me, but then I realized that I really wasn't interested, that everything having to do with him bored me to tears, that what I really wanted was for him to go and let me study in peace, I had a lot of studying to do that afternoon. And then he said it made him sad to travel and see the world without me, that he'd always thought I would come everywhere with him, and he named countries like Libya, Ethiopia, Zaire, and cities like Barcelona, Florence, Avignon, and then I couldn't help asking him what his countries had to do with his cities, and he said: everything, they have everything to do with each other, and I told him that when I was a biologist I would have the time to see those cities and countries, and the money too, because I didn't plan to travel around the world hitchhiking or sleeping just anywhere. And then he said: I don't plan to *see* them, I plan to *live* in them the same way I've lived in Mexico. And I said: well good for you, then, I hope you're happy, live in them and die in them if you want; I'll travel when I have money. Then you won't have the time, he said. I will have the time, I said, you're wrong, I'll be the mistress of my time, I'll do what I like with my time. And he said: you won't be young anymore. He was on the verge of tears as he said it, and seeing him like that, so embittered, made me angry and I shouted at him: what do you care what I do with my life or my youth or where I travel? And then he looked at me and fell into a chair, as if he'd suddenly realized that he was dead tired. He whispered that he loved me, that he would never be able to forget me. Then he got up (twenty seconds after he'd spoken, at most) and slapped my face. The sound echoed through the house. We were on the first floor, but I heard the sound of his hand (when his palm left my cheek) rise up the stairs and enter each of the rooms on the second floor, dropping down through the climbing vines and rolling like glass marbles in the yard. When I could react, I made a fist with my right hand and hit him in the face. He hardly moved. But his arm was fast enough to hit me again. Bastard, I said, faggot, coward, and I launched a clumsy attack, punching, scratching, and kicking. He didn't even try to dodge my blows. Fucking masochist! I screamed at him and I kept hitting him and crying, harder and harder, until through my tears I could only see light and shadows but not a clear picture of the body I was battering. Afterward I sat on the floor, still crying. When I looked up Arturo was beside me. His nose was bleeding, I remember, a little thread of blood running down to his upper lip and from there to the corner of his mouth and down his chin. You hurt me, he said, this hurts. I looked at him and blinked several times. This hurts, he said, and he sighed. And what do you think you did to me? I said. Then he got up and tried to touch my cheek. I jumped back. Don't touch me, I said. I'm sorry, he said. I hope you die, I said. I hope I die, he said, and then he said: I know I'm going to die. He wasn't talking to me. I started to cry again, and the more I cried the more I wanted to cry, and all I could tell him was to leave my house, get out, never set foot there again. I heard him sigh and I closed my eyes. My face was burning, but what I felt was less pain than humiliation. It was as if those two blows had wounded my pride, my dignity as a woman. I knew I would never forgive him. Arturo got up (he was kneeling beside me) and I heard him go into the bathroom. When he came back he was wiping the blood from his nose with a piece of toilet paper.

I told him to leave, I said I never wanted to see him again. He asked me whether I'd calmed down. I'll never be calm around you, I said. Then he turned around, dropped the bloody piece of toilet paper—like the sanitary pad of a drug-addicted whore—and left. I kept crying for a few more minutes. I tried to think about everything that had happened. When I felt better I got up, went to the bathroom, looked at myself in the mirror (my left cheek was red), made myself some coffee, put on music, and went out into the yard to make sure the gate was locked. Then I went to get a few books and settled down in the living room. But I couldn't study so I called a friend from the biology department. Luckily she was home. For a while we talked about various things, I can't remember what now, her boyfriend, I think, and suddenly, as she was talking, I saw the piece of toilet paper that Arturo had used to wipe away his blood. I saw it on the floor, crumpled, white with red streaks, an almost living object, and I felt overwhelmed with nausea. I made up an excuse to get off the phone, telling my friend that I was home alone and someone was knocking at the door. Don't open it, she said, it could be a thief or a rapist, probably both! I won't open the door, I said, I'm just going to see who it is. Does your house have a wall around it? said my friend. An enormous wall, I said. Then I hung up and went through the living room to the kitchen. When I got there, I didn't know what to do. I went into the downstairs bathroom. I took some toilet paper and came back to the living room. The bloody toilet paper was still there but I wouldn't have been surprised to find it under a chair now, or under the dining room table. With the toilet paper in my hand I covered Arturo's bloody toilet paper and then I pinched it in two fingers, carried it to the toilet, and pulled the chain.

# 6

Rafael Barrios, Café Quito, Calle Bucareli, Mexico City DF, May 1977. Our visceral realist activities after Ulises Lima and Arturo Belano left: automatic writing, exquisite corpses, solo performances with no spectators, *contraintes*, two-handed writing, three-handed writing, masturbatory writing (we wrote with the right hand and masturbated with the left, or vice versa if we were left-handed), madrigals, poem-novels, sonnets always ending with the same word, three-word messages written on walls ("This is it," "Laura, my love," etc.), outrageous diaries, mail-poetry, projective verse, conversational poetry, antipoetry, Brazilian concrete poetry (written in Portuguese cribbed from the dictionary), poems in hard-boiled prose (detective stories told with great economy, the last verse revealing the solution or not), parables, fables, theater of the absurd, pop art, haikus, epigrams (actually imitations of or variations on Catullus, almost all by Moctezuma Rodríguez), desperado poetry (Western ballads), Georgian poetry, poetry of experience, beat poetry, apocryphal poems by bpNichol, John Giorno, John Cage (*A Year from Monday*), Ted Berrigan, Brother Antoninus, Armand Schwerner (*The Tablets*), lettrist poetry, calligrams, electric poetry (Bulteau, Messagier), bloody poetry (three deaths at least), pornographic poetry (heterosexual, homosexual, or bisexual, with no relation to the poet's personal preference), apocryphal poems by the Colombian Nadaístas, Peruvian Horazerianos, Uruguayan Cataleptics, Ecuadorian Tzantzicos, Brazilian cannibals, Nô theater of the proletariat . . . We even put out a magazine . . . We kept moving . . . We kept moving . . . We did what we could . . . But nothing turned out right.

---

**Joaquín Font, El Reposo Mental Health Clinic, Camino Desierto de los Leones, on the outskirts of Mexico City DF, March 1977.** Sometimes I think about Laura Damián. Not often. Four or five times a day. Eight or sixteen times if I can't sleep, which makes sense since there's room for a lot of memories in a twenty-four-hour day. But usually I only think of her four or five times, and each memory, each memory capsule, is approximately two minutes long, although I can't say for sure because a little while ago someone stole my watch, and keeping time on one's own is risky.

When I was young I had a friend called Dolores. Dolores Pacheco. She really did know how to keep time. I wanted to go to bed with her. I want you to make me see stars, Dolores, I said to her one day. How long do you think stars last? she said. What do you mean? I asked. How long does one of your orgasms last? she said. Long enough, I said. But how long? I don't know, I said. A long time. You ask funny questions, Dolores. How long is a long time? she persisted. Then I assured her that I had never timed an orgasm, and she said pretend you're having an orgasm now, Quim, close your eyes and imagine that you're coming. With you? I said, seeing my chance. Whoever you want, she said, just imagine it, all right? Let's do it, I said. Fine, she said, when you start, raise your hand. Then I closed my eyes, imagined myself screwing Dolores, and raised my hand. And then I heard her voice saying: one Mississippi, two Mississippi, three Mississippi, four Mississippi, and unable to keep from laughing anymore, I opened my eyes and asked her what she was doing. I'm timing you, she said. Have you come yet? I don't know, I said, it's usually longer. Don't lie to me, Quim, she said, most orgasms are over by four Mississippi. Try again and you'll see. And I closed my eyes and at first I imagined myself screwing Dolores, but then I didn't imagine myself with anyone. Instead, I was in a riverboat, in a white, sterile room very much like the one I'm in now, and from the walls, from a hidden megaphone, Dolores's count came dripping down: one Mississippi, two Mississippi, as if someone were radioing me from shore and I couldn't reply, although deep in my heart all I wanted was to answer, to say: do you read me? I'm fine, I'm alive, I want to come back. And when I opened my eyes Dolores said: that's how you time an orgasm, each Mississippi is a second and no orgasm lasts more than six seconds. We never ended up fucking, Dolores and I, but we were good friends, and when she got married (this was after she graduated) I went to her wedding, and when I congratulated her I said: may your Mississippis be full of joy. The groom, who had been an architecture student like the two of us, but was a year ahead, or had graduated a little while before us, overheard me and thought I was referring to their honeymoon, which of course they were going to spend in the United States. A long time has passed since then. It's been a long time since I thought about Dolores. Dolores taught me to time things.

Now I time my memories of Laura Damián. Sitting on the floor, I begin: one Mississippi, two Mississippi, three Mississippi, four Mississippi, five Mississippi, six Mississippi, and Laura Damián's face, Laura Damián's long hair, settle in my vacant mind for fifty Mississippis or one hundred and fifty Mississippis, until I can't stand it anymore and I open my mouth and—ahh—let my breath out all at once or I spit on the walls. And I'm alone again, I'm empty. The echo of the word *Mississippi* bounces around in my cranial vault, the image of Laura's body destroyed by a killer car fading again, Laura's eyes open in the sky of Mexico City, no, in the sky of Colonia Roma, Colonia Hipódromo–La Condesa, Colonia Juárez, Colonia Cuauhtémoc, Laura's eyes illuminating the greens and sepias and all the shades of brick and stone of Coyoacán. And then I stop and take a deep breath or two, as if I'm having an attack, and I whisper go away, Laura Damián. Go away, Laura Damián. And then at last her face grows dim and my room isn't Laura Damián's face anymore but a room in a modern asylum, with every modern convenience, and the eyes watching me are the nurses' eyes again and not Laura Damián's (she has eyes in the back of her head!), and if no moonface of a watch glows on my wrist it's not because Laura has taken it, not because Laura has made me swallow it, but because it's been stolen by the lunatics you see running around here, these poor Mexican lunatics of ours, these ignoramuses who strike out or cry but who don't know a thing.

**Amadeo Salvatierra, Calle República de Venezuela, near the Palacio de la Inquisición, Mexico City DF, January 1976.** When I found my copy of *Caborca* I cradled it in my arms, I gazed at it and closed my eyes, gentlemen, because no one is made of stone. And then I opened my eyes and kept rummaging through my papers and came up with Manuel's broadsheet, the *Actual no. 1*, that he pasted on the walls of Puebla in 1921, the one where he talks about the "Mexican actualist avant garde," terrible sounding, isn't it? but wonderful too. That's also where he says "my madness never figured in any budget," ah, the life of leisure, "my madness never figured in any budget." But there are nice things too, like when he says: "I exert all the young poets, painters, and sculptors of Mexico, those who have yet to be tainted by the coffered gold of government sinecures, those who have yet to be corrupted by the crooked praise of official criticism and the applause of a crass and concupiscent public, those who have yet to lick the plates at the culinary celebrations of Enrique González Martínez, I exert all of them to make art with the steady drip of their intellectual menses. All those of good faith, all those who haven't yet crumbled in the sad, mephitic efflorescence of our nationalist media with its stink of *pulquerías* and the dying embers of fried food, all are exerted in the name of the Mexican actualist avant-garde to come and fight alongside us in the resplendent ranks of the *decouvert* . . ." That Manuel had a silver tongue. A silver tongue! Now, some of the words I don't understand. For example: *exert*. He must have meant summon, call, convoke, even command, let's see, let's look it up in the dictionary. That's right. *Exert* means something else. But you never know, it might have been a printer's error, and where it says *exert* it should say *exhort*, which would be very like Manuel, or at least the Manuel I knew back then. Or it might be a Latinism or a neologism, who can say. Or a term fallen into disuse. And that's what I told the boys. I said: boys, this was what Manuel Maples Arce's prose was like, hurtling and incendiary, full of words that got us hot and bothered, prose that might not mean anything to you now, but that in its day captivated generals of the Revolution, stalwart men who had seen death and who had killed and who when they read or heard Manuel's words were stopped in their tracks, stopped cold, as if to say what the hell is this, prose that promised poetry like the sea, the sea in the skies of Mexico. But where was I? I had my only copy of *Caborca* under my arm, the *Actual no. 1* in my left hand, and in my right my glass of Los Suicidas mezcal, and as I drank I read to them from that distant year of 1921 and we discussed it all, the passages and the mezcal, what a lovely way to read and drink, at leisure and among friends (young people have always been my friends), and when there was only a little bit left I poured a last round of Los Suicidas, saying a mental goodbye to that old elixir of mine, and I read the last part of the *Actual*, the Directory of the Avant-Garde, which in its time (and afterward, certainly, and after that too) came as such a surprise to insiders and outsiders, creators and scholars. The directory began with the names of Rafael Cansinos-Assens and Ramón Gómez de la Serna. Strange, isn't it? Cansinos-Assens and Gómez de la Serna, as if Borges and Manuel had been in telepathic communication, wouldn't you say? (The Argentinian, you know, reviewed Manuel's 1922 book, *Andamios interiors*.) And it went on like this: Rafael Lasso de la Vega. Guillermo de Torre. Jorge Luis Borges. Cleotilde Luisi. (Who was Cleotilde Luisi?) Vicente Ruiz Huidobro. A countryman of yours, I said to one of the boys. Gerardo Diego. Eugenio Montes. Pedro Garfias. Lucía Sánchez Saornil. J. Rivas Panedas. Ernesto López Parra. Juan Larrea. Joaquín de la Escosura. José de Ciria y Escalante. César A. Comet. Isac del Vando Villar. As you see it, with a single *a*. Probably another printer's error. Adriano del Valle. Juan Las. What a name. Mauricio Bacarisse. Rogelio Buendía. Vicente Risco. Pedro Raida. Antonio Espina. Adolfo Salazar. Miguel Romero Martínez. Ciriquiain Caitarro. Another clunker. Antonio M. Cubero. Joaquín Edwards. He must be a countryman of mine too, said one of the boys. Pedro Iglesias. Joaquín de Aroca. León Felipe. Eliodoro Puche. Prieto Romero. Correa Calderón. Look, I said, all we're getting are the last names now. That has to be a bad sign. Francisco Vighi. Hugo Mayo. Bartolomé Galíndez. Juan Ramón Jiménez. Ramón del Valle-Inclán. José Ortega y Gasset. What in the world is Don José doing on this list! Alfonso Reyes. José Juan Tablada. Diego Rivera. David Alfaro Siqueiros. Mario de Zayas. José D. Frías. Fermín Revueltas. Silvestre Revueltas. P. Echeverría. Atl. The great Dr. Atl, I presume. J. Torres-García. Rafael P. Barradas. J. Salvat Papasseit. José María Yenoy. Jean Epstein. Jean Richard Bloch. Pierre Brune. Do you know who he is? Marie Blanchard. Corneau. Farrey. Here I think Manuel was just pulling names out of a hat. Fournier. Riou. In fact, I'd bet my life on it. Mme. Ghy Lohem. Bloody hell, pardon me. Marie Laurencin. Here things start to improve. Dunozer de Segonzac. Worse again. What French son of a bitch was pulling Manuel's leg? Or did he find the name in some magazine? Honneger. Georges Auric. Ozenfant. Alberto Gleizes. Pierre Reverdy. Out of the swamp at last. Juan Gris. Nicolás Beauduin. William Speth. Jean Paulhan. Guillaume Apollinaire. Cypien. Max Jacob. Jorge Braque. Survage. Coris. Tristan Tzara. Francisco Picabia. Jorge Ribemont-Dessaigne. Renée Dunan. Archipenko. Soupault. Bretón. Paul Élouard. Marcel Duchamp. And here the boys and I agreed that it was arbitrary, to say the least, to call Francis Picabia Francisco and Georges Braque Jorge Braque and not to call Marcel del Campo Marcelo or Paul Éluard Pablo, Éluard without the *o*, as every lover of French poetry knows. Not to mention Breton with an accent. And the Directory of the Avant-Garde continued with its heroes and errors: Frankel. Sernen. Erik Satie. Elie Faure. Pablo Picasso. Walter Bonrad Arensberg. Celine Arnauld. Walter Pach. Bruce. Please! Morgan Russel. Marc Chagall. Herr Baader. Max Ernst. Christian Schaad. Lipchitz. Ortiz de Zárate. Correia d'Araujo. Jacobsen. Schkold. Adam Fischer. Mme. Fischer. Peer Kroogh. Alf Rolfsen. Jeauneiet. Piet Mondrian. Torstenson. Mme. Alika. Ostrom. Geline. Salto. Weber. Wuster. Kokodika. Kandinsky. Steremberg (com. de B. A. de Moscou). The parenthetical reference is Manuel's, of course. As if people would know perfectly well who all the others were, said one of the boys. Herr Baader, for example, or Coris, or that Kokodika who sounds like Kokoschka, or Riou, or Adam and Mme. Fisher. And why write *Moscou* and not *Moscow*? I wondered out loud. But on we go. After the commissioner of Moskva there was no lack of Russians. Mme. Lunacharsky. Erhenbourg. Taline. Konchalowsky. Machkoff. Mme. Ekster. Wlle Monate. Marewna. Larionow. Gondiarowa. Belova. Sontine. With Soutine surely hidden behind the *n*. Daiiblet. Doesburg. Raynal. Zahn. Derain. Walterowua Zur = Mueklen. He's the best of the lot, no doubt about it. Or she is, because who's to know (in Mexico at least) whether Walterowua Zur = Mueklen is male or female. Jean Cocteau. Pierre Albert Birot. Metsinger. Jean Charlot. Maurice Reynal. Pieux. F. T. Marinetti. G. P. Lucinni. Paolo Buzzi. A. Palazzeschi. Enrique Cavacchioli. Libero Altomare. Which for some reason, I don't know why, my memory is failing me, boys, sounds like Alberto Savinio to me. Luciano Folgore. What a pretty name, don't you think? there was a division of parachutists in the Duce's army called Folgore. A bunch of queers who got their asses kicked by the Australians. E. Cardile. G. Carrieri. F. Mansella Fontini. Auro d'Alba. Mario Betuda. Armando Mazza. M. Boccioni. C. D. Carrá. G. Severini. Balilla Pratella. Cangiullo. Corra. Mariano. Boccioni. It's not me repeating myself, it's Manuel or his wretched printers. Fessy. Setimelli. Carli. Ochsé. Linati. Tita Rosa. Saint-Point. Divoire. Martini. Moretti. Pirandello. Tozzi. Evola. Ardengo. Sarcinio. Tovolato. Daubler. Doesburg. Broglio. Utrillo. Fabri. Vatrignat. Liege. Norah Borges. Savory. Gimmi. Van Gogh. Grunewald. Derain. Cauconnet. Boussingautl. Marquet. Gernez. Fobeen. Delaunay. Kurk. Schwitters. Kurt Schwitters, said one of the boys, the Mexican, as if he'd just found his twin brother lost in linotype hell. Heyniche. Klem. Who might've been Klee. Zirner. Gino. Devil take him, could anything be more obscure! Galli. Bottai. Ciocatto. George Bellows. Giorgio de Chirico. Modigliani. Cantarelli. Soficci. Carena. And that was where the directory ended, with the ominous word *etc.* after *Carena*. And when I had finished reading that long list, the boys kneeled or stood at attention, I swear I can't remember which and anyway it doesn't matter, they stood at attention like soldiers or kneeled like true believers, and they drank the last drops of Los Suicidas mezcal in honor of all those strange or familiar names, remembered or forgotten even by their own grandchildren. And I looked at those two boys who just a minute ago had seemed so serious, standing there at attention before me, saluting the flag or their fallen companions, and I too raised my glass and drained it, toasting all our dead.

**Felipe Müller, Bar Céntrico, Calle Tallers, Barcelona, May 1977.** Arturo Belano stayed with his mother when he came to Barcelona. His mother had been living here for a few years. She was sick. She had hyperthyroidism, and she'd lost so much weight that she looked like a walking skeleton.

I was living at my brother's house at the time, on Calle Junta de Comercio, which was full of Chileans. Arturo's mother was living here on Tallers, where I live now, in this same place with no shower and the crapper in the hall. When I got to Barcelona I brought her a book of poetry that Arturo had published in Mexico. She looked at it and murmured something, I don't know what, something that made no sense. She wasn't well. Because of the hyperthyroidism she was constantly running back and forth in a fever and she cried a lot. Her eyes seemed to bulge out of their sockets. Her hands shook. Sometimes she had asthma attacks, but she smoked a pack a day. She smoked black tobacco, like Carmen, Arturo's younger sister, who lived with her mother but spent almost all day out. Carmen worked at Telefónica, cleaning, and she was dating an Andalusian who belonged to the Communist Party. Carmen was a Trotskyite when I met her in Mexico and she still was, but she was dating the Andalusian anyway—an Andalusian who was, if not a committed Stalinist, then very much a committed Brezhnevist, which under the circumstances was essentially the same thing. In any case, he was a bitter enemy of the Trotskyites, so things between them must have stayed pretty lively.

In my letters to Arturo I explained all of this. I told him that his mother wasn't well. I told him that she was wasting away, that she had no money, that this city was killing her. Sometimes I pestered him because I didn't know what else to do, telling him that he had to help her somehow, either send money or bring her back to Mexico. Sometimes Arturo's replies were the kind of thing you don't know whether to take seriously or not. Once he wrote: "Tell them to hang in there. I'll be there soon to take care of everything. But for now they have to hang in there." Such gall. My reply was that she (singular) couldn't hang in there. His sister was perfectly fine, as far as I could tell, although she fought with her mother every day, but unless he did something about his mother right away he would lose the woman who'd brought him into this world. Around that time I'd loaned Arturo's mother all the money I had left, about two hundred dollars, the remainder of a poetry prize I'd won in Mexico in 1975, which was how I bought my ticket to Barcelona in the first place. I didn't tell him that, of course. Although I think his mother did. She wrote him a letter every three days: I guess it was the hyperthyroidism. Anyway, the two hundred dollars was enough to pay her rent, but that was pretty much it. One day I got a letter from Jacinto Requena saying, among other things, that Arturo didn't read his mother's letters. That dumb jerk Requena meant it as a joke, but that was the last straw and I wrote Arturo a letter with nothing in it about literature and plenty about money matters, health, and family problems. I heard back from him right away (say what you like about Arturo, but he never lets a letter go unanswered) and he wrote that he'd already sent his mother money and that he was about to do something even better, he was going to get her a job, because his mother's problem was that she'd always worked and it was fucking her up to feel useless. I wanted to tell him unemployment was high in Barcelona and besides his mother was in no shape to work, if she showed up for a job she would probably frighten her bosses because she was so thin, so horribly thin that she looked more like an Auschwitz survivor than anything else, but I didn't. I decided to give him a break, give *myself* a break, and talk to him about poetry: Leopoldo

203

María Panero, Félix de Azúa, Gimferrer, Martínez Sarrión, poets he and I liked, and Carlos Edmundo de Ory, the creator of postism, with whom I had recently begun to correspond.

One afternoon Arturo's mother came to my brother's house looking for me. She said that her son had sent her the most complicated letter. She showed it to me. Inside the envelope was Arturo's letter and a letter of introduction to the Catalan novelist Juan Marsé, written by the Ecuadorian novelist Vargas Pardo. What his mother had to do, Arturo explained in the letter, was go to Juan Marsé's house, near the Sagrada Familia, and give Marsé Vargas Pardo's introduction. The introduction was on the brief side. The first few lines were a greeting to Marsé, mentioning (in a confused way) what seemed to have been a festive incident on a street near Plaza Garibaldi. Then came a rather cursory introduction of Arturo, and then, immediately, the really important part: the plight of the poet's mother, the request that Marsé do whatever was in his power to find her a job. We're going to meet Juan Marsé! said Arturo's mother. You could see she was happy and proud of what her son had done. I had my doubts. She wanted me to go with her to visit Marsé. If I go alone, she said, I'll be too nervous and I won't know what to say, but you're a writer and if things go wrong you can help me out.

I wasn't thrilled by the idea, but I agreed to go with her. One afternoon we went. Arturo's mother fixed herself up a little more than usual, but she was still in terrible shape. We got on the subway at Plaza Catalonia and got off at the Sagrada Familia. Just before we arrived she felt an asthma attack coming on and had to use her inhaler. Juan Marsé himself came to the door. We greeted him and Arturo's mother explained what she wanted. She made a mess of it, talking about "needs" and "crises" and "socially engaged poetry" and "Chile" and "illness" and "regrettable situations." I thought she'd lost it. Juan Marsé looked at the envelope she was holding out and let us in. Would you like something to drink? he said. No, very kind of you, said Arturo's mother. No, thank you, I said. Then Marsé began to read Vargas Pardo's letter and asked us whether we knew him. He's a friend of my son's, said Arturo's mother. I think he was at my house once, but no, I never met him. I said I didn't know him either. An excellent person, Vargas Pardo, murmured Marsé. And has it been a long time since you lived in Chile? he asked Arturo's mother. Many, many years, yes, so many I can hardly recall. Then Arturo's mother started to talk about Chile and Mexico and Marsé started to talk about Mexico and I don't know when it happened but suddenly they were *tú*-ing each other, laughing. I was laughing too. Marsé probably told some kind of joke. As it happens, he said, I know of a person who has something that might interest you. It isn't a job but a scholarship, a scholarship to study special education. Special education? said Arturo's mother. Well, said Marsé, I think that's what it's called. It has to do with teaching the mentally disabled, or children with Down syndrome. Oh, I'd love that, said Arturo's mother. After a while we left. Call me tomorrow, said Marsé from the door.

On the trip back we couldn't stop laughing. Arturo's mother thought Juan Marsé was handsome, with beautiful eyes, a wonderful man, and so nice and forthright. It had been a long time since I saw her so happy. The next day she called him and Marsé gave her the number of the woman who handled the scholarships. A week later, Arturo's mother was studying to teach the mentally disabled, autistic children, people with Down syndrome, at a school in Barcelona, where she worked as a student teacher while she studied. The scholarship was for three years, renewable from year to year depending on her grades. A little while later she went into the hospital to get her thyroid treated. At first we thought she would have to have an operation, but she didn't. So when Arturo got to Barcelona his mother was much better. The scholarship wasn't lavish but she could get by, and she even had the money to buy all kinds of chocolate, because she knew Arturo liked chocolate, and European chocolate, as everybody knows, is infinitely better than the chocolate you get in Mexico.

# 7

**Simone Darrieux, Rue des Petites Écuries, Paris, July 1977.** When Ulises Lima got to Paris, the only people he knew were a Peruvian poet who'd been living in exile in Mexico and me. I'd only met him once, at Café Quito, one night when I had a date with Arturo Belano. The three of us talked for a while, the time it took us to drink our coffee, and then Arturo and I left.

I did know Arturo well, though I haven't seen him since then and I'll probably never see him again. What was I doing in Mexico? Studying anthropology, in theory. In practice I was traveling, seeing the country. I went to lots of parties too. It's incredible how much free time Mexicans have. Of course, the money didn't stretch far enough for my purposes (I was on scholarship), so I got a job with a photographer, Jimmy Cetina, whom I met at a party at a hotel, the Vasco de Quiroga on Calle Londres, I think. My finances improved considerably. Jimmy did artistic nudes, as he called them, though they were really soft porn, full frontals and provocative poses, or strip-tease sequences, all in his studio at the top of a building on Bucareli.

I can't remember now how I met Arturo, maybe it was after a photo session in Jimmy Cetina's building, maybe at a bar, maybe it was a party. It might have been at the pizza place run by an American whom everybody called Jerry Lewis. In Mexico people meet in the most unlikely places. Anyway, we met and we hit it off, although it was almost a year before we slept together.

He was interested in all things French. In that sense, he was a little naïve. For example, he thought that I, who was studying anthropology, must necessarily know the work of Max Jacob (the name rang a bell, but that was all), and when I told him no, when I told him French girls read other things (in my case, Agatha Christie), he simply didn't believe me. He thought I was kidding. But he was considerate, I mean, he always seemed to be thinking in terms of literature, but he wasn't a fanatic, he didn't look down on you if you'd never in your life read Jacques Rigaut, he even liked Agatha Christie too, and sometimes we would spend hours talking about one of her novels, going over the puzzles (I have a terrible memory, but his was excellent), reconstructing those impossible murders.

I don't know what it was that attracted me to him. One day I brought him with me to the apartment where I lived with three other anthropology students, an American from Colorado and two French girls, and finally, at four in the morning, we ended up in bed. I'd warned him earlier about one of my quirks. I told him, half serious, half joking (we were laughing in the garden of the Museum of Modern Art, where the sculptures are, horrible sculptures): Arturo, never sleep with me, because I'm a masochist. What do you mean by that? he said. That I like to be hit when I'm making love, that's all. Then Arturo stopped laughing. Are you serious? he said. Completely serious, I said. And how do you like to be hit? he said. I like to be slapped, I said, hit in the face, spanked, that kind of thing. Hard? he said. No, not very hard, I said. You must not screw much in Mexico, he said, after thinking awhile. I asked what made him say that. The bruises, Miss Marple, he said, I've never seen a mark on you. Of course I have sex, I replied, I'm a masochist, not an animal. Arturo laughed. I think he thought I was joking. So that night, or that morning, actually, when we ended up in my bed, he was very gentle with me and I couldn't bring myself to stop him, if he wanted to lick me all over and kiss me softly, let him, but soon I noticed that he wasn't getting hard, and I took him in my hand and stroked him for a while, but nothing happened, and then I asked him, whispering in his ear, whether something was bothering him, and he said no, he was fine, and we kept touching each other for a while longer, but it was clear that he wasn't going to get it up, and then I said this is no good, stop trying, that's enough, if you're not in the mood, you're not in the mood, and he lit a cigarette (he smoked a kind called Bali, such a funny name) and then he started to talk about the last movie he'd seen, and then he got up and paced around the room naked, smoking and looking at my things, and then he sat on the floor, beside the bed, and started to look through my pictures, some of Jimmy Cetina's artistic shots that I don't know why I'd kept, because I'm stupid, probably, and I asked him whether they turned him on, and he said no but that they were all right, that I looked *all right*, you're very beautiful, Simone, he said, and it was then, I don't know why, that it occurred to me to tell him to get in bed, to get on top of me and slap me on the cheeks or the ass a little, and he looked at me and said I can't do that, Simone, and then he corrected himself and said: that's another thing I can't do, Simone, but I said come on, be brave, get in bed, and he got in, and I turned over and raised my buttocks and said: just take it slowly, pretend it's a game, and he gave me the first blow and I buried my face in the pillow, I haven't read Rigaut, I said, or Max Jacob, or boring Banville, Baudelaire, Catulle Mendès, or Corbiere, required reading, but I have read the Marquis de Sade. Oh really? he said. Yes, I said, stroking his dick. He had started slapping me on the ass as if he meant it. What have you read by the Marquis de Sade? *Philosophy in the Boudoir*, I said. And *Justine*? Naturally, I said. And *Juliette*? Of course. By then I was wet and moaning and Arturo's dick was as stiff as a rod, so I turned around, spread my legs and told him to put it in, but no more, not to move until I told him to. It was delicious to feel him inside of me. Hit me, I said. On the face, on the cheeks. Put your fingers in my mouth. He hit me. Harder! I said. He hit me harder. Now start to move, I said. For a few seconds the only sounds in the room were my moans and the blows. Then he started to moan too.

We made love until dawn. When we were done he lit a Bali and asked me whether I'd read the Marquis de Sade's plays. I said I hadn't, that it was the first I'd heard that de Sade wrote plays. Not only did he write plays, said Arturo, he wrote lots of letters to theater impresarios urging them to stage what he'd written. But of course, no one dared to put on anything by him, since they would have ended up in prison (we laughed), although the incredible thing is that the marquis persisted, making all kinds of calculations in his letters, down to how much should be spent on wardrobe, and the saddest thing of all is that his figures add up, they're good! the plays would have made money. But were they pornographic? I asked. No, said Arturo, they were philosophical, with some sex.

We were lovers for a while. Three months, to be exact, the time I had left before I went back to Paris. We didn't make love every night. We didn't see each other every night. But we did it every way possible. He tied me up, hit me, sodomized me. He never left a mark, except a red-dened ass, which says something about how gentle he was. A little bit longer and I would have ended up getting used to him. Needing him, in other words, and he would've ended up getting used to me. But we didn't give ourselves time. We were just friends. We talked about the Marquis de Sade, Agatha Christie, life in general. When I met him he was a Mexican like any other Mexican, but toward the end he felt more and more like a foreigner. Once I said: you Mexicans are like this or that, and he said I'm not Mexican, Simone, I'm Chilean, a little sadly, it's true, but like he meant it.

So when Ulises Lima showed up at my place and said I'm a friend of Arturo Belano's, I felt a rush of happiness, although later, when I found out that Arturo was in Europe too and hadn't even had the courtesy to send me a postcard, I was annoyed. By then I had an essentially boring, bureaucratic job at the anthropology department at the Université Paris-Nord, and with Ulises there at least I could practice my Spanish, which was getting a little rusty.

Ulises Lima lived on the Rue des Eaux. Once, just once, I went to visit him there. I'd never seen a worse *chambre de bonne*. It had one tiny window, which didn't open and looked out onto a dark, filthy airshaft. There was hardly room for a bed and a kind of ramshackle nursery table. There was no wardrobe or closet, so his clothes were still in suitcases or strewn around the room. When I came in I felt like throwing up. I asked him how much he paid for it. When he told me, I realized that someone was ripping him off. Whoever found you this room cheated you, I told him, this is a dump, the city is full of better rooms. I'm sure it is, he said, but then he argued that he didn't plan to stay long in Paris and he didn't want to waste time looking for anything better.

We didn't see each other often, and when we did it was always his doing. Sometimes he'd call and other times he just showed up at my building and asked if I felt like a walk, or coffee, or a movie. I usually said I was busy, studying or working on something for the department, but sometimes I agreed and we'd take a walk. We always ended up at a bar on the Rue de la Lune, eating pasta and drinking wine and talking about Mexico. He usually paid, which is odd now that I think about it, since as far as I know he wasn't working. He read a lot. He always had several books under his arm, all in French, though truth be told he was far from mastering the language (as I said, we made a point of speaking

Spanish). One night he told me his plans. He was going to spend some time in Paris and then head for Israel. I smiled in shock and disbelief when he told me. Why Israel? Because he had a friend there. That's what he said. Is that the only reason? I asked incredulously. The only one.

As a matter of fact, nothing he did ever seemed to be planned out.

What was he like as a person? He was laid-back, calm, somewhat distant but not cold. Actually, he could be very warm, unlike Arturo, who was intense and sometimes seemed to hate everybody. Not Ulises. He was respectful. Ironic but respectful. He accepted people for what they were and never seemed to be trying to invade your privacy, which was often not the case with Latin Americans, in my experience.

**Hipólito Garcés, Avenue Marcel Proust, Paris, August 1977.** When my buddy Ulises Lima showed up in Paris I was thrilled, honest to God. I found him a nice little *chambre* on the Rue des Eaux, close to where I was living. From Marcel Proust to his place it was hardly any distance at all. You went left, toward Avenue René Boylesve, then turned onto Charles Dickens, and you were on the Rue des Eaux. So we were practically next door, as they say. I had a hot plate in my room and I cooked every day, and Ulises would come eat at my place. But I said: you've got to let me have a little something for it, *pues*. And he said: Polito, I'll give you money, don't worry, that seems fair, since you buy the food and you cook it too. How much do you want? And I said give me one hundred dollars, *pues*, Ulises, and that'll be the end of it. And he said that he didn't have any dollars left, all he had were francs, so that was what he gave me. He had the cash and he was a trusting guy.

One day, though, he said: Polito, I'm eating worse every day, how can a goddamn plate of rice cost so much? I explained to him that rice in France was expensive, not like in Mexico or Peru, here a kilo of rice costs an arm and a leg, *pues*, Ulises, I told him. He gave me this look, in the brooding kind of way Mexicans do, and he said all right, but at least buy a can of tomato sauce because I'm sick of eating white rice. Of course, I said, and I'll buy wine too, which I forgot because I was in a hurry, but you have to give me a little more money. He gave it to me and the next day I made him his plate of rice with tomato sauce and poured him a glass of red wine. But the next day the wine was gone (I drank it, I admit) and two days later the tomato sauce ran out and he was back to eating plain white rice. And then I made macaroni. Let's see, I'm trying to remember. Then I made lentils, which have lots of iron and are nutritious. And when the lentils were gone I made chickpeas. And then I made white rice again. And one day Ulises stood up and half jokingly let me have it. Polito, he said, I get the feeling you're pulling a fast one. You make the plainest and most expensive food in Paris. No, man, I told him, no, *mi causita*, you have no idea how expensive things are, but the next day he didn't come to eat. Three days went by and there was no sign of him. After that I stopped by his room on the Rue des Eaux. He wasn't there. But I had to see him, so I sat in the hall waiting for him to get home.

He showed up around three in the morning. And when he saw me in the hall, in the dark of that long, nasty-smelling hall, he stopped and stood where he was, about twenty feet from me, with his legs braced, like he was expecting me to attack him. But the funny thing was that he was quiet too, he didn't say a word. Holy shit, I thought, old Ulises is pissed and he's going to disemfuckingbowel me right here in this hallway. So I thought it over and stayed where I was. What kind of threat is a shadow on the floor? And I called him by name, Ulises, *causita*, it's me, Polito, and he says Polito! what the hell are you doing here this time of night, Polito, and then I realized that he hadn't known who I was before and I thought who is this motherfucker *expecting*? Who did he think I was? And I swear on my mother's grave that right then I was more afraid than before, I don't know why, it must have been how late it was, or that gloomy hall, or my poet's imagination running away with me. Shit, I actually started to shake. I thought I saw another shadow behind Ulises Lima's shadow in the hall. By then, frankly, I was afraid to go down the eight flights of stairs to get out of that spooky place. And yet all I wanted was to run away. But at that moment my fear of being left alone was even stronger. When I got up, one of my legs had a cramp, and I asked Ulises if I could come in. Then he seemed to wake up, and he said of course, Polito, and he opened the door. When we were inside, with the light on, I felt the blood start to circulate in my veins again, and like a heartless bastard, I showed him the books I'd brought. Ulises looked at them one by one and said they were all right, though I know he was dying to have them. I brought them to sell to you, I said. How much do you want for them? he said. I named some crazy sum, to see what would happen.

Ulises looked at me and said all right, then he put his hand in his pocket and paid me, and stood there looking at me without saying anything. All right, man, I said, well, I'm going now. Should I have a delicious meal waiting for you tomorrow? No, he said, don't expect me. But you will come one of these days, won't you? Remember that if you don't eat you'll starve to death, I said. I'm not coming again, Polito, he said. I don't know what was wrong with me. Inside I was scared shitless (the idea of heading out, walking down the hall, going down the stairs, was killing me), but on the outside I started to talk. Fuck, suddenly I was talking, *hearing myself talk*, like my voice wasn't mine and the bitch had taken off rambling on its own. I said you have no right, Ulises, with the money I've spent on provisions, if you could see all the good things I've bought, and what do I do with them now? do they rot? do I shove everything down my own throat, Ulises? Is that what you want me to do? What if I get indigestion or stomach cramps from stuffing my face? Answer me, *pues*, Ulises, don't pretend you can't hear me. That kind of thing. No matter that inside of me I was saying to myself shut up, *pues*, Polito, you're going too far, this could get ugly, don't push it, shithead—on the outside, in the kind of half-asleep state I was in, my face and lips numb, my tongue flapping loose, the words (words that for once I didn't want to speak!) kept coming out and I heard myself say: what kind of friend are you, Ulises? when I spoiled you like you were more than my buddy, like you were my own brother, *causita*, my little brother, goddamn it, Ulises, and now you turn your back on me like this. Etc., etc. Why go on? All I can say is that I talked and talked, and Ulises, who stood facing me in that room, so small it seemed more like a coffin, never once took his eyes off me, perfectly still, never doing what I assumed he'd do, what I was afraid he'd do, just standing there like he was letting me dig myself into a hole, like he was saying to himself Polito has two minutes left, a minute and a half, one minute, Polito's got fifty seconds left, poor guy, ten seconds. And I swear it was like I was seeing each and every hair on my body, as if while my eyes were open, another pair of eyes, closed eyes, were scanning every inch of my skin and counting up each hair, eyes that could see more when they were closed than my open eyes could see. I know that doesn't make any fucking sense. And then I couldn't take it anymore and I collapsed on the bed like a slut and I said: Ulises, I feel like shit, Ulises, man, my life is a disaster, I don't know what's wrong with me, I try to do things right but everything turns out wrong, I should go back to Peru, this city is fucking killing me, I'm not the same person I used to be, and on and on I went, letting out everything that was torturing me inside, with my face in the blankets, in Ulises's blankets, I have no idea where they came from but they smelled bad, not just the typical unwashed smell of a *chambre de bonne*, and not like Ulises, but like something else, like death, an ominous smell that suddenly wormed its way into my brain and made me sit up, holy shit, Ulises, where did you get these blankets, *causita*, from the morgue? And Ulises was still standing there, not moving, listening to me, and then I thought this is my chance to go and I got up and reached out my hand and touched his shoulder. It was like touching a statue.


**Roberto Rosas, Rue de Passy, Paris, September 1977.** There were twelve rooms in our attic apartment. Eight of them were occupied by Latin Americans: one Chilean, Ricardito Barrientos; one Argentinian couple, Sofía Pellegrini and Miguelito Sabotinski; and the rest of us Peruvians, all poets, all at war with one another.

We liked to call our attic the Passy Commune or Passy Shantytown.

We were always arguing and our favorite topics, or pretty much our only topics, were politics and literature. Ricardito Barrientos's room had been rented before by Polito Garcés, who was Peruvian and a poet too, but one day, after an emergency meeting, we decided to give him an ultimatum: Either you leave here this very week motherfucker or we'll kick you down the stairs, take a shit in your bed, put rat poison in your wine, or come up with something worse. Luckily Polito listened to us. If he hadn't I don't know what would've happened.

One day he came by, though, shuffling along as always, going into one room after another asking to borrow money (money he would never return), getting somebody to offer him a little coffee here, a drop of maté there (Sofía Pellegrini hated him like the plague), asking to borrow books, saying that he'd seen Bryce Echenique that week, or Julio Ramón Ribeyro, or that he'd had tea with Hinostroza. The first time you might believe him, the second time you might laugh, but after you'd heard the same lies over and over all you felt was disgust, pity, and alarm because it was clear that Polito wasn't right in the head. Who is, when you get right down to it? Still, none of us is as crazy as Polito.

Anyway, one day he came by, some evening when almost all of us happened to be around (I know because I heard him knock on other doors, I heard that voice of his, that unmistakable "how's it, *causita*"), and after a while his shadow fell across the threshold of my room, like he was afraid to come in without being asked, and then I said—and maybe I said it too abruptly—what do you want, motherfucker? and he laughed his little jackass laugh and said *ay*, Robertito, it's been a long time, man, I'm glad to see you haven't changed, look, I've got a poet here with me who I want you to meet, a buddy from Mexico.

Only then did I realize that there was someone beside him. A dark, strong, Indian-looking guy. A guy with eyes that seemed sort of liquefied and blurry at the same time, and a doctor's smile, an unusual smile at the Passy Commune, where we all tended to have the smiles of folk musicians or lawyers.

It was Ulises Lima. That's how I met him. We became friends. Paris friends. He was nothing like Polito, of course. If he had been, we couldn't have been friends.

I don't remember how long he lived in Paris. I know we saw a lot of each other, even though we had very different personalities. But one day he told me he was leaving. How come, man? I asked, because as far as I knew he loved the city. I think I'm not well, he said, smiling. But is it anything serious? No, nothing serious, he said, just a nuisance. Well, I said, then that's all right, let's have a drink to celebrate. To Mexico! I said, raising my glass. I'm not going back to Mexico, he said, I'm going to Barcelona. What do you mean, man? I said. I have a friend there, and I'll stay at his place for a while. That was all he said and I didn't ask any more questions. Then we went out for more wine and sat drinking near the Porte de Bir Hakeim while I told him about my latest romantic adventures. But his mind was elsewhere, so we started to talk about poetry for a change, a subject I enjoy less and less these days.

I remember Ulises liked the young French poets. I can testify to that. We, the Passy Shantytown, thought they were disgusting. Spoiled brats or drug addicts. You have to understand, Ulises, I would say to him, we're revolutionaries, we've seen the insides of the jails of Latin America. So how can we care about poetry like that? And the bastard didn't say anything, just laughed. Once he took me to meet Michel Bulteau. Ulises spoke terrible French, so I had to do most of the talking. Then I met Mathieu Messagier, Jean-Jacques Faussot, and Adeline, Bulteau's companion.

I didn't hit it off with any of them. I asked Faussot whether he could get one of my articles published in the magazine where he worked, this shitty little pop magazine, and he said he'd have to read the article first. A few days later I brought it to him and he didn't like it. I asked Messagier for the address of a French poet, a "grand old man of French letters" who had supposedly met Martín Adán on a trip he took to Lima in the forties, but Messagier wouldn't give it to me. He tried to tell me that the poet was wary of visitors. I'm not going to borrow money from him, I said, I just want to interview him, but it made no difference, it was out of the question. Finally I told Bulteau that I was going to translate him. He liked that and made no objection. I was joking, of course. But then I thought maybe it wasn't such a bad idea. And in fact, I set to work a few nights later. The poem I chose was "Sang de satin." It had never occurred to me before to translate poetry, although I'm a poet and poets are supposed to translate other poets. But no one had translated me, so why should I translate anyone else? Well, so it goes. This time it didn't seem like such a bad idea. Maybe it was because of Ulises, whose influence was making me question old assumptions. Maybe it just seemed like time to do something I'd never done before. I don't know. All I know is that I told Bulteau that I planned to translate him and I planned to publish my translation (*publish* is the key word) in a nonexistent Peruvian magazine (I made up the name), a magazine that counted Westphalen among its contributors, that's what I told him, and he was happy to agree, although I think he had no idea who Westphalen was, I might as well have said that the magazine published Huamán Poma, or Salazar Bondy. Anyway, I set to work.

I don't remember whether Ulises had already left or was still around. "Sang de satin." From the start I had trouble with that shitty poem. How to translate the title? "Satin Blood" or "Blood of Satin"? I thought about it for more than a week. And it was then that I was suddenly overcome by the full horror of Paris, the full horror of the French language, the poetry scene, our state as unwanted guests, the sad, hopeless state of South Americans lost in Europe, lost in the world, and then I realized that I wasn't going to be able to finish translating "Satin Blood" or "Blood of Satin," I knew that if I did I would end up murdering Bulteau in his study on the Rue de Téhéran and then fleeing Paris like an outlaw. So in the end I decided not to go through with it and when Ulises Lima left (I can't remember exactly when), that was the end of my dealings with the French poets.

**Simone Darrieux, Rue des Petites Écuries, Paris, September 1977.** He never found anything remotely resembling a job. Honestly, I don't know what he lived on. He had money when he got here, that I know for a fact. The first few times we met he was always the one to pay, for coffee, calvados, a few glasses of wine, but he ran out of money fast and as far as I know he had no source of income.

Once he told me that he'd found a five-thousand-franc note in the street. After that, he said, he walked with his eyes on the ground.

After a while he found another bill.

He had some Peruvian friends who gave him work occasionally, a group of Peruvian poets, probably poets in name only, since as everyone knows living in Paris wears you down and erodes your vocation if it isn't ironclad. It coarsens you, it pushes you into oblivion. At least that happens to a lot of the Latin Americans I know. I'm not trying to say it was true of Ulises, but it was definitely true of the Peruvians. They had a kind of cleaning cooperative. They waxed office floors, washed windows, that kind of thing, and Ulises helped them out when one of the cooperative was sick or away from the city. Mostly he filled in when someone was sick, since the Peruvians didn't travel much, although in the summer some of them went off to harvest grapes in the Roussillon. They would leave in groups of two or three, sometimes they traveled alone, and before they left they would say they were off to the Costa Brava for a vacation. I saw them three times. They were miserable human beings. More than one of them tried to get me into bed.

With what you make, I said to Ulises once, you hardly manage to keep from starving. How do you expect to ever get to Israel? There's time, he answered, and that was the last we talked about money. Actually, now that I think about it, it's hard to say what kind of conversations we had. Just as with Arturo it was always clear (we talked about literature and sex, basically), with Ulises the boundaries were vague. Maybe this was because we saw each other so infrequently (although in his own way he was loyal to our friendship, loyal to my phone number). Maybe it was because he seemed to be, or was, someone who made no demands.


**Sofía Pellegrini, sitting in the Jardins du Trocadero, Paris, September 1977.** They called him the Christ of the Rue des Eaux and they all made fun of him, even Roberto Rosas, who claimed to be his best friend in Paris. They laughed at him because he was dumb, basically, or so they said. They used to say only a complete moron could let himself be fooled more than three times by Polito Garcés, but they were forgetting that Polito had fooled them too. The Christ of the Rue des Eaux. No, I never went to see his place. I know people said horrible things about it, that it was a filthy hole, that the worst junk in Paris piled up there: trash, magazines, newspapers, books he stole from bookstores, and that all of it soon began to smell like the place and then rotted, blossomed, turned all kinds of crazy colors. They said he could spend whole days without eating a thing, months without a visit to the public baths, but I doubt it because I never saw him looking especially dirty. Anyway, I didn't know him well, I wasn't his friend, but one day he came to our attic in Passy and there was no one home, just me, and I was in bad shape, I was depressed, I had been fighting with my boyfriend, things weren't going well for me, when he showed up I was crying in my *chambre*, the others had gone to the film society or one of their political meetings (they were all activists and revolutionaries), and Ulises Lima walked down the hallway and didn't knock on any of the doors, as if he knew beforehand that no one would be there, and he headed straight for my *chambre*, where I was sitting alone on the bed, staring at the wall, and he came in (he was clean, he smelled good) and stood there next to me, not saying anything, all he said was hello, Sofía, and he stayed there until I stopped crying. And that's why I remember him fondly.


**Simone Darrieux, Rue des Petites Écuries, Paris, September 1977.** Ulises Lima showered at my house. I was never thrilled about it. I don't like to use a towel after somebody else, especially if we aren't intimate in some way, physically and even emotionally, but still I let him use my shower, then I would gather up the towels and put them in the machine.

It helped that he tried to be neat in my apartment. In his own way, but he tried and that's what counts. After I shower I scrub the bathtub and pick the hair out of the drain. It may seem trivial but it drives me up the wall. I hate to find clumps of hair clogging the drain, especially if it isn't mine. Then I pick up the towels I've used and fold them and leave them on the bidet until I have time to put them in the machine. The first few times he came he even brought his own soap, but I told him he didn't have to, that he should feel free to use my soap and shampoo but that he shouldn't even think about touching my sponge.

He was always very formal. He usually called the day before to ask whether it was a good time for him to come, checking to make sure I wouldn't have guests or plans, then we would set a time, and the next day he would arrive right when he said he would, then we'd talk a little and he would head into the bathroom. Then any number of days might go by before I heard from him again, sometimes a week, sometimes two or even three. In the meantime he must have showered at the public baths.

Once, at the bar on the Rue de la Lune, he told me that he liked the public baths where foreigners went to bathe, black people from Francophone Africa or the Maghreb. I pointed out that poor students went there too. That's true, he said, but especially foreigners. And once, I remember, he asked me whether I had ever been to the public baths in Mexico. Of course I hadn't. They're the real thing, he said. They have saunas, Turkish baths, steam baths. Some of the ones here do too, I told him, but they're more expensive. Not in Mexico, he said. In Mexico they're cheap. I'd never thought twice about Mexican public baths, to be honest. Don't tell me you went to those baths, I said. No, not really, he said. Only once or twice.

He was a strange person. He wrote in the margins of books. I'm glad I never lent him any of mine. Why? Because I don't like people to write in my books. You won't believe this, but he used to shower with a book. I swear. He read in the shower. How do I know? Easy. Almost all his books were wet. At first I thought it was the rain. Ulises was a big walker. He hardly ever took the metro. He walked back and forth across Paris and when it rained he got soaked because he never stopped to wait for it to clear up. So his books, at least the ones he read most often, were always a little warped, sort of stiff, and I thought it was from the rain. But one day I noticed that he went into the bathroom with a dry book and when he came out the book was wet. That day my curiosity got the better of me. I went up to him and pulled the book away from him. Not only was the cover wet, some of the pages were too, and so were the notes in the margins, some maybe even written under the spray, the water making the ink run, and then I said, for God's sake, I can't believe it, you read in the shower! have you gone crazy? and he said he couldn't help it but at least he only read poetry (and I didn't understand why he said he only read poetry, not at the time, but now I do: he meant that he only read two or three pages, not a whole book), and then I started to laugh, I threw myself on the sofa, writhing in laughter, and he started to laugh too, both of us laughed for I don't know how long.

**Michel Bulteau, Rue de Téhéran, Paris, January 1978.** I don't know how he got my phone number, but one night, it must have been after midnight, he called me at home. He asked for Michel Bulteau. I said: this is Michel Bulteau. He said: this is Ulises Lima. Silence. I said: yes? He said: I'm glad I caught you at home, I hope you weren't asleep. I said: no, no I wasn't asleep. Silence. He said: I'd like to see you. I said: now? He said: all right, yes, now, I can come to your place if you want. I said: where are you? but he misunderstood me, and said: I'm Mexican. Then I remembered, very vaguely, that I had received a magazine from Mexico. Still, the name Ulises Lima didn't ring any bells. I said: have you ever heard of the Question Marks? He said: no, I've never heard them. I said: I think they're Mexican. He said: the Question Marks? Who are the Question Marks? I said: a rock group, of course. He said: do they wear masks when they play? At first I didn't understand what he'd said. Masks? No, of course they don't wear masks. Why would they? Are there rock groups in Mexico that perform in masks? He said: sometimes. I said: it sounds ridiculous, but it might be interesting. Where are you calling me from? Your hotel? He said: no, from the street. I said: do you know how to get to the metro station Miromesnil? He said: sure, no problem. I said: twenty minutes. He said: I'm on my way, and hung up. As I was putting on my jacket I thought: but I don't know what he looks like! What do Mexican poets look like? I don't know a single one! All I've seen is a picture of Octavio Paz! But this poet, I sensed, would definitely not look like Octavio Paz. Then I thought about the Question Marks, and Elliot Murphie, and something Elliot had told me when I was in New York, about the Mexican Death's-Head, a guy they called the Mexican Death's-Head, who I only saw from a distance at a bar on Franklin Street and Broadway. The Mexican Death's-Head was a musician but all I saw was a shadow, and I asked Elliot what it was about the guy he wanted to show me, and Elliot said: he's a kind of worm, he has worm eyes and he talks like a worm. How do worms talk? In doublespeak, said Elliot. All right. Clear enough. And why is he called the Mexican Death's-Head? I asked. But Elliot wasn't listening to me anymore or he was talking to someone else, so I just assumed this guy must be Mexican or have spent time in Mexico at some point in his life, in addition to being as thin as a rail. But I didn't see his face, just his shadow as it crossed the bar. A shadow empty of metaphor, evoking nothing, a shadow that was only a shadow with no wish to be anything else. So I put on my black jacket, combed my hair, and went out thinking about the stranger who had called me and the Mexican Death's-Head I'd seen in New York. It's only a few minutes from Rue Téhéran to the Miromesnil metro station, walking fairly quickly, but you have to cross Boulevard Haussmann and then head along Avenue Percier and part of Rue la Boétie, streets that at that time of night are mostly lifeless, as if starting at ten they were bombarded with X-rays, and then I thought that it might have been better to meet the stranger at the Monceau metro station, so that I would've had to walk in the opposite direction, from Rue Téhéran to Rue de Monceau, on to Avenue Ruysdaël and then Avenue Ferdousi, which crosses the Parc de Monceau, because at that time of night it's full of junkies and dealers and sad policemen beamed in from other worlds, the languid gloom of the park leading up to the Place de la République Dominicaine, an auspicious place for a meeting with the Mexican Death's-Head. But I'd chosen my path and I followed it to the steps of the Rue de Miromesnil station, which was deserted and immaculate. I confess that the metro steps had never seemed so suggestive, and at the same time so inscrutable. And yet they looked the same as ever. I realized immediately that this was an aura I'd conjured up myself by agreeing to meet a stranger at such an ungodly hour, which isn't something I'd normally do. And yet I'm not in the habit of ignoring the call of fate. There I was and that was all that mattered. But except for a clerk who was reading a book and must have been waiting for someone, there was no one on the stairs. So I started down. I'd made up my mind to wait five minutes, then leave and forget the whole thing. At the first turn I came upon an old woman wrapped in rags and cardboard, sleeping or pretending to sleep. A few feet farther on, watching the old woman as if she were a snake, I saw a man with long black hair whose features may have been what you'd call Mexican, though I really wouldn't know. I stopped and took a good look at him. He was shorter than me and he was wearing a worn leather jacket, carrying four or five books under his arm. All at once he seemed to awake and he fixed me with his gaze. It was him, beyond a doubt. He came up and offered me his hand. His grip was peculiar. As if, as we shook, he threw in Masonic code and signals from the Mexican underworld. A tickling and morphologically peculiar handshake, in any case, as if the hand shaking mine had no skin or were only a sheath, a tattooed sheath. But never mind his hand. I said that it was a beautiful night and we should go outside and walk. It's as if it were still summer, I said. He followed me in silence. For a moment I was afraid he wouldn't say a word the entire time we were together. I looked at his books. One of them was my *Ether-Mouth*, another was by Claude Pelieu, and the rest might have been by Mexican authors I'd never heard of. I asked him how long he'd been in Paris. A long time, he said. His French was terrible. I suggested that we speak in English and he agreed. We walked along the Rue de Miromesnil to the Faubourg St. Honoré. Our strides were long and rapid, as if we were late to an important meeting. I'm not the kind of person who likes to walk. And yet that night we walked nonstop, at top speed, along the Faubourg St. Honoré to the Rue Boissy d'Anglas and on to the Champs-Élyseés, where we turned right again, continuing on to the Avenue Churchill and turning left, the vague shadow of the Grand Palais behind us, making straight for the Pont Alexandre III, our pace never slackening, while in occasionally unintelligible English the Mexican reeled off a story that I had trouble following, a story of lost poets and lost magazines and works no one had ever heard of, in the middle of a landscape that might have been California or Arizona or some Mexican region bordering those states, a real or imaginary place, bleached by the sun and lost in the past, forgotten, or at least no longer of the slightest importance here, in Paris, in the 1970s. A story from the edge of civilization, I said. And he said yes, yes, I guess so, yes. And then I said to him: so you've never heard the Question Marks? And he said no, he'd never heard them. And then I said that he had to hear them someday, because they were very good, but really I only said that because I didn't know what else to say.

# 8

**Amadeo Salvatierra, Calle República de Venezuela, near the Palacio de la Inquisición, Mexico City DF, January 1976.** I said to them: boys, the Los Suicidas mezcal is gone, that's an undeniable, incontrovertible fact, so why doesn't one of you go down and buy me a bottle of Sauza? and one of them, the Mexican, said: I'll go, Amadeo, and he was already on his way to the door when I stopped him and said wait a minute, you're forgetting the money, my friend, and he looked at me and said don't even think about it, Amadeo, we'll get this one. Such nice boys. I did give him some instructions before he left, though: I told him to head down Venezuela to Brasil, then turn right and walk up to Calle Honduras, to the Plaza de Santa Catarina, and turn left, then walk until he came to Chile and then turn right again and keep on as if he were going to La Lagunilla market, and there, on the left side of the street, he would find the bar La Guerrerense, next to the hardware store El Buen Tono, you couldn't miss it, and at La Guerrerense he should say that I, the scribe Amadeo Salvatierra, had sent him, and he should hurry. Then, as I was going through some papers, the other boy got up from his seat and started to examine my library. In fact, I didn't see him, I just heard him, stepping forward, pulling out a book, putting it back. I heard the noise his finger made as he ran it along the spines of my books! But I couldn't see him. I was sitting down again, I had put my money back in my wallet, and with shaky hands (once you reach a certain age drinking isn't what it used to be), I was going through my old, yellowing papers. My head was bent and my vision was blurred and the Chilean boy moved silently around my library and all I heard was the sound of his index finger or his little finger, such a need that boy had to touch everything, skimming like lightning along the spines of my massive tomes, his finger a buzz of flesh and leather, of skin and pasteboard, a sound pleasing to the ear and sleep inducing, and I must really have fallen asleep because suddenly I closed my eyes (or maybe they'd been closed for a while) and I saw the Plaza de Santo Domingo with its archways, Calle Venezuela, the Palacio de la Inquisición, the Cantina Las Dos Estrellas on Calle Loreto, the Cafetería La Sevillana on Justo Sierra, the Cantina Mi Oficina on Misionero near Pino Suárez, where men in uniform and dogs and women weren't allowed in, with the exception of one woman, the only woman who ever went there, and I saw that woman walking those streets again, down Loreto, down Soledad, down Correo Mayor, down Moneda, I saw her hurry across the Zócalo, ah, what a sight, a woman in her twenties in the 1920s crossing the Zócalo as fast as if she were late to meet a lover or on her way to some little job in one of the stores downtown, a woman modestly dressed in cheap but pretty clothes, her hair jet-black, her back straight, her legs not very long but unutterably graceful like all young women's legs, whether they be skinny, fat, or shapely—sweet, determined little legs, and feet clad in shoes with no heel or the lowest possible heel, cheap but pretty and most of all comfortable, as if they were made for walking fast, for meeting someone or getting to work, although I know she isn't meeting anyone, nor is she expected at any job. So where is she going? Or is she going nowhere at all, and is this the way she always walks? By now the woman has crossed the Zócalo and she's walking along Monte Piedad to Tacuba, where the crowds are thicker and she can't walk as fast anymore, and she turns down Tacuba, slowing, and for an instant the throngs hide her from sight, but then she appears again, there she is, walking toward the Alameda, or maybe she's stopping somewhere nearer by, maybe she's headed to the post office, because now I can clearly see papers in her hands, they could be letters, but she doesn't go into the post office, she crosses the street to the Alameda and stops, as if she's trying to catch her breath, and then she keeps walking, at the same pace, through the gardens, under the trees, and just as there are women who see the future, I see the past, Mexico's past, and I see the back of this woman walking out of my dream, and I say to her: where are you going, Cesárea? where are you going, Cesárea Tinajero?

**Felipe Müller, Bar Céntrico, Calle Tallers, Barcelona, January 1978.**
For me, 1977 was the year I moved in with my girlfriend. We had both

just turned twenty. We found an apartment on Calle Tallers and went to live there. I was doing proofreading for a publishing house and she had a scholarship at the same school where Arturo Belano's mother was on scholarship. In fact, it was Arturo's mother who introduced us. Nineteen seventy-seven was also the year we traveled to Paris. We stayed in Ulises Lima's *chambre de bonne*. Ulises, I have to say, wasn't doing so well. The room was a dump. Between the two of us, my girlfriend and I tidied things up a little bit, but no matter how much we swept and mopped there was something there that couldn't be scrubbed away. At night (my girlfriend slept in the bed and Ulises and I slept on the floor) there was something shiny on the ceiling, a glow that came from the only window (which was crusted with dirt) and spread over the walls and ceiling like a tide of seaweed. When we got back to Barcelona we discovered that we had scabies. It was a blow. The only person we could have gotten it from was Ulises. Why didn't he warn us? my girlfriend complained. Maybe he didn't know, I said. But then I thought back on those days in Paris and I saw Ulises scratching himself, drinking wine straight out of the bottle and scratching himself, and the image convinced me my girlfriend was right. He knew it and he kept it to himself. For a while I held a grudge against him because of the scabies, but then it stopped mattering so much and we even laughed about it. Our problem was curing ourselves. We didn't have a shower at our apartment and we had to wash at least once a day with sulfur soap and then use a special cream, Sarnatín. So besides being a good year, 1977 was also the year when for a month or a month and a half we were constantly visiting friends who had showers. One of those friends was Arturo Belano. He didn't just have a shower, he had an enormous claw-foot bathtub that could easily fit three people. The problem was, Arturo didn't live alone, he lived with seven or eight other people, in a kind of urban commune, and some of them didn't like my girlfriend and me showering at their house. Well, it wasn't as if we really showered there much, in the end. Nineteen seventy-seven was the year Arturo Belano found work as a night watchman at a campground. Once I went to visit him. They called him the sheriff, and that made him laugh. I think that was the summer when the two of us broke with visceral realism. We were publishing a magazine in Barcelona, a magazine with hardly any funding and almost no distribution, and we wrote a letter announcing our resignation from visceral realism. We didn't repudiate anything, we didn't bad-mouth our friends in Mexico, we just said we weren't members of the group anymore. Mostly we were busy working and trying to get by.

**Mary Watson, Sutherland Place, London, May 1978.** In the summer of 1977 I traveled to France with my friend Hugh Marks. At the time I was reading literature at Oxford and I was living on a tiny scholarship. Hugh was on the dole. We weren't lovers, just friends. The truth is, we left London together that summer because we'd each been through a bad relationship, and we knew nothing like that could ever happen between us. Hugh had been dumped by a horrible Scottish girl. I had been dumped by a boy from university, someone who was always surrounded by girls and whom I thought I was in love with.

Our money ran out in Paris, but we weren't ready to go home, so we made our way out of the city somehow and hitched south. Near Orléans we were picked up by a camper van. The driver was German and his name was Hans. He was heading south too, with his wife, a Frenchwoman called Monique, and their little boy. Hans had long hair and a bushy beard. He looked like a blond Rasputin, and he'd been all the way around the world.

A little while later we picked up Steve, from Leicester, who worked in a nursery school, and a few miles on we picked up John, from London, who was out of work, like Hugh. It was a big van and there was plenty of room for all of us. Besides—I noticed this immediately—Hans liked to have company, people he could talk to and tell his stories to. Monique didn't seem quite as comfortable having so many strangers around, but she did what Hans told her to do and anyway she was busy taking care of the boy.

Just before we got to Carcassonne, Hans told us that he had business in a town in the Roussillon, and that if we wanted he could find good work for all of us. Hugh and I thought this was fantastic and we said yes straightaway. Steve and John asked what kind of work it was. Hans said we'd be picking grapes on land that belonged to one of Monique's uncles. And when we had finished picking her uncle's grapes we could go on our way with plenty of money, since while we were working our food and lodging would be free. When Hans finished we all agreed that it sounded like a good deal and we turned off the main road and made our way through one tiny village after another, all surrounded by vineyards, down rough tracks, a place like a labyrinth, I said to Hugh, a place (and this I didn't say) that in other circumstances would have frightened or repelled me. If, for example, I'd been alone instead of with Hugh, and Steve and John too. But I wasn't alone, luckily. I was with friends. Hugh is like a brother. And Steve and I hit it off right away too. John and Hans were another story. John was a kind of zombie and I didn't like him much. Hans was pure brute force, a megalomaniac, but you could count on him, or that's what I thought at the time.

When we got to Monique's uncle's it turned out there wouldn't be any work for a month yet. It must have been midnight when Hans gathered us all inside the van and explained the situation. The news wasn't good, he said, but he had an emergency solution. Let's not split up, he said, let's go to Spain and pick oranges. And if that falls through, we'll wait, but in Spain, where everything's cheaper. We told him we had no money and hardly anything left to eat. There was no way we could last for a month. At most, we had enough for three more days. Then Hans told us not to worry about money. He said he would cover our expenses until we were working. In exchange for what? said John, but Hans didn't answer. Sometimes he pretended that he didn't speak English. To the rest of us it really seemed like something heaven-sent. We told him we liked the idea. It was early August, and none of us wanted to go back to England just yet.

That night we slept in an empty house that belonged to Monique's uncle (there were at most thirty houses in the town, according to Hans, and half of them were the uncle's), and the next morning we headed south. Before we reached Perpignan we picked up another hitchhiker, a slightly chubby blond girl from Paris called Erica, and after a few minutes' discussion she decided to join our group. That is, come along to Valencia, work for a month picking oranges, then head back up to the Roussillon village in the middle of nowhere and work in the grape harvest with us. Like us, she didn't have much money, so the German would have to pay her keep too. Once Erica joined us, there was no more space in the van, and Hans told us he wouldn't stop for any more hitchhikers.

All day we drove south. Our group was cheerful but after so many hours on the road the main thing we wanted was a bath and a hot meal and nine or ten hours of solid sleep. The only one still going strong was Hans, who never stopped talking and telling stories about things that had happened to him or people he knew. The worst place in the van was the front passenger seat, meaning the seat next to Hans, and we all took turns there. When it was my turn we talked about Berlin, where I had lived the year I was nineteen. In fact, I was the only passenger who spoke some German, and Hans took the chance to speak his native language. We didn't talk about German literature, though, which is a subject I find fascinating, but politics, which always ends up boring me.

When we crossed the border Steve took my place and I took one of the back seats, where little Udo was sleeping, and from there I went on listening to Hans's endless talk, his plans to change the world. I think I've never met a stranger who was so generous to me and yet whom I disliked so much.

Hans was maddening, and an awful driver too. We got lost a few times, and spent hours driving all over some mountain, not knowing how to get back to the road that would take us to Barcelona. When we finally got there, Hans insisted that we go and see the Sagrada Familia. It was late, and we were all hungry and not in the mood to gaze at cathedrals, beautiful as they might be, but Hans was in charge and after driving in countless circles around the city we got there at last. We all thought it was pretty (except for John, who didn't have much appreciation for any kind of art), although we would certainly rather have stopped at a good restaurant and had something to eat. But Hans said the safest thing to eat in Spain was fruit, and he left us there, sitting on a bench in the plaza looking at the Sagrada Familia, and went off with Monique and their little boy in search of a fruit stall. When he hadn't returned after half an hour, as we watched the pink Barcelona sunset, Hugh said that he was probably lost. Erica said that the chances were just as good that he'd abandoned us. In front of a church, she added, like orphans. John, who didn't say much and when he did usually came out with something stupid, said that it was perfectly possible that at that very moment Hans and Monique were eating a hot meal in a good restaurant. Steve and I didn't say anything, but considering all the possibilities, I think it was John's theory that struck us as closest to the truth.

Around nine, when we were beginning to despair, we saw the van appear. Hans and Monique handed us each an apple, a banana, and an orange, and then he told us that he'd been parleying with the natives and in his opinion it was best that we postpone for the moment the trip to Valencia we had planned. If I'm remembering right, he said, there are some fairly reasonable campsites outside of Barcelona. For a modest daily sum we can rest for a few days, swim, sunbathe. It goes without saying that we all agreed, and we begged to go there straightaway. Monique, I remember, never said a word.

It still took us three hours to work out how to get out of the city. During that time Hans told us that when he was doing his military service, at a base near Lüneburg, he got lost at the controls of a tank and his superiors almost court-martialed him. Driving a tank, he said, is a lot more complicated than driving a van, I can tell you that, kids.

At last we made it out of the city and onto a four-lane highway. The campsites are grouped together in the same area, said Hans, tell me when you see them. The road was dark and all we could see to either side of it were factories and undeveloped land, and, farther back, some very tall, dimly lit buildings, seemingly set there at random and looking as if they were falling into premature ruin. A little later, however, we were in the woods and we spotted the first campsite.

But nothing was quite to Hans's liking, and since he was the one paying, we drove on through the woods until we saw a sign with a solitary blue star jutting out from amid some pine branches. I don't remember what time it was. The only thing I know is that it was late, and that all of us, including little Udo, were awake when Hans braked in front of the bar blocking the road. Then we saw somebody, or somebody's shadow, lifting the bar, and Hans got out of the van and went into the campsite office, followed by the man who had let us in. A little while later he came out again and leaned in the driver's window. The news he had to report was that the campsite didn't have tents to rent. We made some rapid calculations. Erica, Steve, and John didn't have a tent. Hugh and I both did. We decided that Erica and I would sleep in one tent and Steve, John, and Hugh would sleep in the other. Hans, Monique, and the boy would sleep in the van. Then Hans went back into the office, signed some papers, and got behind the wheel. The man who had let us in got on a very small bicycle and led us down ghostly streets, flanked by old caravans, to a corner of the campsite. We were so tired that we all went to sleep immediately, not even showering first.

The next day we spent on the beach, and that night, after dinner, we went for a drink on the terrace of the campsite bar. When I got there, Hugh and Steve were talking to the watchman we'd seen the night before. I sat next to Monique and Erica and surveyed our surroundings.

The bar, faithful reflection of the campsite, was almost empty. Three enormous pines grew out of the cement and in some places the roots had lifted the floor as if it were a rug. For an instant I wondered what I was really doing there. Nothing seemed to make sense. At some point that night Steve and the night watchman started to read poems. Where had Steve found them? Later, some Germans joined us (they bought us a round of drinks) and one did a perfect imitation of Donald Duck. Toward the end of the night, I remember seeing Hans arguing with the watchman. He was speaking in Spanish and seemed increasingly upset. I watched them for a while. At one moment I thought he was going to start crying. The night watchman seemed calm, though, or at least he wasn't waving his arms or making wild gestures.

As I was swimming the next day, still not recovered from drinking the night before, I saw him again. He was the only person on the beach, and he was sitting on the sand, fully dressed, reading the paper. As I came out of the water, I waved. He looked up and waved back. He was very pale and his hair was a mess, as if he had just woken up. That night, since we had nothing else to do, we got together at the bar again. John went to choose songs on the jukebox. Erica and Steve sat by themselves at a table some distance away. The Germans from the night before had left and we were the only ones on the terrace. Later the night watchman came. At four in the morning only Hugh, the watchman, and I were left. Then Hugh left and the night watchman and I went off to have sex.

The cabin where he spent the night was so small that anyone who wasn't a child or a dwarf couldn't lie down full-length inside it. We tried to make love on our knees, but it was too uncomfortable. Later we tried to do it sitting in a chair. Finally we ended up laughing, not having fucked. When the sun came up he walked me to my tent and then he left. I asked him where he lived. In Barcelona, he said. We have to go to Barcelona together, I said.

The next day the night watchman got to the campsite very early, long before his shift began, and we spent some time at the beach together and then we went walking to Castelldefels. That night we all got together on the terrace again, although the bar closed early, probably before ten. We looked like refugees. Hans had gone in the van to buy bread and then Monique made salami sandwiches for everyone. Before the bar closed, we bought beer. Hans gathered us around his table and said that we would move on to Valencia in a few days. I'm doing what I can for the group, he said. This campsite is dying, he added, staring at the night watchman. That night there was no jukebox, so Hans and Monique brought out a cassette player and for a while we listened to their favorite music. Then Hans and the night watchman got into an argument again. They were speaking in Spanish, but every so often Hans would translate what he was saying into German for me, adding remarks about the way the night watchman saw things. The conversation struck me as boring and I left them alone. While I was dancing with Hugh, though, I turned to look at them, and Hans was on the verge of tears again, as he had been the night before.

What do you think they're talking about? asked Hugh. Stupid things, probably, I said. Those two hate each other, Hugh said. They hardly know each other, I said, but later I thought about what he had said and I decided that he was right.

The next morning, before nine, the night watchman came to get me in my tent and we took the train from Castelldefels to Sitges. We spent the whole day in the town. As we were eating cheese sandwiches on the beach, I told him that the year before I'd written a letter to Graham Greene. He seemed surprised. Why Graham Greene? he said. I like Graham Greene, I said. I would never have thought so, he said, I still have a lot to learn. Don't you like Graham Greene? I said. I haven't read much by him, he said. What did you say to him in your letter? I told him things about my life and Oxford, I said. I haven't read many novels, he said, but I have read lots of poetry. Then he asked me whether Graham Greene had answered my letter. Yes, I said, he wrote me a very short but nice reply. A novelist from the country I'm from lives here in Sitges and I visited him once, he said. Which novelist? I asked, although I might as well have saved myself the trouble because I've read hardly any Latin American novelists. The night watchman said a name I've forgotten and then said that his novelist, like Graham Greene, had been very nice to him. So why did you go to see him? I asked. I don't know, he said, I didn't have anything to say to him and in fact I hardly opened my mouth once. You didn't say anything the whole time you were there? I didn't go alone, he said, I went with a friend, and he talked. But didn't you say anything to your novelist? Didn't you ask him any questions? No, said the night watchman, he seemed depressed and a little bit sick and I didn't want to bother him. I can't believe you didn't ask him anything, I said. He asked me something, the night watchman said, watching me curiously. What? I said. He asked me whether I had seen a film that was made in Mexico of one of his novels. And had you seen it? Actually, I had, he said, it so happened that I had seen it and liked it too. The problem was that I hadn't read the novel, and so I didn't know how faithful the film was to the text. And what did you say to him? I said. I didn't tell him I hadn't read it, he said. But you did tell him that you'd seen the movie, I said. What do you think? he said. Then I imagined him sitting opposite a novelist with Graham Greene's face and I thought he couldn't have said anything. You didn't tell him, I said. I did tell him, he said.

Two days later we packed up and left for Valencia. When I said goodbye to the night watchman I thought it would be the last time I saw him. As we drove, when it was my turn to sit next to Hans and talk to him, I asked him what they had argued about. You didn't like him, I said. Why? Hans was silent for a while, which was rare for him, thinking how to answer me. Then he just said he didn't know.

We were in Valencia for a week, going back and forth from one place to another, sleeping in the van and looking for work on the orange plantations, but we couldn't find anything. Little Udo got ill and we took him to the hospital. He only had a cold with a slight fever, aggravated by our living conditions. As a result, Monique's mood soured and for the first time I saw her get angry with Hans. One night we talked about leaving the van so that Hans and his family could continue on alone in peace, but Hans told us he couldn't let us go off on our own, and we realized he was right. The problem, as always, was money.

When we got back to Castelldefels it was pouring with rain and the campsite was flooded. It was midnight. The night watchman recognized the van and came out to meet us. I was sitting in one of the back seats and I saw how he looked in, trying to find me, and then he asked Hans where Mary was. Next he said that if he let us put the tents up they would probably flood, so he led us to a kind of wood-and-brick cabin at the other end of the site, a cabin built in the most haphazard way, with at least eight rooms, and we spent the night there. To save money, Hans and Monique drove to the beach. The cabin had no electricity and the night watchman went looking for candles in a room that was used to store cleaning supplies. He couldn't find them and we had to use cigarette lighters to see. The next morning he turned up at the cabin with a man in his fifties with wavy white hair, who said hello and then started to talk to the night watchman. Afterward, he told us that he was the owner of the campsite and that he was going to let us stay free for a week.

The van appeared that afternoon. Monique was driving, with Udo in one of the back seats. We told her that we were fine and they should come and stay with us, that it was free and there was plenty of room for everyone, but she told us that Hans had talked to her uncle in the south of France on the phone and the best thing would be for us all to go there right away. We asked her where Hans was, and she said he had business in Barcelona to take care of.

We spent one more night at the campsite. The next morning Hans turned up and told us that everything was settled, we could stay at one of Monique's uncle's houses until the grape harvest started, doing nothing and getting a tan. Then he pulled Hugh, Steve, and me aside and said that he didn't want John in the group. He's a pervert, he said. To my surprise, Hugh and Steve agreed. I said I couldn't care less whether John stayed with us or not. But who was going to tell him? We'll do it all together, the proper way, said Hans. That was the last straw, as far as I was concerned, and I decided to have no part in it. Before they left I informed them that I was going to stay in Barcelona for a few days with the night watchman, and I would see them a week later, in the town.

Hans made no objection but before he left he told me to be careful. He's bad news, he said. The night watchman? In what way? In every way, he said. The next morning I went to Barcelona. The night watchman lived in an enormous apartment on the Gran Vía with his mother and his mother's friend, a man twenty years younger than her. They only used the rooms at either end of the apartment. His mother and her lover lived at the back, in a room overlooking the courtyard, and he lived at the front, in a room with a balcony on the Gran Vía. In between there were at least six empty rooms, where the presence of the former inhabitants could be felt amid the dust and spiderwebs. John spent two nights in one of those rooms. The night watchman had asked me why John hadn't left with the others, and when I told him he looked thoughtful and the next morning he had brought John home with him.

Then John took the train to England and the night watchman started to work only at weekends, which meant we had more time to spend together. Those were a nice few days. We got up late, had breakfast in a local bar, a cup of tea for me and coffee or coffee with a shot of brandy for him, and then we spent our time wandering around the city until we were tired and had to come home. Of course, there were difficulties, the main one being that I didn't like him to spend his money on me. One afternoon, when we were in a bookshop, I asked him what he wanted and bought it for him. It was the only present I gave him. He chose a collection by a Spanish poet named De Ory; that name I do remember.

Ten days later I left Barcelona. He came to see me off at the station. I gave him my address in London and the address of the town in the Roussillon where we would be working, in case he felt like coming. Still, when we said goodbye I was almost sure I'd never see him again.

Alone for the first time in a long while, I found the train journey extremely pleasant. I felt comfortable in my own skin. I had time to think about my life, my plans, what I wanted and didn't want. Almost instantly I realized that being alone was not something that would bother me anymore. From Perpignan I took a bus that dropped me off at a crossroads, and from there I walked to Planèzes, where my traveling companions were presumably waiting for me. I got there a little before sunset, and the sight of the rolling vineyards, an intense greenish brown, made me feel even more at peace, if possible. When I got to Planèzes, however, the looks on people's faces didn't bode well. That night Hugh brought me up to date on everything that had happened while I'd been away. For reasons unknown, Hans had fought with Erica and now they weren't speaking. For a few days Steve and Erica had talked about the possibility of leaving, but then Steve fought with Erica too, and their escape plans were shelved. To top it all off, little Udo had been ill again and Monique and Hans had almost come to blows over him. According to Hugh, she wanted to take him to a hospital in Perpignan, and he was against the idea, arguing that hospitals made more people ill than they cured. The next morning Monique's eyes were swollen from crying, or maybe from Hans hitting her. Little Udo, in any case, had recovered on his own or been cured by the herbal potions his father gave him to drink. As far as Hugh was concerned, he said that he was spending most of his time drunk, since there was lots of wine and it was free.

During dinner that night, I didn't notice any alarming signs of tension, and the next day, as if everyone had only been waiting for me, the grape harvest began. Most of us worked cutting grapes. Hans and Hugh worked as porters. Monique drove the car that carried the grapes to a nearby village cooperative's presses. In addition to Hans's group, there were three Spaniards and two French girls with whom I soon became friends.

The work was exhausting and possibly the only good thing about it was that after the working day no one felt like fighting. Still, there were plenty of sources of friction. One afternoon Hugh, Steve, and I told Hans that we needed at least two more workers. He agreed but said that it was impossible. When we asked why, he said it was because he had contracted with Monique's uncle to finish the harvest with eleven workers, and not a single person more.

In the evenings, after our jobs were done, we usually went to the river to wash. The water was cold, but the river was deep enough to swim in and that was how we warmed up. Then we would soap ourselves, wash our hair, and go home for dinner. The three Spaniards were staying in another house and they led a separate life, except when we invited them to eat with us. The two French girls lived in the next village (where the cooperative was) and every night they rode home on their motorcycles. One was called Marie-Josette and the other was called Marie-France.

One night, when we had all had too much to drink, Hans told us that he had lived in a Danish commune, the biggest and best organized commune in the world. I don't know how long he talked. Sometimes he got excited and banged the table, or stood up, and sitting there we watched him grow, stretching to exaggerated heights, like an ogre, an ogre to whom we were bound by his generosity and our lack of money. Another night, when everyone was asleep, I heard him talking to Monique. She and Hans had the room above mine and that night they must have left the window open. Whatever the case, I heard them. They were speaking in French, and Hans was saying that he couldn't help it, that was all, he couldn't help it, and Monique was saying yes, he could, he had to try. I couldn't hear the rest.

One afternoon, when we were about to finish work, the night watchman turned up in Planèzes, and I was so happy to see him I told him that I loved him, and that he should be careful. I don't know why I said that, but seeing him walk down the main street, I had the sense that certain danger was looming over all of us.

Surprisingly, he said that he loved me too and that he wanted to live with me. He seemed happy. Tired—he'd arrived after hitching around almost the whole *département*—but happy. That afternoon, I remember, everyone except Hans and Monique went for a swim in the river, and when we took our clothes off and jumped in the night watchman stayed on the bank, fully clothed, in fact with too much on, as if he were cold despite how hot it was. And then something happened that might seem unimportant but in which I sensed the hand of something: fate or God. While we were in the water three migrant workers appeared on the bridge and stopped for a long time to watch us, watch Erica and me. They were two older men and a teenager, maybe grandfather, father, and son, dressed in ragged work clothes, and finally one of them said something in Spanish and the night watchman answered them. I could see their faces looking down and his face looking up (the sky was very blue), and after the first few words, more were exchanged. They were all talking, the three migrant workers and the night watchman. At first it seemed like questions and answers and then just like small talk, three people on a bridge and a tramp underneath it having a simple conversation, and it all went on while we, Steve, Erica, Hugh, and I, were washing and swimming back and forth, like swans or ducks, theoretically removed from the conversation in Spanish but partly the object of it, Erica and me in particular being a source of visual pleasure and expectation. But soon the migrant workers left (without waiting for us to get out of the water), and they said *adiós*, a word I do understand in Spanish, of course, and the night watchman said goodbye to them too, and that was as far as it went.

That night, during dinner, we all got drunk. I was drunk too, but not as drunk as everyone else. I remember that Hugh was shouting Dionysius, Dionysius. I remember that Erica, who was sitting next to me at the long table, grabbed me by the chin and kissed me on the mouth.

I was sure something bad was going to happen.

I told the night watchman we should go to bed. He ignored me. He was talking, in his terrible English mixed with French, about a friend who had disappeared in the Roussillon. Nice way to look for your friend, said Hugh, drinking with strangers. You aren't strangers, the night watchman said. Then they all started to sing, Hugh, Erica, Steve, and the night watchman, a Rolling Stones song, I think. A little later the two Spaniards who worked with us turned up. I don't know who had gone to get them. And all this time I was thinking: something bad is going to happen, something bad is going to happen, but I didn't know what it would be or what I could do to prevent it, except drag the night watchman to my room and make love with him or convince him to go to sleep.

Then Hans came out of his room (he and Monique had gone to bed early, soon after dinner) and asked us not to make so much noise. I remember this happened several times. Hans would open the door, look at us one by one, and tell us that it was late, that the noise was keeping him up, that we had to work the next day. And I remember that no one paid the slightest bit of attention. When he came out they would say yes, yes, Hans, we'll be quiet now, but when the door closed behind him they would immediately start shouting and laughing again. And then Hans opened the door, his nakedness covered only by a pair of white briefs, his long blond hair wild, and he said that the party was over, that we should get out that instant and go to our rooms. And the night watchman stood up and said: look, Hans, stop being an idiot, or something like that. I remember that Hugh and Steve laughed, whether at the look on Hans's face or at how awkward the sentence was in English. And Hans stopped for an instant, confused, and then roared: how dare you? that was all, and rushed at the night watchman. There was quite a distance between them, and we were all able to watch him in great detail, a seminaked colossus crossing the room at a near run, coming straight at my poor friend.

But then something happened that no one expected. The watchman didn't move from where he was sitting, remaining calm as the mass of flesh hurtled across the room toward him, and when Hans was just a few inches away a knife appeared in his right hand (in his delicate right hand, so different from a grape cutter's hand) and the knife rose until it was just under Hans's beard, in fact just barely embedded in its outer fringes, which stopped Hans cold, and Hans said, what is this? What kind of joke is this? in German, and Erica screamed, and the door, the door that Monique and little Udo were behind, opened a crack and Monique's head appeared chastely, Monique herself possibly naked. And then the night watchman started to walk forward in the direction from which Hans had come barreling, and the knife, I could see clearly since I was only a few feet away, slid into Hans's beard, and Hans began to retreat, and although to me it seemed as if they crossed the whole room back to the door behind which Monique was hiding, they actually only took three steps, maybe two, and then they stopped and the night watchman lowered the knife, looked Hans in the eye, and turned his back on him.

According to Hugh, that was the moment when Hans should have tackled him and overpowered him, but the truth is he stood still, not even noticing that Steve had come up to him and offered him a glass of wine, although he drank it like someone gulping air.

And then the night watchman turned and insulted him. He called him a Nazi, saying what were you trying to do to me, Nazi? And Hans looked him in the eye and muttered something and balled his fists and then we all thought he would lunge at the night watchman, this time nothing would stop him, but he controlled himself, Monique said something, he turned and answered her, Hugh went over to the night watchman and dragged him to a chair, probably poured him more wine.

The next thing I remember is that we all left the house and started to walk the streets of Planèzes in search of the moon. We were looking up at the sky: the moon was hidden by big black clouds. But the wind pushed the clouds eastward and the moon appeared (we screamed) and then disappeared again. At some point I thought we seemed like ghosts. I said to the night watchman: let's go home, I want to sleep, I'm tired, but he ignored me.

He was talking about someone who had disappeared and he was laughing and making jokes that no one understood. When the last houses were behind us, I thought it was time to go back, that if I didn't go back I wouldn't be able to get up the next day. I went over to the night watchman and gave him a kiss. A good-night kiss.

When I got back to the house all the lights were out and it was completely silent. I went over to a window and opened it. No one made a sound. Then I went up to my room, undressed, and got into bed.

When I woke up, the night watchman was sleeping beside me. I said goodbye and went to work with everyone else. He didn't respond, lying there as if he were dead. A smell of vomit floated in the room. By the time we got back, at noon, he was gone. I found a note on my bed, in which he apologized for his behavior the night before and said that I should come to Barcelona whenever I wanted, that he would be there waiting for me.

That morning Hugh told me what had happened the night before. According to him, after I left, the night watchman went crazy. They were close to the river and he kept saying someone was calling him, a voice on the other side of the river. And no matter how many times Hugh told him no one was there, that the only sound was the noise of the water,

and even that was faint, he kept insisting there was someone down below, on the other side of the river, waiting for him. I thought he was joking, said Hugh, but when I wasn't paying attention he went running
downhill, in the pitch darkness, toward what he thought was the river,
plunging blindly through scrub and brambles. According to Hugh, by
then only he and the two Spaniards we had invited to our party were left
from the original group. And when he took off downhill all three went
after him, but much more slowly, because it was very dark and the slope
was so steep that stumbling would have meant a fall and broken bones,
so he soon disappeared from sight.

Hugh thought he intended to throw himself into the river. But the
likeliest thing, he said, was that he would pitch headfirst onto a stone,
plentiful as they were, or trip over a fallen branch, or end up tangled in
a thornbush. When they reached the bottom they found him sitting in
the grass, waiting for them. And here comes the strangest part, said
Hugh, as I came up behind him he whirled around and in less than a
second I was on the ground, he was on top of me and his hands were
around my throat. According to him, it all happened so fast that he
didn't even have time to be afraid, but the night watchman really was
strangling him and the two Spaniards had gone off somewhere and
couldn't see or hear him and anyway, with his hands around his neck
(hands so unlike our hands at the time, which were all full of cuts),
Hugh couldn't make a sound, wasn't even able to shout for help, was
struck dumb.

He could've killed me, said Hugh, but the night watchman suddenly
realized what he was doing and let him go, saying he was sorry. Hugh
could see his face (the moon had come out again) and he realized that it
was, in his words, bathed in tears. And here comes the strangest part of
his story: when the night watchman let him go and said he was sorry,
Hugh started to cry too, because, according to him, he suddenly remembered the girl who had left him, the Scottish girl; he suddenly realized
that no one was waiting for him in England (except for his parents); he
suddenly understood something he wasn't able to explain to me, or
could only explain poorly.

Then the Spaniards turned up, smoking a joint, and they asked
Hugh and the night watchman why they were crying, and they both
started to laugh, and the Spaniards, such decent, normal people, said

Hugh, understood everything without having to be told and passed them the joint and then the four of them headed back together.

And how do you feel now? I asked him. I feel fine, he said, ready for the harvest to be over and to go home. And what do you think about the night watchman? I asked. I don't know, he said, that's your problem, you're the one who has to think about that.

When the work ended, a week later, I went back to England with Hugh. My original idea was to travel south again, to Barcelona, but when the harvest was over I was too tired, too ill, and I decided that the best thing would be to go back to my parents' house in London and maybe visit the doctor.

I spent two weeks at home with my parents, two empty weeks, not seeing any of my friends. The doctor said I was "physically exhausted," prescribed some vitamins, and sent me to the optician. He said I needed glasses. A little while later I moved to 25 Cowley Road, Oxford, and I wrote the night watchman several letters. I told him all about everything: how I felt, what the doctor had said, how I wore glasses now, how as soon as I had made some money I was planning to come to Barcelona to visit him, that I loved him. I must have sent six or seven letters in a relatively short period of time. Then term started, I met someone else, and I stopped thinking about him.

**Alain Lebert, Bar Chez Raoul, Port-Vendres, France, December 1978.** Back then I was living like I was in the Resistance. I had my cave and I read *Libération* in Raoul's bar. I wasn't alone. There were others like me and we hardly ever got bored. At night we talked politics and shot pool. Or we talked about the tourist season that had just ended. Each of us remembered the stupid things the others had done, the holes we'd dug ourselves into, and we laughed our heads off on the terrace of Raoul's bar, watching the sailboats or the stars, very bright stars that announced the arrival of the bad months, the months of hard work and cold. Then, drunk, we each headed off on our own, or in pairs. Me: to my cave outside of town, near the rocks of El Borrado. I have no idea why it's called that I never bothered to ask. Lately I've noticed a disturbing tendency in myself to accept things the way they are. Anyway, as I was saying, each night I'd go back alone to my cave, walking like I was already asleep, and when I got there I'd light a candle, in case I'd gotten turned around. There are more than ten caves at El Borrado and half had people in them, but I never ended up in the wrong one. Then I'd climb into my Canadian Impetuous Extraprotector sleeping bag and start to think about life, about the things you see happen right in front of you, things that sometimes you understand and other times (most of the time) you don't, and then that thought would lead to another, and that other thought would lead to one more, and then, without realizing it, I'd be asleep and flying along or crawling, whatever.

In the morning, El Borrado was like a commuter town. Especially in the summer. Every cave had people in it, sometimes four or more, and around ten o'clock everyone would start to come out, saying good morning, Juliette, good morning, Pierrot, and if you stayed in your cave, tucked away in your sleeping bag, you could hear them talking about the sea, the brightness of the sea, and then a noise like the clanking of pans, like somebody boiling water on a camp stove, and you could even hear the click of lighters and a wrinkled pack of Gauloises being passed from hand to hand, and you could hear the ah-ahs and the oh-ohs and the oh-la-las, and of course there was always some idiot talking about the weather. But over it all what you really heard was the noise of the sea, the sound of the waves breaking against the rocks of El Borrado. Then, as summer ended, the caves emptied, and there were only five of us left, then four, and then just three, the Pirate, Mahmoud, and me. And by then the Pirate and I had found work on the *Isobel* and the skipper told us we could bring our gear and move into the crew's quarters. It was nice of him to offer, but we didn't want to take him up on it right away, since we had privacy in the caves and our own space, while belowdecks it was like sleeping in a coffin and the Pirate and I had gotten used to the comforts of sleeping in the open air.

In the middle of September we started to go out on the Gulf of Lion and sometimes it was all right and other times it was a bust, which in terms of money meant that on the average day, if we were lucky, we made enough to pay our tab, and on bad days Raoul had to give us our toothpicks on credit. The bad streak got to be so worrisome that one night, out at sea, the skipper said maybe the Pirate was bad luck and everything was his fault. He just came out and said it, the way somebody might say it was raining, or he was hungry. And then the other fishermen said that if that was the way it was, why not throw the Pirate overboard right there, and then say at port that he was so drunk he'd fallen in? We were all talking about it for a while, half joking and half serious. Good thing the Pirate was too drunk to realize what the rest of us were saying. Around that time, too, the gendarmerie bastards came to see me at the cave. I was supposed to stand trial in a town near Albi for having ripped off a supermarket. This had happened two years before and all I'd taken was a loaf of bread, some cheese, and a can of tuna. But you can't outrun the long arm of the law. Every night I'd get drunk with my friends at Raoul's and shoot my mouth off about the police (even if I recognized some gendarme at the next table, drinking his pastis), society, and the way the justice system was always on your back, and I would read articles out loud from the magazine *Hard Times*. The people who sat at my table were fishermen, professional and amateur, and lots of young guys like me, city boys, summer fauna, washed up in Port-Vendres until further notice. One night, a girl whose name was Marguerite and whom I wanted to sleep with started to read a poem by Robert Desnos. I didn't know who the fuck Robert Desnos was, but other people at my table did, and anyway the poem was good, it got to you. We were sitting at an outside table, and lights were shining in the windows of the houses in town, but there wasn't even a cat on the streets and all we could hear was the sound of our own voices and a faraway car on the road to the station, and we were alone, or so we thought, but we hadn't seen (or at least I hadn't seen) the guy sitting at the farthest table. And it was after Marguerite read us the poem by Desnos—in that moment of silence after you hear something truly beautiful, the kind of moment that can last a second or two or your whole life, because there's something for everyone on this cruel earth—that the guy across the café got up and came over and asked Marguerite to read another poem. Then he asked if he could join us, and when we said sure, why not, he went to get his coffee from his table and then he emerged from the dark (because Raoul is always saving on electricity) and sat down with us and started to drink wine like us and bought us a couple of rounds, although he didn't look like he had money, but we were all broke so what could we do? we let him pay.

Around four in the morning we said our good nights. The Pirate and I headed for El Borrado. On our way out of Port-Vendres, we walked along quickly, singing as we walked. Then, where the road stops being a road and turns into a path that winds through the rocks to the caves, we slowed down, because even drunk as we were, we both knew one false step in the dark could be fatal with the waves breaking down below. There's usually plenty of noise along that path at night, but on this particular night it was mostly quiet, and for a while all we could hear was the sound of our footsteps and the gentle surf on the rocks. But then I heard a different kind of noise and I don't know why but I got the feeling there was someone behind us. I stopped and turned around, and looked into the dark, but I didn't see anything. A few feet ahead of me, the Pirate had stopped too and was standing there listening. Neither of us spoke, or even moved, and we just waited. From very far away came the whisper of a car and a muffled laugh, as if the driver had lost his mind. And still we didn't hear the noise that I'd heard, which was the sound of footsteps. It must have been a ghost, I heard the Pirate say, and we both started walking again. At the time, it was just him and me in the caves, because Mahmoud's cousin or uncle had come to get him so he could help get ready for the harvest in some village near Montpellier. Before we went to bed the Pirate and I smoked a cigarette, looking out to sea. Then we said good night and went off to our caves. I spent a while thinking about my stuff, the trip I had to make to Albi, the *Isobel*'s bad streak, Marguerite and the Desnos poems, an article about the Baader-Meinhof group I'd read that morning in *Libération*. Just when my eyes were closing I heard it again, the footsteps coming closer, stopping, the shadowy figure that made the footsteps and watched the dark mouths of caves. It wasn't the Pirate, that much I knew, I knew the Pirate's walk and it wasn't him. But I was too tired to get out of my sleeping bag or maybe I was already asleep and still hearing the footsteps, and at any rate, I thought that whoever was making the noise was no threat to me, no threat to the Pirate, and if it was somebody looking for a fight then he'd find one, but for that to happen he would have to come right into our caves and I knew that the stranger wouldn't come in. I knew he was just looking for an empty cave of his own where he could sleep.

The next morning I found him. He was sitting on a flat rock like a chair, watching the sea and smoking a cigarette. It was the stranger from Raoul's, and when he saw me come out of my cave he got up and offered me his hand. I don't like strangers to touch me before I've washed my face. So I stood there staring at him and tried to follow what he was saying, but all I could catch were stray words: "comfort," "nightmare," "girl." Then I headed off to Madame Francinet's orchard, where there's a well, and he stayed where he was, smoking his cigarette. When I got back he was still smoking (he smoked like a fiend) and when he saw me he got up again and said: Alain, let me buy you breakfast. I didn't remember telling him my name. As we were leaving El Borrado I asked how he'd found the caves, who had told him that there were caves at El Borrado where you could sleep. He said it was Marguerite, he called her the Desnos reader. He said that when the Pirate and I left he stayed behind with Marguerite and François and asked if there was somewhere he could spend the night. And Marguerite had told him that there were some empty caves outside of town where the Pirate and I lived. The rest was simple. He ran and caught up with us and then he chose a cave, and unrolled his sleeping bag, and that was it. When I asked him how he'd made his way across the rocks, where the road is so bad it isn't even a road, he said it hadn't been so hard, we were ahead of him and all he did was follow in our footsteps.

That morning we had coffee and croissants for breakfast at Raoul's, and the stranger told me his name was Arturo Belano and he was looking for a friend. I asked who his friend was and why he was looking for him here, in Port-Vendres. He took the last francs out of his pocket, ordered two cognacs, and started to talk. He said his friend had been living with another friend, his friend was waiting for something, a job, maybe, I can't remember, and his friend's friend had kicked his friend out of the house, and then when Belano heard about it he went looking for him. Where does your friend live? I said. He doesn't have a home, he said. And where do you live? I said. In a cave, he said, but he was smiling, like he was kidding. In the end, it turned out that he was staying with a professor at the University of Perpignan, in Collioure, nearby. You can see Collioure from El Borrado. And then I asked him how he'd learned that his friend had been kicked out. And he said: my friend's friend told me. And I asked: the same one who kicked him out? And he said: that's right. And I said: in other words, first he kicks him out and then he tells you? And he said: what happened was, he got scared. And I asked: what was it that scared this so-called friend? And he said: that my friend might kill himself. And I said: so you mean that even though he thought your friend might kill himself, this friend of your friend goes and kicks him out? And he said: that's right, I couldn't have put it better myself. And by then he and I were laughing and half drunk, and when he left, with his little pack over his shoulder, when he left to go hitchhiking around the closest towns, well, by then we were pretty good friends. We'd had lunch together (the Pirate joined us a little later), and I'd told him how unfairly I was being treated by the judges in Albi, and where we worked, and when it started to get dark he left and a week went by before I saw him again. And he still hadn't found his friend, but I think he'd more or less given up on it by then. We bought a bottle of wine and took a stroll around the port and he told me that a year ago he'd worked unloading ships. This time he was only here for a few hours. He was dressed better than before. He asked me how things were going with my case in Albi. He also asked me about the Pirate and the caves. He wanted to know if we were still living there. I told him no, that we'd moved to the boat, not so much because of the cold, which was creeping in, as for financial reasons. We didn't have a franc and on the boat we at least got hot meals. A little while later, he left. According to the Pirate, the guy was in love with me. You're crazy, I said. Why else would he come to Port-Vendres? What does he want here?

Halfway through October he showed up again. I was stretched out on my bunk daydreaming when I heard someone outside saying my name. When I went out on deck I saw him sitting on one of the piles. How's it going, Lebert, he said. I went down to say hello and we lit cigarettes. It was a cold morning, there was a light fog, and no one was around. Everybody, I guessed, must be at Raoul's. In the distance you could hear the sound of winches where a boat was being loaded. Let's get some breakfast, he said. All right, let's get some breakfast, I said. But neither of us moved. We saw a person walking toward us from the seawall. Belano smiled. Fuck, he said, it's Ulises Lima. We were quiet, waiting for him, until he got to where we were. Ulises Lima was shorter than Belano but sturdier. He was carrying a little pack over his shoulder like Belano. As soon as they saw each other they started to talk in Spanish, although their greeting, the way they greeted each other, was casual, flat. I told them I was heading over to Raoul's. Belano said all right, we'll come by later, and I left them there, talking.

The crew of the *Isobel* were all at the bar. They were looking gloomy, for good reason, although if you ask me it only makes it worse to get depressed when things are going badly. So I came in, took a look around to see who was there, made a joke in a loud voice or made fun of them, and then I ordered coffee and a croissant and a cognac and started to read *Libération* from the day before, since François usually bought it and left it at the bar. I was reading an article about the Yuyu of Zaire when Belano and his friend came in and headed over to my table. They ordered four croissants and the disappeared Ulises Lima ate all four. Then they ordered three ham and cheese sandwiches, one for me. I remember that Lima had a strange voice. He spoke French better than his friend. I don't know what we talked about, maybe the Yuyu of Zaire. All I know is that at a certain moment in the conversation Belano asked me if I could find work for Lima. I wanted to laugh. All of us here are looking for work, I said. No, said Belano, I'm talking about a job on the boat. On the *Isobel*? But it's the *Isobel*'s crew that's looking for work! I said. Exactly, said Belano. So there has to be a free spot. And in fact, two of the fishermen from the *Isobel* had found construction jobs in Perpignan, which would keep them busy for at least a week. We'd have to talk to the skipper, I said. Lebert, said Belano, I'm sure you can get my friend the job. There's no money in it, I said. But there's a bunk, said Belano. The problem is, I doubt your friend knows anything about fishing or boats, I said. Of course he does, said Belano, don't you, Ulises? A shitload, said Ulises. I sat there looking at them because it was obvious it wasn't true, all you had to do was look at their faces, but then I asked myself who was I to be so sure what people did. I've never been in America. What do I know about the fishermen over there?

That same morning I went to talk to the skipper and I told him I had a new crew member for him, and the skipper said: all right, Lebert, he can take Amidou's bunk, but only for a week. And when I got back to Raoul's there was a bottle of wine on Belano and Lima's table, and then Raoul brought out three plates of fish soup. It was pretty mediocre soup, but Belano and Lima kept going on about how it was French cooking at its best. I don't know if they were making fun of Raoul or themselves or if they were serious. I think they were serious. Then we ate a salad with boiled fish, and it was the same thing all over again, compliments to the chef, what a salad, what a classic Provençal salad, when it was obvious that it was hardly decent for Roussillon. But Raoul was happy and anyway they were paying cash, so what more could he ask? Then François and Marguerite came in and we invited them to sit with us and Belano made everyone eat dessert and then he ordered a bottle of champagne, but Raoul didn't have champagne and he had to settle for another bottle of wine, and a couple of the fishermen from the *Isobel* who were at the bar came over to our table and I introduced them to Lima. I said: this guy is going to work with us, he's a sailor from Mexico, yes sir, said Belano, the Flying Dutchman of Lake Pátzcuaro, and the fishermen said hello to Lima and shook his hand, although something about Lima's hand struck them as odd, of course it wasn't a fisherman's hand, that's something you notice right away, but they must have thought the same thing I did, which was who knows what the fishermen are like in a country that far away. The Fisher of Souls of the Casa del Lago of Chapultepec, said Belano, and things went on like that, if I'm remembering right, until six in the afternoon. Then Belano paid, said goodbye to everyone, and left for Collioure.

That night Lima slept on the *Isobel* with us. The next day was a bad day. It dawned cloudy and we spent all morning and part of the afternoon getting our tackle in order. Lima was assigned to clean the hold. It smelled so bad down below that we all avoided the job, the stink of rotten fish so strong it could knock a man off his feet, but the Mexican stuck it out. I think the skipper did it to test him. He told him to clean the hold. And I said: pretend you're doing it and come back up on deck in two minutes. But Lima went down and stayed there for more than an hour. At lunchtime the Pirate made a fish stew and Lima wouldn't eat it. Eat, eat, said the Pirate, but Lima said he wasn't hungry. He sat resting for a while, away from us, as if he was afraid he'd throw up if he watched us eat, and then he went back down into the hold. The next day, at three in the morning, we set out to sea. A few hours were all it took for us to realize that Lima had never been on a boat in his life. Let's just hope he doesn't fall overboard, said the skipper. Everybody looked at Lima, who was trying his best but didn't know how to do anything, and at the Pirate, who was already drunk, and all they could do was shrug their shoulders, without complaining, although I'm sure that at that moment they were envying their two fellow workers who'd managed to find construction jobs in Perpignan. I remember the day was overcast, with rain clouds rolling in from the southeast, but then the wind changed and the clouds lifted. At twelve we brought in the nets and there was practically nothing in them. At lunch we were all in a miserable mood. I remember Lima asked me how long things had been like this and I told him it had been at least a month. As a joke the Pirate suggested we set the boat on fire, and the skipper said that if he heard anything like that from him again he'd punch his lights out. Then we set sail northeast and in the afternoon we dropped the nets again in a place we'd never fished before. None of us was putting much into it, I remember, except the Pirate, who by that time of day was completely drunk and babbling in the control room, talking about a gun he'd stashed away someplace or staring for a long time at the blade of a kitchen knife and then looking around for the skipper and saying that every man had his limits, that kind of thing.

When it began to get dark we realized the nets were full. We hauled them in and there were more fish in the hold than on all the previous days combined. Suddenly we started to work like crazy. We kept heading northeast and we kept dropping the nets and bringing them in again full of fish. Even the Pirate did his best. We kept it up all night and all morning, not sleeping, following the shoal of fish as it moved toward the eastern end of the gulf. At six in the afternoon on the second day the hold was overflowing, something none of us had ever seen before, although the skipper said that ten years ago he'd seen a catch that was almost as big. When we got back to Port-Vendres, few of us could believe what had happened. We unloaded, slept a little, and went out again. This time we couldn't find the big shoal, but the fishing was very good. Those two weeks you could say we lived more at sea than in port. Afterward everything went back to normal, but we knew that we were rich, because our pay was a percentage of the catch. Then the Mexican said that he was finished, that he had enough money now to do what he needed to do and he was leaving. The Pirate and I asked him what he needed to do. Travel, he said. With what I've earned I can buy a plane ticket to Israel. I bet there's a girl waiting for you there, the Pirate said. More or less, said the Mexican. Then I went with him to talk to the skipper. The skipper didn't have the money yet. The fish-processing plants take a while to pay, especially if it's such a big haul, and Lima had to hang around a few more days. But he didn't want to sleep on the *Isobel* anymore. He disappeared for a couple of days. When I saw him again he told me he'd been to Paris. He'd hitchhiked there and back. That night the Pirate and I bought him dinner at Raoul's, and then he came to sleep on the boat even though he knew we were leaving Port-Vendres at four in the morning for the Gulf of Lion, trying to find that incredible shoal. We were at sea for two days and the fishing was only average.

After that, Lima decided he'd rather spend the time until he was paid sleeping in one of the El Borrado caves. The Pirate and I went with him one afternoon and showed him which caves were the best, where the well was, which path he should take at night so he wouldn't fall over the cliff: basically, the secrets of gracious living al fresco. When we weren't at sea we saw him at Raoul's. Lima made friends with Marguerite and François and a German in his forties, Rudolph, who worked in and around Port-Vendres doing odd jobs and who claimed he'd been a soldier in the Wehrmacht when he was ten and been given the Iron Cross. When everyone expressed disbelief, he brought out the medal and showed it to whoever wanted to see it: a blackened, rusty iron cross. And then he spat on it and swore in German and French. He held the medal ten inches from his face and talked to it like it was a dwarf and made faces at it and then he put it down and spat on it with rage or disgust. One night I said to him: if you hate the fucking medal so much why don't you fucking throw it in the fucking ocean? Then Rudolph got quiet, he seemed ashamed, and he put the Iron Cross away in his pocket.

And one morning we got our pay at last and that same morning Belano showed up again and we celebrated the Mexican's trip to Israel. Near midnight, the Pirate and I went with them to the station. Lima was taking the twelve o'clock train to Paris and from Paris he'd catch the first flight to Tel Aviv. I swear there wasn't a soul at the station. We sat on a bench outside, and a little while later the Pirate fell asleep. Well, said Belano, I get the feeling this is the last time we'll see each other. We'd been quiet for a long time and his voice startled me. I thought he was talking to me, but when Lima answered him in Spanish, I realized he wasn't. They talked for a while. Then the train came, the train from Cerbère, and Lima got up and said goodbye to me. Thank you for teaching me how to work on a boat, Lebert, that was what he said. He didn't want to wake the Pirate. Belano went with him to the train. I watched them shake hands and then the train left. That night Belano slept at El Borrado and the Pirate and I went to the *Isobel*. The next day Belano was gone from Port-Vendres.

# 9

**Amadeo Salvatierra, Calle República de Venezuela, near the Palacio de la Inquisición, Mexico City DF, January 1976.** Then I heard voices. They were talking to me, saying: Señor Salvatierra, Amadeo, are you all right? I opened my eyes and there were the two boys, one of them with the bottle of Sauza in his hand. I said: it's nothing, boys, I just drifted off. At my age sleep takes you when you least expect it and never when it should, I mean at midnight, when you're in your bed, which is just when the damn thing disappears or plays hard to get, and leaves old people wide awake. But I don't mind not being able to sleep because then I spend hours reading and sometimes I even have time to go through my papers. The trouble is I end up falling asleep anywhere, even at work, which is bad for my reputation. Don't worry, Amadeo, said the boys, if you want to take a nap, go ahead and take one, we can come back another day. No, boys, I'm all right now, I said, let's see, where's that tequila? And then one of them opened the bottle and poured forth the nectar of the gods into our respective glasses, the same ones we'd been drinking from before, which some consider a sign of slovenliness and others the ultimate refinement, since when the glass is, shall we say, glazed with mezcal, the tequila is more at ease, like a naked woman in a fur coat. *Salud*, then! I said. *Salud*, they said. Then I pulled out the magazine I still had under my arm and waved it before their eyes. Oh, those boys: they both grabbed for it, but they were too slow. This is the first and last issue of *Caborca*, I told them, Cesárea's magazine, the official organ, as they say, of visceral realism. Naturally, most of the contributors weren't members of the group. Here's Manuel, here's Germán, there's nothing by Arqueles, here's Salvador Gallardo, look: here's Salvador

Novo, here's Pablito Lezcano, here's Encarnación Guzmán Arredondo, here's yours truly, and next come the foreigners: Tristan Tzara, André Breton, and Philippe Soupault, eh? what a trio. And then I did let them take the magazine from me and it was with great satisfaction that I watched the two of them bury their heads in those old octavo pages, Cesárea's magazine, though cosmopolites that they were, the first thing they turned to were the translations, the poems by Tzara, Breton, and Soupault, in translations by Pablito Lezcano, Cesárea Tinajero, and yours truly, respectively. If I remember correctly, the poems were "The White Swamp," "The White Night," and "Dawn and the City," which Cesárea wanted to translate as "The White City," but I refused to let her. Why did I refuse? Well, because it was wrong, gentlemen. Dawn and the city is one thing and a white city is another, and that's where I put my foot down, no matter how fond I was of Cesárea back then. Not as fond as I should have been, I grant you, but truly fond of her all the same. Our French certainly left much to be desired, except maybe Pablito's. Believe it or not, I've lost my French completely, but we still translated, Cesárea in a slapdash way, if you don't mind my saying so, reinventing the poem however she happened to see fit, while I stuck slavishly to the ineffable spirit as well as the letter of the original. Naturally, we made mistakes, the poems wound up battered like piñatas, and on top of it all, believe me, we had ideas of our own, opinions of our own. For example, Soupault's poem and me. To put it simply: as far as I was concerned, Soupault was the greatest French poet of the century, the one who would go farthest, you understand, and now it's been years and years since I've heard a word about him, even though as far as I know he's still alive. Meanwhile, I knew nothing about Éluard and look how far he's gotten, every prize but the Nobel, yes? Did Aragon get a Nobel? No, I suppose not. They gave one to Char, I think, but he probably wasn't writing poetry at the time. What about Saint John Perse? I have no opinion on the subject. They couldn't possibly have given one to Tristan Tzara. The strange turns life takes! Then the boys started to read Manuel, List, Salvador Novo (they loved him!), me (no, don't read me, I said, it's too depressing, a waste of time), Encarnación, Pablito. Who was this Encarnación Guzmán? they asked. Who was this Pablito Lezcano, who translated Tzara and wrote like Marinetti and supposedly spoke French like a scholarship student at the Alliance Française? It was as if I'd returned to life, as if night had stopped in its tracks, peeked through the blinds, and said: Señor Salvatierra, Amadeo, you have my permission, get out there and declaim until you're hoarse—I mean, what I'm trying to say is that I didn't feel sleepy at all anymore, it was as if the tequila I'd just swallowed had met up with the Los Suicidas in my guts, in my obsidian liver, and was bowing down to it, as well it should, since certain class distinctions still exist. So we poured another round and then I started to tell them stories about Pablito Lezcano and Encarnación Guzmán. They didn't like Encarnación's two poems, they were very frank with me, the poems didn't hold water, and goodness, as it happened, that was close enough to what I thought and believed, that poor Encarnación was included in *Caborca* less because she was any good than because Cesárea had a weakness for her, the weakness of one poetess for another, though who knows what Cesárea saw in Encarnación or exactly what kind of compromises she made for Encarnación's sake or for her own sake. It's a normal part of Mexican literary life, publishing one's friends. And Encarnación may not have been a good poet (as I myself wasn't), she may not even have been a poet at all, good or bad (as I myself wasn't, alas), but she was a good friend of Cesárea's. And Cesárea would have taken bread or tortilla from her own mouth to feed her friends! So I talked to them about Encarnación Guzmán. I told them that she was born in Mexico City in 1903, approximately, according to my calculations, and that she met Cesárea outside of a movie theater, don't laugh, it's true, I don't know what the movie was, though it must have been something sad, maybe with Chaplin in it, but anyway, both of them were crying as they came out and they looked at each other and started to laugh, Cesárea probably raucously, she had her own peculiar sense of humor, it would erupt, just a spark or a glance and bam! all of a sudden Cesárea would be rolling on the ground laughing, and Encarnación, well, Encarnación probably laughed more discreetly. At the time, Cesárea was living in a tenement on Calle Las Cruces and Encarnación was living with an aunt (the poor thing had lost her father and mother), on Calle Delicias, I think. The two of them worked long days, Cesárea at the office of *mi general* Diego Carvajal, a general who had befriended the stridentists, although he didn't know a goddamn thing about literature, that's the truth, and Encarnación as a salesgirl in a dress shop on Niño Perdido. Who knows why they became friends, what they saw in each other. Cesárea didn't have a thing in the world, but one look at her told you that she was a woman who knew what she wanted. Encarnación was the complete opposite, very pretty, certainly, and always well dressed (Cesárea would put on the first thing she could find and sometimes she even wore a peasant's shawl), but insecure and fragile as a porcelain statuette in the middle of a bar fight. Her voice was, how to put it? piping, a slight voice, not forceful at all, though she raised it so that others could hear her, the poor thing being accustomed since she was a child to doubting her powers of speech, a shrill voice, essentially, and an extremely unpleasant one, which I only heard again many years later, in a movie theater, as it happened, watching a cartoon short in which a cat or a dog or maybe a little mouse, you know how clever those gringos are at animated pictures, talked just like Encarnación Guzmán. If she had been dumb, I think more than one of us would have fallen in love with her, but with that voice it was impossible. Besides, she had no talent. It was Cesárea who brought her to one of our meetings one day, when we were all stridentists or stridentist sympathizers. At first people liked her. So long as she was quiet, I mean. Germán probably flirted with her, and I might have too. But she was always distant and shy and stuck close to Cesárea. In time, however, she grew more confident, and one night she began to voice her opinions, offering criticism and making suggestions. And Manuel had no choice but to put her in her place. Encarnación, he said, you don't know the first thing about poetry, so why don't you be quiet? And that caused quite a hullaballoo. Cesárea, who would melt into the background when Encarnación was talking, as if she wasn't there, got up from her seat and told Manuel that that was no way to speak to a woman. But haven't you heard the silly things she's been saying? said Manuel. I heard, said Cesárea, who, remote as she might seem, never missed a single thing her friend and protégée did or said, and I still think an apology is in order. Well, then, I apologize, said Manuel, but from now on she'd better keep her mouth shut. Arqueles and Germán agreed with him. If she can't say anything worth saying, she shouldn't talk, was their argument. That shows a lack of respect, said Cesárea, depriving someone of her right to speak. Encarnación wasn't at the next meeting, and neither was Cesárea. The meetings were informal and no one missed them, or so it seemed. Only when the meeting was over and Pablito Lezcano and I set off along the streets of the city center, reciting the verse of the reactionary Tablada, did I realize that she hadn't been there, and also how little I knew about Cesárea Tinajero.

**Joaquín Font, El Reposo Mental Health Clinic, Camino Desierto de los Leones, on the outskirts of Mexico City DF, March 1979.** One day a strange man came to visit me. That's what I remember about the year 1978. I didn't get many visitors, just my daughter and a woman and another girl who said she was my daughter too, and who was remarkably pretty. This man had never been to see me before. I received him in the yard, facing north. Even though all the lunatics face south or west, I was facing north and that was how I received him. The stranger said good morning, Quim, how are you today? And I answered that I was the same as I'd been yesterday and the day before and then I asked him whether the architecture studio where I used to work had sent him, since the way he looked or talked was vaguely familiar to me. Then the stranger laughed and said how can you not remember me, man, can you possibly be serious? And I laughed too, to put him at ease, and I said yes, of course, my question was perfectly sincere. And then the stranger said I'm Damián, your friend Álvaro Damián. And then he said: we've known each other for years, man, how can this be? And to relax him, or so he wouldn't be sad, I said yes, now I remember. And he smiled (although his eyes didn't look happy) and he said that's better, Quim, it was as if he'd adopted the voice and concerns of my doctors and nurses. And when he left I guess I forgot him, because a month later he came back and he said I've been here before, I remember this asylum, the urinals are over there, this yard faces north. And the next month he said to me: I've been visiting you for more than two years, man, can't you try just a little harder to remember me? So I made an effort and the next time he came I said how are you, Mr. Álvaro Damián, and he smiled but his eyes were still sad, as if he were seeing everything from the vantage point of a great sorrow.

**Jacinto Requena, Café Quito, Calle Bucareli, Mexico City DF, March 1979.** It was really strange. I know it's just a coincidence, but sometimes these things make you think. When I told Rafael about it, he said it was all in my head. I said: have you realized, now that Ulises and Arturo don't live in Mexico anymore, there seem to be more poets? What do you mean more poets? said Rafael. Poets our age, I said, poets born in 1954, 1955, 1956. How do you know that? said Rafael. Well, I said, I get around, I read magazines, I go to poetry readings, I read book reviews, sometimes I even listen to reviews on the radio. And how do you make time for so many things now that you have a kid? said Rafael. Franz loves to listen to the radio, I said. I turn on the radio and he falls asleep. Are they reading poetry on the radio? said Rafael. He was surprised. Yes, I said. There's poetry on the radio and in magazines. It's like an explosion. And every day a new publishing house pops up that publishes new poets. And all of this right after Ulises left. Strange, isn't it? It doesn't seem strange to me at all, said Rafael. A sudden blossoming, the flowering of a hundred schools for no good reason, I said, and it just happens to be when Ulises is gone. Doesn't it seem like too much of a coincidence to you? Most of them are terrible poets, said Rafael, suck-ups to Paz, Efraín, Josemilio, and the peasant poets, complete garbage. I'm not saying that they aren't, I said, or that they are. It's the number of them that bothers me, the appearance of so many of them, and so suddenly. There's even some guy who's putting together an anthology of all the poets in Mexico. Yes, said Rafael, I already knew that. (I already knew he knew.) And he isn't going to include any of my poems, said Rafael. How do you know? I asked. A friend told me so, said Rafael, the guy doesn't want anything to do with the visceral realists. Then I said that what he'd said wasn't entirely true, because even if the asshole who was putting together the anthology had excluded Ulises Lima, he hadn't excluded María and Angélica Font or Ernesto San Epifanio or me. He does want poems from us, I said. Rafael didn't answer. We were walking along Misterios, and Rafael gazed toward the horizon, as if he could actually see it, although where it would have been there were houses, clouds of smoke, the afternoon haze of Mexico City. So are all of you going to be in the anthology? said Rafael after a long silence. I don't know about María and Angélica, I said, it's been a long time since I've seen them. Ernesto almost definitely will be. And I definitely won't be. So why won't you . . . ? said Rafael, but I didn't let him finish the question. Because I'm a visceral realist, I said, and if that asshole won't take Ulises, he's not getting me either.

---

**Luis Sebastián Rosado, a dark office, Colonia Coyoacán, Mexico City DF, March 1979.** Yes, it's an odd phenomenon, but its causes are very different from those put forward just a bit naïvely by Jacinto Requena. There really was a demographic explosion of poets in Mexico. This became clear beginning, say, in January 1977. Or January 1976. It's impossible to put an exact date on it. Among the various contributing factors, the most obvious are the country's more or less steady economic growth (from 1960 to the present day), the consolidation of the middle class, and an increasingly well-structured university, especially in the humanities.

Let's take a closer look at this new horde of poets, of which I'm a part, agewise at least. The great majority are students. A large percentage published their first poems in magazines associated with the university or the Ministry of Education, and their first books with university-affiliated publishing houses. A large percentage have also mastered (in a manner of speaking) a second language in addition to Spanish—usually English, or to a lesser extent French—and translate poets writing in those languages, nor is there any shortage of fledgling translators from the Italian, the Portuguese, or the German. Some combine work as amateur editors with their poetic endeavors, which in turn leads to the proliferation of various often valuable projects of an editorial nature. There are probably more young poets in Mexico now than there've ever been. Does this mean that poets under thirty today, say, are better than those who occupied that age bracket in the sixties? May we conceivably discover the equals of Becerra, José Emilio Pacheco, or Homero Aridjis among some of our most rabidly contemporary poets? That remains to be seen.

And yet Ismael Humberto Zarco's project strikes me as perfect. It was about time to bring out an anthology of young Mexican poets with the same high standards as Monsiváis's *La poesía mexicana del siglo XX*, memorable in so many ways! Or like *Poesía en movimiento*, the exemplary and paradigmatic work undertaken by Octavio Paz, Alí Chumacero, José Emilio Pacheco, and Homero Aridjis. I must admit that in a certain sense I felt flattered when Ismael Humberto Zarco called me at home and said: Luis Sebastián, I need your advice. Of course, advice or not, I knew for a fact that I was already included in the anthology, as a matter of course, you might say (the only thing I didn't know was how many of my poems would be selected), as were my friends, so my visit chez Zarco was initially only in an advisory capacity, in the event that some detail had escaped Zarco, meaning in this particular case some

255

magazine, some publication from the provinces, a name or two that the totalizing zeal of the Zarconian endeavor couldn't permit itself the luxury of overlooking.

But in the scant three days between Ismael Humberto's call and my visit, I happened to learn the number of poets the anthologist planned to include, an excessive number no matter how you looked at it, democratic but hardly realistic, remarkable as an experiment but mediocre as a crucible of poetry. And the devil tempted me, putting ideas in my head during the days between Zarco's call and our meeting, as if the wait (but what wait, my God?) were the Desert and my visit the instant when one opens one's eyes and sees one's Savior. And for those three days I was tortured by doubts. Or Doubts. But it was a torture, this I saw clearly, that brought satisfaction as well as suffering and doubt (or Doubt), as if the flames were a simultaneous source of pain and pleasure.

My idea, or my temptation, was this: to suggest to Zarco that he include Luscious Skin in the anthology. The numbers were in my favor, but everything else was against me. The rashness of this plan, I admit, at first seemed completely insane. I was literally scaring myself. Then it seemed completely pathetic. And later, when I was finally able to get a little distance from it and judge it more coolly (though only in a manner of speaking, of course), it struck me as noble and sad, and I seriously feared for my mental well-being. I did, at least, have the tact or cunning not to announce my plan to the principal interested party, in other words Luscious Skin, whom I saw three times a month, or twice a month, or sometimes only once or not at all, since his absences tended to be long and his appearances unexpected. Our relationship, from the time of our second and transcendental encounter at Emilito Laguna's studio, had followed an irregular course, occasionally in the ascendant (especially as far as I was concerned), and occasionally nonexistent.

We usually saw each other at an empty apartment that my family owned in Nápoles, although the way we met was much more complicated. Luscious Skin would call me at my parents' house and since I was almost never home he would leave a message, calling himself Estéfano. The name, I swear, was not something I suggested. According to him it was an homage to Stéphane Mallarmé, an author he had only heard of (like almost everything, incidentally) but whom he thought of as one of my tutelary spirits, by who knows what kind of strange mental association. Essentially, the name under which he left his messages was a kind of tribute to what he believed I held most dear. In other words, the false name concealed an attraction, a desire, a real need (I don't dare call it love) for me or of me, which, as the months went by and after endless contemplation, I realized filled me with rejoicing.

After he left his messages we would meet at the Glorieta de Insurgentes, at the entrance to a macrobiotic store. Then we would lose ourselves in the city, in coffee shops and bars to the north, near La Villa, where I didn't know anyone and where Luscious Skin had no qualms about introducing me to friends of his, male and female, who would show up in the most unexpected places and whose looks spoke more of a penitentiary Mexico than of otherness, although otherness, as I tried to explain to him, could take many forms. (Like the Holy Spirit, said Luscious Skin, that noble savage.) When night came, we took shelter like two pilgrims in cheap rooms or the lowliest hotels, though there was a certain splendor to them (at the risk of waxing romantic, I'd even say a certain *hope*), places in La Bondojito or on the edges of Talismán. Our relationship was spectral. I don't want to talk about love, and I'm reluctant to talk about desire. We had only a few things in common: some films, some folkloric figurines, the way he liked to tell tales of desperation, the way I liked to listen to them.

Sometimes, inevitably, he would give me one of the magazines published by the visceral realists. I never saw a poem of his in any of them. In fact, when it occurred to me to talk to Zarco about his poetry I had only two poems by Luscious Skin, both of them unpublished. One was a bad imitation of a bad poem by Ginsberg. The other was a prose poem that Torri wouldn't have disapproved of, a strange poem, in which he talked vaguely about hotels and fights. I imagined it was inspired by me.

The night before my meeting with Zarco I could hardly sleep. I felt like a Mexican Juliet, trapped in a sordid struggle between Montagues and Capulets. My relationship with Luscious Skin was secret, at least to the extent that the situation was under my control. By this I don't mean that no one in my circle of friends knew about my homosexuality, which I kept quiet but didn't hide. What they didn't know was that I was involved with a visceral realist (though Luscious Skin was hardly your typical visceral realist). How would Albertito Moore take the news that I was recommending Luscious Skin for the anthology? What would Pepín

Morado say? Would Adolfito Olmo think I'd gone crazy? And Ismael Humberto himself, so cold, so sarcastic, so apparently *above it all*, would he not see my suggestion as a betrayal?

So when I went to visit Ismael Humberto Zarco and showed him those two poems, which I came bearing like two precious objects, I was inwardly prepared to be asked all kinds of difficult questions. And so I was, since Ismael Humberto is no fool and he realized immediately that my protégé was from the wrong side of the fence, as they say. Luckily (Ismael Humberto is no fool, but he isn't God either), he didn't connect him to the visceral realists.

I fought hard for Luscious Skin's prose poem. I argued that since the anthology could hardly be called selective in terms of the number of poets published, it should make no difference to him whether we included something my friend had written. The anthologist was unyielding. He planned to publish more than two hundred young poets, most represented by a single poem, but not Luscious Skin.

At one point in our discussion he asked me the name of my protégé. I don't know his name, I said, exhausted and ashamed.

When I saw Luscious Skin again, in a moment of weakness I told him about my failed efforts to get one of his poems into Zarco's forthcoming book. In the way he looked at me, I saw something like gratitude. Then he asked me whether Pancho and Moctezuma Rodríguez were included in Ismael Humberto's anthology. No, I said, I don't think so. What about Jacinto Requena and Rafael Barrios? They're not either, I said. María and Angélica Font? No. Ernesto San Epifanio? I shook my head, although actually I didn't know, the name didn't sound familiar. And what about Ulises Lima? I looked steadily into his dark eyes and said no. Then it's better if I'm not in it either, he said.


**Angélica Font, Calle Colima, Colonia Condesa, Mexico City DF, April 1979.** At the end of 1977 Ernesto San Epifanio was admitted to the hospital to have a hole drilled in his skull so that he could be operated on for a brain aneurysm. A week later, they had to go back in because apparently they'd left something inside his head. The doctors had very little hope for this second operation. If they didn't operate he would die, and if they did operate he would die anyway, although his odds were slightly better. That was my understanding of it and I was the only person who was with him the entire time. Me and his mother, although somehow his mother doesn't count because her daily visits to the hospital turned her into the invisible woman: whenever she was there she was so quiet that even though she really did come into the room, even though she sat beside the bed, she never seemed to cross the threshold, or ever quite finish crossing the threshold, this tiny figure framed by the white opening of the doorway.

My sister María came a few times too. And Juanito Dávila, alias El Johnny, Ernesto's last love. The rest were brothers and sisters, aunts, people I didn't know, connected to my friend only by the most unlikely family ties.

No writers came, or poets, or ex-lovers.

The second operation lasted more than five hours. I fell asleep in the waiting room and dreamed of Laura Damián. Laura had come looking for Ernesto and then the two of us went for a walk in a eucalyptus forest. I don't know whether there really is such a thing, because I've never been in a eucalyptus forest, but the one in my dream was horrible. The leaves were silver and when they brushed my arm they left a dark, sticky mark. The ground was soft, like the needle-carpeted ground in pine forests, although the forest in my dream was a eucalyptus forest. The trunks of all the trees, without exception, were rotten and their stink was unbearable.

When I woke up in the waiting room there was no one there and I started to cry. How could it be that Ernesto San Epifanio was dying alone in a hospital in Mexico City? How could it be that I was the only person there, waiting for someone to tell me whether he had died or survived a terrible operation? When I was done crying I think I fell asleep again. When I woke up Ernesto's mother was beside me murmuring something I couldn't understand. It took me a while to realize that she was just praying. Then a nurse came in and said that everything had gone well. The operation was a success, she explained.

A few days later Ernesto was discharged and went home. I had never been to his house before. We always saw each other at my house or at other friends' houses. But from then on I began to visit him at home.

The first few days he didn't even talk. He looked around and blinked but didn't talk. He didn't seem to hear anything either. And yet the doctor had recommended that we talk to him, that we treat him as if nothing had happened. So I did. The first day I looked in his bookcase for a book

I knew for sure that he liked and I started to read it out loud. It was Valéry's *Cemetery by the Sea,* and he didn't show the slightest sign that he recognized it. I read it and he looked at the ceiling or the walls or my face, and his real self wasn't there. Then I read him a collection of poems by Salvador Novo and the same thing happened. His mother came into the room and touched my shoulder. Don't wear yourself out, miss, she said.

Little by little, however, he began to distinguish sounds, bodies. One afternoon he recognized me. Angélica, he said, and he smiled. I had never seen such a horrible, pathetic, crooked smile. I started to cry. But he didn't seem to notice that I was crying and kept smiling. He looked like a corpse. The trephination scars weren't hidden by his hair yet, which was maddeningly slow to grow back.

A little later he started to talk. He had a very high-pitched, thin little voice, like a flute. Gradually it grew stronger, but no less shrill. In any case, it wasn't Ernesto's voice, that I was sure of. It was like the voice of a feebleminded adolescent, an ignorant adolescent on his deathbed. His vocabulary was limited. He had a hard time coming up with the words for some things.

One afternoon I got to his house and his mother let me in and then led me to her room, in such a state of agitation that at first I thought my friend must have taken a turn for the worse. But it was a motherly flurry of happiness. He's cured, she told me. I didn't understand what she meant. I thought she was talking about Ernesto's voice or saying that Ernesto's mind had gotten sharper. How is he cured? I said, trying to get her to let go of my arms. It took her a while to say what she meant, but in the end she had to come out with it. Ernesto isn't a fairy anymore, miss, she said. Ernesto isn't what? I said. At that moment his father came into the room, and after asking us what we were doing in there, he declared that his son had finally been cured of his homosexuality. He didn't say it in those exact words, and I didn't want to answer or ask any more questions, so I got out of that horrible room as quickly as I could. Still, before I went into Ernesto's room, I heard his mother say: every cloud has a silver lining.

Of course, Ernesto was still a homosexual even though sometimes he didn't remember very well what that meant. Sexuality, for him, had become something remote, something he knew was pleasurable and exciting, but remote. One day Juanito Dávila called me to say that he was

going north, to work, and that I should tell Ernesto goodbye for him because he didn't have the heart. From then on there were no more lovers
in Ernesto's life. His voice changed a little, but not enough: he didn't
speak, he wailed or moaned, and when he did, everyone except for his
mother and me—his father and the neighbors paying their endless obligatory visits—would flee, which was ultimately a relief, so much so that
once I thought Ernesto was wailing on purpose to drive away all that terrible politeness.

As the months went by, I began to leave more time between my visits too. Having gone to see him every day when he was just out of the
hospital, I visited less frequently once he started to talk and walk up and
down the hall. And yet I called him every night, no matter where I was.
We had some crazy conversations. Sometimes I was the one who would
talk on and on, telling stories, true stories, although they went barely
skin-deep, about the sophisticated Mexico City life (a way of forgetting
that we lived in Mexico) that I was getting to know back then, the parties,
the drugs I took, the men I slept with, and other times he was the one
who would talk, reading stories to me that he'd cut out of the paper that
day (a new hobby, probably suggested by the therapists who were treating
him, who knows), telling me what he'd had to eat, the people who'd
come to visit, something his mother had said that he'd saved up for the
end of the conversation. One afternoon I told him that Ismael Humberto
Zarco had chosen one of his poems for his anthology, which had just
come out. What poem? said that little bird voice of his, that Gillette
blade of a voice that tore at my heart. I had the book beside me. I told
him. Did I write that poem? he said. It struck me that he was joking, why
I'm not sure, maybe because his voice sounded so much deeper than
usual. His jokes had been like that before, innocent, almost impossible
to distinguish from whatever else he was saying. But he wasn't joking.
That week I found time that I didn't have and went to see him. A friend,
a new friend, drove me to his house but didn't want to come in. Wait for
me here, I said, this neighborhood is dangerous and when we come back
we might find ourselves without a car. It seemed strange to him, but he
didn't say anything. Around that time, I had developed a well-deserved
reputation in the circles I moved in for being eccentric. As it happened,
I was right: recently Ernesto's neighborhood had been going downhill.
As if the aftereffects of his operation were visible in the streets, in the
people without work, the petty thieves who would come out at seven in

the evening to sit in the sun, like zombies (or messengers with no message or an untranslatable message) automatically primed to kill another evening in Mexico City.

Ernesto hardly paid any attention to the book, of course. He looked for his poem and said: oh. I don't know if he suddenly recognized it or if he was confused. Then he started to tell me the same kind of things he told me on the phone.

When I came out my friend was standing beside the car smoking a cigarette. I asked whether anything had happened while I was gone. Nothing, he said, it's dead quiet out here. But it couldn't have been so quiet because his hair was disheveled and his hands were shaking.

I never saw Ernesto again.

One night he called me and recited a poem by Richard Belfer. One night I called him, from Los Angeles, and told him that I was sleeping with the theater director Francisco Segura, aka La Vieja Segura, who was at least twenty years older than me. How exciting, said Ernesto. La Vieja must be an intelligent man. He's talented, not intelligent, I said. What's the difference? he said. I sat there thinking how to answer and he waited for me to speak and for a few seconds neither of us said anything. I wish I could be with you, I told him before I said goodbye. Me too, said that voice like a bird from another dimension. A few days later his mother called and told me that he had died. An easy death, she said, while he was sitting at home in a chair in the sun. He fell asleep like a little angel. What time of day did he die? I asked. At about five, after lunch.

Of his old friends, I was the only one who went to his burial, in one of the patchwork cemeteries on the north side of the city. I didn't see any poets, ex-lovers, or editors of literary magazines. Lots of relatives and family friends and possibly every single one of the neighbors. Before I left the cemetery, two teenagers came up to me and tried to lead me somewhere. I thought they were going to rape me. Only then did I feel rage and pain at Ernesto's death. I pulled a switchblade out of my purse and said: I'll kill you, you little creeps. They went running and I chased them for a while down two or three cemetery streets. When I finally stopped, another funeral procession appeared. I put the knife in my bag and watched as they lifted the coffin into its niche, very carefully. I think it was a child. But I couldn't say for sure. Then I left the cemetery and went to have drinks with a friend at a bar downtown.

# 10

**Norman Bolzman, sitting on a bench in Edith Wolfson Park, Tel Aviv, October 1979.** I've always been sensitive to the pain of others, always tried to feel a part of everyone else's suffering. I'm Jewish, a Mexican Jew, and I know the history of my two peoples. That says it all, I think. I'm not trying to justify myself. I'm just trying to tell a story. Maybe I'm also trying to understand its hidden workings, workings I wasn't aware of at the time but that weigh on me now. Still, my story won't be as coherent as I'd like. And my role in it will flicker like a speck of dust between the light and the dark, between laughter and tears, exactly like a Mexican soap opera or a Yiddish melodrama.

Everything began last February. It was a gray afternoon, fine as a shroud, the kind that brings a shudder to the skies of Tel Aviv. Someone rang the bell of our apartment on Hashomer Street. When I opened the door, the poet Ulises Lima, leader of the self-proclaimed visceral realists, was standing there before me. I can't say I knew him, in fact I'd only met him once, but Claudia used to tell me stories about him, and Daniel read me one of his poems once. Literature isn't my specialty. It may be that I was never able to appreciate the quality of his work. In any case, the man in front of me looked less like a poet than a bum.

We didn't get off to a good start, I admit. Claudia and Daniel were at the university and I had to study, so I let him in, made him a cup of tea, and then went into my room and shut the door. For a minute everything seemed back to normal. I immersed myself in the philosophers of the Marburg School (Natorp, Cohen, Cassirer, Lange) and in some commentaries on Solomon Maimon, indirectly devastating to the Marburg philosophers. But after a while, it might have been twenty minutes or two hours, my mind went blank and in the middle of that whiteness the face of Ulises Lima, the recent arrival, began to take shape, and even though in my mind everything was white it took me a long time, I don't know how long, to make out his features precisely, as if Ulises's face were getting darker instead of brightening in the light.

When I came out he was sprawled in an armchair, asleep. I stood there watching him for a while. Then I went back into my room and tried to concentrate on my work. I couldn't. I should have gone out, but it seemed wrong to leave him alone. I thought about waking him up. I thought that maybe I should follow his example and go to sleep too, but I was too afraid or too embarassed, I can't say which. At last I took a book from the shelf, Natorp's *Religion at the Limits of Humanity,* and sat facing him on the sofa.

It was around ten when Claudia and Daniel came in. I had cramps in both legs and my whole body ached. Worse, nothing I'd read had made any sense, but when I saw them come in the door I somehow managed to raise my finger to my lips, why I don't know, maybe because I didn't want Ulises to wake up before Claudia and I could talk, maybe because I'd grown used to hearing the steady rhythm of his breath while he was sleeping. But when Claudia, after a few seconds of hesitation, saw Ulises in the armchair, it was all for nothing. The first thing she said was *carajo* or *bolas* or *cámara* or *chale,* because even though Claudia was born in Argentina and came to Mexico when she was sixteen, deep down she's always felt Mexican. Or so she says, who knows. And Ulises woke up with a start and the first thing he saw was Claudia smiling at him from less than a foot away, and then he saw Daniel, and Daniel was smiling too. What a surprise.

That night we went out to dinner in his honor. At first I said that I really couldn't go, that I had to finish with my Marburg School, but Claudia wouldn't let me get out of it. Don't even think about it, Norman, let's not start. Dinner was fun, despite my fears. Ulises told us about his adventures and we all laughed, or rather he told Claudia about his adventures, but in such a charming way, in spite of how sad everything he was telling us really was, that we all laughed, which is the best you can do at times like that. Then we went walking home along Arlozorov, taking deep breaths of fresh air. Daniel and I were ahead, quite a long way ahead, and Claudia and Ulises were behind, talking as if they were in Mexico City again and they had all the time in the world. And when

Daniel told me not to walk so fast, asking why I was in such a hurry, I quickly changed the subject, asking him what he'd been doing, telling him the first thing that came to mind about crazy old Solomon Maimon, anything to put off what was coming next, the moment I was afraid of. I would happily have run away that night. I wish I had.

When we got to the apartment we still had time for a cup of tea. Then Daniel looked at the three of us and said he was going to bed. When I heard his door close I said the same thing and went into my room. Lying on my bed with the light off, I heard Claudia talking to Ulises for a while. Then the door opened and Claudia turned on the light, asked me whether I had class the next day, and started to undress. I asked her where Ulises Lima was. Sleeping on the sofa, she said. I asked her what she'd told him. I didn't tell him anything, she answered. Then I undressed too, got in bed, and squeezed my eyes shut.

For two weeks a new order reigned in our house. Or at least that was how it seemed to me, deeply disturbed as I was by small details that perhaps I hadn't noticed before.

Claudia, who for the first few days tried to ignore the new situation, finally came to terms with reality too, and said that she was beginning to feel suffocated. On the morning of the second day he was with us, while Claudia was brushing her teeth, Ulises told her that he loved her. Claudia's answer was that she already knew. I came here because of you, Ulises said, I came because I love you. Claudia's answer was that he could have written her a letter. Ulises found that highly encouraging, and he wrote a poem that he read to Claudia at lunch. When I got up discreetly from the table, not wanting to hear it, Claudia asked me to stay and Daniel seconded the request. The poem was essentially a collection of fragments about a Mediterranean city, Tel Aviv, I guess, and a bum or a mendicant poet. I thought it was beautiful and I told him so. Daniel agreed. Claudia was quiet for a few minutes, with a thoughtful expression on her face, and then she said that we were right, she wished she could write such beautiful poems. For a minute I thought everything would work out, that we were all going to be able to get along, and I volunteered to go buy a bottle of wine. But Claudia said that the next day she had to be at the university first thing, and ten minutes later she had shut herself in our room. Ulises, Daniel, and I talked for a while and had another cup of tea, then each of us went to his room. Around three I got up to go to the bathroom and as I tiptoed through the living room I heard Ulises crying. I don't think he realized I was there. He was lying facedown, I guess. From where I was, he was just a shape on the sofa, a shape covered with a blanket and an old coat, a heap, a lump of flesh, a shadowy figure, heaving and pathetic.

I didn't tell Claudia. In fact, it was around then that I first began to hide things from her, keep parts of the story from her, lie to her. As far as our daily lives as students were concerned, things didn't change at all for her, or if they did she did her best not to let it show. When Ulises first came to Tel Aviv, Daniel was his constant companion, but after two or three weeks Daniel had to buckle down again too, or risk jeopardizing his exams. Little by little, I became the only one still available to Ulises. But I was busy with neo-Kantianism, the Marburg School, Solomon Maimon, and my head was a mess because each night, when I got up to pee, I'd find Ulises crying in the dark, and that wasn't the worst of it, the worst was that some nights I thought: today I'll *see* him cry—see his face, I mean, because until then I'd only heard him, and who could be sure that what I was hearing was crying, and not, for example, the heavy breathing of someone in the middle of jerking off? And when I thought about seeing his face, I imagined it raised in the dark, a face bathed in tears, a face touched by the light of the moon filtering through the living room windows. And that face was so desolate that from the very moment I sat up in bed in the dark, listening to Claudia's raspy breathing beside me, a weight like a rock settled on my heart and I felt like crying too. And sometimes I spent a long time sitting there in bed, repressing my urge to go to the bathroom, repressing my urge to cry, all for fear that it would happen that night, that he would lift his face in the dark and I would see it.

Not to mention sex, my sex life, which was shot from the day he came through the door of our apartment. I just couldn't do it. Or I mean I could, but I didn't want to. The first time we tried, on the third night, I think, Claudia asked what was wrong with me. Nothing's wrong, I said, why do you ask? Because you're as silent as the dead, she said. And that was how I felt, not like the dead but like a reluctant guest in the world of the dead. I had to stay quiet. Not moan, not cry out, not pant, come with extreme circumspection. And even Claudia's moans, which used to arouse me so much, became unbearable. They made me frantic (although I was always careful not to let her know), they grated in my ears, and I tried to muffle them by covering her mouth with my hand or my lips. In a word, making love became torture, something that by the third or fourth time I would do anything to avoid or postpone. I was always the last to go to bed. I would stay up with Ulises (who never seemed to get tired anyway) and we would talk about anything. I would ask him to read me what he'd written that day, not caring whether it was poems in which his love for Claudia was painfully obvious. I liked them anyway. Of course, I preferred the other ones, the ones in which he talked about the new things he saw each day when he was left alone and went out to wander Tel Aviv, Giv'at Rokach, Har Shalom, the alleyways of the old port city of Jaffa, the university campus, or Yarkon Park, or the ones in which he remembered Mexico, Mexico City, so far away, or the ones that were formal experiments, or seemed to me like formal experiments. Any of them, except the ones about Claudia. But not for my sake, not because they might hurt me, or her, but because I was trying to avoid the proximity of *his* pain, *his* mulish stubbornness, *his* profound stupidity. One night I told him. I said: Ulises, why are you doing this to yourself? He pretended not to hear me, giving me a sidelong look (which made me remember, as at least a hundred other thoughts flashed through my mind, the look of a dog I'd had when I was a boy in Colonia Polanco, the dog my parents put to sleep when suddenly it started to bite), and then he kept on talking as if I hadn't said a word.

That night, when I went to bed, I made love to Claudia as she slept, and when I was at last able to reach the proper state of arousal, which wasn't easy, I moaned or cried out.

Then there was the question of money. Claudia, Daniel, and I were in school and we each received a monthly allowance from our parents. In Daniel's case this allowance was barely enough to live on. In Claudia's case it was more generous. Mine fell somewhere in between. If we pooled our money, we could pay for the apartment, our classes, and our food and have enough for the movies or the theater or to buy books in Spanish at the Cervantes Bookstore, on Zamenhof. But having Ulises there upset everything, because after a week he had hardly any money left and all of a sudden we had another mouth to feed, as the sociologists say. Still, as far as I was concerned, it was no big deal. I was prepared to give up certain luxuries. Daniel didn't care either, although he continued to live his life exactly as he had before. It was Claudia—who would've thought?—who chafed at the new situation. At first she tackled the problem coolly and practically. One night she told Ulises that he needed to look for work or ask to have money sent from Mexico. I remember that Ulises sat there looking at her with a lopsided smile and then said he would look for work. The next night, during dinner, Claudia asked if he'd found work. Not yet, said Ulises. But did you go out and look? asked Claudia. Ulises was washing the dishes and he didn't turn around when he said yes, he'd gone out and looked but had no luck. I was sitting at the head of the table and I could see his face in profile, and it looked to me like he was smiling. Fuck, I thought, he's smiling, smiling out of sheer happiness. As if Claudia were his wife, a nagging wife, a wife who worried about her husband finding work, and he liked that. That night I told Claudia to leave him alone, that he was already having a hard enough time without her getting on his case about work. Anyway, I said, what kind of job do you expect him to find in Tel Aviv? as a construction worker? a porter at the market? a dishwasher? What do you know, Claudia said to me.

It was the same story the next night, of course, and the next, and each time Claudia was more tyrannical, hounding him, goading him, backing him into a corner, and Ulises always responded in the same way, calmly, resignedly, and, yes, happily. Whenever we were at the university he would go out and look for work, asking here or there but never finding anything, although the next day he would try again. And it got to the point that after dinner Claudia would spread the paper on the table and look for job listings, writing them down on a piece of paper and telling Ulises where he had to go, which bus to take or which was the shortest way to walk, because Ulises didn't always have money for the bus and Claudia said it wasn't necessary to give him money because he liked to walk, and when Daniel or I would say but how can he walk to Ha'Argazim, for example, or Yoreh Street, or Petah Tikva or Rosh Ha'ayin, where they needed construction workers, she would tell us (in front of him, as he watched her and smiled like a whipped husband, but a husband, still) about his wanderings around Mexico City, how he would walk from UNAM to Ciudad Satélite, and at night too, which was almost like from one end of Israel to the other. And things kept getting worse. Ulises had no money left now and no job either, and one night Claudia came home in a rage, saying that her friend Isabel Gorkin had seen Ulises sleeping in Tel Aviv North, the train station, or begging on Avenue Hamelech George or along the Gan Meir, then saying that this was unacceptable, emphasizing the word *unacceptable* in a particular way, as if begging in Mexico City were permissible, but not in Tel Aviv, and worst of all was that she said this to Daniel and me, but with Ulises right there, sitting in his place at the table, listening as if he were the invisible man, and then Claudia said that Ulises was lying to us, that he wasn't looking for work at all, and that we had to decide what we were going to do about it.

That night Daniel shut himself in his room earlier than usual and a few minutes later I followed his example, although I didn't go to my room (the room I shared with Claudia) but outside, where I could wander around and breathe freely, far from the harpy I was in love with. When I got back, around twelve, the first thing I heard when I opened the door was music, a song by Cat Stevens that Claudia especially liked, and then voices. Something about the voices made me keep quiet and not walk on into the living room. It was Claudia's voice and then Ulises's voice, but not their normal, everyday voices, or at least not Claudia's everyday voice. It didn't take me long to realize that they were reading poems. They were listening to Cat Stevens and reading short poems, deadpan and sad, luminous and ambiguous, slow and quick as lightning, poems about a cat rubbing itself up against Baudelaire's legs and a cat, maybe the same cat, rubbing itself up against the legs of an insane asylum! (Later I found out that they were poems by Richard Brautigan translated by Ulises.) When I came into the living room, Ulises raised his head and smiled at me. Without saying anything, I sat down next to them, rolled a cigarette, and told them to please continue. When we went to bed I asked Claudia what had happened. Sometimes Ulises makes me crazy, that's all, she said.

A week later, Ulises left Tel Aviv. When she said goodbye to him, Claudia shed a few tears and then she shut herself in the bathroom for a long time. One night, not even three days later, he called us from the Walter Scholem kibbutz. One of Daniel's cousins, Mexican like us, lived there, and the kibbutz members had taken Ulises in. He told us that he was working in an olive oil factory. How are you liking it? asked Claudia. Not much, said Ulises, it's boring work. A little while later Daniel's cousin called and said that Ulises had been kicked out. Why? Because he wouldn't work. We almost had a fire because of him, said Daniel's cousin. And where is he now? asked Daniel, but his cousin had no idea, in fact, that was why he was calling us, to find out where Ulises was so that he could make him pay the hundred-dollar tab he had run up at the kibbutz store. We spent a few nights waiting for him to show up, but Ulises didn't come. What did arrive was a letter from Jerusalem. I swear on my honor or whatever, it was completely unintelligible. The sole fact that it reached us is proof of the excellence of the Israeli postal service, no question about it. It was addressed to Claudia, but the apartment number wasn't right and the street name contained three misspellings, which was a kind of record. That was on the outside. Inside, it was worse. The letter, as I said, was impossible to read, although it was written in Spanish, or at least that was the conclusion Daniel and I came to. But it might just as well have been written in Aramaic. About that, about Aramaic, I remember something strange. That night, as Daniel and I tried to decipher the letter, Claudia, who after glancing at it showed not the slightest interest in knowing what it said, told us a story that Ulises had told her a long time ago, when both of them lived in Mexico City. According to Ulises, said Claudia, that famous parable about Jesus, the one about the rich man, the camel, and the eye of the needle, might have been the result of an error. In Greek, Claudia said that Ulises had said (but since when did Ulises know Greek?) there existed the word *káun-dos*, camel, in which the *n* (*eta*) read almost just like an *i*, and the word *káuidos*, cable, cord, heavy rope, in which the *i* (*iota*) is read *i*. Which led him to wonder, since Matthew and Luke were based on Mark, whether the possible error or misprint might not have had its origin in Mark or in the work of a scribe immediately posterior to Mark. The only objection to this theory, said Claudia, repeating what Ulises had said, was that Luke, who knew Greek well, would have corrected the error. And yet, Luke knew Greek but not the Jewish world, and he might have supposed that the "camel" passing through or failing to pass through the eye of the needle was a proverb of Hebrew or Aramaic origin. The funny thing, according to Ulises, is that there was another possible source for the error: according to Herr Professor Pinchas Lapide (what a name, said Claudia), of the University of Frankfurt, scholar of Hebrew and Aramaic, there were proverbs in Galilean Aramaic that used the noun *gamta*, ship's cable, and if one of the consonants were carelessly written, as is often the case in Hebrew and Aramaic manuscripts, it would be easy to read *gamal*, or camel, especially considering that vowels weren't written in Aramaic and ancient Hebrew and had to be inferred. Which leaves us, Claudia said that Ulises had said, with a less poetic and more realistic parable. It's easier for a ship's cable or a thick rope to pass through the eye of a needle than for a rich man to enter the kingdom of heaven. And which parable did he like better? asked Daniel. The two of us knew the answer, but we waited for Claudia to tell us. The one with the error, of course.

A week later we got a postcard from Hebron. And then another from the shores of the Dead Sea. And then a third from Eilat, in which he told us that he had found work as a waiter at a hotel. After that, and for a long time, we didn't hear anything. Deep down, I knew the waiter job wouldn't last long and I knew that traveling indefinitely around Israel without a cent in your pocket could be dangerous, but I didn't say anything to the others, although I suppose Daniel and Claudia knew it too. Sometimes we would talk about him during dinner. How do you think he's doing in Eilat? Claudia would ask. He's so lucky to be in Eilat! Daniel would say. We could go visit him next weekend, I would say. And immediately we would tacitly change the subject. At the time I was reading Wittgenstein's *Tractatus*, and everything I saw or did only heightened my sense of vulnerability. I remember that I got sick and spent a few days in bed and Claudia, always so perceptive, took the *Tractatus* away and hid it in Daniel's room, giving me instead one of the novels that she liked to read, *The Endless Rose*, by a Frenchman called J.M.G. Arcimboldi.

One night, as we were having dinner, I started to think about Ulises, and almost without my realizing it a few tears slid down my cheeks. What's wrong? said Claudia. I answered that if Ulises got sick he wouldn't have anyone to take care of him, the way she and Daniel were taking care of me. Then I thanked them and broke down. Ulises is as strong as a . . . as a warthog, said Claudia, and Daniel laughed. Claudia's remark, her simile, hurt me, and I asked her whether she'd become insensitive to everything. Claudia didn't answer and started to make me tea with lemon. We've condemned Ulises to the Desert! I exclaimed. As Daniel was telling me not to exaggerate, I heard the spoon, which Claudia's fingers were holding, clicking and stirring in the glass, mixing the liquid and the layer of honey, and then I couldn't take it anymore and I asked her, I begged her to look at me when I was talking, because I was talking to her, not to Daniel, because I wanted her to be the one to give me an explanation or console me, not Daniel. And then Claudia turned around, put the tea in front of me, sat in her usual chair, and said what do you want me to say? I think this is crazy talk, all that philosophy is affecting your brain. And then Daniel said something like my God, yes, in the last two weeks you've been wallowing in Wittgenstein, Bergson, Keyserling (who frankly I don't know how you can stand), Pico della Mirandola, that Louis Claude guy (he meant Louis Claude de Saint-Martin, author of *The Man of Aspiration*), crazy racist Otto Weininger, and I don't want to know how many others. And you haven't even touched my novel, added Claudia. At that moment I made a mistake and asked her how she could be so insensitive. When Claudia looked at me I realized that I had fucked up, but by then it was too late. The whole room shook when Claudia began to speak. She said that I should never say that again. She said that the next time I said it our relationship would be over. She said that it wasn't a sign of insensitivity not to worry excessively about Ulises Lima's escapades. She said her older brother had died in Argentina, possibly tortured by the police or the army, and that really was serious. She said that her older brother had fought in the ranks of the ERP and had believed in a continentwide American Revolution, and that was serious. She said that if she or her family had been in Argentina during the crackdown they might be dead now. She said all of that and then she started to cry. That's two of us now, I said. We didn't hug, as I would have liked, but we squeezed hands under the table and then Daniel suggested that we all go out and take a walk, but Claudia told him not to be silly, I was still sick, and that it would be best if we all had more tea and then went to bed.

A month later, Ulises Lima showed up. With him was a huge guy, almost six and a half feet tall, dressed in all kinds of rags, an Austrian Ulises had met in Beersheba. We put the two of them up in the living room for three days. The Austrian slept on the floor, Ulises on the sofa. The guy's name was Heimito. We never knew his last name, and he hardly ever said a word. He spoke English with Ulises, but only enough to get by. We had never met anyone with a name like that, although Claudia said there was a writer called Heimito von Doderer, Austrian too, although she wasn't sure. At first glance Ulises's Heimito seemed retarded, or borderline retarded. But they really did get along well.

When they left we went to the airport to see them off. Until then Ulises had seemed calm, in control of himself, indifferent. Now he suddenly turned sad, although *sad* isn't the right word. Glum, maybe. The night before he left we were talking and I told him I was happy I'd gotten to know him. Me too, said Ulises. The day he left, when Ulises and Heimito had already gone through security and we couldn't see them anymore, Claudia started to cry and for a minute I thought that she loved him—in her way, of course—but I soon gave up that idea.

# 11

Amadeo Salvatierra, Calle República de Venezuela, near the Palacio de la Inquisición, Mexico City DF, January 1976. For a while after that we didn't see Cesárea Tinajero at any of our meetings. It sounds odd, it sounded odd to admit it, but we missed her. Each time Maples Arce visited General Diego Carvajal he would ask Cesárea when she thought she'd stop being angry. But Cesárea turned a deaf ear. Once I went with Manuel and I spent a while talking to her. Rather than literature, we talked about politics and dancing, which Cesárea loved. In those days, boys, I said to them, there were dance halls all over Mexico City, the grandest in the center, but plenty in the outlying neighborhoods too, in Tacubaya, Colonia Observatorio! Colonia Coyoacán! Tlalpan to the south and Colonia Lindavista to the north! And Cesárea was one of those fanatics who would travel the city from one end to the other to get to a dance, although as I remember she liked the ones in the center best. She went alone. That is, before she met Encarnación Guzmán. That's something no one thinks twice about today, but in those days it led to all kinds of misunderstandings. Once, for reasons I can't recall, possibly because she asked me to, I took her to a dance. It was in a tent erected in a vacant lot near La Lagunilla. Before we went in I said: I'm your date, Cesárea, but don't make me dance, because I don't know how, and I don't want to learn. Cesárea laughed and said nothing. What a feeling, boys, what a rush of sensations. I remember the little round tables made of some light metal, like aluminum, although it can't have been aluminum. The dance floor was a crooked square, a raised platform of planks, and the orchestra was a quintet or sextet that would just as soon launch into a *ranchera* as a polka or a *danzón*. I ordered two sodas, and when I got back to our table Cesárea wasn't there anymore. Where have you got to? I wondered. And then I saw her. Where do you think she was? That's right, on the dance floor, dancing alone, something I'm sure is normal in this day and age, nothing out of the ordinary, times change, but back then it was the next best thing to an open provocation. So there I was with a serious dilemma on my hands, boys, I said to them. And they said: what did you do, Amadeo? And I said, *ay*, boys, what would you have done in my place? I got out on the dance floor and started to dance. And did you learn to dance on the spot, Amadeo? they said. Well, the truth is, I did, it was as if the music had been waiting for me all my life, waiting twenty-six years, like Penelope waiting for Ulysses, yes? and suddenly all the obstacles and all my qualms were a thing of the past and I was moving and smiling and watching Cesárea, what a pretty woman, and the way she danced! you could tell it was something she did all the time, if you closed your eyes out there on the floor you could imagine her dancing at home, or on her way out of work, or as she made herself her *cafecito de olla*, or as she read, but I didn't close my eyes, boys, I looked at Cesárea with my eyes wide open and I smiled at her and she was looking at me and smiling too, the two of us as happy as can be, so happy that for a moment I thought of giving her a kiss, but in the end I didn't dare, since things were good between us the way they were, after all, and I never had a one-track mind. It's all in the first step, as they say, and that's how it was for me with dancing, boys, all in the first step, and then I couldn't find a way to put an end to it. There was a time, but this was many years later, after Cesárea had disappeared and the fervor of youth had faded, when all my ambitions in life were centered on my biweekly visits to the dance halls. I'm talking about my thirties, boys, then my forties, and even a good slice of my fifties. At first I went with my wife. She didn't understand why I liked to dance so much, but she went with me. We had a good time. Later, after she died, I went alone. And I had a good time then too, although the flavor or the aftertaste of the places was different, and the music was different. I certainly didn't go there to drink or seek companionship, as my sons believed, Francisco Salvatierra and Carlos Manuel Salvatierra, a professor and a lawyer, two good boys whom I love dearly although I don't see them much, they have their own families now and too many problems, I suppose, but anyway I've already done all I can for them, given them a good education, which is more than my parents did for me, so now they're on their own. What was I saying? That my sons thought I went to the dance halls in search of a friendly face? Ultimately, they may have been right. But to my way of thinking, that wasn't what got me out the door each Saturday night. I went for the dancing and in some sense I went for Cesárea, or rather for Cesárea's ghost, which was still dancing around those places that always seemed to be on their last legs. Do you like to dance, boys? I said. And they said, it depends, Amadeo, it depends who we're dancing with, not alone, that's for sure. Oh, those boys. And then I asked them whether there were still dance halls in Mexico and they said that there were, though not many, or at least they didn't know of many, but that they existed. Some, according to them, were called *funk joints*, such a strange name, and the music that got them moving was modern music. Gringo music, you mean, I said, and they said: no, Amadeo, modern music made by Mexican musicians, Mexican bands, and then they started to name names, each one stranger than the next. Yes, I remember some of them. Las Vísceras de los Cristeros, that one I remember for obvious reasons. Los Caifanes de Marte, Los Asesinos de Angélica María, Involución Proletaria, strange names that made us laugh and argue. Why Los Asesinos de Angélica María, when Angélica María seems like such a nice girl? I said. And they: Angélica María is extremely nice, Amadeo, it must be an homage, not a threat, and I: isn't *Los Caifanes* a film starring Anel? And they: Anel and María Félix's son, Amadeo, you're so up to date. And I: I may be old, but I'm no fool. Enriquito Álvarez Félix, yes sir, an upstanding young man. And they: you have a fucking amazing memory, Amadeo, let's toast to that. And I: Involución Proletaria? who are they when they're at home? And they: they're the bastard offspring of Fidel Velásquez, Amadeo, they're new workers hailing back to a preindustrial age. And I: I don't give a rat's ass about Fidel Velásquez, boys, the one who always inspired us was Flores Magón. And they: *salud*, Amadeo. And I: *salud*. And they: *viva* Flores Magón, Amadeo. And I: *viva*, feeling a sharp pain in my stomach as I thought about the old days and how late it was, that time when night sinks into night, though never all of a sudden, the white-footed Mexico City night, a night that endlessly announces her arrival, I'm coming, I'm coming, but is a long time coming, as if she too, the devil, had stayed behind to watch the sunset, the incomparable sunsets of Mexico, the peacock sunsets, as Cesárea would say when Cesárea lived here and was our friend. And then it was as if I could see Cesárea in General Diego Carvajal's office, sitting at her desk with her shiny typewriter in front of her, talking to the general's bodyguards, who usually spent their off-hours there too, lounging in the armchairs or leaning in the doorways as the general raised his voice in his office, and Cesárea, to keep them busy or because she really needed their help, sent them to run errands or to look for a certain book at Don Julio Nodier's bookstore, some book she needed to consult for an idea or two, or a quote or two, for the general's speeches, which according to Manuel she usually wrote herself. Incredible speeches, boys, I said, speeches that circulated all over Mexico and were printed in the papers all over the country, Monterrey and Guadalajara, Veracruz and Tampico. Sometimes we read them aloud at our meetings at the café. And Cesárea wrote them at the general's office, and in the most peculiar fashion: as she smoked and talked to the general's bodyguards or to Manuel or me, talking and typing the speeches all at once. The talent of that woman, boys. Have you ever tried such a thing? I have, and it's impossible, something only a few natural writers or journalists can do, be talking about politics, for example, and at the same time writing a little article on gardening or spondaic hexameters (which I can tell you, boys, are a rare phenomenon). And that was how she spent her days at the general's office, and when she had finished her work, sometimes quite late at night, she would say goodbye to everyone, gather up her things, and leave on her own, although often someone would offer to accompany her, sometimes the general himself, Diego Carvajal, the big man, the grand pooh-bah, but Cesárea wouldn't hear of it: certainly not, here are the papers from the attorney general's office, General (she called him General, not *mi general*, as the rest of us did), and here are the ones from the government of Veracruz and here are the Jalapa letters and here is tomorrow's speech, and then she would leave and no one would see her until the next day. Haven't I told you anything about *mi general* Diego Carvajal, boys? In my day he was *the* patron of the arts. What a man. You had to have seen him. He was on the short side, and thin, and even then he must already have been close to fifty, but more than once I saw him stand up all alone to some of Congressman Martínez Zamora's gunmen, saw how he looked them straight in the eye, never reaching for the Colt in his underarm holster, though it's true his jacket was unbuttoned, and I saw how the gunmen shriveled under his gaze and then I saw them back away, murmuring excuse me, *mi general*, the congressman must have made a mistake, *mi general*. An honest-to-God man if ever there was one, General Diego Carvajal, and a lover of literature and the arts, although as he said himself, he didn't learn to read until he was eighteen years old. The life he led, boys! I said. If I started to tell you about him I could keep going all night and we would need more tequila, it would take a whole carton of Los Suicidas mezcal for me to be able to give you some idea of that black hole in the Mexican firmament. That blazing black hole! Jet-black, they said. Jet-black, that's right, boys, I said, jet-black. And one of them said I'll go right now and buy another bottle of tequila. And I said off you go, and drawing energy from the past I got up and hauled myself (like lightning, or the idea of lightning) along the dark hallways of my apartment to the kitchen, and I opened all the cupboards in search of an unlikely bottle of Los Suicidas, although I knew very well there weren't any left, muttering and cursing, rummaging among the cans of soup that my sons bring me every so often, among the useless junk, finally accepting the bitter truth, up to my ears in ghosts, and I chose some little things to stave off hunger: a few packages of peanuts, a can of chipotle chilies, a package of crackers, and I brought them back at the speed of a World War I cruiser, a cruiser lost in the mists of some river or delta, I don't know, lost, anyway, since the truth is that my steps didn't lead to the living room but to my bedroom. For goodness's sake, Amadeo, I said to myself, you must be drunker than you thought, lost in the fog, with only a little paper lantern hanging from my forward guns, but I didn't panic and I found the way, step by step, tinkling my little bell, ship on the river, warship lost at the mouth of the river of history, and the honest truth is that by then I was walking as if I were doing that heel-toe dance step, whether it's still something anyone does I don't know, I hope not, touching the heel of the left foot to the toe of the right and then the heel of the right foot to the toe of the left, a ridiculous step but one that had its day, don't ask me when, probably while Miguel Alemán was president, I danced it at some point, we've all done foolish things, and then I heard the door slam and then voices and I said to myself Amadeo stop being an ass and make your way toward the voices, part the mists of this river with your rust-eaten prow and return to your friends, and that's what I did, and I made it to the front room, my arms overflowing with snacks, and the boys were in the front room, sitting there waiting for me, and one of them had bought two bottles of tequila. Ah, what a relief to come into the light, even when it's a shadowy half-light, what a relief to come where it's clear.


**Lisandro Morales, *pulquería* La Saeta Mexicana, near La Villa, Mexico City DF, January 1980.** When Arturo Belano's book finally came out, Belano was already a phantom author and I was about to become a phantom publisher. I knew it would happen. There are writers who are jinxes, bad luck, and you'd better steer clear of them whether you believe in bad luck or not. Even if you're a positivist or a Marxist, you have to avoid those people like the plague. And I say this from the bottom of my heart: you have to trust your instincts. I knew I was playing with fire by publishing that boy's book. I got burned and I'm not complaining, but it's never a bad idea to reflect a little on what went wrong, since other people's stories can always be of service to somebody else. Now I drink a lot, I spend the day at the bar, I park my car far from where I live, and when I get home I take a look around just so no collection agent can take me by surprise.

At night I can't sleep and I drink more. I have well-founded suspicions that a hired killer is after me. Maybe two. I was already a widower before the disaster, thank God, so at least I have the consolation of having spared my poor wife this ordeal, this journey through the shadows that awaits all editors in the end. And even if some nights I can't help asking why this had to happen to me, to me of all people, deep down I've accepted my fate. Being alone makes us stronger. So said Nietzsche (I published a paperback edition of his selected quotes in 1969, when the terrible crime of Tlatelolco was still smoldering, and incidentally, it was a huge success) or maybe Flores Magón. We published a small militant biography of him by a law student that didn't do too badly.

Being alone makes us stronger. That's the honest truth. But it's cold comfort, since even if I wanted company no one will come near me anymore. Not that bastard Vargas Pardo, who works for another house now, though with a lesser title than when he worked for me, and not a single one of all those literary types who basked in my reflected glory back in the day. No one wants to walk alongside a moving target. No one wants to walk alongside a man who already bears the stink of carrion. At least now I know what I only intuited before: there's a hired killer after every publisher. This killer may be distinguished, he may be illiterate, but he's in the pay of the darkest interests. And sometimes—oh, the cosmic irony—those interests, so vain and foolish, are our own.

I don't bear Vargas Pardo any grudge. Sometimes I even remember him with a certain fondness. And deep down I don't believe the people who tell me that my company went under because of the magazine that I so blithely placed in his hands. I know my bad luck came from elsewhere. Of course, Vargas Pardo played a part in my downfall with his criminal naïveté, but in the end it wasn't his fault. He thought he was doing the right thing, and I don't blame him. Sometimes, when I've had too much to drink, I find myself cursing him, him and all those literary types who've forgotten me, and the hired killers waiting for me in the dark, and even the typesetters, lost in glory or anonymity, but then I relax and I can't help laughing. You have to live your life, that's all there is to it. A drunk I met the other day on my way out of the bar La Mala Senda told me so. Literature is crap.


**Joaquín Font, El Reposo Mental Health Clinic, Camino Desierto de los Leones, on the outskirts of Mexico City DF, April 1980.** Two months ago, Álvaro Damián came to see me and said he had something to tell me. Tell me, then, I said, have a seat and let's hear it. The prize is finished, he said. What prize? I said. The Laura Damián prize for young poets, he said. I had no idea what he was talking about, but I played along with him. And why is that, Álvaro, I said, why is that? Because I've run out of money, he said, I've lost everything.

Easy come, easy go, I would have liked to say (I've always been a staunch anticapitalist), but I didn't say anything because the poor man looked tired and his face was so sad.

We talked for a long time. I think we talked about the weather and the nice views from the asylum. He would say: it looks like it'll be hot today. I would say: yes. Then we'd sit there in silence, or I'd sing to myself and he'd be silent, until all at once he'd say (for example): look, a butterfly. And I would say: yes, there are quite a lot of them. And after we'd gone on like that for a while, talking or reading the paper together (although that particular day we didn't read the paper), Álvaro Damián said: I had to tell you. And I said: what did you have to tell me, Álvaro? And he said: that the Laura Damián prize was finished. I would've liked to ask him why, why he felt the need to tell me in particular, but then I thought that many people, especially here, had many things to tell me, and although the urge to share was something I couldn't quite understand, I accepted it completely, since there was no harm in listening.

And then Álvaro Damián left and twenty days later my daughter came to visit me, and she said Dad, I shouldn't tell you this but I think it's best that you know. And I said: tell, tell, I'm all ears. And she said: Álvaro Damián shot himself in the head. And I said: how could Álvarito do such a terrible thing? And she said: business was going badly for him, he was ruined, he'd already lost practically everything he had. And I said: but he could have come to live at the asylum with me. And my daughter laughed and said things weren't that easy. And when she left I began to think about Álvaro Damián and the Laura Damián prize, which was finished, and the madmen of El Reposo, where no one has a place to lay his head, and about the month of April, not so much cruel as disastrous, and that's when I knew beyond a doubt that everything was about to go from bad to worse.

# 12

Heimito Künst, in bed in his attic apartment on the Stuckgasse, Vienna, May 1980. I was in jail with my good friend Ulises in Beersheba, where the Jews make their atomic bombs. I knew everything, but I didn't know anything. I watched, what else could I do? I watched from the rocks, sunburned, until I was so hungry and thirsty I couldn't stand it and then I dragged myself to the desert café and ordered a Coca-Cola and a hamburger made of ground beef, although hamburgers made only of beef are no good, I know that and so does everybody else in the world.

One day I drank five Coca-Colas and suddenly I felt sick, as if the sun had filtered down into my Cokes and I'd drunk it without realizing. I had a fever. I couldn't stand it, but I did stand it. I hid behind a yellow rock and waited for the sun to go down and then I curled up in a ball and fell asleep. I kept having dreams all night. I thought they were touching me with their fingers. But dreams don't have fingers, they have fists, so it must have been scorpions. My burns still stung. When I woke up the sun hadn't risen yet. I looked for the scorpions before they could hide under the rocks. I couldn't find a single one! All the more reason to stay awake and worry. And that's what I did. But then I had to go because I needed to eat and drink. So I got up, I'd been on my knees, and headed for the desert café, but the waiter wouldn't bring me anything.

Why won't you bring me what I order? I asked him. Isn't my money good, as good as anybody else's money? He pretended not to hear me, and maybe he couldn't hear me, that was what I thought. Maybe I'd lost my voice after keeping watch in the desert for so long among the rocks and the scorpions, and now I wasn't really talking, although I thought I was. But then whose voice were my ears hearing if not mine? I thought.

How can I have been struck dumb and still hear myself? I thought. Then they told me to leave. Somebody spat at my feet. They tried to provoke me. But I'm not easily provoked. I have experience. I refused to listen to what they were saying to me. If you won't sell me meat then an Arab will, I said, and I left the café, taking my time.

For hours I looked for an Arab. It was as if every Arab had vanished into thin air. At last, without realizing it, I ended up right back where I'd come from, next to the yellow stone. It was nighttime and it was cold, thank God, but I couldn't sleep, I was hungry and there was no water left in my canteen. What do I do? I asked myself. What do I do now, Blessed Virgin? From far away came the muffled sound of the machines the Jews used to make their atomic bombs. When I woke up, I was unbearably hungry. The Beersheba Jews were still working in their secret installations, but I couldn't keep spying on them without so much as a crust of bread. My whole body ached. My neck and my arms were sunburned. It had been I don't know how many days since I took a shit. But I could still walk! I could still jump and move my arms like windmills! So I got up and my shadow got up with me (the two of us had been kneeling, praying) and I set off toward the desert café. I think I started to sing. That's how I am. I walk. I sing. When I woke up, I was in a jail cell. Someone had brought my backpack and tossed it beside my cot. One of my eyes hurt, my chin hurt, my burns stung. Someone had kicked me in the gut, I think, but my gut didn't hurt.

Water, I said. It was dark in the cell. I listened for the sound of the Jews' machines, but I couldn't hear anything. Water, I said, I'm thirsty. Something moved in the dark. A scorpion? I thought. A giant scorpion? I thought. A hand gripped me by the back of the neck. It tugged. Then I felt the rim of a cup on my lips and then the water. Then I slept and I dreamed of Franz-Josefs-Kai and the Aspern Bridge. When I opened my eyes I saw Ulises in the other cot. He was awake, staring at the ceiling, thinking. I greeted him in English. Good morning, I said. Good morning, he replied. Do they give you food in this jail? I asked. They give you food, he answered. I got up and looked for my shoes. I had them on. I decided to take a walk around the cell. I decided to explore. The ceiling was dark, blackened. Damp or soot. Possibly both. The walls were white. There were inscriptions on them, I saw. Drawings on the wall to my left and writing on the wall to my right. The Koran? Messages? News of the underground factory? In the back wall there was a window. On the other side of the window there was a yard. On the other side of the yard was the desert. In the fourth wall there was a door. The door was made of bars, and through the bars there was a corridor. There was no one in the corridor. I turned and went over to my good friend Ulises. My name is Heimito, I said, and I'm from Vienna. He said that his name was Ulises Lima and that he was from Mexico City.

A little while later, they brought us breakfast. Where are we? I asked the guard. In the factory? But the guard left us the food and went away. I wolfed mine down. My good friend Ulises gave me half his breakfast and I ate that too. I could have gone on eating all morning. Then I started to reconnoiter the cell. I started to reconnoiter the inscriptions on the walls. The drawings. It was hopeless. The messages were indecipherable. I took a pen out of my backpack and kneeled by the wall on the right. I drew a dwarf with an enormous penis. An erect penis. Then I drew another dwarf with an enormous penis. Then I drew a breast. Then I wrote: Heimito K. Then I got tired and went back to my cot. My good friend Ulises had gone to sleep, so I tried not to make noise so I wouldn't wake him up. I got in bed and started to think. I thought about the under-ground factories where the Jews built their atomic bombs. I thought about a soccer match. I thought about a mountain. It was cold and snow-ing. I thought about the scorpions. I thought about a plate full of sausages. I thought about the church in the Alpen Garten, near the Jacquingasse. I fell asleep. I woke up. I fell asleep again. I slept until I heard my good friend Ulises's voice. Then I woke up again. A guard pushed us along the corridor. We came out into the yard. I think the sun recognized me immediately. My bones hurt. But not the burns, so I walked and did some exercise. My good friend Ulises sat against the wall quietly, not moving, as I swung my arms and raised my knees. I heard laughter. A few Arabs, sitting on the ground in the corner, were laugh-ing. I ignored them. One two, one two, one two. I worked the stiffness out of my joints. When I glanced at the shady corner again, the Arabs were gone. I got down on the ground. I kneeled. For a second I thought about staying like that. On my knees. But then I got down on the ground and did five push-ups. I did ten push-ups. I did fifteen push-ups. My whole body hurt. When I got up I saw that the Arabs were sitting on the ground around my good friend Ulises. I walked toward them. Slowly. Thinking. Maybe they weren't trying to hurt him. Maybe they were

Mexicans lost in Beersheba. When my good friend Ulises saw me, he said: let there be peace. And I understood.

I sat on the ground next to him, with my back against the wall, and for a second my blue eyes met the dark eyes of the Arabs. I was panting. I panted hard and closed my eyes! I heard my good friend Ulises speaking English, but I couldn't understand what he was saying. The Arabs were speaking English, but I couldn't understand what they were saying. My good friend Ulises laughed. The Arabs laughed. I understood their laughter and I stopped panting. I fell asleep. When I woke up, my good friend Ulises and I were alone. A guard led us to our cell. They brought us food. With my meal they brought two tablets. For the fever, they said. I didn't take them. My good friend Ulises told me to throw them down the hole. But where does that hole lead? To the sewers, said my good friend Ulises. How can I be sure? What if it leads to a warehouse? And what if everything ends up on a huge, wet table where even the smallest things we throw away are cataloged? I crushed the tablets between my fingers and threw the powder out the window. We went to sleep. When I woke up, my good friend Ulises was reading. I asked him what book he was reading. Ezra Pound's *Selected Poems*. Read something to me, I said. I didn't understand any of it. I stopped trying. They came for me and questioned me. They looked at my passport. They asked me questions. They laughed. When I got back to my cell I got down on the floor and did push-ups. Three, nine, twelve. Then I sat on the floor, by the wall on my right, and I drew a dwarf with an enormous penis. When I was done, I drew another one. And then I drew the stuff coming out of one of the penises. And then I didn't feel like drawing anymore and I started to study the other inscriptions. Left to right and right to left. I don't understand Arabic. My good friend Ulises didn't either. Still, I read. I found some words. I racked my brains. The burns on my neck started to hurt again. Words. Words. My good friend Ulises gave me water. I felt his hands under my arms, pulling me, hauling me up. Then I fell asleep.

When I woke up, the guard took us to the showers. He gave us each a piece of soap and told us to shower. This guard seemed to be a friend of Ulises's. They didn't speak English together. They spoke Spanish. I kept careful watch. The Jews are always trying to trick you. I was sorry to have to keep watch, but it was my duty. When something is your duty, there's nothing you can do about it. As I washed my face I pretended to close my eyes. I pretended to fall. I pretended to exercise. But the only thing I was really doing was taking a look at my good friend Ulises's penis. He wasn't circumcised. I was sorry I'd made a mistake, sorry I'd doubted him. But I only did what I had to do. That night they gave us soup. And vegetable stew. My good friend Ulises gave me half his food. Why won't you eat? I said. It's good. You have to feed yourself. You have to exercise. I'm not hungry, he said, you eat. When the lights went out, the moon came into our cell. I looked out the window. In the desert, past the yard, the hyenas were singing. A small, dark, restless group. Darker than the night. And they were laughing too. I felt a tickle in the soles of my feet. Don't mess with me, I thought.

The next day, after breakfast, they let us go. The guard who spoke Spanish walked my good friend Ulises to the bus stop for the bus to Jerusalem. They talked. The guard told stories and my good friend Ulises listened, then Ulises told a story. The guard bought a lemon ice cream for Ulises and an orange ice cream for himself. Then he looked at me and asked me whether I wanted an ice cream too. Do you want an ice cream too, poor bastard? he asked. Chocolate, I said. When I had the ice cream in my hand I felt in my pockets for coins. I felt in my left-hand pockets with my left hand, and in my right-hand pockets with my right hand. I handed him a few coins. The Jew looked at them. The sun was melting the tip of his orange ice cream. I went back the way I'd come. I walked away from the bus stop. I walked away from the road and the desert café. It was a little farther to my rock. Quickly. Quickly. When I got there I leaned on my rock and took a breath. I looked for my maps and my drawings and I couldn't find anything. There was only the heat and the noise the scorpions make in their holes. *Bzzzz.* I dropped to the ground and kneeled. There wasn't a cloud in the sky. Or a bird. What could I do but watch? I hid among the rocks and listened for the sounds of Beersheba, but all I could hear was the sound of the air, a puff of hot dust that burned my face. And then I heard my good friend Ulises's voice calling me, Heimito, Heimito, where are you, Heimito? And I knew I couldn't hide. Not even if I wanted to. And I came out of the rocks, with my backpack in one hand, and I followed my good friend Ulises, who was calling me to the path that fate had determined for me. Villages. Vacant lots. Jerusalem. In Jerusalem I sent a telegram to Vienna asking for money. I demanded my money, my inheritance money. We begged. In front of hotels. In the places where tourists went. We slept in the street.

Or in church doorways. We ate soup from the Armenian brothers, bread from the Palestinian brothers.

I told my good friend Ulises what I'd seen. About the Jews' diabolical plans. He said: sleep, Heimito. Then my money came. We bought two airplane tickets and then we didn't have any money left. That was all the money I had. Lies. I wrote a postcard from Tel Aviv and demanded it all. We flew. From up above I saw the sea. The surface of the sea is a trick, I thought. The only real mirage. Fata morgana, said my good friend Ulises. In Vienna it was raining. But we're not sugar cubes! We took a taxi to Landesgerichtsstrasse and Lichtenfelsgasse. When we got there I punched the taxi driver in the back of the neck and we walked away. First along the Josefstädter Strasse, quickly, then along the Strozzigasse, then the Zeltgasse, then the Piaristengasse, then Lerchenfelder Strasse, then Neubaugasse, then Siebensterngasse, to Stuckgasse, where I live. Then we walked up five floors. Quickly. But I didn't have the key. I had lost the key to my apartment in the Negev. Relax, Heimito, said my good friend Ulises, let's check your pockets. We checked them. One by one. Nothing. The backpack. Nothing. The clothes in the backpack. Nothing. My key, lost in the Negev. Then I remembered the spare key. There's a spare key, I said. What do you know, said my good friend Ulises. He was breathing hard. He was sprawled on the floor, his back against my door. I was kneeling. Then I got up and thought about the spare key and went to the window at the end of the hallway. Through the window there was a view of an inner courtyard of cement and the roofs of the Kirchengasse. I opened the window and the rain got my face wet. Outside, in a little hole, was the key. When I pulled my hand back there were wisps of cobweb on my fingers.

We lived in Vienna. It rained a little more each day. The first two days we didn't leave the apartment. I went out. But not much. Only to buy bread and coffee. My good friend Ulises stayed in his sleeping bag, reading or looking out the window. We ate bread. It was all we ate. I was hungry. On the third night, my good friend Ulises got up, washed his face, combed his hair, and we went out. In front of the Figarohaus I went up to a man and hit him in the face. My good friend Ulises searched his pockets as I held him. Then we went off along Graben and lost ourselves on small, busy streets. In a bar on the Gonzagagasse, my good friend Ulises wanted a beer. I ordered an orange Fanta and made a phone call from the phone booth at the bar, asking for my money, the money that is legally mine. Then we went to see my friends on the Aspern Bridge, but no one was there and we walked home.

The next day we bought sausages and ham and pâté and more bread. We went out every day. We took the subway. In the Rossauer Lände station I ran into Udo Möller. He was having a beer and he looked at me like I was a scorpion. Who is this, he said, pointing to my good friend Ulises. He's a friend, I said. Where did you find him? said Udo Möller. In Beersheba, I said. We took one train to Heiligenstadt and then we took the Schnellbahn to Hernals. Is he Jewish? said Udo Möller. He isn't Jewish, he's not circumcised, I said. We walked in the rain. We were walking to the garage of some guy called Rudi. Udo Möller talked to me in German, but he never took his eyes off my good friend Ulises. It struck me that we were walking into a trap and I stopped. Only then did I see clearly that they wanted to kill my good friend Ulises. And I stopped. I said that I had just realized we had things to do. What things? said Udo Möller. Things, I said. Shopping. We're almost there, said Udo Möller. No, I said, we have things to do. It will just be a minute, said Udo Möller. No! I said. The rain was running down my nose and into my eyes. With the tip of my tongue I licked the rain and said no. Then I turned around and told my good friend Ulises to follow me and Udo Möller started to follow us. Come on, we're almost there, come with me, Heimito, it'll just be a minute. No!

That week we pawned the television and a clock that used to belong to my mother. We took the subway at Neubaugasse, walked along Stephansplatz, and went out on Vorgartenstrasse or the Donauinsel. We spent hours watching the river. The surface of the river. Sometimes we saw cardboard boxes floating on the water. Which brought back terrible memories for me. Sometimes we got off the train in Praterstern and walked around the station. We followed people. We never did anything. It's too dangerous, said my good friend Ulises, it isn't worth the risk. We were hungry. There were days when we didn't leave the house. I did push-ups: ten, twenty, thirty. My good friend Ulises watched, still in his sleeping bag, a book in his hands. But mostly I looked out the window. The gray sky. And sometimes I looked toward Israel. One night, as I was drawing in my notebook, my good friend Ulises asked me: what were you doing in Israel, Heimito? I told him. Searching, searching. The word *searching* alongside the house and the elephant that I had drawn. And what were you doing, my good friend Ulises? Nothing, he said.

When it stopped raining we went out again. We found a man in the Stadtpark station and followed him. On the Johannesgasse, my good friend Ulises grabbed his arm and as the man looked to see who was grabbing him I slammed my fist into the back of his neck. Sometimes we would go to the Neubaugasse post office, close to home, so my good friend Ulises could mail his letters. On the way back we would pass the Rembrandt Theater and my good friend Ulises could spend five minutes looking at it. Sometimes I would leave him in front of the theater and go make phone calls from a bar! The same answer! They wouldn't give me my money! When I came back my good friend Ulises would be there, looking at the Rembrandt Theater. Then I would sigh in relief and we would go home to eat. Once we ran into three of my friends. We were walking along the Franz-Josefs-Kai toward Julius-Raab-Platz, and all of a sudden, there they were. As if they had been invisible up until then. Trackers. Beaters. They said hello to me. They said my name. One of them stepped in front of me. Gunther, the strongest one. Another one moved to my left. Another moved to my good friend Ulises's right. We couldn't walk. We could turn around and run, but we couldn't move forward. It's been a long time, Heimito, said Gunther. It's been a long time, Heimito, they all said. No! We don't have time. But there was nowhere for us to run.

We strolled. We walked. We went to see Julius the policeman. They asked whether my good friend Ulises understood German. Whether he knew the secret. He doesn't understand German, I said, he doesn't know any secrets. But he's smart, they said. He isn't smart, I said, he's nice, he only sleeps and reads and he doesn't exercise. We wanted to leave. There's nothing to say! We're busy! I said. My good friend Ulises looked at them and nodded. Now I was the one standing still like a statue. My good friend Ulises looked around Julius's room, walking around and looking at everything. He wouldn't stay still. Drawings. Gunther was getting more and more nervous. We're busy and we want to leave! I said. Then Gunther grabbed Ulises by the shoulders and said why are you scuttling around like a crab? Stop it! And Julius said: the rat is nervous. My good friend Ulises moved away and Gunther pulled out his brass knuckles. Don't touch him, I said, I'll be getting my inheritance in a week. And Gunther put his brass knuckles back in his pocket and pushed my good friend Ulises into a corner. Then we talked about propaganda. They showed me papers and photographs. I was in one of the photographs, from behind. It's me, I said, this is an old picture. They showed me new pictures, new papers. A photograph of a forest, a cabin in the forest, a gentle slope. I know this place, I said. Of course you know it, Heimito, said Julius. Then came more words and more words and more papers and more photographs. All old! Silence, cunning. I didn't say a thing. Then we left and went walking home. Gunther and Peter walked along with us for a while. But my good friend Ulises and I were silent. Cunning. We walked and walked. Gunther and Peter got on the subway and my good friend Ulises and I walked and walked. Without talking. Before we got home we went into a church. The Ulrichkirche on the Burggasse. I went into a church and my good friend Ulises followed me, keeping watch over me!

I tried to pray. I tried to stop thinking about the photographs. That night we ate bread and my good friend Ulises asked me about my father, my friends, my travels. The next day we didn't go out. But the day after that we did go out because my good friend Ulises had to go to the post office, and once we were out we decided not to go home but to walk. Are you nervous, Heimito? said my good friend Ulises. No, I'm not nervous, I said. Why do you keep looking over your shoulder? Why are you looking from side to side? It never hurts to stay alert, I answered. We didn't have any money. We found an old man in Esterhazy Park. He was feeding the pigeons, but the pigeons were ignoring his crumbs. I came up behind him and punched him in the head. My good friend Ulises went through his pockets but he didn't find any money, only coins and breadcrumbs and a wallet that we took. There was a photograph in the wallet. The old man looks like my father, I said. We tossed the wallet into a mailbox. Then for two days we didn't leave the house, until all we had left were crumbs. So we went to visit Julius the policeman. We went out with him. We went to a bar on the Favoritenstrasse and listened to him talk. I looked at the table, the surface of the table and the drops of spilled Coca-Cola. Ulises spoke English with Julius the policeman and told him that there were more pyramids in Mexico than in Egypt, and bigger ones. When I lifted my eyes from the table I saw Gunther and Peter near the door. I blinked and they disappeared. But half an hour later they came by our table and sat down with us.

That night I talked to my good friend Ulises and told him I knew of a house in the country, a wooden cabin at the foot of a gentle hill covered in pine trees. I told him that I never wanted to see my friends again.

Then we talked about Israel, about the jail in Beersheba, about the desert, about the yellow rocks, and about the scorpions that only came out at night, when they couldn't be seen by the human eye. Maybe we should go back, said my good friend Ulises. The Jews would kill me for sure, I said. They wouldn't do anything to you, said my good friend Ulises. The Jews would kill me, I said. Then my good friend Ulises put a dirty towel over his head, but he still seemed to be looking out the window. I sat there watching him for a while and wondering how he knew they wouldn't do anything to me. I got down on my knees and crossed my arms. Ten, fifteen, twenty squats. Until I got bored and started to draw.

The next day we went back to the bar on the Favoritenstrasse. Julius the policeman and six of his friends were there. We took the subway at Taubstummengasse and got out at Praterstern. I heard somebody howling. We ran. We were sweating. The next day one of my friends was watching the house. I told my good friend Ulises. But he couldn't see anything. That night we combed our hair, washed our faces, and went out. At the bar on the Favoritenstrasse, Julius the policeman talked to us about dignity, evolution, the great Darwin and the great Nietzsche. I translated so that my good friend Ulises could understand what he was saying, although I didn't understand any of it. The prayer of the bones, said Julius. The yearning for health. The virtue of danger. The tenacity of the forgotten. Bravo, said my good friend Ulises. Bravo, said everyone else. The limits of memory. The wisdom of plants. The eye of parasites. The agility of the earth. The merit of the soldier. The cunning of the giant. The hole of the will. Magnificent, said my good friend Ulises in German. Extraordinary. We drank. I didn't want beer, but they put a mug in front of me and said drink, Heimito, it won't hurt you. We drank and we sang. My good friend Ulises sang a few lines in Spanish and my friends watched him like wolves and laughed. But they didn't understand what my good friend Ulises was singing! Neither did I! We drank and sang. Every so often Julius the policeman would say dignity, honor, memory. They put a mug and then another mug in front of me. With one eye I watched the beer trembling in the mugs and with the other eye I watched my friends. They weren't drinking. For each mug they drank, I drank four. Drink, Heimito, it won't hurt you, they said. They were buying Ulises drinks too. Drink, little Mexican, they said, it won't hurt you. And we sang. Songs about the house in the country, at the foot of the little hill. And Julius the policeman said: home, native land, homeland. The owner of the bar came over to drink with us. I saw how he winked at Gunther. I saw how Gunther winked at him. I saw how he avoided looking into the corner where my good friend Ulises was sitting. Drink, Heimito, they said to me, it won't hurt you. And Julius the policeman smiled, flattered, and said thank you, thank you, of course, of course, it's nothing, please. Extraordinary. Ruthless. And then he said: decency, duty, betrayal, punishment. And they congratulated him again, but this time only a few people were smiling.

Afterward we all left together. Like a cluster. Like the fingers of a steel hand. Like a gauntlet in the wind. But outside we began to separate. Into smaller and smaller groups. Farther and farther apart. Until we lost sight of the others. It was Udo and four other friends in our group. Walking toward the Belvedere. Along the Karolinengasse and then the Belvederegasse. Some talked and others didn't, preferring to watch the ground beneath their feet. Hands in their pockets. Collars turned up. And I said to my good friend Ulises: do you know what we're doing here? And my good friend Ulises said that he was getting an idea, more or less. And we crossed the Prinz Eugen Strasse and I asked my good friend Ulises what kind of idea that was. And he said: more or less the same idea you're getting, Heimito, more or less the same idea. The others didn't understand English or if any of them did, they were pretending not to. When we went into the park I started to pray. What are you whispering, Heimito? said Udo, who was next to me. No, no, no, I said as the tree branches that we were parting brushed my face and hair. Then I looked up and didn't see a single star. We came to a clearing: everything was deep green, even the shadows of Udo and my friends. We stood there quietly, our legs braced, and the lights danced behind the trees and plants, distant, remote. The brass knuckles came out of my friends' pockets. No one said a word! Or if they did say anything I didn't hear it. But I don't think they did. We had stopped in a secret place and there was no need to talk! I don't think we even looked at each other! It made me feel like shouting! But then I saw that my good friend Ulises had taken something out of his jacket pocket and was hurling himself at Udo. I moved too. I grabbed one of my friends by the neck and punched him in the forehead. I was hit from behind. One, two, one, two. Someone else hit me from the front. The metallic taste of his brass knuckles was on my lips. But I managed to hold on to one of my friends by the shoulder and with a sharp movement I shook off the one who was on my back. I think I broke someone's rib. I felt a wave of heat. I heard Udo shouting, calling for help. I broke a nose. Let's go, Heimito, said my good friend Ulises. I looked for him and couldn't find him. Where are you? I said. Here, Heimito, here, calm down. I stopped hitting. In the clearing there were two bodies on the grass. The others were gone. I was covered in sweat and couldn't think. Rest for a minute, said my good friend Ulises. I kneeled with my arms flung wide. I watched my good friend Ulises go over to the bodies on the ground. For a moment I thought he was going to slit their throats. He still had the knife in his hand, and I thought let God's will be done. But my good friend Ulises didn't raise his weapon against the fallen. He went through their pockets and felt their necks and put his ear to their mouths and said: we haven't killed anyone, Heimito, we can go. I cleaned my bloody face with one of my friends' shirts. I smoothed my hair. I got up. I was sweating like a pig. My legs were as heavy as an elephant's! But still, I ran and ran, and then I walked, and I even whistled until at last we came out of the park. We walked along Jacquingasse to Rennweg. And then along Marrokanergasse to the Konzerthaus. And then along Lisztstrasse to Lothringerstrasse. We spent the next few days on our own. But we went out. One afternoon we saw Gunther. He watched us from a distance and then he went away. We ignored him. One morning we saw two of my friends. They were on a corner and when they saw us they left. One afternoon, on Kärtner Strasse, my good friend Ulises saw a woman from behind and went up to her. I saw her too, but I didn't go up to her. I stayed thirty feet away, then thirty-five, then fifty, then seventy-five. And I saw how my good friend Ulises called out and put his hand on the woman's shoulder, and how she turned around and my good friend Ulises excused himself and the woman kept walking.

Every day we went to the post office. We took walks that ended at Esterhazy Platz or the Stiftskaserne. Sometimes my friends followed us. Always at a distance! One night we found a man in the Schadekgasse and followed him. He went into the park. He was an old man, well dressed. My good friend Ulises came up beside him and I punched him in the back of the neck. We went through his pockets. That night we ate at a bar close to home. Then I got up from the table and made a phone call. My inheritance, my money, I said, and from the other end of the line someone said: no, no, no. Then the police came and took us to the

Bandgasse station. They took off our handcuffs and interrogated us. Questions, questions. I said: I have nothing to say. When they took me to the cell Ulises wasn't there. The next morning my lawyer came. I said: Mr. Lawyer, you look like a statue abandoned in the forest, and he laughed. When he stopped laughing, he said: no more joking from now on, Heimito. Where is my good friend Ulises? I said. Your accomplice is under arrest, Heimito, said my lawyer. Is he alone? I said. Of course, said my lawyer, and then I stopped shaking. If my good friend Ulises was alone, nothing could happen to him.

That night I dreamed about a yellow rock and a black rock. The next day I saw my good friend Ulises in the courtyard. We talked. He asked me how I was. Fine, I said, I exercise, I do push-ups, sit-ups, I shadow-box. Don't shadowbox, he said. How are you, I said. Fine, he said, they treat me well, the food is good. The food is good! I said. Then they interrogated me again. Questions, questions. I don't know anything, I said. Heimito, tell us what you know, they said. Then I told them about the Jews who were working to build an atomic bomb in Beersheba and about the scorpions that only came out at night. And they said that they would show me pictures and when I saw the pictures I said: they're dead, these are pictures of dead people! and I wouldn't talk to them anymore. That night I saw my good friend Ulises in the corridor. My lawyer said: nothing bad will happen to you, Heimito, nothing bad can happen to you, that's the law, you'll go live in the country. And my good friend Ulises? I said. He'll stay here for a while longer. Until his situation is resolved. That night I dreamed about a white rock and the sky of Beersheba, dazzling as a crystal goblet. The next day I saw my good friend Ulises in the courtyard. The courtyard was covered in a green film but neither one of us seemed to care. We were both wearing new clothes. We could have been brothers. He said: everything is working out, Heimito. Your father is going to take charge of you. And what about you? I said. I'm going back to France, said my good friend Ulises. The Austrian police are paying for my ticket to the border. And when will you come back? I said. I can't come back until 1984, he said. The year of Big Brother. But we don't have brothers, I said. So it would seem, he said. Is the devil's spit green? I asked all of a sudden. It might be, Heimito, he answered, but I'd guess it's colorless. Then he sat on the ground and I started to do my exercises. I ran, I did push-ups, I did squats. When I was done my good friend Ulises had gotten up and was talking to another prisoner. For a minute I thought we were in Beersheba and that the cloudy sky was just a trick of the Jewish engineers. But then I slapped my face and said to myself no, we're in Vienna and my good friend Ulises is leaving tomorrow and he won't be able to come back for a long time and maybe soon I'll see my father. When I went back over to him the other prisoner left. We talked for a while. Take care of yourself, he said when they came to get him, stay in shape, Heimito. See you soon, I said, and then I never saw him again.

**María Font, Calle Montes, near the Monumento a la Revolución, Mexico City DF, February 1981.** When Ulises came back to Mexico, I had just moved in here. I was in love with a guy who taught high school math. Things between us had been rocky at first because he was married and I thought he would never leave his wife, but one day he called me at my parents' house and told me to find a place where we could live together. He couldn't stand his wife anymore and they were about to separate. He was married and had two children, and he said his wife used the children to blackmail him. The conversation we had wasn't especially reassuring — in fact quite the contrary — but the next morning I really did start looking for a place where the two of us could live, even if it was only temporary.

Of course, money was a problem. He had his salary but he had to keep paying rent on the house where his children lived and contribute money each month to pay for their keep, tuition, etc. And I didn't have a job and all I could count on was an allowance that one of my mother's sisters was giving me to finish my studies in dance and painting. So I had to dip into my savings, borrow from my mother, and not look for anything too expensive. After three days, Xóchitl told me that there was a vacant room in the hotel where she and Requena lived. I moved in right away.

The room was big, with a bathroom and a kitchen, and it was right above Xóchitl and Requena's room.

That very night the math teacher came to see me and we made love until dawn. The next day, however, he didn't show up, and even when I tried calling him a few times at school, I couldn't reach him. Two days later I saw him again and I accepted all the explanations he was willing to give me. That was more or less how things went during the first and then the second week of my new life on Calle Montes. The math teacher would show up every four days, more or less, and we would be together until dawn and the start of a new workday. Then he would disappear.

Naturally, we didn't only make love. We talked too. He would tell me things about his children. Once, talking to me about the littlest girl, he started to cry, and finally he said that he didn't understand any of it. What's to understand? I said. He looked at me as if I'd said something idiotic, as if I were too young to know what he meant, and didn't answer. Otherwise, my life was more or less the same as it had always been. I went to class, found a (miserably paid) job as a proofreader at a publishing house, saw my friends, and took long walks around the city. Xóchitl and I grew closer, in large part because we were now neighbors. In the evenings, when the math teacher wasn't around, I would go down to her room and we would talk or play with the little boy. Requena was almost never there (although he, at least, came home every night) and Xóchitl and I would talk about the things that mattered to us, women's things, unconstrained by the presence of men. As was only natural, the subject of our first conversations was the math teacher and his strange ideas about how a new relationship should work. According to Xóchitl, the guy was ultimately a gutless jerk who was afraid to leave his wife. In my opinion, it had much more to do with his sensitivity, his desire not to hurt anyone unnecessarily, than with real fear. Privately, I was surprised how firmly Xóchitl took my side, and not the side of the math teacher's wife.

Sometimes we would go to the park with little Franz. One night when the math teacher was there, I invited them to dinner. The math teacher wanted us to be alone, but Xóchitl had asked to be introduced to him, and I thought this was the perfect occasion. It was the first dinner I had given in what I now thought of as my new home, and although the meal itself was simple, a big salad, cheeses, and wine, Requena and Xóchitl showed up punctually and Xóchitl was wearing her best dress. The math teacher was trying to be nice, which I appreciated, but I don't know whether it was the meagerness of the food (in those days I was into low-calorie eating) or the abundance of wine, but the dinner was a disaster. When my friends left, the math teacher called them parasites, saying that they were the kind of element that paralyzes society and keeps a country from ever making any progress. I said that I was just like them and he replied that it wasn't true, that I studied and worked whereas they didn't do anything. They're poets, I argued. The math teacher looked me in the eyes and repeated the word *poet* several times. Lazy slobs is what they are, he said, and bad parents. Who goes out to eat and leaves their child alone at home? That night, as we were making love, I thought about little Franz sleeping in the room downstairs as his parents drank wine and ate cheese in my room, and I felt empty and irresponsible. Not much later, maybe a day or two afterward, Requena told me that Ulises Lima had come back to Mexico.

One afternoon, as I was reading, I heard Xóchitl calling me, banging on her ceiling with a broomstick. I leaned out the window. Ulises is here, said Xóchitl, do you want to come down? I went downstairs. There was Ulises. I wasn't especially thrilled to see him. Everything he and Belano had meant to me was too remote now. He talked about his travels. I thought there was too much literature in his telling of them. As he was talking I started to play with little Franz. Then Ulises said he had to go see the Rodríguez brothers and asked whether we wanted to go with him. Xóchitl and I looked at each other. If you want to go, I'll watch the kid, I said. Before I left, Ulises asked me about Angélica. She's home, I said, call her. I can't say why, but my attitude was generally hostile. When they left, Xóchitl winked at me. That night the math teacher didn't come. I fed little Franz in my room and then I took him downstairs, got him into his pajamas, and put him to bed, where he soon fell asleep. I chose a book from the shelf and sat reading beside the window, watching the headlights of the cars going by on Calle Montes. I read and thought.

At midnight, Requena came home. He asked me what I was doing there and where Xóchitl was. I told him she had gone to a meeting of visceral realists at the Rodríguez brothers' house. After he checked on his son, Requena asked me whether I'd eaten. I told him I hadn't. I'd forgotten to eat. But I gave the boy his supper, I said.

Requena opened the refrigerator and took out a small pot that he put on the stove. It was rice soup. He asked me whether I wanted any. What I really wanted was not to go back to my lonely room, so I said I'd have a little. We spoke in lowered voices so as not to wake up little Franz. How are your dance classes going? he said. How are your painting classes going? Requena had only been in my room once, the night of the dinner, and he'd liked my paintings. Everything's fine, I said. And your poetry? I haven't written for a long time, I said. Me neither, he said. The rice soup was very spicy. I asked him whether Xóchitl always cooked like that. Always, he said, it must be a family tradition.

For a while we looked at each other without saying anything, and we looked out the window too, and at Franz's bed and the unevenly painted walls. Then Requena started to talk about Ulises and his return to Mexico. My mouth and my stomach were burning, and then I realized that my face was burning too. I thought he would stay in Europe forever, I heard Requena saying. I don't know why I started to think about Xóchitl's father just then, whom I had only seen once, as he was leaving the room. When I saw him I took a step backward, because I thought he was a frightening-looking man. He's my father, said Xóchitl when she saw the expression of alarm on my face. He nodded to me, and left. Visceral realism is dead, said Requena, we should forget about it and make something new. A Mexican section of surrealism, I murmured. I need something to drink, I said. I watched Requena get up and open the refrigerator, the yellow light streaking across the floor to the legs of little Franz's bed. I saw a ball and some tiny slippers, though they were too big to belong to the boy, and I thought about Xóchitl's feet, much smaller than mine. Did you notice anything new about Ulises? said Requena. I drank some cold water. I didn't notice anything, I said. Requena got up and opened the window to clear the cigarette smoke. He acts crazy, said Requena, like he's out of his head. I heard a noise from little Franz's bed. Does he talk in his sleep? I asked. No, it's from outside, said Requena. I went over to the window and looked up toward my room. The light was off. Then I felt Requena's hands on my waist and I didn't move. He didn't move either. After a while he pulled down my pants and I felt his penis between my buttocks. We didn't say anything to each other. When we were done we sat down at the table again and lit cigarettes. Will you tell Xóchitl? said Requena. Do you want me to tell her? I said. I'd rather you didn't, he said.

I left at two in the morning and Xóchitl still hadn't come home. The next day, when I got back from my painting classes, Xóchitl came to my room to get me. I went with her to the supermarket. As we were shopping she told me that Ulises Lima and Pancho Rodríguez had fought. Visceral realism is dead, said Xóchitl, if only you'd been there . . . I told her that I didn't write poetry anymore, and I didn't want to have anything to do with poets either. When we got back, Xóchitl asked me in. She hadn't made the bed, and the dishes from the night before, the dishes

Requena and I had used, were piled unwashed in the sink along with Xóchitl and Franz's lunch dishes.

That night the math teacher didn't come either. I called my sister from a public phone. I didn't have anything to say but I needed to talk to someone and I didn't feel like being in Xóchitl's room again. I caught her on her way out. She was going to the theater. What do you want? she said. Do you need money? We made conversation for a while, then before we hung up I asked her whether she knew that Ulises Lima was back in Mexico. She hadn't heard. She didn't care. We said goodbye and hung up. Then I called the math teacher's house. His wife answered the phone. Hello? she said. I was silent. Answer, you goddamn fucking bitch, she said. I hung up gently and went home. Two days later Xóchitl told me that Catalina O'Hara was having a party where all the visceral realists might get together and see whether it was possible to start the group up again, put out a magazine, plan new activities. She asked me whether I planned to go. I said no, but that if she wanted to go I would watch Franz. That night Requena and I made love again, for a long time, from the moment the boy fell asleep until three in the morning, approximately, and for a moment I thought that he was the one I loved, not the stupid math teacher.

The next day Xóchitl told me how the meeting had gone. Like a zombie movie. In her opinion, visceral realism was finished, which was too bad because the poems she was writing now, she said, were really visceral realist poems. I listened to her without saying anything. Then I asked about Ulises. He's the boss, said Xóchitl, but he's on his own. After that, there were no more visceral realist meetings, and Xóchitl didn't ask me to watch her son at night again. My relationship with the math teacher was over, but we still slept together every once in a while and I still kept calling his house, out of masochism, I guess, or worse, because I was bored. One day, though, we talked about everything that was or wasn't happening between us, and after that we stopped seeing each other. When he left he seemed relieved. I thought about moving out of the room on Calle Montes and going back to live at my mother's house. In the end I decided not to leave, to stay there for good.

# 13

Rafael Barrios, sitting in his living room, Jackson Street, San Diego, California, March 1981. Have you seen *Easy Rider*? That's right, the movie with Dennis Hopper, Peter Fonda, and Jack Nicholson. That was basically what we were like back then. But especially Ulises Lima and Arturo Belano, before they left for Europe. Like Dennis Hopper and his doppelgänger: two dark figures, moving fast and full of energy. And it's not that I have anything against Peter Fonda but neither of them looked like him. Müller looked like Peter Fonda. Those two, on the other hand, looked just like Dennis Hopper and that was creepy and seductive, creepy and seductive to those of us who knew them, I mean, those of us who were their friends. And this isn't a judgment of Peter Fonda. I like Peter Fonda. Whenever that movie he made with Frank Sinatra's daughter and Bruce Dern is on TV I watch it, even if I have to stay up till four in the morning. But neither of them looked like him. And they really did look like Dennis Hopper. It was as if they were consciously imitating him. Two Dennis Hoppers walking the streets of Mexico City. A Mr. Hopper spiraling from east to west, like a double black cloud, until (inevitably) they vanished without a trace on the other side of the city, the side where there was no way out. And sometimes I'd look at them and even though I liked them a lot I'd think, what kind of act is this? what kind of scam or collective suicide is this? And one night, a little before New Year's Day 1976, before they left for Sonora, I realized it was their way of playing politics, a way that isn't my way anymore and that at the time I didn't understand. Their way might have been good or bad, right or wrong, but it was their way of playing politics, of politically influencing reality. I'm sorry if what I'm saying doesn't make sense. Lately I've been feeling a little bit confused.

**Barbara Patterson, in her kitchen, Jackson Street, San Diego, California, March 1981.** Dennis Hopper? Politics? That son of a bitch! That piece of butt-hair-crusted shit! What does that dumbfuck know about politics? I was the one who said: take up politics, Rafael, take up some noble cause, goddamn it, you're a freaking man of the people, and the bastard would look at me like I was shit, some piece of trash, like he was looking down from some imaginary height, and he would say: cool it, Barbarita, it's not so easy, and then he'd go to sleep and I'd have to go out to work and then school, I was busy all day, basically, I'm *still* busy all day, back and forth from the university to work (I waitress at a burger place on Reston Avenue), and when I came home Rafael would be asleep, the dishes in the sink, the floor dirty, crumbs in the kitchen (but no food for me, the deadbeat!), the house a pit, like a pack of baboons had been through, and then I'd have to start to clean, sweep, cook, then go out shopping to stock the refrigerator, and when Rafael woke up I'd ask him: have you written, Rafael? have you started your novel about Chicano life in San Diego? and Rafael would look at me like he was watching me on TV and say: I wrote a poem, Barbarita, and then I would give up and say all right, asshole, read it to me, and Rafael would open a couple of beers and hand me one (the bastard knows I shouldn't drink beer), then read me the goddamn poem. And it must be because deep down I still love him that the poem would make me cry almost without me realizing it (only if it was good), and when Rafael was done reading my face would be wet and shiny and he would come closer to me and I could smell him, he smelled like a Mexican, the bastard, and we would hold each other very gently, and then, but maybe half an hour later, we would start to make love, and then Rafael would say to me: what are we going to eat, baby? and I would get up, without getting dressed, and go into the kitchen and make him his eggs with ham and bacon, and as I cooked I would think about literature and politics and I would remember the time when Rafael and I were still living in Mexico and we went to see a Cuban poet, let's go see him, Rafael, I said, you're a man of the people and that faggot will have to recognize how talented

301

you are whether he wants to or not, and Rafael said: but I'm a visceral realist, Barbarita, and I said don't be a dumb shit, your goddamn balls are visceral realist, will you face the fucking truth for once in your life, darling? so Rafael and I went to see the great lyric poet of the Revolution, and all the Mexican poets Rafael hated most (the poets Belano and Lima hated most, that is) had been there, it was funny because both of us could tell it by the smell, the Cuban's hotel room *smelled* like the peasant poets, like the poets from the magazine *El Delfín Proletario*, like Huerta's wife, like the Mexican Stalinists, like the shitty revolutionaries who cash a government check every two weeks, but anyway, what I said to myself and what I tried to tell Rafael telepathically was: don't blow it now, don't fuck this up, and the Havana guy was nice to us, a little tired, a little sad, but basically nice, and Rafael talked about the young Mexican poets but not about the visceral realists (before we went in I told him I'd kill him if he did) and I even came up on the spot with a plan for a magazine that, I said, the University of San Diego was going to fund, and the Cuban was interested in that, interested in Rafael's poems, interested in my fucking nonexistent magazine, and suddenly, when our visit was almost over, the Cuban, who at this point seemed more asleep than awake, suddenly asked us about visceral realism. I don't know how to explain it. The room in that fucking hotel. The silence and the distant elevators. The smell of the previous visitors. The Cuban's eyes, closing from sleep or boredom or liquor. His unexpected words, as if spoken by a man under hypnosis, a man mesmerized. It made me give a little scream, just a little scream but it sounded like a shot. It must have been nerves, that's what I told them. Then the three of us were silent for a while, the Cuban surely wondering who this hysterical gringa must be, Rafael wondering whether or not to talk about the group, and me saying over and over to myself you stupid fucking bitch, one of these days you're going to have to sew your fucking mouth shut. And then, as I imagined myself sitting in my closet at home, with a giant scab for a mouth, reading the stories of *El llano en llamas* over and over again, I heard Rafael talking about the visceral realists, I heard the fucking Cuban asking question after question, I heard Rafael saying yes, saying maybe, talking about the birth pangs of communism, I heard the Cuban proposing manifestos, proclamations, repostulations, greater ideological clarity, and then I couldn't restrain myself anymore and I opened my mouth and said that those days were over now, now Rafael was only speaking for himself, like the good poet he was, and then Rafael said be quiet, Barbarita, and I said don't tell me to be quiet, you bum, and the Cuban said oh, women, and tried to step in with his rotten, revolting macho bullshit, and I said shit, shit, shit, we just want to be published by the Casa de las Américas on our own merits, and then the Cuban looked at me very seriously and said of course, the Casa de las Américas *always* publishes people on their merits. As long as it suits them, I said, and Rafael said Jesus, Barbarita, the maestro will get the wrong idea, and I said the fucking maestro can think whatever he fucking wants, but the past is the past, Rafael, and your future is your future, right? and then the Cuban looked at me even more seriously, his eyes seeming to say sweetheart, if we were in Moscow you'd end up in a mental ward, but at the same time (I noticed this too) as if he were thinking, well, what does it matter, madness is madness is madness, and sadness too, and at the end of the day the three of us are Americans, children of Caliban, lost in the great American wilderness, and I think that touched me, to see a spark of understanding, a spark of tolerance in the eyes of that powerful man, as if he were saying don't take it to heart, Barbara, I know how these things are, and then, like an idiot, I smiled, and Rafael took out his poems, some fifty loose-leaf pages, and said here are my poems, friend, and the Cuban took his poems and thanked him, and then right away he and Rafael got up, as if in slow motion, like a flash of lightning, or twin flashes, or a flash and its shadow, but in slow motion, and in that fraction of a second I thought: everything is all right, I hope everything will be all right, and I saw myself swimming on a Havana beach and I saw Rafael by my side, a little distance away, talking to some American journalists, people from New York, from San Francisco, talking about LITERATURE, talking about POLITICS, at the gates of paradise.

**José "Zopilote" Colina, Café Quito, Avenida Bucareli, Mexico City DF, March 1981.** This was the closest those deadbeats got to politics. Once when I was at *El Nacional*, in 1975 or thereabouts, Arturo Belano, Ulises Lima, and Felipe Müller were there waiting for Don Juan Rejano to see them. Suddenly in walks this blonde, not bad looking either (and I'm an expert), and she cuts right in front of all the lousy poets who're sitting there crowded together like flies in the little room where Don Juan Rejano worked. No one complained, of course (they might have been poor but they were gentlemen, the dipshits, and anyway, what the fuck could they say?), so the blonde goes up to Don Juan's desk and gives him a bunch of paper, some translations, I think I heard her say (I have excellent hearing), and Don Juan, God bless him, men like him are few and far between, gives her a big smile and says how are you, Verónica (the oily Spanish son of a bitch, he treated the rest of us like dirt), what good wind brings you here? and this Verónica gives him the translations and they talk for a while, or actually Verónica talks to the old man and Don Juan nods, like he's hypnotized, and then the blond girl takes her check, puts it in her purse, turns on her heel, and vanishes down the filthy rotten hallway, and then, as the rest of us are drooling, Don Giovanni sits there for a minute sort of dazed and lost in thought, and Arturo Belano, who was somebody he always trusted and who was sitting closest to him, says: what is it, Don Juan, what's the matter? and Don Rejas, as if emerging from a fucking dream or a fucking nightmare looks him in the eye and says: do you know who that girl was? speaking with a Spanish-from-Spain accent too, which was a bad sign, since not only did Rejano have a rotten temper, he usually spoke with a Mexican accent, as none of you would have any reason to know, poor old guy, the shitty luck he had at the end, but anyway, he says do you know who that girl was, Arturo? and Belano says no sir, but she looked nice. Who was she? Trotsky's great-granddaughter! says Don Rejas, none other than Lev Davidovich's great-granddaughter Verónica Volkow (or was it granddaughter? no, great-granddaughter, I think), and then, sorry I keep losing my place, Belano said far out and went running after Verónica Volkow, and Lima hurried after Belano, and the kid Müller stayed for a minute to pick up their checks and then he was off like a shot too, and Rejano watched them disappear down the Hall of Filth and he smiled as if to himself, as if to say lousy little fuckers, and I think he must have been thinking about the Spanish Civil War, his dead friends, his long years of exile, maybe he was even thinking of his years as a Communist Party militant, although that was an odd fit with Trotsky's great-granddaughter, but that was Don Rejas, basically a sentimental guy, a good guy, and then he came back down to planet Earth, to the lousy editorial department of the *Revista Mexicana de Cultura, El Nacional's* cultural supplement, and everyone who was crowded into the stuffy room and languishing in the dark hallway snapped back to reality with him and we all got our checks.

Later, after I'd come to terms with Don Giovanni over a piece about a painter buddy of mine and gone out with two guys from the paper, all ready to start drinking early, I saw them through the windows of a café, I think it was La Estrella Errante, but I can't remember. Verónica Volkow was with them. They'd caught up with her and asked her out for a drink. I watched them for a while, standing on the sidewalk while the guys I was with decided where to go. They seemed happy: Belano, Lima, Müller, and Trotsky's great-granddaughter. Through the windows I watched them laugh, watched them fall all over the place laughing. They were probably never going to see her again. The Volkow girl was clearly a society type and those guys were going to end up at Lecumberri or Alcatraz, it was written all over them. I don't know what was wrong with me, I swear. I felt tenderhearted and Zopilote Colina never goes soft like that. The bastards were laughing with Verónica Volkow, but they were laughing with Leon Trotsky too. It was the closest they would ever get to the Bolsheviks. It was probably the closest they would ever want to get. I thought about Don Ivan Rejanovich, and I felt my chest swell with sadness. But with happiness too, goddamn it. The strangest things happened at *La Nacional* on payday.

**Verónica Volkow, with a female friend and two male friends, International Departures, Mexico City DF airport, April 1981.** Mr. José Colinas was mistaken when he said that I would never see the Chilean citizens Arturo Belano and Felipe Müller and their friend, my fellow Mexican citizen Ulises Lima, again. If the incidents he describes, with scant regard for the truth, occurred in 1975, it was probably a year later that I saw the young men in question again. If I'm not mistaken, it was in May or June 1976, on what must have been a clear night, even a bright night, the kind of night that year after year makes Mexicans and bewildered foreign visitors move slowly, with great caution, and that I personally find stimulating but decidedly sad.

There isn't much to tell. It was outside a movie theater on Reforma, the day of the opening of some film, American or European, I can't remember.

It might even have been by a Mexican director.

I was with friends and suddenly, I don't know how, I saw them. They were sitting on the stairs, smoking and talking. They had already seen me, but they hadn't come over to say hello. The truth is that they looked like bums, glaringly out of place there, at the entrance to the theater, among well-dressed, clean-shaven people who edged away as they climbed the stairs. It was as if they were afraid that one of them might reach out his hand and grope them. At least one of them seemed to me to be under the influence of some kind of drug. I think it was Belano. The other one, Ulises Lima, I think, was reading and writing in the margins of a book, singing softly to himself. The third one (no, it definitely wasn't Müller, Müller was tall and blond and this person was short and dark) looked at me and smiled as if he knew me. I had no choice but to nod in return, and when my friends were distracted I went over and said hello. Ulises Lima said hello back, although he didn't get up from the stairs. Belano did get up, like a robot, but he looked at me as if he didn't recognize me. The third one said you're Verónica Volkow and he mentioned some poems of mine that had recently been published in a magazine. He was the only one who seemed to feel like talking. Please God, I thought, don't let him talk to me about Trotsky, but he didn't talk about Trotsky, he talked about poetry, saying something about a magazine he was publishing with a mutual friend (a mutual friend? horrible!) and then he said other things that I didn't understand.

As I was about to go—I was only with them for a minute—Belano looked at me more carefully and recognized me. Ah, Verónica Volkow, he said, and what seemed to me like an enigmatic smile appeared on his face. How's the poetry going? he said. I didn't know how to answer such a stupid question and I shrugged my shoulders. I heard one of my friends calling me and I said I had to go. Belano held out his hand and I shook it. The third one gave me a kiss on the cheek. For a moment I thought he'd have been perfectly capable of leaving his friends there on the stairs and joining my group. See you later, Verónica, he said. Ulises Lima didn't get up. As I was going into the theater I saw them for the last time. A fourth person had arrived and was talking to them. I think it was the painter Pérez Camarga, but I can't say for sure. In any case, he was nicely dressed, well groomed, and he seemed nervous about something. Later, on my way out of the theater, I saw Pérez Camarga or the person who looked like him, but I didn't see the three poets, by which I deduced that they'd been there on the stairs waiting for that fourth person and that after their brief encounter they'd left.

———

**Alfonso Pérez Camarga, Calle Toledo, Mexico City DF, June 1981.**
Belano and Lima weren't revolutionaries. They weren't writers. Sometimes they wrote poetry, but I don't think they were poets either. They
sold drugs. Marijuana, mostly, although they also had a stock of shrooms
in glass jars, little baby-food jars, and although at first it looked disgusting, like a tiny turd floating in amniotic fluid in a glass container, we
ended up getting used to those fucking shrooms and that's what we usually ordered, shrooms from Oaxaca, shrooms from Tamaulipas, shrooms
from La Huasteca in Veracruz or Potosí, or wherever they were from.
Shrooms to do at our parties or in *petit comité*. Who were we? Painters
like me, architects like poor Quim Font (in fact, he was the one who introduced them to us, never suspecting the relationship we would soon
strike up, or at least that's what I'd like to think). Because beneath it all
those kids were shrewd businessmen. When I met them (at poor Quim's
house), we talked about poetry and painting. Mexican poetry and painting, I mean (is there any other kind?). But before long, we were talking
about drugs. And from drugs we moved on to business. And after a few
minutes they had taken me out into the garden, and I was under a poplar
tree, sampling their marijuana. First-class? Was it ever. Like nothing I'd
tasted for a long time. And that was how I became their client. And
meanwhile I talked them up to various painter and architect friends of
mine for free, and they became clients of Lima and Belano too. Well,
from a certain point of view, it was an improvement, even a relief. They
were at least *clean*, I guess. And you could talk to them about art while
you were doing the deal. And we trusted them not to blackmail us or set
us up. You know, none of the shit that small-time dealers pull. And they
were more or less discreet (or so we thought) and punctual, and they had
connections, you could call them and say I need fifty grams of Acapulco
Gold for tomorrow because I'm throwing a surprise party, and all they
would ask you was where and when, they didn't even mention money, although of course they never had anything to complain about in that
regard, we paid what they asked without argument, which is always nice
in a customer, don't you think? And everything went perfectly smoothly.
Sometimes, of course, we had disagreements. It was mostly our fault. We
were too trusting, and as everybody knows, some people are better kept at
arm's length. But our democratic spirit got the best of us, and when there
was a party or an especially boring meeting, for example, we would invite
them in, pour them drinks, ask them to tell us more about where exactly

the stuff that we were about to ingest or smoke came from, that kind of thing, innocent questions, in no way meant to be offensive, and they drank our liquor and ate our food, but—how to put it?—in an absent way, maybe, or a cold way, as if they were there but not there, or as if we were insects or cows that they bled each night and that it made sense to keep comfortably alive but without the slightest hint of closeness, warmth, or affection. And even though we were usually drunk or high, we noticed, and sometimes, to annoy them, we forced them to listen to what we had to say, our opinions, what we really thought about them. Of course, we never considered them to be real poets. Much less revolutionaries. They were salesmen, and that was all. We respected Octavio Paz, for example, and they held him in utter contempt, willfully ignorant. That's just unacceptable, don't you think? Once, I don't know why, they said something about Tamayo, something negative about Tamayo, and that was the last straw, I can't remember the context, and in fact I don't even know where it was, maybe at my house, maybe not, it doesn't matter, but someone was talking about Tamayo and José Luis Cuevas, and one of us praised José Luis's toughness, the power and courage that each and every one of his works radiates, saying how lucky we were to be his fellow citizens and contemporaries, and then Lima or Belano (the two of them were sitting in a corner, that's how I remember them, in a corner waiting for their money) said that Cuevas's courage, or his toughness, or his energy, I don't know which, was all bluff, and that declaration cast a sudden chill over us, made a cold indignation rise in us, if you know what I mean. We almost ate them alive. I mean, sometimes it was funny to hear them talk. They really seemed like two extraterrestrials. But as they got more comfortable, as you got to know them or started to *listen* to them more carefully, their pose seemed more sad than anything else, offputting. They weren't poets, certainly, and they weren't revolutionaries. I don't even think they were sexualized. What do I mean by that? Just that sex didn't seem to interest them (the only thing that interested them was the money they could squeeze out of us), nor did poetry or politics, although their look seemed modeled on the hackneyed archetype of the young leftist poet. But sex didn't interest them, I know that for a fact. How do I know? From a friend, an architect friend who tried to have sex with one of them. Belano, probably. And at the moment of truth nothing happened. Limp dicks.

# 14

**Hugo Montero, having a beer at the bar La Mala Senda, Calle Pensador Mexicano, Mexico City DF, May 1982.** There was a free spot, and I said to myself, why don't I get my buddy Ulises Lima into the Nicaragua group? This happened in January, so it was a good way to start the year. Also, I'd heard that Lima was in bad shape, and I thought that a little field trip to the Revolution would cheer anybody up. So I got the papers in order without consulting anyone and I put Ulises on the plane to Managua. Of course, I had no idea that I was signing my own death warrant. If I'd known, Ulises Lima would never have left Mexico City, but sometimes I'm like that, impulsive, and in the end what's meant to be will be, because we're puppets in the hands of fate, aren't we?

Well, anyway, as I was saying: I put Ulises on the plane, and even before we took off I think I got a whiff of what our little trip might have in store for me. My boss, the poet Álamo, was the head of the Mexican delegation, and when he saw Ulises he turned pale and called me aside. What's that idiot doing here, Montero? he said. He's coming with us to Managua, I replied. I'd rather not repeat the rest of what Álamo said, because I'm really not a bad person. But I thought: if you didn't want him on the trip, you lazy bastard, why didn't you take care of the invitations yourself? why didn't *you* take the trouble to call everyone who was supposed to come? Álamo had personally invited his best buddies, namely the peasant-poet gang. And then he had personally invited his favorite suck-ups, and then the heavyweights, or literary lights, all local champions in their respective divisions of Mexican literature, but as always, no one has any sense of etiquette in this country, and two or three assholes canceled at the last minute and I was the one who had to fill the gaps, or

*rellenar las ausencias,* as Neruda puts it. And that was when I thought of
Lima. I'd heard from who knows who that he was back in Mexico and
that he was having a shitty time of it, and I'm the kind of guy who'll help
a person out when I can, what can you do, Mexico made me this way
and that's all there is to it.

Now, of course, I'm out of a job and sometimes, when I'm in a certain mood, when I wake up with a hangover and it's one of those apoca-
lyptic Mexico City mornings, I think that I did the wrong thing, that I
could have invited someone else, in a word, that I fucked up, but most of
the time I'm not sorry. And there we were on the plane, as I was saying,
Álamo having just found out that Ulises was crashing our junket, and I
said: relax, maestro, nothing will happen, you have my word, and then
Álamo gave me a hard look, a scorching look, if that doesn't sound too
ridiculous, and said: all right, Montero, it's your problem, let's see how
you deal with it. And I said: the Mexican pavilion will float above the
fray, boss! Peace and calm. Don't you worry about a thing. And by then
we were already on our way to Managua through the blackest of black
skies, and the writers of the delegation were drinking as if they knew or
suspected or had been tipped off that the plane was going down, and I
was walking back and forth, up and down the aisle, greeting all the atten-
dees, passing out sheets printed with the Declaration of Mexican Writers, a statement that Álamo and the peasant poets had composed in
support of their sister country of Nicaragua and that I'd typed up (and
corrected, I don't mind saying), so that those who weren't familiar with
it, which was most people, could read it, and those who hadn't given it
their stamp of approval, which was only a few, could scrawl their names
under the heading "We the undersigned," or in other words right under
the signatures of Álamo and the peasant poets, the five horsemen of the
apocalypse. And then, as I was collecting the missing signatures, I remembered Ulises Lima. I saw him slouched in his seat with his head
hanging down, and I thought he must be sick or asleep, but whatever it
was, he had his eyes closed and he was grimacing, like someone in the
middle of a nightmare, I thought. And then I thought, this guy isn't going to sign the declaration just like that, and for a second, as the plane
lurched from side to side and everyone's worst fears seemed about to be
confirmed, I weighed the possibility of not asking for his signature, of
completely ignoring him, since, after all, I'd gotten him on the trip as a
friendly favor, because he wasn't doing well, or so I'd been told, not so

that he would pledge his allegiance to some group or other, but then it occurred to me that Álamo and the peasant poets would go over the "We the undersigned" with a magnifying glass and I'd be the one to pay if his name was missing. And doubt, as Othon says, lodged itself in my mind. And then I went over to Ulises and touched his arm and he opened his eyes immediately, like he was a goddamn robot I had awoken by activating some hidden mechanism in his flesh, and he looked at me as if he didn't know me but did recognize me, if that makes sense (I guess it doesn't), and then I sat down next to him and I said look, Ulises, we have a problem, all the poets here have signed this stupid thing that's supposed to show their solidarity with Nicaraguan writers and the people of Nicaragua, and your signature is the only one I still don't have, but if you don't want to sign, it's no big deal, I think I can fix things, and then he said, in a voice that broke my heart: let me read it, and at first I didn't know what the fuck he was talking about and when I realized I handed him a copy of the declaration and I watched him, what's the word, immerse himself in it? something like that, and I said: I'll be back in a minute, Ulises, I'm going to take a stroll around the plane since you never know when the captain might need my help, and meanwhile you sit there and read, take your time and don't feel pressured, if you want to sign you can, and if you don't, then don't, and with that I got up and went back to the prow of the plane, it's called the prow, isn't it? well, anyway, the front part, and I spent more time handing out the fucking declaration and chatting away with the cream of Mexican and Latin American literature (there were several writers on the trip who were living in exile in Mexico: three Argentinians, one Chilean, a Guatemalan, and two Uruguayans), who by this point were beginning to show the first signs of inebriation, and when I got back to Ulises's place, I found the signed declaration, the paper neatly folded on the empty seat, and Ulises, sitting up very straight, though with his eyes closed again, as if he were suffering horribly, but also as if he were enduring his suffering with great dignity. And that was the last I saw of him until we reached Managua.

I don't know what he did for the first few days. All I know is that he didn't go to a single reading, meeting, or roundtable discussion. Every once in a while I would think of him, fuck, the things he was missing. History in the making, as they say, one endless party. I remember that I went to his hotel room to look for him on the day that Ernesto Cardenal had a reception for us at the Ministry of Culture, but he wasn't there and at the desk they told me that he hadn't been back for a few nights. What can you do, I said to myself, he must be off boozing somewhere or with some Nicaraguan friend or whatever, I was busy, I had to take care of the whole Mexican delegation and I couldn't spend all day looking for Ulises Lima, I'd already done enough getting him on the trip in the first place. So I washed my hands of him and the days went by, as Vallejo says, and I remember that one afternoon Álamo came up to me and said Montero, where the fuck is your friend? because it's been a long time since I've seen him. And then I thought: shit, it's true, isn't it? Ulises had disappeared. Frankly, it took me a little while to grasp the situation in front of me, the array of dire and not so dire possibilities that suddenly ranged themselves before me with a dull thud. I thought: he must be somewhere, and although I can't say I forgot all about him a second later, you might say I shelved the problem. But Álamo didn't shelve it and that night, during a Nicaraguan-Mexican poets' fellowship dinner, he asked me again where the hell Ulises Lima had gone. To make matters worse, one of Cardenal's fucking protégés who had studied in Mexico knew Ulises, and when he heard that Ulises was part of the delegation he insisted on seeing him, so he could greet the father of visceral realism, he said. He was a short, dark, balding little Nicaraguan guy who looked familiar to me, maybe I'd even organized one of his readings at Bellas Artes years ago, I don't know, it struck me that he was half kidding, mostly because of the way he said what he did about the father of visceral realism, like he was mocking Ulises, getting his kicks there in front of the Mexican poets who, I have to say, laughed as if they were in on the joke, even Álamo laughed, in part because it was funny and in part to observe the protocols of hell, unlike the Nics, who mostly laughed because everybody else was laughing or because they felt they had to. It takes all kinds, especially in this business.

And when I was finally able to get away from all those annoying bastards it was already after midnight and the next day I had to herd everyone back to Mexico City and the truth is that I suddenly felt tired, kind of queasy, almost sick but not quite, so I decided to have a nightcap at the hotel bar, where they served more or less decent drinks, not like at other places in Managua where the stuff was pure poison, I don't know what the Sandinistas are waiting for to do something about it. And at the hotel bar I ran into Don Pancracio Montesol, who had come with the Mexican delegation even though he was Guatemalan, among other things because there was no Guatemalan delegation and because he'd been living in Mexico for at least thirty years. And Don Pancracio saw me hitting the bottle and at first he didn't say anything, but then he leaned over and said Montero, my boy, you look a little worried tonight, is it girl trouble? So he said, more or less. And I said if only, Don Pancracio, I'm just tired, a lame answer no matter how you look at it, since it's much better to be tired than to be pining away for some girl, but that was what I said, and Don Pancracio must have noticed that something was wrong because I'm usually a little less incoherent, so he leaped from his stool—I was shocked by how nimble he was—and crossed the space between us, settling himself on the stool beside me with a graceful hop. What's wrong, then? he said. I've lost a member of the delegation, I answered. Don Pancracio looked at me like I was dense and then ordered a double scotch. For a while the two of us sat there in silence, drinking and looking out the windows at the dark space that was the city of Managua, the perfect city to lose yourself in, literally, I mean, a city that only its mailmen could find their way around, and where in fact the Mexican delegation had gotten lost more than once, I can vouch for that. For the first time in a long time, I think, I started to feel comfortable. A few minutes later a kid showed up, a really skinny kid who headed straight for Don Pancracio to ask for his autograph. He had one of Don Pancracio's books with him, published by Mortiz, worn and dog-eared. I heard him stammering and then he left. In a kind of sepulchral voice Don Pancracio mentioned his host of admirers. Then his small legion of plagiarizers. And finally his basketball-team's-worth of critics. And he also mentioned Giacomo Moreno-Rizzo, the Mexican-Venetian, who obviously wasn't part of our delegation, although when Don Pancracio said his name, I got the idea, idiot that I am, that Moreno-Rizzo was there, that he had just come into the bar, which was entirely unlikely since our delegation, despite all its faults, was solidly leftist, and Moreno-Rizzo, as everybody knows, is one of Paz's hangers-on. And Don Pancracio mentioned, or alluded to, Moreno-Rizzo's dogged efforts to surreptitiously imitate him, Don Pancracio. But Moreno-Rizzo couldn't help sounding prim and thuggish at the same time, typical of Europeans stranded in America, forced to make superficial gestures of bravado in order to survive in a hostile environment, whereas Don Pancracio's prose, my prose, said Don Pancracio, was the prose of a legitimate descendant of Reyes, if he did say so himself, natural foe of Moreno-Rizzo's brand of chilly fakery. Then Don Pancracio said: so which Mexican writer are you missing? His voice startled me. Someone called Ulises Lima, I said, feeling my skin erupt in goose bumps. Ah, said Don Pancracio. And how long has he been missing? I have no idea, I confessed, maybe since the first day. Don Pancracio was silent again. Signaling to the bartender, he ordered another scotch. After all, the Ministry of Education was paying. No, not since the first day, said Don Pancracio, who's the quiet type but very observant. I passed him in the hotel on the first day of our stay, and the second day too, so he hadn't left by then, although it's true I don't remember seeing him anywhere else. Is he a poet? Of course, he must be, he said without waiting for me to answer. And that was the last time you saw him, on the second day? I said. The second night, said Don Pancracio. Yes, that was the last time. And now what do I do? I said. Stop moping, said Don Pancracio, all poets get lost at some point or another. Just report his disappearance to the police. The Sandinista police, he specified. But I didn't have the balls to call the police. Sandinista or Somozan, the police is always the police, and whether it was the alcohol or the night outside the windows, I didn't have the guts to rat Ulises out like that.

It was a decision I'd later regret, since the next morning, before we left for the airport, Álamo came up with the idea of gathering the whole delegation in the hotel lobby, supposedly for a final rundown of our stay in Managua but really to raise a last glass in the sun. And when all of us had left no doubt about our undying solidarity with the Nicaraguan people and were on our way to our rooms to pick up our suitcases, Álamo, together with one of the peasant poets, came over and asked if Ulises Lima had ever shown up. I had no choice but to tell him that he hadn't, unless Ulises was in his room at that very moment, asleep. Let's settle this right now, said Álamo, and he got in the elevator, followed by the peasant poet and me. In Ulises Lima's room we found the poet Aurelio Pradera, an elegant stylist, who confessed what I already knew, which was that Ulises had been there for the first two days but then vanished. And why didn't you tell Hugo? bellowed Álamo. The explanations that followed weren't very clear. Álamo tore at his hair. Aurelio Pradera said that he didn't understand why he was being blamed when he'd had to endure a whole night of Ulises talking in his sleep, which in his opinion was just as bad. The peasant poet sat on the bed where the cause of the commotion should supposedly have slept and started to flip through a literary magazine. A little later I realized that another of the peasant poets had graced us with his presence and that behind him, on the threshold, was Don Pancracio Montesol, mute spectator of the drama unfolding within the four walls of Room 405. Of course, as I at once realized, I'd been relieved of the duties of managing director of the Mexican delegation. In the emergency this role fell to Julio Labarca, the Marxist theoretician of the peasant poets, who took charge of the situation with a vigor that I was far from feeling myself.

His first decision was to call the police, then he convened an emergency meeting of what he called the "thinking minds" of the delegation, in other words, the writers who every so often wrote opinion pieces, essays, or reviews of political books (the "creative minds" were the poets or the fiction writers like Don Pancracio, and there was also the category of "hotheads," the novices and beginners like Aurelio Pradera and maybe Ulises Lima himself, and the "thinking-creative minds," the crème de la crème, consisting of just two peasant poets, Labarca first among them), and after a brisk, forthright evaluation of the new situation fostered or created by the incident, and of the incident itself, they came to the conclusion that the best thing for the delegation would be to stick to the original schedule, or in other words to depart without delay that very day and leave the Lima affair in the hands of the proper authorities.

Truly extraordinary things were said about the political repercussions that the disappearance of a Mexican poet in Nicaragua might entail, but then, keeping in mind that very few people knew Ulises Lima and that of the few people who did, half weren't speaking to him, the level of alarm dropped several degrees. Somebody even raised the possibility that his disappearance might pass unnoticed.

After a while the police showed up and Álamo, Labarca, and I spent some time talking to one of them who called himself an inspector and whom Labarca immediately began to address as "comrade," "comrade" this and "comrade" that, but for a policeman he was actually nice and sympathetic, although he didn't tell us anything that we hadn't already thought of ourselves. He asked us about the habits of the "comrade writer." Of course, we told him that we weren't familiar with Ulises's habits. He wanted to know whether Ulises had any "peculiarity" or "weakness." Álamo said that one never knew, the profession was as diverse as humanity itself, and humanity, as we well knew, was a conglomeration of weaknesses. Seconding Álamo (in his own way), Labarca said

315

that Ulises might be a degenerate and he might not. Degenerate in what sense? the Sandinista inspector wanted to know. That I can't say for sure, said Labarca. To be honest, I don't know him. I didn't even see him on the plane. He was on the same plane we were on, wasn't he? Of course, Julio, said Álamo. And then Álamo passed the ball to me: you know him, Montero (the quantity of suppressed rage in those words!), tell us what he's like. I immediately washed my hands of it all. I told the whole story again, from beginning to end, to the manifest boredom of Álamo and Labarca and the sincere interest of the inspector. When I was done he said ah, the lives you writers lead. Then he wanted to know why there'd been writers who hadn't wanted to travel to Managua. For personal reasons, said Labarca. Not because they were hostile to our revolution? How can you think such a thing, certainly not, said Labarca. Which writers didn't want to come? said the inspector. Álamo and Labarca looked at each other, then at me. I opened my big mouth and told him the names. Well, what do you know, said Labarca, so Marco Antonio was invited too? Yes, said Álamo, I thought it was a good idea. And why wasn't I consulted? said Labarca. I mentioned it to Emilio and he said it was all right, said Álamo, annoyed at Labarca for questioning his authority in front of me. So this Marco Antonio, who is he? said the inspector. A poet, said Álamo, flatly. But what kind of poet? the inspector wanted to know. A surrealist poet, said Álamo. A surrealist and a PRI-ist, specified Labarca. A lyric poet, I said. The inspector nodded his head several times, as if to say I see, although it was clear to us that he didn't understand shit. And this lyric poet didn't want to show his support for the Sandinista revolution? Well, said Labarca, that's a strong way to put it. He couldn't make it, I guess, said Álamo. Although you know Marco Antonio, said Labarca, and he laughed for the first time. Álamo took out his pack of Delicados and offered it around. Labarca and I each took one, but the inspector waved them away and lit a Cuban cigarette. These are stronger, he said with a clear hint of irony. It was as if he were saying: we revolutionaries smoke strong tobacco, real men smoke strong tobacco, those of us with a stake in objective reality smoke real tobacco. Stronger than a Delicados? said Labarca. Black tobacco, comrades, genuine tobacco. Álamo laughed under his breath and said: it's hard to believe we've lost a poet, but what he really meant was: what do you know about tobacco, you stupid son of a bitch? You can kiss my ass with your Cuban tobacco, said Labarca almost without batting an eye. What did you say, comrade? said the inspector. That I don't give a shit about Cuban tobacco. Where Del-icados are lit, let the rest be put out. Álamo laughed again and the in-spector seemed to hesitate between turning pale with rage and looking confused. I assume, comrade, that you mean what I think you mean, he said. That's right, I do, you heard me. No one turns his nose up at a Del-icados, said Labarca. Oh, Julio's a bad boy, murmured Álamo, looking at me to hide his barely suppressed laughter from the inspector. And on what grounds do you say that? said the inspector, wreathed in a cloud of smoke. I could see that things were taking a new tone. Labarca raised a hand and waved it back and forth a few inches from the inspector's nose, as if he were slapping him. Don't blow smoke in my face, man, he said, do you mind? This time the inspector definitely turned pale, as if the strong scent of his own tobacco had made him sick. For fuck's sake, show a little respect, comrade, you almost hit me in the nose. If you call that a nose, said Labarca to Álamo, unruffled. If you can't tell the smell of a Delicados from a bundle of vulgar Cuban weed then your nose is failing you, comrade, which hardly matters in and of itself, but in the case of a smoker or a policeman is worrisome, to say the least. A Delicados, you see, Julio, is blond tobacco, said Álamo, overcome by laughter. And the paper is sweet too, said Labarca, which is something you only find in parts of China. And in Mexico, Julio, said Álamo. And in Mexico, of course, said Labarca. The inspector gave them a look of pure hatred, then abruptly put out his cigarette and said in an altered voice that he would have to file a missing person report and that such a procedure could only be carried out at the police station. He seemed ready to arrest us all. Well, what are we waiting for, said Labarca, let's go to the station, comrade. Montero, he said to me on his way out, give the minister of culture a call for me. Okay, Julio, I said. The inspector seemed to hesi-tate for a few seconds. Labarca and Álamo were in the lobby. The in-spector looked at me as if asking for advice. I mimed handcuffed wrists, but he didn't get it. Before he left, he said: they'll be back in less than ten minutes. I shrugged my shoulders and turned away. After a while Don Pancracio Montesol showed up, wearing a spotless white guayabera and carrying a plastic bag from the Gigante supermarket in Colonia Chapul-tepec, full of books. Are matters on the way to being resolved, Montero, my boy? My dear friend Don Pancracio, I said, matters are exactly where they were last night and the night before last. We've lost poor Ulises Lima, and like it or not, it's my fault for having dragged him here.

Don Pancracio, as usual, didn't make the slightest effort to console me and for a few minutes the two of us sat in silence, him drinking his penultimate whiskey and me with my head in my hands, sucking down a daiquiri with a straw and unsuccessfully trying to imagine Ulises Lima with no money and no friends, alone in that ravaged country, as we heard the calls and shouts of the members of our delegation who were roaming the adjoining rooms like stray dogs or wounded parrots. Do you know what the worst thing about literature is? said Don Pancracio. I knew, but I pretended I didn't. What? I said. That you end up being friends with writers. And friendship, treasure though it may be, destroys your critical sense. Once, said Don Pancracio, Monteforte Toledo dropped this riddle in my lap: a poet is lost in a city on the verge of collapse, with no money, or friends, or anyone to turn to. And of course, he neither wants nor plans to turn to anyone. For several days he roams the city and the country, eating nothing, or eating scraps. He's even stopped writing. Or he writes in his head: in other words, he hallucinates. All signs point to an imminent death. His drastic disappearance foreshadows it. And yet the poet doesn't die. How is he saved? Etc., etc. It sounded like Borges, but I didn't tell him so. His fellow writers already pester him enough about whether he's stealing from Borges here or stealing from Borges there, whether he's stealing from him in a good way or stealing from him in a clumsy way, as López Velarde would have said. What I did was listen to Don Pancracio and then follow his example. In other words, I kept my mouth shut. And then a guy came to tell me that the van that was taking us to the airport was in front of the hotel, and I said all right, let's go, but first I looked over at Don Pancracio, who had already gotten down from his stool and was watching me with a smile on his face, as if I'd discovered the answer to the riddle, but obviously I hadn't discovered or figured out or guessed anything, and anyway I didn't give a damn, so I said: this riddle your friend asked you, what was the answer, Don Pancracio? And then Don Pancracio looked at me and said: what friend? Your friend, whoever it was, Miguel Ángel Asturias, the riddle about the poet who's lost and survives. Oh, that, said Don Pancracio as if he were waking up, the truth is I don't remember anymore, but don't worry, the poet doesn't die, he loses everything, but he doesn't die.

What thou lovest well remains, said someone who was standing nearby and had overheard us, a light-skinned guy in a double-breasted suit and red tie who was the official poet of San Luis Potosí, and right

318

there, as if his words had been the starting pistol shot, or in this case the departing shot, major chaos broke out, with Mexican and Nicaraguan writers autographing books for each other, and there was more chaos in the van, which was too small for all of us who were leaving and those who were seeing us off, so that we had to call three taxis to provide additional logistical support for our deployment. It goes without saying that I was the last person to leave the hotel. Before I did, I made a few phone calls and left a letter for Ulises Lima on the highly unlikely chance that he might show up there. In the letter I advised him to head straight to the Mexican embassy where they would take care of getting him back to Mexico. I also called the police station and spoke to Álamo and Labarca, who assured me that we would meet at the airport. Then I got my suitcases, called a taxi, and left.

# 15

Jacinto Requena, Café Quito, Calle Bucareli, Mexico City, July 1982.
I went to see Ulises Lima off at the airport when he left for Managua,
partly because I still couldn't believe he'd been invited and partly because I didn't have anything else to do that morning, and I went to meet
him when he came back too, more than anything just to see his face and
so we could have a laugh together, but when I caught sight of the writers
who'd been on the trip, neatly lined up in two rows, I couldn't pick out
his figure (which was unmistakeable) even though I looked and looked.

There were Álamo and Labarca, Padilla and Byron Hernández, Vil-
laplata and our old acquaintance Logiacomo, Sala and the poetess Carmen Prieto, sinister Pérez Hernández and sublime Montesol, but not
Ulises.

My first thought was that he'd fallen asleep on the plane and that
he'd show up soon escorted by two stewardesses and with a hangover of
Homerian proportions. At least that's what I wanted to think, since I'm
pretty slow to panic, although to be honest, I had a bad feeling the moment I saw that group of intellectuals returning tired and content.

Bringing up the end of the line, loaded down with several carry-ons,
was Hugo Montero. I remember that I waved to him but he didn't see
me, or didn't recognize me, or pretended not to recognize me. When all
the writers had left I saw Logiacomo, who seemed reluctant to leave the
airport, and I went up to say hello, trying not to show how worried I was.
He was with another Argentinian, a tall, fat guy with a little goatee, no
one I knew. They were talking about money. Or at least I heard the word
*dollars* a few times, followed by multiple, tremulous exclamation points.
After I said hello, Logiacomo's initial tactic was to act as if he didn't re-

member me, but then he had to accept the inevitable. I asked him about Ulises. He looked at me in horror. There was disapproval in his gaze too, as if I were parading around the airport with my fly open or an oozing sore on my cheek.

It was the other Argentinian who spoke. He said: that asshole made us look like a bunch of idiots. Is he your friend? I looked at him and then I looked at Logiacomo, who was watching for someone in the waiting area, and I didn't know whether to laugh or be serious. The other Argentinian said: a person has to show a little more responsibility (he was talking to Logiacomo, not even looking at me). If I run into him I swear I'll nail his balls to the wall. But what happened? I murmured with my best smile (that is, my worst). Where's Ulises? The other Argentinian said something about the literary lumpen proletariat. What are you talking about? I said. Then Logiacomo spoke, to calm us down, I guess. Ulises disappeared, he said. What do you mean he disappeared? Ask Montero, we just found out about it. It took me longer than it should have to realize that Ulises hadn't disappeared during the flight home (in my imagination I saw him get up from his seat, go down the aisle, pass a stewardess who smiles at him, go into the toilet, lock the door, and *disappear*) but in Managua, during the Mexican delegation's visit. And that was all. The next day I went to see Montero at Bellas Artes and he told me that because of Ulises he was going to lose his job.


**Xóchitl García, Calle Montes, near the Monumento a la Revolución, Mexico City DF, July 1982.** Someone had to call Ulises's mother, I mean, it was the least we could do, but Jacinto didn't have the heart to tell her that her son had disappeared in Nicaragua, even though I said it's probably not such a big deal, Jacinto, you know Ulises, you're his friend, you know what he's like, but Jacinto said that he'd disappeared, end of story, just like Ambrose Bierce and the English poets who died in the Spanish Civil War and Pushkin, except that in Pushkin's case his wife, Pushkin's wife, I mean, was Reality, the Frenchman who killed Pushkin was the Contras, the snows of St. Petersburg were the empty spaces Ulises Lima left in his wake, his lethargy, I mean, and his laziness and lack of common sense, and the seconds in the duel were Mexican Poetry or Latin American Poetry, which, in the form of the Solidarity Delegation, were silent witnesses to the death of one of the best poets of our day.

That was what Jacinto said, but he still wouldn't call Ulises's mother, and I said: let's see, let's examine the situation, the last thing that woman cares about is whether her son is a Pushkin or an Ambrose Bierce. I put myself in her shoes, I'm a mother, and if someday some bastard kills Franz (God forbid), then I'm not going to be thinking that the great Mexican (or Latin American) poet is dead, I'm going to be writhing in pain and anguish and I won't be having the first thought about literature, I can promise you that, because I'm a mother and I know about sleepless nights and the fears and worries that come with having a brat of your own. The best thing we could do, I swear, is to call her or go see her in Ciudad Satélite and tell her what we know about her son. And Jacinto said: she probably already knows, Montero probably already told her. And I said: how can you be so sure? And then Jacinto was quiet and I said: it hasn't even come out in the papers, no one has said anything, it's as if Ulises never went to Central America. And Jacinto said: that's true. And I said: there's nothing you or I can do, because no one will pay attention to us, but I'm sure they'll listen to his mother. They'll tell her to get lost, said Jacinto, and all we'll do is give her more to worry about, more to think about, when she's better off the way she is. What you don't know can't hurt you, he said, preparing food for Franz and pacing around the house, what you don't know can't hurt you, living in ignorance is almost like living in bliss.

And then I said: how can you call yourself a Marxist, Jacinto, how can you call yourself a poet, when you say things like that? Do you plan to make revolution with clichés? And Jacinto answered that frankly there was no way he was planning to make revolution anymore, but that if some night he happened to be in the mood, then making it with clichés and the lyrics of sappy love songs wouldn't be such a bad idea, and he also said that it was as if I was the one who'd gotten lost in Nicaragua, I was so upset, and who's to say, he said, that Ulises *did* get lost in Nicaragua, he might not have gotten lost at all, he might have decided to stay of his own free will, since after all, Nicaragua must be like what we dreamed about in 1975, the country where we all wanted to live. And then I thought about the year 1975, before Franz was born, and I tried to remember what Ulises was like back then and what Arturo Belano was like, but all I could remember clearly was Jacinto's face, his gap-toothed angel smile, and it made me feel so fondly toward him, made me feel like hugging him right then and there, him and Franz, and telling the two of them that I loved them very much, but right away I remembered Ulises's mother and I thought that no one had the right not to tell her where her son was, she'd already suffered enough, the poor woman, and I insisted again that he call her, call her, Jacinto, and tell her everything you know, but Jacinto said that it wasn't his responsibility, that he wasn't one to speculate on the basis of vague news, and then I said: stay with Franz for a little while, I'll be right back, and he was quiet, watching me without saying anything, and when I picked up my bag and opened the door he said: at least try not to be alarmist. And I said: all I'm going to tell her is that her son isn't in Mexico anymore.

**Rafael Barrios, in the bathroom of his house, Jackson Street, San Diego, California, September 1982.** Jacinto and I wrote each other occasionally. He was the one who let me know about Ulises's disappearance. But he didn't give me the news in a letter. He called me from his friend Efrén Hernández's house, which meant that it was serious, or at least that he thought it was serious. Efrén is a young poet who wants to write poetry like the visceral realists used to write. I don't know him. He showed up after I'd moved to California, but according to Jacinto, the kid isn't a bad writer. Send me some of his poems, I said, but Jacinto only sends letters, so I don't know whether he writes well or not, whether he writes visceral realist poetry or not, though to be honest, of course, I don't know what that means, visceral realist poetry. Maybe what Ulises Lima writes. I don't know. All I know is that no one in Mexico has heard of us anymore and those who have heard of us make fun of us (we're the example of what not to do), and maybe they're not all wrong. So it's always nice (or at least appreciated) to come across a young poet who writes or wants to write in the visceral realist style. And this poet's name was Efrén Hernández and it was from his phone, or actually his parents' phone, that Jacinto Requena called to tell me that Ulises Lima had disappeared. I listened to the story and then I said: he hasn't disappeared, he decided to stay in Nicaragua, which is a whole different thing. And he said: if he had decided to stay in Nicaragua, he would have told us so, I went to see him off at the airport and he had no intention of not coming back. I said: cool it, man, it's like you don't know Ulises. And he said: he's disappeared, Rafael, believe me, he didn't even say a thing to his mother, you don't want to know the hard time she's giving the assholes at

Bellas Artes. I said: holy smoke. And he said: she thinks the peasant poets killed her son. I said: holy shit. And he said: you can say that again. Anytime somebody touches a mother's child she turns into a lioness. At least that's what Xóchitl says.

**Barbara Patterson, in the kitchen of her house, Jackson Street, San Diego, California, October 1982.** Our life was miserable but when Rafael heard that Ulises Lima hadn't come back from a trip to Nicaragua it became twice as miserable.

One day I said things can't go on like this. Rafael wasn't doing anything. He didn't work, he didn't write, he didn't help me clean the house, he didn't do the shopping, all he did was take showers (because if nothing else, Rafael is clean, like practically all fucking Mexicans) and watch TV until dawn or go out for beers or play soccer with the fucking Chicanos in the neighborhood. When I came home, there he'd be at the door, sitting on the steps or on the ground, in an Américas T-shirt that stank of sweat, drinking his Tecate and shooting the shit with his friends, this little group of brain-dead teenagers who called him Poet Man (which he didn't seem to mind) and who he'd be with until I'd made our fucking dinner. Then Rafael would say goodbye to them, and they would say sure thing, Poet Man, see you later, Poet Man, we'll catch you tomorrow, Poet Man, and only then would he come into the house.

I was seething with rage, I really was, absolute fury, and I would happily have poisoned his goddamn scrambled eggs, but I restrained myself. I counted to ten. I told myself he was going through a bad patch. The problem was, I knew the bad patch had already been going on too long, four years, to be precise, and although there were plenty of good moments, there were more bad ones and my patience was almost at its limit. But I kept trying, and I would ask how was your day (stupid question) and he would say (what could he say?) fine, okay, so-so. And I would ask: what do you talk about with those kids? And he would say: I tell them stories, I teach them life lessons. Then we would be quiet with the TV on, each of us absorbed in our own scrambled eggs, our pieces of lettuce, our tomato slices, and I would think what life lessons are you talking about, you poor bastard, you poor jerk, what lessons did you ever learn, you pathetic leech, you pathetic loser, you fucking *asshole*, if it weren't for me you'd be sleeping under a bridge. But I didn't say anything, I just looked at him, and that was all. Although even my glances seemed to bother him. He would say: what are you looking at, white girl, what are you scheming? And then I would force a dumb smile, not answering, and start to clear the plates.

**Luis Sebastián Rosado, a dark office, Calle Cravioto, Colonia Coyoacán, Mexico City DF, March 1983.** One afternoon, he called me. How did you get my number? I asked. I had just moved out of my parents' house and it had been a long time since I'd seen him. A moment came when I thought that our relationship was killing me and I decided to make a clean break. I stopped seeing him, I stopped showing up when we were supposed to meet, and it didn't take him long to disappear. He lost interest, he went in search of new adventures, but still, deep down (as I always knew I would), I yearned for him to call, to come looking for me, to miss me. But Luscious Skin didn't come looking for me and for a while, a year or so, we were completely out of touch. So it was a pleasant surprise when he called. How did you get my number? I asked. I called your parents and they gave it to me, he said, I've been trying to call you all day, you're never home. I sighed. I would've preferred it if he'd had a harder time finding me. But Luscious Skin was talking as if we'd just seen each other last week, so that was that. We talked for a while. He asked how I'd been, he mentioned that he'd seen a poem of mine in *Espejo de México* and a story in an anthology of young Mexican writers that had just come out. I asked whether he'd liked the story. I had only recently taken up the difficult art of storytelling and my steps were still unsure. He told me he hadn't read it. I took a look at the book when I saw your name, but I didn't read it, I don't have any money, he said. Then he stopped talking, I stopped talking, and for a while we were both silent, listening to the muted humming and crackling of Mexico City's public telephones. I remember that I was quiet, smiling and thinking about Luscious Skin's face, also smiling, imagining him standing on some sidewalk in the Zona Rosa or Reforma, with his little black knapsack hanging over his shoulder, brushing his ass sheathed in worn, tight denim, a full-lipped smile sketched with surgical precision on an angular face without an ounce of fat, like a young Maya priest, and then I couldn't bear it anymore (I felt tears come to my eyes) and before he could ask for it I gave him my address (which he must have already had) and told him to come right away, and he laughed, a happy laugh, and he said it would take him more than two hours from where he was, and I said it didn't matter, I would make some dinner in the meantime, and I'd be waiting for him. Narratively speaking, that was the moment to hang up and dance for joy, but Luscious Skin always waited until the coins ran out, and he didn't hang up. Luis Sebastián, he said, I have something very important to tell you. You can tell me when you get here, I said. It's something I wanted to tell you a long time ago, he said. His voice sounded unusually forlorn. At that moment I began to suspect that something was going on, that Luscious Skin hadn't called me just because he wanted to see me, or because he needed money. What is it? I said, what's wrong? I heard the last coin fall into the bowels of the public phone, the sound of leaves, the wind whipping dead leaves, a sound like cables tangling and untangling and then slipping apart in the void. Poetic misery. Remember there was something I wanted to tell you and in the end I didn't? he said, his voice sounding perfectly normal. When? I heard myself ask stupidly. A while ago, said Luscious Skin. I told him I didn't remember and then I argued that it didn't matter, he could tell me when he got there. I'm going out to do some shopping, I'll see you soon, I said, but Luscious Skin didn't hang up. And if he wasn't going to hang up, how could I? So I waited and listened and even encouraged him to talk. And then he brought up Ulises Lima, saying that Lima had gotten lost somewhere in Managua (I wasn't surprised, half the world was going to Managua), but that actually he wasn't lost, he was hiding, or in other words, everyone thought (who was *everyone*? I wanted to ask, his *friends*, his *readers*, the *critics* who've been assiduously following his work?) that he was lost, but that he knew he wasn't lost, he was really hiding. Why would Ulises Lima want to hide? I asked. That's what it all comes down to, said Luscious Skin. I talked to you about this a while ago, remember? No, I said in a tiny voice. When? Years ago, the first time we slept together, he said. I felt shivers, a twisting in my gut; my testicles contracted. It was an effort to speak. How do you expect me to remember? I whispered. Now I was even more eager to see him. I suggested that he take a taxi. He said that he didn't have any money. I promised that I would pay, that I would be waiting for him outside. Luscious Skin was about to say something else when the line went dead.

I thought about taking a shower but decided to save it for when he got there. I spent a while straightening things up, and then I changed my shirt and went outside to wait. It was more than half an hour, and all I did the entire time was try to remember the first time we made love.

When he got out of the taxi he looked much thinner than he had the last time I'd seen him, vastly thinner and more worn down than in my memories, but he was still Luscious Skin and I was happy to see him. I held out my hand but he didn't take it, instead he hurled himself at me and hugged me. The rest was more or less the way I'd imagined it, the way I'd wished. There was nothing disappointing about it.

At three in the morning we got up and I made us a second supper, this time a cold one, and I poured us some whiskey. We were both hungry and thirsty. Then, as we were eating, Luscious Skin started to talk more about Ulises Lima's disappearance. He had a wild theory that didn't stand up to the slightest scrutiny. According to him, Ulises was fleeing from an organization (or that's the way it sounded at first) that wanted to kill him, so when he ended up in Managua he decided not to come back. No matter how you looked at it, it was an unlikely story. Everything had begun, according to Luscious Skin, with a trip that Lima and his friend Belano took up north, at the beginning of 1976. After that trip they both went on the run. First they fled to Mexico City together, and then to Europe, separately. When I asked him what the founders of visceral realism were doing in Sonora, Luscious Skin said they'd gone to look for Cesárea Tinajero. After he'd spent several years in Europe, Lima had returned to Mexico. Maybe he thought the whole thing had been forgotten, but the killers showed up one night after a meeting where Lima had been trying to reunite the visceral realists, and he had to run away again. When I asked Luscious Skin why anyone would want to kill Lima, he said he didn't know. You didn't travel with him, did you? Luscious Skin said he hadn't. Then how do you know all this? Who told you this story? Lima? Luscious Skin said no, it was María Font who'd told him (he explained who María Font was), and she'd gotten it from her father. Then he told me that María Font's father was in an insane asylum. Under ordinary circumstances, I would have started to laugh right there, but when Luscious Skin told me that the person who'd started the rumor was a madman, a shiver ran up my spine. And I felt pity too, and I knew I was in love.

That night we talked until dawn. At eight in the morning I had to go to the university. I left Luscious Skin copies of the keys to the house and I asked him to wait till I came back. From the university I called Albertito Moore and asked him whether he remembered Ulises Lima. His reply was vague. He did and he didn't. Who was Ulises Lima? A lost lover? I said goodbye and hung up. Next I called Zarco and asked him the same question. This time the reply was much more emphatic: a lunatic, said Ismael Humberto. He's a poet, I said. More or less, said Zarco. He traveled to Managua with a delegation of Mexican writers and got lost, I said. It must have been the delegation of peasant poets, said Zarco. And he didn't come back with them, he disappeared, I said. That's the kind of thing that happens to these people, said Zarco. That's it? I said. Sure, said Zarco, there's nothing else to it. When I got home, Luscious Skin was sleeping. My latest book of poetry was open next to him. That night, as we ate dinner, I suggested that he stay with me for a few days. That's what I was planning to do, said Luscious Skin, but I wanted you to be the one who asked. A little later he brought over a suitcase with all his belongings in it. He had nothing: two shirts, a serape that he'd stolen from a musician, some socks, a portable radio, a notebook he used to keep a kind of diary, and not much else. So I gave him an old pair of pants that were maybe a little tight on him but that he loved, plus three new shirts that my mother had just bought me, and one night, on my way home from work, I went to a shoe store and bought him some boots.

Our life together was brief but happy. For thirty-five days we lived together and each night we made love and talked until late and ate meals that he cooked. Usually they were complicated or sometimes they were simple but they were always tasty. One night he told me that the first time he had sex he was ten years old. I didn't want him to tell me anything else. I remember looking away, at a Pérez Camarga print hanging on the wall, and I prayed that his first time had been with a teenager, or a kid, and that he hadn't been raped. Another night, or maybe the same night, he told me that he'd come to Mexico City when he was eighteen, with no money, no clothes, no friends to turn to, and that he'd had a rough time of it, until a journalist friend he'd had sex with let him sleep in *El Nacional*'s paper warehouse. Since I was there, he said, I thought I was fated be a journalist, and for a while he tried to write articles that no one would publish. Then he lived with a woman and had a child and a long string of jobs, none of them permanent. He even worked as a street hawker around Azcapotzalco, but he ended up in a knife fight with his supplier and he quit. One night, when he was inside of me, I asked him whether he had ever killed anyone. I didn't mean to ask the question, I didn't want to hear his answer, whether it was true or a lie, and I bit my lips. He said that he had and thrust even harder, and I cried when I came.

During that time no one came to see me and I stopped visiting anyone, I told some people I didn't feel well, and others that I was working on something that required utter solitude and unbroken concentration. The truth is, I did write a little while Luscious Skin was living with me, five or six short poems. They aren't bad. I'll probably never publish them, but you never know. The visceral realists always appeared in the stories he told me and although at first it bothered me when he talked about them, little by little I got used to it and when he didn't happen to mention them, I was the one to ask: where were the Rodríguez brothers when you were in the house on Calzada Camarones? where did Rafael Barrios live when you lived in the Niño Perdido hotel? and then he would reshuffle the pieces of his story and talk to me about those shadowy figures, his occasional brothers-in-arms, the ghosts populating his vast freedom, his vast desolation.

One night he talked to me about Cesárea Tinajero again. I told him that Lima and Belano had probably made her up to justify their trip to Sonora. I remember that we were lying naked in bed, the window open to the skies of Coyoacán, and that Luscious Skin turned on his side and pulled me to him, my erect cock seeking his testicles, his scrotum, his still flaccid cock, and then Luscious Skin said ñero (he had never addressed me in that vulgar way before), he said ñero and grabbed me by the shoulders, and he said it wasn't like that, Cesárea Tinajero existed, she might still exist, and then he was quiet, but watching me, his eyes open in the dark as my erect penis lightly tapped his testicles. And then I asked him how Belano and Lima had heard of Cesárea Tinajero, a purely perfunctory question, and he said that it was in an interview, that in those days Belano and Lima didn't have any money and they started to do interviews for a magazine, a corrupt magazine under the sway of the peasant poets or soon to be under the sway of the peasant poets, but then as now, said Luscious Skin, there was no way not to be part of one of the two camps, what camps are you talking about? I whispered, my penis rising up his scrotum and its tip touching the base of his penis, which was beginning to swell, the peasant poets' camp or Octavio Paz's camp, he said, and just as he was saying "Octavio Paz's camp" his hand moved from my shoulder to the back of my neck, since there could be no doubt

329

that I belonged to Octavio Paz's camp, although the scene was more nuanced than that, but at any rate, the visceral realists weren't part of any camp, not the neo-PRI-ists or the champions of otherness, the neo-Stalinists or the aesthetes, those who drew a government salary or those who lived off the university, the sellers or the buyers, those who clung to tradition or those who masked ignorance with arrogance, the whites or the blacks, the Latin Americanists or the cosmopolites. But what matters is that they did these interviews (was it for *Plural*? was it for *Plural* after Octavio Paz was forced out?), and although I asked how those two could need money when they made a living selling drugs, the point is that according to Luscious Skin they needed the money and they went to interview some old men who nobody remembered, the stridentists: Manuel Maples Arce, born in 1900 and died in 1981, Arqueles Vela, born in 1899 and died in 1977, and Germán List Arzubide, born in 1898 and probably died recently too, or maybe not, I have no idea, it's not as if it makes much difference to me, since from a literary point of view the stridentists were a contemptible group, comical without intending to be. And one of the stridentists, at some point in his interview, mentioned Cesárea Tinajero, and then I told Luscious Skin that I would find out what had happened to Cesárea Tinajero. Then we made love, but it was like doing it with someone who's there but isn't there, someone who's gently drifting away and whose gestures of farewell we aren't able to decipher.

Soon afterward, Luscious Skin left. Earlier, I'd spoken to some friends, people who specialized in the history of Mexican literature, and no one could tell me anything about the existence of a poet from the 1920s by that name. One night Luscious Skin admitted that Belano and Lima might have made her up. Now both of them have disappeared, he said, and no one can ask them anything. I tried to console him: they'll show up, I said, everyone who leaves Mexico ends up coming back someday. He didn't seem very convinced, and one morning, while I was at work, he went away, without even leaving me a note goodbye. He took some money too, not much, money that I kept in one of my desk drawers in case he needed something when I wasn't there, and a pair of pants, several shirts, and a novel by Fernando del Paso.

For days all I did was think about him and wait for a phone call that never came. The only person from my circle whom I'd seen during his stay was Albertito Moore, when Luscious Skin and I went to the movies one night and bumped into him on our way out. Although it was a brief encounter and we hardly spoke, Albertito immediately suspected the real reason I'd been holed up and making excuses not to see anyone. When I realized that Luscious Skin wasn't coming back, I called him and told him the whole story. What seemed to interest him most was Ulises Lima's disappearance in Managua. We talked for a long time and his conclusion was that everyone was slowly but surely going insane. Albertito doesn't sympathize with the Sandinista cause, although it can't be said that he's pro-Somozan either.

# 16

Amadeo Salvatierra, Calle República de Venezuela, near the Palacio de la Inquisición, Mexico City DF, January 1976. Luckily, the boys weren't in a hurry. I put the snacks on a little table, we opened the cans of chipotle chilies, I passed out toothpicks, we poured the tequila, and our eyes met. Where were we, boys? I said, and they said: in the middle of the full-length portrait of General Diego Carvajal, patron of the arts and Cesárea Tinajero's boss, while outside, in the street, sirens began to wail, first police sirens and then ambulance sirens. I thought about the dead and the wounded and I said to myself that that was *mi general*, dead and wounded all at once, just as Cesárea was a blank and I was a tipsy, excitable old man. Then I told the boys that *boss* was just a manner of speaking, that you had to have known Cesárea to realize that she could never in her life have had a boss or what you might call a steady job. Cesárea was a stenographer, as I've said. That was what she did, and she was a good secretary, but her personality, her eccentricities, perhaps, outweighed her skills, and if it hadn't been for Manuel getting her the job with *mi general*, poor Cesárea would have been consigned by fate to wander the sinister underbelly of Mexico City. And then I asked them again whether it was really true (really and honestly true) that they had never heard of General Diego Carvajal. And they said no, Amadeo, never, what was he? Obregonista or Carrancista? one of Plutarco Elías Calles's men or a real revolutionary? A real revolutionary, I said in the saddest voice in the world, but also one of Obregón's men. There's no such thing as purity, boys, don't fool yourselves, life is shit, *mi general* was a wounded man and a dead man all at once, and he was brave. And then I started to talk about the night when Manuel told us his plan for an avant-garde city, Stridentopolis, and how we laughed when we heard him, thinking it was a joke, but it wasn't a joke, no, Stridentopolis was a possible city (possible at least in the tortuous pathways of the imagination) that Manuel planned to erect in Jalapa with the help of a general, General Diego Carvajal is going to help us build it, he said, and then some of us asked him who the hell that was (just as the boys asked me the night they were here) and Manuel told us the general's story, a story, boys, I told them, that could be the story of so many men who fought and made a name for themselves in our revolution, men who went naked into the whirlwind of history and came out dressed in the most glittering and terrible rags, like *mi general* Diego Carvajal, who went in illiterate and came out convinced that Picasso and Marinetti were the prophets of something, of what he wasn't sure—never was, boys—but we aren't much surer of anything ourselves. One afternoon we went to his office to meet him. This was a little before Cesárea joined the stridentists. At first the general was slightly chilly, at first he kept his distance. He didn't get up to greet us and while Manuel was introducing us all he hardly said a word. But he did look us each in the eye, as if he wanted to see deep into our minds or our souls. I thought: how could Manuel have become friends with this man? because at first glance the general was no different from any of the other soldiers who had washed up in Mexico City on the tides of revolution. He had the look of an intense, serious, distrustful, violent person, which is to say, nobody you would associate with poetry, although I know perfectly well that there've been poets who were intense and serious and distrustful and even violent, take Díaz Mirón, for example, but don't get me started, because sometimes I can't help thinking that poets and politicians, especially in Mexico, are one and the same, or at least I'd say that they drink from the same trough. But back then I was young, too young and idealistic, which is to say I was pure, and that kind of business affected me deeply, so I can't say that I liked General Diego Carvajal right away. But then something very simple happened and everything changed. After he'd pierced us with his gaze and sat through Manuel's preliminaries looking half bored and half alert, the general summoned one of his bodyguards, a Yaqui Indian he called Equitativo, and ordered him to bring tequila, bread, and cheese. And that was all, that was the magic wand the general waved to win our hearts. The way I've told it, it sounds silly, even to me it sounds silly, but back then, just by clearing the papers off his desk and telling us not to be shy and to pull up our chairs, the general demolished any reservations or prejudices we might have had, and all of us, as you can imagine, gathered around the table and started to drink and eat bread and cheese, which, according to *mi general*, was a French custom, and Manuel seconded him there (and everywhere), of course it was a French custom, a common habit at the hole-in-the-wall taverns off the Boulevard du Temple and around the Faubourg St. Denis, and Manuel and *mi general* Diego Carvajal got to talking about Paris and the bread and cheese that people ate in Paris, and the tequila that people drank in Paris and how you could hardly believe how well people drank, how well the goddamn Parisians around the Marché aux Puces could drink, as if in Paris, or so I thought, everything happened *around* some street or place and never *on* a specific street or *in* a specific place, and this was because, as I later discovered, Manuel had never been to the City of Light, and neither had *mi general*, although both of them, I don't know why, professed a fondness or passion for that faraway and presumably intoxicating metropolis that struck me as worthy of better objects. And now that we've reached this point, allow me to digress: years later, some time after Manuel had let our friendship lapse, I read in the paper one morning that he was leaving for Europe. The poet Manuel Maples Arce, the item said, will depart from Veracruz en route to Le Havre. It didn't say the father of stridentism is going to Europe or the leading Mexican poet of the avant-garde is leaving for the Old World, but simply: the poet Manuel Maples Arce. And maybe it didn't even say poet, maybe the note said Mr. Maples Arce, bachelor of arts, is bound for a French port, where he will continue his trip to Italian soil by other means (by train, by runaway carriage!), in order to assume the duties of consul or vice-consul or cultural attaché at the Mexican embassy in Rome. Well. My memory isn't what it used to be. There are things I forget, I admit it. But that morning, when I read those few lines and learned that Manuel would see Paris at last, I was happy, I felt my chest swell with happiness, even though Manuel didn't consider himself my friend anymore, even though stridentism was dead, even though life might have changed us so much that we'd have had trouble recognizing each other on the street. I thought about Manuel and I thought about Paris, which I've never seen but which I've visited once or twice in dreams, and it seemed to me that his trip vindicated us and, in some inexplicable way, did us justice. Of course, *mi general* Diego Carvajal never left Mexico. He was killed in 1930, in a shootout still shrouded in mystery, in the inner courtyard of the Rojo y Negro, a brothel, which in those days was on Calle Costa Rica, a few blocks from here, under the direct protection of a bigwig at the Ministry of the Interior, or so it was said. Killed in the firefight were *mi general* Diego Carvajal, one of his bodyguards, three gunmen from the state of Durango, and Rosario Contreras, a whore said to be Spanish who was famous in those days. I went to the burial and on my way out of the cemetery I ran into List Arzubide. According to List (who in his day traveled to Europe too), they had laid a trap for *mi general* for political reasons, which was the exact opposite of what the newspapers said, the press inclining toward a brothel skirmish or a crime of passion with Rosario Contreras in a leading role. According to List, who was personally familiar with the brothel, *mi general* liked to screw in the most out-of-the-way room, which wasn't very big but had the advantage of being at the back of the house, far from the noise, near this courtyard where there was a fountain. And after screwing, *mi general* liked to go out into the courtyard to smoke a cigarette and think about postcoital sadness, that vexing sadness of the flesh, and about all the books he hadn't read. And according to List, the killers stationed themselves in the hallway leading to the main rooms, and there they commanded every corner of the courtyard. Which suggests that they knew *mi general*'s habits. And they waited and waited, as *mi general* screwed Rosario Contreras, a whore by avocation, or so I understood, since she'd had plenty of retirement offers and she'd always chosen her freedom. Stranger things have happened. And as the story goes, it was a long and meticulous screwing, as if the cherubs or cupids wanted Rosario and *mi general* to fully enjoy their last lovemaking, or their last here on the Mexican part of planet Earth, at least. And so the hours went by, with Rosario and *mi general* engaged in what young people and not so young people today call a lay, or a ride, or a tumble, or a poke, or a balling, or a plowing, or a roll in the hay, or a few laps around the track, although this run would have to last them through all eternity. And meanwhile the killers waited, getting bored, but what they didn't expect was that *mi general*, who was a creature of habit, would come out into the courtyard with his pistol in his belt or his pocket or tucked between his trousers and his belly. And when *mi general* finally came out at last to smoke his cigarette, the shooting began. According to List, *mi general*'s bodyguard had already been butchered without further ado, so when the dance began it was three to one and on top of that the killers had the advantage of surprise. But *mi general* Diego Carvajal was all man and he still had good reflexes too, and things didn't go their way. The first shots struck him, but he had the gumption to pull out his pistol and fire back. According to List, *mi general* could have kept them at bay indefinitely, because if the killers were staked out in an unbeatable position, the spot where *mi general* had taken cover behind the fountain was just as good, and neither side dared to make the first move. But then Rosario Contreras came out of her room, roused by the noise, and a bullet killed her. The rest is unclear: *mi general* probably ran to help her, to escort her to safety, or maybe he realized that she was dead and his rage got the better of his good judgment and he rose and strode toward the killers with guns blazing. That's how Mexican generals used to die, boys, I said, what do you think? And they said: we don't know what to think, Amadeo, it sounds like a movie. And then I started to think again about Stridentopolis, about its museums and bars, its open-air theaters and newspapers, its schools and its dormitories for traveling poets, dormitories where Borges and Tristan Tzara, Huidobro and André Breton would sleep. And I saw *mi general* talking to us again. I saw him making plans, I saw him drinking, standing at the window, I saw him receiving Cesárea Tinajero, who had come in with a letter of recommendation from Manuel, I saw him reading a little book by Tablada, maybe the one where Don José Juan says: "Under fearful skies / keening for the only star / the song of the nightingale." Which is as if to say, boys, I said, that I saw our struggles and dreams all tangled up in the same failure, and that failure was called joy.

**Joaquín Font, psychiatric hospital La Fortaleza, Tlalnepantla, Mexico City, March 1983.** Now that I'm surrounded by penniless lunatics, hardly anyone comes to see me. And yet my psychiatrist tells me I'm getting a little better every day. My psychiatrist is called José Manuel, which I think is a nice name. When I tell him so he laughs. It's a very romantic name, I say, a name that would make any girl fall in love with you. It's a shame he's almost never here when my daughter comes to visit, because visiting days are Saturday and Sunday, and those are the days my psychiatrist doesn't work, except for one Saturday and Sunday each month when he's on duty. If you could see my daughter, I tell him, you'd fall in love with her. Oh, Don Joaquín, he says. But I persist: if you saw her you'd drop at her feet like a wounded bird, José Manuel, and you'd suddenly understand all kinds of things that you don't understand right now. Like what, for example? he says, trying to sound as if he's not paying attention, as if he's politely indifferent, but I know deep down he's very interested. Like what, for example? Then I opt for silence. Sometimes silence is best. Descending into the catacombs of Mexico City again to pray in silence. The courtyards of this jail are perfect for silence. Rectangular and hexagonal, as if designed by the great Garábito, they all converge on the big courtyard, an expanse the size of three soccer fields, bordered by a nameless street where the Tlalnepantla bus goes by, full of workers and people with nothing better to do than stare wide-eyed at the madmen roaming the courtyard in the uniform of La Fortaleza, or half naked, or in their shabby street clothes, these last being the recent arrivals who haven't been able to find themselves uniforms, let alone uniforms in the proper size, since very few here wear uniforms that fit. This big courtyard is the natural abode of silence, although the first time I saw it I thought the noise and clamor of the lunatics might become unbearable and it took me a while to get up the courage to set foot on that steppe. But soon I realized that if there was a place anywhere in La Fortaleza where sound bounded away like a frightened rabbit, it was the big courtyard protected by a tall fence from the nameless street, while the people outside drove right by, safe inside their vehicles, since real pedestrians were rare, although sometimes the confused family member of some lunatic or people who preferred not to enter by the main door would stop outside the fence for just a minute, and then go on their way. At the far end of the courtyard, near the buildings, are the tables where the lunatics usually spend a few minutes visiting with their families, who bring them bananas or apples or oranges. In any case, they don't stay there long, because when the sun is out it's unbearably hot and when the wind blows, the madmen who never get visitors shelter under the eaves. When my daughter comes to visit I tell her we should stay in the visitors' hall or go out into one of the hexagonal courtyards, although I know that she finds the visitors' hall and the small courtyards unsettling and sinister. But things happen in the big courtyard that I don't want my daughter to see (a sign, according to my psychiatrist, that I'm definitely on the road to recovery), as well as other things that for now I'd rather keep to myself. Anyway, I have to tread carefully and never let down my guard. The other day (a month ago), my daughter told me that Ulises Lima had disappeared. I know, I said. How do you know? she said. Oh dear. I read it in the paper, I said. But it wasn't in any of the papers! she said. Well then, I must have dreamed it, I said. What I didn't say was that a lunatic from the big courtyard had told me about it two weeks ago. A lunatic whose real name I don't even know. Everyone calls him Chucho or Chuchito (his name is probably Jesús, but I prefer to avoid all religious references, which are beside the point and only poison the silence of the big courtyard), this Chucho or Chuchito came up to me, as he often does, since in the courtyard we all approach each other and retreat, those of us who are doped up and those who are well on the way to recovery, and when he passed me he whispered: Ulises has disappeared. The next day I saw him again (maybe I was unconsciously seeking him out), and I walked toward him, my steps very slow, very patient, so slow that sometimes the people going by in buses on the street may get the idea that we don't move, but we do, I have no doubt that we do, and when he saw me his lips began to tremble, as if just seeing me triggered some urgent message, and as he passed me I heard the same words again: Ulises has disappeared. And only then did I realize that he meant Ulises Lima, the young visceral realist poet whom I'd seen for the last time behind the wheel of my shiny Ford Impala in the first minutes of 1976, and I realized that black clouds had begun to cover the sky again, that above Mexico's white clouds the black clouds drifted, impossibly heavy and terrifyingly imperious, and that I had to be careful and take refuge in pretense and silence.

**Xóchitl García, Calle Montes, near the Monumento a la Revolución, Mexico City DF, January 1984.** When Jacinto and I separated, my father told me that if Jacinto gave me any trouble I should let him know and he'd take care of everything. Sometimes my father would look at Franz and say: he's so blond, wondering (I'm sure, though he never said so) how the boy could possibly have ended up with hair that color when everyone in my family is dark and so is Jacinto. My father adored Franz. My little blond boy, he would say, where's my little blond boy? and Franz loved him too. He would come on Saturdays or Sundays and take

Franz out for a walk. When they came back I would make him a cup of black coffee and he would sit silently at the table watching Franz or reading the paper, and then he would leave.

I think he thought that Franz wasn't Jacinto's son and sometimes that made me a little bit angry and other times I thought it was funny. As it happened, my breakup with Jacinto wasn't difficult at all, so there was nothing to tell my father. Even if it had been bad I might not have told him anything. Jacinto would come by every two weeks to see Franz. Sometimes he would pick him up and drop him off and then leave, and we would hardly talk, but other times he would stay for a while when he came back to drop him off. He'd ask me about my life, and I'd ask him about his life, and we might talk until two or three in the morning, about things that had happened to us and the books we'd read. I think that Jacinto was afraid of my father and that was why he didn't come more often, for fear of running into him. He didn't know that by that time my father was very sick and would've had a hard time hurting anyone. But my father had quite a reputation and even though nobody knew for sure where he worked, his look was unmistakable and it said I'm with the secret police, so watch yourself, I'm a Mexican cop, so watch yourself. And if his face was haggard because he was sick or if he moved more slowly, that hardly mattered, it only made him that much more threatening. One night he stayed for dinner. I was in an excellent mood and I wanted to eat with my father and see him and see Franz, I wanted to see them together, talk. I can't remember now what I made, a simple meal, I'm sure. As we ate I asked him why he'd become a policeman. I don't know whether it was a serious question, it just occurred to me that I'd never asked him, and that if I waited any longer it might be too late. He answered that he didn't know. Wouldn't you have liked to be something else? I said. He said yes. What would you have liked to be? I said. A peasant, he said, and I laughed, but when he left I couldn't stop thinking about it and my good mood went away.

In those days the person I became very close friends with was María. María was still living upstairs, and although she had boyfriends off and on (some nights I could hear her as if the ceiling was made of paper), since her breakup with the math teacher she'd been living alone, a circumstance (living alone, that is) that had done a lot to change her. I know what I'm talking about because I've been living alone since I was eighteen. Although come to think of it, I've never really lived alone, because first I lived with Jacinto and now I live with Franz. Maybe what I meant was living independently, without family. Anyway, María and I became even closer friends. Or we became real friends, because before that we hadn't been real friends, I guess, and our friendship was based on other people, not ourselves. When Jacinto and I separated, I got into poetry. I started to read and write poetry as if it were the most important thing in the world. Before that, I had written a few little poems and I used to think I read a lot, but when he left I started to read and write for real. I didn't have lots of time, but I made time where I could.

Around then I'd gotten my job as a cashier at a Gigante, thanks to my father, who'd talked to a friend who had a friend who was the manager of the Gigante in Colonia San Rafael. And María was working as a secretary at one of the offices of the Instituto Nacional de Bellas Artes. During the day, Franz would go to school and a fifteen-year-old girl who made her spending money that way would go pick him up for me and take him to a park or watch him at home till I got back from work. At night, after dinner, María would come down to my room or I'd go upstairs and read her the poems I'd written that day, at Gigante or while I was heating up Franz's dinner, or the night before, while I watched Franz sleep. The television had been a bad habit of mine when I lived with Jacinto. Now I only turned it on when there was big news and I wanted to find out what was going on, and sometimes not even then. What I did, as I was saying, was sit at the table, which had been moved and was over by the window now, and start to read and write poems until my eyes closed, I was so sleepy. I would rewrite my poems as many as ten or fifteen times. When I saw Jacinto, he would read them and give me his opinion, but my real reader was María. Finally I would type them up and put them in a folder that kept growing day by day, to my satisfaction and delight, since it was like concrete proof that my struggle wasn't in vain.

After Jacinto left it was a long time before I slept with another man, and my only passion, besides Franz, was poetry. The complete opposite of María, who had stopped writing and brought home a new lover each week. I met three or four of them. Sometimes I'd say: what do you see in that guy, *mana*, he's not right for you, if worse comes to worst, he'll end up hitting you, but María said that she knew how to handle things, and the truth is she did, although more than once I was so scared by the shouting I had to go running up to her room and tell her lover that he'd better leave right away or I'd call my father, who was in the secret police, and then he'd really be sorry. Fucking police sluts, I remember one of them shouted at us from the middle of the street, and María and I both burst out laughing on the other side of the glass. But most of the time she didn't have serious problems. The poetry problem was different. Why don't you write anymore, *mana*? I asked her once and she answered that she didn't feel like it, that was all, she just didn't feel like it.

**Luis Sebastián Rosado, a dark study, Calle Cravioto, Colonia Coyoacán, Mexico City DF, February 1984.** One morning, Albertito Moore called me at work and told me that he'd had the worst night of his life. At first I thought he was talking about some wild party, but then he stammered, he hesitated, and I heard something else underneath the words he was saying. What's going on? I said. I had a terrible night, said Albertito, you can't imagine. For a moment I thought he was going to cry, but suddenly, before he said anything, I realized that I'd be the one who cried, that inevitably it would be me who cried. What's going on? I said. Your friend, said Albertito, got Julita in trouble. Luscious Skin, I said. That's right, said Albertito, I didn't know. What's going on? I said. I was up all night, Julita was up all night, she called me at ten last night, the police were at her apartment and she didn't want our parents to know, said Albertito. What's going on? I said. This country is a fucking mess, said Albertito. The police don't do what they're supposed to do and neither do the hospitals or the morgues or the funeral homes. That guy had Julita's address and the police had the nerve to question her for more than three hours. What's going on? I said. And worst of all, said Albertito, is that then Julita wanted to go see him, she went crazy, and the god-damn policemen, who at first had wanted to arrest her, told her that they could give her a ride to the morgue themselves, they probably would have raped her in some dark alley, but Julita was beside herself and she wouldn't listen to reason and she was about to head out when I put my foot down, me and the lawyer I'd brought with me (you know Sergio García Fuentes, don't you), and said that there was no way she was going anywhere alone. That pissed them off, and they started to ask questions again. What they wanted to know, basically, was the name of the deceased. Then I thought of you, I thought that you might know his real name, but of course I didn't say anything. The same thought occurred to Julita, but that girl is a wild thing and she only said what she wanted to say. I guess the police haven't been to see you. What's going on? I said. But when the police left, Julita couldn't sleep, and there were the three of us, Julita, poor García Fuentes, and me, scouring police stations and morgues so we could identify your friend's body. Finally, thanks to some friend of García Fuentes, we found him at the Camarones police station. Julita recognized him right away even though half his face was blown off. What's going on? I said. Take it easy, said Albertito. García Fuentes's friend told us that the police had killed him in a shootout in Tlalnepantla. The police were after some narcos, and they had the address of a boardinghouse on the way to Tlalnepantla. When they got there the people in the house put up a fight and the police killed all of them, including your friend. The awful part of it is that when they tried to identify Luscious Skin all they could find was Julita's address. He didn't have a record, no one knew his name or alias, and the only clue was my sister's address. It seems the others were known criminals. What's going on? I said. So no one knows what his name is and Julita loses it, she starts to cry, she uncovers the corpse, she says Luscious Skin, she screams Luscious Skin right there in the morgue for anyone to hear, and García Fuentes takes her by the shoulders, puts his arms around her, you know García Fuentes has always been a little in love with Julita, and then there I was face-to-face with the corpse, not a pleasant sight, I can tell you, he didn't look very luscious anymore, because even though it hadn't been that long since he was killed, his skin was ashen, and he was bruised all over, as if he'd been beaten, and he had an enormous scar from his neck to his crotch, although the expression on his face was almost calm, that dead person calm that isn't really calm, that isn't really anything at all, just dead flesh with no memories. What's going on? I said. It was seven in the morning before we left the police station. They asked us if we were going to take charge of the body. I said no, that they could do what they wanted with it. He'd only been my sister's off-and-on-again lover, after all, and then García Fuentes slipped something to one of the officials to make sure that they wouldn't bother Julita again. Later, as we were having breakfast, I asked Julita how long she'd been seeing the guy and she said that after he lived with you for a while he started seeing her. But how did he find you? I asked her. It seems he got the phone number out of your address book. She didn't know he was dealing drugs. She thought that he lived on air, on the money he got from people like you or her. When you get mixed up with people like that you always end up with dirty hands, I said, and Julita started to cry and García Fuentes told me not to make a fuss, that it was all over now. What's going on? I said. Nothing's happening, it's all over, said Albertito, but I didn't get any sleep, and I couldn't take the day off either, because we're swamped at the office.

# 17

Jacinto Requena, Café Quito, Calle Bucareli, Mexico City DF, September 1985. Two years after he disappeared in Managua, Ulises Lima came back to Mexico. Not many people saw him after that, and when anyone did it was almost always by accident. For most, he was dead as a person and a poet.

I saw him a few times. The first time I ran into him on Madero and the second time I went to see him at his place. He was living in a tenement in Colonia Guerrero. He only went there to sleep. He made his living selling marijuana. He didn't have much money and the little he did have he gave to the woman who lived with him. Her name was Lola and she had a son. This Lola seemed pretty tough: she was from the south, from Chiapas, or maybe Guatemala, she liked dancing, she dressed like a punk, and she was always in a bad mood. But the kid was nice and Ulises seemed to have taken a shine to him.

One day I asked him where he'd been. He told me that he'd traveled along a river that connects Mexico and Central America. As far as I know, there is no such river. But he told me he'd traveled along this river and that now he could say he knew its twists and tributaries. A river of trees or a river of sand or a river of trees that in certain stretches became a river of sand. A constant flow of people without work, of the poor and starving, drugs and suffering. A river of clouds he'd sailed on for twelve months, where he'd found countless islands and outposts, although not all the islands were settled, and sometimes he thought he'd stay and live on one of them forever or that he'd die there.

Of all the islands he'd visited, two stood out. The island of the past, he said, where the only time was past time and the inhabitants were bored and more or less happy, but where the weight of illusion was so great that the island sank a little deeper into the river every day. And the island of the future, where the only time was the future, and the inhabitants were planners and strivers, such strivers, said Ulises, that they were likely to end up devouring one another.

After that it was a long time before I saw him again. I was trying to move in different circles, I had other interests, I had to look for work, I had to give Xóchitl a little money, and I had other friends too.

**Joaquín Font, psychiatric hospital La Fortaleza, Tlalnepantla, Mexico City DF, September 1985.** The day of the earthquake I saw Laura Damián again. It had been a long time since I'd had such a vision. I saw things, I saw ideas, above all I saw pain, but I didn't see Laura Damián, the hazy figure of Laura Damián, her lips all-knowing and all-seeing, saying that everything was fine, despite the evidence to the contrary. Fine in Mexico, I conjecture, or fine in Mexican homes, or fine in Mexican heads. The tranquilizers were to blame, although at La Fortaleza, to economize, they only give a pill or two to each inmate, and then only to the most deranged. So maybe it wasn't the tranquilizers. The point is that I hadn't seen her in a long time, and when the earth began to shake, I saw her. And then after the disaster I knew everything was all right. Or maybe at the moment of the disaster everything suddenly made itself all right, to keep from dying. A few days later, my daughter came to see me. Did you hear about the earthquake? she asked. Of course I did, I said. Have many people died? No, not many, said my daughter, but enough. Have many of our friends died? None, as far as I know, said my daughter. The few friends we have left don't need the help of any Mexican earthquake to die, I said. Sometimes I think you aren't crazy, said my daughter. I'm not crazy, I said, just confused. But you've been confused for a long time, said my daughter. Time is an illusion, I said, and I thought about people I hadn't seen for a long time and even people I'd never seen. I'd get you out of here if I could, said my daughter. There's no rush, I said, and I thought about the earthquakes of Mexico marching toward us out of the past, trudging on beggars' feet, straight toward eternity or Mexican nothingness. If it were up to me, I'd get you out of here today, said my daughter. Don't worry, I said, you must have problems enough of your own. My daughter just looked at me and didn't say any-

345

thing. During the earthquake the sufferers of La Fortaleza fell out of their beds, those who weren't tied down, I said, and there was no one to keep guard over the wards because the nurses went out into the highway and some left for the city to see what had happened to their families. For a few hours the lunatics were free to do what they wanted. And what did they do? asked my daughter. Not much. Some started to pray, others went out into the courtyards, and most kept sleeping, in their beds or on the floor. That was lucky, said my daughter. And what did you do? I asked out of politeness. Nothing, I went down to a friend's apartment and the three of us were there together. Who? I said. My friend, her son, and me. And none of our friends died? None, said my daughter. Are you sure? I'm absolutely sure. We're so different, I said. Why? said my daughter. Because without having left La Fortaleza, I know that more than one friend must have been crushed to death in the earthquake. No one died, said my daughter. Never mind, never mind, I said. For a while we were silent, watching the lunatics of La Fortaleza, who wandered about like little birds, seraphs, and cherubs, their hair crusted with shit. Such despair, said my daughter, or that's what I thought I heard. I think she started to cry but I tried not to pay attention and I managed not to. Do you remember Laura Damián? I said. I hardly knew her, she said, and you hardly knew her either. I was very close friends with her father, I said. A lunatic kneeled and began to vomit beside a metal door. You only became friends with her father after Laura's death, said my daughter. No, I said, I was friends with Álvaro Damián before the tragedy. Well, said my daughter, let's not argue about it. Then she spent a while telling me about all the rescue work that was going on in the city, and the work she was taking part in or had taken part in or would have liked to take part in (or had watched from a distance), and she also told me that her mother was talking about leaving Mexico City for good. That interested me. To go where? I said. To Puebla, said my daughter. I would've liked to ask her what they planned to do with me, but thinking about Puebla I forgot to. Then my daughter left and I was alone with Laura Damián, with Laura and the lunatics of La Fortaleza, and her voice, her invisible lips, told me not to worry, that if my wife went to Puebla she would stay by my side and no one would ever turn me out of the asylum and if someday they did, she would come with me. Oh, Laura, I sighed. And then Laura asked me, pretending as if she didn't know, how the young poets of Mexico were faring, whether my daughter had brought me news of their long, bloody march. And I told her they were fine. I lied, saying: they're fine, almost everyone is publishing, the earthquake will give them years of material. Don't talk to me about the earthquake, said Laura Damián, talk to me about poetry, what else did your daughter tell you? And then I felt tired, deeply tired, and I said everything's fine, Laura, everyone is fine. And do people still read my poems? she said. They still read them, I said. Don't lie to me, Quim, said Laura. I'm not lying to you, I said, and I closed my eyes.

When I opened them the circle of madmen who roved the court-yards of La Fortaleza had closed around me. Anyone else would have shouted in terror, begun wailing prayers, torn off all his clothes, and started to run like an American football player gone mad, withering un-der the gaze of the myriad eyes spinning like unmoored planets. But not me. The madmen circled around me and I kept as quiet as Rodin's thinker and watched them, and then I looked at the ground and I saw red ants and black ants locked in combat and I didn't say or do anything. The sky was very blue. The earth was light brown, with little stones and clumps of dirt. The clouds were white and drifting westward. Then I looked at the madmen who were stumbling here and there like pawns of an even madder fate, and I closed my eyes again.

**Xóchitl García, Calle Montes, near the Monumento a la Revolución, Mexico City DF, January 1986.** The funny thing was when I tried to publish. For a long time I wrote and revised and rewrote and threw lots of poems away, but there came a day when I was ready to publish and I started to send my poems to magazines and cultural supplements. María warned me. They aren't going to answer, she said, they aren't even going to read your work. You should go in person and ask for a response face-to-face. So that's what I did. At some places they wouldn't see me. But at other places they would, and I got to talk to the deputy editor or the head of the books section. They would ask me things about my life, what I read, what I'd published so far, what workshops I'd been in, what college classes I'd taken. I was naïve: I told them about my dealings with the vis-ceral realists. Most of the people I talked to didn't have any idea who the visceral realists were, but the mention of the group piqued their interest. The visceral realists? Who were they? Then I would explain, more or less, the brief history of visceral realism and they would smile. A few of them scrawled down a name or some other note. A few asked for further explanations, and then they'd thank me and say they'd call or that I should come by in two weeks and they would let me know. Others, the minority, remembered Ulises Lima and Arturo Belano, but only vaguely. For example, they didn't know that Ulises was alive and that Belano didn't live in Mexico City anymore, but they had known them, they remembered the scenes Ulises and Arturo used to make, hassling the poets at readings, they remembered the way they were against everything, they remembered their friendship with Efraín Huerta, and they looked at me as if I were an alien, and they said, so you were a visceral realist, were you? and then they would say they were sorry, but they couldn't publish a single one of my poems. According to María, when I turned to her in growing disappointment, this was normal. Mexican literature, probably more than any other Latin American literature, was like that, a strict sect. Forgiveness was hard to come by. But I'm not asking to be forgiven for anything, I'd say. I know, she'd say, but if you want to publish you'd better never mention the visceral realists again.

Still, I didn't give up. I was tired of working at Gigante and I thought my poetry deserved a little attention at least, if not respect. As time went by I discovered other magazines, not the ones I'd have wanted to publish in, but different ones, the inevitable magazines that spring up in a city of sixteen million. The publishers or editors were terrible men and women, people who had crept out of the sewers, you could tell just by looking, a mix of ousted officials and repentant killers. But they had never heard of visceral realism and had no interest at all in being told the story. Their notion of literature ended (and probably began) with Vasconcelos, although it was easy to guess the admiration they felt for Mariano Azuela, Yáñez, Martín Luis Guzmán, authors they probably knew only by reputation. One of these magazines was called *Tamal*, and its editor was a man named Fernando López Tapia. It was there that I published my first poem, in the two-page arts section, and López Tapia personally handed me the check for the amount I'd made. That night, after I cashed it, María, Franz, and I celebrated by going to the movies and then eating at a restaurant downtown. I was tired of cheap meals and I wanted to give myself a treat. From then on I stopped writing poems, at least I stopped writing as many as before, and I started to write articles, stories about Mexico City, pieces about gardens that very few people knew existed anymore, items about colonial houses, reports on specific subway lines, and everything or almost everything I wrote was published. Fernando López Tapia fit me into the magazine wherever he could, and on Saturdays, instead of going with Franz to Chapultepec, I would take him to the magazine's offices and while he banged on a typewriter I would help *Tamal*'s few staff members put together the next issue, which was always a problem, since we had a hard time getting the magazine out on schedule.

I learned to do layouts and edit, and sometimes I even chose the photographs. And everybody loved Franz too. Of course, I didn't make enough at the magazine to quit my job at Gigante, but even so it was nice for me, since while I was working at the supermarket, especially when the work was particularly annoying (Friday afternoons, for example, or Monday mornings), I would think about my next article, about the story I was planning to write on the peddlers of Coyoacán, or the fire-eaters of La Villa, or whatever it might be, and the time would fly. One day Fernando López Tapia asked me to write profiles of some low-level politicians, friends of his, I guess, or friends of friends, but I refused. I can only write about things I feel connected to, I said, and he replied: what's so interesting about the houses of the Colonia 10 de Mayo? I didn't know what to say, but I stood firm. One night Fernando López Tapia invited me out to dinner. I asked María to keep an eye on Franz and we went to a restaurant in Roma Sur. To be honest, I was expecting something better, more sophisticated, but I had lots of fun during dinner, although I hardly ate a thing. That night I slept with the publisher of *Tamal*. It'd been a long time since I'd had sex with anyone, and it wasn't exactly a pleasurable experience. We did it again a week later. And then the following week. Sometimes, to be honest, it was excruciating to stay up all night and then go to work early in the morning and spend hours stickering products like a sleepwalker. But I wanted to live my life. Deep down I knew that I *had* to live my life.

One night Fernando López Tapia showed up on Calle Montes. He said he wanted to see where I lived. I introduced him to María, who treated him coldly at first, as if she were a princess and poor Fernando were an illiterate peasant. Luckily, I don't think he even noticed how rude she was. He was always a perfect gentleman. I liked that. After a while María went up to her room and I was left alone with Franz and Fernando. Then Fernando told me that he'd come because he wanted to see me, and then he said now he had seen me but he wanted to keep on seeing me. It was silly, but I liked that he said it. Later I went up to get María and the four of us went out to dinner. We laughed a lot that night. A week later I took some of María's poems to *Tamal*, and they published them. If your friend writes, said Fernando López Tapia, tell her that the pages of our magazine are at her disposal. The problem, as I soon discovered, was that for all her college studies, María hardly knew how to write prose: properly punctuated, grammatically correct prose without poetic pretensions, I mean. So for several days she tried to write an article on dance, but no matter how hard she tried and how much I helped her, she couldn't do it. What she came up with in the end was a very good poem that she called "Dance in Mexico." After she gave it to me to read, she filed it away with her other poems and forgot all about it. María was a powerful poet, definitely better than me, for example, but she had no idea how to write prose. It was too bad, but that put an end to her chances of being a regular contributor to *Tamal*. I don't think it made much difference to her, in any case, since she turned up her nose at the magazine, as if it were beneath her. But that's María for you, and I love her the way she is.

My relationship with Fernando López Tapia lasted a while longer. He was married, as I suspected from the start, with two children, the older one twenty, and he wasn't about to separate from his wife (I wouldn't have let him, anyway). I went with him to business dinners now and then. He would introduce me as his most productive writer. I really tried to be that, and there were weeks when, with Gigante on the one hand and the magazine on the other, I barely averaged three hours of sleep a night. But I didn't care because things were going well for me, just the way I wanted them to go, and even though I didn't want to publish any more of my own poems in *Tamal*, what I did was literally take over the arts pages and publish poems by Jacinto and other friends who didn't have a venue for their work. And I learned a lot. I learned everything there is to learn about editing a magazine in Mexico City. I learned to lay out pages, negotiate with advertisers, deal with the printers, talk to people who were theoretically important. Of course, no one knew that I worked at Gigante. Everyone thought I lived on what Fernando López Tapia paid me or that I was a college student, I, who'd never been to college, who'd never even finished high school. And that had its appealing side. It was like living the Cinderella story, and even when I had to return to Gigante and turn back into a salesgirl or cashier, I didn't mind and somehow I found the strength to do both jobs well, the one at *Tamal* because I liked it and I was learning, and the one at Gigante because I had to take care of Franz, I had to buy him clothes and school supplies, and pay for our room on Calle Montes, because my father, poor man, was having a hard time and couldn't give me rent money anymore, and Jacinto didn't even have enough money for himself. The bottom line was, I had to work and bring up Franz all on my own. And that was what I was doing, and I was writing and learning too.

One day Fernando López Tapia told me he had to talk to me. When I went in to see him he said that he wanted us to live together. I thought he was kidding, because sometimes Fernando gets in these moods, wanting to live with everybody in the world, and I assumed we'd probably go to a hotel that night and make love and he would get over wanting to set me up in an apartment. But this time he was serious. Of course, he had no intention of leaving his wife, at least not all of a sudden, but gradually, in a series of done deeds, as he put it. For days we talked about the possibility. Or rather, Fernando talked to me, laying out the pros and cons, and I listened and thought carefully. When I told him no, he seemed crushed, and for a few days he was angry at me. By then I had started to send my pieces to other magazines. Most places turned them down, but a few accepted them. Things got worse with Fernando, I'm not sure why. He criticized everything I did and when we slept together he was even rough with me. Other times he would be sweet, giving me presents and crying at the least little thing, and by the end of the night he'd be dead drunk.

Seeing my name published in other magazines was a great thing. It gave me a feeling of security and I began to distance myself from Fernando López Tapia and *Tamal*. At first it wasn't easy, but I was already used to hardships and they didn't faze me. Then I found work as a copy editor at a newspaper and I quit Gigante. We celebrated my last day with a dinner attended by Jacinto, María, Franz, and me. That night, while we were eating, Fernando López Tapia came to see me but I wouldn't let him in. He was shouting in the street for a while and then he left. Franz and Jacinto watched him from the window and laughed. They're so alike. María and I didn't want to look and we pretended (though maybe we weren't quite pretending) to be in hysterics. What we were really doing was staring into each other's eyes and saying everything we had to say without speaking a word.

I remember that we had the lights off and that Fernando's shouts drifted up muffled from outside, they were desperate shouts, and that then we didn't hear anything, he's leaving, said Franz, they're taking him away, and that then María and I looked at each other, not pretending anymore but serious, tired but ready to go on, and that after a few seconds I got up and turned on the light.

**Amadeo Salvatierra, Calle República de Venezuela, near the Palacio de la Inquisición, Mexico City DF, January 1976.** And then one of the boys asked me: where are Cesárea Tinajero's poems? and I emerged from the swamp of *mi general* Diego Carvajal's death or the boiling soup of his memory, an inedible, mysterious soup that's poised above our fates, it seems to me, like Damocles' sword or an advertisement for tequila, and I said: on the last page, boys. And I looked at their fresh, attentive faces and I watched their hands turn those old pages and then I peered into their faces again and they looked at me too and they said: we aren't losing you, are we, Amadeo? do you feel all right, Amadeo? do you want us to make you some coffee, Amadeo? and I thought oh, hell, I must be drunker than I thought, and I got up and walked unsteadily over to the front room mirror and looked myself in the face. I was still myself. Not the self I'd gotten used to, for better or for worse, but myself. And then I said, boys, what I need isn't coffee but a little more tequila, and when they'd brought me my cup and filled it and I'd drunk, I could separate myself from the confounded quicksilver of the mirror I was leaning against, or what I mean is, I could peel my hands off the glass of that old mirror (noticing, all the same, how my fingerprints lingered like ten tiny faces speaking in unison and so quickly that I couldn't make out their words). And when I had sat back down in my chair I asked them again what they thought, now that they had a real poem by Cesárea Tinajero herself in front of them, with no talk in the way, the poem and nothing else, and they looked at me and then, holding the magazine between them, they plunged back into that puddle from the 1920s, that closed eye full of dust, and they said gee, Amadeo, is this the only thing of hers you have? is this her only published poem? and I said, or maybe I whispered: why yes, boys, that's all there is. And I added, as if to gauge what they really felt: disappointing, isn't it? But I don't think they even heard me, they had their heads close together and they were looking at the

352

poem, and one of them, the Chilean, seemed thoughtful, while his friend, the Mexican, was smiling. It's impossible to discourage those boys, I thought, and then I stopped watching them and I stopped talking and I stretched, *crack, crack*, and one of them lifted his gaze at the sound and looked at me as if to make sure I hadn't fallen to pieces, and then he went back to Cesárea, and I yawned or sighed and for a second, distant images passed before my eyes of Cesárea and her friends walking down a street in the north of Mexico City, and I saw myself among her friends, how curious, and I yawned again, and then one of the boys broke the silence and said in a clear and pleasant voice that it was interesting, and right away the other one agreed. Not only was it interesting, he said, he'd already seen it when he was little. How? I said. In a dream, said the boy, I couldn't have been more than seven, and I had a fever. Cesárea Tinajero's poem? Had he seen it when he was seven years old? And did he understand it? Did he know what it meant? Because it had to mean something, didn't it? And the boys looked at me and said no, Amadeo, a poem doesn't necessarily have to mean anything, except that it's a poem, although this one, Cesárea's, might not even be that. So I said let me see it and I reached out my hand like someone begging and they put the only issue of *Caborca* left in the world into my cramped fingers. And I saw the poem that I'd seen so many times:

Sión

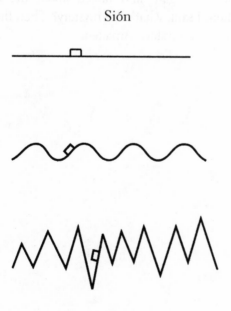

And I asked the boys, I said, boys, what do you make of this poem? I said, boys, I've been looking at it for more than forty years and I've never understood a goddamn thing. Really. I might as well tell you the truth. And they said: it's a joke, Amadeo, the poem is a joke covering up something more serious. But what does it mean? I said. Let us think a little, Amadeo, they said. Of course, please do, I said. Then one of them got up and went to the bathroom and the other one got up and went to the kitchen, and I fell into a doze as, like Pedro Páramo, they wandered the hell of my house, or the hell of memories my house had become, and I let them do as they liked and I fell into a doze, because by then it was very late and we'd had a lot to drink, although from time to time I'd hear them walking, as if they were moving to stretch their legs, and every once in a while I would hear them talking, asking and telling each other who knows what, some serious things, I suppose, since there were long silences between question and answer, and other less serious things, because they would laugh, oh, those boys, I thought, oh, what an interesting evening, it's been so long since I drank so much and talked so much and remembered so much and had such a good time. When I opened my eyes again the boys had turned on the light and there was a cup of steaming coffee in front of me. Drink this, they said. At your orders, I said. I remember that while I was drinking the coffee the boys sat down across from me again and talked about the other pieces in *Caborca*. Well, then, I said, what's the mystery? Then the boys looked at me and said: there is no mystery, Amadeo.

# 18

Joaquín Font, Calle Colima, Colonia Condesa, Mexico City DF, August 1987. Freedom is like a prime number. When I got home everything had changed. My wife didn't live here anymore and my daughter Angélica was sleeping in my bedroom now with her partner, a theater director a few years older than me. My son, meanwhile, had taken over the little house in the garden which he shared with a girl with Indian features. Both he and Angélica worked full-time, although they didn't make much money. My daughter María was living in a hotel near the Monumento a la Revolución and almost never saw her sister and brother. My wife, it seemed, had remarried. The theater director turned out to be quite a considerate person. He had been a friend of La Vieja Segura, or a disciple of his, I couldn't say for sure, and he didn't have much money or luck, but he hoped to direct a play someday that would catapult him to fame and fortune. At night, as we ate dinner, he liked to talk about that. My son's girlfriend, on the other hand, hardly said a word. I liked her.

The first night I slept in the living room. I put a blanket on the sofa, lay down, and closed my eyes. The noises were the same as ever. But no, I was wrong. There was something that made them different and prevented me from sleeping, so I spent my nights sitting on the sofa with the television on and my eyes half shut. Then I moved into my son's old room and that cheered me up. I suppose it was because the room still retained a certain air of happy, carefree adolescence. I don't know. In any case, after three days the room only smelled like me, in other words, like old age and madness, and everything went back to the way it was before. I got depressed and didn't know what to do. Silently, I waited in that empty house for the hours to go by until one of my children would come back from work and we could exchange a few words. Sometimes someone would call and I would answer. Hello? Who is this? No one knew me and I didn't know anyone.

A week after I came home I started to take walks around the neighborhood. At first they were short walks: once around the block and that was it. Little by little, though, I grew more daring, and my outings, at first tentative, took me farther and farther afield. The neighborhood had changed. I was mugged two different times. The first time, it was kids with kitchen knives, and the second time, some older guys who beat me up when they didn't find any money in my pockets. But I don't feel pain anymore and I didn't care. That's one of the things I learned at La Fortaleza. That night, Lola, my son's girlfriend, put iodine on my cuts and scrapes and warned me that there were certain places I shouldn't go. I told her that I didn't care whether I got beaten up every so often. Do you like it? she said. I don't, I said. If I were beaten up every day I wouldn't like it.

One night the theater director said that the Instituto Nacional de Bellas Artes was going to give him a grant. We celebrated. My son and his girlfriend went out to buy a bottle of tequila and my daughter and the director made a gala dinner, although the truth is neither of them knew how to cook. I don't remember what they made. Food. I ate everything. But it wasn't very good. The person who did that kind of thing well was my wife, but she was living somewhere else now and she wasn't interested in impromptu dinners like this. I sat at the table and started to shake. I remember that my daughter looked at me and asked whether I felt sick. I'm just cold, I said, and it was true. With the years I've become the kind of person who's always cold. A little glass of tequila would have helped, but I can't drink tequila or any kind of alcohol. So I shivered and ate and listened to what they were saying. They were talking about a better future. They were talking about silly things, but what they were really talking about was a better future, and although that future didn't include my son and his girlfriend or me, we smiled too and talked and made our plans.

A week later the department that was supposed to award the grant was closed because of budget cuts and the theater director ended up with nothing.

I realized that it was time for me to take action. I took action. I called a few old friends. At first no one remembered me. Where have you been? they said. Where have you come from? What kind of life have you been leading? I told them that I'd just returned from abroad. I've been traveling around the Mediterranean, I've lived in Italy and in Istanbul. I've been looking at buildings in Cairo, so suggestive architecturally. Suggestive? Yes, of hell. Like the Tlatelolco towers, but with less green space. Like Ciudad Satélite, but without running water. Like Netzahualcóyotl. All of us architects deserve to be shot. I've been in Tunis and Marrakech. In Marseille. In Venice. In Florence. In Naples. Lucky you, Quim, but why did you come back? Mexico is going straight to hell. You've probably been following the news. Yes, I've been keeping up, I told them. There's been no shortage of reports. My daughters sent Mexican newspapers to the hotels where I was living. But Mexico is my country, and I missed it. There's no place like this. Don't fuck with me, Quim, you can't be serious. I'm completely serious. Completely serious? I swear, completely serious. Some mornings, as I ate my breakfast watching the Mediterranean and those little sailboats that Europeans like to sail, I'd get tears in my eyes thinking of Mexico City, thinking about breakfast in Mexico City, and I knew that sooner or later I'd have to return. And one of my friends might say: but wait, weren't you in a mental hospital? And I would say yes, but that was years ago. In fact, it was when I left the mental hospital that I went abroad. Doctor's orders. And my friends would laugh at this or at other quips, since I told the story differently each time and they would say oh, Quim, and then I would seize my chance and ask them whether they knew of any work for me, a little job at some architecture firm, anything at all, a part-time job, to help me get used to the idea that I had to find something full-time, and then they would answer that the employment situation was terrible, that firms were closing one after another, that Andrés del Toro had left town for Miami and that Refugio Ortiz de Montesinos had set up shop in Houston, just to give me some idea, they said, and I got the idea, but I kept calling and abusing their patience and telling the story of my adventures in happier parts of the world.

All of this persistence finally landed me a job as a draftsman in the studio of an architect I didn't know. He was a kid who was just starting out, and when he discovered that I was an architect, not a draftsman, he took a liking to me. At night, when we closed the little office, we would go to a bar in Ampliación Popocatépetl, near Calle Cabrera. The bar was called El Destino and we would sit there talking about architecture and politics (the kid was a Trotskyite) and travel and women. His name was Juan Arenas. He had a partner I hardly ever saw, a fat guy in his forties who was an architect too but he looked more like he belonged to the secret police and hardly ever showed up at the studio. So the firm essentially consisted of Juan Arenas and me, and since we had hardly anything to do and we liked to talk, we spent most of the day talking. At night he would give me a ride home and as we crossed a Mexico City like a fading nightmare, I would sometimes think that Juan Arenas was my happier reincarnation.

One day I invited him to the house for lunch. It was a Sunday. No one was home and I made him soup and an omelet. We ate in the kitchen. It was nice to be there, listening to the birds that came to peck in the garden and watching Juan Arenas, a simple, unpretentious boy who ate with a hearty appetite. He lived alone. He wasn't from Mexico City but Ciudad Madero, and sometimes he felt lost in the capital. Later my daughter and her partner came home and found us watching TV and playing cards. I think that Juan Arenas liked my daughter from the start, and after that he visited often. Sometimes I would dream that we were all living together in the house on Calle Colima, my two daughters, my son, the theater director, Lola, and Juan Arenas. Not my wife. I didn't see her living with us. But things never turn out the way you see them in dreams, and one day Juan Arenas and his partner closed the office and vanished without saying where they were going.

Once again I had to call my old friends and ask for favors. I'd learned from experience that it was better to look for a job as a draftsman than as an architect, and so I soon found myself working hard again. This time it was at a firm in Coyoacán. One night, my bosses invited me to a party. The alternative was to head for the nearest metro stop and return to what would surely be an empty house, so I accepted and went. The party was at a house not far from mine. For a few minutes it seemed familiar to me and I thought I'd been there before, but then I realized I hadn't, that it was just that all houses of a certain period in a certain neighborhood were as alike as two peas in a pod, and then I relaxed and went straight into the kitchen to find something to eat because I hadn't had a bite since breakfast. I don't know what came over me, but all of a sudden I felt very hungry, which was unusual for me. Very hungry and very much like crying and very happy.

And then I rushed into the kitchen and in the kitchen were two men and a woman, who were talking animatedly about someone who had died. And I took a ham sandwich and ate it and then I had two gulps of Coca-Cola to wash it down. The bread was somehow dry. But the sandwich was delicious, so I took another one, this time a cheese sandwich, and I ate it little by little, not all at once, chewing carefully and smiling the way I used to smile so many years ago. And the trio who were talking, the two men and the woman, looked at me and saw my smile and smiled at me, and then I moved a little closer to them and I heard what they were saying: they were talking about a corpse and a burial, about a friend of mine, an architect, who had died, and at that moment it seemed appropriate for me to say that I'd known him. That was all. They were talking about a dead man whom I'd known, and then they started to talk about other things, I guess, because I didn't stay but went out into the garden, a garden of rosebushes and fir trees, and I went over to the wrought-iron gate and began to watch the traffic. And then I saw my old '74 Impala go by, looking worse for the wear, its paint peeling and with dents on the fender and doors, moving very slowly, at a crawl, as if it were looking for me along the night streets of Mexico City, and it had such an effect on me that then I did start to shake, grabbing the rails of the gate so I wouldn't fall, and sure enough, I didn't fall, but my glasses fell off, my glasses slipped off my nose and dropped onto a shrub or a plant or a rosebush, I don't know, I just heard the noise and I knew they hadn't broken, and then I thought that if I bent down to get them, by the time I got up the Impala would be gone, but if I didn't I wouldn't be able to see who was driving that ghost car, the car I'd lost in the final hours of 1975, the early hours of 1976. And if I couldn't see who was driving it, what good would it do to have seen it? And then something even more surprising occurred to me. I thought: my glasses have fallen off. I thought: until a moment ago I didn't know I wore glasses. I thought: now I can perceive change. And knowing that now I knew I needed glasses to see, I was afraid, and I bent down and found my glasses (what a difference between having them on and not having them on!) and I stood up and the Impala was still there, which makes me think that I must have moved as fast as only certain madmen can, and I saw the Impala, and with my glasses, the glasses that until just then I hadn't known I possessed, I peered into the darkness, searching for the driver's face, half eager and half afraid, because I thought that I would see Cesárea Tinajero, the lost poet, at the wheel of my lost Impala, I thought that Cesárea Tinajero was emerging from the past to bring me back the car I'd loved most in my life, the car that had meant the most to me and that I'd had the least time to enjoy. But it wasn't Cesárea who was driving it. In fact, no one was driving my ghost Impala! Or so I thought. But then I realized that cars don't drive themselves and that some poor, short, severely depressed little man was probably driving that beat-up Impala, and I returned to the party bowed down by an enormous weight.

When I was halfway there, though, I had an idea and I turned around, but the Impala was no longer in the street, visible or invisible, now you see it, now you don't. The street had become a jigsaw of shadows with several pieces missing, and one of the pieces missing, oddly enough, was me. My Impala was gone. And in some sense that I couldn't quite understand, I was gone too. My Impala was back inside my head again. I was back inside my head again.

Then, humbled and confused and in a burst of utter Mexicanness, I knew that we were ruled by fate and that we would all drown in the storm, and I knew that only the cleverest, myself certainly not included, would stay afloat much longer.


**Andrés Ramírez, Bar El Cuerno de Oro, Calle Avenir, Barcelona, December 1988.** I was destined to be a failure, Belano, take my word for it. I left Chile on a long-ago day of 1975, on March 5 at eight p.m., to be precise, hidden in the hold of the cargo ship *Napoli*. In other words, as a common stowaway, with no idea of my final destination. I'll spare you the variously unpleasant details of the crossing. Put it this way: I was thirteen years younger than I am now and in my neighborhood in Santiago (La Cisterna, that is), my friends knew me as Mighty Mouse, after the funny, crime-fighting little animal that did so much to brighten the afternoons when we were children. In short, the man you see before you was prepared to put up with every hardship of such a voyage. At least physically, as they say. Never mind the hunger, the fear, the seasickness, the uncertainty of what lay ahead, alternately dim or terrifying. There was always some charitable soul who would venture down to the bilge with a piece of bread, a bottle of wine, a little bowl of spaghetti Bolognese. Besides, I had all the time in the world to think, something nearly impossible in my previous life, since as we all know, in modern cities it doesn't pay to be idle. And so I was able to examine my childhood (when you're stuck in the bottom of a boat it's best to do these things in an organized way) in more or less the time it took us to reach the Panama Canal. From then on, or in other words as long as it took us to cross the Atlantic (*ay*, already so far from my beloved country and even my continent, not that I'd seen much of it, but I felt a deep affection for it all the same), I set out to dissect what had become of my youth. And I concluded that everything had to change, even if I wasn't sure just then how to go about it or what path to take. Really, though, I was only killing time, keeping up my strength and my spirits, since I was already near the end of my rope after so many days in that damp, echoing darkness, which I wouldn't wish on my worst enemy. Then one morning we docked in Lisbon and my thoughts took a new tack. Naturally, my first impulse was to disembark then and there, but one of the Italian sailors who sometimes fed me explained that a person in my position would have trouble at the Portuguese borders, by sea or by land. So I had to sit tight, and for two days that seemed like two weeks, all I could do was listen to the voices in the ship's hold, which hung open like the jaws of a whale. There, in my barrel, I got sicker and more impatient with each passing moment, shaking with chills that struck at random intervals. Then finally one night we set sail and left behind the industrious Portuguese capital that I envisioned, in my fever dreams, as a black city, with people dressed in black and houses built of mahogany or black marble or stone, maybe because while I was crouched there, burning up and half asleep, I thought of Eusebio, the Black Panther of the team that fought so valiantly in the England World Cup of '66, in which we Chileans were treated so unfairly.

Back on the open seas, we rounded the Iberian peninsula, and I was still sick, so sick that one night two Italians brought me up on deck so that I could get some air and I saw lights in the distance and I asked what they were, what part of the world those lights belonged to (the world that seemed so unfriendly), and the Italians said Africa—the way you might say *beak*, or the way you might say *apple*—and then I really started to shake, my fever felt like an epileptic seizure, but it was only a fever, and then the Italians left me sitting on the deck and moved to one side, like people leaving a sickroom to smoke a cigarette, and I heard one Italian say to the other: if he dies on us we'd better throw him overboard, and the other Italian answered: all right, all right, but he won't die. And although I didn't speak Italian I understood that clearly, since both of our languages were Romance languages, as a scholar would say. I know you've been in similar situations, Belano, so I won't go on too long. Fear or the will to live, the survival instinct, gave me strength that I didn't know I had, and I said to the Italians I'm all right, I'm not going to die, what's the next port? Then I dragged myself back down into the hold, curled up in my corner, and slept.

By the time we got to Barcelona I was better. On our second night in port I snuck off the ship and went walking out of the harbor like any night-shift worker. I had the clothes on my back, plus ten dollars I'd brought with me from Santiago hidden in one of my socks. Life has many wonderful moments, and they come in all shapes and sizes, but I'll never forget Barcelona's Ramblas or the side streets opening up to me that night like the arms of a girl you've never seen before but who you know is the love of your life. In three hours, I swear, I had a job. If a Chilean has strong arms and isn't lazy, he can make a living anywhere, my father told me when I went to say goodbye. I would have liked to punch the old son of a bitch in the face, but that's another story, so why dwell on it? The point is, on that unforgettable night I was already washing dishes by the time I lost the rocking sensation of the long crossing. This was at a place called La Tía Joaquina, on Calle Escudillers. Around five in the morning, tired but happy, I left the bar and headed for the Pensión Conchi (what a name!), which had been recommended by one of the waiters at La Tía Joaquina, a kid from Murcia who was also staying at that dump.

I spent two days at the Pensión Conchi, then they made me leave in a hurry when I refused to show papers so I could be registered with the police, and I spent a week at La Tía Joaquina, just long enough for the real dishwasher to recover from a bad case of the flu. Over the next few days I made the rounds of other boardinghouses, on Calle Hospital, Calle Pintor Fortuny, Calle Boquería, until I found one on Junta de Comercio, the Pensión Amelia, such a nice, pretty name, where they didn't ask me for papers as long as I shared my room with two others and whenever the police came by I hid myself in a wardrobe with a false back and didn't complain.

As you can imagine, my first weeks in Europe were spent looking for work and working, because I had to pay for my lodging each week. Also because on solid ground my appetite, which had been hibernating during the crossing, was back and much more voracious than I remembered. But as I walked from place to place, say from the boardinghouse to work or from the restaurant to the boardinghouse, something began to happen to me that had never happened before. It didn't take me long to realize. Modesty aside, I've always been alert if nothing else, and I notice what's happening to me. It was a simple thing, anyway, although at first I admit it worried me. It would've worried you too. To give you an idea: I would be walking along the Ramblas, say, happy as can be, thinking the normal thoughts of a normal man and all of a sudden numbers would start to dance in my head. First 1, for example, then 0, then 1, then 1 again, then 0, then another 0, then back to 1, and so on. At first I chalked it up to all the time I'd spent trapped in the belly of the *Napoli*. But the truth is I felt fine, I was eating fine, I had normal bowel movements, I slept my six or seven hours like a baby, and my head didn't hurt at all, so it couldn't be that. Then I wondered whether it might be the change of scenery, which in this case was a change of country, continent, hemisphere, customs, everything. Then, of course, I blamed it on nerves. There have been some cases of insanity in my family, and of delirium tremens too, nobody's perfect. But none of these explanations were convincing, and little by little I adapted. I got used to the numbers. I didn't have much time to dwell on the matter, because the solution wasn't long in coming, and it came all of a sudden. One afternoon, another guy in the kitchen gave me an extra ticket he had for the soccer pools. I don't know why, but I didn't feel like filling it out at work and I took it with me to the boardinghouse. That night, as I was heading home along the half-deserted Ramblas, the numbers started to come, and right off the bat, I connected them with the ticket. I went into a bar on the Rambla Santa Mónica and asked for coffee and a pencil. But then the numbers stopped. My mind was blank! When I went out they started up again. I saw an open newsstand, 0, I saw a tree, 1, I saw two drunks, 2, and so on, until the fourteen scores were filled in. But I didn't have a pen to write them down in the street, so instead of heading to my boardinghouse, I walked down to the end of the Rambla and then back up again, as if I'd just gotten out of bed and I had the whole night ahead of me. A newsstand man near the Mercado de San José sold me a pen. When I paused to buy it the numbers stopped and I felt like I was teetering on the edge of a cliff. Then I walked back up the Rambla and my mind was blank. Moments like that are rough, let me tell you. Suddenly, the numbers returned and I pulled out my ticket and started to write them down. 0 was

X, you didn't have to be a genius to figure that out, 1 was 1, and 2, which hardly appeared anyway or flickered in my head, was 2. Easy, right? By the time I got to the Plaza Catalonia metro stop my ticket was complete. Then the devil tempted me and I went slowly back down toward the Rambla Santa Mónica again, like a sleepwalker or a lunatic, with the ticket a fraction of an inch from my face, checking to see whether the numbers that kept appearing matched the ones written on my lucky little piece of paper. Not one bit! The same way you see the night sky, I saw the 0, the 1, and the 2, but the sequence was different, the figures came faster, and when I passed the Liceo, a number appeared that I had never seen before: 3. I stopped agonizing over it and went to bed. That night, as I was undressing in the dark room, listening to the snoring of the two bastards I had for roommates, it occurred to me that I was going crazy, which struck me as so funny that I had to sit down on the bed and cover my mouth to keep from laughing out loud.

The next day I turned in my ticket, and three days later I was one of nine people who had a match for all fourteen. The first thing I thought, and you had to have been through this yourself to know how it felt, was that they wouldn't give me the money because I was in Spain illegally. So that same day I went to see a lawyer and told him everything. The shyster—Mr. Martínez was his name, and he was from Lora del Río— congratulated me on my good luck and then went on to reassure me. In Spain, he said, a child of the Americas is never a foreigner, although it was true that I had entered the country in an irregular fashion, and that would have to be fixed. Then he called a journalist at *La Vanguardia*, who asked me a few questions and took some pictures of me. By the next day I was famous. I was in two or three papers, at least. Stowaway Wins Pool, they said. I kept the clippings and sent them to Santiago. I gave some radio interviews. In a week, we'd straightened out my situation, and in three months I went from being an undocumented alien to being a legal resident with no work permit, while Martínez negotiated a better deal for me. The prize amounted to 950,000 pesetas, which was real money back then, and even after the lawyer bled me for 200,000, the truth is that in those days I felt rich: rich, famous, and free to do as I pleased. The first few days I toyed with the idea of packing my suitcases and returning to Chile. With the money I had, I could've started a business in Santiago, but in the end I decided to exchange 100,000 pesetas for dollars, send my mother the money, and stay in Barcelona, which now seemed to be opening up to me like a flower, if you'll pardon the expression. This was 1975, anyway, and things in Chile were looking ugly, so I got over my doubts and decided to stay the course. At the consulate, after some resistance requiring a certain amount of tact and money on my part, they agreed to give me a passport. I didn't change boardinghouses, but I asked for a bigger, brighter room of my own (which they gave me in a heartbeat, what can I say? fate had made me the darling of Casa Amelia), quit working as a dishwasher, and began nosing around for a job that would be a good match for my interests. I took my own sweet time. I'd sleep until twelve or one. Then I'd go eat at a restaurant on Calle Fernando or another place on Calle Joaquín Costa, waited on by the nicest pair of twins, and after that I would wander around Barcelona, from Plaza Catalonia to Paseo Colón, from Paralelo to Vía Layetana, having coffee at sidewalk cafés and wine and little dishes of squid at bars, reading the sports page and pondering my next step, though in my innermost self I already knew what it would be, even if my education in the Chilean schools (and granted, I never actually spent much time in class) made me reluctant to lay it out on the table. And while I was at it, I'll tell you, I even thought about that bastard Descartes. Just to give you some idea. Descartes, Andrés Bello, Arturo Prat, the men who left their mark on our long, narrow strip of land. But you can't turn your back on the truth and one afternoon I stopped beating around the bush and admitted to myself that what I really wanted was to win another soccer pool, not look for work, win another pool by any means possible, but preferably the way I knew best. Don't look at me like I'm crazy, because of course I realized that my hope, or my dream, as Lucho Gatica would say, was irrational, even highly irrational—look, what mechanism or syndrome was making those figures appear so clearly in my head? who was dictating them to me? did I believe in visions? was I an ignorant person, a superstitious person come to this corner of the Mediterranean from the farthest reaches of the Third World? or was it possible that everything that was happening to me and everything that had happened to me was just a lucky combination of fate and the delirium of a man driven halfway out of his mind by a god-awful crossing that no travel agency would dare to offer?

Those were days of deep soul-searching. And yet, at the same time, I have to admit, nothing mattered to me (it's a contradiction, but that's the way it was) and as the days went by I stopped reading and responding to the generous job offerings in *La Vanguardia*, and although the numbers had fled from me ever since the prize (as a result of the shock, I presume), I tried to figure out what to do, and one afternoon, as I was feeding the pigeons in Parque de la Ciudadela, I thought I'd found the solution. If the numbers wouldn't come to me, I'd go after them in their den and drag them out by hook or by crook.

I tried several methods, which for professional reasons I should probably spare you. You say no? All right, then, I won't spare you. I started with street numbers. For example, I would walk along Calle Oleguer and Calle Cadena and note down the numbers on the doors as I went. The ones to my right were 1s, the ones to my left were 2s, and the people who looked me straight in the face as I passed were the Xs. It didn't work. I tried playing dice by myself in a bar on Calle Princesa, a place that doesn't exist anymore called La Cruz del Sur, run in those days by an Argentinian friend. That didn't work either. Other times I would lie in bed, my mind blank, and in desperation I would order the numbers to come back, but I couldn't think, couldn't call up the 1, which in my madness I equated with cash and shelter. Ninety days after I'd won the pool, and after I'd spent more than fifty thousand pesetas on huge, futile multiple bets, I got it. I had to change neighborhoods. It was that simple. The numbers of the Old City were exhausted, at least for me, and it was time to move on. I started to roam the Ensanche, a strange neighborhood that until then I had only eyed from Plaza Catalonia, never daring to cross the boundary of Ronda Universidad, or at least not consciously, thereby exposing my senses to the neighborhood magic and walking unguarded, all eyes, defenseless; in short, the antenna man.

The first few days I just walked up the Paseo de Gracia and down Balmes, but on the days after that I ventured onto side streets, Diputación, Consejo de Ciento, Aragón, Valencia, Mallorca, Provenza, Rosellón, and Córcega. The secret of those streets is the way they can be dazzling and somehow familiar, homey, all at once. When I would get to Diagonal, that was always the end of my walk, which sometimes followed a straight line and other times an endless series of zigzags. As you might imagine, I didn't just look lost. I looked like a crazy person. Lucky for me Barcelona prided itself on its tolerance in those days, as of course it still does. Naturally, I'd bought myself new gear. I was crazy all right, but not crazy enough to think I could pass unnoticed in clothes that reeked of a boardinghouse in Distrito 5. When I went out walking, I sported a white shirt, a tie with the Harvard logo, a sky-blue V-neck sweater, and pleated black pants. The only old things were my moccasins, because when it comes to walking, I've always favored comfort over elegance.

For the first three days, nothing happened. The numbers were conspicuous in their absence, as they say. But something in me resisted giving up the area I had so randomly chosen. On the fourth day, as I walked up Balmes, I raised my eyes skyward and saw the following inscription on a church tower: *Ora et labora*. I couldn't tell you exactly what it was that drew me to that inscription, but I really did feel something. I had a premonition. I knew I was close to the source of what beckoned to me and tormented me, the thing I desired with such unhealthy intensity. As I walked along, on the other side of the tower I read: *Tempus breve est*. Several pictures next to the inscriptions caught my eye, making me think of mathematics and geometry. It was like seeing the face of an angel. From then on that church became the center of my wanderings, although I strictly forbade myself to go inside.

One morning, just as I'd been hoping, the numbers came back. The sequences didn't make any sense at first, but it didn't take me long to see the logic in them. The secret was to follow their lead. That week I played three soccer pools (with four doubles) and bought two lottery tickets. As you can imagine, I was unsure of my strategy. I won one pool with thirteen matches. The lottery was a bust. The next week I tried again, this time restricting myself to the pools. I matched fourteen and took home fifteen million. Life changes so fast! In a heartbeat, I had more money than I'd ever dreamed of. I bought a bar on Calle del Carmen and sent for my mother and sister. I didn't go in person because all of a sudden I got scared. What if my plane crashed? What if the soldiers in Chile killed me? The truth is, I didn't even have the strength to leave Pensión Amelia, and for a week I didn't go out. I just sat there, waited on hand and foot, chained to the phone, talking very little because I was afraid I'd do something stupid that would land me in a mental hospital. In the end I was spooked by the powers that I myself had called up. My mother's arrival helped me relax. There's nobody like your mother when you're feeling down! Also, my mother hit it off right away with the owner of the boardinghouse and before you knew it, everybody was eating *empanadas de horno* and *pastel de choclo*, which my mother made to spoil me. While she was at it, she spoiled all the castaways holed up there. They were good people, mostly, except for a few bad seeds, sullen types who worked hard and kept a jealous eye on me. But I was the soul of amiability! Then I started to do business. After the bar on Calle del Carmen there was a restaurant on Calle Mallorca, an elegant place where the local office workers came for breakfast and lunch. After a while we started turning a huge profit. With my family there I couldn't keep living in the boardinghouse, so I bought myself an apartment on Sepúlveda and Viladomat and had a big housewarming party. The women from the boardinghouse, who had cried when I left, cried again when I made a speech welcoming them to my new home. My mother couldn't believe it. So much good luck all at once! It was different with my sister. Now that there was money, she gave herself airs she'd never given herself before. Or if she had I never noticed. I put her to work as a cashier at the restaurant on Calle Mallorca, but after a few months I was in the position of having to choose between someone who'd become a hopeless snob and all the rest of my employees, and, even worse, a good slice of my clientele. So I got her out of there and set her up in a salon on Calle Luna, close enough to our place, across Ronda San Antonio. Of course, all of this time I kept searching for the numbers, but it was as if they'd vanished as soon as I came into my fortune. I had money, I had businesses, and above all I had lots of work, so I hardly felt the loss, at least in the first few months. Later, when things began to settle down, when the excitement wore off, and I went back to the streets of Distrito 5, where people went about the real business of life and death, I started to think about the numbers again and I came up with the wildest, most ridiculous hypotheses trying to explain the miracle that I'd called down on myself. But I was thinking about it too much, and that was bad too. Late some nights, I admit, I even scared myself, so whatever you imagine won't be far from the truth.

Part of what I was afraid of, when I had these thoughts, was the possibility of losing, of playing and losing everything that I'd won and held on to by dint of hard work. But what scared me even more, I swear, was poking into the nature of my luck. Like a good Chilean, the desire to get ahead gnawed at me, but like the Mighty Mouse I once was—like the Mighty Mouse I still am, deep down—prudence held me back. A little voice said to me: don't tempt fate, you lucky bastard, be happy with what you've got. One night I dreamed about the church on Calle Balmes, and I saw that little message, which this time I thought I understood: *Tempus breve est, Ora et labora.* We aren't given much time on this earth. We have to pray and work, not go pushing our luck with soccer pools. That was all. I woke up sure I'd learned my lesson. Then Franco died, and there was the transition, then democracy. This country began to change at a pace that was something to behold, something you could hardly believe your eyes were seeing. It's such a wonderful thing to live in a democracy. I applied for and received Spanish citizenship, traveled abroad to Paris, London, Rome. Always by train. Have you ever been to London? The channel crossing is a joke. That's no channel, not by a long shot. A little rougher, I guess, than the Golfo de Penas. One morning I woke up in Athens and the sight of the Parthenon brought tears to my eyes. There's nothing like traveling to expand your horizons. But also to cultivate your taste. I saw Israel, Egypt, Tunisia, Morocco. When I was done traveling I returned convinced of one thing: we're nothing. One day a new cook came to work at my restaurant on Calle Mallorca. She was young for the job and not very good at it, but I hired her right away. Her name was Rosa, and the next thing I knew, I'd married her. I wanted to name my first son Caupolicán, but in the end we named him Jordi. Next was a girl, and we named her Montserrat. When I think about my children I feel like crying with happiness. Women are funny: my mother, who was worried about me getting married, ended up being thick as thieves with Rosita. Now my life was perfectly on track, as they say. The *Napoli* and my first days in Barcelona seemed so far away—never mind my misspent youth in La Cisterna! I had a family, a couple of kids I adored, a wife who was perfect for me (but whom I retired from the kitchen of my restaurant the first chance I got, since you can have too much of a good thing), health, money. If you thought about it, there was nothing I didn't have, and yet still, some nights when I was left alone at the restaurant doing the books, with no one around but some waiter I trusted or the dishwasher, whom I couldn't see but could hear hard at work in the kitchen, starting in on his last stack of dirty dishes, I was struck by the strangest ideas, very Chilean ideas, if that makes sense, and then I felt that something was missing and I started to wonder what it could be and after thinking a lot and turning it over and over in my head I always came to the same conclusion: I missed the numbers, I missed the flash of the numbers behind my eyelids, which is like saying that I was missing a purpose or *the* purpose. Or what amounts to the same thing, at least from my perspective: I wanted to *understand* the phenomenon that had jump-started my fortune, the numbers that hadn't lit up my head for so long, and *accept* that reality like a man.

And it was then that I had a dream, and I started to read nonstop, with no thought for myself or my eyes, like someone half crazed, all kinds of books, from my favorite historical biographies to books of occultism or poetry by Neruda. The dream was very simple. Actually, it was more like words than a dream, words that I heard in my sleep, spoken by a voice that wasn't mine. These were the words: *she's laying thousands of eggs.* What do you think of that? I could have been dreaming about ants or bees. But I know it wasn't ants or bees. So who was laying the thousands of eggs? I don't know. All I know is that *she* was alone when she laid them and that the place they were being laid—I apologize if I sound pedantic—was like Plato's cave, a kind of hell or heaven where there are only shadows (lately I've been reading the Greek philosophers). She's laying thousands of eggs, the voice said, and I knew that it was as if it were saying she's laying millions of eggs. And then I understood that my luck was there, nestled in one of those abandoned eggs—but abandoned hopefully, I mean, with hope—in Plato's cave. And that's when I realized that I was probably never going to understand the true nature of my luck, of the money that had rained down on me from the sky. But like a good Chilean I refused to accept this, that there was anything I couldn't know, and I began to read and read, sometimes I'd stay up all night, I didn't mind. I'd get up early to open my bars, I'd work all day, immersed in the true industriousness that a person breathes day and night in Barcelona (sometimes it seems a little obsessive), and I'd close my bars and go over my accounts, and after I'd finished my accounts, I'd start to read, and many times I'd fall asleep in a chair (as Chileans also have a tendency to do), and wake up early in the morning, when the sky in Barcelona is an almost purplish blue, almost violet, a sky that makes you want to sing and cry just to look at it, and after looking up at the sky I would keep reading, without letting myself rest, as if I were about to die and I didn't want to die before I'd understood what was going on around me and over my head and under my feet.

To put it briefly, I sweated blood, although to be honest I didn't notice a thing. A little later I met you, Belano, and I gave you a job. The dishwasher had gotten sick and I had to hire a replacement. I don't remember now who sent you to me, probably some other Chilean. This was around the time I was staying late at the restaurant pretending to be going over my accounts while really I was daydreaming in my chair. One night I went to say hello to you, remember? and I was impressed by how polite you were. It was obvious that you'd read a lot, and traveled a lot, and that you were going through a hard time. We hit it off, and incredibly enough, it wasn't twenty-four hours before I'd opened up to you in a way I hadn't once opened up to anyone in all these years. I told you about my soccer pools (that was common knowledge), but I also told you about the numbers that hammered in my head, my darkest secret. I invited you home to meet my family, and I offered you a steady job at one of my bars. You accepted the invitation (my mother made *empanadas de horno*), but you wouldn't even hear of coming to work for me. You said you didn't see yourself working at a bar for long, because dealing with the public was a thankless task and the burnout factor was high. Anyway, and despite the friction that always exists between employer and employee, I think we became friends. Although you may not have realized it, that was a critical time for me. I had never come so close to the numbers before, or at least not consciously, seeking them out myself instead of letting them come to me. You would be washing dishes in the kitchen of the Cuerno de Oro, Belano, and I would sit at one of the tables near the door, spread out my account books and novels, and close my eyes. Knowing you were there made me that much more fearless, I think. Maybe it was all foolishness. Have you ever heard the theory of Easter Island? According to the theory, Chile is the real Easter Island. You know: to the east we're bordered by the Andes, to the north by the Atacama Desert, to the south by Antarctica, and to the west by the Pacific Ocean. We were born on Easter Island and our moai are ourselves, the Chileans, looking in bewilderment toward the four points of the compass. One night, while you were washing dishes, Belano, I imagined that I was still on board the cargo ship *Napoli*. You must remember that night. I imagined that I was dying in the bowels of the *Napoli*, forgotten by everyone, and in my final delirium I dreamed I'd made it to Barcelona and I was riding astride the shining numbers and that I made money, enough to bring my family here and indulge myself a little, and my dream included my wife, Rosa, and my children and my bars, and then I thought that if I was dreaming so vividly it must be because I was about to die, because I was dying in the hold of the *Napoli*, in that airless, stinking hold, and then I said to myself open your eyes, Andrés, Mighty Mouse, open your eyes! but I was speaking in a voice I didn't recognize, a voice that scared

371

me, to tell the truth, and I couldn't open my eyes, but with my Mighty Mouse ears I heard you, Belano, washing dishes in the kitchen of my bar, and then I said to myself for fuck's sake, Andrés, you can't go off the rails now, if you're dreaming, just keep dreaming, you bastard, and if you aren't dreaming, open your eyes and don't be afraid. And then I opened my eyes and I was in the Cuerno de Oro and the numbers clattered on the walls like radioactivity, an endless swarm of numbers, as if an atomic bomb had finally fallen on Barcelona. If I'd known they were there, I would have kept my eyes shut a little longer, but I opened my eyes, Belano, and I got up from my chair and I went into the kitchen where you were working and when I saw you I felt like telling you the whole story, remember? I was shaky and sweating like a pig, and no one would've believed that my brain was working the best it ever had, better than now, which is maybe why I didn't say anything. I offered you a better job, I made you a rum and Coke and brought it to you, I asked your opinion about some books, but I didn't tell you what had happened.

From that night on I knew that maybe, with a little luck, I could win the pools again, but I didn't play. She's laying thousands of eggs, said the voice in my dream, and one of the eggs dropped down to me. I've had enough of the pools. Business is good. Now you're going to leave and I'd like it if you went away with a good impression of me. A sad impression, maybe, but a good one. I have your last paycheck here and I've added a month or two of paid vacation. Don't say anything, it's already done. You told me once that you didn't have much patience, but I think you were wrong.


**Abel Romero, Café L'Alsatien, Rue de Vaugirard, near the Luxembourg Gardens, Paris, September 1989.** It was at Victor's Café, on Rue St. Sauveur, on September 11 in 1983. A group of masochistic Chileans had gathered to remember that dismal day. There were twenty or thirty of us and we were scattered around inside the café and at the outside tables. Suddenly someone, I don't know who, started to talk about evil, about the crime that had spread its enormous black wing over us. Please! Its enormous black wing! It's clear we Chileans will never learn. Then, as you might expect, an argument broke out and bits of bread even flew from table to table. A mutual friend must have introduced us in the middle of the pandemonium. Or maybe we introduced ourselves, and he seemed to recognize me. Are you a writer? he said. No, I said, I was a policeman under Guatón Hormazábal and now I work for a cooperative, vacuuming offices and cleaning windows. It must be a dangerous job, he said. For people who are afraid of heights it is, I answered, for everyone else it's mostly boring. Then we joined the general conversation. People were talking about evil, about corruption, as I said. Friend Belano made two or three fairly pertinent remarks. I didn't say a word. Everyone drank lots of wine that night, and when we left, without knowing how, I found myself walking with him for several blocks. Then I said what had been going around in my head. Belano, I said, the heart of the matter is knowing whether evil (or sin or crime or whatever you want to call it) is random or purposeful. If it's purposeful, we can fight it, it's hard to defeat, but we have a chance, like two boxers in the same weight class, more or less. If it's random, on the other hand, we're fucked, and we'll just have to hope that God, if He exists, has mercy on us. And that's what it all comes down to.

# 19

Amadeo Salvatierra, Calle República de Venezuela, near the Palacio de la Inquisición, Mexico City DF, January 1976. What do you mean there's no mystery to it? I said. There's no mystery to it, Amadeo, they said. And then they asked: what does the poem mean to you? Nothing, I said, it doesn't mean a thing. So why do you say it's a poem? Well, because Cesárea said so, I remembered. That's the only reason why, because I had Cesárea's word for it. If that woman had told me that a piece of her shit wrapped in a shopping bag was a poem I would have believed it, I said. How modern, said the Chilean, and then he mentioned someone named Manzoni. Alessandro Manzoni? I asked, remembering a translation of *I Promessi Sposi* penned by Remigio López Valle, that upstanding gentleman, and published in Mexico in approximately 1930, I'm not sure, Alessandro Manzoni? but they said: Piero Manzoni! the *arte povera* artist who canned his own shit. Well, what do you know. Art has gone crazy, boys, I said, and they said: it's always been crazy. At that moment I saw something like the shadows of grasshoppers on the walls of the front room, behind the boys and to each side, shadows that slid down from the ceiling and seemed to want to glide across the wallpaper to the kitchen but finally sank into the floor, so I rubbed my eyes and said all right, let's see whether you can explain this poem to me once and for all, because I've been dreaming about it for more than fifty years, give or take a year or two. And the boys rubbed their hands together in sheer excitement, the little angels, and came over to my chair. Let's begin with the title, one of them said. What do you think it means? Zion, Mount Zion in Jerusalem, I said promptly, and also the Swiss city of Sion, Sitten in German, in the canton of Valais. Very good, Amadeo, they said, it's clear you've given it some thought. And which do you choose? Mount Zion, yes? I think so, I said. Obviously, they said. Now let's take the first part of the poem. What do we have? A straight line with a rectangle on it, I said. All right, said the Chilean, forget the rectangle, pretend it doesn't exist. Just look at the straight line. What do you see?

A straight line, I said. What else is there to see, boys? And what does a straight line suggest to you, Amadeo? The horizon, I said. The edge of a table, I said. Peace, said one of them. Yes, peace, calm. All right, then: a horizon and calmness. Now let's look at the second part of the poem:

What do you see, Amadeo? A wavy line, I suppose, what else is there to see? Good, Amadeo, they said, now you see a wavy line. Before, you saw a straight line that made you think of calmness and now you see a wavy line. Does it still suggest calmness to you? I guess not, I said, suddenly seeing what they were getting at, what they wanted me to see. What does the wavy line suggest to you? Hills on the horizon? The sea, waves? Could be, could be. A premonition that the calm will be broken? Movement, change? Hills on the horizon, I said. Maybe waves. Now let's look at the third part of the poem:

We have a jagged line, Amadeo, which might be many things. Shark's teeth, boys? Mountains on the horizon? The western Sierra Madre? Lots of things, really. And then one of them said: when I was little, I couldn't have been more than six, I would dream about these three lines, the straight line, the wavy line, and the jagged line. I don't know why, but back then I slept under the stairs, or at least in a very low-ceilinged room next to the stairs. It might not have been my house, maybe we were only there for a little while, maybe it was my grandparents' house. And each night, after I'd gone to sleep, the straight line would appear. So far so good. The dream was even pleasant. But little by little the scene would start to change and the straight line would become a wavy line. Then I would start to feel sick and get hotter and hotter and lose my sense of things, my sense of stability, and all I wanted was to go back to the straight line. And yet, nine times out of ten, after the wavy line would come the jagged line, and at that point the best way to describe how I felt was as if I were being torn apart, not from the outside but from the inside, a tearing that began in the belly but that I soon felt in my head and my throat too, and the only way I could escape the pain was by waking up, although waking up wasn't exactly easy. Isn't that strange? I said. Yes, they said, it is strange. It really is strange, I said. Sometimes I would wet my bed, said one of them. Dear, dear, I said. Do you understand now? they said. Well, to be honest, I don't, boys, I said. The poem is a joke, they said, it's easy to see, Amadeo, look: add a sail to each of the rectangles, like this:

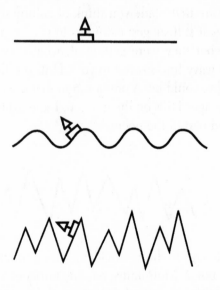

What do we have now? A boat? I said. Exactly, Amadeo, a boat. And hidden behind the title, *Sión*, we have the word *navigation*. And that's all, Amadeo, it's as simple as that, nothing else to it, said the boys and I would have liked to say that they had taken a weight off my mind, that's what I would have liked to say, or that *Sión* could also be a front for *Simón*, a word from the past meaning yes in street slang, but the only thing I did was say well, well, and reach for the bottle of tequila and pour myself a glass, another one. That was all there was left of Cesárea, I thought, a boat on a calm sea, a boat on a choppy sea, and a boat in a storm. For a moment, I can tell you, my head was like a stormy sea and I couldn't hear what the boys were saying, although I did catch some phrases, some stray words, the predictable ones, I suppose: Quetzalcoatl's ship, the nighttime fever of some boy or girl, Captain Ahab's encephalogram or the whale's, the surface of the sea that for sharks is the enormous mouth of hell, the ship without a sail that might also be a coffin, the paradox of the rectangle, the rectangle of consciousness, Einstein's impossible rectangle (in a universe where rectangles are unthinkable), a page by Alfonso Reyes, the desolation of poetry. And then, after I'd drunk my tequila, I filled my cup again and filled theirs, and I said that we should drink to Cesárea, and I saw their eyes, those damn boys were so happy, and the three of us raised our glasses as our little ship was tossed by the gale.

**Edith Oster, sitting on a bench in the Alameda, Mexico City DF, May 1990.** In Mexico, in Mexico City, I only saw him once, outside the María Morillo gallery, in the Zona Rosa, at eleven in the morning. I had come out onto the sidewalk to smoke a cigarette and he was passing by and stopped to say hello. He crossed the street and said I'm Arturo Belano, Claudia's told me about you. Now I know who you are, I said. I was seventeen then, and I liked to read poetry, but I hadn't read anything by him. He didn't look good, he looked like he'd been up all night, but he was handsome. I mean, he seemed handsome to me then, although I wasn't attracted to him. He wasn't my type. Why is he talking to me? I wondered. Why did he cross the street and stop in front of the gallery? I wondered. There was no one inside and I invited him in, but he said that it was nice outside. The two of us stood there, me with a cigarette in my hand and him just a few feet away in a kind of cloud of dust, looking at me. I don't know what we talked about. I think he asked me to come have coffee at the restaurant next door and I told him I couldn't leave the gallery. He asked me whether I liked my job. It's temporary, I said,

I'm quitting next week. Anyway, the pay is really bad. Do you sell a lot of paintings? he said. None yet, I answered, and then we said goodbye and he left. I don't think he was attracted to me, although later he told me that he'd liked me from the first moment he saw me. Back then I was fat or I thought I was fat and I was a nervous wreck. I cried at night and I had an iron will. I was also leading two lives, or a life that was like two lives. On the one hand, I was a philosophy student and I worked temporary jobs like the one at the María Morillo gallery. On the other hand, I was a militant in a Trotskyite party with a clandestine existence that in some confused way I knew served my interests well, although I didn't know what my interests were. One afternoon, when we were handing out leaflets to cars stopped in traffic, I suddenly found myself in front of my mother's Chrysler. Poor thing, the shock almost killed her. And I got so nervous that I handed her the mimeographed sheet and said read this and turned around and left, although as I walked away I heard her say that we would talk at home. We always talked at home. Endless discussions that ended with recommendations, about doctors, movies, books, money, politics.

It was a few years before I saw Arturo Belano again. The first time was in 1976, the second in—1979? 1980? Dates aren't my forte. It was in Barcelona. There's no way I could forget that. I had gone there to live with the painter Abraham Manzur, my partner, boyfriend, friend, fiancé. Before that, I'd lived in Italy, London, and Tel Aviv. One day Abraham called me from Mexico City and told me that he loved me, that he was moving to Barcelona and he wanted me to live with him. I was in Rome then and I wasn't well. I told him yes. We would have a romantic meeting at the airport in Paris and then we would take the train to Barcelona. Abraham had a grant, or something like that, probably his parents had decided it would be good for him to spend a while in Europe and they were bankrolling him. I'm not sure about any of this. Abraham's face is lost to me in a cloud of fog that just keeps getting bigger. Things were going well for Abraham. They'd always gone well for him, actually. He was exactly the same age as me (we were born in the same month of the same year), but while I went back and forth not knowing what I wanted to do, he was completely sure of himself and he had an enormous capacity for work, energy like Picasso, he said, and although sometimes he might be unhappy, or sick and in pain, he would paint every day for five hours straight, eight hours straight, including Saturday and Sunday. He was the first person I made love with. We were both sixteen. Then we were together on and off, we kept breaking up, he never supported my political militancy, I don't mean he was right-wing, just that he wasn't interested in militancy, he probably didn't have time for it, I had other lovers, and he started to go out with a girl called Nora Castro Bilenfeld, and when it looked like they were about to move in together, they broke up, I was in the hospital a few times, my body changed. So I took the train to Paris and waited for Abraham at the airport. After ten hours I realized that he wasn't coming and I left the airport crying, although it was only later that I fully realized I'd been crying. That night I stayed at a cheap hotel in Montparnasse and I spent hours thinking about my life so far and when my body couldn't take it anymore I stopped thinking and lay down in bed, staring at the ceiling, and then I closed my eyes and tried to sleep, but I couldn't, and I was like that for days, unable to sleep, holed up in the hotel, only going out in the morning, eating almost nothing, hardly washing, constipated, with terrible headaches, basically wanting to die.

Until I fell asleep. Then I dreamed that I was traveling to Barcelona and that the trip, in a mysterious, vital way, was like starting my life over from scratch. When I woke up I paid the bill and took the first train to Spain. For the first few days I lived in a boardinghouse on Rambla Capuchinos. I was happy. I bought a canary, two pots of geraniums, and some books. But I needed money and I had to call my mother. When I talked to her I found out that Abraham had been looking for me like crazy all over Paris and that my family had assumed I'd disappeared. My mother asked me whether I'd lost my mind. Then I explained my long wait at the airport and being stood up by Abraham. No one stood you up, darling, my mother said, what happened is that you got the date wrong. It seemed strange that my mother would say that. It sounded like Abraham Manzur's official version of the story. Tell me where you are and Abraham will come get you right away, said my mother. I gave her my address, told her to wire me money, and hung up.

Two days later Abraham showed up at my boardinghouse. Our meeting was cold. I thought he had just come from Paris, but actually he had been living in Barcelona about as long as I had. We ate at a restaurant in the Barri Gòtic, and then he brought me to his place, a few blocks away, near the Plaza Sant Jaume, the apartment of the well-known Catalan-Mexican art dealer Sofía Trompadull, where Abraham could stay as long as he wanted since La Trompadull hardly ever came to Barcelona any-more. The next day we went to get my things at the boardinghouse and I moved in. But there was still a coldness between us. I didn't bear Abra-ham any grudge about being stood up in Paris, which might have been my fault, but I felt distanced from him, as if I'd agreed to be his wife and share his bed, and go to exhibitions and museums and have dinners with Barcelona friends, but nothing else. Months went by like that. One day Daniel Grossman showed up in Barcelona. He knew where Arturo Be-lano was living and he visited him almost every day. One afternoon I went with him. We talked. He remembered me perfectly. The next day I went back to his apartment, but this time I was alone. He took me out to eat at a cheap restaurant and we talked for hours. I think I told him my whole life story. He talked too and told me things I've forgotten now, but still, I did most of the talking.

After that we began to see each other at least twice a week. Once I invited him to my house, if you could call La Trompadull's Barcelona apartment my house, and just before he left, Abraham showed up. I could see that Abraham was jealous. He greeted us, gave me a kiss on the forehead, and then shut himself in his studio, as if that way he would teach Arturo a lesson. When Arturo left I went into his studio and asked him what was wrong. He didn't answer but that night we made love much more violently than usual. I thought for once things might be dif-ferent. But in the end I didn't feel anything. My relationship with Abra-ham, I realized suddenly, was over. I decided to go back to Mexico, study film, reenroll at the university. I talked to my mother and the next day she sent me a ticket for Mexico City. When I told Arturo I was leaving I could see the sadness in his eyes. I thought: he's the only person who'll care that I'm gone. Once (but this happened before I decided to leave Abraham), I told him I was a dancer. He thought I danced in clubs or was a stripper. That struck me as really funny. No, I said, I wish I could dance like that, but modern dance is my thing. Actually, I'd never even *imagined* myself dancing in a club, doing one of those pathetic little numbers and living with shady people, in unsavory places, but when Ar-turo got the wrong idea and said that, for the first time in my life I thought about it and the (imaginary) vistas of the life of a professional dancer seemed attractive to me, even painfully attractive, although then I stopped thinking about it because my life was already complicated enough. I still had two weeks left in Barcelona and I saw him every day.

We talked a lot, almost always about me. I talked about my parents and their separation, about my grandfather, the Mexican underwear king, about my mother, who had inherited his empire, and about my father, who had studied medicine and whom I adored. I talked to him about my weight problems when I was an adolescent (he couldn't believe it because by then I was really skinny), my militancy in the Trotskyite party, the lovers I'd had, my psychoanalysis.

One morning we went to a riding school in Castelldefels whose owner was a friend of Arturo's, and he let us have two horses all day without charging us anything. I had learned to ride at a club in Mexico City, and he'd learned on his own in the south of Chile when he was a boy. The first few feet we rode in step, then I said that we should race. The path was straight and narrow, and then it went up a ridge bordered with pine trees, and down again to a dry riverbed. Past the river was a tunnel and beyond the tunnel was the sea. We galloped. At first he kept his horse close beside mine, but then, I don't know what got into me, I merged with the horse and started to gallop as fast as I could, leaving Arturo behind. At that moment I wouldn't have cared if I died. I knew, I was conscious of the fact, that there were many things I hadn't told him that I probably needed to tell him or should tell him, and I thought that if I died riding or if the horse threw me or if a branch in the pine forest knocked me to the ground, Arturo would know everything I hadn't told him and would understand it without needing to hear it from my lips. But when I crossed the ridge and left the pine forest behind, my desire to die turned into happiness, happiness that I was riding and galloping, happiness that I was feeling the wind on my cheeks. A little later I even felt afraid of falling, because the slope was much steeper than I'd thought, and then I didn't want to die anymore, it wasn't a game and I didn't want to die, at least not just then, and I began to slow down. Then something surprising happened. I saw Arturo shoot past me like an arrow, not stopping, and I saw him look at me and smile, a Cheshire cat smile, although he'd lost a few molars living the crazy life he lived, but it didn't matter, his smile hung there as he and his horse shot toward the dry riverbed, so fast that I thought that both of them, horse and rider, would go tumbling onto the dusty stones, and that when I dismounted and came through the cloud raised by the fall I would find the horse with a broken leg and Arturo next to him with his head a bloody mess, dead, his eyes open, and then I was afraid, and I spurred my horse on, riding down toward the river, but I couldn't see through the dust at first, and when the dust had cleared there was no horse or rider in the riverbed, nothing, just the sound of cars going by on the highway in the distance, hidden behind a patch of trees, and the sun beating down on the dry stones of the riverbed, and everything was like a magic trick, one minute I was with Arturo and the next I was alone again, and then I really was scared, so scared that I didn't dare get off the horse or say anything, all I did was look around and I didn't see any sign of him, as if the earth or air had swallowed him up, and when I was almost about to cry, I saw him, at the entrance to the tunnel, in the shadows, like an evil spirit, watching me without saying anything, and I spurred the horse on toward him and I said you fucking scared me, Arturo, you jerk, and he looked at me in a sad way and although later he laughed to cover it up, it was then, and only then, that I knew he'd fallen in love with me.

The night before I left I went to see him. We talked about the trip. He asked me whether I was sure I was doing the right thing. I told him I wasn't sure, but that I had the ticket and I had to go through with it now. He asked who would take me to the airport. I told him Abraham and a friend. He said I shouldn't leave. No one had ever asked me not to leave the way he asked me. I told him that if he wanted to make love with me (I said: if you want to fuck) we should do it now. It was all very melodramatic. If what you want is to fuck, let's fuck now. Now? he said. Right now, I said, and without waiting for him to say yes or no, I took off my sweater and got undressed. And we didn't make love (or maybe not making love was our way of making love) because he didn't get hard, but we did hold each other and his hands stroked my legs and between my legs, his hands caressed my stomach, my breasts, and when I asked him what was wrong he said: nothing's wrong, Edith, and I thought he didn't like me, that it was my fault, and then he said no, it's not your fault, it's my fault, I can't get it up, or maybe he said it won't get hard or something like that. Then he said: don't worry. And I said: if you aren't worried, I won't worry. And then I told him that I hadn't had my period for almost a year, and that I had medical problems, that I had been sexually assaulted twice, that I was angry and afraid, that I was going to make a film, that I had plans, and as he listened to me he stroked my body and looked at me and suddenly everything that I was telling him seemed stupid to me and I wanted to sleep, sleep with him, on his mattress on the floor of that tiny apartment, and immediately I was asleep, I slept for a long time, a deep peaceful sleep, and when I woke up, daylight was coming in the only window of the apartment and there was the sound of a radio in the distance, the radio of a worker getting ready to go to work, and Arturo was asleep beside me, curled up a little, the blankets pulled up to his ribs, and for a while I lay there watching him and thinking about what my life would be like if I lived with him, but then I decided that I had to be practical and not let myself be carried away by fantasies and I got up carefully and left.

My return to Mexico was miserable. At first I lived in my mother's house and then I rented a little place in Coyoacán and started to take classes at the university. One day I was thinking about Arturo and I decided to call him. When I dialed the number I felt as if I couldn't breathe and I thought I was going to die. A voice told me that Arturo didn't get into work until nine at night, Spanish time. When I hung up, my first impulse was to get into bed and go to sleep. But at almost the same instant I realized that I wouldn't be able to sleep, so I started to read, sweep the house, clean the kitchen, write a letter, think about meaningless things until it was midnight and I called again. This time it was Arturo who answered. We talked for almost fifteen minutes. After that we started to call each other every week. Sometimes I would call him at work and other times he would call me at home. One day I asked him to come and live in Mexico with me. He said he wasn't allowed into the country, that Mexico wouldn't give him a visa. I told him to fly to Guatemala, we could meet in Guatemala and get married there, and then he would be able to get in, no problem. We discussed this possibility for days. He'd been to Guatemala, I hadn't. Some nights I dreamed of Guatemala. One afternoon my mother came to see me and I made the mistake of telling her about it. I told her about my Guatemala dreams and my phone conversations with Arturo. Everything became unnecessarily complicated. My mother reminded me of my health problems, maybe she even started to cry, although I don't think so, or at least I don't remember seeing tears on her face. Another afternoon, my mother and my father came together and begged me to see a famous specialist. I had no choice but to accept since they were the ones giving me money. Luckily, there was no problem with the doctor. Edith is completely recovered, he told them. Still, over the next few days I went to see two other famous specialists and their diagnoses weren't so positive. My friends kept asking what was wrong with me. I told only one of them that

I was in love, and that my love lived in Europe and couldn't come to Mexico to be with me. I talked about Guatemala. My friend pointed out that it would be easier for me to go back to Barcelona. I hadn't thought about that, and when I did, I felt like an idiot. Why not go back to Barcelona? I tried to solve my problems with my parents. I got money for the ticket. I talked to Arturo and told him I was coming. When I got there, he was at the airport. I don't know why, but I wasn't really expecting anyone to be there. Or I was expecting more people, not just Arturo, maybe some of his friends. That was the beginning of my new life in Barcelona.

One afternoon, as I was sleeping, I heard a woman's voice. Right away I knew it was one of Arturo's old lovers. I called her Santa Teresa. She was older than me, probably twenty-eight at least, and people told outrageous stories about her. Then I heard Arturo's voice, saying very quietly that I was asleep. For a few minutes, the two of them went on whispering to each other. Then Arturo asked her something and his old lover said yes. Much later I realized that what Arturo had asked her was whether she wanted to see me sleeping. Santa Teresa said yes. I pretended to be asleep. The curtain that separated the only bedroom from the living room was pulled back and Arturo and Santa Teresita came into the darkness. I didn't want to open my eyes. Afterward, I asked Arturo who'd been in the apartment. He said Santa Teresa's name and showed me some flowers that she'd brought me. If you love each other so much, I thought, you should still be together. But deep down I knew that Arturo and Santa Teresa would never live together again. I didn't know many things, but that I knew for sure. I was absolutely sure he loved me. The first few days of our life together weren't easy. He wasn't used to sharing his little house with anyone and I wasn't used to living so precariously. But we talked, and that got us through the day. We talked to the point of exhaustion, from the moment we got up until the moment we went to bed. And we made love too. Badly and awkwardly the first few days, but it got better every day. Still, I didn't like the way he tried so hard to make me come. I just want you to enjoy yourself, I would say, if you want to come, come, don't wait for me. Then he just wouldn't come (to spite me, I think) and we could spend the whole night screwing and he would say that he liked it that way, not coming, but after a few days his testicles would hurt horribly and he'd have to come even if I couldn't.

Another problem was my smell, the smell of my vagina, the smell when we had sex. I'd always been ashamed of it. Back then it was very strong, and it made its way into every corner of the room where we were fucking. And Arturo's apartment was so small and we made love so often that my smell wasn't confined to the bedroom but seeped into the living room, which was only separated from the bedroom by a curtain, and into the kitchen, a tiny room that didn't even have a door. And the worst of it was that the apartment was in the center of Barcelona, in the old city, and Arturo's friends would stop by every day without calling first, most of them Chileans, although there were Mexicans too, Daniel among them, and I didn't know whether I was more embarrassed by the smell when it was the Chileans, who hardly knew me, or the Mexicans, who in some sense were our mutual friends. Either way, I hated my smell. One night I asked Arturo whether he'd ever slept with a woman who smelled that way. He said no. And I started to cry. Arturo added that he'd never slept with anyone he loved so much either. I didn't believe him. I told him that he must have had a better time with Santa Teresa. He said yes, sexually he'd had a better time, but he loved me more. Then he said that he loved Santa Teresa too, but in a different way. She really loves you, he said. All that love made me feel like throwing up. I made him promise that he wouldn't open the door if some friend of his came by and the smell hadn't gone away yet. He answered that he didn't care whether he never saw anyone again except for me. Of course, I thought he was joking. Then I don't know what happened.

I started to feel bad. We were living on what he made because I'd strictly forbidden my mother to send me money. I didn't want that money. I looked for work in Barcelona and finally I ended up giving private Hebrew classes. My students were very strange Catalans who were studying the Kabbalah or the Torah, from which they drew heterodox conclusions that freaked me out. They would explain them to me over coffee at a bar or tea at their houses once the lesson was over. At night I talked to Arturo about my students. Once Arturo told me that Ulises Lima had his own version of one of Jesus' parables, but either he couldn't explain it very well or I've forgotten it, or, most likely, I wasn't paying much attention when he told it to me. By then, I think Arturo and Ulises's friendship was over. I saw Ulises three times in Mexico, and the last time, when I told him I was going back to Barcelona to live with Arturo, he said I shouldn't go, if I went he would really miss me. At first I didn't understand what he was trying to say, but then I realized that he'd fallen in love with me or something, and I laughed in his face. But Arturo is your friend! I said, and then I started to cry, and when I looked up and saw Ulises, I realized that he was crying too. Or no, not crying, I realized that he was making an effort to cry, that he was forcing tears and some had already risen to his eyes. What am I going to do, all alone? he said. The whole scene was unreal somehow. When I told Arturo about it he laughed and said he couldn't believe it, and then he called his friend a son of a bitch. That was the last time we talked about it, but during that second stay in Barcelona I thought about Ulises and his tears sometimes, and about how lonely he'd claimed he was going to be in Mexico.

One night I made chicken with red mole and Arturo and I ate it with the windows open, because it was very hot, it must have been the middle of summer, and suddenly there was an enormous noise from outside, as if the whole city had turned out for a protest, although actually they weren't protesting anything, just celebrating some soccer victory. I had set the table and taken a lot of trouble with the mole, but the noise from outside was so loud that we couldn't even hear ourselves talk, so we had to close the window. It was hot, and the mole was very spicy. Arturo was sweating, I was sweating, and suddenly everything fell apart again and I started to cry. The strange thing is that when Arturo tried to put his arms around me I was struck by a wave of rage and I started to scream at him. I would have liked to hit him, but instead, all of a sudden, I surprised myself by hitting myself. I was saying: me, me, me, and hitting myself in the chest with my thumb until Arturo caught my hand. Later he said that he was afraid I would break my thumb or hurt my chest or both. Finally I calmed down and we went outside. I needed fresh air, but that night there were millions of people in the streets. The Ramblas were overrun. On some corners we saw big trash bins blocking the way and on other corners kids struggling to flip cars. We saw flags. People were laughing loudly and looking at me in surprise because I was walking with a serious expression on my face, elbowing my way through the crowd, trying to find the fresh air I craved, but the air had disappeared as if all of Barcelona had become a giant bonfire, a dark bonfire full of shadows and shouts and soccer chants. Then we heard the wail of police sirens. More shouts. The sound of breaking glass. We started to run. I think it was then that everything ended between Arturo and me. At night we used to write. He was writing a novel and I was writing my journal and poetry and a movie script. We would write facing each other and drink lots of cups of tea. We weren't writing for publication but to understand ourselves better or just to see how far we could go. And when we weren't writing we talked endlessly about his life and my life, especially mine, although sometimes Arturo told me stories about friends who had died in the guerrilla wars of Latin America, I knew some of them by name, because they'd been on their way through Mexico when I was with the Trotskyites, but most of them I'd never heard of. And we kept making love, although each night I distanced myself a little more, involuntarily, without meaning to, without knowing where I was going. It was the same thing that had already happened to me with Abraham, more or less, except now it was a little worse, now that I didn't have anything.

One night, while we were making love, I told him. I told him that I thought I was going crazy, that I kept having the same symptoms. I talked for a long time. His response surprised me (it was the last time he surprised me). He said that if I was going crazy then he would go crazy too, that he didn't mind going crazy with me. Do you like to tempt fate? I said. It's not fate I'm tempting, he said. I searched for his eyes in the dark and asked whether he was serious. Of course I'm serious, he said, and he pressed his body close to mine. That night I slept peacefully. The next morning I knew I had to leave him, the sooner the better, and at noon I called my mother from Telefónica. In those days, Arturo and his friends didn't pay for the international calls they made. I never knew how they did it. All I knew was that they had more than one method and they had to be swindling Telefónica out of thousands of millions of pesetas. They would find some telephone and hook up a few wires and that was it, they had a connection. The Argentinians were the best at it, hands down, and then the Chileans. I never met a Mexican who knew how to rig a phone, maybe because we weren't ready for the modern world, or maybe because the few Mexicans who lived in Barcelona at the time had enough money so that they didn't need to break the law. The rigged telephones were easy to tell by the lines that formed around them, especially at night. The best and the worst of Latin America came together in those lines, the old revolutionaries and the rapists, the former political prisoners and the hawkers of junk jewelry. When I saw those lines, on my way back from the movies, around the phone booth in Plaza Ramalleras, for example, I would freeze and start to shake, a metallic cold like a security wand running from the back of my neck down to my heels. Adolescents, young women with nursing children, old men and women: what did they think about out there, at midnight or one in the morning, while they waited for a stranger to finish talking, able not to hear but to guess at what was being said, since the person on the phone would gesture or cry or stand there without speaking for a long time, just nodding or shaking his head? What were those people in line waiting for? Were they only hoping that their turn would come soon, that the police wouldn't show up? Was that all? In any case, I distanced myself from that too. I called my mother and asked for money.

One afternoon I told Arturo that I was leaving, that we had to stop living together. He asked me why. I told him I couldn't stand him anymore. What have I done to you? he said. Nothing, I'm the one doing terrible things to myself, I said. I need to be alone. We ended up shouting at each other. I moved to Daniel's apartment. Sometimes Arturo would come by and we'd talk, but each day it was more painful for me to see him. When my mother sent me money I left for good and flew to Rome. At this point I should probably mention my kitten. Before we were living together, a friend or ex-lover of Arturo's had been forced to move unexpectedly and she left him six kittens that her cat had just had. She left him the kittens and took her cat. Arturo kept the kittens for a while, when they were still little. Later, when he realized that his friend or ex-lover was never coming back, he began to look for owners for them. His friends took most of them, except for one gray kitten that no one wanted and I took, which annoyed Abraham, because he was afraid the kitten would claw his canvases. I called her Zia, in memory of another kitten I'd seen one afternoon in Rome. When I left for Mexico, Zia came with me. When I went back to Barcelona to Arturo's apartment, Zia came with me. I think she loved to fly. When I went to stay with Daniel Grossman, naturally I brought Zia with me. And when I caught the flight to Rome, the cat was in a straw bag on my lap. She was going to see Rome at last, the city she was from, namewise at least.

My life in Rome was a disaster. Everything went badly, and worst of all, or at least so I was told later, was that I refused to ask for help. All I had was Zia and all I cared about was taking care of Zia and feeding her. I did read a lot, but when I try to remember what I read a kind of hot, quivery wall gets in the way. Maybe I read Dante in Italian. Maybe Gadda. I don't know. I'd already read them both in Spanish. The only person who had more than a vague indication of my whereabouts was Daniel. I got some letters from him. In one of them he told me that Arturo was shattered by my leaving and each time he saw Daniel he asked about me. Don't give him my address, I said, because he's capable of following me to Rome. I won't give it to him, said Daniel in his next letter. I also heard from him that my mother and father were worried and that they kept calling Barcelona. Don't give them my address, I said, and Daniel promised he wouldn't. His letters were long. My letters were short, almost always postcards. My life in Rome was short and simple. I worked in a shoe store and lived in a boardinghouse on Via della Luce, in Trastevere. At night, when I got home, I would take Zia out for a walk. We usually went to a park behind the church of Sant'Egidio, and as the cat wandered among the plants I would open a book and try to read. I must have read Dante, I guess, or Guido Cavalcanti or Cecco Angiolieri or Cino da Pistoia, but all I remember of what I read is a hot curtain or maybe just a warm curtain fluttering in the slight breeze of Rome at dusk, and plants and trees and the sound of footsteps. One night I met the devil. That's all I remember. I met the devil and I knew I was going to die. The owner of the shoe store saw me come to work with bruises on my neck and watched me for a week. Then he wanted to sleep with me and I refused. One day Zia got lost in the park, not the one behind Sant'Egidio, but another one, on Via Garibaldi, with no trees or lights. Zia just strayed too far and the darkness swallowed her up.

I looked for her until seven in the morning. Until the sun came up and people started slowly heading to work. That day I didn't go to the shoe store. I went to bed, pulled the covers up to my chin, and slept. When I woke up I went out to look for my cat again. I couldn't find her. One night I dreamed of Arturo. The two of us were at the top of an office building, the kind built out of glass and steel, and we opened a window and looked down. It was nighttime. I wasn't planning to jump, but Arturo looked at me and said if you jump, I will too. I wanted to call him an idiot, but I didn't have the strength to insult him.

One day the door of my room opened and I saw my mother and younger brother come in, my brother who'd been a soldier in the Tsahal and who lived most of the year in Israel. They moved me to a hospital in Rome right away, and two days later I was flying back to Mexico. As I found out later, my mother had flown to Barcelona and between her and my brother they had managed to get my address in Rome out of Daniel, after he refused to give it to them at first.

In Mexico I was admitted to a private clinic in Cuernavaca, and the first thing the doctors told my mother was that there was nothing they could do if I didn't make an effort. By then I weighed ninety pounds and I could hardly walk. Then I got on a plane again and was admitted to a clinic in Los Angeles. There I met a Doctor Kalb and gradually we became friends. I weighed seventy-five pounds and in the afternoon I watched television and that was pretty much it. My mother moved into a hotel in downtown Los Angeles, on Sixth Street, and every day she would come to see me. After a month I had gained weight and I was back up to ninety pounds. My mother was very happy and decided to return to Mexico City, to take care of business. With my mother gone, Dr. Kalb and I established a friendship. We talked about food and tranquilizers and other kinds of drugs. We didn't talk much about books because Dr. Kalb only read bestsellers. We talked about film. He'd seen many more movies than I had and he loved movies from the fifties. In the afternoons I'd turn on the television and find some movie so I could discuss it with him later, but the medicine I was taking made me fall asleep halfway through. When I talked to Dr. Kalb he would tell me what had happened in the part I hadn't seen, although by then I'd usually forgotten the part I had seen. My memory of those movies is strange, images and scenes filtered through the lens of my doctor's simple enthusiasm. My mother came most weekends. She would arrive Friday night and return to Mexico City on Sunday night. Once she told me that she was thinking about moving permanently to Los Angeles. Not to the city itself, but to some nice place nearby, like Corona del Mar or Laguna Beach. Then what will happen to the factory? I said. Grandfather wouldn't have wanted you to sell it. Mexico is going to hell, said my mother, sooner or later it'll have to be sold. Sometimes she would show up with some friend of mine whom she'd invited along because, according to the doctors, including Dr. Kalb, it was good for my health to see my "old gang." One Saturday she showed up with Greta, a friend of mine from high school whom I hadn't seen since then. Another Saturday she showed up with a guy I didn't even recognize. You're the one who should be bringing friends and trying to have a good time, I told her one night. When I said things like that my mother would laugh, as if she couldn't believe what she was hearing, or start to cry. Aren't you dating anyone? Don't you have a boyfriend? I asked her. She admitted that she was seeing someone in Mexico City, a man who was divorced like she was, or a widower. I didn't try very hard to get it straight. I guess I didn't really care. After four months I weighed one hundred and five pounds and my mother started to prepare for my transfer to a Mexican clinic. The day before I left, Dr. Kalb came to say goodbye. I gave him my phone number and begged him to call me sometime. When I asked for his number, he claimed something about a move so he wouldn't have to give it to me. I didn't believe him, but I didn't call his bluff either.

We went back to Mexico City. This time I was admitted to a clinic in Colonia Buenos Aires. I had a big room with lots of light, a window overlooking a park, and a television with more than one hundred channels. In the morning I would sit in the park and read novels. In the afternoon I would shut myself in my room and sleep. One day Daniel, who had just gotten back from Barcelona, came to visit me. He wasn't going to be in Mexico for long and as soon as he found out that I was in the hospital he came to see me. I asked him how I looked. He said fine, but thin. The two of us laughed. By then it didn't hurt to laugh anymore, which was a good sign. Before he left I asked him about Arturo. Daniel said he didn't live in Barcelona anymore, or at least he didn't think so, but it had been a while since they stopped seeing each other. A month later I weighed one hundred and ten pounds and I was discharged from the hospital.

Still, my life changed very little. I lived with my mother and I never went out, not because I couldn't but because I didn't want to. My mother gave me her old car, a Mercedes, but the only time I drove it I almost had an accident. Any little thing made me cry. A house seen from the distance, traffic jams, people trapped inside their cars, the daily news. One night Abraham called me from Paris, where he had work in a group show of young Mexican painters. He wanted to talk about my health, but I wouldn't let him. He ended up talking about his painting, the progress he'd made, his successes. When we said goodbye I realized that I'd managed not to shed a single tear. Not long afterward, around the same time my mother decided to move to Los Angeles, I began to lose weight. One day, without having sold the factory, we got on a plane and settled in Laguna Beach. I spent the first two weeks at my old hospital in Los Angeles, undergoing exhaustive tests, and then I joined my mother in a little house on Lincoln Street, in Laguna Beach. My mother had been there before, but visiting was one thing and daily life something entirely different. For a while we would take the car out early in the morning and go looking for some other place we might like. We tried Dana Point, San Clemente, San Onofre, finally ending up in a town called Silverado, like in the movie, on the edge of the Cleveland National Forest, where we rented a two-story house with a yard and bought a police dog that my mother called Hugo, after the friend she'd just left behind in Mexico.

We lived there two years. During that time my mother sold my grandfather's main factory and I was subjected to regular and increasingly routine doctors' appointments. Once a month my mother traveled to Mexico City. When she came back, she would bring me novels, Mexican novels that she knew I liked, old favorites or new books by José Agustín or Gustavo Sainz or even younger writers. But one day I realized that I couldn't read them anymore and little by little the books in Spanish were set aside. Shortly afterward, without warning, my mother showed up with a friend, an engineer called Cabrera who worked for a construction company in Guadalajara. The engineer was a widower and had two children a little older than me who lived in the United States, on the East Coast. He and my mother got along easily, and it seemed like they'd stay together. One night my mother and I talked about sex. I told her that my sexual life was over and after a long argument my mother started to cry and hugged me and said I was her little girl and she'd never leave me. Otherwise, we hardly ever fought. Our life consisted solely of reading, watching television (we never went to the movies), and weekly trips to Los Angeles, where we saw gallery shows or went to concerts. We had no friends in Silverado, except for a Jewish couple in their eighties whom my mother met at the supermarket, or so she told me, and whom we saw every three or four days, just for a few minutes and always at their house. According to my mother, it was our duty to visit them, because old people could have an accident or one of them might die all of a sudden and the other one might not know what to do, something I doubted since the old people had been in a German concentration camp during World War II and were hardly unacquainted with death. But it made my mother happy to help them and I didn't want to argue with her. The couple were called Mr. and Mrs. Schwartz, and they called us the Mexican Ladies.

One weekend when my mother was in Mexico City I went to see them. It was the first time I'd gone alone, and to my surprise I stayed a long time at their house and I enjoyed talking to them. I had lemonade and Mr. and Mrs. Schwartz poured themselves whiskey. At their age it was the best medicine, they claimed. We talked about Europe, which they knew pretty well, and about Mexico, where they'd also been a few times. But the idea they had of Mexico couldn't have been more wrong or superficial. I remember that after we'd been talking for a long time they looked at me and said I was clearly Mexican. Of course I'm Mexican, I said. Still, they were very nice and I started to visit them more often. Sometimes, when they didn't feel well, they would call me and ask me to do their shopping at the supermarket that day or take their clothes to the cleaners or go to the newsstand and buy them a paper. Sometimes they would ask for the *Los Angeles Times* and other times for the local Silverado paper, a four-page flyer devoid of anything of interest. They liked Brahms, whom they thought was both a dreamer and a rationalist, and only very rarely did they watch television. I was the complete opposite. I almost never listened to music and I had the TV on most of the day.

When we'd been living there for over a year, Mr. Schwartz died and my mother and I went with Mrs. Schwartz to the burial at the Jewish cemetery in Los Angeles. We insisted that she come in our car, but Mrs. Schwartz refused, and that morning she drove off behind the hearse in a rented limousine, alone, or at least so my mother and I thought. When we got to the cemetery some guy in his forties, dressed entirely in black and with his head shaved, got out of the car and helped Mrs. Schwartz out as if he was her beau. When they left, the same scene was repeated: Mrs. Schwartz got in the car, then the bald man got in and they left, followed closely by my mother's white Nissan. When we got to Silverado, the limousine stopped in front of the Schwartzes' house and the bald man helped Mrs. Schwartz out, then got back in the limousine, which immediately drove away. Mrs. Schwartz was left alone in the middle of the deserted sidewalk. It's a good thing we followed her, said my mother. We parked the car and went over to her. Mrs. Schwartz seemed lost somehow, gazing down the street after the limousine. We got her inside and my mother made us tea. Until then Mrs. Schwartz had let herself be led, but after the first sip of tea she pushed the cup away and asked for whiskey. My mother looked at me. There was a gleam of triumph in her eyes. Then I asked where the whiskey was and I poured her one. With water or without? Straight up, dear, said Mrs. Schwartz. Ice or no ice? I heard my mother's voice from the kitchen. Straight up! repeated Mrs. Schwartz. After that we grew closer. When my mother went to Mexico I would spend all day at Mrs. Schwartz's house, and sometimes I would even spend the night there. And although Mrs. Schwartz never ate at night, she would prepare a salad and grill a steak and make me eat. She would sit beside me, with her whiskey nearby, and tell me stories about her youth in Europe, when food, she said, was a necessity and a luxury. We listened to records too, and commented on the local news.

During the long and peaceful year of Mrs. Schwartz's widowhood, I met a man in Silverado, a plumber, and slept with him. It wasn't a pleasant experience. The plumber's name was John and he wanted to see me again. I told him no, that once was enough. My refusal didn't convince him and he started to call me every day. Once my mother picked up the phone and they spent a while telling each other off. A week later my mother and I decided to take a vacation in Mexico. We were at the beach and then we went to Mexico City. I don't know why my mother got the idea into her head that I needed to see Abraham. One night he called me and we agreed to meet the next day. By this time, Abraham had left Europe for good and was living in Mexico City, where he had a studio. Things seemed to be going well for him. The studio was in Coyoacán, near his apartment, and after we had dinner he wanted me to see his most recent paintings. I can't say whether I liked them or not. They probably left me cold. They were very large canvases, strongly resembling the work of a Catalan painter Abraham admired, or had admired when he lived in Barcelona, although to be fair, they'd been filtered through his own sensibility: where once there'd been ochers and earth tones, now there were yellows, reds, blues. He also showed me a series of drawings and I liked those a little better. Then we talked about money, or he talked about money, about the instability of the peso, about the possibility of going to live in California, about friends we no longer saw.

Suddenly, out of the blue, he asked me about Arturo Belano. It surprised me because Abraham never asked such direct questions. I told him that I didn't know what had happened to Arturo. I do, he said, do you want me to tell you? First I thought about saying no, but then I told him to go ahead, that I wanted to know. I saw him one night in the Barrio Chino, he said, and at first he didn't recognize me. He was with a blond woman. He looked happy. I said hello to him, since we were in a little dive bar, practically at the same table (here Abraham laughed), and it would have been stupid to pretend I hadn't seen him. It took him a while to recognize me. Then he came closer, almost pushing his face in mine, which made me realize that he was completely drunk (so was I, probably), and asked about you. And what did you say? I told him that you were living in the United States and you were fine. And what did he say? That it was a weight off his shoulders, or something, I guess, that sometimes he thought you were dead. And that was all. He turned back to the blonde and a little later my friends and I left.

Fifteen days later we went back to Silverado. One afternoon I ran into John on the street and I told him that if he kept calling me and bothering me I would kill him. John apologized and said that he'd fallen in love with me, but that he wasn't in love with me anymore and he wouldn't call me again. Around that time, I weighed one hundred and ten pounds and I wasn't losing or gaining weight and my mother was happy. She had a steady relationship with the engineer and they were even talking about getting married, although my mother never sounded as if she meant it. She opened a shop of Mexican handicrafts with a friend in Laguna Beach, and the business didn't bring in much money but it wasn't losing much either, and the social life it gave her was exactly what she wanted. A year after Mr. Schwartz's death Mrs. Schwartz got sick and had to be admitted to a hospital in Los Angeles. The next day I went to see her and she was asleep. The hospital was downtown, on Wilshire Boulevard, near MacArthur Park. My mother had to leave and I wanted to stay and wait until Mrs. Schwartz woke up. The problem was the car, because if my mother left and I didn't, who would take me back to Silverado? After a long discussion in the hallway, my mother said she would come pick me up between nine and ten that night, and if for some unexpected reason she was held up, she would call me at the hospital. Before she left she made me promise that I wouldn't budge. I don't know how much time I spent in Mrs. Schwartz's hospital room. I ate at the hospital cafeteria and struck up a conversation with a nurse. The nurse's name was Rosario Álvarez and she was born in Mexico City. I asked her what life was like in Los Angeles and she said that it was different every day, that sometimes it could be very good and sometimes very bad, but if you worked hard you could get ahead. I asked her how long it had been since she was in Mexico. Too long, she said, I don't have the money to be nostalgic. Then I bought a paper and went back up to Mrs. Schwartz's room. I sat next to the window and looked up the museum and movie listings in the paper. There was a movie on Alvarado Street that I suddenly felt like seeing. It had been a long time since I'd been to the movies and Alvarado Street wasn't far from the hospital. And yet, when I was outside the ticket window I didn't feel like it anymore and I kept walking. Everyone says that Los Angeles isn't a pedestrian city. I walked along Pico Boulevard to Valencia and then turned left and walked along Valencia back to Wilshire Boulevard, a two-hour walk in all, without hurrying, stopping in front of buildings that might have seemed uninteresting or carefully watching the flow of traffic. At ten my mother came back from Laguna Beach and we left. The second time I went to see Mrs. Schwartz, she didn't recognize me. I asked the nurse whether she'd had any visitors. The nurse said that an older woman had come to see her that morning and had left just before I got there. This time I came in the Nissan, because my mother and the engineer, who had just arrived, had taken his car to Laguna Beach. According to the nurse I talked to, Mrs. Schwartz was fading fast. I ate at the hospital and sat in the room for a while, thinking, until six. Then I got in the Nissan and went for a drive around Los Angeles. In the glove compartment there was a map that I consulted carefully before I turned the key in the ignition. Then I started the car and left the hospital. I know I passed the Civic Center, the Music Center, the Dorothy Chandler Pavillion. Then I headed for Echo Park and I merged into traffic on Sunset Boulevard. I don't know how long I was driving. All I know is that I never got out of the Nissan and that in Beverly Hills I got off Highway 101 and meandered along on side roads until I got to Santa Monica. There I got on Interstate 10, or the Santa Monica Freeway, and I headed back downtown, then took Highway 11, passing Wilshire Boulevard, although I couldn't turn off until farther up, at Third Street. When I got back to the hospital it was ten at night and Mrs. Schwartz had died. I was going to ask whether she was alone when she died but then I decided not to ask anything. The body wasn't in the room anymore. I sat next to the window for a while, breathing and recovering from my trip to Santa Monica. A nurse came in and asked me whether I was related to Mrs. Schwartz and what I was doing there. I told her that I was a friend and I was just trying to calm down, that was all. She asked me whether I was calm yet. I said yes. Then I got up and left. I got to Silverado at three in the morning.

A month later my mother married the engineer. The wedding was in Laguna Beach and the engineer's children were there, as well as one of my brothers and the friends my mother had made in California. They lived in Silverado for a while and then my mother sold the shop in Laguna Beach and they went to live in Guadalajara. For a while, I didn't want to leave Silverado. Without my mother, the house seemed much bigger and quieter and cooler than before. Mrs. Schwartz's house was empty for a while. In the afternoons I would get in the Nissan and go to a bar in town and have a coffee or a whiskey and reread some old novels whose plot I'd forgotten. At the bar I met a guy who worked for the Forest Service and we slept together. His name was Perry and he knew a few words of Spanish. One night Perry told me that my vagina had an unusual smell. I didn't answer and he thought he'd offended me. Have I offended you? he said, I'm sorry if I have. But I was thinking about other things, other faces (if it's possible to think about a face), and he hadn't offended me. Most of the time, however, I was alone. Each month there was a check for me from my mother at the bank and I spent my days cleaning the house, sweeping, mopping, going to the supermarket, cooking, washing the dishes, taking care of the yard. I didn't call anyone and the only calls I got were from my mother, and, once a week, from my father or one of my brothers. When I was in the mood, I would go to a bar in the afternoon, and when I wasn't in the mood I would stay home reading beside the window. If I raised my eyes I could see the Schwartzes' empty house from where I sat. One afternoon a car stopped in front of it and a man in a jacket and tie got out. He had keys. He went in and ten minutes later he came out again. He didn't look like a relative of the Schwartzes. A few days later two women and a man came back to visit the house again. When they left, one of the women put a sign out saying that the house was for sale. Then many days went by before anyone came to visit it, but one day at noon, while I was busy in the yard, I heard children shouting and I saw a couple in their thirties going into the house led by one of the women who'd been there before. I knew immediately that they would buy the house and right there in the yard, without taking off my gloves, standing there like a pillar of salt, I decided that the time had come for me to leave too. That night I listened to Debussy and thought about Mexico and then, I don't know why, I thought about my cat Zia and I ended up calling my mother and asking her to get me a job in Mexico City, any job. I told her I'd be leaving soon. A week later my mother and her new husband were in Silverado, and two days later, one Sunday night, I flew to Mexico City. My first job was at a gallery in the Zona Rosa. It didn't pay much, but the work wasn't hard. Then I started to work at a publishing house, the Fondo de Cultura Economica, in the English Philosophy division, and my work life was finally settled.


**Felipe Müller, sitting on a bench in Plaza Martorell, Barcelona, October 1991.** I'm almost sure it was Arturo Belano who told me this story, because he was the only one of us who liked to read science fiction. It's by Theodore Sturgeon, or so Arturo said, although it might be by some other author or even Arturo himself; the name Theodore Sturgeon means nothing to me.

The story, a love story, is about a hugely rich and extremely intelligent girl who one day falls in love with her gardener or her gardener's son or a young tramp who just happens to end up on one of the estates she owns and becomes her gardener. The girl, who's not only rich and smart but also headstrong and a little impulsive, lures him into bed the first chance she gets, and without quite knowing how, falls madly in love with him. The tramp, who's nowhere near as smart as she is and who doesn't have a high school degree but who makes up for it by being angelically pure, falls in love with her too, though naturally not without a few complications. In the first phase of the romance, they live in her palatial mansion, where they spend their time looking at art books, eating exquisite delicacies, watching old movies, and mostly making love all day. Then they live for a while in the gardener's cottage and then on a boat (maybe the kind that cruises the rivers of France, like in the Jean Vigo film) and then they roam the vast expanse of the United States on a couple of Harleys, which was one of the tramp's long-cherished dreams.

As the girl lives out her love, her interests continue to prosper, and since money begets money, she gets richer by the day. Of course, the tramp, who's generally clueless, is decent enough to convince her to devote part of her fortune to good works or charity (which is something the girl has always done anyway, through lawyers and a network of various foundations, though she doesn't tell him so, in order to make him think she's doing it on his account) and then he forgets about it all, because ultimately the tramp has only the vaguest idea of the mass of money that trails like a shadow behind his beloved. Anyway, for a while, months, maybe a year or two, the girl millionaire and her lover are indescribably happy. But one day (or one evening), the tramp falls ill and although the best doctors in the world come to examine him, there's nothing to be done. His health has been ruined by an unhappy childhood, an adolescence plagued with hardships, a troubled life that the short time he's spent with the girl has barely managed to ease or sweeten. Despite all the efforts of science, he dies of cancer.

For a few days the girl seems to lose her mind. She travels all over the globe, takes lovers, immerses herself in dark pursuits. But she ends up coming home, and soon, when it becomes clear that she's more obsessed than ever, she decides to embark on a project that in some way had already begun to take root in her mind just before the tramp's death. A team of scientists moves into the mansion. In record time, the house is doubly transformed, the inside into a sophisticated laboratory, and the outside, the lawns and the gardener's cottage, into a replica of Eden. To shield it all from the gaze of strangers, an extremely high wall is erected around the grounds. Then the work begins. Soon the scientists implant a clone of the tramp in the womb of a whore, who will be generously compensated. Nine months later the whore has a boy, hands him over to the girl, and disappears.

For five years the girl and a team of specialists care for the boy. Then the scientists implant a clone of the girl in her own womb. Nine months later the girl has a child. The laboratory in the mansion is dismantled and the scientists disappear, replaced by teachers, the tutor-specialists who will keep watch from a distance as both children are raised according to a plan previously drawn up by the girl. When everything is set in motion the girl disappears. She travels, she attends society parties again, she plunges headfirst into perilous adventures, takes lovers: her name shines like a star's. But every once in a while, cloaked in the greatest secrecy, she returns to the mansion and observes the children's progress, unseen by them. The clone of the tramp is an exact replica of the man she fell in love with, his purity and innocence intact. Except that now all his needs are met and his childhood is a peaceful succession of games and teachers who instruct him in all he needs to know. The female clone is an exact replica of the girl herself, and her teachers repeat the same successes and failures, the same actions of the past.

The girl, of course, hardly ever lets herself be seen by the children, although occasionally the clone of the tramp, who is never tired of playing and is a bold child, spots her through the lace curtains of the mansion's upper floors and goes running after her, always in vain.

The years pass and the children grow up, becoming more and more inseparable. One day the millionairess falls ill, with whatever, a deadly virus, cancer, and after a purely symbolic struggle, gives in and prepares to die. She's still young, forty-two. Her only heirs are the two clones and she leaves everything ready for them to inherit part of her immense fortune the moment they're married. Then she dies and her lawyers and scientists weep bitterly for her.

The story ends with a meeting of her staff after the reading of the will. Some, the most innocent and farthest from the millionairess's inner circle, ask the questions that Sturgeon guesses readers might ask themselves. What if the clones refuse to marry? What if the boy and girl love each other, as seems indisputable, but their love never goes beyond the strictly fraternal? Will their lives be ruined? Will they be condemned to live together like two prisoners serving life sentences?

Arguments and debates break out. Moral and ethical questions are raised. The oldest lawyer and scientist, however, soon take it upon themselves to clear up all doubts. Even if the boy and girl don't agree to marry, even if they don't fall in love, they'll still be given the money they're due and they'll be free to do as they like. No matter how the relationship between them develops, within a year the scientists will implant a new clone of the tramp in the body of a surrogate, and five years later they'll repeat the operation with a new clone of the millionairess. And when these new clones are twenty-three and eighteen, no matter what their interpersonal relationship might be—in other words, whether they love each other like brother and sister or like lovers—the scientists or the scientists' successors will implant two more clones, and so on until the end of time or until the millionairess's immense fortune is exhausted.

This is where the story ends, with the faces of the millionairess and the tramp silhouetted against the sunset, and then the stars, and then infinite space. A little creepy, isn't it? Sublime, in a way, but creepy too. Like all crazy loves, don't you think? If you add infinity to infinity, you get infinity. If you mix the sublime and the creepy, what you end up with is creepy. Right?

# 20

Xosé Lendoiro, Terme di Traiano, Rome, October 1992. I was no ordinary lawyer. *Lupo ovem commisisti* or *Alter remus aquas, alter tibi radat harenas*: either could be said of me with equal justice. And yet I've preferred to adhere to the Catullian *noli pugnare duobus*. Someday my merits will be recognized.

In those days I was traveling and conducting experiments. My practice as a lawyer or jurist afforded me sufficient income so that I could devote ample time to the noble art of poetry. *Unde habeas quaerit nemo, sed oportet habere*, which, simply put, means that no one inquires as to the source of one's possessions, but possessions are necessary. An essential truth if one wants to devote oneself to one's most secret calling: poets are dazzled by the spectacle of wealth.

But let us return to my experiments. At first, these consisted solely of traveling and observing, although I was soon given to know that my unconscious intention was the attainment of the ideal map of Spain. *Hoc erat in votis*, such were my desires, as the immortal Horace says. Naturally, I had a magazine. I was, if I may say so, the funder and editor, the publisher and star poet. *In petris, herbis vis est, sed maxima verbis*: stones and grass have many virtues, but words have more.

My publication was tax-deductible too, which meant that it was little burden. But why bore you? Details have no place in poetry. That's always been my maxim, along with *Paulo maiora canamus*: let us sing of greater things, as Virgil says. One has to get to the marrow, the pith, the essence. I had a magazine and I headed a firm of lawyers, ambulance chasers and sharks, a firm of not undeserved renown, and during the summers I traveled. Life was good. And yet one day I said to myself,

Xosé, you've been all over the world: *incipit vita nova*. It's time for you to tread the pathways of Spain, though you be no Dante, time for you to tread the roads of this country of ours, so battered and long-suffering and yet still so little known.

I'm a man of action. What's said is done: I bought myself a *roulotte* and off I went. *Vive valeque.* I traveled through Andalusia. Granada is so pretty, Seville so lovely, Cordoba so severe. But I needed to go deeper, get to the source. Doctor of law and criminal lawyer that I was, I couldn't rest until I'd found the right path: the *ius est ars boni et aequi*, the *libertas est potestas faciendi id quod facere iure licet*, the root of the apparition. It was a summer of initiation. I kept repeating to myself, after sweet Horace: *nescit vox missa reverti*, the word, once spoken, cannot be withdrawn. From the legal point of view, the statement has its loopholes. But not for a poet. By the time I returned from that first trip, I was in a state of excitement, and also somewhat confused.

Before long, I separated from my wife. There were no scenes and no one was hurt, since fortunately our daughters were already grown and had the sufficient discernment to understand me, especially the older one. Keep the apartment and the house in Tossa, I said, and let that be the end of it. My wife accepted, surprisingly enough. We put the rest in the hands of a few lawyers she trusted. *In publicis nihil est lege gravius: in privatis firmissimum est testamentum.* Although why I say that I don't know. What do wills have to do with divorce? My nightmares are getting the better of me. In any case, *legum omnes servi sumus, ut liberi esse possimus*, which means that in order to be free, which is our most precious desire, we are all slaves before the law.

Suddenly, I was overflowing with energy. I felt rejuvenated: I stopped smoking, I went running every morning, I participated diligently in three law conferences, two of them held in old European capitals. My magazine didn't go under; on the contrary, the poets who drew sustenance from my largesse closed ranks in manifest sympathy. *Verae amicitiae sempiternae sunt*, I thought, along with the learned Cicero. Then, in a clear instance of overconfidence, I decided to publish a book of my poetry. The printing was expensive and of the four reviews it received, all but one were negative. I blamed everything on Spain and my optimism and the unchanging laws of envy. *Invidia ceu fulmine summa vaporant.*

When summer came I got in the *roulotte* and set out to roam the lands of my elders, or in other words verdant, primeval Galicia. I left in good spirits, at four in the morning, muttering sonnets by the immortal and prickly Quevedo. Once in Galicia I traveled its *rías* and tried its *mostos* and talked to its sailors, since *natura maxime miranda in minimis.* Then I headed for the mountains, for the land of *meigas*, my soul fortified and my senses alert. I slept at campgrounds, because a Guardia Civil sergeant warned me that it was dangerous to camp along back roads or country highways, especially in the summer, because of lowlifes, traveling singers, and partygoers who wandered from one club to another along the foggy night roads. *Qui amat periculum in illo peribit.* The campgrounds weren't bad either, and I was soon calculating the wealth of emotions and passions that I might discover and observe and even catalog in such places, with an eye to my map.

So it was while I was at one of these establishments that what I now regard as the central part of my story took place. Or at least the only part that still preserves intact the happiness and mystery of my whole sad, futile tale. *Mortalium nemo est felix*, says Pliny. And also: *felicitas cui praecipua fuerit homini, non est humani iudici.* But to get to the point. I was at a campground, as I've said, near Castroverde, in the province of Lugo, in a mountainous spot abounding in thickets and shrubs of every sort. I was reading and taking notes and amassing knowledge. *Otium sine litteris mors est et homini vivi sepultura.* Although that may be an exaggeration. In short (and to be honest): I was dying of boredom.

One afternoon, as I was walking in an area that would doubtless be of interest to a paleontologist, the misfortune that I'm about to describe took place. I saw a group of campers coming down the mountain. From the looks of shock on their faces, one didn't need to be a genius to realize that something bad had happened. Gesturing for them to stop, I made them tell me their news. It turned out that the grandson of one of them had fallen down a shaft or pit or chasm up the mountain. My experience as a criminal lawyer told me that we had to act fast, *facta, non verba*, so while half the party continued on its way to the campground, I scaled the steep hill with the others and came to where they claimed the misfortune had occurred.

The chasm was deep, bottomless. One of the campers said that it was called Devil's Mouth. Another said that the locals claimed it was really the dwelling place of the devil or one of his earthly incarnations. I asked what the disappeared child's name was and one of the campers answered: Elifaz. The situation was already strange, but with his answer it

403

became frankly ominous, because it isn't every day that a chasm swallows up a boy with such an unusual name. So it's Elifaz, is it? I said or whispered. That's his name, said the one who'd spoken. The others, uncultured office workers and government clerks from Lugo, looked at me and didn't say anything. I'm a man of thought and reflection, but I'm also a man of action. *Non progredi est regredi*, I remembered. So I went up to the rim of the chasm and shouted the boy's name. A menacing echo was the only answer I got: a shout, *my* shout, returned to me from the depths of the earth, turned into its blood-chilling echo. A shiver ran up my spine, but to hide it I think I laughed, telling my companions that the hole was certainly deep, and suggesting that if we tied all of our belts together we could create a makeshift rope so that one of us, the thinnest, of course, could go down and explore the first few feet of the pit. We conferred. We smoked. No one seconded my proposal. After a while, the people who had continued on to the campground returned with the first reinforcements and the necessary equipment to make the descent. *Homo fervidus et diligens ad omnia est paratus*, I thought.

We roped up a sturdy young man from Castroverde as well as we could, and with five strong men at the other end of the rope, he began his descent, equipped with a flashlight. He soon disappeared from sight. From above, we shouted: what can you see? and from the depths came his ever-fainter reply: nothing! *Patientia vincit omnia*, I advised, and we kept calling. We couldn't see anything, not even the light of the flashlight, although the walls of the cave closest to the surface were sporadically lit with a brief splash of light, as if the boy were pointing the flashlight over his head to check how many feet deep he was. It was then, as we were remarking on the light, that we heard a superhuman howl and we all moved to the edge of the shaft. What happened? we shouted. There was another howl. What happened? What did you see? Did you find him? No one answered from below. A few women started to pray. I wasn't sure whether to be appalled or to let myself be swept up in the phenomenon. *Stultorum plena sunt omnia*, as Cicero points out. A relative of our explorer asked us to haul him up. The five men who were holding the rope couldn't do it and we had to help them. The shout from down below was repeated several times. Finally, after tireless efforts, we managed to get him to the surface.

The young man was alive, and except for tattered jeans and a few scrapes on his arms, he seemed to be all right. To make sure, the women felt his legs. He hadn't broken any bones. What did you see? his relative asked him. He wouldn't answer and covered his face with his hands. That was when I should have taken charge and stepped in, but my position as spectator kept me, how shall I say, bewitched by the play of shadows and useless gestures. Others repeated the question, with slight variations. I may have recalled aloud that *occasiones namque hominem fragilem non faciunt, sed qualis sit ostendunt.* This young fellow was clearly a weak character. Given a swallow of cognac, he offered no resistance and drank as if his life depended on it. What did you see? the group repeated. Then he spoke and only his relative could hear him. The relative asked him the same question again, as if he couldn't believe what he'd heard. The young man replied: I saw the devil.

From that moment on, the rescue group was seized by confusion and anarchy. *Quot capita, tot sententiae*: some said that they had called the Guardia Civil from the campground and the best thing we could do was wait. Others asked about the boy, whether the youth had gotten a glimpse of him or heard him on the way down, and the reply was negative. Most asked what the devil was like, whether the youth had seen all of him or just his face, what he looked like, what color he was, etc. *Rumores fuge*, I said to myself and gazed out at the surrounding countryside. Then the camp watchman and the bulk of the women appeared with another group from the campground, among them the mother of the vanished boy, who hadn't heard what was happening because she'd been watching a game show, as she announced to anyone who would listen. Who's down there? asked the watchman. In silence, someone pointed out the youth, who was still lying in the grass. The mother, helpless, went up to the mouth of the cave and shouted her son's name. No one answered. She shouted again. Then the cave howled, and it was as if it were answering back.

Some people turned pale. Most backed away from the hole, afraid that a foggy hand might suddenly shoot out and drag them down into the depths. More than one person said that a wolf must be living down there. Or a wild dog. Meanwhile, it had gotten dark, and the gas lanterns and flashlights competed in a macabre dance, with that open wound in the mountainside for its magnetic center. People were laughing or speaking in Galician, a language that, uprooted as I was from my origins, I no longer remembered. They kept pointing with trembling hands toward the mouth of the pit. The Guardia Civil hadn't shown up. It was imperative that a decision be made, although everything was in utter confusion. Then I saw the camp watchman tie the rope around his waist and I realized that he was preparing to go down. His behavior, I confess, struck me as admirable, and I went over to congratulate him. Xosé Lendoiro, lawyer and poet, I said as I shook his hand effusively. He looked at me and smiled as if we'd met before. Then, amid general expectation, he started down into that terrible pit.

To be honest, I and many of those gathered there feared the worst. The watchman went down as far as the rope reached. At that point we all thought he would come back up, and for a moment, I think, he pulled from below and we pulled from above and the search stalled in an ignoble series of misunderstandings and shouts. I tried to make peace, *addito salis grano*. If I hadn't had courtroom experience, those angry people would have thrown me down the pit headfirst. Finally, however, I seized control. With no little effort, we managed to communicate with the watchman and decipher what he was shouting. He was asking us to let go of the rope. So we did. More than one of us felt our hearts stop to see the remaining length of rope disappear into the chasm like a rat's tail into a snake's jaws. We told each other that the watchman must know what he was doing.

Suddenly, the night got darker, and the black hole got blacker, if that was possible, and those who minutes before were making brief forays around the edge of the hole, carried away by impatience, stopped, since the possibility of tripping and being swallowed up by the chasm was manifested as sins are sometimes manifested. Fainter and fainter howls escaped from within, as if the devil were retreating into the depths of the earth with his two freshly caught prey. It goes without saying that the wildest hypotheses were making the rounds of our group on the surface. *Vita brevis, ars longa, occasio praeceps, experimentum periculosum, iudicium difficile.* There were those who couldn't stop checking their watches, as if time played a crucial role in this adventure. There were those who were chain-smoking, and others who were attending to the fainting fits of the lost boy's female relatives. There were those who cursed the Guardia Civil for taking so long. Suddenly, as I was watching the stars, it occurred to me that all of this bore an extraordinary resemblance to a story by Don Pío Baroja that I'd read in my years as a law student at the University of Salamanca. The story was called "The Chasm," and in it a little shepherd boy is lost deep inside a mountain. A lad with a rope tied securely around him is lowered in search of the boy, but the howls of the devil scare him away and he comes back up without the boy, whom he hasn't seen but whose moans of pain are clearly audible from outside. The story ends with a scene of complete powerlessness, in which fear vanquishes love, duty, and even the bonds of family. No one in the rescue group (made up, it must be said, of uncouth and supersti-tious Basque shepherds) dares to go down after hearing the stammered story that the first would-be rescuer tells, in which he claims to have seen the devil, or to have felt or sensed or heard him, I forget. *In se semper ar-matus Furor*. In the last scene, the shepherds go home, including the boy's terrified grandfather, and the whole night long (a windy night, I suppose) they can hear the boy's cries from the chasm. That's Don Pío's story. A youthful effort, I think, in which his glorious prose hasn't quite taken wing. A good story, nevertheless. And that was what I thought as behind me human passions roiled and my eyes counted the stars: that the story I was living was just like Baroja's story and that Spain was still Baroja's Spain, in other words a Spain where chasms weren't barricaded and children were still careless and fell into them, where people smoked and fainted in a rather excessive way, and where the Guardia Civil never showed up when it was needed.

And then we heard a shout, not an inarticulate howl but words, something like hey, you up there, hey, you bastards, and although a few fantasists said that it must be the devil, who, still unsated, wanted to carry off someone else, the rest of us crowded around the edge of the pit and saw the light of the watchman's flashlight, a beam like a firefly lost in the darkness of the mind of Polyphemus, and we asked the light whether it was all right but all the voice behind the light said was I'm fine, I'm go-ing to toss the rope up to you, and we heard a scarcely perceptible noise against the walls of the pit, and after several failed attempts the voice said throw me another rope, and a little later we pulled up the boy who had disappeared, roped around the waist and under the armpits. His unex-pected appearance was celebrated with tears and laughter, and when we had untied the boy we threw the rope down and the watchman came up, and the rest of that night, I remember this now that I have nothing to look forward to, was one long party, *O quantum caliginis mentibus nostris obicit magna felicitas*, a Galician party in the mountains, since the campers were Galician civil servants or office workers, and I hailed from those lands too, and the watchman, whom they called the Chilean, since that was his nationality, was also descended from hardworking Galicians, as indicated by his last name, Belano.

In the two further days that I spent there, the watchman and I had long conversations, and above all I was able to share my literary qualms and adventures with him. Then I returned to Barcelona and that was the last I heard of him until he showed up at my office two years later. As is always the way in these cases, he was short of money and out of work, so after taking a good look at him and wondering to myself whether I should kick him out, *supremum vale,* or toss him a line, I settled on the latter option, and told him that for now I could assign him a few reviews for the law school journal, whose literary pages I edited, and later we would see. Then I gave him a copy of my most recent book of poetry and let him know that he should limit himself to reviewing verse, since the fiction reviews were penned by my colleague Jaume Josep, a divorce expert and homosexual of long standing, known by the hordes of ass peddlers in the dives off the Ramblas as the Little Martyr, in reference to his shortness and his weakness for rough trade.

I think it's fair to say that I detected some disappointment in his face, possibly because he was hoping to publish in my literary magazine, which was more than I could offer him just then, since the caliber of the writers was incredibly high. Time hadn't passed for nothing. The elite of the Barcelona literary world, the crème de la crème of the poetry world, were making appearances in my magazine, and there could be no question of me turning soft overnight simply because of two summer days of friendship and an essentially superficial exchange of ideas. *Discat servire glorians ad alta venire.*

That was the beginning, one might say, of the second stage of my relationship with Arturo Belano. I saw him once a month, at my office, where I tended to my literary obligations while dealing with various legal cases, and where (these were different times) the most cultivated and renowned writers and poets of Spain and even Latin America would turn up, the latter stopping by to pay their respects on their way through town. On one occasion or another, I remember that Belano ran into some contributors to the magazine and a guest or two of mine, and that those encounters were less satisfactory than I might have liked. But distracted as I was by work and pleasure, I never bothered to take this up with him, nor did I heed the background noise engendered by such encounters, a noise like a convoy of cars, a swarm of motorcycles, the traffic in hotel parking lots, a noise that was saying be careful, Xosé, live your life, take care of your body, time is short, glory fleeting. In my ignorance I failed to decipher the message or assumed it was meant for him, not me, that noise of impending doom, of something lost in the vastness of Barcelona. These words didn't concern me, I thought they had nothing to do with me but with him, when in reality they were written expressly for me. *Fortuna rerum humanarum domina.*

In some ways, Belano's encounters with the contributors to my magazine weren't devoid of a certain appeal. Once, one of my boys (who later gave up writing and is now quite successfully involved in politics) wanted to hit him. He wasn't serious, of course, although one never knows for sure, but the point is that Belano pretended not to notice: I think he asked something like whether my contributor knew karate (he was a black belt) and then claimed to have a migraine and refused to fight. On such occasions I thoroughly enjoyed myself. I would say: come on, Belano, defend your opinions, argue, stand up to the literary elite, *sine dolo*, and he would say that he had a headache, laugh, ask me to pay him for his monthly law journal assignment, and leave with his tail between his legs.

I should have mistrusted that tail between the legs. I should have thought: what does that tail between the legs mean, *sine ira et studio*. I should have asked myself which animals have tails. I should have consulted books and guides and I should have correctly identified the bushy tail that bristled between the legs of the ex-watchman of the Castroverde campground.

But I didn't, and I kept living. *Errare humanum est, perseverare autem diabolicum.* One day I was at my older daughter's apartment and I heard noises. I have a key, of course: as a matter of fact, it's the apartment where the four of us (my wife, my two daughters, and I) lived before the divorce. After the divorce I bought myself a house in Sarriá, my wife bought herself a penthouse in Plaza Molina where she went to live with my younger daughter, and I decided to give our former apartment to my older daughter, who is herself a poet like me and the main contributor to my magazine. As I was saying, I had a key, although I didn't visit very often, basically just to pick up a book or because the magazine's board meetings were held there. So I went in and I heard noises. Discreetly, as befits a father and a modern man, I peeked into the living room. I didn't see anyone there. The noises were coming from down the hallway. *Non vis esse iracundus? Ne fueris curiosus*, I repeated to myself a few times. And yet I kept creeping around my old apartment. I passed my daughter's room and looked in: nobody was there. I kept walking on tiptoe. Though it was late morning, the apartment was dark. I didn't turn on the light. The noises, I realized then, were coming from the room that used to be mine, a room that also happens to be just as my wife and I left it. I opened the door partway and saw my older daughter in Belano's arms. What he was doing to her struck me as indescribable, at first glance at least. He was dragging her back and forth across the huge expanse of my bed, riding her, rolling her over and over, all in the midst of a hideous series of moans, bellows, brayings, cooings, and obscene noises that gave me goose bumps. *Mille modi Veneris*, I recalled with Ovid, but this was too much. Still, I didn't cross the threshold, standing there frozen, silent, spellbound, as if I were suddenly back at the Castroverde campground and the neo-Galician watchman had gone down into the chasm again and the office workers and I were once more at the mouth of hell. *Magna res est vocis et silentii tempora nosse.* I said nothing. Keeping quiet, I left the way I'd come in. And yet I wasn't able to go far from my old apartment, my daughter's apartment, and my steps led me to a neighborhood café that someone, almost certainly its new owner, had turned into a much more modern place, with shiny plastic chairs and tables. There I ordered a coffee and sat to contemplate the situation. Visions of my daughter behaving like a dog kept coming to me in waves, and each wave left me drenched in sweat, as if I had a fever, so after I finished my coffee I ordered a cognac to see whether something stronger would settle me down. Finally, by the third cognac, I pulled myself together. *Post vinum verba, post imbrem nascitur herba.*

What was born in me, however, wasn't words or poetry, not even a single solitary line, but a great desire for revenge, the determination to get my own back, the firm resolve to make that third-rate Julien Sorel pay for his insolence and gall. *Prima cratera ad sitim pertinet, secunda ad hilaritatem, tertia ad voluptatem, quarta ad insaniam.* The fourth cup brings madness, said Apuleius, and that was what I needed. I realized it at that moment with a clarity that seems touching to me now. The waitress, a girl my daughter's age, was watching me from the other side of the counter. Across from her, having a soda, was a woman who worked as a door-to-door pollster. The two of them were talking animatedly, although from time to time the waitress would turn her gaze in my direction. I raised my hand and ordered a fourth cognac. I don't think it would be an exaggeration to say that the waitress looked sympathetic.

I decided to crush Arturo Belano like a cockroach. For two weeks, unhinged and unbalanced, I would show up at my old apartment, my daughter's apartment, at odd hours. Four times I caught them together again. Twice they were in my bedroom, once they were in my daughter's bedroom, and once they were in the master bathroom. This last time I wasn't able to spy on them, although I could hear them, but the other three times I could see with my own eyes the terrible acts to which they abandoned themselves fervently, recklessly, shamelessly. *Amor tussisque non caelatur*: neither love nor a cough can be concealed. But was it love that they felt for each other? I asked myself more than once, especially as I snuck feverishly out of my apartment after those unspeakable acts that I was obliged to witness as if by a mysterious force. Was it love that Belano felt for my daughter? Was it love that my daughter felt for that cheap imitation of Julien Sorel? *Qui non zelat, non amat*, I said or whispered to myself when it occurred to me, in a burst of clarity, that my behavior was more like that of a jealous lover than a strict father. And yet I wasn't a jealous lover. What was it I felt, then? *Amantes, amentes.* Lovers, lunatics, *dixit* Plato.

As a precautionary measure, I decided to sound them out, to give them one last chance, in my own way. As I feared, my daughter was in love with the Chilean. Are you sure? I asked her. Of course I'm sure, she answered. And what do the two of you plan to do? Nothing, Dad, said my daughter, who bore no resemblance to me in these matters, being in fact almost the complete opposite. She'd turned out a pragmatist like her mother. A little later I spoke to Belano. He came to my office, as he did each month, to deliver a poetry review for the law school journal and collect his payment. So, Belano, I said when I had him in front of me, sitting in a low chair, crushed beneath the legal heft of my diplomas and the burnished weight of the silver-framed photographs of great poets that adorned my sturdy ten-by-five-foot oak table. I think it's time, I said, for you to make the leap. He looked at me blankly. The qualitative leap, I said. After a moment in which we were both silent, I explained what I meant. I wanted him (it was my wish, I said) to make the move from reviewer for the law school magazine to regular contributor to my magazine. I think his only commentary was a rather subdued "wow." As you'll understand, I explained, this is a great responsibility I've assumed. The magazine is gaining in reputation every day. Its contributors include many distinguished Spanish and Latin American poets. You read it, I assume, so you'll have noticed that we've published Pepe de Dios, Ernestina Buscarraons, and Manolo Garcidiego Hijares, not to mention the young blades who make up our team of regular contributors: Gabriel Cataluña, who bids fair to become the great bilingual poet we've all been waiting for, Rafael Logroño, an extremely young but staggeringly powerful poet, Ismael Sevilla, meticulous and elegant, Ezequiel Valencia, a stylist of blazing warmth and cool intelligence capable of composing the most rabidly modern sonnets in Spain today, and last but not least, of course, our two gladiators of poetry criticism, Beni Algeciras, almost always ruthless, and Toni Melilla, professor at the Autónoma and an expert in the poetry of the 1950s. All of them men, I said in conclusion, whom I have the honor to lead and whose names are destined to shine in bronze letters in the literature of this country (the motherland, as you people say) that has opened its arms to you, and in whose company you'll work.

Then I was silent and we watched each other for a while, or rather I watched him, searching his face for any sign that would give away what was going on inside his head, and Belano looked at my pictures, my objets d'art, my diplomas, my paintings, my collection of handcuffs and shackles mostly dating from before 1940 (it was a collection to which my clients usually reacted with interest and a tinge of fear, my legal colleagues with some tasteless joke or remark, and the poets who visited me with admiring fascination), the spines of the few carefully chosen books that I keep in my office, most of them first editions of the nineteenth-century Spanish Romantics. As I was saying, his gaze slithered over my possessions like a small and highly nervous rat. What do you think? I blurted out. Then he looked at me and I realized abruptly that my proposal had fallen on fallow ground. Belano asked me how much I planned to pay him. I looked at him and didn't answer. The arriviste was already calculating his take. He looked at me, waiting for my answer. I watched him, poker-faced. He asked in a stammer whether the pay would be the same as for the law school journal. I sighed. *Emere oportet, quem tibi oboedire velis.* His gaze was clearly that of a frightened rat. I don't pay, I said. Only the greats, the big names, the names with clout. For now, you'll only be assigned a few reviews. Then he moved his head, as if he were reciting: *O cives, cives, quaerenda pecunia primum est, virtus post nummos.* After that he said that he would think about it, and he left. When he closed the door I buried my head in my hands and remained like that for a while, thinking. Deep down I didn't want to hurt him.

It was like sleeping, it was like dreaming, it was like rediscovering my true self: I was a giant. When I woke up I walked to my daughter's apartment ready to have a long father-daughter talk. It had probably been some time since I'd spoken with her, listened to her fears, her concerns, her doubts. *Pro peccato magno paulum supplicii satis est patri.* That night we had dinner at a nice restaurant on Calle Provenza and although we only talked about literature, the giant in me behaved just as I expected it to behave: it was elegant, agreeable, understanding, full of plans, in love with life. The next day I visited my younger daughter and took her to La Floresta, to a friend's house. The giant drove carefully and said funny things. When we parted my daughter gave me a kiss on the cheek.

It was just the beginning, but inside, on the burning life raft of my brain, I was already starting to feel the healing effects of my new attitude. *Homo totiens moritur quotiens emittit suos.* I loved my daughters, and I knew I'd been on the verge of losing them. Maybe, I thought, they've been too much alone, spent too much time with their mother, a docile woman given to carnal abandonment, and now the giant needs to make an appearance, demonstrate that he's alive and thinking of them, that's all. It was such a simple thing that I felt angry (or maybe just sorry) not to have done it before. Meanwhile, the giant's coming did more than help improve my rapport with my daughters. I began to notice a clear change in my daily dealings with clients at the firm: the giant wasn't afraid of anything, he was bold, he came up instantly with the most unexpected strategies, he could fearlessly navigate legal twists and turns with his eyes shut and without the least hesitation. And that's not to mention his dealings with the literary types. There the giant, I realized with true pleasure, was sublime, majestic, a towering mass of sounds and pronouncements, constant affirmation and negation, a fount of life.

I stopped spying on my daughter and her wretched lover. *Odero, si potero. Si non, invitus amabo.* And yet I let the full weight of my authority fall against Belano. I was at peace again. It was the best time of my life.

Now I think about the poems that I could have written and didn't and it makes me want to laugh and cry all at once. But back then, I

413

wasn't thinking about the poems I could write: I was writing them, or I thought I was. Around that time I had a book out: I got one of the most respected publishing houses of the day to publish it for me. I covered all the costs, of course. They just printed the book and distributed it. *Quantum quisque sua nummorum servat in arca, tantum habet ei fidei.* The giant didn't worry about money. Instead, he made it flow, dispensed it, exercised his sovereignty over it fearlessly and unabashedly, just as a giant should.

Regarding money, naturally, I have indelible memories. Memories that glisten like a drunkard in the rain or a sick man in the rain. There was a time when my money was the object of jokes and ridicule, I know that. *Vilius argentum est auro, virtutibus aurum.* I know there was a time, at the beginning of my magazine's run, when my young collaborators mocked the source of my money. You pay poets, it was said, with the money you make from crooked businessmen, embezzlers, drug traffickers, murderers of women and children, money launderers, corrupt politicians. I never dignified this slander with a reply. *Plus augmentantur rumores, quando negantur.* Someone has to defend the murderers, the crooks, the men who want divorces and aren't prepared to surrender all their money to their wives; someone has to defend them. And my firm defended them all, and the giant absolved them and charged them a fair price. That's democracy, you fools, I told them, it's time you understood. For better or for worse. And instead of buying a yacht with the money I made, I started a literary magazine. And although I knew that the money troubled the consciences of some of the young poets of Barcelona and Madrid, when I had a free moment I would come up silently behind them and touch their backs with the tips of my fingers, which were perfectly manicured (no longer, since even my nails are ragged now), and I would whisper in their ears: *non olet.* It doesn't smell. The coins earned in the urinals of Barcelona and Madrid don't smell. The coins earned in the toilets of Zaragoza don't smell. The coins earned in the sewers of Bilbao don't smell. Or if they smell, they smell of money. They smell of what the giant dreams of doing with his money. Then the young poets would understand and nod, even if they didn't entirely follow what I was saying, even if they didn't comprehend every jot and tittle of the terrible, timeless lesson I'd meant to drum into their silly little heads. And if any of them failed to understand, which I doubt, they understood when they saw their pieces published, when they smelled the freshly printed pages, when they saw their names on the cover or in the table of contents. It was then that they got a whiff of what money really smells like: like power, like the gracious gesture of a giant. And then there were no more jokes and they all grew up and followed me.

All except Arturo Belano, and he didn't follow me for the simple reason that he wasn't called. *Sequitur superbos ultor a tergo deus.* And everyone who had followed me embarked on a career in the world of letters or cemented a career already begun but still in its infancy, except for Arturo Belano, who buried himself in a world where everything stank, where everything stank of shit and urine and rot and poverty and sickness, a world where the stink was suffocating and numbing, and where the only thing that didn't stink was my daughter's body. And I didn't lift a finger to put an end to their unnatural relationship, but I bided my time. And one day I discovered (don't ask me how because I've forgotten) that even my daughter, my beautiful older daughter, had begun to smell to that wretched ex-watchman of the Castroverde campground. Her mouth had begun to smell. The smell worked its way into the walls of the apartment where the wretched ex-watchman of the Castroverde campground was living. And my daughter, whose hygiene I refuse to let anyone question, brushed her teeth constantly: when she got up, at midmorning, after lunch, at four in the afternoon, at seven, after dinner, before she went to bed, but there was no way to get rid of the smell, there was no way to eliminate or hide the smell that the watchman scented or sniffed like a cornered animal, and although my daughter rinsed her mouth with Listerine between brushings, the smell persisted. It would go away for a moment only to appear again when it was least expected: at four in the morning, in the watchman's big castaway bed, when he would turn to my daughter in his sleep and screw her. It was an unbearable smell that chipped away at his patience and tact, the smell of money, the smell of poetry, maybe even the smell of love.

My poor daughter. It's my wisdom teeth, she said. My poor daughter. It's my last wisdom tooth coming in. That's why my mouth smells, she would protest, when faced with the increasing coolness of the ex-watchman of the Castroverde campground. Her wisdom tooth! *Numquam aliud natura, aliud sapientia dicit.* One night I invited her to have dinner with me. Just you, I said, although by then she and Belano hardly ever saw each other, but I made it plain: just you, sweetheart. We talked until three in the morning. I talked about the path the giant was blazing, the

415

path that led to real literature. She talked about her wisdom tooth, about the new words that the emerging wisdom tooth was depositing on her tongue. At a literary meeting a little later, almost casually and as if in passing, my daughter informed me that she'd broken things off with Belano, and that after thinking about it carefully, she couldn't take a favorable view of his future inclusion on the magazine's eminent team of reviewers. *Non aetate verum ingenio apiscitur sapientia.*

Innocent darling! At that moment I would have loved to tell her that Belano was never part of the team, which could be seen just by looking through the last ten issues of the magazine. But I didn't say anything. The giant embraced her and forgave her. Life went on. *Urget diem nox et dies noctem.* Julien Sorel was dead.

Around this time, months after Arturo Belano had left our lives for good, I had a dream, and in my dream I heard once again the howl that had emerged from the mouth of the pit at the Castroverde campground. *In se semper armatus Furor,* as Seneca says. I woke up trembling. It was four in the morning, I remember, and instead of going back to sleep, I went to look for the Pío Baroja story "The Chasm" in my library, without quite knowing why. I read it twice before the sun came up, the first time slowly, still lost in the fog of sleep, and the second time at top speed, returning to certain passages that struck me as highly revealing and that I hadn't quite understood. With tears in my eyes, I tried to read it for a third time, but exhaustion overcame the giant and I fell asleep on a chair in the library.

When I woke up, at nine in the morning, all my bones hurt and I'd shrunk at least ten inches. I took a shower, grabbed Don Pío's book, and left for the office. There, *nil sine magno vita labore dedit mortalibus,* after taking care of a few urgent matters, I gave orders that no one disturb me and immersed myself once more in the desolation of "The Chasm." When I finished I closed my eyes and thought about the men's fear. Why didn't anyone climb down to rescue the boy? I asked myself. Why was his own grandfather afraid? I asked. If they thought he was dead, why didn't someone go down to look for his little body, damn it? I asked. Then I closed the book and paced around my office like a caged lion, until I couldn't stand it anymore, and I threw myself on the sofa, curled up as tight as I could, and let my lawyer's tears, poet's tears, and giant's tears flow all at once, mingling in streams of burning magma that instead of calming me pushed me toward the mouth of the pit, toward the gaping crevice, a crevice that I could see with increasing clarity, despite my tears (which cast a veil over the things in my office), and I associated this crevice—I don't know why, since it didn't suit my mood—with a toothless mouth, a mouth full of teeth, a fixed smile, a young girl's gaping sex, an eye watching me from the depths of the earth. The eye was, in some dark sense, innocent, since I knew that it thought no one could see it as long as it couldn't see anyone—absurdly, since it was inevitable that as it kept watch, giants or ex-giants like me were watching it too. I don't know how long I lay there like that. Then I got up, went into the bathroom to wash my face, and told my secretary to cancel all my appointments for the day.

The next few weeks I lived as if in a dream. I did everything correctly, as I always had, but I was no longer living in my own skin. Instead I was watching myself from the outside, *facies tua computat annos*, pitying myself, criticizing myself in the harshest terms, mocking my ridiculous propriety, the manners and empty phrases that I knew wouldn't get me anywhere.

I soon understood how vain all my ambitions had been, the ambitions that trundled the golden labyrinth of the law as well as those I set spinning along the edge of the edge of the cliff of literature. *Interdum lacrimae pondera vocis habent.* I realized what Arturo Belano had known from the moment he saw me: I was a terrible poet.

At least things still functioned when it came to love, I mean I could still get it up, but I'd almost lost my taste for sex: I didn't like to see myself fucking, I didn't like to see myself moving on top of the defenseless body of the woman whom I was seeing at the time (poor innocent soul!). Soon I managed to shake her off. Gradually I began to prefer strangers, girls I picked up in bars or all-night clubs and whom I could confuse, at least at first, with the shameless display of my old giant's powers. Some, I'm sorry to say, could have been my daughters. More than once I came to this realization in situ, which troubled me greatly and made me want to go running outside howling and leaping, though out of respect for the neighbors, I never did. In any case, *amor odit inertes*, I slept with women and made them happy (the gifts I had once lavished on young poets I began to give to wayward girls) and their happiness pushed back the onset of my unhappiness, which came when it was time to sleep and dream, or dream that I was dreaming, about the cries that came from the maw of a chasm in a Galicia that was itself like the maw of a savage beast, a gigantic green mouth open painfully wide under a sky in flames, the sky of a scorched world, a world charred by a World War III that never was or at least never was in my lifetime, and sometimes the wolf was maimed in Galicia, but other times the backdrop of its martyrdom was the Basque country, Asturias, Aragon, even Andalusia! and in my dream, I remember, I would take refuge in Barcelona, a civilized city, but even in Barcelona the wolf howled and writhed in madness and the sky was rent and nothing could be put right.

Who was torturing me?

I asked myself this question more than once.

Who was making the wolf howl morning and night, when I fell exhausted into bed or some unfamiliar armchair?

*Insperata accidunt magis saepe quam quae spes,* I said to myself.

I thought it was the giant.

For a while, I tried to sleep without sleeping. Close just one eye. Sneak down the backstreets of sleep. But great efforts only brought me to the lip of the chasm, *nemo in sese tentat descendere,* and there I would stop and listen: my own snoring in restless sleep, the far-off noises drifting in on the breeze from the street, muffled sounds from the past, the senseless words of the terrified campers, the sound of the footsteps of those who circled the chasm not knowing what to do, the voices announcing the arrival of reinforcements from the campground, a mother weeping (sometimes it was my own mother!), my daughter's garbled words, the sound of the rocks that fell like little guillotine blades when the watchman went down after the boy.

One day I decided to look for Belano. I did it for my own sake, for the sake of my health. The eighties, which had been such a disastrous decade for his continent, seemed to have swallowed him up without a trace. From time to time poets of the right age or nationality, poets who might have known where he lived or what he was doing, would come by the magazine's offices, but the truth is that as time went by his name was blotted out. *Nihil est annis velocius.* When I brought him up with my daughter, I got an address in Ampurdán and a reproachful look. The address belonged to a house where no one had lived for a long time. One particularly desperate night I even called the Castroverde campground. It had closed.

After a while I thought I might get used to living with the demented giant and the howls that came from the chasm night after night. I sought peace, or if not peace, then distraction, in my social life (which I had let go a little, thanks to the wayward girls), in the growth of the magazine, in some official honor that the Generalitat had always begrudged me because I was a Galician immigrant. *Ingrata patria, ne ossa quidem mea habes.* I sought peace in my dealings with poets and the recognition of my peers. I didn't find it. Instead, I found desolation and opposition. I found brittle women who wanted the velvet-glove treatment (and who were all on the far side of fifty!), I found clerks from the Castroverde campground who looked at me like what they were, Galicians frightened in the face of the irremediable, and who only made me feel more like weeping, I found new magazines joining the fray, their existence putting my magazine's existence in constant jeopardy. I sought peace and I didn't find it.

By then I think I could recite Don Pío's story by heart, *periturae parcere chartae,* and still I understood nothing. My life seemed to be progressing through the same realms of mediocrity as usual, but I knew that I was walking in the land of destruction.

At last I contracted a fatal illness and stopped working. In a final effort to regain my lost identity, I tried to secure the City of Barcelona Award for myself. *Contemptu famae contemni virtutes.* Those who knew the state of my health thought I was trying to achieve some kind of posthumous recognition while I was still alive and took me bitterly to task. I was just trying to die as myself, not as an ear on the edge of a chasm. Catalans only understand what suits them.

I made a will. I divided up my worldly goods, which were less plentiful than I'd thought, among the women of my family and two wayward girls of whom I'd grown fond. I hate to imagine the look on my daughters' faces when they find out that they have to share my money with two street lovelies. *Venenum in auro bibitur.* Then I sat in my dark office and I saw the weak flesh and the strong mind passing before me, as if in a diorama, like a husband and wife who hate each other, and I also saw the strong flesh and the weak mind pass by arm in arm, another model couple, and I saw them stroll around a park like the Parque de la Ciudadela (although sometimes it was more like the Gianicolo near the Piazzale Giuseppe Garibaldi), weary yet unwearying, at the pace of cancer patients or prostate sufferers, well dressed, haloed in a kind of horrible dignity, and the strong flesh and the weak mind went from right to left and the weak flesh and the strong mind went from left to right, and each time they crossed paths they acknowledged each other but didn't stop, out of politeness or because they knew each other from other walks, if only slightly, and I thought: my God, talk, talk, speak to each other, dialogue is the key to any door, *ex abundantia cordis os loquitur,* but the weak mind and the strong mind only nodded, and perhaps their consorts did no more than bow their eyelids (eyelids don't bow, Toni Melilla told me one day, but how wrong he was! of course they bow, eyelids can even kneel), proud as bitches, the weak flesh and the strong flesh, steeped together in the crucible of fate, if you'll permit me the expression, an expression that means nothing but is as sweet as a bitch lost on the mountainside.

Then I checked into a clinic in Barcelona, then a clinic in New York, and then one night all my Galician orneriness rose up in me and I pulled off my tubes and got dressed and traveled to Rome, where I was admitted to the Ospedale Britannico, where my friend Dr. Claudio Palermo Rizzi works (he's a poet in the little free time he has), and after submitting to countless tests and indignities (the same ones to which I'd submitted in Barcelona and New York) the diagnosis was that I had only a few days left to live. *Qui fodit foveam, incidet in eam.*

And here I am, without the strength to return to Barcelona, or the courage to leave the hospital for good, although each night I get dressed and go out for a walk under the Roman moon, the moon I first came to know and admire long ago, in a distant past that I naïvely thought was happy and would never be lost and that today I can only call up with a spasm of incredulity. And my steps lead me, unfailingly, along Via Claudia to the Colosseum and then along Viale Domus Aurea to Via Mecenate and then I turn left, past Via Botta, along Via Terme di Traiano, at which point I'm in hell. *Etiam periere ruinae.* And then I listen to the howls that issue like gusts of wind from the mouth of the chasm and by God I make an effort to understand their language but I can't, no matter how I try. The other day I told Claudio about it. Doctor, I said, every night I go out for a walk and I have hallucinations. What do you see? said the poet-physician. I don't see anything, they're auditory hallucinations. So what do you hear? asked the noble Sicilian scion, visibly relieved. Howls, I said. Well, considering your health and sensitivity, it's nothing serious; one could even say it's normal. Cold comfort.

In any case, I don't tell the ineffable Claudio everything that happens to me. *Imperitia confidentiam, eruditio timorem creat.* For example:

I haven't told him that my family is unaware of the state of my health. For example: I haven't told him that I've strictly forbidden them to come and visit me. For example: I haven't told him that I know with absolute certainty that I won't die in his Ospedale Britannico but one night in the middle of the Parco di Traiano, hidden in the shrubs. Will I drag myself, will I be brought by my own powers to my last leafy hiding place or will it be others, Roman hoods, Roman hustlers, Roman psychopaths, who hide my body, their corpus delicti, under the burning bush? In any case, I know I'll die in the baths or the park. I know that the giant or the shadow of the giant will shrink as the howls are unbottled from the Domus Aurea and spread all over Rome, a black and ominous cloud, and I know that the giant will say or whisper: save the boy, and I know that no one will hear his plea.

So much for poetry, the Jezebel that kept me treacherous company all these years. *Olet lucernam.* Now it would be nice to tell a joke or two, but I can only think of one on the spot like this, just one. What's more, it's a Galician joke. Maybe you've heard it before. A man goes walking in the forest. Like me, for example, walking in a forest like the Parco di Traiano or the Terme di Traiano, but a hundred times bigger and more unspoiled. And the man goes walking, I go walking, through the forest and I run into five hundred thousand Galicians who're walking and crying. And then I stop (a kindly giant, an interested giant for the last time) and I ask them why they're crying. And one of the Galicians stops and says: because we're all alone and we're lost.

# 21

Daniel Grossman, sitting on a bench in the Alameda, Mexico City DF, February 1993. It had been years since I'd seen him and when I got back to Mexico the first thing I did was ask about him, about Norman Bolzman, where he was, what he was doing. His parents told me that he was teaching at UNAM and that he spent long stretches at a place he'd rented near Puerto Ángel, a place without a telephone where he holed up to write and think. Then I called other friends. I asked questions. I went out to dinner. That was how I learned that things had ended with Claudia, and Norman was living alone now. One day I saw Claudia at the house of a painter whom the three of us, Claudia, Norman, and I, had known in our teens. In those days, by my calculations, the painter must have been sixteen, at the oldest, and we'd all talked about how great he was going to be. The dinner was delicious, a very Mexican meal, in honor of me, I guess, and my return to Mexico after what had been a pretty long time away, and then Claudia and I went out on the terrace and we were bitching about our host, making fun of him. Claudia was adorable. Remember, she said, how the dipstick used to swear he'd be better than Paalen? Well, he turned out worse than Cuevas! I don't know whether she was serious or not, Claudia never liked Cuevas, but she saw a lot of the painter, Abraham Manzur, Abraham had made a name for himself in the Mexican art world and his paintings sold in the United States, but he certainly wasn't the promising kid he used to be, the kid Claudia and Norman and I had known in Mexico City in the seventies and whom we thought of, a little condescendingly, since he was two or three years younger than us at the age when a few years make a difference, as the incarnation of the artist or the artist's drive. Anyway, Claudia didn't see him that way anymore. And neither did I. What I mean is, we didn't expect anything of him. He was just a short little Mexican Jew, on the chubby side, with lots of friends and lots of money. Like me, in fact, a tall, thin, unemployed Mexican Jew, and like Claudia, a gorgeous Argentinian-Mexican Jew handling PR for the one of the biggest galleries in Mexico City. All of us with our eyes open, all of us locked in a dark passageway, motionless, waiting. But maybe that overstates it.

That night, at least, I didn't overstate or criticize or make fun of the painter, who'd been kind enough to invite me to dinner, even if he had me over only to show off and talk about shows he'd had in Dallas or San Diego, cities that, to hear people tell it, are almost part of Mexico by now. And then I left with Claudia and Claudia's date, a lawyer maybe ten or even fifteen years older than her, a divorced guy with kids in college, the head of the Mexican affiliate of a German company, worried about everything. At this point I can't even remember Claudia's pet name for him, they broke up a little later. Claudia was like that, she still is, none of her boyfriends lasted longer than a year. We didn't really get to talk. We didn't say anything serious, we didn't ask each other the questions we should have asked. All I remember about that night is the meal, which I ate with relish, the works by the painter and some of the painter's friends that were scattered around the painter's cavernous living room, Claudia's smiling face, the dark streets of Mexico City, and the trip, not as short as I thought it would be, back to my parents' house, where I was staying until I started to get things straightened out.

Not long afterward, I left for Puerto Ángel. I made the trip by bus, from Mexico City to Oaxaca and from Oaxaca, on another bus line, to Puerto Ángel, and when I finally got there I was tired, my body ached, and all I wanted was to fall into bed and go to sleep. Norman's place was on the edge of town, in a neighborhood called La Loma. It was a two-story house, the bottom built of cement blocks and the top of wood, with a tiled roof and a small, overgrown yard full of bougainvillea. Norman wasn't expecting me, of course, but when we saw each other I got the feeling that he was the only person who was happy I was back. The feeling of alienation that I'd been trying to shake since I set foot in the Mexico City airport began to fade imperceptibly as the bus headed deeper into Oaxaca, and I relaxed into the certainty that I was in Mexico again and that things could change. Not that I knew whether these changes, if they did come, would be for better or worse, but that's almost always the way with changes, almost always the way it is in Mexico. And Norman's welcome was magnificent, and for five days we swam at the beach, read in the shade on the porch in hammocks that hung from nails and gave way little by little until our backsides touched the floor, drank beer, and took long walks around a part of La Loma where there were lots of cliffs, and also locked fishermen's huts, there on the edge of the woods by the beach, which a thief could have broken into with an expedient kick to one of the walls, a kick that we were sure would knock a hole or make the whole thing collapse.

The fragility of those shacks, though this only occurs to me now, gave me a funny feeling more than once, not of precariousness or poverty but of obscure tenderness and foreboding; I'm probably not making much sense. Norman called the spot the "resort," although during my stay I never saw anyone swimming at the beaches in that part of Puerto Ángel. The water was pretty rough. The rest of the day we spent talking, especially about politics and the state of the country, which we saw from different perspectives but which seemed equally grim to both of us, and then Norman would shut himself in his office and work on an essay on Nietzsche that he was planning to publish in the *Revista del Colegio de México*. Thinking about it now, I realize we actually didn't talk very much. That is, we didn't talk much about ourselves. I might have talked about myself some night. I must have told him about my adventures, my life in Israel and Europe, but we never *talked*.

On my sixth day there, it was a Sunday morning, we left for Mexico City. Norman had to teach at the university on Monday and I had to look for work. We left Puerto Ángel in Norman's white Renault, which he only used when he came to Oaxaca, because in Mexico City he preferred to get around on public transportation. We talked about Nietzsche's *Genealogy of Morals*, how every time Norman reread it he found (to his dismay) more and more points in common between the philosopher and the Nazis who would soon take over Germany. We talked about the weather, about the seasons, which I claimed I was going to miss and which Norman assured me I would soon forget, about the people I'd left behind but with whom I meant to keep in touch by postcard from time to time. I don't remember when we started to talk about Claudia. All I know is that somehow I became aware of it because then I stopped talking and started to listen. He said things had ended between them soon after he started working at the university, which I already knew, and that the breakup wasn't as painful as everybody assumed. You know how she is, he said, and I said yes, I know. Then he said that since then his relationships with women had been relatively cool. Then he laughed. I remember his laugh with utter clarity. There wasn't a car to be seen on the road, just trees, mountains, and sky, and the sound of the Renault cutting through the air. He said that he slept with women, or that he still liked to sleep with women, but that in some way he couldn't understand he was having more and more problems in that regard. What kind of problems? I asked. Problems, problems, said Norman. You can't get it up? I said. Norman laughed. Is that it, you can't get a hard-on? I said. That's a symptom, he said, not a problem. That answers my question, I said, you can't get it up. Norman laughed again. He had the window down and the wind was whipping his hair. He was very tan. He seemed happy. The two of us laughed. Sometimes I can't get a hard-on, he said, but what kind of word is that, hard-on? No, sometimes it won't get hard, but that's just a symptom, and sometimes not even a symptom. Sometimes it's just a joke, he said. I asked him whether he hadn't found anyone in all this time, a question that seemed to answer itself, and Norman said yes, that he'd found someone in a way, but that both he and she, a divorced philosophy professor with two children who for some reason I imagined as ugly, or at least not as beautiful as Claudia, wanted to wait, not take things too fast, a relationship on ice.

Then he talked about children, children in general and the children of Puerto Ángel in particular, asking me what I thought about the children of Puerto Ángel, and the truth is I didn't think *anything* about the children of the town we were leaving behind, I mean I hadn't even noticed them! and then Norman looked at me and said: each time I think about them it centers me. Just like that. It centers me. And I thought: it would be better if he watched the highway instead of me, and I also thought: something's up. But I didn't say anything. I didn't say: drive more carefully, I didn't say: Norman, what's going on? Instead I started to watch the scenery: trees and clouds, mountains, rolling hills, the tropics, with Norman already talking about something else, a dream Claudia had had, when? not long ago, she called him early one morning and told him about it. Evidently they were still close friends. And do you know what the dream was about? he said. Why, *mano*, I asked, do you want me to interpret it for you? A dream about colors, with a battle in the background, a battle drifting away, carrying all interpretations with it as it went. But Norman said: she dreamed about the children we hadn't had. Fuck off, I said. That was the meaning of the dream. So according to you, the battle drifting away is the children you didn't have? More or less, said Norman, that was the shadows fighting. And the colors? They're what's left, said Norman, a shitty abstraction of what's left.

And then I thought about the painter and his abstract paintings, and I don't know why it occurred to me to tell Norman (with whom I'd surely already discussed it while we were in Puerto Ángel) that that asshole Abraham Manzur was playing in the minor leagues, maybe to change the subject, maybe because that was all I had to say just then, at a moment when whatever I said wouldn't make much difference, because it was Norman who was in charge and nothing I could add was going to change that incontrovertible fact, the Renault going over eighty down the deserted road. Did you see his paintings? said Norman. Some, I said. And what did you think of them? said Norman, as if everything we'd talked about in Puerto Ángel had been forgotten. They were all right, I said. And what did Claudia think of them? She didn't tell me what she thought, I said. We kept on like that for a while. Norman started to talk about Mexican painting, the condition of the roads, university politics, the interpretation of dreams, the children of Puerto Ángel, about Nietzsche, and I broke in at long intervals with some monosyllabic remark, some question intended just to get the basic concepts clear, although the truth is that at that point I no longer gave a shit about basic concepts and all I wanted was to get back to Mexico City as soon as possible and never set foot in the state of Oaxaca again in my life.

And then Norman said: Ulises Lima. Do you remember Ulises Lima? Of course I did, how could I have forgotten him? And Norman said: lately I've been thinking about him, as if Ulises Lima were part of his daily reality, or had been part of his life, when I knew for a fact that he'd only been a brief episode, and an annoying episode at that. And then Norman glanced at me, as if he were expecting a wink or a knowing look, but I just said watch the road, be careful, because the Renault was heeling toward the right and we were already on the shoulder, although that didn't seem to bother Norman, because with a jerk of the wheel he had us back in the center, on course, and I looked at him again and I said: so what then? Ulises Lima, the days he spent with us in Tel Aviv, and Norman: didn't you notice anything strange, anything out of the ordinary? ultranormal Norman. And then I said: everything! because that's how Ulises was, and that's secretly how we wanted him to be. Not Norman, who wasn't his friend and who mostly knew him by reputation, but Claudia and I, who back then thought we were going to be writers and would have given anything to belong to that essentially pathetic group, the visceral realists. Youth is a scam.

And then Norman said: it has nothing to do with the visceral realists, asshole, you haven't understood a thing. And I said: well, what does it have to do with, then? And Norman, to my relief, stopped looking at me and concentrated on the road for a few minutes, and then he said: it has to do with life, with what we lose without knowing it, and what we can regain. So what can we regain? I said. What we've lost, said Norman, we can get it back intact. It would've been easy to argue, but instead I opened the window and let the warm air ruffle my hair. The trees were passing by at an incredible speed. What can we regain? I thought, and it struck me that we were going faster and faster and that there weren't many straight lengths of road anymore, but I didn't care, maybe because Norman had always driven carefully and he could talk, watch me, look for cigarettes in the glove compartment, light them, and even glance ahead every once in a while, all without taking his foot off the accelerator. We can get back into the game whenever we want to, I heard him say. Do you remember the days Ulises spent with us in Tel Aviv? Of course I remember, I said. Do you know why he came to Tel Aviv? Goddamn Ulises, of course I know: because he was in love with Claudia, I said. He was madly in love with Claudia, Norman corrected me, so madly that he didn't realize what he had within his grasp. He didn't realize a fucking thing, I said, the truth is, I don't know how he managed not to get himself killed. You're wrong, said Norman (actually, he shouted it), you're wrong, you're wrong, he couldn't have died even if he'd wanted to. Well, he came for Claudia, he came looking for Claudia, I said, and nothing went right. That's true, he came for Claudia, said Norman, laughing. Goddamn Claudia, do you remember how beautiful she was? Of course I remember, I said. And do you remember where Ulises slept while he was staying with us? On the sofa, I said. On the fucking sofa! said Norman. Hypostasis of romantic love. Threshold space. No-man's-land. And then he whispered, so quietly that between the noise of the Renault, which was blasting down the road, and the noise of the wind rushing along my arm and up the left side of my face, I had to work hard to make out his words: some nights, he said, he would cry. What? I said. Some nights, when I got up to go to the bathroom, I would hear him sobbing. Ulises? That's right, didn't you ever hear him? No, I said, when my head hits the pillow I'm out. That's good, said Norman, although the way he said it, it sounded more like too bad, *mano*. And why was he crying? I said. I don't know, said Norman, I never asked, I was just on my way to the bathroom and when I passed the living room I heard him, that's all, he might not even have been crying, he might have been jerking off and what I heard might've been sounds of pleasure, see what I mean? Yes, more or less, I said. But then again he might not have been jerking off, said Norman, or crying. What, then? He might have been sleeping, said Norman, maybe those were the sounds Ulises made in his sleep. He cried in his sleep? Hasn't it ever happened to you? said Norman. Frankly, no, I said. The first few nights I was afraid, said Norman, afraid of standing there in the living room, in the dark, listening to him. But one night I stayed, and then all of a sudden I understood everything. What was there to understand? I said. Everything, the most important thing of all, said Norman, and then he laughed. What Ulises Lima was dreaming? No, no, said Norman, and the Renault leaped forward.

Strangely enough, the leap made me remember the giant Austrian whom Ulises had shown up with a month later, and I said to Norman: do you remember that Austrian kid who was friends with Ulises? And Norman laughed and said of course he did, but that wasn't it, Ulises wasn't the same when he got back to Tel Aviv, or he was the same but he wasn't, he didn't sob at night anymore, he didn't cry, I was watching him and I noticed, or maybe that bastard Ulises had stopped indulging himself, what do I know. And then Norman said: it happened at the beginning, when he was alone and slept in the armchair. It was then and not afterward. All right, sure, I said. A long time before he showed up with the Austrian. And he never said anything? Anything about what? said Norman. For fuck's sake, anything about anything, I said. Then Norman laughed again and said: Ulises was crying because he knew that nothing was over, because he knew he would have to come back to Israel again. The eternal return? Fuck the eternal return! Here and now! But Claudia doesn't live in Israel anymore, I said. Wherever Claudia lives is Israel, said Norman, no matter what fucking place it is, call it whatever you want, Mexico, Israel, France, the United States, planet Earth. Let me see if I understand you, I said, Ulises knew that things were going to end between you and Claudia? And then he could try again? You haven't understood anything! said Norman. I have nothing to do with any of this. Claudia has nothing to do with it. Sometimes even that bastard Ulises has nothing to do with it. The tears are all that count. I guess you're right, I don't understand you, I said.

And then Norman looked at me and I swear he had the same expression on his face that he used to have when he was sixteen or fifteen, the expression he had when we met in high school, when he was much thinner, with his bird face, his longer hair, his brighter eyes, and he had a smile that made you love him instantly, a smile that said here today, gone tomorrow. And that was when the truck came barreling toward us and Norman swerved to miss it and we went flying. Norman went flying, I went flying, glass went flying. And we all ended up where we ended up.

When I woke up I was in a hospital in Puebla and my parents or the shadows of my parents were moving across the walls of the room. Then Claudia came and kissed me on the forehead and spent hours sitting by my bed, or so I'm told. A few days later they told me that Norman had died. A month and a half later I was able to leave the hospital and I went to live with my parents. Every so often, relatives I didn't know and friends I'd forgotten would come to see me. It didn't bother me, but I decided to move out and live by myself. I rented a little house in Colonia Anzures, with a bathroom, kitchen, and one big room, and little by little I began to take long walks around Mexico City. I was limping and sometimes I got lost, but the walking did me good. One morning I started to look for work. I didn't need to, because my parents had told me they'd support me till I was stronger. I went to the university and talked to two of Norman's friends. They seemed surprised to see me there, and then they said Norman was one of the most upstanding people they had ever known. They were both philosophy professors and both supporters of Cuauhtémoc Cárdenas. I asked them what Norman thought about Cárdenas. He supported him, they said, supported him in his own way, like all of us, but he supported him. The truth, I realized then, was that it wasn't Norman's political affiliation I was looking for but something else, something I wasn't even able to formulate clearly to myself. I had dinner with Claudia a few times. I wanted to talk about Norman, wanted to tell Claudia what Norman and I had talked about as we were on our way back from Puerto Ángel, but Claudia said that talking about it made her sad. Anyway, she added, when you were in the hospital all you did was repeat your last conversation with Norman. So what did I say? What everyone says when they're delirious, said Claudia, sometimes you went on and on about the scenery and other times you switched subjects so fast that it was impossible to follow.

No matter how I tried, I couldn't get anything clear. One night, as I was sleeping, Norman appeared to me and told me to relax, that he was fine. Then, but I'm not sure if this was in the dream or when I woke up shouting, I realized that Norman seemed to be in Mexican heaven, not Jewish heaven, let alone philosophy heaven or Marxist heaven. But what was goddamned Mexican heaven? A pretense of happiness? or what lay behind it? empty gestures? or what was hidden (for reasons of survival) behind them? A little later I started to work at an advertising agency. One night, drunk, I tried to call Arturo Belano in Barcelona. At the number I tried, someone told me that no one lived there by that name. I talked to Müller, Arturo's friend, and he told me Arturo was living in Italy. What's he doing in Italy? I said. I don't know, said Müller, working, I guess. When I hung up I started to look for Ulises Lima in Mexico City. I knew I had to find him and ask him what Norman had meant in his last conversation. But looking for someone in Mexico City is easier said than done.

For months I went back and forth, traveling by metro and in crowded buses, calling people I didn't know and didn't want to know. I was mugged three times. At first no one had heard or wanted to hear anything about Ulises Lima. According to some people I talked to, he'd become an alcoholic and a drug addict. A thug who was shunned by his closest friends. According to others, he'd gotten married and was devoting himself full-time to his family. Some said that his wife was of Japanese descent or the only heir of a Chinese family who owned a chain of Chinese cafés in Mexico City. It was all vague and depressing.

One day, at a party, I was introduced to the woman Ulises had lived with for a while. Not the Chinese woman, an earlier one.

She was thin and had hard eyes. We talked for a while, standing in a corner, while her friends did lines of coke. She said she had a son, but that he was the son of another man. All the same, Ulises had been like a father to him.

Like a father to your son? Something like that, she said. Like a father to my son and like a father to me. I watched her carefully. I was afraid that she was making fun of me. Except for her eyes, everything about her radiated helplessness.

Then she talked about drugs, probably the only subject she thought worth discussing, and I asked her whether Ulises Lima used to get high. At first he didn't, she said, he only sold, but while he was with me he started. I asked her whether he wrote. She didn't hear me or maybe she didn't want to answer. I asked her if she knew where to find Ulises. She had no idea. He might be dead, she said.

It was only at that moment that I realized the woman was sick, possibly very sick, and I didn't know what else to say to her, I just wanted to get out of there and forget about her. And yet I stayed with her (or near her, since being in her presence for any length of time was unbearable) until the party ended at dawn. And afterward we even left together and walked a few blocks to the nearest metro station. We got on at Tacubaya. Everyone riding the metro at that time of night seemed sick. She went one way and I went the other.


**Amadeo Salvatierra, Calle República de Venezuela, near the Palacio de la Inquisición, Mexico City DF, January 1976.** We sat in silence for a while. The boys seemed tired and I was tired. So what happened to Encarnación Guzmán? one of them said suddenly. It was the last question I'd expected to hear and yet it was the only question that made it possible for us to go on. I took my time answering. Or maybe first I answered telepathically, as drunk old men often do, and then, in the face of the obvious, I opened my big mouth and said: nothing, boys. Nothing happened to her, just like nothing happened to Pablito Lezcano or me or even Manuel, if it comes to that. Life left us all where we were meant to be or where it was convenient to leave us and then forgot us, which is as it should be. Encarnación got married. She was too pretty to end up an old maid. It came as a surprise when she showed up one afternoon at the café where we met and invited us all to the wedding. Maybe the invitation was a joke and she was really just coming to boast. We congratulated her, of course, saying wonderful, Encarnación, what a lovely surprise, and then we didn't go to her wedding, although maybe one or two of us did. How did Encarnación Guzmán Arredondo's wedding affect Cesárea? Negatively, I suppose, although with Cesárea one never knew how bad things really were, but she wasn't pleased, no question about that. We didn't realize, but in those days everything was sliding inexorably toward the edge of a cliff. Or maybe that's putting it too strongly. In those days we were all sliding downhill. And no one would try to make the climb back up again, except maybe Manuel, in his own way, but otherwise no one else. Miserable goddamn life, isn't it, boys? I said. And they said: I guess so, Amadeo. And then I thought about Pablito Lezcano, who soon afterward would get married too, and whose wedding I did attend (it was a civil ceremony), and I thought about the banquet hosted by the father of the bride, a lavish celebration in a hall that doesn't exist anymore somewhere near Arcos de Belén, on Calle Delicias, I think, with mariachis and speeches before and after the banquet, and I could see Pablito Lezcano, his forehead shiny with sweat, reading a poem dedicated to his bride and his bride's family that from then on would be like his own family, and before he started to read the poem he looked at me and at Cesárea, who was beside me, and he winked at us, as if to say don't worry, my friends, you'll always be my secret family, or so I thought, although I may have been wrong. A few days after Pablito's wedding, Cesárea left Mexico City for good. We ran into each other one afternoon on the way out of a movie theater, which really is a coincidence, isn't it? I'd gone alone and so had Cesárea, and as we walked we talked about the movie. What movie? I don't remember, boys, it would be nice if it had been something with Charlie Chaplin, but the truth is I don't remember. I do remember that we liked it, that much I can tell you, and I also remember that the theater was across from the Alameda, and that Cesárea and I walked through the Alameda first and then toward the center of town, and at some moment I remember I asked her about her life and she told me that she was leaving Mexico City. Then we talked about Pablito's wedding, and at some point in the conversation, Encarnación Guzmán came up. Cesárea had been at her wedding. I asked how it had been, just to say something, and she told me that it was very pretty and moving, those were her words. And sad, like all weddings, I added. No, said Cesárea, which is what I told the boys, weddings aren't sad, Amadeo, she said, they're happy. But I was really only interested in talking about Cesárea, not Encarnación Guzmán. What will happen to your magazine? I said. What will happen to visceral realism? She laughed when I asked her that. I remember her laugh, boys, I said, night was falling over Mexico City and Cesárea laughed like a ghost, like the invisible woman she was about to become, a laugh that made my heart shrink, a laugh that made me want to run away from her and at the same time made me understand beyond the shadow of a doubt that there was no place I could run to. And then it occurred to me to ask where she was going. She won't tell me, I thought, that's Cesárea, she won't want me to know. But she told me: to Sonora, the land she was from, and she said it as naturally as someone else might tell you the time or say good morning. But why, Cesárea? I said. Don't you realize that if you leave now you're going to give up your literary career? Do you have any idea what a wasteland Sonora is? What are you going to do there? Questions like that. Questions a person asks, boys, when he doesn't really know what to say. And Cesárea looked at me as we walked and said that there was nothing left for her here. Have you gone mad? I said. Have you lost your mind, Cesárea? You have your work here, you have your friends, Manuel thinks highly of you, I think highly of you, Germán and Arqueles think highly of you, the general wouldn't know what to do without you. You're a stridentist, body and soul. You'll help us build Stridentopolis, Cesárea, I said. And then she smiled, as if I was telling her a good joke but one she already knew, and she said that she had quit her job a week ago and that anyway she'd always been a visceral realist, not a stridentist. And so am I, I said or shouted, all of us Mexicans are more visceral realists than stridentists, but what does it matter? Stridentism and visceral realism are just two masks to get us to where we really want to go. And where is that? she said. To modernity, Cesárea, I said, to goddamned modernity. And then, only then, I asked her whether it was true she had quit her job with *mi general*. And she said of course it was true. And what did he say? I asked. He went wild, laughed Cesárea. And? That's all, he doesn't believe I'm serious, but if he thinks I'm coming back he'd better wait sitting down, because otherwise he'll get tired. Poor man, I said. Cesárea laughed. Do you have relatives in Sonora? I said. No, I don't think so, she said. So what will you do then? I said. Look for a job and a place to live, said Cesárea. And is that all? I said. Is that all fate has in store for you, Cesárea, my love? I said, although I probably didn't say my love, I may just have thought it. And Cesárea gave me a look, a brief little sideways glance, and said that the search for a place to live and a place to work was the common fate of all mankind. Deep down you're a reactionary, Amadeo, she said (but she said it fondly). And we carried on like that for a while. As if we were arguing, but not arguing. As if we were blaming each other for something, but not blaming each other. And all of a sudden, just before we got to the street where we would part forever, I tried to imagine Cesárea in Sonora, I tried to imagine her in Sonora and I couldn't. I saw the desert or what I imagined the desert to be like back then, because I've never been there, boys, I said, I've seen it over the years in movies or on television, but I've never been there, thanks be to God, and in the desert I saw a spot moving along an endless ribbon and the spot was Cesárea and the ribbon was the road that led to a nameless city or town and then, like a melancholy buzzard, I swooped down and landed my ailing imagination on a rock and I saw Cesárea walking, although it wasn't the same Cesárea I'd known anymore but a different woman, a fat Indian dressed in black under the sun of the Sonora desert, and I said or tried to say goodbye, Cesárea Tinajero, mother of the visceral realists, but only a pitiful croak came out, best regards, dear Cesárea, I tried to say, regards from Pablito Lezcano and Manuel Maples Arce, regards from Arqueles Vela and the incombustible List Arzubide, regards from Encarnación Guzmán and *mi general* Diego Carvajal, but all that came out was a gurgle, as if I were having a heart attack, heaven forbid, or an asthma attack, and then I saw Cesárea again, walking beside me, as sure of herself and determined and brave as ever, and I said: Cesárea, think carefully, don't be foolhardy, watch your step, and she laughed and said: Amadeo, I know what I'm doing, and then we started to talk about politics, which was a topic that Cesárea enjoyed less and less, as if she and politics had gone mad together, she had funny ideas on the subject, saying, for example, that the Mexican Revolution would come in the twenty-second century, nonsense that's no comfort to anyone, is it? and we talked about literature too, about poetry, about the latest Mexico City news, about the gossip from the literary salons, about the things Salvador Novo was writing, about accounts of bullfighters and politicians and chorus girls, subjects that we tacitly agreed didn't bear close scrutiny, or were hard to scrutinize. And then Cesárea stopped as if suddenly she remembered something very important that she'd forgotten, and she was quiet, looking at the ground or the passersby at that time of day, but without seeing them, she was frowning, boys, I said, and then she looked at me, without seeing me at first, then seeing me, and she smiled and said goodbye, Amadeo. And that was the last time I saw her alive. Cool as could be. And that was the end of everything.

# 22

Susana Puig, Calle Josep Tarradellas, Calella de Mar, Catalonia, June 1994. He called me. It had been a long time since I talked to him. He said you have to go to such and such a beach, on such and such a day, at such and such a time. What are you talking about? I said. You have to be there, you have to, he said. Are you crazy? Are you drunk? I said. Please, I'll expect you there, he said, and he repeated the name of the beach and the date and the time. Can't you come to my apartment? I said. We can talk here if that's what you want. I don't want to talk, he said, I don't want to talk anymore, everything's over, it's pointless to talk, he said. I felt like hanging up, but I didn't. I'd just had dinner and I was watching a movie on TV, it was a French movie, I can't remember what it was called or who the director or the actors were, all I remember is that it was about a singer, a sort of hysterical girl, I think, and a pathetic guy she inexplicably falls in love with. I had the volume turned down low, as usual, and while I was talking to him I didn't take my eyes off the TV: rooms, windows, the faces of people whose presence in the movie didn't quite make sense. The table was cleared and there was a book on the sofa, a novel I was planning to start that night when I got tired of the movie and went to bed. Will you come? he said. What for? I said, but I was really thinking about something else, about the singer's stubbornness, about her tears, tears that flowed uncontainably, tears of hatred, although I don't know whether that makes sense. It's hard to cry with hatred, hard to hate someone so much it makes you sob. So you can see me, he said. For the last time, the last time, he insisted. Are you still there? I said. For a moment I thought he'd hung up. It wouldn't be the first time. I was sure he was calling me from a public phone, I could

436

imagine it perfectly, a telephone on the Paseo Marítimo of the town where he lived, which was just twenty minutes from my town by train and fifteen by car, why I started to think about distances that night I don't know, but he couldn't have hung up, I could hear the sound of cars, unless I hadn't closed all the windows and what I was hearing was noise from my own street. Are you there? I said. Yes, he said, will you come? What a pain in the ass! What do you want me to come for if we aren't going to talk? What do you want me to come for when we have nothing left to say to each other? I really don't know, he said, I must be going crazy. I thought the same thing but didn't say so. Have you seen your son? Yes, he said. How is he? Very well, he said, good-looking, getting bigger every day. And your ex-wife? Very well, he said. Why don't you get back together? Don't ask idiotic questions, he said. I mean just as friends, I said, so she can take care of you a little. This seemed to strike him as funny, I heard him laugh, then he said that his wife (he didn't say ex-wife, he said wife) was doing fine now and he didn't want to be the one to ruin things for her. You're too thoughtful, I said. She isn't the one who broke my heart, he said. So sappy! So sentimental! Of course I knew the story by heart.

He told it to me on the third night, as he begged me to give him a shot in the vein of Nolotil, that's exactly what he said, "a shot in the vein," not intravenous, which is essentially the same thing, but different, and of course I gave it to him, go on now, go to sleep, but we always talked, each night for a little longer, until he'd told me the whole story. At the time I thought it was a sad story, not because of the story itself, but because of the way he told it. I can't remember now how long he was in the hospital, maybe ten or twelve days, that's right, I remember that nothing happened between us, sometimes we might have looked at each other more intensely than a patient and a nurse usually do, but that was all. I had just ended a relationship (I can't really call it an engagement) with an intern, so you could say the climate was right, but nothing happened. Fifteen days after he was discharged, I went into a room during one of my shifts and there he was again. I thought I was seeing things! I went up to the bed without making a sound and took a good look from up close. It was him. I checked his chart: he had pancreatitis, although they hadn't put in a nasogastric tube. When I came back into the room (the man in the next bed was dying of cirrhosis and needed constant attention), he opened his eyes and said hello. How are you, Susana, he said. He held out his hand. I don't know why I didn't just shake his hand but instead I bent down and kissed him on the cheek. The next morning the other man died and when I came back he had the room to himself. That night we made love. He was still a little weak, still on an IV, and his pancreas hurt, but we did it, and although later I started to think it had been recklessness on my part, almost criminal recklessness, the truth is I'd never felt so happy at the hospital before, at least not since I got the job, but that was a different kind of happiness, nothing like what I felt when we made love. Of course, I already knew that he'd been married and he had a son (he'd told me so himself the first time he was hospital-ized), although I'd never heard of his wife visiting him in the hospital, but mainly he'd told me the other story, the one that "broke his heart," a tacky story, really, although he had no clue.

Anyone else (a more experienced person, a more practical person) would have known that what we had couldn't last very long, at most the time he was in the hospital, but I got my hopes up and didn't think about the obstacles. It was the first (and only) time that I'd gone to bed with someone so much older than me (sixteen years) and it didn't bother me at all, in fact, I liked it. In bed he was gentle, polite, and sometimes com-pletely wild, I don't mind saying. Although as the days went by and the hospital faded in his memory, he seemed even more distracted and his visits were farther and farther apart. He lived, as I've said, in a town like mine on the coast, just twenty minutes away by train and fifteen by car, and some nights he would show up at my apartment and not leave until the next morning, and other nights I was the one who would drive past my house and keep driving till I got to his town, which was like a trip into the lion's den, because he didn't like visits. He never said so, but I knew it. He lived in a building in the center of town, the back wall right up against the movie theater, so if a horror movie was playing or the sound track was very loud, you could hear the shouts and the high notes from the kitchen, and especially if you'd already seen the movie, you'd more or less know what part it was at, whether they'd found the killer or not, how much longer until the end.

After the last show, the apartment would be plunged into a deep si-lence, as if the building had suddenly dropped into a mine shaft, except that the shaft was liquid somehow, an underwater world, because soon afterward I started to imagine fish, those flat, blind deep-sea fish. Other-wise, the apartment was a disaster: the floor was dirty, the living room was taken up by an enormous table covered with papers, there was room for a couple of chairs and that was all, the bathroom was horrible (do all single men have bathrooms like that? I hope not), there was no washing machine, and the sheets left much to be desired, as did the towels, the kitchen rags, his clothes, basically everything was a wreck, even considering that when we started to date, if we ever really dated, I told him he should bring his dirty clothes to my house and I would throw them in the washing machine, I have a really good one, but he ignored me, he said that he washed his things by hand, one time we went up to the roof, he lived on the second floor and the only other person in the building was the landlady on the first floor, no one lived on the third floor, although some nights, as we made love (or fucked, which is more like what it really was), I heard noises, as if someone on the third floor were moving a chair or bed or walking from the door to the window, which the person didn't open, it must have been the wind, everyone knows how old houses make strange noises, creaking on winter nights, anyway, we went up to the roof and he showed me the sink, a sink made of chipped cement as if someone, some former tenant, had taken a hammer to it in desperation one afternoon, and he said that's where he washed his clothes, by hand, of course, he didn't need a washing machine, and then we stood there looking over the town roofs, there's always something haphazard and pretty about the roofs of the old town, the sea, the seagulls, the church bell tower, everything a pale brown or yellow, like bright earth or bright sand. Later, inevitably, I came to my senses and realized that it was all wrong. You can't love someone who doesn't love you, you can't be with someone just for the sex. I told him it was over between us and he didn't object. It was as if he'd always known it would end that way. But we were still friends and sometimes, on nights when I felt lonely or depressed, I would get in the car and go see him. We would have dinner together and then we would make love, but I wouldn't spend the night at his apartment. Then I met someone else, nothing serious, and that ended too.

Once we argued. Why? I've forgotten. It didn't have anything to do with jealousy, that much I remember. He wasn't jealous at all. For several days he didn't call me and I didn't visit him. I wrote him a letter. I told him that he should grow up, that he should take better care of himself, that his health was fragile (he had sclerosis of the bile duct, a sky-high liver count, extensive ulcerative colitis, he had just recovered from an attack of hyperthyroidism, and every once in a while his teeth hurt!), that he should get his life on track because he was still young, that he should forget the woman who'd "broken his heart," that he should buy a washing machine. I spent a whole afternoon writing it and then I ripped it up and started to cry. Sometime later I received his last phone call.

You want to see me but we aren't going to talk? I said. That's right, he said, that's right, we aren't going to talk, I just need to know you're nearby, but we aren't going to see each other either. Have you gone crazy? No, no, no, he said. It's very simple. But it wasn't very simple. To make a long story short, what he wanted was for me to see him. You won't see me? I said. No, there's no way I'll be able to see you, I've worked it all out very carefully, you have to park the car at the curve by the gas station, on the shoulder, and from there you'll be able to see me, you won't even have to get out of the car. Are you planning to commit suicide, Arturo? I said. I heard him laugh. No suicide, at least not for now, he said. You could hardly hear what he was saying. I have a ticket to Africa. I'm leaving in a few days. Africa, what part of Africa? I said. Tanzania, he said, I've already gotten every vaccine there is. Will you be there? he asked. None of this makes any sense, I said, I don't see the point. There is a point! he said. But not for me, asshole, I said. All you have to do is park your car at the first curve after the gas station and wait. How long? I don't know, five minutes, he said. If you get there when I tell you to, only five minutes. And then what? I said. Then you wait for ten more minutes, then you leave. And that's all. So what about Africa? I said. Africa comes afterward, he said (his voice sounded the same as it always did, a tiny bit ironic, but not the least bit insane), it's the future. The future? Nice future. And what do you plan to do there? I said. His answer was vague, as always. Things, assignments, the usual, is what I think he said, or something like that. When I hung up I didn't know what baffled me most, his invitation or his announcement that he was leaving Spain.

The day of the appointment I followed his instructions word for word. High up on the road, with the car parked on the shoulder, there was a view of almost the whole cove, a little beach where the local nudists came in the summer. To my left was a row of hills and crags with a house poking up every so often, to my right the railroad line, some brush, and then, past a dip in the ground, the beach. It was a gray day and when I got there I couldn't see anyone. At one end of the cove was the bar Los Calamares Felices, a wooden shack painted blue, and not a soul in sight. At the other end were some rocks hiding smaller coves, more sheltered from the public gaze, which was where most of the nudists congregated in summer. I got there half an hour before the specified time. I didn't want to get out of the car, but after waiting for ten minutes and smoking two cigarettes, it became suffocating inside, in every sense of the word. When I opened the door to get out, a car parked in front of Los Calamares Felices. I watched it closely: a man got out, a guy with long, straight hair, presumably young, and after looking all around (except up, toward where I was), he walked behind the bar and vanished from sight. I don't know why I was so nervous. I got back in the car and locked the doors. I was thinking seriously about leaving when a second car parked at the entrance to Los Calamares Felices. A man and a woman got out. After looking at the first car, the man raised his hands to his mouth and shouted or whistled, I don't know, because just then a truck went by and I couldn't hear anything. The man and woman waited for a moment and then they walked toward the beach down a little dirt path. After a while, the first man came out from behind the part of Los Calamares Felices that I couldn't see and walked toward them. They must have known each other, because they shook hands and the woman kissed the first man. Then, in a motion that struck me as excessively slow, the second man's hand pointed to a spot on the beach. Emerging from among the rocks, two men were heading toward the bar, walking just at the line where the waves vanished on the sand. Although they were far away, I recognized one of them as Arturo. I don't know why, but I got out of the car as fast as I could, maybe with the idea that I would go down to the beach, although I realized immediately that to get there I would have to make a huge detour through a pedestrian underpass, and that by the time I got there they might all be gone. So I stayed there beside the car and watched. Arturo and his companion stopped in the middle of the beach. The two men from the cars walked toward them and the woman sat on the sand and waited. When the four met, one of the men, Arturo's companion, set a package on the ground and unwrapped it. Then he stood up and moved back. The first man went over to the package, took something out of it, and moved back too. Then Arturo went over to the package and took something out himself, imitating the previous man. Now Arturo and the first man were each holding a long thing in their hands. The second man went up to the first man and said something. The first man nodded and the second man moved away, but he must have been a little confused because he moved toward the water and a wave washed over his shoes, which made him jump as if he'd been bitten by a piranha and retreat quickly in the opposite direction. The first man didn't even look at him: he was talking to Arturo in what seemed a friendly way, and Arturo was moving his left foot, as if while he was listening he was amusing himself by tracing something, a face or a few numbers, with the tip of his boot in the wet sand. Arturo's companion backed several feet away toward the rocks. The woman got up and went over to the second man, who was sitting on the sand cleaning his shoes. Only Arturo and the first man were left in the middle of the beach. Then they raised what they were holding in their hands and struck them together. At first glance I thought it was walking sticks and I laughed, because I realized that this was what Arturo had wanted me to see: some clowning around, a strange kind of clowning around, but definitely clowning around. But doubt crept into my mind. What if those weren't walking sticks? What if they were swords?


**Guillem Piña, Calle Gaspar Pujol, Andratx, Mallorca, June 1994.** We met in 1977. It's been a long time since then. A lot has happened. Back then I used to buy two newspapers each morning and several magazines. I read everything. I knew everything that was going on. We saw a lot of each other, always on my turf. I think I only went to his place once. We went out to eat together. I paid. It's been a long time since then. Barcelona has changed. Barcelona's architects haven't changed, but Barcelona has. I used to paint every day, not like now, but there were too many parties, too many gatherings, too many friends. Life was exciting. In those days everybody had a magazine and I liked that. I had shows in Paris, New York, Vienna, London. Arturo would disappear for long stretches at a time. He liked my magazine. I would give him back issues, and I gave him a drawing too. I gave it to him framed because I knew he didn't have the money to frame anything. What drawing was it? A sketch for a painting I never finished: *The Other Demoiselles d'Avignon*. I met dealers who were interested in my work. But I wasn't very interested in my work. Around that time I painted three fake Picabias. They were perfect. I sold two and kept one. Painting the fakes, I saw a faint light, but it was a light, which is the important thing. With the money I made I bought a Kandinsky print and a batch of *arte povera*, possibly also forgeries. Sometimes I would get on a plane and fly to Mallorca. I would go see my parents in Andratx and take long walks in the country. Sometimes I would just watch my father, who painted too, when he went out with his canvases and easel, and strange ideas would come to my head. Ideas that were like dead fish or fish on the verge of death at the bottom of the sea. But then I would think about other things. In those days I had a studio in Palma. I moved paintings back and forth. I would bring them from my parents' house to the studio and from the studio to my parents' house. Then I would get bored and fly back to Barcelona. Arturo would come to my house to shower. He didn't have a shower where he was living, obviously, and he would come use mine on Moliner, near Plaza Cardona.

We talked, we never argued. I would show him my paintings and he would say fantastic, I love them, that kind of thing. I've always found that oppressive. I know he meant what he said, but still, I felt oppressed. Then he would be quiet, smoking, and I would make tea or coffee or bring out a bottle of whiskey. I don't know, I don't know, I would think, I might be doing something right, I might be onto something. The visual arts are ultimately incomprehensible. Or they're so comprehensible that nobody, first and foremost myself, will accept the most obvious reading of them. Back then, Arturo was sleeping occasionally with a girlfriend of mine. He didn't know about us. That is, he knew we were friends, how could he not when I was the one who'd introduced them, but what he didn't know was that she was a girlfriend. They slept together every once in a while: once a month, say. I thought it was funny. In some ways he could be very naïve. My friend lived on Calle Denia, not far from where I lived, and I had the key to her apartment and sometimes I would show up there at eight in the morning, looking for something I had forgotten for one of my classes, and I would find Arturo in bed or making breakfast, and he would look at me as if asking himself is she his friend or a girlfriend? I thought it was funny. Good morning, Arturo, I would say, and sometimes I had to make an effort not to laugh. I was sleeping with another friend too, but I slept with her much more often than my friend slept with Arturo. Problems. Life is full of problems, although life was wonderful in Barcelona in those days, and problems were called surprises.

Then came the disenchantment. I was teaching classes at the university and I wasn't happy there. I didn't want to explain my work in theoretical terms. I was teaching classes and my colleagues seemed to fall into two clearly distinct groups: the frauds (the mediocrities and scoundrels), and those who weren't just teaching but were getting somewhere with their art outside of work, for better or for worse. And all of a sudden I realized that I didn't want to belong to either group, and I quit. I started to teach at a high school. What a relief. Was it like being demoted from lieutenant to sergeant? Possibly. Maybe to corporal. Though I didn't feel like a lieutenant or a sergeant or a corporal, but a ditch digger, sewer dredger, a road worker lost or separated from his crew. In retrospect, the passage from one state to another takes on the harsh, brutal overtones of the sudden and irremediable, but of course it all happened much more slowly. I met a millionaire who bought my work, my magazine died of neglect and lack of interest, I started other magazines, I had shows. But none of that exists anymore: the words are more real than the actuality. The truth is that one day it was over and all I had left was my fake Picabia, my only guide, my only handhold. Some unemployed person could reproach me for being incapable of happiness, even though I had everything. I could reproach a murderer for committing murders, and a murderer could reproach a suicide victim for his desperate or enigmatic last act. The truth is that one day it was all over and I took a look around me. I stopped buying so many magazines and newspapers. I stopped having shows. I started to teach my drawing classes at the high school with humility and seriousness and even (although I don't make a big deal about it) a certain sense of humor. Arturo had disappeared from our lives long ago.

I don't know what reasons he had for disappearing. One day he got angry at my friend because he found out that she was a girlfriend, or maybe he slept with my other friend and she said to him you dope, can't you see that Guillem's friend is a *girlfriend*? or something, conversations in bed do oscillate between the cryptic and the transparent. I don't know, not that it matters much. All I know is that he left and for a long time I didn't see him. It certainly wasn't my intent. I try to hold on to my friends. I try to be pleasant and sociable, I try not to rush the passage from comedy to tragedy. Life does a fine job on its own. Anyway, one day Arturo disappeared. The years went by and I didn't see him again. Until one day my friend said: guess who called me tonight. I wish I'd said: Arturo Belano. It would have been funny if I'd guessed it right away, but I said other names and then I gave up. Still, when she said Arturo I was happy. How many years had it been since we'd seen each other? Many years, so many that it was better not to count, not to remember, although I remembered them all, each and every one. So Arturo showed up at my friend's place one day, and she called me and I went over to see him. I hurried, I was running. I don't know why I started to run, but I did. It was almost eleven at night and it was cold and when I got there I saw a guy who was in his forties now, like me, and as I walked toward him I felt like the *Nude Descending a Staircase*, although I wasn't descending any staircase, not that I recall.

After that we met several times. One day he came to my studio. I was sitting there staring at a tiny canvas set beside a canvas that was at least ten feet by seven. Arturo looked at the small painting and the big painting and asked me what they were. What do you think they are? I said. Ossuaries, he said. In fact, they were ossuaries. By that point, I hardly ever painted and I never showed my work. Those who had been lieutenants with me were captains now, or colonels, and one, my dear Miguelito, had even reached the rank of general or field marshal. Others had died of AIDS or drugs or cirrhosis or had simply been given up for lost. I was still a ditch digger. I know that this lends itself to all kinds of interpretations, most of them grim. But my situation wasn't grim at all. I felt reasonably happy, I kept busy, I watched things, I watched myself watch things, I read, I lived a peaceful life. I didn't produce much. That may be important. Arturo, on the other hand, produced a lot. Once I ran into him as I was coming out of the laundry. He was on his way to my house. What are you doing? he said. As you can see, I answered, I'm leaving with clean clothes. Don't you have a washing machine at home? he said. It broke five years ago, I said. That afternoon Arturo went out into the inner courtyard and spent some time looking at my washing machine. I made myself tea (by then I hardly ever drank) and watched him as he examined the washing machine. For a brief moment I thought he was going to fix it. It wouldn't have seemed so remarkable, but it would have made me happy. But in the end, my washing machine was as dead as ever. I told him again about an accident I'd had. I think I told him about it because I saw him eyeing my scars. The accident happened in Mallorca. A car accident. I almost lost both of my arms and my jaw. There were only a few scratches on the rest of my body. Strange accident, wouldn't you say? Very strange, said Arturo. He told me that he'd been in the hospital too, six times in two years. In what country? I asked him. Here, he said, at Valle Hebrón and before that at Josep Trueta in Gerona. So why didn't you let us know? we would've come to see you. Well, it doesn't matter. Once he asked me whether I was depressed. No, I said, sometimes I feel like the *Nude Descending a Staircase,* which can actually be nice when you're with friends and not so nice if you're walking along the Paseo de Gracia, for example, but mostly I feel good.

One day, not long before he disappeared for the last time, he came to my house and said: someone's going to write a bad review of my book. I made him some chamomile tea and didn't say anything, which is the right thing to do, I think, when there's a story to be told, sad or happy. But he was quiet too, and for a while we just sat there, he staring at his tea or the little slice of lemon floating in his tea as I smoked a Ducados. I think I'm one of the few left who still smoke Ducados, or one of the few of my generation, I mean. Even Arturo smokes blond tobacco now. After a while, just to say something, I said: are you going to spend the night in Barcelona? and he shook his head. When he spent the night in Barcelona he stayed at my friend's house (in separate rooms, although it cheapens everything to spell these things out), not with me. Still, we would have dinner together, and sometimes the three of us would go for a drive in my friend's car. Anyway, I asked him whether he was going to spend the night and he said he couldn't, he had to get back to the town where he lived, a town on the coast a little more than an hour away by train. And then the two of us were quiet again, and I started to think about what he'd said about a bad review, and no matter how much I thought about it I had no idea what he meant, so I stopped thinking about it. Instead I waited, which is what the *Nude Descending a Staircase* does, contrary to one's expectation and which is exactly why it has always provoked such a peculiar critical response.

For a while all I heard was the noise Arturo made as he drank his tea, muffled sounds from the street, the elevator going up and down a few times. And suddenly, when I wasn't thinking or hearing anything anymore, I heard him repeat that a critic was going to trounce him. It doesn't really matter, I said. It's a hazard of the trade. It does matter, he said. It's never mattered to you before, I said. Now it does matter to me, he said, I must be getting bourgeois. Then he explained that there were similarities between his last book and his new book that fell into the realm of games that were impossible to decipher. I had read his last book and liked it, and I didn't have any idea what his new book was about, so I didn't have anything to say. All I could ask was: what kind of similarities? Games, Guillem, he said. Games. The fucking *Nude Descending a Staircase*, your fucking fake Picabias, games. So what's the problem? I said. The problem, he said, is that the critic, a guy named Iñaki Echevarne, is a shark. Is he a bad critic? I said. No, he's a good critic, he said, or at least he isn't a bad critic, but he's a fucking shark. And how do you know that he's going to review your new book when it isn't even in bookstores yet? Because the other day, he said, while I was at the publishing house, he called the head of publicity and asked for my last novel. So? I said. So I was sitting there, across from the head of publicity, and she said hello, Iñaki, what a coincidence, Arturo Belano is right here across from me, and that bastard Echevarne didn't say anything. What was he supposed to say? Hello, at least, said Arturo. And since he didn't say anything, you've decided that he's going to tear you apart? I said. Besides, what if he does tear you apart? It doesn't matter! Look, said Arturo, Echevarne fought recently with Aurelio Baca, the Cato of Spanish letters, do you know him? I haven't read him but I know who he is, I said. It was all because of a review Echevarne had written of a book by one of Baca's friends. I don't know whether the criticism was justified or not. I haven't read the book. All I know for sure is that this novelist had Baca to defend him. And Baca's attack on the critic was the kind of thing that brings a person to tears. But I don't have any self-righteous strongman to defend me, absolutely no one, so Echevarne can do whatever he wants to me. Not even Aurelio Baca could defend me, because I make fun of him in my book, not the one that's about to come out but the last one, although I doubt he's ever read me. You make fun of Baca? I made fun of him a little, said Arturo, although I doubt he or anyone else would ever notice. That rules out Baca as a champion, I admitted, thinking that I too had overlooked the passage that was worrying my friend. That's right, said Arturo. Well, let Echevarne lay into you, I said. Who cares? None of this matters. Of all people you should know that. We're all going to die, think about the hereafter. But Echevarne must feel like taking it out on someone, said Arturo. Is he really that bad? I said. No, no, he's very good, said Arturo. Well then? It has nothing to do with that, it's about exercising the muscles, said Arturo. The muscles of the brain? I said. Some kind of muscles, and I'm going to be the punching bag Echevarne trains on for his second or eighth round with Baca, said Arturo. I see, this is an old fight, I said. So what do you have to do with all of it? Nothing, I'm just going to be the punching bag, said Arturo. For a while we sat there without saying anything, thinking, as the elevator went up and down and the noise it made was like the sound of all the years we hadn't seen each other. I'm going to challenge him to a duel, said Arturo at last. Do you want to be my second? That's what he said. I felt as if someone had given me a shot in the arm. First the pinprick, then the liquid going not into my veins but my muscles, an icy liquid that made me shiver. The proposition seemed crazy and unwarranted. You don't challenge a man for something he hasn't done yet, I thought. But then I thought that life (or the specter of life) is constantly challenging us for acts we've never committed, and sometimes for acts we never even thought of committing. My answer was yes and immediately afterward I thought that maybe in the hereafter *Nude Descending a Staircase* or *The Large Glass* really does exist or will exist. And then I thought: what if the review is good? What if Echevarne likes Arturo's novel? Wouldn't it be unfair then, gratuitous, to challenge him to a duel?

Little by little, various questions began to come to mind, but I decided that it wasn't the moment to be sensible. There's a time for everything. The first thing we discussed was the choice of weapon. I suggested balloons filled with red dye. Or a battle of exaggerated sombrero doffing. Arturo insisted that it had to be with sabers. To first blood? I proposed. Grudgingly, although deep down probably in relief, Arturo accepted my suggestion. Then we went looking for the sabers.

My original plan was to buy them in one of those tourist stores that sell everything from blades made in Toledo to samurai swords, but informed of our intentions, my friend said that her late father had left a pair of swords, so we went to look at them and they turned out to be real ones. After giving them a good polish, we decided to use them. Then we looked for the perfect place. I suggested the Parque de la Ciudadela, at midnight, but Arturo preferred a nudist beach halfway between Barcelona and the town where he lived. Then we got Iñaki Echevarne's telephone number and called him. It took us a long time to convince him that it wasn't a joke. Arturo spoke to him three times all together. Finally Iñaki Echevarne said that he agreed and that we should let him know the date and time. The afternoon of the duel we ate at a snack bar in Sant Pol de Mar. Fried cuttlefish and shrimp. My friend (who had come this far with us but wasn't planning to attend the duel), Arturo, and me. The meal, I have to say, was a little gloomy, and while we were eating Arturo pulled out a plane ticket and showed it to us. I thought it would be to Chile or Mexico and that Arturo was, in some sense, bidding farewell to Catalonia and Europe. But the ticket was for a flight to Dar es Salaam with stopovers in Rome and Cairo. Then I realized that my friend had gone completely insane and that if the critic Echevarne didn't kill him with a whack on the head he would be eaten by the black or red ants of Africa.

**Jaume Planells, Bar Salambó, Calle Torrijos, Barcelona, June 1994.** One morning my friend and colleague Iñaki Echevarne called me and said he needed a second for a duel. I was a little hungover, so at first I didn't understand what Iñaki was saying, and anyway he hardly ever calls me, especially at that time of day. Then, when he explained, I thought he was kidding and I went along with him, people are always kidding me, but I don't mind, and anyway Iñaki is a little strange, strange but attractive, the kind of guy women think is really handsome and men think is nice, if slightly intimidating, and whom they secretly admire. Not long ago he'd had a feud with the great Madrid novelist Aurelio Baca, and even though Baca thundered and stormed, hurling abuse at him, Iñaki managed to emerge unscathed from the exchange of hostilities, coming out even with Baca, you might say.

The funny thing is that Iñaki hadn't criticized Baca but a friend of Baca's, so you can only imagine what would've happened if he'd gone after the great man himself. As far as I could tell, the problem was that Baca was a writer on the model of Unamuno, there being no lack of them nowadays, who would launch into some lecture full of cheap moralizing whenever he got the chance, the typical preachy, irate Spanish lecture, and Iñaki was the typical provocative, kamikaze critic who liked making enemies and who had a habit of leaping in with both feet. It was a matter of time before they clashed. Or at least Baca had to clash with Echevarne, call him to order, give him a slap on the wrist, something like that. Underneath, they both fell somewhere along the increasingly vague spectrum we call the left.

So when Iñaki explained to me about the duel, I thought he must be joking. The passions Baca had unleashed couldn't be so powerful that authors were taking justice into their own hands now, and in such a melodramatic way. But Iñaki said it had nothing to do with that. He sounded a little bit confused but he said this was something different and he had to accept the challenge (could he have mentioned the *Nude Descending a Staircase*? but what did Picasso have to do with it?) and I should tell him once and for all whether I was prepared to be his second or not, and he had no time to waste because the duel was taking place that very afternoon.

What could I say but yes, of course I'll do it, tell me where and when, although afterward, when Iñaki hung up, I started to think that maybe I'd just gotten myself mixed up in some serious shit, and that I, who have a pretty nice life and enjoy a good joke every once in a while like any normal guy so long as it doesn't go too far, might be landing myself in one of those messes that never end well. And then, on top of that, I got to thinking (something a person should never, ever do in cases like this), and I came to the conclusion that it was strange to begin with that Iñaki would call me to be his second in a duel, since I'm not exactly one of his best friends. We work for the same newspaper, we run into each other sometimes at the Giardinetto or the Salambó or the bar at Laie, but we're not really what you'd call friends.

And since there were only a few hours left before the duel, I called Iñaki to see whether I could catch him, but no, clearly he'd called me and then gone right out to, I don't know, write his last article or head for the nearest church, so once that had been established, I called Quima Monistrol on her cell phone, it was like a light going off in my head, if I'm with a woman things can't get too ugly, although of course I didn't tell Quima the truth, I said Quima, baby, I need you, Iñaki Echevarne and I are meeting someone and we want you to come with us, and Quima asked when, and I said right now, sweetheart, and Quima said all right, come pick me up at the Corte Inglés, something like that. When I hung up I tried to get in touch with two or three other friends, because all of a sudden I realized that I was much more nervous than I should've been, but no one answered.

At five-thirty I spotted Quima smoking a cigarette on the corner of Plaza Urquinaona and Pau Claris, and after a pretty bold U-turn I had the intrepid reporter in the passenger seat. As hundreds of drivers honked their horns at us and I could see the menacing outline of a cop in the rearview mirror, I stepped on the gas and we headed for the A-19, toward the Maresme. Of course, Quima asked me where I was hiding Iñaki (the man has an amazing effect on women, it must be said), so I had to tell her that he was waiting for us at the bar Los Calamares Felices, outside of Sant Pol de Mar, near a cove that becomes a nudist beach in spring and summer. For the rest of the trip, which took less than twenty minutes (my Peugeot goes like lightning), I was on edge, listening to Quima's stories and unable to find the right moment to tell her the real reason we were going to the Maresme.

To make matters worse, we got lost in Sant Pol. According to some locals, we had to take the road to Calella, but turn left at a gas station after a quarter of a mile, as if we were heading for the mountains, then turn right again and go through a tunnel—but what tunnel?—and come back out onto a beach road, where the place called Los Calamares Felices stood, solitary and desolate. For half an hour Quima and I argued and fought. Finally we found the damn bar. We got there late and for an instant I thought Iñaki wouldn't be there, but the first thing I saw was his red Saab, actually *all* I saw was his red Saab, parked on a strip of sand and scrub, and then the desolate building, the dirty windows of Los Calamares Felices. I parked next to Iñaki's car and honked the horn. Without a word, Quima and I decided to stay in the Peugeot. Soon afterward we saw Iñaki appear from around the other side of the restaurant. He didn't scold us for being late, as I thought he might, and he didn't seem to be angry when he saw Quima. I asked him where his adversary was, and Iñaki smiled and shrugged his shoulders. Then the three of us went walking toward the beach. When Quima heard why we were there (it was Iñaki who explained it to her, clearly and objectively and in just a few words, something I could never have done), she seemed more excited than ever and for a second I was sure everything would turn out all right. The three of us were laughing for a while. There wasn't a soul on the beach. He hasn't come, I heard Quima say, and I thought she sounded a tiny bit disappointed.

From the north end of the beach, two figures emerged from among the rocks. My heart skipped a beat. The last time I was in a fight I was eleven or twelve. Since then I've always avoided acts of violence. There they are, said Quima. Iñaki looked at me and then he looked at the sea and only then did I realize that there was something hopelessly ridiculous about the scene and that its ridiculousness was not unrelated to my presence there. The two figures that had appeared from among the rocks kept walking toward us, along the water's edge, and finally they stopped about three hundred feet away, close enough for us to see that one of them was carrying a package with the points of two swords poking out. Quima had better stay here, said Iñaki. After our companion had finished protesting, the two of us headed slowly toward the pair of madmen. So you're going to go ahead with this farce? I remember I asked as we walked along the sand, so this duel is going to happen for real, not pretend? so you've chosen me to be the witness to this madness? because it was just then that I sensed or had the revelation that Iñaki had chosen me because his real friends (if he had any, maybe Jordi Llovet or some intellectual like that) would have refused point-blank to take part in something so absurd and he knew it and everyone knew it, except for me, the dumb hack, and I also thought: my God, this is all that bastard Baca's fault, if he hadn't attacked Iñaki this wouldn't be happening, and then I couldn't think anymore because we had come up to the other two and one of them said: which of you is Iñaki Echevarne? and then I looked Iñaki in the face, suddenly afraid that he would say it was me (with my nerves in the state they were in, I thought Iñaki might be capable of anything), but Iñaki smiled as if he were delighted and said that he was who he was, and then the other one looked at me and introduced himself: hello, I'm Guillem Piña, the second, and I heard myself saying: hello, I'm Jaume Planells, the other second, and frankly now that I remember it I could puke or laugh my ass off, but what I felt then more than anything else was a sharp pain in my stomach, and cold, because it had suddenly gotten cold and only a few rays of the setting sun lit the beach where in the spring people stripped naked, little coves, rocky inlets, seen only by the passengers on the train along the coast, passengers unmoved by the spectacle, that's democracy and civic spirit for you, in Galicia those same passengers would have stopped the train and climbed down to hack the balls off the nudists, anyway, I was thinking all of this when I said hello, I'm Jaume Planells, the other second.

And then this Guillem Piña unwrapped the package he was carrying and the swords were bared, and I thought the blades even seemed to glow a little bit, steel? bronze? iron? I don't know anything about swords, but I did know enough to realize that they weren't plastic, and then I reached out my hand and touched the blades with my fingertips, metal, of course, and when I pulled back my hand I saw the shine again, a very faint shine, as if they were coming to life, or at least that's what Iñaki's friends would have said if he'd had the guts or the decency to ask them to come with him, and if they'd come, which I thought was unlikely, and it struck me as too much of a coincidence, or in any case too intense a coincidence: the sun going down behind the mountains and the glow of the swords, and only then, at last, was I able to ask (who? I don't know, Piña, maybe Iñaki himself) whether they were really serious, whether the duel was in earnest, and warn them in a loud though not very steady voice that the last thing I wanted was trouble with the police. The rest is a blur. Piña said something in Mallorcan. Then he let Iñaki choose one of the swords. Iñaki took his time, hefting each of them, first one, then the other, then both at the same time, as if he'd done nothing all his life but play musketeers. The swords weren't gleaming anymore. The other guy, the writer with a grievance (but a grievance against whom, and why, if the goddamn offending review hadn't even been published yet?) waited until Iñaki had chosen. The sky was a milky gray and a dense fog was drifting out to sea from the hills and fields. My memories are confused. I think I heard Quima shout: go, Iñaki, or something like that. Then, by common accord, Piña and I retreated, backing away. A little wave wet my pant legs. I remember looking down at my moccasins and cursing. I also remember the feeling I had of indecency, illicitness, because of my wet socks, and the noise they made as I moved. Piña retreated toward the rocks. Quima had gotten up and come a little closer to the duelers. They clashed swords. I remember that I sat on a mound and took off my shoes and was careful to wipe off the wet sand with a handkerchief. Then I tossed the handkerchief away and watched the line of the horizon as it grew darker, until Quima put her hand on my shoulder and with her other hand put into my hand a live, wet, prickly object that it took me a while to identify as my own handkerchief coming back to me, returned to me like a curse.

I remember that I put the handkerchief in a pocket of my blazer. Later Quima would say that Iñaki handled the sword like an expert and the fight went his way from the start. But that's not what I would've said. They were evenly matched at first. Iñaki's swings were on the timid side. All he did was clash swords with his adversary, and he kept backing farther away, out of fear or because he was sizing up the other guy. In contrast, his opponent's blows were increasingly confident. At some point he took a thrust at Iñaki, the first of the fight, gripping the sword and lunging with his right foot and right arm, and the tip of his sword almost touched the seam of Iñaki's pants. It was then that Iñaki seemed to wake from the foolish dream he was in and plunge into another dream where the danger was real. From that moment on, his steps became much more nimble and he moved more quickly, always backing away, although not in a straight line but in circles, so that sometimes I'd see him from the front, other times from the side, and other times from behind. What were the rest of the spectators doing all this time? Quima was sitting on the sand behind me, and every once in a while she would cheer Iñaki on. Piña, meantime, was standing, quite far from where the swordsmen were circling, and his face looked like the face of someone who was used to this kind of thing and also the face of someone who was sleeping.

In a brief moment of lucidity, I was sure that we'd all gone crazy. But then that moment of lucidity was displaced by a supersecond of superlucidity (if I can put it that way), in which I realized that this scene was the logical outcome of our ridiculous lives. It wasn't a punishment but a new wrinkle. It gave us a glimpse of ourselves in our common humanity. It wasn't proof of our idle guilt but a sign of our miraculous and pointless innocence. But that's not it. That's not it. We were still and they were in motion and the sand on the beach was moving, not because of the wind but because of what they were doing and what we were doing, which was nothing, which was watching, and all of that together was the wrinkle, the moment of superlucidity. Then, nothing. My memory has always been mediocre, no better than a reporter needs to do his job. Iñaki attacked the other guy, the other guy attacked Iñaki, I realized they might go on like this for hours, until the swords were heavy in their hands, I got out a cigarette, I didn't have a light, I looked in all my pockets, I got up and went over to Quima, only to learn that she'd quit a long time ago, a year or an eternity. For a moment I considered going to ask Piña for a light, but that seemed excessive. I sat next to Quima and watched the duelers. They were still moving in circles but they were slowing down. I also got the impression that they were talking to each other, but the sound of the waves drowned out their voices. I said to Quima that I thought it was all a farce. You're absolutely wrong, she answered. Then she said that she thought it was very romantic. Strange woman, that Quima. I wanted a cigarette more than before. In the distance, Piña was sitting in the sand like us now, and a trail of cobalt blue smoke issued from his lips. I couldn't take it anymore. I got up and went over to him, going the long way around, to keep out of range of the duelers. A woman was watching us from a hill. She was leaning on the hood of a car and shading her eyes with her hands. I thought she was looking at the sea, but then I realized that she was watching us, of course.

Piña offered me his lighter without a word. I looked at his face: he was crying. I'd felt like talking but now when I saw him I suddenly didn't feel like it. So I went back over to Quima and looked up again at the woman alone on top of the hill and I also watched Iñaki and his opponent, who instead of crossing swords were just pacing and eyeing each other now. When I let myself drop down beside Quima my body made a sound like a sack of sand. Then I saw Iñaki's sword raised higher than prudence or musketeer movies would advise and I saw his opponent's sword advance until its point was a fraction of an inch from Iñaki's heart, and I think, though it can't be, that I saw Iñaki turn pale and I heard Quima say my God, or something like that, and I saw Piña flick his cigarette far away, toward the hill, and I saw that there was no one on the hill anymore, not the woman or the car, and then the other guy abruptly drew back the point of his sword and Iñaki stepped forward and struck him with the flat of his blade on the shoulder, in revenge for the fright he'd given him, I think, and Quima sighed and I sighed and blew smoke rings into the tainted air of that hideous beach and the wind whipped the rings away instantly, before there was time for anything, and Iñaki and his opponent kept going at it like two stupid children.

# 23

Iñaki Echevarne, Bar Giardinetto, Calle Granada del Penedés, Barcelona, July 1994. For a while, Criticism travels side by side with the Work, then Criticism vanishes and it's the Readers who keep pace. The journey may be long or short. Then the Readers die one by one and the Work continues on alone, although a new Criticism and new Readers gradually fall into step with it along its path. Then Criticism dies again and the Readers die again and the Work passes over a trail of bones on its journey toward solitude. To come near the work, to sail in her wake, is a sign of certain death, but new Criticism and new Readers approach her tirelessly and relentlessly and are devoured by time and speed. Finally the Work journeys irremediably alone in the Great Vastness. And one day the Work dies, as all things must die and come to an end: the Sun and the Earth and the Solar System and the Galaxy and the farthest reaches of man's memory. Everything that begins as comedy ends as tragedy.

Aurelio Baca, Feria del Libro, Madrid, July 1994. Not only to myself or before the mirror or at the hour of my death, which I hope will be long in coming, but in the presence of my children and my wife and in the face of the peaceful life I'm building, I must acknowledge: (1) That under Stalin I wouldn't have wasted my youth in the gulag or ended up with a bullet in the back of my head. (2) That in the McCarthy era I wouldn't have lost my job or had to pump gas at a gas station. (3) That under Hitler, however, I would have been one of those who chose the path of exile, and that under Franco I wouldn't have composed sonnets

456

to the caudillo or the Holy Virgin like so many lifelong democrats. One thing is as true as the other. My bravery has its limits, certainly, but so does what I'm willing to swallow. Everything that begins as comedy ends as tragicomedy.

**Pere Ordóñez, Feria del Libro, Madrid, July 1994.** In years past, the writers of Spain (and Latin America) joined the public fray to subvert it, reform it, set it on fire, revolutionize it. The writers of Spain (and of Latin America) were generally from well-to-do families or families of a certain social standing. As soon as they took up the pen, they rejected or chafed at that standing: to write was to renounce, to forsake, sometimes to commit suicide. It meant going against the family. Today, to an ever more alarming degree, the writers of Spain (and Latin America) come from lower-class families, the proletariat and the lumpen proletariat, and they tend to use writing as a means to move a few rungs up the social ladder, as a way to make a place for themselves while being very careful not to overstep any bounds. I'm not saying they're uneducated. They're as well educated as the writers who came before them. Or nearly so. I'm not saying they don't work hard. They work much harder than those earlier writers! But they're also much more vulgar. And they act like businessmen or gangsters. And they don't renounce anything, or they renounce what's easily renounced, and they're very careful not to make enemies, or to choose their enemies from among the defenseless. They are driven to suicide not for the sake of ideas but by rage and madness. Little by little, the doors inexorably open to them. And so literature is what it is. Everything that begins as comedy inevitably ends as comedy.

**Julio Martínez Morales, Feria del Libro, Madrid, July 1994.** I'm going to tell you something about the honor of poets as I stroll now around the Feria del Libro. I'm a poet. I'm a writer. I've made a fair name for myself as a critic. At a guess, $7 \times 3 = 22$ booths, but in fact there are many more. Our sight is limited. And yet I've managed to make a place for myself under the sun of this feria. Left behind are the wrecked cars, the limits of writing, the $3 \times 3 = 9$. It hasn't been easy. Left behind are the A and the E, bleeding to death hanging from a balcony to which I sometimes return in dreams. I'm an educated man: the prisons I know are subtle ones.

And of course poetry and prison have always been neighbors. And yet it's melancholia that's the source of my attraction. Am I in the seventh dream or have I truly heard the cocks crow at the other end of the feria? It might be one thing or it might be another. But cocks crow at dawn, and it's noon now, according to my watch. I wander through the feria and greet my colleagues who are wandering as dreamily as I am. Dreamily × dreamily = a prison in literary heaven. Wandering. Wandering. The honor of poets: the chant we hear as a pallid judgment. I see young faces looking at the books on display and feeling for coins in the depths of pockets as dark as hope. 7 × 1 = 8, I say to myself as I glance out of the corner of my eye at the young readers and a formless image is superimposed on their remote little smiling faces as slowly as an iceberg. We all pass under the balcony where the letters A and E hang and their blood gushes down on us and stains us forever. But the balcony is pallid like us, and pallor never attacks pallor. At the same time, and I say this in my defense, the balcony wanders with us too. Elsewhere this is called mafia. I see an office, I see a computer running, I see a lonely hallway. Pallor × iceberg = a lonely hallway slowly peopled by our own fear, peopled with those who wander the feria of the hallway, looking not for any book but for some certainty to shore up the void of our certainties. Thus we interpret life at moments of the deepest desperation. Herds. Hangmen. The scalpel slices the bodies. A and E × Feria del Libro = other bodies; light as air, incandescent, as if last night my publisher had fucked me up the ass. Dying can seem satisfactory as a response, Blanchot would say. 31 × 31 = 961 good reasons. Yesterday we sacrificed a young South American writer on the town altar. As his blood dripped over the bas-relief of our ambitions I thought about my books and oblivion, and that, at last, made sense. A writer, we've established, shouldn't look like a writer. He should look like a banker, a rich kid who grows up without a care in the world, a mathematics professor, a prison official. Dendriform. Thus, paradoxically, we wander. Our arborescence × the balcony's pallor = the hallway of our triumph. How can young people, readers by antonomasia, not realize that we're liars? All one has to do is look at us! Our imposture is blazoned on our faces! And yet they don't realize, and we can recite with total impunity: 8, 5, 9, 8, 4, 15, 7. And we can wander and greet each other (I, at least, greet everyone, the juries and the hangmen, the benefactors and the students), and we can praise the faggot for his unbridled heterosexuality and the impotent man for his virility and the cuckold for his spotless honor. And no one moans: there is no anguish. Only our nocturnal silence when we crawl on all fours toward the fires that someone has lit for us at a mysterious hour and with incomprehensible finality. We're guided by fate, though we've left nothing to chance. A writer must resemble a censor, our elders told us, and we've followed that marvelous thought to its penultimate consequence. A writer must resemble a newspaper columnist. A writer must resemble a dwarf and MUST survive. If we didn't have to read too, our work would be a point suspended in nothingness, a mandala pared down to a minimum of meaning, our silence, our certainty of standing with one foot dangling on the far side of death. Fantasies. Fantasies. In some lost fold of the past, we wanted to be lions and we're no more than castrated cats. Castrated cats wedded to cats with slit throats. Everything that begins as comedy ends as a cryptographic exercise.

**Pablo del Valle, Feria del Libro, Madrid, July 1994.** I'm going to tell you something about the honor of poets. There was a time when I didn't have money or the name I have now: I was out of work and my name was Pedro García Fernandez. But I was talented and I was friendly. I met a woman. I met many women, but I met one woman especially. This woman, best left unnamed, fell in love with me. She worked for the post office. She was a postal official, I would say when my friends asked me what my girlfriend did. But it was really a euphemism so I wouldn't have to say that she was a mailwoman. We lived together for a while. My girlfriend left for work in the morning and didn't come home until five. I would get up when I heard the soft noise the door made as it closed (she was considerate of my sleep) and start to write. I wrote about lofty things. Gardens, lost castles, that kind of thing. Then, when I got tired, I would read. Pío Baroja, Unamuno, Antonio and Manuel Machado, Azorín. At lunchtime I would go out, to a restaurant where they knew me. In the afternoon, I revised. When she got back from work we would talk for a while, but what did a man of letters and a mailwoman have to say to each other? I would talk about what I'd written, what I was planning to write: a commentary on Manuel Machado, a poem on the Holy Spirit, an essay taking its first sentence from Unamuno: Spain hurts me too. She would talk about the streets she'd been on and the letters she'd delivered. She talked about stamps, some of them very rare, and the faces she'd seen in her long morning carrying letters. Then, when I couldn't take it anymore, I would say goodbye and head out to hit the bars of Madrid. Sometimes I would go to book parties, more for the free drinks and hors d'oeuvres than anything else. I would go to the Casa de América and listen to the smug Latin American writers. I would go to the Ateneo and listen to the contented Spanish writers. Later I would meet up with friends and we would talk about our work or go together to visit the maestro. But over the literary chatter I kept hearing the sound of my girlfriend's sensible shoes as she quietly made her rounds, toting her yellow bag or pulling her yellow cart after her, depending on how much mail she had to deliver that day, and then I'd lose my concentration, and my tongue, which seconds before had been sharp and clever, would turn clumsy, and I'd fall into a sullen, helpless silence that the others, including our maestro, would luckily take as evidence of my pensive, introspective, philosophical nature. Sometimes, on my way home late at night, I would stop in the neighborhood where she worked and retrace her route, I'd mimic her, I'd ape her, marching with a step that was at once soldierly and ghostly. In the end I'd find myself throwing up, in tears, leaning against a tree, asking myself how I could possibly live with a woman like her. I never came up with any answers, at least the ones I came up with never felt true, but in fact I didn't leave her. We lived together for a long time. Sometimes, when I took a break from my writing, I'd console myself that it would be worse if she were a butcher. I would have been happier if she were a policewoman, mostly because it would've been more fashionable. A policewoman was better than a mailwoman. Then I'd keep writing and writing, in a rage or near collapse, and little by little I mastered the rudiments of the trade. And so the years went by and the entire time I lived off my girlfriend. Finally I won the New Voices of the Council of Madrid Prize and overnight I found myself in possession of three million pesetas and an offer to work for one of the capital's most distinguished papers. Hernando García León wrote a rave review of my book. The first and second printings sold out in less than three months. I've been on two television shows, even though I think one of them brought me on to make fun of me. I'm writing my second novel. And I left my girlfriend. I told her we weren't right for each other and that I didn't want to hurt her and that I wished her the best and that she knew she could always count on me if she ever needed anything. Then I packed my books in cardboard boxes, I put my clothes in a suitcase, and

I left. I can't remember which great writer said it, but love smiles on a winner. It wasn't long before I was living with another woman and renting an apartment in Lavapiés, an apartment that I pay for myself, where I'm happy and productive. My current girlfriend is studying English literature and writes poetry. We spend a lot of time talking about books. And sometimes she has great ideas. I think we make a wonderful couple: people look at us and nod their heads. We embody optimism and the future in a certain way, a way that's pragmatic and thoughtful too. Some nights, though, when I'm in my office putting the final touches on my column or revising a few pages of my novel, I hear footsteps in the street, and I think, I could almost swear, that it's the mailwoman out delivering mail at the wrong time of day. I go out onto the balcony and I don't see anyone there or maybe I see some drunk on his way home, vanishing around a corner. Nothing's wrong. There's no one there. But when I go back to my desk, I hear the steps again, and then I know that the mailwoman is working, that even though I can't see her she's making her rounds and she couldn't have picked a worse time. And then I stop working on my column or my chapter and I try to write a poem or spend the rest of the evening writing in my diary, but I can't. The sound of her sensible shoes keeps echoing in my head. You can hardly hear it, and I know how to make it go away: I get up, walk to the bedroom, take off my clothes, and get into bed, where I find my girlfriend's sweet-smelling body. I make love to her, sometimes with great tenderness, sometimes violently, and then I sleep and dream that I'm being inducted into the Academy. Or not. It's just a manner of speaking. Actually, sometimes I dream I'm being inducted into Hell. Or I don't dream anything at all. Or I dream that I've been castrated, and that with the passage of time two tiny testicles, like colorless olives, sprout back between my legs, and I fondle them with a mixture of love and fear and keep them secret. Day chases away the ghosts. Of course, I don't talk to anybody about this. I pay for my relationship with the mailwoman with a few nightmares, a few auditory hallucinations. It could be worse. I can handle it. If I were less sensitive, I'm sure I wouldn't even remember her anymore. Sometimes I actually have the urge to call her, to follow her on her route and watch her at work, for the first time. Sometimes I feel like meeting her at some bar in her neighborhood, which isn't my neighborhood anymore, and asking about her life: whether she has a new lover, whether she's delivered any letters from Malaysia or Tanzania, whether she still gets the same Christmas bonus. But I don't do it. I settle for hearing her footsteps, fainter and fainter. I settle for thinking about the hugeness of the Universe. Everything that begins as comedy ends as a horror movie.

**Marco Antonio Palacios, Feria del Libro, Madrid, July 1994.** Here's something about the honor of poets. I was seventeen and I had a burning desire to be a writer. I prepared myself. But I didn't sit around and wait while I was preparing myself, because I realized that I'd never get ahead by sitting around. Discipline and a kind of ingratiating charm, those are the keys to getting where you want to go. Discipline: writing every morning for at least six hours. Writing every morning and revising in the afternoons and reading like a fiend at night. Charm, or ingratiation: visiting writers at home or going up to them at book parties and telling them exactly what they want to hear. What they desperately want to hear. And being patient, because it doesn't always work. There are assholes who'll give you a pat on the back and then act like they've never seen you before in their lives. There are some hard, cruel, vicious bastards out there. But they aren't all like that. You have to be patient and keep looking. The best are the homosexuals, but be careful: you have to know when to stop and exactly what you want, or you'll end up taking it up the ass for nothing from some random old leftist faggot. Three times out of four it's the same thing with women: the Spanish women writers who might be able to lend you a hand are usually old and ugly. Sometimes it just isn't worth it. The best are the heterosexual men over fifty or approaching old age. Whatever it takes, you must get close to them. You must cultivate a garden in the shadow of their grudges and resentments. You have to study their complete works. That goes without saying. You have to quote them two or three times in every conversation. You have to quote them constantly! You want some advice? Never criticize your mentor's friends. Your mentor's friends are sacred, and a thoughtless remark can throw an entire future off course. You want some advice? Hate foreign novelists with a passion. Rant against them with all your might, especially if they're American, French, or English. Spanish writers hate their contemporaries working in other languages. A negative review of one of them will always make you friends. And keep your mouth shut and your eyes open. And set yourself a clear schedule. Write in the morning, revise in the afternoon, read at night, and spend the rest of your time exercising your diplomacy, stealth, and charm. At seventeen I wanted to be a writer. At twenty I published my first book. Now I'm twenty-four, and sometimes it gives me vertigo, looking back. I've come so far. I've published four books and I make a comfortable living (although to be honest, I've never needed much, just a table, a computer, and books). I write a weekly column for a right-wing Madrid newspaper. Now I preach and curse and castigate various politicians (within limits, of course). Young people who want to make a career in writing see me as an example to follow. Some say I'm an improved version of Aurelio Baca. I don't know. (Spain hurts us both, although at the moment I think it happens to hurt him more.) They might be sincere, but they might also be trying to make me lower my guard and lose my grip. If that's the case, I won't give them the satisfaction: I'm still working as doggedly as ever, still producing, still nurturing my friendships. I'm not even thirty yet and the future is unfolding like a rose, a perfect rose, perfumed and unique. What begins as comedy ends as a triumphal march, wouldn't you say?


**Hernando García León, Feria del Libro, Madrid, July 1994.** Like everything big, it all began with a dream. A little less than a year ago, I took a walk over to one of our most venerable literary cafés and had a conversation with various writers about the plight of our beloved Spain. Amid the usual hubbub, everyone I spoke to declared (and here unanimity isn't suspect) that although my last book may not have sold as well as some of the others, it was one of the most read. That may be so. I don't concern myself with marketing. And yet, behind the curtain of praise, I glimpsed a shadow. I had the praise of my peers, and the youngest even saw me as a great man—and congratulated themselves for it—but behind the curtain of flattery I sensed the breath, the imminence, of something unknown. What was it? I didn't know. A month later, when I found myself in one of the departure lounges at the airport, about to take my leave for a few days from our rancorous Spain, three young men came up to me, tall, slender, and cerulean, and told me in no uncertain terms that my last book had changed their lives. Strange, although they were by no means the first to address me in such a manner. I proceeded on my journey. There was a layover in Rome. In the duty-free shop, an interesting-looking man kept staring at me. His name was Hermann Künst and he was an Austrian traveling on business (I didn't ask what he did) who had been captivated by my last book, which he must have read in Spanish, since as far as I know it hasn't yet been translated into German. He wanted my autograph. His kind words left me speechless. When I got to Nepal, a boy at the hotel who couldn't have been more than fifteen asked me whether I was Hernando García León. I said yes and was about to give him a tip when the lad declared himself a fervent admirer of my work and a little later, almost before I realized it, I found myself signing a worn copy of *Between Bulls and Angels*, in the eighth Spanish printing, to be precise, dated 1986. Regrettably, a mishap occurred just then that has no place in this story but that prevented me from questioning the young reader about the turns or twists of fate that had caused my book to reach his hands. That night I dreamed about Saint John the Baptist. The headless figure drew near the hotel bed and said: go to Nepal, Hernando, and a magnificent book will open its pages to you. But I'm already in Nepal, I replied in the half speech of the sleeping. But Saint John repeated: go to Nepal, Hernando, etc., etc., as if he were my literary agent. The next morning I forgot the dream. On a trip into the mountains of Kathmandu, I ran unexpectedly into a group of tourists from our beleaguered Spain. I was recognized (I was alone, needless to say, meditating behind a rock) and subjected to the usual question-and-answer session, as if we were on a television show. My fellow countrymen's thirst for knowledge is great, obsessive, unquenchable. I signed two books. That night, back at the hotel, I had another dream about Saint John the Baptist, except this time, in a notable variation, he was accompanied by a shadow, a shrouded being who remained at a distance as the headless figure spoke. His message was essentially the same as it had been the night before. He urged me to visit Nepal and promised me the sweet reward of a magnificent book, worthy of the boldest scribe. These dreams recurred night after night for nearly as long as I stayed in the East. I returned to Madrid and after subjecting myself reluctantly to the obligatory interviews, I removed myself to Orejuela de Arganda, a village in the mountains, with the firm intention of embarking on a creative project. I dreamed again of Saint John the Baptist. Hernando, my man, this is too much, I said to myself in the middle of the dream, and with a mental effort that only those who have honed their nerves in the most adverse circumstances can muster, I managed to wake up abruptly. The room was submerged in the fertile silence of the Castilian night. I opened the windows and breathed the pure mountain air, with no nostalgia for that distant past when I smoked two packs a day, although for a tiny fraction of a second I thought to myself that I wouldn't have minded a cigarette. Like a man with no time to lose, I spent my hours of wakefulness sorting through papers, finishing letters, preparing drafts of articles and lectures, the scut work of a successful author, something that those envious, resentful types who don't sell more than a thousand copies of a book will never understand. Then I went back to bed and fell asleep instantly, as usual. Out of a blackness like something painted by Zurbarán, Saint John the Baptist appeared again and fixed me with his gaze. He nodded, and then he said: I'm going now, Hernando, but you won't be left alone. I watched as the landscape brightened little by little, as if a breeze or angelic breath were dissolving the fog and gloom, while still preserving, shall we say, dawn's proper mourning attire. In the background, beside a rocky outcropping some ten feet from my bed, the veiled shadow waited patiently. Who are you? I said. My voice was trembling. I'm about to cry, I thought, overcome with emotion in the midst of my slumbers and on such a somber morning. And yet, steeling myself, I managed to repeat the question: who are you? Then the shadow quivered or shook off the morning dew with an economical movement of its body, or it was simply that my staring eyes made me perceive as a quiver something that wasn't, and after the quiver it began to walk toward my bed on feet that seemed not to touch the ground, and yet I could hear the sound of the stones, the singing of the stones as they rejoiced to feel the soles of those feet on their spines, a rustle and a tinkling all at once, a murmur and a whisper, as if the stones were the grass of the fields and the feet were air or water, and then, with an enormous effort, I raised myself from the bed, and, leaning on an elbow, asked who are you, shadow, what do you want from me, what's hidden under that shawl? and the shadow kept advancing over the field of stones and ash-gray pebbles until it reached my bed, and then it halted and the stones stopped singing or sighing or cooing, and an enormous silence fell over my room and the valley and the mountainside, and I closed my eyes and said to myself courage, Hernando, you've had worse dreams, and I opened my eyes again. And then the shadow removed its shawl or maybe it was only a scarf and there before me stood the Virgin Mary and her light wasn't blinding, as my friend Patricia Fernández-García Errázuriz says, having had various experiences of this kind, but a light pleasing to the eye, a light in harmony with the morning light. And before I was struck dumb I said: what do you wish from your humble servant, Lady? And she said: Hernando, my son, I want you to write a book. The rest of our conversation I can't reveal. But I wrote. I set myself to the task, prepared to sweat blood, and after three months I had three hundred and fifty manuscript pages that I deposited on my editor's desk. The title: *The New Age and the Iberian Ladder*. Today, they tell me, it's sold more than a thousand copies. I haven't signed them all, of course, because I'm not Superman. Everything that begins as comedy inevitably ends as mystery.

**Pelayo Barrendoaín, Feria del Libro, Madrid, July 1994.** First: here I am, doped, the antidepressants coming out of my ears, walking around this feria that's supposedly so nice, where Hernando García León has all kinds of readers, and Baca, the diametrical opposite of García León but just as revered, has all kinds of readers, and even my old friend Pere Ordóñez has some readers, and even I, why beat around the bush, why not just say so, even I have my share of readers too, the burnouts, the whipped, the people with little lithium bombs in their heads, rivers of Prozac, lakes of Epaminol, dead seas of Rohypnol, stoppered wells of Tranquimazín, my brothers and sisters, those who feed on my madness to nourish their madness. And here I am with my nurse, although instead of a nurse she might be a social worker, a special education teacher, maybe even a lawyer. In any case here I am with a woman who seems to be my nurse, or at least one might draw that conclusion seeing how quick she is to offer me the miracle pills, the bombs that go off in my brain and stop me from doing anything crazy. She walks beside me and her graceful shadow brushes my spreading, heavy shadow when I turn. My shadow seems ashamed to flow beside her shadow, but look again and you see it's perfectly happy that way. My shadow, the Yogi Bear of the third millennium, and her shadow, disciple of Hypatia. And it's precisely then that I'm happy to be here, more than anything because my nurse likes to see so many books all together and likes to walk alongside the most famous madman of so-called Spanish poetry or so-called Spanish literature. And that's when I realize I'm laughing mysteriously or singing mysteriously under my breath and she asks me why I'm laughing or why I'm singing and I tell her I'm laughing because the whole thing seems ludicrous to me, because Hernando García León pretending to be Saint John the Baptist or Saint Ignatius Loyola or the sainted Escrivá is ridiculous, and because the great struggle of all these writers for recognition and readers, hunkered down in their respective asbestos booths, is ludicrous. And she looks at me and asks why I'm singing. And I tell her it's my poems, that my singing is poems I'm thinking up or trying to memorize. And then my nurse smiles and nods, satisfied with my answers, and it's at times like this, when the crowd is enormous and the crush begins to seem faintly menacing (we're near Aurelio Baca's booth, she tells me), that her hand seeks and easily finds my hand, and hand in hand we slowly traverse the patches of blazing sun and icy shade, her shadow dragging my shadow after it but especially her body dragging my body. And although what I told her isn't true (I smile to keep from howling, I sing so I won't pray or curse), my explanation is more than good enough for my nurse, which doesn't say much for her skills as a psychologist but says plenty for her zest for life, her yearning to enjoy the sun shining on Retiro Park, her irrepressible desire to be happy. And that's when I think about things that from a certain perspective might not seem very poetic, like unemployment (my nurse has just been rescued from unemployment, thanks to me being crazy), and also the lost time rising before my eyes like a single red balloon that floats up and up until it makes me cry, Daedalus mourning the fate of Icarus, Daedalus doomed, and then I come back down to planet Earth, to the Feria del Libro, and try to give her a half smile, just for her, but she's not the one who sees, it's my readers, the whipped, the massacred, the madmen who feed on my madness and who'll end up doing away with me or my infinite patience, it's my critics who see me, those who want to have their pictures taken with me but wouldn't be able to stand my presence for more than eight hours straight, it's the writer–television hosts, those who love how crazy Barrendoaín is and at the same time gravely shake their heads. She doesn't see, she never sees, the fool, the idiot, the innocent, this woman who's come too late, who's interested in literature with no idea of the hells lurking beneath the tainted or pristine pages, who loves flowers and doesn't realize there's a monster in the bottom of the vase, who strolls around the Feria del Libro and drags me around behind her, who smiles at the photographers when they point their cameras at me, who drags my shadow along, and her shadow too, the ignorant, the dispossessed, the disinherited, who will outlive me and is my only consolation. Everything that begins as comedy ends as a dirge in the void.


**Felipe Müller, Bar Céntrico, Calle Tallers, Barcelona, September 1995.** This is an airport story. Arturo told it to me in the Barcelona airport. It's the story of two writers. Nebulous, in the end. Stories told in airports are soon forgotten, unless they're love stories, and this one isn't. I think we'd met the writers. At least he had. In Barcelona, Paris, Mexico? That I don't know. One of the writers was from Peru, the other was Cuban, although I'm not one hundred percent sure of that either. When he told me the story, Arturo not only knew where they were from, he also told me their names. But I wasn't paying much attention. I think, at least I'd guess, that they were of our generation, which means they were born in the 1950s. Their fates, according to Arturo, and this I do remember clearly, were instructive. The Peruvian was a Marxist, or at least his reading followed those lines: he was acquainted with Gramsci, Lukacs, Althusser. But he had also read Hegel, Kant, some of the Greeks. The Cuban was a happy storyteller. That should be capitalized: a Happy Storyteller. Instead of theory, he read novelists, poets, short story writers. Both of them, the Peruvian and the Cuban, were born into poor families, working-class in the one case, peasants in the other. Both grew up happy, with a talent for happiness. Each had the will to be happy. Arturo said that they must both have been beautiful children. Well, I think all children are beautiful. They discovered their literary callings early on, of course: the Peruvian wrote poems and the Cuban wrote stories. Both believed in the revolution and freedom, like pretty much every Latin American writer born in the fifties. Then they grew up and experienced the full flush of success: their books were published, all the critics unanimously praised them, they were hailed as the continent's top young writers, one in poetry and the other in fiction, and although it was never spoken everyone began to await their definitive works. But then the same thing happened to them that almost always happens to the best Latin American writers or the best of the writers born in the fifties: the trinity of youth, love, and death was revealed to them, like an epiphany. How did this vision affect their works? At first, in a scarcely perceptible way: as if a sheet of glass lying on top of another sheet of glass were shifted slightly.

Only a few friends noticed. Then, inescapably, they headed for catastrophe or the abyss. The Peruvian received a grant and left Lima. For a while he traveled through Latin America, but he soon set off for Barcelona and then Paris. Arturo met him in Mexico, I think, but it was in Barcelona that they became close. In those days everything seemed to point to a meteoric career, and yet with very few exceptions, Spanish editors and writers showed no interest in his work. Who can say why? Then he left for Paris, where he made contact with a student group of Peruvian Maoists. According to Arturo, the Peruvian had always been a Maoist, a playful and irresponsible Maoist, a salon Maoist, but in Paris he let himself be convinced, one way or another, that he was the reincarnation of Mariátegui, the hammer or the anvil, I don't remember which, scourge of the paper tigers roaming in Latin America. Why did Belano think it was all just a game for his Peruvian friend? Well, he had reason enough: one day the Peruvian might write pages of revolting propaganda and the next day an almost illegible essay on Octavio Paz full of flattery and praise of the Mexican poet. For a Maoist, that showed a certain lack of seriousness. It wasn't consistent. Actually, the Peruvian had always been hopeless as an essayist, it didn't matter if he was playing spokesman of the dispossessed or extolling Paz's poetry. And yet he was still a good poet, occasionally very good. Daring, innovative. One day, the Peruvian decided to return to Peru. Maybe he thought the moment had come for the new Mariátegui to return to his native soil, or maybe he just wanted to use what was left of his grant to live somewhere cheaper and set to work on his new projects without interruption. But he was unlucky. He had hardly set foot in the Lima airport when the Shining Path rose up as if it had been waiting for him. Here, suddenly, was a force to be reckoned with, a force that threatened to spread all over Peru. Clearly, the Peruvian couldn't retreat to a little town in the mountains to write. That was when everything started to go wrong. The bright hope of Peruvian letters disappeared and was replaced by someone who was increasingly afraid, increasingly unbalanced, someone who couldn't get over having traded Barcelona and Paris for Lima, where the only people who didn't despise his poetry loathed him as a revisionist or a traitorous dog, and where, in the eyes of the police, he had been one of the ideologues of the millenarian guerrilla movement (which, in a certain way, was true). In other words, the Peruvian suddenly found himself stranded in a country where he might just as easily be assassinated by the police as by the

Shining Path. Both groups had more than sufficient cause; both felt affronted by what he had written. From that moment on, everything he did to save himself brought him irrevocably closer to destruction. To make a long story short: the Peruvian came unglued. The former admirer of the Gang of Four and the Cultural Revolution was transformed into a believer in the theories of Madame Blavatsky. He returned to the Catholic church. He became a fervent follower of John Paul II and a bitter enemy of liberation theology. And yet the police refused to believe in this metamorphosis and he remained on file as a potential threat. His poet friends, on the other hand, those who expected something of him, did believe him and stopped speaking to him. It wasn't long before his wife left him too. But the Peruvian persisted in his madness and stood his ground, digging in his heels. He wasn't making any money, of course. He went to live with his father, who supported him. When his father died, his mother supported him. And of course, he never stopped writing or turning out huge, uneven books punctuated by occasional moments of brilliant, shaky humor. Years later, he would sometimes boast that he'd been chaste since 1985. Also: he lost any hint of shame, composure, or discretion. He went over the top (notably over the top, that is, since this is Latin American writers we're talking about) in his praise of others and he completely lost his sense of the ridiculous in complimenting himself. And yet, every once in a while he wrote beautiful poems. According to Arturo, the Peruvian believed that the two greatest American poets were Whitman and himself. A strange case. The Cuban was a different story. He was gay and the revolutionary authorities weren't prepared to tolerate homosexuals, so after a brief moment of glory during which he wrote two excellent novels (also brief), it wasn't long before he was dragged through the shit and madness that passes for a revolution. Gradually, they began to take away what little he had. He lost his job, no one would publish him, he was pressured to become a police informer, he was followed, his mail was intercepted, in the end they threw him in jail. It seems the revolutionaries had two aims: to cure the Cuban of his homosexuality and, once he was cured, to persuade him to work for his country. Both were a joke. The Cuban held out. Like all good (or bad) Latin Americans, he wasn't afraid of the police or poverty or not being published. He had countless adventures on the island. He survived it all and kept his wits about him. One day he escaped. He made it to the United States. His books began to be published. He started to work even harder

470

than before, if possible, but he and Miami weren't made for each other. He headed to New York. He had lovers. He got AIDS. In Cuba they went so far as to say: you see, if he'd stayed here, he wouldn't have died. For a while he was in Spain. His last days were hard: he wanted to finish the book he was writing and he could barely type. Still, he finished it. Sometimes he would sit at the window of his New York apartment and think about what he could have done and what, in the end, he did. His last days were days of loneliness, suffering, and rage at what he had lost forever. He didn't want to die in a hospital. That's what Arturo told me as we were waiting for the plane that would carry him away from Spain forever. The dream of Revolution, a hot nightmare. You and I are Chilean, I told him, and none of this is our fault. He looked at me and didn't answer. Then he laughed. He gave me a kiss on each cheek and left. Everything that begins as comedy ends as a comic monologue, but we aren't laughing anymore.

# 24

Clara Cabeza, Parque Hundido, Mexico City DF, October 1995. I was Octavio Paz's secretary. You can't imagine how much work it was. Writing letters, finding impossible-to-find manuscripts, calling contributors to the magazine, tracking down books that had ceased to exist outside of one or two North American universities. After two years of working for Don Octavio I had a chronic headache that set in around eleven in the morning and wouldn't go away until six in the evening, no matter how many aspirin I took. In general, I preferred the tasks that were most like housework, making breakfast or helping the maid with lunch. That was work I enjoyed, and it was also a rest for my tortured mind. I usually got to the house around seven in the morning, before the traffic got too bad, or at least before it was as terrible as at rush hour, and I would prepare coffee, tea, orange juice, two pieces of toast, a simple breakfast, and then take the tray into Don Octavio's bedroom and say Don Octavio, wake up, it's a new day. But Señora María José would be the first to open her eyes and she was always cheerful when she woke up, her voice coming out of the darkness and saying: leave breakfast on the bedside table, Clara, and I would say good morning, Señora, it's a new day. Then I would go back to the kitchen and make my own breakfast, something light like the señores' breakfast, coffee, orange juice, a piece of toast or two with jam, and then I would go into the library and get to work.

You don't know the stacks of letters Don Octavio received and how hard it was to file them. As you can imagine, people wrote to him from every corner of the globe, all kinds of people, from other Nobel laureates to young English or Italian or French poets. I'm not saying that Don Octavio answered every letter, he probably only answered fifteen or twenty percent of them, but the rest still had to be classified and filed, don't ask me why, I'd have been happy to throw them away. At least the filing system was simple: we sorted them by nationality, and when a writer's nationality wasn't clear (this was often the case with letters written in Spanish, English, or French), we sorted them by language. Sometimes, while I was going through the mail, I would start to think about the workdays of the secretaries of pop singers or rock stars, and I would wonder whether they had to deal with as many letters as I did. Maybe so, but I'm sure they didn't get letters in as many languages. Sometimes Don Octavio would even receive letters in Chinese, which says it all. When that happened, I had to put the letters aside in a separate little pile that we called *marginalia excentricorum*, which Don Octavio would go through once a week. Then, but this only happened very occasionally, he would say Clarita, take the car and go see my friend Nagahiro. All right, Don Octavio, I would say, but it wasn't as simple as he made it sound. First I would spend all morning calling this Nagahiro and when I reached him at last, I would say Don Nagahiro, I have a few little things for you to translate, and we would make a date for some day that week. Sometimes I would send the papers to him by mail or messenger, but when it was important, which I could tell by the expression on Don Octavio's face, I would go in person and not leave Señor Nagahiro's side until he had at least given me a brief summary of what the papers or letter said, a summary that I would take down in shorthand in my little notebook and then type out later, print, and leave on Don Octavio's desk, on the left side, so that if he wanted he could take a look at it and satisfy his curiosity.

And then there were the letters that Don Octavio sent. That really was exasperating work, because he would write quite a number each week, say sixteen more or less, to the unlikeliest places in the world, which was an astounding thing to see, because one had to ask how the man had made so many friends in so many different places, even mismatched places like Trieste and Sydney, Cordoba and Helsinki, Naples and Bocas del Toro (Panama), Limoges and New Delhi, Glasgow and Monterrey. And he had words of encouragement for everyone, or one of those thoughts that he would mutter to himself and that I suppose gave the recipient something to think about and mull over. It would be wrong to reveal what he said in his letters, so all I'll say is that he talked about more or less the same things he talks about in his essays and poems:

pretty things, somber things, and otherness, which is something I've thought about a lot, like many Mexican intellectuals, I suppose, and have never quite been able to figure out. Another thing I did, and willingly, was act as nurse, since I happened to have taken a few first aid courses. By then, Don Octavio wasn't what you might call healthy and he had to take pills every day, and since he always had other things on his mind, he would forget when he had to take them, and then it would all be a muddle, did I take this one at noon, didn't I take that one at eight this morning, anyway, a confusion that I'm proud to say I put an end to, since I even made sure he took what he was supposed to take when I wasn't there, like clockwork. In order to do that, I would call him from my apartment or wherever I happened to be and ask the maid: has Don Octavio taken his eight o'clock pills yet? and the maid would go and see, and if the pills that I'd left ready in a plastic container were still there, then I would tell her: give them to him and make him take them. Sometimes I would speak to the señora instead of the maid, but just the same, I'd say: has Don Octavio taken his medicine? and Señora María José would laugh and say oh Clarisa, she called me Clarisa sometimes, I don't know why, one of these days you'll make me jealous, and when Señora María José said that I would blush a little and somehow be afraid that she would see me blushing, can you imagine? as if she could see anything when we were talking on the phone! but I still kept calling and insisting that he take his pills on time, because otherwise how were they supposed to do him any good?

Another thing I did was keep Don Octavio's calendar, which was full of social engagements, everything from parties and conferences to invitations and art openings to birthday parties and the awarding of honorary doctorates. The truth is that if he'd gone to all of those events the poor man wouldn't have been able to write a single line of poetry, never mind his essays. So when I had prepared his calendar he and Señora María José would go over it with a fine-tooth comb and rule things out, and sometimes I would watch them from my little corner and say to myself: that's right, Don Octavio, punish them with your indifference.

And then came the era of Parque Hundido, a place that isn't one bit interesting, if you want my opinion. Maybe it used to be, but today it's become a jungle swarming with thieves, rapists, drunks, and disreputable women.

It happened like this. One morning, when I'd just gotten to the house and it wasn't even eight yet, I found Don Octavio up already, waiting for me in the kitchen. As soon as he saw me, he said: I'll trouble you to take me for a drive, Clarita, in your car. What do you think of that? As if I'd ever refused to do anything he asked me to do. So I said: just tell me where you'd like to go, Don Octavio. But he motioned to me without saying anything, and we went outside. He settled himself beside me in the car, which incidentally is only a Volkswagen, so it isn't very comfortable. When I saw him sitting there with that absent look of his, I felt a little sorry that I didn't have a better vehicle to offer him, although I didn't say anything because it also occurred to me that if I apologized he might take it as a kind of reproach, since after all he was the one who paid me and if I didn't have enough money for a better car a person could say it was his fault, which is something I'd never even have dreamed of suggesting. So I was quiet, concealing my thoughts as best I could, and I started the car. We took the first streets at random. Then we drove around Coyoacán, and finally turned up Insurgentes. When Parque Hundido appeared, he ordered me to park wherever I could. Then we got out of the car and after Don Octavio took a look around, he walked into the park, which at that time of day wasn't exactly crowded but wasn't empty either. This must bring back some memory for him, I thought. The farther we walked, the lonelier it became. I noticed that through carelessness or laziness or lack of funds or shameless irresponsibility, the park had been left in a shocking state of neglect. Once we were deep in the park we sat on a bench and Don Octavio looked up at the treetops or the sky and then he murmured some words that I didn't understand. Before we left I had grabbed the pills and a little bottle of water and since it was time for him to take them and we were sitting down now, I gave them to him. Don Octavio looked at me as if I'd gone mad but he swallowed the pills without complaint. Then he said: you stay here, Clarita, and he got up and went walking along a little dirt path scattered with pine needles, and I did as he said. It was nice to sit there, I have to admit. Sometimes, along other paths, I would see the figures of maids taking a shortcut or students who had decided not to go to class that morning. The air was breathable, the pollution wouldn't be so bad that day, and from time to time I think I even heard a bird chirp. Meanwhile, Don Octavio was walking. He walked in wider and wider circles and sometimes he would step off the path onto the grass, grass that was sickly from having been trampled so often and that the gardeners probably didn't even tend anymore.

It was then that I saw the man. He was walking in circles too and his steps took him along the same path, but in the opposite direction, so that he would have to pass Don Octavio. For me, it was as if an alarm had gone off in my chest. I got up and tensed all my muscles in case it would be necessary for me to intervene, since I happened to have taken a course in karate and judo a few years before with Doctor Ken Takeshi, whose real name was Jesús García Pedraza and who had been a member of the federal police. But it wasn't necessary: when the man passed Don Octavio he didn't even raise his head. So I stayed where I was and this is what I saw: Don Octavio, when he passed the man, stopped and stood still as if he were thinking, then he started to walk again, but this time he wasn't moving as aimlessly or as nonchalantly as he had been a few minutes before but rather seemed to be calculating the moment that the two trajectories, his and the stranger's, would cross again. And when the stranger passed Don Octavio once more, Don Octavio turned and stood there staring at him with real curiosity. The stranger looked at Don Octavio too, and I would say that he recognized him, which is hardly surprising, since everybody, and when I say everybody, I mean literally everybody, knows who he is. On our way home Don Octavio's mood had altered notably. His eyes were brighter and he was more energetic, as if the long morning walk had given him new strength. I remember that at some point during the trip he recited some very pretty lines of poetry in English and I asked him who the poet was and he said a name, it must have been the name of an English poet, I forget what it was, and then, as if to change the subject, he asked me why I'd been so nervous, and I remember that at first I didn't answer, maybe I just exclaimed oh, Don Octavio, and then I explained that Parque Hundido was hardly a peaceful spot, a place where one could walk and think without fear of being attacked by ruffians. And then Don Octavio looked at me and said in a voice that seemed to come straight from the heart of a wolf: no one attacks me, not even the president of the Republic. And he said it with such certainty that I believed him and thought it best not to say anything else.

The next day, Don Octavio was waiting for me when I got to the house. We left without speaking a word and I drove, silly me, toward

Coyoacán, but when Don Octavio noticed he told me to head for Parque Hundido without further delay. The story repeated itself. Don Octavio left me sitting on a bench and started to walk in circles in the same place he had the day before. Before that, I gave him his pills and he took them without a fuss. A little while later the other man showed up. When Don Octavio saw him he couldn't help looking at me from the distance as if to say: you see, Clarita, everything I do is for a reason. The stranger looked at me too and then he looked at Don Octavio and for a second it seemed to me that he wavered, his steps faltering and becoming more hesitant. But he didn't turn around, as I began to fear he might, and he and Don Octavio set off again and passed each other again and each time they passed each other they would raise their eyes from the ground and look each other in the face and I realized that at first both of them were wary of each other, but by the third time around they were immersed in their own thoughts and didn't even look at each other when they crossed paths. And I think it was then that it occurred to me that neither of the two was speaking, I mean, neither one was muttering *words*, but numbers, that the two of them were counting something, maybe not their steps, which is the only thing I can think of now that makes sense, but something like that, random numbers, possibly, adding or subtracting, multiplying or dividing. When we left, Don Octavio was tired. His eyes were shining, those beautiful eyes of his, but otherwise he looked as if he had just run a race. I confess that for a moment I was worried and I thought that if something happened to him it would be my fault. I imagined Don Octavio having a heart attack, I imagined him dead, and then I imagined all the Mexican writers who love him so much (especially the poets) surrounding me in the visitors' lounge at the hospital where Don Octavio has his checkups and asking me with frankly hostile stares what in the world I'd done to the only Mexican Nobel laureate, how Don Octavio could possibly have been expiring in Parque Hundido, such an unpoetic spot, and so far from my boss's urban haunts. And in my imagination I didn't know what answer to give them, except to tell them the truth, which at the same time I knew wasn't going to convince them, so why bother, better to say nothing, and that's what I was thinking, driving along the increasingly unbearable streets of Mexico City and imagining myself plunged into situations full of blame and recrimination, when I heard Don Octavio say let's go to the university, Clarita, there's something I need to ask a friend. And although at that moment Don Octavio looked the same as he always had, as in command of himself as ever, the truth is that I could no longer rid myself of a nagging worry, the weight of dark foreboding. Especially when at five that afternoon Don Octavio called me into his library and asked me to make a list of Mexican poets born since 1950, a request no stranger than many others, it's true, but highly disturbing given the matter we were involved in. I think Don Octavio realized how nervous I was, which wouldn't have been particularly difficult since my hands were shaking. I felt like a little bird in the middle of a storm. Half an hour later he called for me again and when I came he looked me in the eyes and asked me whether I trusted him. What a question, Don Octavio, I said, the things that occur to you. And he repeated the question, as if he hadn't heard me. Of course I do, I said, I trust you more than anyone. Then he said: not a word to a single person about anything I tell you here or what you've seen or what you'll see tomorrow. Agreed? I swear on my mother's grave, may she rest in peace, I said. And then he made a gesture as if he were shooing away flies and he said I know that boy. Really? I said. And he said: many years ago, Clarita, a group of radical leftist lunatics planned to kidnap me. I can't believe it, Don Octavio, I said and I started trembling all over again. Well, they did, he said, such are the vicissitudes of life as a public figure, Clarita, stop shaking, pour yourself a whiskey or whatever you like, but calm down. And that man is one of the terrorists? I said. I think so, he said. And what in the world did they want to kidnap you for, Don Octavio? I said. It's a mystery to me, he said, maybe they were offended because I didn't pay them any attention. It's possible, I said, people bear grudges for all kinds of silly reasons. But maybe that wasn't what it was about, maybe it was just a joke. A fine joke, I said. In any case, they never actually tried to kidnap me, he said, but they announced it with great fanfare, and so I got wind of it. And when you found out, what did you do? I said. Nothing, Clarita, I laughed a little and then I forgot about them forever, he said.

The next morning we returned to Parque Hundido. I'd had a bad night, unable to sleep, such a nervous wreck that even reading Amado Nervo couldn't soothe me (incidentally, I would never admit to Don Octavio that I'd been reading Amado Nervo, I'd mention Don Carlos Pellicer or Don José Gorostiza, and of course I have read them, but you tell me what point there is reading Pellicer or Gorostiza when you're trying to relax, or with luck even fall asleep, when really it's better not to read

478

anything at all, even Amado Nervo, it's better to watch television, the stupider the show, the better), and I had huge circles under my eyes that makeup couldn't hide and even my voice was a little hoarse, as if the night before I'd smoked a pack of cigarettes or had too much to drink. But Don Octavio didn't notice a thing and he got in the Volkswagen and we left for Parque Hundido, without speaking a word, as if we'd been doing it all our lives, which was exactly one of those things that drove me wild, that ability of human beings to adapt to anything, instantly. In other words: if I stopped and thought calmly, which was the proper thing to do, and said to myself that we'd only been to Parque Hundido twice, and this was the third time, well, I could hardly believe it, because it really did seem as if we'd been there many times, and if I admitted that we'd only been there twice, then it was worse, because it made me want to scream or drive my Volkswagen into a wall, so I had to get control of myself and concentrate on the steering wheel and not think about Parque Hundido or the stranger who visited it when we did. In short, not only was I haggard that morning, with circles under my eyes, I was irrationally upset. And yet what happened that morning was very different from what I'd expected.

We got to Parque Hundido. That much is clear. We walked into the park and sat on the same bench as always, under the shelter of a big, leafy tree, although I suppose it was as sick as all the trees in Mexico City. And then, instead of leaving me alone on the bench as he had before, Don Octavio asked me whether I'd completed the task he'd given me yesterday, and I said yes, Don Octavio, I made a list of lots of names, and he smiled and asked whether I'd memorized the names and I looked at him as if to ask whether he was serious and took the list out of my bag and showed it to him and he said: Clarita, find out who that boy is. That was all he said. And I got up like an idiot and went to wait for the stranger, and to pass the time I started to walk until I realized that I was following the same path Don Octavio had taken on the two previous days and then I stopped walking, not daring to look at him, my gaze fixed on the spot where the stranger whose identity I was supposed to discover should appear. And the stranger appeared, at the same time as he had twice before, and he started to walk. And then, not wanting to prolong matters any further, I went up to him and asked him who he was and he said I'm Ulises Lima, the visceral realist poet, none other than the second-to-last visceral realist poet left in Mexico, and to be honest, what can I say, his name didn't ring any bells, although the night before, on Don Octavio's orders, I'd gone through the indexes of more than ten anthologies of recent and not so recent poetry, among them the famous Zarco anthology that catalogs more than five hundred young poets. But his name didn't ring any bells. And then I said: do you know who that gentleman is sitting over there? And he said: yes, I know. And I said (I had to be sure): who is he? And he said: it's Octavio Paz. And I said: do you want to come sit with him for a while? And he shrugged his shoulders or made a similar gesture that I interpreted as a yes and both of us went walking toward the bench from which Don Octavio was following our every move with great interest. When I reached him I thought that it wouldn't hurt to make a formal introduction, so I said: Don Octavio Paz, the visceral realist poet Ulises Lima. And then Don Octavio, as he motioned for Lima to take a seat, said: visceral realist, visceral realist (as if the name was familiar to him), wasn't that Cesárea Tinajero's circle? And Lima sat down beside Don Octavio and sighed or made a strange noise with his lungs and said yes, that was what Cesárea Tinajero's circle was called. For a minute or so they were silent, looking at each other. An excruciating minute, to be honest. In the distance, past some bushes, I saw two bums. I think I got a little nervous, which foolishly led me to ask Don Octavio what the group was and whether he had known them. I might just as well have remarked on the weather. And then Don Octavio looked at me with those pretty eyes of his and said Clarita, back in the days of the visceral realists I would hardly have been ten years old, this was around 1924, wasn't it? he said, addressing Lima. And Lima said yes, more or less, the 1920s, but he said it with such sadness in his voice, with such . . . emotion, or feeling, that I thought it was the saddest voice I would ever hear. I think I even felt ill. Don Octavio's eyes and the stranger's voice and the morning and Parque Hundido, such a seedy place, isn't it? so neglected, wounded me in the depths of my being, just how, I couldn't say. So I left them to talk in peace and moved several feet away, to the nearest bench, with the excuse that I had to look over the next day's schedule, and I brought along the list I'd made of the names of Mexican poets from recent generations and I went through it from beginning to end, and I can promise you that Ulises Lima was nowhere on it. How long did they talk? Not long. And yet from where I was sitting it was clear that it was a leisurely, calm, polite conversation. Then the poet Ulises Lima got up, shook Don Octavio's hand, and left. I watched him walk off toward one of the park exits. The bums I had seen in the shrubbery, three of them now, were moving toward us. Let's go, Clarita, I heard Don Octavio say.

The next day, as I expected, we didn't go to Parque Hundido. Don Octavio got up at ten and worked on an article to be published in the next issue of his magazine. There were moments when I felt like asking him more about our little three-day adventure, but something inside of me (my common sense, probably) made me give up that idea. Things had happened the way they'd happened and if I, who was the only witness, didn't know what had gone on, it was best that I not know. Approximately a week later, Don Octavio went away with the señora to give a series of lectures at an American university. I didn't go with them, of course. One morning, while he was away, I went to Parque Hundido with the hope or fear of seeing Ulises Lima appear again. The only difference this time was that I didn't sit in plain view of everyone but hid behind some bushes, though with a perfect view of the clearing where Don Octavio and the stranger had met for the first time. For the first few minutes of my wait, my heart raced. I was freezing cold, and yet when I touched my cheeks I had the feeling that my face was about to explode. Then came disappointment, and when I left the park at around ten, it could even be said that I felt happy. Don't ask me why, I couldn't tell you.

**María Teresa Solsona Ribot, Jordi's Gym, Calle Josep Tarradellas, Malgrat, Catalonia, December 1995.** It's a sad story, but when I think about it, it makes me laugh. I needed to rent a room in my apartment and he was the first person to show up, and although I don't entirely trust South Americans, he seemed like a good guy and I said he could have it. He paid me two months in advance and went into his room and closed the door. Back then I was in every championship and demonstration in Catalonia and I also had a job as a waitress at the pub La Sirena, which is in the touristy part of Malgrat, by the sea. When I asked him what he did, he told me he was a writer, and I don't know why but I got the idea that he must work at some newspaper, and back then I had what you might call a special weakness for reporters. So I decided to be on my best behavior, and the first night he spent at my place I went to his room, knocked on the door, and invited him to have dinner with me and Pepe at a Pakistani bar. Pepe and I weren't going to eat anything at the bar, of course, a salad, maybe, but we were friends of the owner, Mr. John, and that lends a certain cachet.

That night I found out that he didn't work for any newspaper but wrote novels. That got Pepe excited, because Pepe is a mystery novel fanatic and they had plenty to talk about. Meanwhile, I picked at my salad and watched him, sizing him up as he talked or listened to Pepe. He ate well and he was polite, to start with. Then, the more you watched him, other things began to appear, things that slipped away like those fish that come close to the shore when the water is shallow and you see dark things (darker than the water) moving very quickly past your legs.

The next day Pepe went back to Barcelona to compete in Mister Olympia Catalan and didn't come back. That same morning, very early, the writer and I met in the living room while I was doing my exercises. I do them every day. First thing in the morning in high season, because I have less time then and I have to make the most of the day. So there I was, in the living room, doing push-ups on the floor, and he comes in and says good morning, Teresa, and then he goes into the bathroom, I think I didn't even answer him or maybe I grunted, I'm not used to being interrupted, and then I heard his footsteps again, the bathroom or kitchen door closing, and a little later I heard him asking me whether I'd like a cup of tea. I said I would and for a while we stared at each other. I think he'd never seen a woman like me. Do you want to exercise a little? I said. I said it just for the sake of saying something, of course. He didn't look well and he was already smoking. As I expected, he said no. People only take an interest in their health when they end up in the hospital. He left a cup of tea on the table and shut himself in his room. A little later I heard the sound of his typewriter. That was the last we saw of each other that day. The next morning, however, he appeared in the living room again at six in the morning and offered to make me breakfast. I don't eat or drink anything at that time of day, but it made me feel sort of, I don't know, bad to say no, so I let him make me another cup of tea, and I told him that while he was at it he could look in the cupboard for some jars of Amino Ultra and Burner that I should have had the night before but had forgotten about. What, I said, haven't you ever seen a chick like me? No, he said, never. He was pretty honest, but it was the kind of honesty that makes you not know whether to feel offended or flattered.

That afternoon, when my shift was over, I went to get him and said we should go out. He said that he would rather stay home and work. I'll buy you a drink, I said. He thanked me and said no. The next morning we had breakfast together. I was doing my exercises and wondering to myself where he was because it was already seven forty-five and he still hadn't come out. When I start to do my exercises I usually let my mind wander. At first I think about something specific, like my job or my competitions, but then my head starts to do its own thing and I might start thinking about where I'll be a year from now or I might just as easily end up thinking about my childhood. That morning I was thinking about Manoli Salabert, who won whatever there was to win wherever she went, and I was wondering how she did it, when suddenly I heard his door open and a little later I heard his voice asking me whether I wanted tea. Of course I want tea, I said. When he brought it I got up and sat at the table with him. That time we spent maybe two hours talking, until nine-thirty, when I had to leave in a hurry for the pub, because the manager, who's a friend of mine, had asked me to settle something with the cleaning lady. We talked about all kinds of things. I asked him what he was writing. He said a book. I asked him whether it was a romance. He didn't know what to answer. I asked him again and he said he didn't know. Man, I said, if you don't know, who the fuck will? Or maybe it wasn't until later that night that I said that, when we had gotten a little more relaxed around each other. Anyway, love was a subject I enjoyed and we talked about that till I had to leave. I said I could tell him a thing or two about love. That I'd been involved with this guy Nani, the top bodybuilder in Gerona, and that after that experience I felt qualified to teach a course. He asked me how long it had been since we broke up. About four months, I said. Did he leave you? he said. Yes, I admitted, he left me. But now you're going out with Pepe, he said. I explained that Pepe was a good person, a sweetheart, he wouldn't hurt a fly. But it isn't the same, I said. Arturo had a habit that I'm not sure whether to call good or bad. He would listen and not take sides. I like it when people express their opinions, even if I don't agree with them. One afternoon I invited him to come to La Sirena. He said he didn't drink and so he felt sort of dumb hanging out in a pub. I'll make you an herbal tea, I said. He didn't come and I stopped inviting him. I'm outgoing and friendly, but I don't like to be a pest.

A while later he showed up at the pub, though, and I made him his chamomile tea myself. After that he came every day. Rosita, the other waitress, thought there was something going on between us. When she said that it made me laugh. I thought about it for a while and it made me laugh even more. How could there be anything between Arturo and me! But then, for no good reason, I thought about it again and I realized I *wanted* to be his girlfriend. Until then I'd only dealt with two South Americans, both basically assholes, and I didn't have any desire to go through that again. And I'd never known any novelists. Here was this guy from South America and he was a writer and suddenly I wanted to be his girlfriend. Anyway, it's better to share an apartment with a boyfriend than a stranger. But it wasn't just practical reasons that made me want to be his girlfriend. It was how I felt, I didn't ask myself why. He needed someone too, I could see that right away. One morning I asked him to tell me something about himself. I was always the one who talked. That time he didn't tell me anything, but he said I could ask him whatever I wanted. I found out that he'd been living near Malgrat and that he'd recently given up his place. He didn't say why. I found out he was divorced and had a son. His son lived in Arenys de Mar. Once a week, on Saturdays, he would go see him. Sometimes we took the train together. I would go into Barcelona, to see Pepe or my friends at Muscle Gym, and he would go to Arenys to see his son. One night, as he was having his chamomile tea at La Sirena, I asked him how old he was. Over forty, he said, but he didn't look it. I would have guessed thirty-five at most, which is what I said. After that, even though he hadn't asked, I told him how old I was. Thirty-five. Then he smiled at me. I didn't like that smile at all. He smiled at me like someone with a kind of complex, or someone who doesn't give a shit. Anyway, it was a smile I didn't like. I'm basically a fighter. I try to stay positive. Things don't *have* to be bad or inevitable. That night, after that smile, I don't know why but I said that I didn't have kids even though I would've loved to have them, and that I had never been married either, and I didn't have much money, which was obvious, but that I thought life could be a pretty thing, a beautiful thing, and a person had to try to live a happy life. I don't know why I said all that corny stuff. I regretted it immediately. Naturally, all he said was of course, of course, like he was talking to a moron. Still, we talked. More and more. In the mornings, over breakfast, and at night, when he came to La Sirena, once he finished his workday. Or took a break, because I guess writers are always working: I remember hearing the sound of his typewriter at four in the morning in my sleep. And we talked about everything. Once, while he was watching me lift weights, he asked me why I'd gotten into bodybuilding. Because I like it, I answered. Since when? he said. Since I was fifteen, I said. Do you think there's something wrong with it? Does it seem unfeminine to you? Does it seem weird? No, he said, but there aren't many girls like you. I tell you, sometimes he drove me crazy. I should have answered that I was a woman, not a girl, but instead I told him there were more and more women doing what I did. Then, I don't know why, I told him about the time two summers ago that Pepe suggested that we perform in Gramanet, at a club in Gramanet. They gave us all stage names. They called me Lady Samson. I had to strike poses on the go-go girls' platform and also lift weights. That was all. But I didn't like the name. I'm no Lady Samson, I'm Teresa Solsona Ribot, period. But it was an opportunity, it paid all right, and Pepe said that some guy who scouted for models for the special-interest magazines might show up any night. In the end no one showed up, or if they did nobody told me. Still, it was a job, and I did it. What was it that you didn't like about the job? he asked me. Well, I answered, thinking about it for a while, what I didn't like was the stage name they gave me. It's not that I'm against stage names, but I think that if someone's going to take a different name she should have the right to choose it. I would never have called myself Lady Samson. I don't see myself as a Lady Samson. It's a cheap, sleazy name. Anyway, I wouldn't have chosen it. What name would you have chosen? Kim, I said. After Kim Basinger? he said. I knew he was going to say that. No, I said, after Kim Chizevsky. And who's Kim Chizevsky? A champion in the sport, I said.

Later on that night, I showed him a photo album I had with pictures in it of Kim Chizevsky and Lenda Murray, who's perfect, and Sue Price and Laura Creavalle and Debbie Muggli and Michele Ralabate and Natalia Murnikoviene, and then we went out walking around Malgrat. It was too bad we didn't have a car. If we did we could've gone someplace else, to some club in Lloret, for example, I know lots of people in Lloret. Well, I know lots of people everywhere. As I said before: I'm sociable, I'm a person who likes to be happy, and where do you find happiness if not in people? Anyway, that's how we became friends. Friends is the word for it. We respected each other and we had our own lives, but we talked more every day. What I mean is, it became a habit for us to talk. I was usually the one who started it, I don't know why, maybe because he was a writer. And then, democratically, he would follow. I found out a lot about his life. His wife had left him, he adored his son, at one time he'd had lots of friends but now he had hardly any. One night he told me that he'd been involved with a girl in Andalusia. I listened patiently and then I told him that life was long and there were many women in the world. That was where we had our first important difference of opinion. He said no, that for him there weren't lots, and then he quoted a poem that I begged him to write down on a page in my order pad so I could learn it by heart. The poem was by some French guy. It said more or less that the flesh was sad and that he, the poet who was writing the poem, had already read all the books. I don't know what to think, I said to him, I haven't read much, but it still seems impossible to me that anyone, no matter how much he read, could've read every book in the world. There must be so many of them, and I don't mean every single book, good and bad, just the good ones. There must be stacks of them! Enough so you could spend twenty-four hours a day reading! And that's not to mention the bad ones, since there must be more bad ones than good ones, and at least a few of those, like anything, must be good and worth reading. And then we started to talk about this "sad flesh." What did he mean by that? That he'd already fucked all the women in the world? That just like he'd read every book in the world he'd slept with every woman? I'm sorry, Arturo, I said, but that poem is total bullshit. Neither of those things is possible. And he started to laugh, you could see he thought it was funny to talk to me, and he said that it *was* possible. No it isn't, I said, the person who wrote that is full of shit. He probably hardly slept with anybody, I can tell you that for a fact. And I'm sure he didn't read all those books he bragged about reading either. There were a few more things I would've liked to say, but it was hard to keep up the conversation because I was always having to come out from behind the bar to wait on people. Arturo was sitting on a stool and when I came out I would look at his back or neck, poor thing, or I would search for his face in the mirror behind the shelves holding the bottles. And then I finished my shift. That night I got off at three in the morning, and we went walking home. At some point I suggested that we go to an after-hours club on the coast road, but he said that he was tired, so we went home, and as we walked I asked him, as if I had accepted his argument, what a person was supposed to do after reading everything and sleeping with everyone, according to the French poet, of course, and he said travel, go away, and I said well, as far as traveling is concerned, you never even go as far as Pineda, and he didn't say anything back.

Strangely enough, after that night I couldn't forget the poem. I won't say I thought about it constantly, but I thought about it a lot. I still thought it was bullshit, but I couldn't get it out of my head. One night when Arturo didn't come to La Sirena I went to Barcelona. Sometimes I get like that: I can't help myself. I came back the next day at ten in the morning, in terrible shape. When I got home he was in his room with the door shut. I got in bed and went to sleep listening to the sound of his typewriter. At noon he knocked on my door and when I didn't answer he came in and asked me whether I was all right. Aren't you going to work today? he said. Fuck work. I'll make you some tea, he said. Before he brought it to me I got up, got dressed, put on sunglasses, and went to sit in the living room. I thought I was going to throw up, but I didn't. I had a bruise on my cheek that there was no way to hide and I was waiting for him to ask me about it. But he didn't ask me anything. It was a miracle I didn't get fired from La Sirena that time. That night I wanted to go out for drinks with some friends and Arturo came too. We were at a pub on the Paseo Marítimo and then I met some other friends and we partied some more in Blanes and Lloret. At some point during the night I told Arturo to stop fooling around and devote himself to the things he really loved, which were his son and his novels. If that's what you care about most, devote yourself to them, I said. He both liked and didn't like to talk about his son. He showed me a picture of the kid, who must have been about five and looked just like his father. You're such a lucky bastard, I said. Yes, I'm very lucky, he said. Then why leave, you dumbass? Why risk your health, when you know it isn't good? Why don't you settle down and work and be happy with your son and find yourself a woman who'll really love you? It's a funny thing: he wasn't drunk, but he was acting like he was. He said other people's drunkenness had a psychological effect on him. Or maybe I was so drunk that I couldn't tell the difference between someone who was drunk and someone who wasn't.

Did you used to get drunk? I asked him one morning. Of course I did, he said, like everybody else, although usually I preferred being sober. I could have guessed that, I said.

One night I got in a fight with a guy who came on to me. It was at La Sirena. The guy was rude and I asked him whether he wanted to come outside and repeat what he'd said. I didn't notice that there were people

487

with him. The guy followed me out and I got him in an armlock and threw him. His friends came after me, but my manager and Arturo talked them out of it. Until then I hadn't been noticing anything, but when I saw Arturo and my manager, I don't know what it was but I felt free, that was the main thing, and I also felt loved, embraced, protected, I felt like I was a worthwhile person and that made me happy. And then Pepe just happened to show up a little later that same night, and by five in the morning we were making love, and that really was the best. Total happiness. While we were in bed, I closed my eyes and thought about everything that had happened that night, all the violent things and then all the nice things and how the nice things had overcome the violent things, and without having to get too violent, the nice things, I mean, and I was thinking about all of that and whispering other things in Pepe's ear, and suddenly, bam, I started to think about Arturo, I *heard* the sound of his typewriter and instead of including that image, instead of saying to myself "Arturo is fine too," instead of saying to myself "we're all fine, the world's still turning," instead of that, as I was saying, I started to think about my roommate and his state of mind and I made a decision that I would help him. And the next morning, as Pepe and I were doing stretches and Arturo was watching us, sitting in the same place he always sat, I went on the attack. I don't know what I said to him. Maybe that he should take the day off, since he was his own boss, and go spend the day with his son. And if I said that I must have been so insistent that in the end Arturo let himself be convinced and Pepe said Arturo could come with him, that he'd give him a ride to Arenys.

That night Arturo didn't show up at La Sirena.

I was on my way home at three in the morning when I ran into him at one of the public phones on the Paseo Marítimo. I spotted him from a distance. A group of drunk tourists were hanging around the phone next to his, which didn't seem to be working. A car was parked at the curb, with the doors open and the music cranked up all the way. As I came closer (I was with Cristina), I got a better look at Arturo. Long before I could see his face (he was standing with his back to me, wedged into the booth) I knew that he was crying or about to cry. Could he possibly have gotten drunk? Could he be high? That's what I was wondering as I hurried toward him, ahead of Cristina. For a second, when I got to where he was and the tourists were giving me weird looks, I thought maybe it wasn't him after all. He was wearing a Hawaiian shirt I'd never seen before. I touched him on the shoulder. Arturo, I said, I thought you must be staying in Arenys tonight. He turned around and said hello. Then he hung up the phone and started to talk to me and Cristina, who'd caught up with me by now. I noticed that he had forgotten to take his change out of the slot. It was more than fifteen hundred pesetas. That night, when we were alone, I asked him how things had gone in Arenys. He said fine. His wife was living with a Basque guy and seemed happy, and his son was fine. So what else? I said. That's all, he said. So who were you calling? Arturo looked at me and smiled. That fucking Andalusian? I said. That bitch who's brainwashed you? Yes, he said. And did you talk to her? Only for a little while, he said, the English guys wouldn't shut up and it was annoying. So if you weren't talking to her anymore what the hell were you doing there, hanging on to the phone? I said. He shrugged his shoulders. He thought about it for a second, then he said he was getting ready to call her again. Call her from here, I said. No, he said, my calls are long and then you'll have a big phone bill. You pay your part and I'll pay mine, I told him gently. No, he said. By the time the bill comes I'll be in Africa. My God, you're such an idiot, I said, go on, just call, I'm going to take a bath, let me know when you're done.

I remember that I took a shower, then I put lotion on all over and I even had time to do a few exercises in front of the steamed-up bathroom mirror. When I came out Arturo was sitting at the table with chamomile tea and a cup of tea with milk for me, covered with a saucer so it wouldn't get cold. Did you call her? Yes, he said. And what happened? She hung up on me, he said. Her loss, I said. He snorted. To change the subject I asked him how his book was going. Fine, he said. Can I see it? Can I go in your room and look at it? He looked at me and said yes. His room wasn't clean, but it wasn't filthy either. Unmade bed, clothes on the floor, a few books scattered around. More or less like mine. He'd set up his typewriter next to the window, on a little table. I sat down and started to look through his papers. I didn't understand any of what he'd written, of course, but I wasn't expecting to. I know the secret of life isn't in books. But I also know that it's good to read, that it can be instructive, or relaxing: we agree about that. He read books, I read magazines like *Muscle* or *Muscle & Fitness* or *Bodyfitness*. Then we started to talk about his great love. That's what I called her, to make fun of him, your great love, a girl he'd known a long time ago, when she was eighteen, and who he'd seen again not long ago. His trips back to Catalonia had always been disastrous. The first time, he said, the train almost went off the tracks. The second time he came back sick with a temperature of a hundred and four, huddled sweating on the bunk, wrapped in blankets and his coat. And this girl let you get on the train knowing you were that sick? I said as I looked at his things, he really had so few things. She doesn't love you, Arturo, I thought. Forget her, I said. I had to leave, he said, I had to come see my son. I'd like to meet him, I said. I've already shown you his picture, he said. I just don't understand it, I said. What don't you understand? he said. I never would've let a sick friend get on a train with a temperature of a hundred and four, even if I didn't love him anymore, even if I wasn't in love with him, I said. First, I would've taken care of him and made sure he got better, at least a little bit better, and then I would've let him go. Sometimes I feel so guilty, I thought, but the strangest thing is I don't know why, I don't know what I've done wrong to make me feel that way. You're a good person, he said. So you like bad people? I said. The first time she was afraid to come and live with me, he said, she was only eighteen. Stop right there, I said, or you're going to piss me off. That girl is a coward, I thought, and you're an idiot. There's nothing left for me here, he said. Why are you being so melodramatic? I loved her, he said. Stop! I said, I can't keep listening to this ridiculousness. That night we talked some more about the fucking Andalusian and Arturo's son. Do you need money? I said. Are you leaving because you don't have money? Because you aren't making enough? I'll lend you money. Don't pay me this month's rent. Or next month's. Don't pay me until you have more than enough. Do you have money for medicine? Have you been going to the doctor? Do you have money to buy your son toys? I can give you a loan. I have a friend who works at a toy store. I have a friend who's an aide at an outpatient clinic. There's a solution for everything.

The next morning he told me the story of the Andalusian all over again. It looked like he hadn't slept. It's the last time I'll be with anyone, he said. Why should it be the last time? I said. Are you dead, or what? Arturo, sometimes you drive me up the wall.

The story of the Andalusian girl was very simple. He met her when she was eighteen. That much I already knew. Then she broke up with him, but in a letter, and he had a funny feeling, as if the relationship had never really ended. Every once in a while she would call him. The years went by. They had their own lives, they got by as best they could. Arturo

490

met another woman, he fell in love, got married, had a child, was separated. Then he got sick. He almost died: he had some kind of problem with his pancreas, his liver was a wreck, he had an ulcerated colon. One day he called the girl. It had been a long time since they talked, and that day, maybe because he was in bad shape and felt sad, he called her. Years had gone by and the girl wasn't at the number he had anymore, so he had to track her down. It didn't take him long to find her new number and he reached her. The bitch was in more or less the same shape he was in, if that. They were in touch again. It was as if no time had passed. Arturo went south. He was still recovering, but he decided to go and see her. She was in an essentially similar situation. There was nothing physically wrong with her, but when Arturo got there she was in bed because her head was a mess. According to the girl, she was going crazy: she saw rats, she heard rats scratching around in the walls of her room, she had horrible dreams and she couldn't sleep, she hated going out. She was separated too. Her marriage had been a disaster too, and so had her lovers. They managed to stand each other for a week. It was that time, on Arturo's way back to Catalonia, that the Talgo almost went off the rails. According to Arturo, the engineer stopped in the middle of nowhere and the ticket takers got off the train and walked along the tracks until they found a loose plate, a piece on the bottom of the train that was coming off. I frankly don't understand how they didn't notice it before. Either Arturo didn't explain it very well or all the workers on that train were drunk. The only passenger who got off the train and walked along the tracks, according to Arturo, was Arturo himself. Maybe it was at that moment, as the ticket inspectors were looking for the plate or sheet coming loose from the underside of the train, that he started to go crazy and think about escape. But the worst came later: after five days in Catalonia, Arturo began to think about going back, or realize that he had no choice but to go back. During that time he talked to the Andalusian girl at least once a day and sometimes as often as seven times. Usually, they argued. Other times they talked about how much they missed each other. He spent a fortune on phone calls. Finally, before even a week had gone by, he got on another train and went back. No matter how much Arturo tried to sugarcoat it, this last trip was just as disastrous as the first, if not worse. The only thing he was sure about was that he loved the fucking Andalusian. Then he got sick and came back to Catalonia or the Andalusian girl kicked him out or he couldn't take it anymore and decided to come back or whatever it was, but the bottom line is, he was sick and the girl let him get on the train with a temperature of a hundred and four, something I would never have done to my worst enemy, Arturo, I said, even if I don't have any enemies. And he said: we had to get away from each other, we were devouring each other. Don't give me that, I said. That girl never loved you. That girl has a screw loose, and you must like that, but she never really loved you. And another day, when I saw him again at the bar in La Sirena, I said to him: what matters is your son and your health. Worry about your son and worry about your health, and stop getting yourself in these messes. It's hard to believe that such a smart guy could be so dumb.

Then I was at a bodybuilding championship, a minor championship in La Bisbal, where I came in second, which made me really happy, and I hooked up with this guy Juanma Pacheco, who was from Seville and worked as a bouncer at the club where the championship was held and used to be a bodybuilder. When I got back to Malgrat, Arturo wasn't there. I found a note on his door informing me that he would be gone for three days. He didn't say where, but I assumed he'd gone to see his son. Later, thinking about it, I realized that he didn't need to be gone for three days to see his son. When he got back four days later, he looked as happy as I'd ever seen him. I didn't want to ask him where he'd been, and he didn't tell me. He just showed up one night at La Sirena and we started to talk as if we'd just seen each other that morning. He stayed at the pub until closing time and then we walked home. I felt like talking and I suggested that we go have a couple of drinks at a bar that a friend of mine owned, but he said he'd rather go home. Still, we didn't hurry. At that time of night there's hardly anyone on the Paseo Marítimo and it's nice out, with the breeze from the sea and music drifting from the few places that are still open. I felt like talking and I told him about Juanma Pacheco. What do you think? I said when I was finished. He has a good name, he said. His real name is Juan Manuel, I said. I guessed that, he said. I think I'm in love, I said. He lit a cigarette and sat on a bench on the Paseo. I sat down beside him and kept talking. At that moment I even understood, or thought I understood, all of Arturo's insanities, the crazy things he'd done and the things he was about to do, and I would've liked to go to Africa too that night while we were watching the sea and the lights in the distance, the little trawlers; I felt capable of anything and especially of leaving for somewhere far away. I wish it would storm, I said. Don't say that, he said, it could start raining any minute. I laughed. What've you been doing for the last few days? I asked him. Nothing, he said, thinking, watching movies. What movies did you see? *The Shining*, he said. What an awful movie, I said, I saw it years ago and afterward I couldn't sleep. I saw it years ago too, said Arturo, and I was up all night. It's a great movie, I said. It's very good, he said. We were quiet for a while, watching the sea. There was no moon and the lights of the fishing boats were gone. Do you remember the novel that Torrance was writing? Arturo said suddenly. Torrance who? I said. The bad guy in the movie, in *The Shining*, Jack Nicholson. That's right, the son of a bitch was writing a novel, I said, although the truth is I hardly remembered. More than five hundred pages long, said Arturo, and he spat toward the beach. I'd never seen him spit. Excuse me, there's something wrong with my stomach, he said. Don't worry about it, I said. He'd written more than five hundred pages and all he'd done was endlessly copy a single sentence, in every possible way: capitalized, lowercase, double-columned, underlined, always the same sentence, nothing else. And what was the sentence? Don't you remember? No, I don't, I have a terrible memory, all I remember is the ax, and that the boy and his mother are saved at the end of the movie. All work and no play makes Jack a dull boy, said Arturo. He was crazy, I said, and at that moment I stopped watching the sea and turned toward Arturo, beside me, and he looked like he was about to collapse. It might have been a good novel, he said. Don't scare me, I said, how could it be a good novel when it was just one sentence repeated over and over again? That shows a lack of respect for the reader. Life is shitty enough without being stuck buying a book where all it says is "All work and no play . . ." It would be like me serving tea instead of whiskey, it would be false advertising but it would just be rude too, don't you think? Your common sense amazes me, Teresa, he said. Have you looked at what I write? he asked. I only go into your room when you invite me in, I lied. Then he told me about a dream, or maybe it was the next morning, while he watched me doing my daily exercises, sitting at the table with his chamomile tea and with that look on his face as if he hadn't slept for a week.

I thought it was a nice dream and that's why I remember it. Arturo was an Arab boy who goes hand in hand with his little brother to an Indonesian outpost to launch a transoceanic communications cable. Two Indonesian soldiers wait on him. Arturo is dressed like an Arab. In the dream he must be twelve years old, his little brother maybe six or seven. His mother watches from a distance, but then her presence fades. Arturo and his little brother are left alone, although both are wearing those wide, short, sharply curved Arab knives on their belts. Together they haul the cable, which looks handcrafted or homemade. And they're also carrying a barrel of a thick, greenish-brown liquid, which is the money to pay the Indonesians. As they wait, Arturo's little brother asks him how many feet long the cable is. Not feet, says Arturo, miles! The soldiers' hut is built of wood and it's on the shore. As they wait, another Arab, an older guy, cuts in front of them in line, and although Arturo's first impulse is to insult him or at least accuse him of being rude, first checking to see whether his curved sword is in place, he soon gives up the idea when the older Arab begins to tell a story to the Indonesian soldiers and to anyone else who wants to listen. The story is about a party in Sicily. Arturo told me that when he and his little brother heard it they felt happy, they felt thrilled, as if the other man was reciting a poem. In Sicily there's a glacier made of sand. A motley crowd of spectators watch it from a safe distance, except for two men: the first climbs to the top of a hill where the glacier is balanced, and the other stands at the foot of the hill and waits. Then the one on top starts to move or dance or stamp on the ground and the top layer of the glacier begins to crumble, sending down big masses of sand that fall toward the man below. He doesn't move. For a moment it looks as if he'll be buried in sand, but at the last instant he leaps aside and is saved. That was the dream. The sky in Indonesia was almost green, the sky in Sicily almost white. It had been a long time since Arturo had such a good dream. Maybe the Indonesia and the Sicily he dreamed of were on another planet. In my opinion, I said, that dream means your luck is about to change. From now on, things will go your way. Do you know who your little brother in the dream was? I can guess, he said. It was your son! When I said that, Arturo smiled. Days later, though, he brought up the Andalusian girl again. I wasn't feeling well and I told him to fuck off. Now I know I shouldn't have, even if it didn't really matter. I think I talked to him about life's responsibilities, the things I believed in and clung to in order to keep breathing. It must have seemed like I was angry at him, but I wasn't. He didn't get angry at me. That night he didn't come home to sleep. I remember because it was the first night that Juanma Pacheco came to see me. He had time off every fifteen days and he came to Malgrat wanting to make the most of it. We

494

went into my room and tried to make love. I couldn't do it. I tried several times, but I couldn't. Maybe it was because of Juanma's muscles, which were flabby since he hadn't been to the gym for so long. Whatever it was, it was probably my fault. I kept getting up to go into the kitchen for a drink of water. One of those times, I don't know why, I went into Arturo's room. On the table was his typewriter and a neat stack of paper. Before I flipped through the sheets I thought about *The Shining* and it gave me the shivers. But Arturo wasn't crazy, I knew that. Then I walked around the room, opened the window, sat on the bed, heard footsteps in the hall. Juanma Pacheco's face appeared around the door. He asked me if anything was wrong. Nothing, it's all right, I said, I'm thinking, and then I saw the packed suitcases and I knew he was going to leave.

He gave me four books that I still haven't read. A week later we said goodbye, and I went with him to the station.

# 25

Jacobo Urenda, Rue du Cherche-Midi, Paris, June 1996. This is a hard story to tell. It seems easy, but scratch the surface and you realize it isn't easy at all. Every story about that place is hard. I travel to Africa at least three times a year, usually to the hot spots, and when I get back to Paris it's as if I'm still dreaming and I can't wake up, although you might think that Latin Americans were less affected by horror than anyone else, at least in theory.

That was where I met Arturo Belano, in the Luanda post office, on a hot afternoon when I had nothing better to do than spend a fortune on calls to Paris. He was at the fax window going head to head with the guy acting as manager, who was trying to overcharge him, and I backed him up. By coincidence, it turned out we were both from the Southern Cone, him from Chile and me from Argentina, and we decided to spend the rest of the day together. I might have been the one to suggest it, I've always been a sociable person, I like to talk and get to know other people, and I'm not a bad listener, although sometimes when I seem to be listening I'm actually thinking my own thoughts.

We soon realized that we had more in common than we expected. At least I realized it, and I guess Belano did too, not that we said anything, or patted each other on the back. We'd both been born around the same time, we'd both split from our respective countries when what happened happened, we both liked Cortázar, we both liked Borges, neither of us had much money, and we both spoke shitty Portuguese. Basically, we were the typical forty-something Latin American guys who find themselves in an African country on the edge of the abyss or the edge of collapse, whichever you want to call it. The only difference was that when I

496

finished my work (I'm a photographer for the La Luna Agency) I was going back to Paris, and when poor Belano finished his work he was going to stick around.

But why, man? I asked him at some point during the night, why don't you come with me to Europe? I even went so far as to offer to lend him the money for the ticket if he didn't have it, which is the kind of thing you say when you're very drunk and the night is not just foreign but also big, very big, so big that if you don't look out it'll swallow you up, you and everyone around you, but that's something you wouldn't know anything about, you people who've never been to Africa. I do know. Belano did too. Both of us were freelancers. I worked for La Luna, as I've said, Belano as a stringer for a Madrid newspaper that paid him next to nothing for his pieces. And although he didn't tell me just then why he wasn't going to leave, we sat there comfortably together until we were carried by the night or by inertia (so to speak, since real inertia in Luanda made you hide under your cot) to a kind of private club belonging to this guy João Alves, a two-hundred-fifty-pound African. There we ran into some people we knew: reporters and photographers, cops and pimps, and we kept talking. Or maybe not. Maybe we went our separate ways there, maybe I lost sight of him in the cigarette smoke like so many people you meet when you're out on a job, people you talk to and then lose sight of. In Paris, it's different. People drift away, people dwindle, and you have time to say goodbye, even if you'd rather not. Not in Africa. People *talk* there, people tell you their *problems*, and then they vanish in a cloud of smoke, the way Belano vanished that night, without warning. And you never even consider the possibility of running into X or Y again at the airport. The possibility exists, I'm not saying it doesn't, but you don't consider it. So that night, when Belano disappeared, I stopped thinking about him, stopped thinking about loaning him money, and drank and danced and then I fell asleep in a chair and when I woke up with a start (more out of fear than because I was hungover, since I was afraid I'd been robbed, not being in the habit of going to places like João Alves's) it was already morning and I went outside to stretch my legs and there he was, in the yard, smoking a cigarette and waiting for me.

Yes, it was quite the gesture.

After that, we saw each other every day. Sometimes I'd buy him dinner and sometimes he'd buy dinner for me. It was cheap, he wasn't the kind of person who ate much. Each morning he'd have his little chamomile tea and when there wasn't any chamomile he'd order linden or mint or whatever herbal tea they had, he never touched coffee or black tea and he didn't eat anything fried. He was like a Muslim, he wouldn't touch pork or drink alcohol and he always carried around lots of pills. *Che* Belano, I said to him one day, you're like a walking drugstore, and he gave this bitter laugh, as if to say don't hassle me, Urenda, I'm not in the mood. As for women, he got along without them, as far as I know. One night the American reporter Joe Rademacher invited some of us to a dance in the neighborhood of Pará to celebrate the end of his mission to Angola. The dance was behind a private house, in a courtyard of packed dirt, and it was wonderful how many girls were there. Like modern men, we had all brought plenty of condoms, except for Belano, who joined us at the last minute, mostly because I insisted. I won't say he didn't dance, because in fact he did, but when I started to ask him whether he had condoms or if he wanted some of mine, he cut me off, saying: Urenda, I have no need of such things, or words to that effect, which leads me to believe he limited himself to dancing.

When I went back to Paris, he stayed in Luanda and was planning to head for the interior, which still seethed with armed, lawless gangs. We had one final conversation before I left. His story didn't really hang together. On the one hand, I got the sense that life meant nothing to him, that he'd taken the job so he could die a picturesque death, a death that was out of the ordinary, the usual bullshit. My generation all overdosed on Marx and Rimbaud. (I don't mean this as an excuse, at least not the way you think, and I'm not here to judge anyone's reading habits.) On the other hand, and this is what puzzled me, he took good care of himself. He took his little pills religiously each day. Once I went with him to a drugstore in Luanda in search of something resembling Ursochol, which is ursodeoxycholic acid, and which was more or less what kept his sclerotic bile duct functioning, as I understood it. When it came to these things, Belano behaved as if his health were extremely important to him. I watched him go into that drugstore speaking his abysmal Portuguese and scan the shelves, first in alphabetical order and then at random, and when we left, without the lousy ursodeoxycholic acid, I said to him *che* Belano, don't worry (because he had such a dire look on his face), I'll send you some as soon as I get to Paris, and then he said: you can't without a prescription, and I started to laugh, and I thought this man wants to live, there's no way he's planning to die.

But it wasn't as simple as that. He needed medicine, that was a fact. Not just Ursochol, but also mesalazine, and omeprazole, and the first two had to be taken daily, four mesalazine for his colitis and six Ursochol for his sclerosis. He could do without the omeprazole, I'm not sure whether he took it for a duodenal ulcer or a gastric ulcer or acid reflux or what, but he didn't take it every day. The funny thing, if this makes any sense, is that he *worried* about getting his medicine, worried about eating something that might bring on an attack of pancreatitis (he'd had three already, in Europe, not Angola; if he had an attack in Angola he would die for sure), I mean, he actually worried about his health, and yet when we talked, talked man to man, I guess you'd say, which sounds terrible but what else do you call a dismal conversation like that, he insinuated that he was there to get himself killed, which I suppose isn't the same as being there to kill yourself or to commit suicide, since you aren't taking the trouble to do it yourself, although in the end it's just as disturbing.

When I got back to Paris, I told Simone about it—that's my wife's name, she's French—and she asked me what Belano was like, asked me to describe him physically, in full detail, and then she said she understood him. How can you understand him? I didn't understand him. It was my second night back, we were in bed with the lights out, and that was when I told her everything. So what about the medicine, have you bought it? said Simone. No, not yet. Well, buy it first thing tomorrow and send it right away. I will, I said, but I kept thinking that there was something wrong with the story. In Africa you're always coming across strange stories. Do you think it's possible that someone could travel to such a faraway place in search of death? I asked my wife. It's perfectly possible, she said. Even a forty-year-old man? I said. If he has a spirit of adventure, it's perfectly possible, said my wife. Unlike most Parisian women, who tend to be practical and thrifty, she's always had a romantic streak. So I bought him the medicine, sent it to Luanda, and soon afterward received a postcard thanking me. I calculated that what I'd sent would last him twenty days. What would he do after that? I supposed he would return to Europe or die in Angola. And that was the last thought I gave it.

Months later I ran into him at the Grand Hotel in Kigali, where I was staying and where he came every once in a while to use the fax. We greeted each other effusively. I asked whether he was still working for the same paper in Madrid and he said he was, plus a couple of South American magazines, which brought in a little more money. He'd stopped wanting to die, but he was too broke to get back to Catalonia. That night we had dinner together at the house where he was living (Belano never stayed at hotels like the other foreign journalists, he'd rent a room or a bed or a corner of some private house where they'd let him stay for cheap) and we talked about Angola. He told me he'd been in Huambo, he'd traveled the Cuanza River, he'd been in Cuito Cuanavale and in Uíge, the pieces he'd written had gone over well, and he'd made it to Rwanda overland, first heading from Luanda to Kinshasa and then on to Kisangani, sometimes along the Congo River and other times along the treacherous forest roads, and then on to Kigali, in total more than thirty days of nonstop traveling. The terrain itself would have made this next to impossible, never mind the political situation. When he was done talking I couldn't tell whether to believe him or not. On the face of it, it was incredible. Also, he told it with a half smile that inclined you to doubt him.

I asked about his health. He said he'd come down with diarrhea in Angola, but now he was all right. I told him that my photographs were selling better and better. If he wanted, I said, and this time I think I meant it, I could lend him money, but he wouldn't hear of it. Then, despite myself, I asked him about the great death quest and he told me it made him laugh now to think about it and that I'd see real death, the be-all and end-all, up close the next day. He was, what's the word, changed. He could go for days at a time without taking his pills. He seemed calmer. Happy too, when I saw him, because he'd just received medicine from Barcelona. Who sent it to you? I asked him, a woman? No, he said, a friend. His name is Iñaki Echevarne, we had a duel. A fight? I said. No, a duel. And who won? I don't know which of us killed the other, said Belano. Fantastic! I said. Yes, he said.

Meanwhile, he'd clearly taken charge of his surroundings, or begun to, which is something I could never do. Nobody can, really, except the big media correspondents who have plenty of backup, and the rare freelancer who does without by making lots of friends and by simply *getting* it, how to maneuver in the African environment.

Physically, he was thinner than he'd been in Angola, skin and bones, in fact, but he looked healthy, not sick. Or that's how he looked to me, anyway, in the middle of so much death. His hair was longer, he probably cut it himself, and he had on the same clothes he'd worn in Angola, though they were filthier now and falling apart. He'd picked up the lingo, I could tell that right away, the language of a country where life was worth nothing and talk—along with money—was ultimately the key to everything.

The next day I went to the refugee camps and when I got back he was gone. At the hotel there was a note wishing me luck and asking me, if it wasn't too much trouble, to send him medicine when I got back to Paris. His address was included with the note. I went looking for him. He wasn't there.

My wife wasn't surprised at all when I told her. But Simone, I said, there was one chance in a million that I would see him again. These things happen, was all she said. The next day she asked whether I was planning to send him the medicine. I already had.

That time I didn't stay long in Paris. I went back to Africa, sure I'd run into Belano, but our paths didn't cross, and although I asked the veteran correspondents about him, none of them knew him. The few who remembered him had no idea where he might have gone. And the same thing happened on the next trip, and the next. Did you see him? my wife would ask when I got back. I didn't see him, I would reply, maybe he went back to Barcelona or back home. Or somewhere else, said my wife. Could be, I'd say, we'll never know.

Until I ended up in Liberia. Do you know where Liberia is? That's right, on the west coast of Africa, more or less between Sierra Leone and Ivory Coast. Good. But do you know who rules the country? the right or the left? I'm willing to bet you don't.

I got to Monrovia in April on a ship from Freetown, Sierra Leone. It had been chartered by a humanitarian organization, the name of which escapes me now, on a mission to evacuate hundreds of Europeans who were waiting at the American embassy—the only reasonably safe place in Monrovia, according to anyone who'd been there or gotten firsthand news of what was going on. These ultimately turned out to be Pakistanis, Hindus, North Africans, and the odd black Englishman. The other Europeans, if I can put it that way, had gotten out long before, and only their secretaries were left. For a Latin American it was odd to associate an American embassy with safety, it seemed a contradiction in terms, but times had changed, and why shouldn't the embassy be safe? I figured I might end up there myself. Still, the information struck me as a bad omen, a clear sign that everything would go wrong.

A band of Liberian soldiers, none of them over twenty, escorted us to a three-story building on New Africa Avenue, the Liberian version of the old Ritz Hotel or the old Crillon. It was run now by an organization of international journalists I'd never heard of. The hotel, called the Center for Press Correspondents, was one of the few things that worked in the capital, thanks in no small part to the presence of five U.S. marines. They stood guard now and then but spent most of their time in the lobby, drinking with the American TV correspondents and playing go-between for the journalists and a group of young Mandingo soldiers whom the journalists employed as guides and bodyguards on outings to Monrovia's hot zones, or, rarely and on a whim, to areas outside the capital, the nameless villages (though they all had names and had once had people, children, work) which, mostly according to hearsay or the reports we saw each night on CNN, were a faithful reflection of the end of the world, human insanity, the evil nestled in every heart.

The Center for Press Correspondents also functioned as a hotel, which meant we had to sign the register our first day there. I was already drinking whiskey and talking to two French friends when my turn came, and I don't know why, but I found myself flipping back, looking for a name. With no surprise, I found Arturo Belano's.

He'd been there two weeks. He had arrived at the same time as a group of Germans, two men and a woman from a Frankfurt newspaper. I tried to get in touch with him immediately and couldn't find him. A Mexican reporter told me that it had been seven days since he showed up at the Center. If I wanted news of him I should ask at the American embassy. I thought back on our now-distant conversation in Angola, about his death wish, and it occurred to me that he might be about to get what he wanted. The Germans, I was told, had already left. Reluctantly, knowing inside I had no other choice, I went looking for him at the embassy. No one could tell me anything, but I got a few photos out of it. The streets of Monrovia, the embassy courtyards, some faces. On my way back to the Center I ran into an Austrian who knew a German who'd seen Belano before he left. This German, however, spent all day out, making the most of the daylight, and there was nothing to do but wait. I remember it was around seven when some French colleagues and I got a poker game going, and that we stocked up on candles in preparation for the blackouts that usually came at sunset, or so we were told. But the lights didn't go out and the players soon sank into a general state of apathy. I remember we drank and talked about Rwanda and Zaire and the last movies we'd seen in Paris. The German got back at midnight, by which time I was alone in the lobby of that ghost-filled Ritz, and Jimmy, a young mercenary (but in whose pay?) serving as doorman and bartender, let me know that Herr Linke, the photographer, was on his way to his room.

I caught up with him on the stairs.

Linke could speak only the most rudimentary English, didn't understand a word of French, and had a decent face. When I was able to make him understand that I was looking for news of my friend Arturo Belano, he asked me politely (more or less, despite the faces he made to get his message across) to wait for him in the lobby or the bar, informing me that he needed to shower and would be down right away. He was gone for more than twenty minutes and when he came back he smelled of lotion and disinfectant. We talked for a long time, in fits and starts. Linke didn't drink, and he said this was why he'd noticed Arturo Belano, because back then the Center for Press Correspondents was swarming with journalists, many more than now, and they all got deliberately drunk each night, including some famous talking heads, people who should behave responsibly and set an example, according to Linke, and who ended up being sick from the balconies. Arturo Belano didn't drink and that led to their striking up a conversation. Linke remembered him spending three days total at the Center, going out each morning and coming back at midday or dusk. Once, but this was in the company of two Americans, he spent the night away trying to interview George Kensey, Roosevelt Johnson's youngest and bloodiest general, an ethnic Krahn, but the guide accompanying them was a Mandingo who not unreasonably got scared and abandoned them in the eastern part of Monrovia, and it took them all night to get back to the hotel. The next day Arturo Belano slept until very late, according to Linke, and two days later he left Monrovia with the same Americans who had tried to interview Kensey. Presumably they went north. Before Belano left, Linke gave him a little packet of cough drops made by a natural products company in Bern—at least I think that's what he was trying to say. He hadn't seen him since.

I asked him the names of the Americans. He knew one of them: Ray Pasteur. I thought he was joking and asked him to repeat it, I might have laughed, but the German was serious. Besides, he was too tired to joke around. Before he went to bed he took a little piece of paper out of the back pocket of his jeans and wrote it down for me: Ray Pasteur. I think he's from New York, he said. The next day Linke moved to the American embassy to try to get out of Liberia and I went with him to see if they'd had word of Ray Pasteur, but the place was total chaos and it seemed pointless to insist. When I left, Linke was in the embassy garden taking photos. I took one of him and he took one of me. In my shot, Linke is standing with his camera in his hand, looking at the ground, as if something shiny in the grass has suddenly caught his attention, drawing his eyes away from the lens. The expression on his face is calm, sad and calm. In the one he took of me, my Nikon is hanging around my neck and I'm staring into the camera (I think). I may have smiled and made the V-for-victory sign.

Three days later, it was my turn to try to leave, but I couldn't get out. Ostensibly, an embassy official informed me, the situation was improving, but the transport chaos was inversely related to the country's political stabilization. I left the embassy not entirely convinced. I went looking for Linke among the hundreds of residents roaming the grounds and couldn't find him. I ran into a new party of journalists who had just arrived from Freetown, and several who, God knows how, had reached Monrovia by helicopter from somewhere in Ivory Coast. Most, like me, were already thinking of leaving and stopped by the embassy each day to look for a berth on one of the ships to Sierra Leone.

It was then, when there was nothing left to do, when we had already written and photographed everything imaginable, that someone proposed that a few of us take a trip to the interior. Most, of course, turned down the offer. A Frenchman from *Paris Match* accepted. So did an Italian from Reuters, and me. The trip was organized by one of the guys who worked in the kitchen at the Center and who, besides making a few bucks, wanted to have a look at his town, which he hadn't been back to in six months, even though it was only fifteen or twenty miles from Monrovia. During the trip (we were in a dilapidated Chevy driven by a friend of the cook, armed with an assault rifle and two grenades) the cook told us that he was ethnic Mano and his wife was ethnic Gio, friends of the Mandingo (the driver was Mandingo) and enemies of the Krahn, whom he accused of being cannibals, and that he didn't know whether his family was dead or alive. Shit, said the Frenchman, we should go back. But we were already halfway there and the Italian and I were happy, using up the last of our film.

And so, without crossing a single checkpoint, we passed through the town of Summers and the hamlet of Thomas Creek, the Saint Paul River occasionally appearing to our left and other times lost from sight. The road was bad. At times it ran through the forest, what may have been old rubber plantations, and at times along the plain. From the plain one could guess at more than see the gently sloping hills rising in the south. Only once did we cross a river, a tributary of the Saint Paul, over a wooden bridge in perfect condition, and the only thing presenting itself to the camera's eye was nature, nothing I would call lush, or even exotic, so I don't know why it reminded me of a trip I made as a boy to Corrientes, but I even said as much, I said to Luigi: this looks like Argentina, saying it in French, which was the language in which the three of us communicated, and the guy from *Paris Match* looked at me and said that he hoped it only *looked* like Argentina, which frankly disconcerted me, because I wasn't even talking to him, was I? and what did he mean? that Argentina was even wilder and more dangerous than Liberia? that if the Liberians were Argentinians we would've been dead by now? I don't know. In any case his remark completely broke the spell for me and I would have liked to have it out with him then and there, but I know from experience that kind of argument gets you nowhere, and anyway the Frenchman was already annoyed by our majority decision not to go back and he had to let off steam somehow, not being satisfied by his constant grumbling about the poor black guys who just wanted to make a few dollars and see their families again. So I pretended not to have heard him, although mentally I wished him a monkey fucking, and I kept talking to Luigi, explaining things that until that moment I thought I'd forgotten, I don't know, the names of the trees, for example, which to me looked like the old Corrientes trees and had the same names as the Corrientes trees, although they obviously weren't the Corrientes trees. And I guess my enthusiasm made me seem brilliant, or in any case much more brilliant than I am, and even funny, to judge by Luigi's laughter and the occasional laughter of our companions, and it was in an atmosphere of relaxed camaraderie, excluding the Frenchman Jean-Pierre, of course, who was increasingly sulky, that we left behind those ever so Corrientes-like trees and entered a treeless stretch, only brush, bushes that were somehow sickly, and a silence split from time to time by the call of a solitary bird, a bird that called and called and received no answer, and then we started to get nervous, Luigi and I, but by then we were too close to our goal to turn back, and we kept going.

The shots began soon after the village came into sight. It all happened very fast. We never saw the shooters and the firing didn't last longer than a minute, but by the time we came around the bend and were in Black Creek proper, my friend Luigi was dead and the arm of the guy who worked at the center was bleeding and he was whimpering quietly, crouched under the passenger seat.

We too had automatically dropped to the floor of the Chevy.

I remember perfectly well what I did: I tried to revive Luigi, I gave him mouth-to-mouth resuscitation and then CPR, until the Frenchman touched my shoulder and pointed with a trembling, dirty forefinger at the Italian's left temple, where there was a hole the size of an olive. By the time I realized that Luigi was dead there were no shots to be heard and the silence was only broken by the air displaced by the Chevy as it drove and by the sound of the tires flattening the stones and pebbles on the road into town.

We stopped in what seemed to be Black Creek's main square. Our guide turned and told us that he was going to look for his family. A bandage made of strips of his own shirt was tied around his wounded arm. I supposed that he had made it himself, or the driver had, but I could hardly imagine when, unless their perception of time had suddenly diverged from ours. Shortly after the guide left, four old men appeared, surely drawn by the noise of the Chevy. Without saying a word, they stood there looking at us, sheltered under the eaves of a house in ruins. They were thin and moved with the parsimony of the sick, one of them naked like some of Kensey and Roosevelt Johnson's Krahn guerrillas, although it was clear that the old man was no guerrilla. Like us, they seemed to have just woken up. The driver saw them and remained sitting at the wheel, sweating and smoking and occasionally glancing at his watch. After a while he opened the door and made a sign to the old men, who responded without moving from under the protection of the eaves, and then he got out of the car and started to examine the engine. When he came back he launched into a series of incomprehensible explanations, as if the car were ours. Basically, what he was saying was that the front end was as full of holes as a sieve. The Frenchman shrugged his shoulders and shifted Luigi so that he could sit beside him. I thought he was having an asthma attack, but otherwise he seemed calm. Mentally, I thanked him for it, because if there's anything I hate it's a hysterical Frenchman. Later an adolescent girl appeared, looked at us, and kept walking. We watched her disappear down one of the narrow little streets that ran into the square. When she was gone the silence was absolute and only by listening as hard as we could were we able to hear something like the glare of the sun on the roof of the car. There wasn't the slightest breeze.

We're fucked, said the Frenchman. He said it in a friendly way, so I pointed out that it had been a long time since the shooting had stopped and probably it was only a few people who had ambushed us, maybe a couple of bandits who were as scared as we were. That's bullshit, said the Frenchman, this village is empty. Only then did I realize that there was no one else in the square and see that it wasn't normal and that the Frenchman was probably right. Instead of being afraid, I was angry.

I got out of the car and urinated lengthily against the nearest wall. Then I went over to the Chevy, took a look at the engine, and didn't see anything that would prevent us from getting out of there the same way we'd come. I took several pictures of poor Luigi. The Frenchman and the driver watched me without saying anything. Then Jean-Pierre, as if he'd considered it carefully, requested that I take a picture of him. I did as he asked without protest. I photographed him and the driver and then I asked the driver to photograph Jean-Pierre and me, and then I told Jean-Pierre to photograph me with Luigi, but he refused, saying he thought it was the height of morbidity, and the friendship that had begun to grow between us was shattered again. I think I swore at him. I think he swore at me. Then the two of us got back in the Chevy, Jean-Pierre next to the driver and me next to Luigi. We must have been there for more than an hour. During that time Jean-Pierre and I suggested more than once that we should forget the cook and hightail it out of there, but the driver refused to listen.

At some point during the wait, I think I fell into a brief, uneasy sleep, but it was sleep nonetheless, and I probably dreamed about Luigi and a terrible toothache. The pain was worse than the certainty that the Italian was dead. When I woke up, covered in sweat, I saw Jean-Pierre sleeping with his head on the driver's shoulder while the driver smoked another cigarette, staring straight ahead at the funereal yellow of the deserted square, his rifle lying across his knees.

Finally our guide appeared.

Walking beside him was a thin woman whom we at first took for his mother but who turned out to be his wife, and a boy of about eight, dressed in a red shirt and blue shorts. We're going to have to leave Luigi, said Jean-Pierre, there isn't room for everybody. For a few minutes we argued. The guide and the driver were on Jean-Pierre's side and in the end I had to give in. I hung Luigi's cameras around my neck and emptied his pockets. Between the driver and me we lifted him out of the Chevy and laid him in the shade of a kind of thatch. The guide's wife said something in her language. It was the first time she had spoken, and Jean-Pierre turned to look at her and asked the cook to translate. At first the cook was reluctant, but then he said that his wife had said that it would be better to put the body inside one of the houses on the square. Why? Jean-Pierre and I asked in unison. So silent and serene was the woman that although she was ravaged, she had a queenly air, or so it seemed to us at that moment. Because the dogs will eat it there, she said, pointing to where the body lay. Jean-Pierre and I looked at each other and laughed, of course, said the Frenchman, why didn't we think of that, naturally. So we lifted Luigi's body again and after the driver had kicked in the weakest-looking door, we carried the body into a room with a packed-earth floor. The room was piled with mats and empty cardboard boxes, and its smell was so unbearable that we left the Italian and got out as fast as we could.

When the driver started the Chevy we all jumped, except for the old men who were still watching us from under the eaves. Where are we going? said Jean-Pierre. The driver made a gesture as if to say that we shouldn't bother him or that he didn't know. We're taking a different road, said the guide. Only then did I notice the boy: he had wrapped his arms around his father's legs and was asleep. Let's go where they say, I said to Jean-Pierre.

For a while we drove the deserted streets of the village. When we left the square we headed down a straight street, then we turned left and the Chevy inched forward, almost scraping the walls of the houses and the eaves of the thatch roofs, until we came out into an open space where there was a big, single-story zinc shed, as big as a warehouse. On its side we could read "CE-RE-PA, Ltd.," in big red letters, and below that:

"toy factory, Black Creek & Brownsville." This shitty town is called Brownsville, not Black Creek, I heard Jean-Pierre say. The driver, the guide, and I corrected him without turning our gaze from the shed. The town was Black Creek, and Brownsville was probably a little farther east, but for no good reason Jean-Pierre kept saying that we were in Brownsville, not Black Creek, which had been the deal. The Chevy crossed the open space and started down a road that ran through dense forest. Now we really are in Africa, I said to Jean-Pierre, trying vainly to raise his spirits, but he only replied with some incoherent remark about the toy factory we had just passed.

The trip lasted only fifteen minutes. The Chevy stopped three times and the driver said that the engine, with luck, wouldn't make it past Brownsville, and that was if we were lucky. Brownsville, as we would soon find out, was scarcely thirty houses in a clearing. We got there after driving over four bare hills. Like Black Creek, the town was half deserted. Our Chevy, with "press" written on the windshield, attracted the attention of the only inhabitants, who waved to us from the door of a wooden house, long like a factory shed, the biggest in the town. Two armed men appeared on the threshold and started to shout at us. The car stopped a few hundred feet away and the driver and guide got out to talk. As they moved toward the house I remember Jean-Pierre said to me that if we wanted to save ourselves we should run into the woods. I asked the woman who the men were. She said that they were Mandingo. The boy was asleep with his head in her lap, a little thread of saliva escaping from between his lips. I told Jean-Pierre that we were among friends, at least in theory. The Frenchman made a sarcastic reply, but physically I could see the calm (a liquid calm) spread over every wrinkle of his face. I remember it and it makes me feel bad, but at the time I was glad. The guide and the driver were laughing with the strangers. Then three more people came out of the long house, also armed to the teeth, and stood there staring at us as the guide and the driver came back to the car accompanied by the first two men. Shots sounded in the distance and Jean-Pierre and I ducked our heads. Then I rose, got out of the car, and greeted them, and one of the black men greeted me and the other hardly looked at me, busy as he was lifting the hood of the Chevy and checking the irreparably dead engine and then I thought that they weren't going to kill us and I looked toward the long house and I saw six or seven armed men and among them I saw two white guys walking toward us. One of them had a beard and was carrying two cameras bandolier-style, a fellow photographer, that much was obvious, although at that moment, while he was still at a distance, I was unaware of the fame that preceded him everywhere he went, by which I mean that I knew his name and his work, like everyone in the business, but I had never seen him in person, not even in a photograph. The other was Arturo Belano.

I'm Jacobo Urenda, I said, trembling, I don't know whether you remember me.

He remembered me. How could he not? But I was so far gone then that I wasn't sure he would remember anything, let alone me. By that I don't exactly mean he had changed. In fact, he hadn't changed at all. He was the same guy I'd known in Luanda and Kigali. Maybe I was the one who had changed, I don't know, but the point is it seemed to me that nothing could be the same as before, and that included Belano and his memory. For a moment my nerves almost betrayed me. I think Belano noticed and he clapped me on the back and said my name. Then we shook hands. Mine, I noticed with horror, were stained with blood. Belano's, and this I also noticed with a sensation akin to horror, were immaculate.

I introduced him to Jean-Pierre and he introduced me to the photographer. It was Emilio López Lobo, the Magnum photographer from Madrid, one of the living legends of the profession. I don't know whether Jean-Pierre had heard of him (Jean-Pierre Boisson, from *Paris Match*, said Jean-Pierre without turning a hair, which probably meant that he didn't recognize the name or that under the circumstances he didn't give a damn about meeting the great man), but I'd heard of him, I'm a photographer, and for us López Lobo was what Don DeLillo is to writers, a phenomenon, a chaser of front-page shots, an adventurer, a man who'd won every prize Europe had to offer and photographed every kind of human stupidity and recklessness. When it was my turn to shake his hand, I said: Jacobo Urenda, from La Luna, and López Lobo smiled. He was very thin, probably somewhere in his forties, like the rest of us, and he seemed drunk or exhausted or about to fall apart, or all three things at once.

Soldiers and civilians were gathered inside the house. At first glance, it was hard to tell them apart. The smell inside was bittersweet and damp, a smell of expectancy and fatigue. My first impulse was to go outside for a breath of fresh air, but Belano informed me that it was better not to show yourself too often, since there were Krahn snipers posted in the hills who'd blow your head off. Lucky for us, they got tired of keeping watch all day and they weren't good shots either, though this I only learned later.

The house, two long rooms, was furnished only with three rows of uneven shelves, some metal and others wood, all empty. The floor was of packed dirt. Belano explained the situation we were in. According to the soldiers, the Krahn who were surrounding Brownsville and the men who'd attacked us at Black Creek were the advance troops of General Kensey's force, and Kensey was positioning his people to attack Kakata and Harbel and then march toward the neighborhoods of Monrovia that Roosevelt Johnson still controlled. The soldiers were planning to leave the next morning for Thomas Creek, where, according to them, one of Taylor's generals, Tim Early, was stationed. The soldiers' plan, as Belano and I soon agreed, was desperate and would never work. If it was true that Kensey was regrouping his people in the area, the Mandingo soldiers wouldn't have the slightest chance of making their way back to their own side. The civilians, who, unusually for Africa, seemed to be led by a woman, had come up with a much better plan. Some planned to stay in Brownsville to wait and see what happened. Others, the majority, planned to head northeast with the Mandingo woman, cross the Saint Paul, and reach the Brewerville road. The plan, the civilians' plan, that is, wasn't outrageous, although in Monrovia I'd heard talk about killings on the road between Brewerville and Bopolu. The lethal stretch, however, was farther east, closer to Bopolu than Brewerville. After listening to them, Belano, Jean-Pierre, and I decided to go with them. If we managed to reach Brewerville, we were saved, according to Belano. A ten-mile walk through old rubber plantations and tropical jungle lay ahead of us, not to mention the river crossing, but when we made it to the road we would only be five miles from Brewerville and then it was only fifteen miles to Monrovia along a road that was surely still in the hands of Taylor's soldiers. We would leave the next morning, shortly after the Mandingo soldiers went off in the opposite direction to face certain death.

I didn't sleep that night.

First I talked to Belano, then I spent a while talking to our guide, and then I talked to Arturo again, and López Lobo. This must have been between ten and eleven, and by that time it was difficult to move around the house, which was plunged into utter darkness, a darkness broken only by the glow of the cigarettes that some people were smoking to stave off fear and insomnia. In the doorway I saw the shadows of two soldiers squatting, keeping guard, who didn't turn when I went up to them. I also saw the stars and the outline of the hills and once again I was reminded of my childhood. It must have been because I associate my childhood with the country. Then I moved back into the house, feeling my way along the shelves, but I couldn't find my spot. It was probably twelve when I lit a cigarette and prepared to sleep. I know I was happy (or I know I thought I was happy) because the next day we would start back to Monrovia. I know I was happy because I was in the middle of an adventure and I felt alive. So I started to think about my wife and my home and then I started to think about Belano, how well he looked, what good shape he seemed to be in, better than in Angola, when he wanted to die, and better than in Kigali, when he didn't want to die anymore but couldn't get off this godforsaken continent, and when I'd finished the cigarette I pulled out another one, which really was the last, and to cheer myself up I even started to sing very softly to myself or in my head, a song by Atahualpa Yupanqui, my God, Atahualpa Yupanqui, and only then did I realize that I was extremely nervous and that if I wanted to sleep what I needed was to talk, and then I got up and took a few blind steps, first in deathly silence (for a fraction of a second I thought we were all dead, that the hope sustaining us was only an illusion, and I had the urge to go running out the door of that foul-smelling house), then I heard the sound of snoring, the barely audible whispering of those who were still awake and talking in the dark in Gio or Mano, Mandingo or Krahn, English, Spanish.

All languages seemed detestable to me just then.

To say that now is silly, I know. All those languages, all that whispering, simply a vicarious way of preserving our identity for an uncertain length of time. Ultimately, the truth is that I don't know why they seemed detestable, maybe because in an absurd way I was lost somewhere in those two long rooms, lost in a region I didn't know, a country I didn't know, a continent I didn't know, on a strange, elongated planet, or maybe because I knew I should get some sleep and I couldn't. And then I felt for the wall and sat on the floor and opened my eyes extrawide trying and trying to see something, and then I curled up on the floor and closed my eyes and prayed to God (in whom I don't believe) that I wouldn't get sick, because there was a long walk ahead of me the next day, and then I fell asleep.

When I woke up it must have been close to four in the morning.

A few feet from me, Belano and López Lobo were talking. I saw the light of their cigarettes, and my first impulse was to get up and go to them. I wanted to share in the uncertainty of what the next day would bring, join the two shadows I glimpsed behind the cigarettes even if I had to crawl or go on my knees. But I didn't. Something in the tone of their voices stopped me, something in the angle of their shadows, shadows sometimes dense, squat, warlike, and sometimes fragmented, dispersed, as if the bodies that cast them had already disappeared.

So I controlled myself and pretended to be asleep and listened.

López Lobo and Belano talked until just before dawn. To transcribe what they said is in some way to detract from what I felt as I listened to them.

First they talked about people's names and they said incomprehensible things, their voices like the voices of two conspirators or two gladiators, speaking softly and agreeing on almost everything, although Belano's voice dominated and his arguments (which I heard in bits and pieces, as if half of what they said was carried away by some sound current inside that long house, or blocked by randomly placed screens) were belligerent, raw, it was unforgivable to be called López Lobo, unforgivable to be called Belano, that sort of thing, although I might be wrong and the subject of the conversation might have been something else entirely. Then they talked about other things: the names of cities, the names of women, the titles of books. Belano said: we're all afraid of going under. Then he was quiet and only then did I realize that López Lobo had hardly said anything and Belano had talked too much. For an instant I thought they were going to sleep, and I prepared to do the same. All my bones hurt. The day had been overwhelming. Just at that moment I heard their voices again.

At first I couldn't understand anything, maybe because I had changed position or because they were speaking more softly. I turned over. One of them was smoking. I made out Belano's voice again. He was saying that when he got to Africa, he too had wanted to be killed. He told stories about Angola and Rwanda that I already knew, that all of us here more or less know. Then López Lobo's voice interrupted him. He asked (I could hear him perfectly clearly) why he'd wanted to die back then. I couldn't hear Belano's answer, but I guessed it, which isn't so impressive, since in a way I already knew. He had lost something and he wanted to die, that was all. Then I heard Belano laugh and I imagined that he was laughing about what he'd lost, his great loss, laughing at himself and other things, things I knew nothing about and didn't want to know anything about. López Lobo didn't laugh. I think he said: well, for God's sake, something like that. Then they were both silent.

Later, though how much later I can't say, I heard López Lobo's voice, maybe asking the time. What time is it? Someone moved beside me. Someone stirred restlessly in his sleep and López Lobo spoke a few guttural words, as if he were once again asking what time it was, but this time, I'm sure, he was asking something else.

Belano said it's four in the morning. At that moment I accepted that I wasn't going to be able to sleep. Then López Lobo started to talk and his speech went on until dawn, only very occasionally interrupted by questions from Belano that I couldn't hear.

He said that he'd had two children and a wife, like Belano, like everyone, and a house and books. Then he said something I didn't catch. Maybe he talked about happiness. He mentioned streets, metro stops, telephone numbers. As if he were looking for someone. Then silence. Someone coughed. López Lobo repeated that he'd had a wife and two children. A generally satisfactory life. Something like that. Anti-Franco activism and a youth, in the seventies, in which there was no lack of sex or friendship. He became a photographer by chance. He didn't take his fame or prestige or anything else very seriously. He was in love when he got married. His life was what is usually described as a happy life. One day, he and his wife happened to discover that their oldest son was sick. He was a very clever boy, said López Lobo. What he had was serious, a tropical disease, and of course López Lobo thought the boy must have caught it from him. Still, after performing the appropriate tests, the doctors couldn't find even a trace of the disease in López Lobo's blood. For a while, López Lobo pursued the possible carriers of the disease within the child's limited circle and found nothing. Finally, he lost his mind.

He and his wife sold their house in Madrid and went to live in the United States, leaving with the sick child and the healthy child. The hospital where the boy was admitted was expensive and the treatment was long and López Lobo had to go back to work, so his wife stayed with the boys and he took on freelance assignments. He was in many places, he said, but he always returned to New York. Sometimes the boy would be better, as if he were beating the disease, and other times his health would plateau or decline. Sometimes López Lobo would sit in a chair in the sick boy's room and dream about his two sons, seeing their faces close together, smiling and defenseless, and then, without knowing why, he knew that he, López Lobo, must cease to exist. His wife had rented an apartment on West Eighty-first Street, and the healthy child attended a nearby school. One day, while he was waiting in Paris for a visa to an Arab country, he got a call telling him that the sick boy had taken a turn for the worse. He dropped what he was doing and caught the first flight to New York. When he got to the hospital everything seemed submerged in a kind of hideous normality and that's when he knew the end had come. Three days later the boy died. He dealt with the arrangements for the cremation himself, because his wife was devastated. Up until this point, López Lobo's account was more or less intelligible. The rest is just one sentence, one scene after another. I'll try to string them together.

The very day the boy died, or a day later, López Lobo's wife's parents arrived in New York. One afternoon they had an argument. They were in the bar of a hotel on Broadway, near Eighty-first Street, everyone together, López Lobo's in-laws, his younger son, and his wife, and López Lobo started to cry and said that he loved his two sons and that it was his fault his older son had died. Although maybe he didn't say anything and there was no argument and all of this only took place in López Lobo's mind. Then López Lobo got drunk and left the boy's ashes in a New York City subway car and then he went back to Paris without saying anything to anyone. A month later he learned that his wife had returned to Madrid and wanted a divorce. López Lobo signed the papers and thought it had all been a dream.

Much later I heard Belano's voice asking when "the tragedy" had occurred. It sounded to me like the voice of a Chilean peasant. Two months ago, answered López Lobo. And then Belano asked him what had happened to the other boy, the healthy one. He lives with his mother, answered López Lobo.

By then I could make out their silhouettes where they sat leaning against the wall. Both of them were smoking and both looked tired, but I might have gotten that impression because I was tired myself. López Lobo wasn't talking anymore. Only Belano was talking, as he had been at the beginning, and surprisingly, he was telling his own story, a story that made no sense, telling it over and over, with the difference that each time he told it he condensed it a little more, until at last all he was saying was: I wanted to die, but I realized it was better not to. Only then did I fully understand that López Lobo was going to go with the soldiers the next day, not the civilians, and that Belano wasn't going to let him die alone.

I think I fell asleep.

At least, I think I slept for a few minutes. When I woke up, the light of the new day had begun to filter into the house. I heard snores, sighs, people talking in their sleep. Then I saw the soldiers getting ready to leave. López Lobo and Belano were with them. I got up and told Belano not to go. Belano shrugged his shoulders. López Lobo's face was impassive. He knows he's going to die and now he's calm, I thought. Belano's face, meanwhile, looked like the face of a madman: in a matter of seconds, terrible fear and fierce happiness coursed across it. I grabbed his arm and without thinking went walking outside with him.

It was a gorgeous morning, of an airy blueness that gave you goose bumps. López Lobo and the soldiers watched us go and didn't say anything. Belano was smiling. I remember that we walked toward our useless Chevy and that I told him several times that what he planned to do was insane. I heard your conversation last night, I confessed, and everything makes me think your friend is crazy. Belano didn't interrupt: he looked toward the forest and the hills that surrounded Brownsville and every so often he nodded. When we got to the Chevy I remembered the snipers and I felt a stirring of panic. It seemed absurd. I opened one of the doors and we got in the car. Belano noticed Luigi's blood soaked into the fabric but he didn't say anything, and I didn't think it was the right moment to explain. For a while we sat there in silence. I had my face hidden in my hands. Then Belano asked me whether I'd realized how young the soldiers were. They're all fucking kids, I answered, and they kill each other like they're playing. Still, there's something nice about it, said Belano, looking out the window at the forest trapped between the fog and the light. I asked him why he was going with López Lobo. So he won't be alone, he answered. That much I already knew, I was hoping for a different answer, something conclusive, but I didn't say anything. I felt very sad. I wanted to say something else and couldn't find the words. Then we got out of the car and went back to the long house. Belano took his things and left with the soldiers and the Spanish photographer. I went with him to the door. Jean-Pierre was beside me and he looked at Belano in confusion. The soldiers were already beginning to head off and we said goodbye to him right there. Jean-Pierre shook his hand and I hugged him. López Lobo had gone on ahead and Jean-Pierre and I realized that he didn't want to say goodbye to us. Then Belano started to run, as if at the last moment he thought the column would leave without him. He caught up with López Lobo, and it looked to me as if they started to talk, as if they were laughing, as if they were off on an excursion, and then they crossed the clearing and were lost in the underbrush.

Our own trip back to Monrovia was almost without incident. It was long and grueling, but we didn't run into soldiers from either camp. We got to Brewerville at dusk. There we said goodbye to most of the people who'd come with us and the next morning a van from a humanitarian organization took us back to Monrovia. Jean-Pierre was out of Liberia in less than a day. I spent two more weeks there. The cook, his wife, and their son, with whom I became friendly, moved into the Center. The woman worked making beds and sweeping the floor and sometimes I would look out the window of my room and see the boy playing with other children or with the soldiers who were guarding the hotel. I never saw the driver again, but he made it to Monrovia alive, which is some consolation. It goes without saying that for the rest of my time there I tried to track down Belano, find out what had happened in the Brownsville–Black Creek–Thomas Creek area, but I couldn't get any straight answers. According to some, the territory was now under the control of Kensey's armed bands, and according to others, troops under a nineteen-year-old general, General Lebon I think was his name, had managed to reestablish Taylor's control over all the territory between Kakata and Monrovia, which included Brownsville and Black Creek. But I never found out whether this was true or false. One day I went to hear a speech at a place near the American embassy. The speech was given by a General Wellman, and in his own way, he tried to explain the situation in the country. At the end, anyone could ask whatever they wanted. When everyone had left or gotten tired of asking questions that we somehow knew were pointless, I asked him about General Kensey, about General Lebon, about the situation in the towns of Brownsville and Black Creek, about the fates of photographer Emilio López Lobo, from Spain, and journalist Arturo Belano, from Chile. General Wellman gave me a long look before he answered (but he gave everyone the same look, maybe he was nearsighted and didn't know where to get himself a pair of glasses). In as few words as possible, he said that according to his reports General Kensey had been dead for a week. Lebon's troops had killed him. General Lebon, in turn, was also dead, in his case at the hands of a gang of highwaymen, in one of the eastern neighborhoods of Monrovia. So far as Black Creek was concerned, he said: "Peace reigns in Black Creek." Literally. And he had never heard of the settlement of Brownsville, though he pretended otherwise.

Two days later I left Liberia and never went back.

# 26

Ernesto García Grajales, Universidad de Pachuca, Pachuca, Mexico, December 1996. In all humbleness, sir, I can say that I'm the only expert on the visceral realists in Mexico, and if pressed, the world. God willing, I plan to publish a book about them. Professor Reyes Arévalo has told me that the university press might bring it out. Of course, Professor Reyes Arévalo had never heard of the visceral realists. Deep down he would have preferred a monograph on the Mexican modernists or an annotated edition of Manuel Pérez Garabito, the Pachucan poet par excellence. But by dint of perseverance, I've managed to convince him that there's nothing wrong with studying certain aspects of our most fiercely modern poetry. And in the process, we'll bring Pachuca to the threshold of the twenty-first century. Yes, you could say I'm the foremost scholar in the field, the definitive authority, but that's not saying much. I'm probably the only person who cares. Hardly anyone even remembers the visceral realists anymore. Many of them are dead. Others have disappeared and no one knows what happened to them. But some are still active. Jacinto Requena, for example, is a film critic now and runs the Pachuca film society. He's the one who first got me interested in the group. María Font lives in Mexico City. She never married. She writes, but she doesn't publish. Ernesto San Epifanio died. Xóchitl García works for Mexico City newspaper magazines and Sunday supplements. I don't think she writes poetry anymore. Rafael Barrios disappeared in the United States. I don't know whether he's still around. Angélica Font recently published her second collection of poetry, only thirty pages long, not a bad book, in a very elegant edition. Luscious Skin died. Pancho Rodríguez died. Emma Méndez committed suicide. Moctezuma Rodríguez is involved in politics. I've heard that Felipe Müller is still in Barcelona, married and with a kid. He seems to be happy. Every so often his buddies over here publish some poem he's written. Ulises Lima still lives in Mexico City. I went to see him last break. A real spectacle. To tell you the truth, I was even a little scared at first. The entire time I was with him he called me Professor. But *mano*, I said to him, I'm younger than you, so why don't we call each other by our first names? Whatever you say, Professor, he replied. What a character. About Arturo Belano I know nothing. No, I never met Belano. Yes, several of them. I never met Müller or Pancho Rodríguez or Luscious Skin. Or Rafael Barrios either. Juan García Madero? No, the name doesn't ring a bell. He never belonged to the group. Of course I'm sure. Man, if I tell you so as the reigning expert on the subject, it's because that's the way it is. They were all so young. I have their magazines, their pamphlets, documents you can't find any-place. There was a seventeen-year-old kid, but he wasn't called García Madero. Let's see . . . his name was Bustamante. He only published one poem in a mimeographed magazine that came out in Mexico City, no more than twenty copies of the first issue, and that was the only issue there ever was. And he wasn't Mexican, but Chilean, like Belano and Müller, the son of exiles. No, as far as I know this Bustamante doesn't write poetry anymore. But he belonged to the group. The Mexico City visceral realists. Yes, because there had already been another group of visceral realists, in the 1920s. The northern visceral realists. You didn't know that? Well, they existed. Although talk about undocumented. No, it wasn't a coincidence. More like an homage. A gesture. A response. Who knows. Anyway, these are labyrinths I prefer not to lose myself in. I limit myself to the material at hand and let readers and scholars draw their own conclusions. I think my little book will do well. Worst-case sce-nario, I'll be bringing Pachuca into the modern age.

**Amadeo Salvatierra, Calle Venezuela, near the Palacio de la Inquisi-ción, Mexico City, January 1976.** Everyone forgot her, boys, except me, I said. Now that we're old and past hope maybe a few remember her, but back then everyone forgot her and then they started to forget themselves, which is what happens when you forget your friends. Except for me. Or that's how it seems to me now. I kept her magazine and I kept her mem-ory alive. Possibly my life was suited to it. Like so many Mexicans, I too gave up poetry. Like so many thousands of Mexicans, I too turned my back on poetry. Like so many hundreds of thousands of Mexicans, I too, when the moment came, stopped writing and reading poetry. From then on, my life proceeded along the drabbest course you can imagine. I did everything, I did whatever I could. One day I found myself writing letters, incomprehensible documents under the arcades of the Plaza Santo Domingo. It was a job like any other, at least no worse than other jobs I'd had, but it didn't take me long to realize that I was going to be there forever, chained to my typewriter, pen, and blank sheets of paper. It isn't bad work. Sometimes I even laugh. I write everything from love letters to petitions, legal appeals, financial claims, pleas sent by the desperate to the prisons of the Republic. And it gives me time to talk to my colleagues, scribes as tenacious as me (we're an endangered species), or to read the latest marvels of our literature. Mexican poetry is hopeless: the other day I read that one of our most cultivated poets thought that the *Pensil Florido* was a colored pencil, not a garden or a park full of flowers, even an oasis. *Pensil* also means dangling, hanging, suspended. Did you know that, boys, I said, did you know that, or have I put my foot in it? And the boys looked at each other and said yes, but in a way that might also have meant no. I had no news of Cesárea. One day, at a bar, I struck up a friendship with an old man from Sonora. The old man knew Hermosillo and Cananea and Nogales very well, and I asked him whether he had ever heard of Cesárea Tinajero. He said no. I don't know what I must have said to him, but he got the idea that I was talking about my wife or my sister or my daughter. When he said so, it occurred to me that really I had hardly known Cesárea. And now, boys, you tell me that Maples Arce talked to you about her. Or that List or Arqueles did, it doesn't matter. Who gave you my address? I said. List or Arqueles or Manuel, it doesn't matter. And the boys looked at me or maybe they didn't look at me, day had been dawning for a while now, waves of noise from Calle Venezuela were coming into the apartment, and at that moment I saw that one of the boys had fallen asleep sitting on the sofa, but with his back very straight, as if he were awake, and the other one had begun to leaf through Cesárea's magazine, but he seemed to be sleeping too. And then I said, boys, it looks as if day is here, it looks as if the sun has risen. And the one who was asleep opened his big mouth and said yes, Amadeo. The one who was awake, meanwhile, paid no attention to me, still leafing through the magazine, still with a half smile on his lips, as if he were dreaming of a girl just out of reach, while his eyes scanned the only poem by Cesárea Tinajero that existed in Mexico. My mind was spinning from fatigue and the alcohol I'd drunk and suddenly I got the idea that it was the one who was awake who'd spoken. And I said: are you a ventriloquist, boy? And the one who was asleep said no, Amadeo, or maybe he said negative, Amadeo, or maybe *nel* or *nelson* or *nelazo*, or maybe he said no sir or not likely or not a chance, or maybe he just said he wasn't. And the one who was awake looked at me, gripping the magazine as if he was afraid someone would take it from him, and then he looked away and kept reading, as if, I thought then, there was anything to read in Cesárea Tinajero's wretched magazine. I lowered my gaze and nodded. Don't be shy now, Amadeo, said one of them. I didn't want to look at them. But I did. And I saw two boys, one awake and the other asleep, and the one who was asleep said don't worry, Amadeo, we'll find Cesárea for you even if we have to look under every stone in the north. And I opened my eyes as wide as I could and looked at them and I said: I'm not worried, boys, don't do it for my sake. And the one who was asleep said: it's no trouble, Amadeo, it's a pleasure. And I insisted: don't do it for me. And the one who was asleep laughed or made a noise in his throat that could have been a laugh, a gurgle, or a purr, or maybe he was about to choke, and he said: we're not doing it for you, Amadeo, we're doing it for Mexico, for Latin America, for the Third World, for our girl-friends, because we feel like doing it. Were they joking? Weren't they joking? And then the one who was sleeping breathed in a very strange way, as if he were breathing with his bones, and he said: we're going to find Cesárea Tinajero and we're going to find the Complete Works of Cesárea Tinajero. And the truth is that then I felt a shiver and I looked at the one who was awake, who was still studying the only poem in the world by Cesárea Tinajero, and I said to him: I think something's wrong with your friend. And the one who was reading raised his eyes and looked at me as if I were behind a window or he were on the other side of a window, and said: relax, nothing's wrong. Goddamn psychotic boys! As if speaking in one's sleep were nothing! As if making promises in one's sleep were nothing! And then I looked at the walls of my front room, my books, my photographs, the stains on the ceiling, and then I looked at them and I saw them as if through a window, one of them with his eyes open and the other with his eyes shut, but both of them looking, looking out? looking in? I don't know, all I know is that their faces had turned pale, as if they were at the North Pole, and I told them so, and the one who was sleeping breathed noisily and said: it's more as if the North Pole had descended on Mexico City, Amadeo, that's what he said, and I asked: boys, are you cold? a rhetorical question, or a practical question, because if the answer was yes, I was determined to make them coffee right away, but ultimately it was really a rhetorical question, if they were cold all they had to do was move away from the window, and then I said: boys, is it worth it? is it worth it? is it really worth it? and the one who was asleep said *Simonel*. Then I got up (all my bones creaked) and went to the window by the dining room table and opened it, and then I went to what was, strictly speaking, the front room window, and opened it, and then I shuffled over to the switch and turned out the light.

# III

# THE SONORA DESERT

## (1976)

## JANUARY 1

Today I realized that what I wrote yesterday I really wrote today: everything from December 31 I wrote on January 1, i.e., today, and what I wrote on December 30 I wrote on the 31st, i.e., yesterday. What I write today I'm really writing tomorrow, which for me will be today and yesterday, and also, in some sense, tomorrow: an invisible day. But enough of that.

## JANUARY 2

We were on our way out of Mexico City. To entertain my friends, I asked them some tricky questions, questions that were problems too, and enigmas (especially in the Mexican literary world of today), even riddles. I started with an easy one: what is free verse? I said. My voice echoed inside the car as if I were speaking into a microphone.

"Something with no fixed number of syllables," said Belano.

"And what else?"

"Something that doesn't rhyme," said Lima.

"And what else?"

"Something with no regular placement of stresses," said Lima.

"Good. Now a harder one. What is a tetrastich?"

"What?" said Lupe beside me.

"A metrical system of four verses," said Belano.

"And a syncope?"

"Oh, Jesus," said Lima.

"I don't know," said Belano. "Something syncopated?"

"Cold, cold. Do you give up?"

Lima's eyes were fixed on the rearview mirror. Belano looked at me for a second, then he looked past me. Lupe was looking behind us too. I didn't want to look.

"A syncope," I said, "is the omission of one or several phonemes within a word. For example: *bosun* for *boatswain, o'er* for *over*. All right. Moving along. Now an easy one. What's a sestina?"

"Six six-line stanzas," said Lima.

"And what else?" I said.

Lima and Belano said something I couldn't hear. Their voices seemed to drift inside the Impala. Well, there is something else, I said. And I told them what it was. And then I asked them whether they knew what a gly-conic was (it's a verse in classical meter that can be defined as a log-aoedic tetrapody catalectic *in syllabam*), and a hemiepes (which is the first foot of a dactylic hexameter, in Greek meter), or phonosymbolism (which is the independent emotional significance that the phonic elements of a word or verse can assume). And Belano and Lima didn't know a single answer, never mind Lupe. So I asked them whether they knew what an epanorthosis was, which is a figure of logic that consists of restating what's been said to qualify or amend or even contradict it, and I also asked them whether they knew what a pythiambic was (they didn't), or a mimiambic (they didn't), or a homeoteleuton (they didn't), or a paragoge (they did, and they thought that all Mexican and most Latin American poets were paragogic), and then I asked them whether they knew what a hapax or hapax legomenon was, and since they didn't know, I told them. It's a technical term used in lexicography or works of textual criticism to indicate an expression that appears just once in a language, oeuvre, or text. And that gave us something to think about for a while.

"Ask us an easier one," said Belano.

"All right. What's a zéjel?"

"Fuck, I don't know, I don't know anything," said Belano.

"What about you, Ulises?"

"It sounds like Arabic to me."

"And you, Lupe?"

Lupe looked at me and didn't say anything. I couldn't help laughing, probably because I was so nervous, but even so, I explained what a zéjel was. And when I had stopped laughing I told Lupe that I wasn't laughing at her or her ignorance (or lack of sophistication) but at all of us.

"All right, what's a Saturnian?"

"No idea," said Belano.

"Saturnian?" said Lupe.

"And a chiasmus?" I said.

"A what?" said Lupe.

Without closing my eyes, and at the same time as I was seeing every-one, I saw the car speeding like an arrow along the roads leading out of Mexico City. I felt as if we were floating on air.

"What is a Saturnian?" said Lima.

"Easy. An old Latin verse form whose principles of versification are unclear. Some think it was quantitative, others that it was accentual. If the first hypothesis is accepted, the Saturnian can be broken down into an iambic dimeter catalectic and an ithyphallic, although other varia-tions exist. If the accentual explanation is accepted, it's made up of two hemistiches, the first with three tonic accents and the second with two."

"Which poets used the Saturnian?" said Belano.

"Livius Andronicus and Naevius. Religious and commemorative poetry."

"You know a lot," said Lupe.

"He really does," said Belano.

I was seized by laughter again, laughter that was expelled instantly from the car. Orphan, I thought.

"It's just a question of memory. I memorize the definitions, that's all."

"You haven't told us what a chiasmus is yet," said Lima.

"Chiasmus, chiasmus, chiasmus . . . Well, a chiasmus is the presenta-tion of the elements of two sequences in reverse order."

It was nighttime. The night of January 1. The early morning hours of January 1. I looked back and it didn't seem as if anyone was following us.

"All right, how about this," I said. "What's a proceleusmatic?"

"You made that one up, García Madero," said Belano.

"No. It's a foot in classical meter consisting of four short syllables. It doesn't have a set rhythm and may therefore be considered a simple met-rical figure. What about a molossus?"

"You really did make that one up," said Belano.

"No, I swear. A molossus, in classical meter, is a foot consisting of three long syllables across six beats. The ictus can fall on the first and third syllables or only on the second. It has to be combined with other feet to form meter."

"What's an ictus?" said Belano.

Lima opened his mouth and closed it again.

"An ictus," I said, "is the downbeat, the temporal stress. Now I should say something about the arsis, which is the accented part of the Latin metrical foot, which means the syllable on which the ictus falls, but let's continue with the questions instead. Here's an easy one for you, something everyone can get. What's a bisyllable?"

"A two-syllable line," said Belano.

"Very good. About time," I said. "Two syllables long. Very rare and also the shortest possible line in Spanish meter. It almost always appears linked to longer verses. Now a harder one. What's an asclepiad?"

"No idea," said Belano.

"Asclepiad?" said Lima.

"It comes from Asclepiades of Samos, who used it most often, although Sappho and Alcaeus used it too. It takes two forms: the lesser asclepiad, which is made up of twelve syllables distributed in two Aeolic cola (or elements), the first consisting of a spondee, a dactyl, and a long syllable, the second of a dactyl and a trochaic dipode catalectic. The greater asclepiad is a verse of sixteen syllables formed by the insertion of a dactylic dipode catalectic *in syllabam* between two Aeolic cola."

We were almost out of Mexico City. We were going over eighty miles an hour.

"What is an epanalepsis?"

"No idea," I heard my friends say.

The car headed down dark avenues, through neighborhoods with no lights, down streets where there were only women and children. Then we swept through neighborhoods that were still celebrating New Year's Eve. Belano and Lima were looking forward, at the road. Lupe's head was resting against the window. She seemed to have fallen asleep.

"And what's an epanadiplosis?" No one answered me. "It's a syntactic figure consisting of the repetition of a word at the beginning and end of a sentence, line, or series of lines. An example is García Lorca's "Green oh how I love you green."

For a while I was quiet and I looked out the window. I had the feeling that Lima was lost, but at least no one was behind us.

"Keep going," said Belano, "we'll get one."

"What is a catachresis?" I said.

"That one I used to know, but I've forgotten," said Lima.

"It's a metaphor that's become part of common everyday speech and is no longer perceived as a metaphor. For example: needle's eye, bottle-neck. And an Archilochian?"

"That one I do know," said Belano. "It has to be the meter that Archilochus used."

"Great poet," said Lima.

"But what is it?" I said.

"I don't know. I can recite a poem by Archilochus, but I don't know what an Archilochian is," said Belano.

So I told them that an Archilochian was a two-line stanza (dystich), and that it could take various forms. The first consisted of a dactylic hexameter followed by a dactylic trimeter catalectic *in syllabam*. The second . . . but then I began to fall asleep and I listened to myself talk or to my voice echoing inside the Impala saying things like iambic dimeter or dactylic tetrameter or trochaic dimeter catalectic. And then I heard Belano reciting:

Heart, my heart, so battered with misfortune far beyond your
    strength,
up, and face the men who hate us. Bare your chest to the assault
of the enemy, and fight them off. Stand fast among the beam-
    like spears.
Give no ground; and if you beat them, do not brag in open show,
nor, if they beat you, run home and lie down on your bed
    and cry.

And then I opened my eyes with a great effort and Lima asked whether the poem was by Archilochus. Belano said *simón*, and Lima said what a great poet or what a fucking amazing poet. Then Belano turned around and explained to Lupe (as if she cared) who Archilochus of Paros had been, a poet and mercenary who lived in Greece around 650 B.C., and Lupe didn't say anything, which I thought was an appropriate re-sponse. Then I sat there half asleep, my head against the window, and lis-tened to Belano and Lima talking about a poet who fled the battlefield, caring nothing about the shame and dishonor that the act would bring upon him, in fact boasting of it. And then I started to dream about some-one crossing a field of bones, and the person in question had no face, or at least I couldn't see his face because I was watching him from a dis-tance. I was at the foot of a hill and there was hardly any air in the valley.

The person was naked and had long hair and at first I thought it was Archilochus but it really could have been anyone. When I opened my eyes it was still night and we had left Mexico City.

"Where are we?" I said.

"On the road to Querétaro," said Lima.

Lupe was awake too, and she was watching the dark countryside with eyes like insects.

"What are you watching?" I said.

"Alberto's car," she said.

"No one's following us," said Belano.

"Alberto's like a dog. He has my smell and he'll find me," said Lupe.

Belano and Lima laughed.

"How will he be able to find you when I've been doing ninety-five miles an hour ever since we left Mexico City?" said Lima.

"Before the sun comes up," said Lupe.

"All right," I said, "what's an aubade?"

Neither Belano nor Lima made a sound. I imagined they were thinking about Alberto, so I started to think about him too. Lupe laughed. Her insect eyes sought me:

"All right, Mr. Know-It-All, can you tell me what a *prix* is?"

"A toke of weed," said Belano without turning around.

"And what is *muy carranza*?"

"Something very old," said Belano.

"And *lurias*?"

"Let me answer," I said, because all the questions were really for me.

"All right," said Belano.

"I don't know," I said after thinking for a while.

"Do you know?" said Lima.

"I guess not," said Belano.

"Crazy," said Lima.

"That's right, crazy. And *jincho*?"

None of the three of us knew it.

"It's so easy. *Jincho* is Indian," said Lupe, laughing. "And what is *la grandiosa*?"

"Jail," said Lima.

"And what is *Javier*?"

A convoy of five freight trucks passed in the left lane heading toward Mexico City. Each truck looked like a burned arm. For an instant there was only the noise of the trucks and the smell of charred flesh. Then the road was plunged into darkness again.

"What's *Javier?*" said Belano.

"The police," said Lupe. "And *macha chacha?*"

"Marijuana," said Belano.

"This one is for Garcia Madero," said Lupe. "What's a *guacho de orégano?*"

Belano and Lima looked at each other and smiled. Lupe's insect eyes weren't watching me but the shadows unfurling threateningly out the back window. In the distance I saw the lights of one car, then another.

"I don't know," I said, as I imagined Alberto's face: a giant nose coming after us.

"A gold watch," said Lupe.

"What about a *carcamán?*" I said.

"A car," said Lupe.

I closed my eyes: I didn't want to see Lupe's eyes and I rested my head against the window. In my dreams I saw the black *carcamán*, unstoppable, Alberto's nose riding in it with a couple of off-duty policemen ready to beat the shit out of us.

"What's a *rufo?*" said Lupe.

We didn't answer.

"A car," said Lupe, and she laughed.

"All right, Lupe, how about this one, what's *la manicure?*" said Belano.

"Easy. The mental hospital," said Lupe.

For a moment it seemed impossible to me that I'd ever made love with a girl like Lupe.

"And what does *dar cuello* mean?" said Lupe.

"I don't know, I give up," said Belano without looking at her.

"The same thing as *dar caña,*" said Lupe, "but different. When you *dar cuello* you wipe somebody out, and when you *dar caña* you might be wiping somebody out, but you might also be fucking." Her voice sounded as ominous as if she had said *antibacchian* or *palimbacchian.*

"And what does it mean if you *dar labiada*, Lupe?" said Lima.

I thought about something sexual, about Lupe's pussy, which I'd only touched and not seen, about María's pussy and Rosario's pussy. I think we were going more than one hundred and ten.

"To give someone a chance, of course," said Lupe, and she looked at me as if she could guess what I was thinking. "What did you think it was, García Madero?" she said.

"What does *de empalme* mean?" said Belano.

"Something that's funny but hurts because it's true," said Lupe, undaunted.

"And a *chavo giratorio?*"

"A pothead," said Lupe.

"And a *coprero?*"

"A cokehead," said Lupe.

"And *echar pira?*" said Belano.

Lupe looked at him and then at me. I could feel the insects hopping from her eyes and landing on my knees, one on each knee. A white Impala just like ours shot past heading for Mexico City. As it disappeared through the back window it honked several times, wishing us luck.

"*Echar pira?*" said Lima. "I don't know."

"When more than one man rapes a woman," said Lupe.

"Gang rape, that's right, you know them all, Lupe," said Belano.

"And do you know what it means if you say somebody's *entrado en la rifa?*" said Lupe.

"Of course I know," said Belano. "It means you've already gotten involved in the problem, you're mixed up in it whether you want to be or not. It can also be taken as a veiled threat."

"Or not so veiled," said Lupe.

"So what would you say?" said Belano. "Have we *entrado en la rifa* or not?"

"All the way," said Lupe.

The lights of the cars that were following us suddenly disappeared. I had the feeling that we were the only people on the road in Mexico at that hour. But a few minutes later, I saw the lights again in the distance. There were two cars, and the distance separating them from us seemed to have decreased. I looked forward. There were insects smashed on the windshield. Lima was driving with both hands on the wheel and the car was vibrating as if we'd turned onto a dirt road.

"What is an epicede?" I said.

No one answered.

For a while we were all silent as the Impala sped forward in the dark.

"Tell us what an epicede is," said Belano without turning around.

"It's an elegy, recited in the presence of the dead," I said. "Not to be confused with the threnody. The epicede took the form of a choral dialogue. The meter used was the dactylo-epitrite, and later elegiac verse."

No reply.

"Fuck, this goddamn road is pretty," said Belano after a while.

"Ask us more questions," said Lima. "How would you define a threnody, García Madero?"

"Just like an epicede, except that it wasn't recited in the presence of the dead."

"More questions," said Belano.

"What's an alcaic?" I said.

My voice sounded strange, as if it wasn't I who'd spoken.

"A stanza of four alcaic verses," said Lima, "two hendecasyllables, one endecasyllable, and one decasyllable. The Greek poet Alcaeus used it, which is where the name comes from."

"It isn't two hendecasyllables," I said. "It's two decasyllables, one endecasyllable, and a trochaic decasyllable."

"Maybe," said Lima. "Who cares."

I watched Belano light a cigarette with the car lighter.

"Who introduced the alcaic stanza into Latin poetry?" I said.

"Man, everyone knows that," said Lima. "Do you know, Arturo?"

Belano had the lighter in his hand and he was staring at it, although his cigarette was already lit.

"Of course," he said.

"Who?" I said.

"Horace," said Belano, and he slid the lighter into its socket and then rolled down the window. The air ruffled my hair and Lupe's.


JANUARY 3

We had breakfast at a gas station outside of Culiacán, huevos rancheros, fried eggs with ham, eggs with bacon, and poached eggs. We each drank two cups of coffee and Lupe had a big glass of orange juice. We ordered four ham and cheese sandwiches for the road. Then Lupe went into the women's room, and Belano, Lima, and I went into the men's room, where we proceeded to wash our faces, hands, and necks, and use the facilities. When we came out the sky was a deep blue, as blue as I'd ever seen it, and there were lots of cars driving north. Lupe was nowhere to be seen, so after waiting a prudent amount of time, we went looking for her in the ladies' room. We found her brushing her teeth. She looked at us and we left without a word. Next to Lupe, bent over the other sink, was a woman in her fifties, brushing long black hair that fell to her waist.

Belano said we had to go into Culiacán to buy toothbrushes. Lima shrugged and said he didn't care. I said that I thought we had no time to lose, although actually time was the only thing we had more than enough of. In the end, Belano got his way. In a supermarket on the outskirts of Culiacán we bought toothbrushes and other personal hygiene things that we would need and then we turned around and left without going into the city.

## JANUARY 4

We passed through Navojoa, Ciudad Obregón, and Hermosillo like ghosts. We were in Sonora, although I'd felt as if we were in Sonora ever since Sinaloa. Sometimes we saw pitahayas, nopals, or saguaros rising alongside the road in the noonday glare. In the Hermosillo municipal library, Belano, Lima, and I searched for traces of Cesárea Tinajero. We couldn't find anything. When we got back to the car Lupe was asleep on the backseat and two men were standing on the sidewalk, motionless, watching her. Belano thought it might be Alberto and one of his friends and we separated to approach them. Lupe's dress had ridden up around her hips and the men were masturbating, their hands in their pockets. Get lost, said Arturo, and they went, turning to watch us as they retreated. Then we were in Caborca. If that's what Cesárea's magazine was called, it must have been for some reason, said Belano. Caborca is a little town northwest of Hermosillo. To get there we took the federal highway to Santa Ana and from Santa Ana we turned west along a paved road. We passed through Pueblo Nuevo and Altar. Before we got to Caborca we saw a turnoff and a sign with the name of another town: Pitiquito. But we drove on and got to Caborca, where we wandered around the town hall and the church, talking to everyone, searching in vain for someone who could tell us something about Cesárea Tinajero until night fell and we got in the car again, because Caborca didn't even have a boardinghouse or a little hotel where we could stay (and if it did we couldn't find it). So that night we slept in the car and when we woke up

536

we headed back to Caborca, got gas, and drove to Pitiquito. I have a hunch, said Belano. In Pitiquito we had a good meal and we went to see the church of San Diego del Pitiquito, from the outside, because Lupe said she didn't want to go in and we didn't really feel like it either.


JANUARY 5

We're heading northeast, along a good road, as far as Cananea, then south along a dirt road to Bacanuchi, and then on to 16 de Septiembre and Arizpe. I've stopped going along with Belano and Lima to ask questions. I stay in the car with Lupe or we get a beer. In Arizpe the road is better again and we head down to Banámichi and Huépac. From Huépac we head back up to Banámichi, this time without stopping, and return to Arizpe, turning east along a hellish dirt track to Los Hoyos, and from Los Hoyos, along a much better road, to Nacozari de García.

On the way out of Nacozari a patrolman stops us and asks for the car's papers. Are you from Nacozari, officer? Lupe asks him. The patrolman looks at her and says no, why would she think that, he's from Hermosillo. Belano and Lima laugh. They get out to stretch their legs. Then Lupe gets out and she and Arturo whisper to each other a little. The other officer gets out of his car too and comes over to talk to his partner, who is busy deciphering Quim's papers and Lima's driver's license. The two officers watch Lupe, who has walked a few yards away from the road, into a stony yellow landscape with darker patches, minuscule plants colored a nauseating brownish-purple-green. The brown, green, and purple of permanent exposure to an eclipse.

So where are you from? says the second officer. From Mexico City, I hear Belano answer. *Mexiquillos?* says the patrolman. More or less, says Belano, with a smile that frightens me. Who is this jerk? I think, but I'm thinking about Belano, not the policeman, and about Lima too, who's leaning on the hood of the car and staring at a point on the horizon, between the clouds and the quebrachos.

Then the policeman returns our papers and Lima and Belano ask him the shortest way to Santa Teresa. The second patrolman goes back to his car and gets out a map. When we leave the patrolmen wave goodbye. The paved road soon becomes a dirt road again. There are no cars, just a pickup truck every once in a while loaded with sacks or men. We pass towns called Aribabi, Huachinera, Bacerac, and Bavispe before we realize that we're lost. Just before dark a town suddenly appears in the distance that might or might not be Villaviciosa, but it's too much effort to find the way there. For the first time, Belano and Lima look nervous. Lupe is immune to the pull of the town. As far as I'm concerned, I don't know what to think: I might feel strange things, I might just want to sleep, I might be dreaming for all I know. Then we turn down another terrible road that seems to go on forever. Belano and Lima want me to ask them tough questions. I assume they mean questions about meter, rhetoric, and style. I ask them one and then I fall asleep. Lupe's sleeping too. In the time it takes me to fall asleep, I hear Belano and Lima talking. They talk about Mexico City, about Laura Damián and Laura Jáuregui, about a poet I've never heard of before, and they laugh, apparently the poet is a nice guy, a good person, they talk about people who are publishing magazines and who I gather are naïve or unsophisticated or just desperate. I like to hear them talk. Belano talks more than Lima, but both of them laugh a lot. They also talk about Quim's Impala. Sometimes, when there are lots of potholes in the road, the car jumps in a way that Belano doesn't think is normal. Lima thinks it's the noise the engine makes that isn't normal. Before I fall into a deep sleep I realize that neither of them knows anything about cars. When I wake up we're in Santa Teresa. Belano and Lima are smoking and the Impala is circling around the city center.

We check into a hotel, the Hotel Juárez, on Calle Juárez, Lupe taking one room and the three of us taking another. The only window in our room looks onto an alley. At the end of the alley, which runs into Calle Juárez, there's a gathering of shadowy figures who talk in low voices, although every so often someone curses or starts to shout for no reason, and after a prolonged period of observation, I see one of the shadows raise an arm and point at the window I'm watching from. At the other end of the alley, trash piles up, and it's even darker, if possible, although among the buildings one stands out, one that's a little more brightly lit. It's the back of the Hotel Santa Elena, with a tiny door that no one uses, except for a kitchen worker who comes out once with a trash can and stops beside the door when he goes back in, craning his neck to watch the traffic on Calle Juárez.

Belano and Lima spent all morning at the Municipal Registry Office, the census office, a few churches, the Santa Teresa Library, the university archives, and the archives of the only newspaper here, *El Centinela de Santa Teresa*. We met for lunch in the main square, next to an odd statue commemorating the victory of the locals over the French. In the afternoon, Belano and Lima are resuming their search. They have a meeting, they said, with the number one man in the literature department at the university, a jerk named Horacio Guerra, who is (surprise!) the spitting image of Octavio Paz, but in miniature, and that goes for his name too, if you think about it, said Belano, so tell me, García Madero, did Horace live in the same era as Caesar Augustus? I told him I didn't know. Let me think, I said. But they were in a rush and they started to talk about other things and when they went off I was left alone with Lupe again, and I thought about taking her to the movies, but since Lima and Belano had the money and I'd forgotten to ask them for some we couldn't go, and we had to settle for walking around Santa Teresa and window-shopping at the stores in the center and then going back to the hotel and watching television in a room off the lobby. There we met two little old ladies who, after staring at us for a while, asked us whether we were husband and wife. Lupe said yes. I had no choice but to play along, though the whole time I was thinking about what Belano and Lima had asked me, whether Horace had lived in the same era as Caesar Augustus, and I thought he had, my instinct would've been to say yes, but I also had the feeling that Horace wasn't exactly a champion of Augustus, and Lupe was talking to the old ladies, snoopy old ladies, as it turned out, and I don't know why but I kept thinking about Augustus and Horace and listening with my left ear to the soap opera that was on TV and with my right ear to Lupe and the old ladies talking, and suddenly my memory went *plumph*, like a soft wall collapsing, and I saw Horace fighting *against* Augustus or Octavian and for Brutus and Cassius, who had murdered Caesar and wanted to bring back the Republic, shit, it couldn't have been weirder if I had dropped acid, I saw Horace, twenty-four at Philippi, only a little older than Belano or Lima and just seven years older than me, and that bastard Horace, who was staring into the distance, suddenly turned around and looked at me! Hello, García Madero, he said in Latin, although I don't understand a fucking word of Latin,

I'm Horace, born in Venusia in 65 B.C., son of a freed slave (the most loving father anyone could ask for), appointed tribune under Brutus, ready to march into battle, the Battle of Philippi, which we'll lose but which I'm destined to fight, the Battle of Philippi, where the fate of mankind is at stake, and then one of the old ladies touched my arm and asked me what had brought me to the city of Santa Teresa, and I saw Lupe's smiling eyes and the eyes of the other old lady, which were shooting sparks as she watched Lupe and me, and I answered that we were on our honeymoon, our honeymoon, ma'am, I said, and then I got up and told Lupe to follow me and we went to her room where we fucked like crazy or as if we were going to die the next morning, until it got dark and we heard the voices of Lima and Belano, who had come back to their room and were talking, talking, talking.

## JANUARY 7

Now we know for sure: Cesárea Tinajero was here. There was no trace of her at the registry, or the university, or the parish archives, or the library, where for some reason the archives of the old Santa Teresa hospital, now called the General Sepúlveda Hospital after the Revolutionary hero, are stored. And yet, at the *Centinela de Santa Teresa* they let Belano and Lima comb through the morgue and in the news from 1928 there was a June 6 mention of a bullfighter named Pepe Avellaneda, who fought two bulls from Don José Forcat's stock in the Santa Teresa bullring with considerable success (two ears) and of whom there's a profile and interview in the June 11, 1928, issue, in which it says, among other things, that Pepe Avellaneda was traveling in the company of a woman named Cesárea Tinaja [*sic*], formerly of Mexico City. There are no photographs with the piece, but the local reporter describes her as "tall, attractive, and reserved," although I frankly have no idea what he could mean by that, unless he's saying it to emphasize the difference between the woman and the bullfighter she was accompanying, who is described, somewhat bluntly, as a little man, no more than five feet tall, very thin, with a big dented skull, a description that reminds Belano and Lima of a Hemingway bullfighter (Hemingway's an author I unfortunately haven't read), the typical brave and luckless Hemingway bullfighter, more sad than anything else, deathly sad, although I wouldn't dare say as much with so little to go on, and anyway Cesárea Tinajero is one thing and Cesárea

Tinaja is another, which is something my friends refuse to admit, chalking it up it to a misprint, a bad transcription, or the reporter's faulty hearing, and maybe even an intentional slip on Cesárea Tinajero's part, saying her name wrong, a joke, a modest way of hiding a modest clue.

The rest of the article is unremarkable. Pepe Avellaneda talks about bullfighting, saying incomprehensible or incongruous things, but so mildly that he never sounds pedantic. A final clue: the July 10 issue of the *Centinela de Santa Teresa* announces the departure of the bullfighter (and presumably his companion) for Sonoyta, where he will share billing in the ring with Jesús Ortiz Pacheco, bullfighter from Monterrey. So Cesárea and Avellaneda were in Santa Teresa for about a month, evidently doing nothing, seeing the local sights or holed up in their hotel. In any case, according to Lima and Belano we now had someone who knew Cesárea, who knew her well, and who plausibly still lived in Sonora, although with bullfighters you never know. Their response to my argument that Avellaneda might be dead was that we would still have his family and friends. So now we were looking for Cesárea and the bullfighter. They told outrageous stories about Horacio Guerra. They said again that he was exactly like Octavio Paz. Considering the short time they'd spent with him I don't know how they could know so much about him, but they said that his acolytes in this lost corner of Sonora were carbon copies of Paz's acolytes. As if in this forgotten province, forgotten poets, essayists, and professors were simulating the mass-media actions of their idols.

At first, they said, Guerra was extremely interested in knowing who Cesárea Tinajero was, but his interest evaporated when Belano and Lima explained the avant-garde nature of her work, and how little of it there was.


JANUARY 8

We didn't find anything in Sonoyta. On our way back we stopped in Caborca again. Belano insisted it couldn't be just a coincidence that Cesárea had named her magazine after it. But once again we found nothing to suggest that the poet had ever been there.

In the archives of the Hermosillo paper, on the other hand, we stumbled on our first day of searching upon the announcement of Pepe Avellaneda's death. On the fragile old sheets we read that the bullfighter had died in the Agua Prieta bullring, charged by the bull as he prepared to deliver the coup de grâce, a thing at which Avellaneda had never excelled given how short he was: no matter the size of the bull, he had to leap to kill it and as he leaped his little body was unprotected, vulnerable to the beast's slightest lunge.

It didn't take him long to die. Avellaneda bled to death in his hotel room at the Agua Prieta Excelsior, and two days later he was buried in the Agua Prieta cemetery. There was no service. The mayor, the top municipal authorities, and the Monterrey bullfighter Jesús Ortiz Pacheco attended the burial, as did some aficionados who had seen Avellaneda die and wanted to pay their last respects. The story raised two or three lingering questions and convinced us to visit Agua Prieta.

First of all, according to Belano, the reporter was probably going by hearsay. It was possible, of course, that the main Hermosillo newspaper had a correspondent in Agua Prieta and that this correspondent had sent in his account of the tragic event by telegraph, but what was clear (though why I don't know, incidentally) was that here, in Hermosillo, the story had been embellished, lengthened, polished, made more literary. A question: who sat in the vigil over Avellaneda's body? A curious detail: who was the bullfighter Ortiz Pacheco, whose shadow seemed to cling to Avellaneda's? Was he touring Sonora with Avellaneda or was his presence in Agua Prieta purely coincidental? As we feared, we found no other news of Avellaneda in the Hermosillo archives, as if once the death of the bullfighter had been witnessed, he had fallen into absolute oblivion, which, after all, was only natural. The vein of information was exhausted. So we made our way to the Peña Taurina Pilo Yáñez, located in the old part of the city, a family bar with a faintly Spanish air where the Hermosillo tauromachy fanatics gathered. No one there knew anything about a pint-size bullfighter called Pepe Avellaneda, but when we told them that he was active in the 1920s, and the name of the bullring where he was killed, they referred us to a little old man who knew everything about the bullfighter Ortiz Pacheco (again!) although his favorite was Pilo Yáñez, Sultan of Caborca (Caborca yet again), a nickname that we, unfamiliar with the labyrinthine byways of Mexican bullfighting, thought seemed more fitting for a boxer.

The old man's name was Jesús Pintado and he remembered Pepe Avellaneda, Pepín Avellaneda, he called him, a bullfighter who never had much luck but was braver than most, from Sonora, possibly, or maybe Sinaloa or Chihuahua, although he made his name in Sonora, which meant that he was Sonoran by adoption if nothing else, killed in Agua Prieta on a bill he shared with Ortiz Pacheco and Efrén Salazar, during Agua Prieta's big fiesta, in May 1930. Señor Pintado, do you know whether he had any family? asked Belano. The old man didn't know. Do you know whether he traveled with a woman? The old man laughed and looked at Lupe. All of them traveled with women or picked them up along the way, he said. In those days, men were wild and some of the women were too. But you don't know? said Belano. The old man didn't know. Is Ortiz Pacheco alive? said Belano. The old man said yes. Do you know where we could find him, Señor Pintado? The old man said the bullfighter had a ranch near El Cuatro. What's that, said Belano, a town, a road, a restaurant? The old man looked at us as if he had suddenly recognized us from somewhere, then he said it was a town.

### JANUARY 9

To make the trip go faster, I started to draw pictures, puzzles that I was taught in school a long time ago. Although there are no cowboys here. No one wears a cowboy hat here. Here there's only desert, and towns like mirages, and bare hills.

"What's this?" I said.

Lupe looked at the drawing as if she didn't feel like playing, and was silent. Belano and Lima didn't know either.

"An elegiac verse?" said Lima.

"No. A Mexican seen from above," I said. "And this one?"

"A Mexican smoking a pipe," said Lupe.

"And this one?"

"A Mexican on a tricycle," said Lupe. "A Mexican boy on a tricycle."
"And this one?"

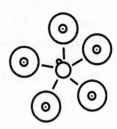

"Five Mexicans peeing in a urinal," said Lima.
"And this one?"

"A Mexican on a bicycle," said Lupe.
"Or a Mexican on a tightrope," said Lima.
"And this one?"

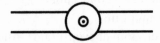

"A Mexican on a bridge," said Lima.
"And this one?"

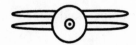

"A Mexican skiing," said Lupe.
"And this one?"

"A Mexican about to draw his guns," said Lupe.
"Jesus, Lupe, you know them all," said Belano.
"And you don't know a single one," said Lupe.
"That's because I'm not Mexican," said Belano.
"And this one?" I said, showing the drawing to Lima first and then to the others.

"A Mexican going up a ladder," said Lupe.
"And this one?"

"Gee, that's a hard one," said Lupe.
For a while my friends stopped laughing and looked at the picture and I watched the landscape. I saw something in the distance that looked like a tree. When we passed it I realized it was a plant: an enormous dead plant.
"We give up," said Lupe.
"It's a Mexican frying an egg," I said. "And this one?"

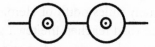

"Two Mexicans on one of those bicycles for two," said Lupe.
"Or two Mexicans on a tightrope," said Lima.
"Here's a hard one for you," I said.

"Easy: a buzzard wearing a cowboy hat," said Lupe.
"And this one?"

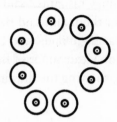

"Eight Mexicans talking," said Lima.
"Eight Mexicans sleeping," said Lupe.
"Or even eight Mexicans watching an invisible cockfight," I said.
"And this one?"

"Four Mexicans keeping vigil over a body," said Belano.

**JANUARY 10**

The trip to El Cuatro didn't go smoothly. We spent almost the whole day on the road, first looking for El Cuatro, which according to what we'd been told was about ninety miles north of Hermosillo along the federal highway, and then, once we'd reached the town of Benjamín Hill, a left turn east along a dirt road where we got lost and came back out on the highway again, this time six miles south of Benjamín Hill, which made us think that El Cuatro didn't exist, until we took the turn at Benjamín Hill again (actually, to get to El Cuatro it's better to take the first left, the one that's six miles from Benjamín Hill) and drove and drove through landscapes that looked lunar sometimes and other times revealed patches of green, always desolate, and then we came to a town called Félix Gómez and there a man planted himself in front of our car with his legs braced and his hands on his hips and cursed us and then other people told us that to get to El Cuatro we had to go a certain way and then turn another way and then we got to a town called El Oasis, which in no way resembled an oasis but rather seemed to sum up all the misery of the desert in its storefronts and then we came out on the highway again and then Lima said that the Sonora desert was a shithole and Lupe said that if they had let her drive we would've been there a long time ago, to which Lima responded by hitting the brake and getting out and telling Lupe to take the wheel. I don't know what happened then, but we all got out of the Impala and stretched our legs. In the distance we could see the highway and some cars heading north, probably to Tijuana and the United States, and others heading south, toward Hermosillo or Guadalajara or Mexico City, and then we started to talk about Mexico City and bask in the sun (comparing our tanned forearms) and smoke and talk about Mexico City and Lupe said that she didn't miss anybody anymore. When she said it I realized that strangely enough I didn't miss anyone either, although I was careful not to say so. Then they all got back in, except for me. I entertained myself by tossing clumps of dirt as far as I could in no particular direction, and although I could hear them calling me I didn't turn my head or make the slightest move toward heading back, until Belano said: García Madero, either get in or stay here, and then I turned around and started to walk toward the Impala, having gotten pretty far away without meaning to, and as I returned I thought how dirty Quim's car looked, imagining Quim seeing his Impala through my eyes or María seeing her father's Impala through my eyes and it really wasn't a pretty sight. Its color had almost vanished under a layer of desert dust.

Then we went back to El Oasis and Félix Gómez and we made it to El Cuatro at last, in the municipality of Trincheras, and we had lunch there and asked the waiter and the people at the next table whether they knew where the ex-bullfighter Ortiz Pacheco's ranch was, but they had never heard of him, so we decided to wander around the town, Lupe and I in silence and Belano and Lima talking nonstop, but not about Ortiz Pacheco or Avellaneda or Cesárea Tinajero, but about Mexico City gossip or Latin American books or magazines they'd read just before setting off on this meandering road trip, or movies. Basically, they talked about things that struck me as frivolous, and possibly Lupe too, because both of us were quiet, and after lots of asking we found a man in the market (which was deserted at that hour) who had three cardboard boxes full of chicks and was able to tell us how to get to Ortiz Pacheco's ranch. So we got back in the Impala and set off again.

Halfway down the road from El Cuatro to Trincheras we were supposed to turn left, onto a track that skirted the slopes of a hill shaped like a quail, but when we took the turn, all the hills, every raised bit of ground, even the desert, looked quail-shaped, like quail in different positions, so we wandered down tracks that couldn't even be called dirt roads, battering the car and ourselves too, until the track ended and a house, a building that looked like an eighteenth-century mission, suddenly appeared through the dust, and an old man came out to meet us and told us that this was in fact the bullfighter Ortiz Pacheco's ranch, La Buena Vida, and that he himself (but he only said this after watching us closely for a while) was the bullfighter Ortiz Pacheco.

That night we enjoyed the old matador's hospitality. Ortiz Pacheco was seventy-nine and had a memory fortified by life in the country, according to him, or the desert, according to us. He remembered Pepe Avellaneda (Pepín Avellaneda, the saddest little man I ever saw, he said) perfectly well, and he remembered the afternoon when Avellaneda was killed in the Agua Prieta bullring. He was at the wake, which was held in the parlor at the hotel, where nearly every living soul in Agua Prieta stopped by to offer a final farewell, and at the burial, which was a gathering of multitudes, a dark end to an epic fiesta, he said. Naturally, he remembered the woman who was with Avellaneda. A tall woman, the way short men tend to like them, quiet, though not out of shyness or prudence, but as if she had no choice, as if she were sick and couldn't speak. Was she Avellaneda's lover? No doubt about that. Not his better half, because Avellaneda was married and his wife, whom he'd left long before, lived in Los Mochis, Sinaloa. According to Ortiz Pacheco, the bullfighter sent her money every month or two (or whenever he damn well could). In those days, bullfighting wasn't the way it is now with even the novices getting rich. Anyway, back then Avellaneda was living with this woman. He couldn't remember her name, but he knew that she came from Mexico City and that she was an educated woman, a typist or a stenographer. When Belano said Cesárea's name, Ortiz Pacheco said yes, that was it. Was she the kind of woman who was interested in bulls? asked Lupe. I don't know, said Ortiz Pacheco, maybe she was and maybe she wasn't, but when someone is with a bullfighter, in the long run they end up liking that world. In any case, Ortiz Pacheco had only seen Cesárea twice, the last time in Agua Prieta, which probably meant they hadn't been lovers for long. Still, she exerted an obvious influence on Pepín Avellaneda, according to Ortiz Pacheco.

The night before he died, for example, as the two bullfighters were drinking at a bar in Agua Prieta and just before they both returned to the hotel, Avellaneda started to talk about Aztlán. At first he spoke as if he were telling a secret, as if he didn't really want to talk, but as the minutes went by he grew more and more excited. Ortiz Pacheco didn't even know what Aztlán meant, never having heard the word before in his life. So Avellaneda explained it to him from the beginning, telling him about the sacred city of the first Mexicans, the city of legend, the undiscovered city, Plato's true Atlantis, and when they got back to the hotel, half drunk, Ortiz Pacheco thought that only Cesárea could be responsible for such wild ideas. She was alone most of the time during the wake, shut in her room or sitting in a corner of the Excelsior's hall, which was done up like a funeral parlor. No women offered her their condolences. Only the men, and in private, since it hadn't escaped anyone that she was just the mistress. She didn't say a word at the burial. There were speeches by the town treasurer, who was also what you might call the official poet of Agua Prieta, and the president of the bullfighting society, but she didn't speak. Nor, according to Ortiz Pacheco, was she seen to shed a single tear. Though she did commission the mason to carve some words on Avellaneda's tombstone, what they were, Ortiz Pacheco couldn't remember, strange words, in any case, in the same style as Aztlán, he seemed to recall, and surely invented by her for the occasion. Invented, not requested, was what he said. Belano and Lima asked him what the words were. Ortiz Pacheco thought for a while but finally said he'd forgotten them.

That night we slept at the ranch. Belano and Lima slept in the main room (there were many bedrooms, but they were all uninhabitable), Lupe and I in the car. I woke up just as the sun was rising and took a piss in the yard, watching the first pale yellow (but also blue) lights slipping stealthily across the desert. I lit a cigarette and spent a while watching the horizon and breathing. In the distance I thought I spotted a plume of dust, but then I realized it was just a low cloud. Low and motionless. It seemed strange not to hear any animal sounds. And yet every once in a while, if you paid attention, you could hear a bird singing. When I turned around, Lupe was watching me from one of the windows of the Impala. Her short black hair was a mess and she seemed thinner than before, as if she were turning invisible, as if the morning were painlessly dissolving her, but at the same time she seemed more beautiful than ever.

We went into the house together. In the main room, we found Lima, Belano, and Ortiz Pacheco, each in a leather armchair. The old bullfighter was wrapped in a serape and he was asleep with a startled expression on his face. As Lupe made coffee, I woke my friends. I was afraid to wake Ortiz Pacheco. I think he's dead, I whispered. Belano stretched, his joints cracking. He said it had been a long time since he slept so well and then he took it upon himself to wake our host. As we were having breakfast, Ortiz Pacheco said that he'd had a strange dream. Did you dream about your friend Avellaneda? said Belano. No, not at all, said Ortiz Pacheco, I dreamed that I was ten years old and my family was moving from Monterrey to Hermosillo. In those days that must have been a very long trip, said Lima. Very long, yes, said Ortiz Pacheco, but happy.

JANUARY 11

We went to Agua Prieta, to the Agua Prieta cemetery. From La Buena Vida to Trincheras first, and then from Trincheras to Pueblo Nuevo, Santa Ana, San Ignacio, Ímuris, Cananea, and Agua Prieta, right on the Arizona border.

On the other side of the border was Douglas, an American town, and in between was customs and the border police. On the other side of Douglas, about forty miles northwest, was Tombstone, where the best American gunmen once gathered. As we were eating at a coffee shop, we heard two stories: one demonstrating the value of all things Mexican and the other the value of all things American. In one, the protagonist was from Agua Prieta, and in the other he was from Tombstone.

When the man who was telling the stories, a guy with long gray-streaked hair who talked as if his head hurt, left the coffee shop, the man who'd been listening started to laugh for no apparent reason, or as if he'd needed a couple of minutes to make sense of the stories he'd heard. Really, it was just two jokes. In the first, the sheriff and one of his deputies take a prisoner from his cell and lead him far out into the country to kill him. The prisoner knows what's happening and is more or less resigned to his fate. It's a harsh winter, day is dawning, and prisoner and executioners alike are complaining of the cold in the desert. At a certain moment, though, the prisoner starts to laugh, and the sheriff says what the hell's so funny, has he forgotten that he's about to be killed and buried where no one can find him? has he lost his mind? And the prisoner says, and this is the punch line, that he's laughing because in a few minutes he won't be cold, but the lawmen will have to walk back.

The other story tells of the execution of Colonel Guadalupe Sánchez, prodigal son of Agua Prieta, who at the moment he faced the firing squad asked, as a last wish, to smoke a cigar. The commanding officer granted him his wish. He was given his last Havana. Guadalupe Sánchez lit it calmly and began to smoke in a leisurely manner, savoring it and watching the sun come up (because like the Tombstone story, this one takes place at dawn, maybe even unfolding on the same morning, the morning of May 15, 1912), and, wreathed in smoke, Colonel Sánchez was so relaxed, so unruffled, so serene, that the ash stayed glued to the cigar, which might have been the colonel's intention, to see for himself if his pulse would quicken, if in the end his hand would shake and show he'd lost his nerve, but he finished the Havana and the ash didn't fall. Then Colonel Sánchez tossed away the butt and said whenever you like.

That was the story.

When the recipient of the stories stopped laughing, Belano asked himself a few questions out loud: is the prisoner who's going to die outside of Tombstone from Tombstone? or just the sheriff and his deputy? was Colonel Guadalupe Sánchez from Agua Prieta? was the commander of the firing squad from Agua Prieta? why did they kill the Tombstone prisoner like a dog? why did they kill *mi coronel* [sic] Lupe Sánchez like a dog? Everyone in the coffee shop was looking at him, but no one said anything. Lima took him by the shoulder and said: come on, man, let's go. Belano looked at him with a smile and put a few bills on the counter. Then we left for the cemetery and went looking for the gravestone of Pepe Avellaneda, who was killed because he was gored by a bull or because he was too short and clumsy with his sword, a gravestone with an epitaph written by Cesárea Tinajero, and no matter how long we looked, we couldn't find it. The Agua Prieta cemetery was the closest thing we'd seen to a labyrinth, and the cemetery's veteran gravedigger, the only one who knew exactly where each dead person was buried, was away on vacation or out sick.

JANUARY 12

So if you travel with a bullfighter, in the long run you end up liking that world? said Lupe. I guess so, said Belano. And if you're with a policeman, do you end up liking the policeman's world? I guess so, said Belano. And if you're with a pimp, do you end up liking the pimp's world? Belano didn't answer. Strange, because he always tries to answer every question, even when no answer is needed or the question is beside the point. Lima, on the other hand, talks less and less, just driving the Impala with an absent look on his face. Blind as we are, I think we haven't noticed how Lupe is beginning to change.

JANUARY 13

Today we called Mexico City for the first time. Belano talked to Quim Font. Quim said Lupe's pimp knew where we were and was coming after us. Belano said that was impossible. Alberto had followed us to the edge of the city and we'd managed to lose him there. Yes, said Quim, but then he came back here and threatened to kill me if I didn't tell him where you were going. I took the phone and told him I wanted to talk to María. I heard Quim's voice. He was crying. Hello? I said. I want to talk to María. Is that you, García Madero? sobbed Quim. I thought you'd have gone home. I'm here, I said. I thought I heard Quim sniff. Belano and Lima were talking in low voices. They had moved away from the phone and looked worried. Lupe stayed close to me, close to the phone, as if she were cold, even though it wasn't cold. She had her back turned to me, and she was looking toward the gas station where we'd parked. Take the first bus and come back to Mexico City, I heard Quim say. If you don't have money I'll send it to you. We have more than enough money, I said. Is María there? No one's here, I'm alone, sobbed Quim. For a while we were both silent. How is my car? that voice from another world said suddenly. Fine, I said, everything's fine. We're getting closer to finding Cesárea Tinajero, I lied. Who's Cesárea Tinajero? said Quim.

552

## JANUARY 14

We bought clothes in Hermosillo and a bathing suit for each of us. Then we went to pick up Belano at the library (where he'd spent the morning, in the firm belief that a poet always leaves a written trail, a belief borne out by none of the evidence so far) and went to the beach. We paid for two rooms at a boardinghouse in Bahía Kino. The sea is dark blue. It was the first time Lupe had seen it.

## JANUARY 15

An excursion: our Impala set off down the road that dangles along one side of the Gulf of California, to Punta Chueca, across from the island of Tiburón. Then we went on to El Dólar, across from the island of Patos. Lying on a deserted beach, we spent hours smoking weed. Punta Chueca–Tiburón, Dólar-Patos: they're only names, of course, but they fill my soul with dread, as one of Amado Nervo's contemporaries might say. What is it about those names that makes me feel so upset, sad, fatalistic, that makes me look at Lupe as if she were the last woman on earth? A little before nightfall we headed farther north, to where Desemboque rises. Darkness in my soul. I think I actually shuddered. And then we turned around and went back to Bahía Kino along a dark road. Every so often we'd pass a pickup full of Seri fishermen singing one of their songs.

## JANUARY 16

Belano has bought a knife.

## JANUARY 17

Back in Agua Prieta. We left Bahía Kino at eight in the morning. The route we took was from Bahía Kino to Punta Chueca, Punta Chueca to El Dólar, El Dólar to Desemboque, Desemboque to Las Estrellas, and Las Estrellas to Trincheras. About one hundred and fifty miles along terrible roads. If we had taken the Bahía Kino–El Triunfo–Hermosillo route, the highway from Hermosillo to San Ignacio, and then the road to Cananea and Agua Prieta, we would almost certainly have had a more comfortable trip and gotten there sooner. And yet we all decided that it was better to travel along roads without much traffic, or with no traffic at all, and we liked the idea of stopping at La Buena Vida again. But we got lost in the triangle between El Cuatro, Trincheras, and La Ciénaga and finally we decided to drive all the way to Trincheras and visit the old bullfighter another time.

When we parked the Impala at the gates of the Agua Prieta cemetery, it was starting to get dark. Belano and Lima rang the bell for the watchman. After a while, a man with a face so sun-beaten that it looked black came to the door. He was wearing glasses and had a big scar on the left side of his face. He asked us what we wanted. Belano said that we were looking for the gravedigger Andrés González Ahumada. The man looked at us and asked who we were and what we wanted him for. Belano said it was about the bullfighter Pepe Avellaneda's grave. We want to see it, we said. I'm Andrés González Ahumada, said the gravedigger, and this is hardly the time of day to visit a cemetery. Please? said Lupe. And why are you so interested, if you don't mind my asking? said the gravedigger. Belano went up to the bars and spent a few minutes conferring with the man in a low voice. The gravedigger nodded several times and then he went into his little hut and came out again with an enormous key he used to let us in. We followed him along the cemetery's main path, a walk lined with cypresses and old oaks. When we turned down the side paths, however, we saw some cactuses native to the region: choyas and sahuesos and a nopal or two, as if to remind the dead that they were in Sonora and not some other place.

This is the bullfighter Pepe Avellaneda's grave, said the gravedigger, gesturing toward a niche in a neglected corner. Belano and Lima went over and tried to read the inscription, but the niche was four levels up and night was already falling over the cemetery paths. There were no flowers at any of the graves, except one where four plastic carnations hung, and most of the inscriptions were covered in dust. Then Belano interlaced his fingers, making a little seat or stirrup, and Lima stepped up, pressing his face to the glass over Avellaneda's photograph. What he did next was wipe the plaque with his hand and read the inscription aloud: "José Avellaneda Tinajero, matador, Nogales 1903–Agua Prieta 1930." Is that all? I heard Belano say. That's all, replied Lima's voice, hoarser than ever. Then he jumped down and did as Belano had done, making a step with his hands so that Belano could climb up. Give me the lighter, Lupe, I heard Belano say. Lupe went up to the pathetic figure composed of my two friends and without saying anything handed him a box of matches. What about my lighter? said Belano. I don't have it, *mano*, said Lupe, in a sweet voice that I still wasn't used to. Belano lit a match and held it up to the niche. When it went out he lit another, and then another. Lupe was leaning against the wall across from him, her long legs crossed. She was staring at the ground, looking pensive. Lima was staring at the ground too, but his face only expressed the effort of supporting Belano's weight. After using up seven matches and burning the tips of his fingers a few times, Belano gave up and got down. We walked back out toward the gate of the Agua Prieta cemetery without speaking. There, by the door, Belano gave the gravedigger a few bills and we left.

### JANUARY 18

In Santa Teresa, when we went into a café with a big mirror behind the bar, I realized how much we had changed. Belano hasn't shaved for days. Lima doesn't need to shave, but he probably hasn't combed his hair since around the time Belano stopped shaving. I'm all skin and bones (I've been screwing three times a night, on average). Only Lupe looks good, or anyway better than she did when we left Mexico City.

### JANUARY 19

Was Cesárea Tinajero the dead bullfighter's cousin? Was she a distant relative? Did she ask them to put her own last name on the plaque, give Avellaneda her own name, as a way of saying this man is mine? Did she add her name to the bullfighter's name as a joke? A way of saying *Cesárea Tinajero was here*? It hardly matters. Today we called Mexico City again. All quiet at Quim's. Belano talked to Quim, Lima talked to Quim. When I tried to talk the phone went dead, although we had plenty of coins. I got the impression that Quim didn't want to talk to me and that he hung up. Then Belano called his father and Lima called his mother and then Belano called Laura Jáuregui. The first two conversations were relatively long, formal, and the last was very short. Only Lupe and I didn't call anyone in Mexico City, as if we didn't feel like it or didn't have anyone to talk to.

This morning, while we were eating breakfast at a café in Nogales, we saw Alberto behind the wheel of his Camaro. He was wearing a shirt the same color as the car, bright yellow, and next to him was a guy in a leather jacket who looked like a cop. Lupe recognized him right away: she turned pale and said Alberto's here. She didn't let her fear show, but I knew she was afraid. Lima followed Lupe's gaze and said yes, it was Alberto and one of his buddies. Belano watched the car go by through the big café windows and told us we were hallucinating. I saw Alberto perfectly clearly. Let's get out of here now, I said. Belano looked at us and said no way. First we would go to the Nogales library and then head back to Hermosillo to continue our search, as we had planned. Lima agreed. I like your stubbornness, man, he said. So they finished their breakfasts (neither Lupe nor I could eat anything else) and then we left the café, got in the Impala, and dropped Belano off at the door to the library. Be brave, for fuck's sake, don't go imagining things, he said before disappearing. Lima watched the library door for a while, as if trying to come up with a reply, and then he started the car. You saw him, Ulises, said Lupe, it was him. I think so, said Lima. What will we do if he finds me? said Lupe. Lima didn't answer. We parked the car on a deserted street, in a middle-class neighborhood, with no bars or stores in sight except for a fruit stand, and Lupe started to tell us stories from her childhood and then I started to tell stories about when I was a boy too, just to kill time, and although Ulises didn't open his mouth once and started to read a book, still sitting behind the wheel, you could tell he was listening because every so often he would raise his eyes and look at us and smile. At noon we went to pick up Belano. Lima parked close to a nearby plaza and said that I should go to the library. He would stay with Lupe and the Impala in case Alberto showed up and they had to get out of there fast. I walked the four blocks to the library quickly, looking straight ahead the whole way. I found Belano sitting at a long wooden table, stained dark by the passage of time, with several bound volumes of the Nogales local paper. He was the only person in the library, and when I got there he raised his head and motioned for me to come and sit next to him.

## JANUARY 21

The only image I took away from the Nogales newspaper's obituary of Pepín Avellaneda is of Cesárea Tinajero walking along a dreary desert road hand in hand with her little bullfighter, a little bullfighter who's struggling not to keep shrinking, who's struggling to grow, and who in fact begins to grow little by little, say until he reaches five and a half feet, then disappears.

## JANUARY 22

In El Cubo. To get from Nogales to El Cubo you have to take the highway to Santa Ana and head west, from Santa Ana to Pueblo Nuevo, Pueblo Nuevo to Altar, Altar to Caborca, Caborca to San Isidro, then take the road to Sonoyta, on the Arizona border, but turn off onto a dirt road before you get there and go about fifteen or twenty miles. The Nogales newspaper talked about "his faithful companion, a devoted teacher in El Cubo." In the town we went to the school, and one glance was enough to tell us that it had been built after 1940. Cesárea Tinajero couldn't have taught here. Though if we dug around under it, we might be able to find the old school.

We talked to the teacher. She teaches the children Spanish and Pápago. The Pápagos live in Arizona and Sonora. We asked the teacher whether she was Pápago. No, she isn't. I'm from Guaymas, she tells us, and my grandfather was a Mayo. We ask her why she teaches Pápago. So the language won't be lost, she tells us. There are only two hundred Pápagos left in Mexico. You're right, that's not many, we admit. In Arizona there are almost sixteen thousand, but only two hundred in Mexico. And how many Pápagos are left in El Cubo? About twenty, says the teacher, but it doesn't matter, I'll keep teaching. Then she explains that the Pápagos don't call themselves that. They call themselves O'Odham and the Pimas call themselves Óob and the Seris call themselves Konkáak. We tell her that we were in Bahía Kino, in Punta Chueca, and El Dólar and we heard the fishermen singing Seri songs. The teacher is surprised. There are seven hundred Konkáak, she says, if that, and they don't fish. Well, these fishermen had learned a Seri song, we say. Maybe, says the teacher, but more likely they fooled you. Later she invited us to her house for dinner. She lives alone. We asked her whether she wouldn't like to live in Hermosillo or Mexico City. She said no. She likes this place. Then we went to see an old Pápago woman who lived half a mile from El Cubo. The old woman's house was adobe. It consisted of three rooms, two empty and one in which she lived with her animals. And yet the smell was hardly noticeable, swept away by the desert wind that came in through the glassless windows.

The teacher explained to the old woman in her language that we wanted news of Cesárea Tinajero. The old woman listened to the teacher and looked at us and said: huh. Belano and Lima looked at each other for a second and I knew they were wondering whether the old woman's *huh* meant something different in Pápago or whether it meant what we thought it did. A good person, said the old woman. She lived with a good man. Both of them good. The teacher looked at us and smiled. What was the man like? said Belano, gesturing to indicate differ-ent heights. Medium tall, said the old woman, skinny, medium tall, light-colored eyes. Light like this? said Belano, picking an almond-colored branch from the wall. Light like that, said the old woman. Medium tall like this? said Belano, holding up his index finger to a level suggesting someone on the short side. Medium tall, that's right, said the old woman. And what about Cesárea Tinajero? said Belano. Alone, said the old woman, she left with her man and came back alone. How long was she here? As long as the school, good teacher, said the old woman. A year? said Belano. The old woman looked through Belano and Lima, as if she didn't see them. She looked sympathetically at Lupe, asking her something in Pápago. The teacher translated: which of these men is yours? Lupe smiled. She was behind me and I couldn't see her, but I knew she was smiling. She said: none of them. She didn't have a man ei-ther, said the old woman. One day she went away with him and later she came back alone. Was she still teaching? said Belano. The old woman said something in Pápago. She lived in the school, translated the teacher, but she didn't teach anymore. Things are better now, said the old woman. Don't be so sure, said the teacher. And then what hap-pened? The old woman spoke in Pápago, stringing together words that only the teacher understood, but she looked at us and at last she smiled. She lived in the school for a while and then she left, said the teacher. It seems she lost weight, was very thin, but I'm not sure, the old woman gets things mixed up sometimes, said the teacher. Though considering that she wasn't working, that she didn't have a salary, it seems only natural that she would lose weight, said the teacher. She must not have had much money for food. She ate, said the old woman suddenly, and we all jumped. I gave her food, my mother gave her food. She was skin and bones. Her eyes sunken. She looked like a coral snake. A coral snake? said Belano. *Micruroides euryxanthus*, said the teacher. Poisonous. So clearly you were good friends, said Belano. And when did she leave? After a while, said the old woman, without specifying how much time she meant. For the Pápagos, said the teacher, measuring time is as meaningless as measuring eternity. And how was she when she left? said Belano. Thin as a coral snake, said the old woman.

Later, a little before dusk, the old woman came with us to El Cubo to show us the house where Cesárea Tinajero had lived. It was near some corrals that were so old they were falling apart, the wood of the cross-pieces rotten, next to what must have been a toolshed, although it was empty now. The house was small, with a dried-up yard to one side, and when we got there we could see light through its only front window. Should we knock? said Belano. There's no point, said Lima. So we went walking back again, through the hills, to the old Pápago woman's house, and thanked her for everything, and then we said good night and headed back alone to El Cubo, although really she was the one who was left alone.

That night we slept at the teacher's house. After we ate, Lima settled down to read William Blake, Belano and the teacher took a walk in the desert and went into her room when they got back, and after Lupe and I washed the dishes, we went out to smoke a cigarette while we watched the stars, and made love in the Impala. When we came back into the house we found Lima asleep on the floor with the book in his hands and a familiar murmur coming from the teacher's room, indicating that neither she nor Belano would appear again for the rest of the night. So we covered Lima with a blanket, made a bed for ourselves on the floor, and turned out the light. At eight in the morning the teacher went into her room and woke up Belano. The bathroom was an outhouse in the backyard. When I returned, the windows were open and there was *café de olla* on the table.

We said goodbye outside. The teacher didn't want us to give her a ride to the school. When we got back to Hermosillo, I had the feeling that not only had I already been over every inch of this fucking land, but that I'd been born here.

We've been to the Sonora Cultural Institute, the National Indian Institute, the Bureau of Folk Culture (Sonora Regional Branch), the National Education Counsel, the Records Office of the Ministry of Education (Sonora Region), and the Peña Taurina Pilo Yáñez for the second time. Only at the last was anybody friendly.

Traces of Cesárea Tinajero keep appearing and disappearing. The sky in Hermosillo is bloodred. Belano was asked for papers, his papers, when he requested the old registers of rural teachers, which had to contain a record of Cesárea's destination after she left El Cubo. Belano's papers weren't in order. A secretary at the university told him that at the very least he could be deported. Where? shouted Belano. Back to your country, young man, said the secretary. Are you illiterate? said Belano, didn't you read here that I'm Chilean? You might as well shoot me in the head! They called the police and we went running. I had no idea that Belano was here illegally.

JANUARY 24

Belano is more nervous every day and Lima is more withdrawn. Today we saw Alberto and his policeman friend. Belano didn't see him or didn't want to see him. Lima did see him, but he doesn't care. Only Lupe and I are worried (very worried) about the inevitable showdown with her former pimp. It's no big deal, said Belano, to put an end to the discussion. After all, there are twice as many of us as there are of them. I was such a nervous wreck that I started to laugh. I'm not a coward, but I'm not suicidal either. They're armed, said Lupe. So am I, said Belano. In the afternoon they sent me to the Records Office. I said that I was writing an article for a Mexico City magazine about the rural schools in Sonora in the 1930s. Such a young reporter, said the secretaries, who were painting their nails. I found the following clue: Cesárea Tinajero had been a teacher from 1930 to 1936. Her first posting was El Cubo. Then she taught in Hermosillo, Pitiquito, Bábaco, and Santa Teresa. After that she was no longer part of the teaching force of the state of Sonora.

## JANUARY 25

According to Lupe, Alberto already knows where we are, what boarding-house we're staying at, and what car we're driving. He's just waiting for the right moment to launch a surprise attack. We went to see the Her-mosillo school where Cesárea had worked. We asked about old teachers from the 1930s. They gave us the former principal's address. His house was next door to what was once the state penitentiary. It's a three-story stone building with a tower that rises above the other guard towers and inspires a feeling of dread. A work of architecture built to last, said the principal.

## JANUARY 26

We drove to Pitiquito. Today Belano said that it might be best to go back to Mexico City. Lima doesn't care one way or the other. He says that at first he got tired of driving so much, but now he's gotten to like it. Even when he's asleep he dreams about driving Quim's Impala along these roads. Lupe doesn't talk about going back to Mexico City but she says that the best thing would be to hide. I don't want to be separated from her. I don't have plans either. Onward, then, says Belano. His hands, I notice when I lean over the front seat to ask him for a cigarette, are shaking.

## JANUARY 27

We didn't find anything in Pitiquito. For a while we were stopped in the car on the road to Caborca that leads to the turnoff for El Cubo, trying to decide whether we should visit the teacher again or not. Belano had the final say and we waited patiently, watching the road, the few cars that passed every so often, the very white clouds blown over on the wind from the Pacific. Until Belano said let's go to Bábaco and Lima started the car without saying a word and turned right and we drove off.

The trip was long and took us places we'd never been, although I, at least, still had the constant feeling of having seen it all before. From Pi-tiquito we drove to Santa Ana and turned onto the highway. We took the highway to Hermosillo. From Hermosillo we took the road east to Maza-tán, and from Mazatán to La Estrella. That was where the paved road ended, and we continued along dirt roads to Bacanora, Sahuaripa, and Bábaco. From the Bábaco school they sent us back to Sahuaripa, which was the municipal seat and supposedly the place where we could find the record books. But it was as if the Bábaco school, the school from the 1930s, had been swept away by a hurricane. We slept in the car again, like in the beginning. Night noises: wolf spiders, scorpions, centipedes, tarantulas, black widows, desert toads. All poisonous, all deadly. At moments the presence (or the imminence, I should say) of Alberto is as real as the night noises. Outside of Bábaco, where we've returned for no particular reason, we talk before we go to sleep about anything but Alberto. We keep the headlights on. We talk about Mexico City, about French poetry. Then Lima turns out the lights. Bábaco is dark too.


JANUARY 28

What if we find Alberto in Santa Teresa?


JANUARY 29

This is what we find: a teacher who's still working tells us that she knew Cesárea. They met in 1936, when our interlocutor was twenty. She had just been given the job and Cesárea had only been working at the school for a few months, so it was natural that they became friends. She didn't know the story of the bullfighter, or any other man. When Cesárea quit her job it took the teacher a while to understand it, but she accepted it as one of her friend's peculiarities.

For a while Cesárea disappeared: for months, maybe a year. But one morning the teacher saw her outside the school and they resumed their friendship. Back then Cesárea was thirty-five or thirty-six and the teacher considered her a spinster, although she regrets it now. Cesárea found work at the first canning factory in Santa Teresa. She lived in a room on Calle Rubén Darío, which at the time was in a remote neighborhood, dangerous or at least unsuitable for a woman. Did she know that Cesárea was a poet? She didn't. When both of them were working at the school, she often saw Cesárea write, sitting in her empty classroom, in a thick notebook with black covers that she always carried with her. She imagined it was a diary. During the time Cesárea worked at the canning factory, when they met in the center of Santa Teresa to go to the movies or to go shopping, when she was late she often found Cesárea writing in a notebook with black covers, like the previous one, but smaller, a notebook that looked like a prayer book and in which her friend's tiny handwriting flowed like a stampede of insects. Cesárea never read anything to her. Once she asked her what she was writing about and Cesárea said a Greek woman. The Greek woman's name was Hypatia. Sometime later the teacher looked up the name in the encyclopedia and learned that Hypatia was an Alexandrian philosopher killed by Christians in 415. The thought occured to her, maybe impulsively, that Cesárea identified with Hypatia. She didn't ask Cesárea anything else, or if she did, she had forgotten by now.

We wanted to know whether Cesárea read and whether the teacher remembered the names of any books. In fact, she did read a lot, but the teacher couldn't remember a single one of the books that Cesárea borrowed from the library and carried around with her. She worked at the canning factory from eight in the morning until six at night, so it wasn't as if she had much time to read, but the teacher imagined that she stole hours from sleep to spend reading. Then the canning factory had to close and for a while Cesárea was out of work. This was around 1945. One night, after the movies, the teacher went with her to her room. By then the teacher was married and saw Cesárea less often. She'd only been to her room on Calle Rubén Darío once before. Her husband, although he was a saint, wasn't happy about her friendship with Cesárea. In those days Calle Rubén Darío was like a sewer where all the dregs of Santa Teresa washed up. There were a couple of bars where at least once a week there was a fight that ended in bloodshed; the tenement rooms were occupied by out-of-work laborers or peasants who had just immigrated to the city; few of the children had any schooling. The teacher knew that because Cesárea herself had brought a few of them to the school to be enrolled. Some prostitutes and their pimps lived there too. It wasn't a proper street for a decent woman (maybe it was Cesárea's living there that had prejudiced the teacher's husband against her), and if the teacher hadn't realized it before, it was because the first time she went there was before she was married, when she was, in her own words, innocent and heedless.

But this second visit was different. The poverty and neglect of Calle Rubén Darío tumbled down on her like a death threat. The room where Cesárea lived was clean and neat, as one would expect of the room of a former teacher, but something emanated from it that weighed on her heart. The room was painful proof of the nearly impossible distance between her and her friend. It wasn't that it was untidy or smelled bad (as Belano wondered), or that Cesárea's poverty had surpassed the limits of gentility, or that the filth of Calle Rubén Darío extended into every corner, but something subtler, as if reality were skewed inside that lost room, or even worse, as if over time someone (who but Cesárea?) had imperceptibly turned her back on reality. Or, worst of all, had twisted it on purpose.

What did the teacher see? She saw a wrought-iron bed, a table strewn with papers holding more than twenty notebooks with black covers stacked in two piles, she saw Cesárea's few dresses hanging from a cord that stretched from one side of the room to the other, an Indian rug, a little paraffin burner sitting on a night table, three library books (she couldn't remember their titles), a pair of flat-heeled shoes, black stockings peeking out from under the bed, a leather suitcase in the corner, a black straw hat hanging from a tiny rack nailed behind the door, and food: she saw a chunk of bread, she saw a jar of coffee and another of sugar, she saw a half-eaten chocolate bar that Cesárea offered her and she refused, and she saw the weapon: a switchblade with a horn handle and the word *Caborca* engraved on the blade. And when she asked Cesárea why she needed a knife, Cesárea answered that she was under threat of death and then she laughed, a laugh, the teacher remembers, that echoed past the walls of the room and the stairs until it reached the street, where it died. At that moment it seemed to the teacher as if a sudden, perfectly orchestrated silence fell over Calle Rubén Darío: radios were turned down, the chatter of the living was suddenly muted, and only Cesárea's voice was left. And then the teacher saw or thought she saw a plan of the canning factory pinned to the wall. And as she was listening to what Cesárea had to tell her, in words that were neither faltering nor rushed, words that the teacher would rather have forgotten, but that she remembers perfectly well and even understands, understands now anyway, her eyes were drawn to the plan of the factory, a plan that Cesárea had drawn with great attention to certain details, leaving other parts shadowy or vague, complete with notations in the margins, although sometimes what was written was illegible and other times it was all in capital letters and even followed by exclamation marks, as if

564

Cesárea were seeing herself in her hand-drawn map, or seeing facets of herself that she had until then overlooked. And then the teacher had to sit down on the edge of the bed, although she didn't want to, and close her eyes and listen to what Cesárea was saying. And even though she was feeling worse and worse, she had the courage to ask Cesárea why she had drawn the plan. And Cesárea said something about days to come, although the teacher imagined that if Cesárea had spent time on that senseless plan it was simply because she lived such a lonely life. But Cesárea spoke of times to come and the teacher, to change the subject, asked her what times she meant and when they would be. And Cesárea named a date, sometime around the year 2600. Two thousand six hundred and something. And then, when the teacher couldn't help but laugh at such a random date, a smothered little laugh that could scarcely be heard, Cesárea laughed again, although this time the thunder of her laughter remained within the confines of her own room.

From that moment on, the teacher recalled, the tension in the air of Cesárea's room, or the tension that she imagined in the air, faded until it went away. Then she left and didn't see Cesárea again until two weeks later. That was when Cesárea told her that she was leaving Santa Teresa. She had brought the teacher a going-away present, one of the notebooks with black covers, possibly the thinnest of them all. Do you still have it? asked Belano. No, she didn't have it anymore. Her husband had read it and thrown it away. Or it had simply gotten lost. The house she lived in now wasn't the same one she'd been living in then, and small things often get lost in moves. But did you read the notebook? said Belano. Yes, she'd read it. It was mostly notes on the Mexican educational system, some very sensible and others completely inappropriate. Cesárea hated Secretary of Education Vasconcelos, although sometimes her hatred seemed more like love. There was a plan for general literacy, which the teacher could hardly make out because it was so chaotic, followed by reading lists for childhood, adolescence, and young adulthood, lists that were contradictory when they weren't plainly opposed. For example: two of the books on the first children's reading list were La Fontaine and Aesop's *Fables*. On the second list, La Fontaine disappeared. On the third list there was a popular book about gangster life in the United States, a book that might (though only might) be appropriate for adolescents, but never for children, which in turn vanished from the fourth list, replaced by a collection of medieval tales. Stevenson's *Treasure Island* and Martí's *The Golden Age* remained on all the lists, though they were books that the teacher considered most appropriate for adolescents.

After that, it was a long time before the teacher had any news of Cesárea. How long? said Belano. Years, said the teacher. Until one day she saw her again. It was during Santa Teresa's fiesta, when the city filled with peddlers from every corner of the state.

Cesárea was behind a stand selling medicinal herbs. The teacher walked right past her, but since she was with her husband and another couple she was ashamed to say hello. Or maybe it wasn't shame but shyness. And it might not even have been shame or shyness: she simply wasn't sure whether this woman selling herbs could be her old friend. Cesárea didn't recognize her either. She was sitting behind her table, a plank resting on four wooden boxes, and she was talking to a woman about the goods for sale. She had changed physically: now she was fat, hugely fat, and although the teacher didn't see a single gray hair amid the black, she had wrinkles around her eyes and deep circles under them, as if the journey she had made to Santa Teresa, to Santa Teresa's fiesta, had taken her months, even years.

The next day the teacher came back alone and saw her again. Cesárea was standing up and she looked much bigger than the teacher remembered. She must have weighed three hundred pounds and she was wearing an ankle-length gray skirt that accentuated her fatness. Her naked arms were like logs. Her neck had disappeared behind a giant's double chin, but her head was still Cesárea Tinajero's noble head: big, with prominent bones, her skull arched and her forehead wide and smooth. This time the teacher went up to her and said good morning. Cesárea looked at her and didn't recognize her, or pretended not to. It's me, said the teacher, your friend Flora Castañeda. When she heard the name, Cesárea frowned and got up. She moved around the plank of herbs and came up close to the teacher as if she couldn't see her well from a distance. She put her hands (two claws, according to the teacher) on her shoulders and for a few seconds she scrutinized her face. Oh, Cesárea, what a terrible memory you have, said the teacher, to say something. Only then did Cesárea smile (foolishly, according to the teacher) and say of course, how could she forget her. Then they talked for a while, the two of them sitting behind the table, the teacher on a wooden folding chair and Cesárea on a box, as if the two of them were tending the little herb stall together. And although the teacher realized immediately that they had very little to say to each other, she told Cesárea that she had three children now and that she was still working at the school, and remarked on thoroughly unimportant things that had happened in Santa Teresa. And then she thought about asking Cesárea whether she had married and had children, but she couldn't formulate the question because she could see for herself that Cesárea hadn't married and didn't have children, so she just asked her where she lived, and Cesárea said sometimes in Villaviciosa and other times in El Palito. The teacher knew where Villaviciosa was, although she'd never been there, but it was the first time she'd heard of El Palito. She asked her where the town was and Cesárea said that it was in Arizona. Then the teacher laughed. She said she had always suspected that Cesárea would end up living in the United States. And that was all. They parted. The next day the teacher didn't go to the market and she spent her idle hours wondering whether it would be a good idea to invite Cesárea over for lunch. She discussed it with her husband, they fought, she won. The next day, first thing, she went back to the market, but when she got there Cesárea's stall was occupied by a woman selling kerchiefs. She never saw her again.

Belano asked her whether she thought Cesárea was dead. Possibly, said the teacher.

And that was all. Belano and Lima were pensive for hours after the interview. We got rooms at the Hotel Juárez. At dusk the four of us met in Lima and Belano's room and talked about what to do. According to Belano, first we should go to Villaviciosa, then we could decide whether we wanted to go back to Mexico City or on to El Palito. The problem with El Palito was that he couldn't enter the United States. Why not? asked Lupe. Because I'm Chilean, he said. They won't let me in either, said Lupe, and I'm not Chilean. And García Madero won't get in either. Why not me? I said. Does anyone have a passport? said Lupe. No one did, except for Belano. That night Lupe went to the movies. When she got back to the hotel she said that she wasn't going back to Mexico City. So what will you do? said Belano. Live in Sonora or cross over into the United States.

Last night they found us. Lupe and I were in our room, fucking, when the door opened and Ulises Lima came in. Get dressed fast, he said, Alberto is in the lobby talking to Arturo. We did as he ordered without saying a word. We put our things in plastic bags and went down to the first floor, trying not to make a sound. We went out the back door. The alley was dark. Let's get the car, said Lima. There wasn't a soul on Avenida Juárez. We walked three blocks from the hotel, to the place where the Impala was parked. Lima was afraid that there would be someone there, but the spot was deserted and we started the car. We passed the Hotel Juárez. Part of the lobby and the lit-up window of the hotel bar were visible from the street. There was Belano, and across from him was Alberto. We didn't see Alberto's policeman friend anywhere. Belano didn't see us either and Lima thought it wasn't a good idea to honk the horn. We drove around the block. The sidekick, Lupe said, had probably gone up to our rooms. Lima shook his head. A yellow light was falling on Belano and Alberto's heads. Belano was talking, but it might just as well have been Alberto. They didn't seem angry. When we drove by again, they'd each lit a cigarette. They were drinking beer and smoking. They looked like friends. Belano was talking: he moved his left hand as if he was tracing a castle or the silhouette of a woman. Alberto never took his eyes off him and sometimes he smiled. Honk the horn, I said. We drove around the block once more. When the Hotel Juárez appeared again, Belano looked out the window and Alberto lifted a can of Tecate to his lips. A man and a woman were arguing at the main entrance to the hotel. Alberto's policeman friend was watching them, leaning on the hood of a car some thirty feet away. Lima honked the horn three times and slowed down. Belano had already seen us. He turned around, got up close to Alberto, and said something. Alberto grabbed him by the shirt. Belano pushed him and went running. By the time he reached the hotel door the cop was heading toward him and reaching into his jacket. Lima honked the horn three more times and stopped the Impala sixty feet from the Hotel Juárez. The policeman pulled out a gun and Belano kept running. Lupe opened the car door. Alberto appeared on the sidewalk outside the hotel with a gun in his hand. I had been hoping he was carrying the knife. As Belano got into the car, Lima took off and we sped away along the dimly lit streets of Santa Teresa. Somehow we ended up heading in the direction of Villaviciosa, which we thought was a good sign. By around three in the morning we were completely lost. We got out of the car to stretch our legs. There wasn't a single light anywhere. I'd never seen so many stars in the sky.

We slept in the Impala. We woke up at eight the next morning, freezing cold. We've been driving and driving around the desert without coming to a town or even a miserable ranch. Sometimes we get lost in the bare hills. Sometimes the road runs between crags and ravines and then we drop down to the desert again. The imperial troops were here in 1865 and 1866. Just the mention of Maximilian's army can crack us up. Belano and Lima, who already knew something about the history of Sonora before they came here, say there was a Belgian colonel who tried to capture Santa Teresa. A Belgian at the head of a Belgian regiment. It cracks us up. A Belgian-Mexican regiment. Of course, they got lost, although the Santa Teresa historians prefer to think they were defeated by the town's militia. Hilarious. There's also a record of a skirmish in Villaviciosa, possibly between the Belgian rearguard and the villagers. It's a story that Lima and Belano know well. They talk about Rimbaud. If only we'd followed our instincts, they say. Hilarious.

At six in the evening we come upon a house by the side of the road. They give us tortillas and beans, for which we pay a hefty sum, and fresh water that we drink straight from a gourd. Without moving, the peasants watch us while we eat. Where is Villaviciosa? On the other side of those hills, they tell us.


JANUARY 31

We've found Cesárea Tinajero. In turn, Alberto and the policeman found us. Everything was much simpler than I ever imagined it would be, but I never imagined anything like this. The town of Villaviciosa is a ghost town. The northern Mexican town of lost assassins, the closest thing to Aztlán, said Lima. I don't know. It's more like a town of the tired or the bored.

The houses are adobe, although the houses here almost all have front yards and backyards and some yards are cement, which is strange and unlike the houses every other place we've been this crazy month. The trees in the town are dying. As far as I could see, there are two bars, a grocery store, and nothing else. The rest is houses. Business is done in the street, on a curb in the plaza, or under the arches of the biggest building in town, the mayor's house, where no one seems to live.

Finding Cesárea wasn't hard. We asked about her and were sent to the washing troughs, on the east side of town. The troughs are made of stone and they're set in such a way that the water flows from the height of the first one and runs down a little wooden channel, enough for ten women's washing. When we arrived there were only three washerwomen there. Cesárea was in the middle and we recognized her right away. Seen from behind, leaning over the trough, there was nothing poetic about her. She looked like a rock or an elephant. Her rear end was enormous and it moved to the rhythm set by her arms, two oak trunks, as she rinsed the clothes and wrung them out. Her hair was long, it fell all the way to her waist. She was barefoot. When we called her she turned around calmly and faced us. The other two washerwomen turned around too. For an instant Cesárea and her companions watched us without saying anything: the one to her right was probably about thirty, but she could just as easily have been forty or fifty. The one to her left couldn't have been more than twenty. Cesárea's eyes were black and they seemed to absorb all the sun in the yard. I looked at Lima, who had stopped smiling. Belano blinked as if he had a grain of sand in his eye. At some point, exactly when I can't say, we started to walk to Cesárea Tinajero's house. I remember that as we headed down little streets under the relentless sun, Belano attempted an explanation, or several explanations. I remember his silence after that. Then I know that someone led me into a dark, cool room and that I threw myself down on a mattress and slept. When I woke up, Lupe was beside me, asleep, her arms and legs twined around my body. It took me a while to realize where I was. I heard voices and got up. In the next room Cesárea and my friends were talking. When I came in no one looked at me. I remember that I sat on the floor and lit a cigarette. Bunches of herbs tied with sisal hung on the walls of the room. Belano and Lima were smoking, but what I smelled wasn't tobacco.

Cesárea was sitting near the only window and every so often she would look out, up at the sky, and then I don't know why, but I could have cried too, although I didn't. We were there for a long time. At some moment Lupe came into the room and sat down beside me without saying anything. Later the five of us got up and went out into the yellow, almost white street. It must have been near dusk, although the heat still came in waves. We walked to where we had left the car. Along the way we saw only two people: an old man carrying a transistor radio in one hand and a ten-year-old boy who was smoking. It was blazing hot inside the Impala. Belano and Lima got in front. I was sandwiched between Lupe and the immense humanity of Cesárea Tinajero. Then the car crept complaining along the dirt streets of Villaviciosa until we reached the road.

We were outside of town when we saw a car coming from the opposite direction. We were probably the only two cars for miles around. For a second I thought we were going to collide, but Lima pulled over to one side and braked. A dust cloud settled around our prematurely aged Impala. Someone swore. It might have been Cesárea. I felt Lupe's body pressing against mine. When the dust cloud vanished, Alberto and the cop had gotten out of the other car and were aiming their guns at us.

I felt sick: I couldn't hear what they were saying, but I saw their mouths move and I guessed that they were ordering us to get out. They're insulting us, I heard Belano say incredulously. Sons of bitches, said Lima.

FEBRUARY 1

This is what happened. Belano opened the door on his side and got out. Lima opened the door on his side and got out. Cesárea Tinajero looked at Lupe and me and told us not to move. That no matter what happened we shouldn't get out of the car. She didn't say it in those words, but that was what she meant. I know it because it was the first and last time she spoke to me. Don't move, she said, and then she opened the door on her side and stepped out.

Through the window I watched Belano walk forward smoking, with his other hand in his pocket. Beside him I saw Ulises Lima, and a little farther back, rocking like a phantom battleship, I saw Cesárea Tinajero's armor-plated back. What happened next is a blur. I guess Alberto swore at them and asked them to hand over Lupe, I guess Belano told him to come get her, she was all his. Maybe then Cesárea said that they were going to kill us. The policeman laughed and said no, they only wanted the little slut. Belano shrugged his shoulders. Lima looked at the ground. Then Alberto directed his hawkish gaze at the Impala and searched for us, to no avail. I guess the setting sun's reflection shielded us from view. Belano gestured toward us with the hand that was holding the cigarette.

Lupe shook as if the cigarette's ember were a miniature sun. There they are, man, they're all yours. All right, then, I'll go check on my woman, said Alberto. Lupe's body clung to my body and although her body and my body were pliant, everything began to creak. Her former pimp only managed to take two steps. As he passed Belano, Belano was on top of him.

With one hand he seized Alberto's gun arm. His other hand shot out of his pocket, gripping the knife he'd bought in Caborca. Before the two of them tumbled to the ground, Belano had buried the knife in Alberto's chest. I remember that the policeman opened his mouth very wide, as if all the oxygen had suddenly vanished from the desert, as if he couldn't believe that a few students were putting up a fight. Then I watched Ulises Lima tackle him. I heard a shot and ducked. When I raised my head in the backseat again, I saw the policeman and Lima rolling on the ground until they came to a stop at the edge of the road, the policeman on top of Ulises, the gun in the policeman's hand aimed at Ulises's head, and I saw Cesárea, I saw the huge bulk of Cesárea Tinajero, who could hardly run but was running, toppling onto them, and I heard two more shots and I got out of the car. I had trouble moving Cesárea's body off the bodies of the policeman and my friend.

All three of them were covered in blood, but only Cesárea was dead. She had a bullet hole in her chest. The policeman was bleeding from an abdominal wound and Lima had a scratch on his right arm. I picked up the gun that had killed Cesárea and wounded the other two and stuck it in my belt. As I helped Ulises up, I saw Lupe sobbing next to Cesárea's body. Ulises told me that he couldn't move his left arm. I think it's broken, he said. I asked him whether it hurt. It doesn't hurt, he said. Then it isn't broken. Where the fuck is Arturo? said Lima. Lupe stopped sobbing instantly and looked behind her: about thirty feet away, sitting astride the pimp's motionless body, we saw Belano. Are you all right? cried Lima. Belano got up without answering. He shook the dust off and took a few shaky steps. His hair was stuck to his face with sweat and he kept rubbing his eyelids because the drops falling from his forehead and eyebrows were getting in his eyes. When he kneeled beside Cesárea's body I realized that his nose and lips were bleeding. What are we going to do now? I thought, but I didn't say anything. Instead I started to walk to work the stiffness out of my frozen limbs (but why frozen?) and for a while I watched Alberto's body and the lonely road that led to Villaviciosa. Every so often I heard the moans of the policeman, who was begging us to take him to a hospital.

When I turned around I saw Lima and Belano talking, leaning on the Camaro. I heard Belano say that we'd fucked up, that we'd found Cesárea only to bring her death. Then I didn't hear anything until someone touched my shoulder and told me to get in the car. The Impala and the Camaro drove off the road and into the desert. A little before dark they stopped again and we got out. The sky was full of stars and you couldn't see a thing. I heard Belano and Lima talking. I heard the moans of the policeman, who was dying. Then I didn't hear anything. I know I closed my eyes. Later Belano called me and between the two of us we put Alberto's and the policeman's bodies in the trunk of the Camaro and Cesárea's body in the backseat. Moving Cesárea's body took us forever. Then we got in the Impala and smoked and slept or thought until morning came at last.

Then Belano and Lima told us that it would be better if we separated. They were leaving us Quim's Impala. They would take the Camaro and the bodies. Belano laughed for the first time: a fair deal, he said. Now will you go back to Mexico City? he asked Lupe. I don't know, said Lupe. Everything went wrong, I'm sorry, said Belano. I think he was saying it to me, not Lupe. But now we'll try to fix it, said Lima. He laughed too. I asked them what they planned to do with Cesárea. Belano shrugged his shoulders. They had no choice but to bury her with Alberto and the policeman, he said. Unless we wanted to spend some time in jail. No, no, said Lupe. You know we don't, I said. We hugged and Lupe and I got in the Impala. I watched Lima try to get in on the driver's side of the Camaro, but Belano stopped him. I watched them talk for a while. Then I watched Lima get in on the passenger side and Belano take the wheel. For the longest time nothing happened. Two cars sitting in the middle of the desert. Can you make it back to the road, García Madero? said Belano. Of course, I said. Then I watched the Camaro start, hesitantly, and for a while the two cars bumped together through the desert. Then we separated. I headed off in search of the road and Belano turned west.

## FEBRUARY 2

I don't know whether today is February 2nd or 3rd. It might be the 4th, or even the 5th or 6th. But it's all the same to me. This is our threnody.

## FEBRUARY 3

Lupe told me that we're the last visceral realists left in Mexico. I was lying on the floor, smoking, and I looked at her. Give me a break, I said.

## FEBRUARY 4

Sometimes I start to think and I imagine Belano and Lima digging a pit in the desert for hours. Then, when it gets dark, I imagine them leaving and losing themselves in Hermosillo, where they abandon the Camaro on some random street. That's as far as my imagination takes me. I know they were planning to travel back to Mexico City by bus. I know they expected to meet us there. But neither Lupe nor I feels like going back. See you in Mexico City, they said. See you in Mexico City, I said before the cars parted ways in the desert. They gave us half the money they had left. Then, when we were alone, I gave half to Lupe. Just in case. Last night we came back to Villaviciosa and slept in Cesárea Tinajero's house. I looked for her notebooks. They were in plain sight, in the same room I'd slept in the first time we were here. The house doesn't have electricity. Today we had breakfast at one of the bars. People looked at us and didn't say anything. According to Lupe, we could stay here as long as we wanted.

## FEBRUARY 5

Last night I dreamed that Belano and Lima abandoned Alberto's Camaro on a beach in Bahía Kino and then headed out to sea and swam to Baja California. I asked them why they wanted to go to Baja and they answered: to escape, and then they vanished from sight behind a big wave. When I told her the dream, Lupe said it was silly, that I shouldn't worry, that Lima and Belano were probably fine. In the afternoon we went to eat at another bar. The same people were there. No one has said anything to us about living in Cesárea's house. No one seems bothered by our presence in town.

## FEBRUARY 6

Sometimes I think about the fight as if it were a dream. I see Cesárea Tinajero's back again like a stern emerging from a centuries-old shipwreck. All over again, I see her throwing herself on the policeman and Ulises Lima. I see her taking a bullet in the chest. Finally I see her shooting the policeman or deflecting the last shot. I see her die and I feel the weight of her body. Then I think. I think that Cesárea may have had nothing to do with the policeman's death. Next I think about Belano and Lima, one digging a grave for three people, the other watching the work with his right arm bandaged, and then I imagine that it was Lima who wounded the policeman, that the policeman was distracted when Cesárea attacked him and Ulises saw his chance and grabbed the gun and aimed it at the policeman's gut. Sometimes, for a change, I try to think about Alberto's death, but I can't. I hope they buried them with their guns. Or buried the guns in another hole in the desert. Whatever they did, I hope they got rid of the guns! I remember that when I lifted Alberto's body into the trunk I checked his pockets. I was looking for the knife that he used to measure his penis. I didn't find it. Sometimes, for a change, I think about Quim and his Impala, which I guess he'll probably never see again. Sometimes it makes me laugh. Other times it doesn't.

## FEBRUARY 7

The food is cheap here. But there isn't any work.

## FEBRUARY 8

I've read Cesárea's notebooks. When I found them I thought sooner or later I would mail them to Mexico City, to Lima or Belano. Now I know I won't. There's no sense in doing it. Every cop in Sonora must be after my friends.

**FEBRUARY 9**

Back in the Impala, back to the desert. I've been happy in this town. Before we left, Lupe said that we could come back to Villaviciosa whenever we wanted. Why? I said. Because the people accept us. They're killers, just like us. We aren't killers, I say. The people here aren't either, it's just a manner of speaking, says Lupe. Someday the police will catch Belano and Lima, but they'll never find us. Oh, Lupe, how I love you, but how wrong you are.

**FEBRUARY 10**

Cucurpe, Tuape, Meresichic, Opodepe.

**FEBRUARY 11**

Carbó, El Oasis, Félix Gómez, El Cuatro, Trincheras, La Ciénaga.

**FEBRUARY 12**

Bamuri, Pitiquito, Caborca, San Juan, Las Maravillas, Las Calenturas.

**FEBRUARY 13**

What's outside the window?

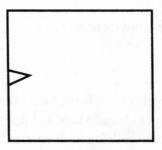

A star.

**FEBRUARY 14**

What's outside the window?
A sheet.

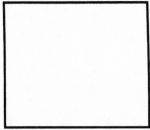

**FEBRUARY 15**

What's outside the window?